Guardians
of Justice

Patrick Riddle

outskirts
press

Outskirts Press, Inc.
http://www.outskirtspress.com

Paperback ISBN: 978-1-9772-3811-5

*"Last night I dreamed a deadly dream
beyond the Isle of Skye,*

I saw a dead man win the fight and I think that man was I."

From the song "The Battle of Otterburn"

PROLOGUE

Here's the thing about baby boomers–love us or hate us, we changed the world. Think about it. Did anyone ever use the words "lactose intolerant" before we came along?

By 1972, there were 75 million of us between the ages of 8 and 26, depending on who was keeping score. Actually, the more accurate way to think about it was to place the boomers into two groups. The real boomers were born between 1945 and 1957 and the shadow boomers came along between 1958 and 1964.

The real boomers are the ones who God and history will hold accountable for all the chaos. We were the ones who basically dumped our entire culture. At least most of it.

Our parents drummed into our skulls that we were the best and the brightest generation that the world had ever produced, not in small part because of their sacrifices in World War II and Korea and also so that we would never have to suffer through a great depression like they had and could go to college or at least get a damned good job. Hell, many of our parents hadn't even graduated high school. We believed them on the smart part. We were smarter. A lot smarter.

Smart enough so that even as teenagers and young adults we knew pretty much that all cultural mores and icons were subject to scrutiny and were presumed guilty of being either racist, stupid, or at least archaic. *Never Trust Anyone over 30*, *God is Dead*, and *Hell No, We Won't Go* became our battle cries. At least for some of us. And, our parents became ashamed of us–so what.

Many of us discovered drugs. Why not? The fact that our parents didn't use them was reason enough to try them. Actually I blame the whole thing (since none of us really like to take any blame ourselves) on birth control pills, and the fact that any girl could get them without her parents' permission. Up until that time, we were a little more cautious about who we laid down with, because we didn't want to get married, which in those days you had to do if you got the girl "knocked up". With birth control pills, which of course we believed were 100% effective, all restraints were gone.

By 1972, the country was torn apart by the Vietnam War, the civil rights movement, and the social experimentation by the boomers with sex and drugs. The pill and abortion were here to stay. All of this with a backdrop of general distrust for all authority by a portion, but not all, of the world's best and brightest generation. At least that's what we thought.

This had manifested itself into the criminal justice system as well. Drug possession, even for marijuana, could result in felony convictions and prison time, a horrifying thought to the parents of college kids caught using and selling drugs to their frat brothers.

A new examination was in order of the entire criminal justice system. Police began to be portrayed as "pigs" trampling over the Constitutional rights of the accused rather than protecting the innocent and the victims.

Everyday a new study spewed out of academia suggesting a new reform or program was needed to prevent crime, because as all good, right thinking people of our age knew, it was the inequity of the circumstances of one's birth or social standing that caused most of the crime in the first place. Poverty, racism, and unequal education were the root causes. Given a level playing field, most crime could be prevented.

It was stupid to have a prison system that merely housed prisoners and punished them with hard labor. Reform was what was necessary. Pour into these underprivileged retches enough training, education, and employment opportunities in the time you had them confined, and you would get back a model citizen with a recidivist rate that would almost vanish. A drug addict needed a drug program, not incarceration. A thief and a robber needed training and a job to quit stealing. And for sure, the death penalty had to go. Everyone knew that only the poor people of color were the ones getting executed anyway. After all, we were in the eighth year of President Lyndon Johnson's War on Poverty which was the federally directed application of resources to expand government's role in social welfare programs from education to healthcare. While we hadn't licked poverty yet, we had certainly put a great many people to work manning the new government programs that were now in place to lick it.

But even with the chaos and the war, in 1972 there seemed to be plenty of money and opportunity. As the old saying goes, you can't make an omelette without breaking eggs. Our parents would come around.

━━━◖◍◗━━━

Chapter 1

The last thing Elizabeth Van Houten remembered around 10:00 a.m. on that sunny cloudless, cool November day was Eddie Reno tearing at her hair as he roughly tried to kiss her. The last thing she would ever regret was letting him into her car after the accident.

In her terror, when he grabbed her right breast, she found the strength to punch him in the stomach. As she did she felt the gun. But Reno was far too quick, and after his fist connected solidly with her chin, just to make sure, he slammed her head into the driver's side doorpost of her Volkswagen Beetle. Then dragging her unconscious body into the peach orchard, he proceeded to violently rape her.

Had Reno been a remotely normal person, he might have felt a sense of shame or even panic that something so simple as a minor fender bender had gotten so out of hand. But Reno was a true sociopath, and without a hint of remorse, when it was all over, he pointed his snub nose .38 caliber revolver at Elizabeth's forehead and squeezed the trigger. Then almost casually he lifted the blonde, twenty-four-year old 's lifeless body, now minus the back of her head, into the Beetle and drove away. Unseen, or so he thought.

Taking only country roads, which wound through endless walnut, cherry, and apple orchards, Eddie Reno soon arrived at the small farm community of Linden, some ten miles east of Stockton, California. Finding the cherry tree lined road he was searching for, he turned left onto it.

By the time he reached the trailer, parked a quarter of a mile down the rough dirt road, Reno's damaged Corvette, and his passenger from the earlier accident, were already there.

"What's going on, Eddie?" the man asked, emerging from the trailer, and glancing at the damaged car.

Reno pointed. "We gotta get rid of it."

"Why?"

"Because it and the chick need to disappear."

The man's eyes widened. "The broad's in the car?"

Reno nodded. "Back seat." He gestured toward some old farm buildings. "Get a backhoe."

"You thinking of burying her here twenty feet down?"

Reno grinned. "Why not? Who'd find her here?"

"Look man, I want nothing to do with this," said the man who was stupid enough to get involved with a sicko like Eddie Reno, now feeling the cold realization of what he was involved in beginning to creep over him. He began to turn away.

"Too late for that, buddy," Reno replied, making him stop. "A classy Stockton broad is dead, and you were with me. I get caught, you know who will find out."

"Jesus Christ, Eddie," cried the other man.

Reno took a step forward. "I ain't got time to argue. I gotta get outta here. If you don't want to backhoe the bitch, think of something else."

Five miles away, deep in a forty-acre walnut orchard, Carlo DeBennedetti was on his tractor, getting set to pull down a dead walnut tree with a thick chain, when he saw a blue VW Beetle turn onto the private road next to his orchard and head slowly toward the river.

Can't anyone read the damn no-trespassing sign? he thought.

If circumstances had been different, DeBennedetti would have pursued the vehicle and given the dark skinned driver a good tongue-lashing. But he still had to get the tree down and get cleaned up.

Who gets married at five o'clock on a Friday? he was thinking as he turned his attention back to the tree. *Stupid cousin Enzio, that's who.*

San Joaquin County Courthouse, Stockton, California
Later That Afternoon

After easing his '65 Mustang convertible, a passing-the-bar gift from his parents, into a metered parking space at the side of the courthouse, Joe Larsen still had an hour to kill before his interview appointment with the Public Defender's Office. It wasn't really an interview. More of a formality, since his heart-specialist father had already wired it up with the grateful patient who just happened to be the Public Defender of San Joaquin County.

Beggars can't be choosers, Larsen thought, looking up at the recently built seven-storey building. The remainder of Weber Avenue appeared much older and the elms lining one side of the street just beginning to lose their leaves, made the downtown area appear more charming than it really was. It reminded Larsen of the old San Francisco business district, some eighty miles away, where his father had an office.

Leaving his "pride and joy" at the curb, Larsen entered the courthouse, wondering why the address for the Public

Defender's Office didn't match, and made his way to a court-room. It became clearly apparent as he took a seat on a back row theater-style seat that the black-robed judge, his clerk and an armed uniformed deputy were already bored stiff with the proceedings. They were all but ignoring the sniffling, well-dressed forty something woman in the witness box. Except for traffic court in Oakland to fight a ticket, Larsen had never been in an actual courtroom before, but it didn't take him long to realize that the woman's tears were faked. That would explain the Judge's ambivalence, but not why, unlike traffic court, he was the only spectator to this family feud. "So this is where I am going to be working", thought Larsen as he sat there listening to the woman going on and on about why she needed more money from her philandering former husband.

As the husband's lawyer, dressed in an expensive looking checkered suit, continued with his cross-examination of the tearful wife, Larsen was beginning to think that his overbearing father had a point. The doctor had expected Larsen to follow in his footsteps; into the world of San Francisco medicine and society, and had been very disappointed when he hadn't. In Larsen's own defense, he'd inherited many of his mother's artistic genes and had a zero aptitude for science and chemistry. Therefore, Med school was out. As far as Larsen was concerned, becoming an attorney worked for three reasons; First and foremost, it pissed off his father; second, he never had to look at a science book again, and thirdly, he could actually get admitted to a second tier law school in the Bay area with his mediocre grades and some juice from daddy.

"...Each side to pay their own costs," the judge announced, jolting Larsen from his thoughts.

From the reaction of both parties, including their respective lawyers, the judge's ruling did not go down well. After much shouting and posturing, the irate husband was finally hustled out of court by his attorney. They were the last to leave.

From his walnut paneled bench, the judge then noticed Larsen

"You lost, son?" he asked.

"Ah, no, sir. Just watching," Larsen replied, immediately getting to his feet.

The judge chuckled. "We don't get many observers in family disputes." He said eyeing Larsen carefully. "What's with the new suit?"

Larsen explained.

"There seems to be no end to you new fellows," the judge said when Larsen finished his explanation. "I wonder where Hawthorne finds it in his budget to keep hiring." He hesitated. "Well, good luck young man."

"Thank you, sir. You wouldn't know where the office is located?"

"Across from the Owl Club on San Joaquin Street. You'll love it," he chuckled."

⸻⸺◈⸺⸻

THE SAN JOAQUIN PUBLIC DEFENDER'S OFFICE, SAN JOAQUIN STREET, STOCKTON, CALIFORNIA
A SHORT TIME LATER THAT SAME DAY

The narrow dilapidated building, recently converted from an old skidrow transient hotel, sat directly across from The Owl Club, an ancient dump of a bar that announced

'Schlitz' in old neon from its single barred window. On a similar barred window of the tiny Italian deli next door were painted the words 'Angelina and Ferrari,' and as Larsen peered in he decided that three customers at one time would swamp the place. His parents' bedroom was bigger. Beyond the Owl Club, things seemed to get incrementally worse. The shoe repairer and dry cleaners, opposite a Mexican restaurant, whose name Larsen couldn't begin to pronounce, along with the corner liquor store, all looked faded and tired.

Inside the public defender's office building things were no better. A converted three floor transient hotel with furnishings that were a mishmash of linoleum covered floors and recently slapped on paint, all of which could have been selected by Helen Keller. It was all lipstick on a pig as far as Larsen was concerned. He wondered how county offices could be located in such a dump.

"So what did you think of our Judge Stock?" Bradley Hawthorne, III, asked, after Larsen told him that he had killed some time in the judge's court waiting for his interview.

"He seemed okay to me," Larsen replied. "But what do I know." He was getting the distinct impression that Hawthorne didn't care much for the judge.

"Well, you seem like an observant young man, and I'm sure you'll develop some impressions soon enough," Hawthorne added with a movie star grin that could be turned on like a switch. His perfectly manicured nails drumming the desk blotter also grabbed Larsen's attention. They were space capsule clean, and Larsen didn't think for a moment that this was the type of town for manicuring men's nails.

Already have, he thought, as Hawthorne leaned back in his large executive chair. The once expensive desk was now old and worn, but didn't come close to matching the fake wood paneling and cheap carpet. As far as Larsen was concerned, everything in the small office appeared not only oversized but also out of place. Like Hawthorne. From his neatly trimmed grey hair to his tailored brown suit and extra shiny shoes, he was manufactured perfect. Except for his nose. Larsen recognized a drinker's nose when he saw one. His father had such a nose; red with deep blue veins coursing like a road map of Brooklyn. There was no mistaking that Hawthorne liked his drink, making Larsen wonder if Hawthorne and his old man had more than just a doctor-patient relationship.

"You come with high recommendations," Hawthorne continued, getting to his feet. "Incidentally, how are your parents?"

"Just fine." *Should I get up? Is the interview over? What high recommendations?* Larsen was only too aware that he didn't have high recommendations from anybody including his ex-girlfriend.

Hawthorne maneuvered around the desk. "Let's meet the fellows, then. Tomorrow we have a woman starting for the first time."

For a big pear-shaped man, he moved lightly down the hallway to begin their tour. The old kitchen was now converted to the library and next to the waiting room was Hawthorne's office. Jack Fletcher, the assistant public defender, occupied the office next door.

Fletcher gave Larsen a weak-gripped handshake. Similarly dressed to Hawthorne and also in his early fifties, he appeared to have an addiction to framing everything from pictures to diplomas. Plastering his walls were everything from his college diploma to his certificate of participation in the San Joaquin County Bar Association, plus numerous photographs with Hawthorne and Fletcher, and people Larsen didn't recognize. Although the desk was only slightly less ostentatious for the surroundings than Hawthorne's.

Across the hall were three interview rooms with nothing more than gun-metal grey desks and two chairs. The six investigators, who were housed in the basement like so many rats, used the rooms to interview the out-of-custody public defender clients. This was the secret of the operation, Hawthorne explained. The soon to be fourteen attorneys would defend ten thousand or so cases that year. Each of the defendants would be initially interviewed by an investigator sometime between their first arraignment and their next court appearance. This left the attorneys free to make a jillion court appearances, and cut 10,000 deals.

The in-custodies were easy. The San Joaquin County Jail was in the middle of nowhere, some twenty minutes south of the office, and had its own attorney-client interview rooms. There the investigator would go over the charges and police reports, then write a one or two page synopsis of each defendant's statements. They almost always began with 'Defendant denies charges.'

The out-of-custodies were a different matter. Whether bailed, or released on their on recognizance, the court ordered those assigned to the public defender to make an appointment and be interviewed before their next court appearance. Each one was handed a map and a telephone number that frequently got thrown away. Consequently, less than half the defendants were actually interviewed on time. At the next court appearance, whomever appeared with them, usually had to do it on the fly, scribbling notes on a file cover.

In the secretarial pool, converted from the old hotel dining room, the chitchat immediately subsided and the clack of electric typewriters dribbled to a stop as, to Larsen's horror, Hawthorne introduced him as a prominent San Francisco doctor's son who would be starting on Monday.

Interview over? Larsen thought.

With barely enough room for desks and chairs, and no windows for ventilation, a thick blue haze surrounded the eight young women, all of whom seemed to be smoking. Through the smog, Larsen saw enormous amounts of paper being processed, as cigarettes burned in ashtrays. Although he was there less than a minute, Larsen felt he'd been scanned and appraised. Another interview over.

The library was filled with shelves of red, blue and brown books, none of which Larsen had ever seen before. The tables formed a large rectangle in the center of the room and were strewn with paper, legal pads, and cups of coffee. Wearing Levis and flannel shirts, the two young male "interns" were introduced to Larsen, along with Beaumont Henderson who sat at the head of a table in a creaky, brown leather swivel, high-back desk chair in front of another stack of books held in place by busts of Plato and Socrates on each end.

"Our prize law clerk," Hawthorne nodded at Henderson.

Henderson, known by everyone in the office as "Merlin," took Larsen's hand in a vice-like grip that befitted his tall, athletic frame. His long curly blonde hair, full beard and mustache perfectly complimented his Levis and tie-died t-shirt.

He peered at Hawthorne through wire rimmed, Coke bottle thick glasses. "You starting him here, boss?"

"Not at this time," Hawthorne replied. "We need two bodies in muni court, so I'm starting Larsen and the woman in there part-time, and part-time with you. Get them on suppression motions right away."

Before Henderson could comment, Hawthorne hustled Larsen away to the second floor hallway.

The king showing off the castle to a prospective knight, Larsen was thinking as he followed in Hawthorne's wake.

"Got a sec, Stanley?" Hawthorne asked at the first open door, and not waiting for a reply, he pushed Larsen inside the spartan room. The only adornment, if you discounted the unhealthy looking Ficus, was a poster of Che Guevera, taped at an annoying angle to the cheap paneling.

Stanley Latchman remained seated behind a grey metal desk, half hidden by three stacks of beige legal folders piled on the fake wood formica top. In his mid-twenties, Latchman was slightly built with a parrot-like nose and pointed chin. Although he smiled, his eyes remained cold and calculating. Larsen instantly disliked him.

Hawthorne didn't seem to notice that Latchman hadn't stood or offered to shake Larsen's hand. "Mr. Larsen will be joining you half time, starting next week," he said with another fake smile. "A young lady is interviewing tomorrow and she will also start. I'm going to have them follow you for the first week, when they aren't in the library."

Latchman didn't comment, but his sullen expression spoke volumes.

Office after office, the tour continued. Each one with the same lousy decor; posters instead of paintings, all looking like they had come from the same Berkeley book store. However, the occupants, mostly nondescript guys in suits or sport coats, had hung the obligatory framed Supreme Court Shingle and the Law School Diploma.

By the time they reached the third floor, Larsen was beginning to have doubts as to whether he really wanted to join their little club. Not that he had a choice. No one else was beating a path to his door.

Hawthorne lost his fake smile as he entered the first office. The three occupants, so far as Larsen could tell from his limited exposure, were all "anti-Hawthornes."

Leaning back in an ancient swivel rocker, his feet perched on an equally old and distressed oak desk, whose items looked as though they been laid out using a T-square, was Jacob 'Snake' Sanderson. With an L.A. Dodger batting helmet perched above his Norwegian features, Larsen was not surprised to see a framed picture of L.A. Dodger pitcher, Don Sutton, featured prominently on the wall behind him. However, he was surprised at the inscription. 'To Snake, Homosexually Yours, Don.'

Larsen tried to ignore the inscription as he studied the two other occupants. Opposite Sanderson, Anthony J. Borelli wore a black sweatshirt with 'Pete's Auto Wreckers,' in gold lettering splashed across the front. His thick hands held a list of names, as he peered at them through large, black framed glasses resting on a distinct Roman nose. With his mustache and thick curly hair, he was a picture of relaxed good humor.

His companion, Francisco 'Frankie' Sanchez was neatly dressed in pressed khakis, short-sleeved white shirt and light blue tie adorned with a scantily clad flamenco dancer.

Hawthorne quickly introduced them, but Larsen was more intent in soaking up the surroundings. Not only did the office have a window, but also just outside the window, on a flat-topped tar paper roof over some of the offices on the second floor below, there sat a rusty metal table and faded beach umbrella, flanked by two mismatched plastic strapped sun loungers.

"Who are you starting him with?" Sanderson asked.

Hawthorne hesitated. "I was thinking Stanley for a week or so."

"That's bullshit, boss," Sanderson continued. "Let him come with me, next week. In case you forgot, I've still got misdemeanors and traffic before you stuff me into juvie. He can take over my calendar when I go."

"We'll see."

Borelli finally looked up, swivelling his sturdy five-foot, six inch frame. "Screw that. What position does he play?"

"I don't know, Anthony," Hawthorne replied. "I told you we can't use sports aptitude as a hiring criteria." He turned to Larsen. "Do you play baseball, Mr. Larsen?"

"Shortstop," Larsen replied to Borelli, finally taking his eyes off the large Ursula Andress 'Dr. No' poster.

"Well, well, we may have some pig shit luck here." He said placing the list on Sanderson's desk, next to an ivory chess set with a game in progress. "You any good?"

"I can kick it around a little. How good do I have to be?" *So that explains the coatrack being used as a second wardrobe, and the smelly gym clothes,* Larsen thought.

"He takes this crap serious", said Sanderson eyeing Larson like a professional scout. "You like basketball? We play every noon."

"Where?"

"Kid's gym at the old Catholic Church down the street. No hot water, no heat, but the rent is right," Sanderson added.

"I thought I was your shortstop," Sanchez said.

"You were the shortstop, you stone handed son-of-a-bitch," Borelli replied. "You're my new center fielder since the boss didn't see fit to take my request for an outfielder seriously."

"Any word on Mr. Hunter's jury?" Hawthorne asked, trying to change the subject.

"Not yet," Sanderson said. "But we were just about to

go over. You know Wally ain't keeping a jury past five."

"How long have they been out?" Hawthorne continued.

"Since eleven."

"Maybe they're hung?"

"Maybe," Borelli replied. "Mike was concerned about one of them. Bartender with a cop for a father. Deputy sheriff actually. Stuck out at the jail for the last decade."

Hawthorne couldn't hide his annoyance. "He kept a law enforcement officer's child on the jury? What was he thinking? Cardinal rule that."

"Mike knows what he's doing. Why don't you leave the new meat with us. We'll take him over and show him around."

Hawthorne checked his watch before facing Larsen. "Okay then. I'll leave you in capable hands. See you Monday. Eight-o-clock. Check with my secretary Alice, and she'll point you in the right direction."

Without waiting for a reply, he left the room.

"What the hell was he doing keeping that broad on the jury?" Borelli asked Sanderson quietly.

"Hell if I know," Sanderson replied. "But let's get over there."

"Let me turn my line in first," Borelli added.

—————⊂«◍»⊃—————

San Joaquin County Courthouse, Stockton, California
A short time later

It was 4:50 p.m., when they entered the courthouse,

now accompanied by two of the pool secretaries and a couple of the third floor attorneys.

One of them, Jim 'Spread' Harris, a former Navy JAG lawyer, got his name not from his beer-kegged body shape, but from the fact he could quote the point spread on any professional game played that day or week. The 'line' Borelli had turned in was Spread's odds on all the upcoming NFL games. Most of the public defenders, DAs, and court bailiffs bet with Harris, who took a modest "administrative fee" for taking the action.

Peter Rothman, the second attorney, was a reed skinny guy with glasses. They were rarely removed if he wanted to see anything smaller than a refrigerator, especially when he played baseball.

Department Three was on the third floor of the courthouse where most of the Superior Courts were located. These courts handled all criminal felonies and civil matters worth more than twenty-five thousand dollars, as well as juvenile and family matters.

This particular Superior Court was the personal domain of Presiding Judge Wallace Hollins. Originally from the Deep South, 'Wally' as the boys called him, was an imposing figure on and off the bench. Impatient and demanding, especially if a criminal defendant who was obviously guilty pled not guilty, he ran his court by a rigid set of personal rules that all counsel were expected to know. Having little use for defense lawyers, he hated his calendar cluttered with cases where the outcome was obvious. Consequently, smart criminal lawyers tried to avoid Hollins like the plague.

Unlike Larsen's earlier experience, this courtroom was full of people, and as the group took their seats in a back row, the jury was just filing in.

"Guilty," Rothman hissed to Sanderson.

"How the hell would you know," Sanderson hissed back. "The last time you won a case, Jesus hadn't even been tried."

"One of Rothman's family represented Jesus, the way I heard it," Borelli said quietly, while attempting to get the attention of defense attorney, Michael Hunter.

"All the more reason that I know and appreciate the look on their faces," replied Rothman. "See, no eye contact with the defendant. Sure sign."

"Yeah, but they're all looking at Michael," Borelli said.

Sanderson gestured at a female juror, who was glancing nervously at the wall clock. "Not the good looking skirt in the fourth hole."

Borelli finally got Michael's attention.

His reply was a shrug as he mouthed "talk to them."

"Not again," Rothman whined. "I hate talking to jurors after a trial. Who does that besides Michael?"

"Shut up and make sure you take notes, this time," Borelli snapped.

Although Michael had started the practice, Sanderson and Borelli now also quizzed their juries immediately as they left the courtroom. Most juries wanted to talk. They found it cathartic. Beyond the obvious on how and why they'd voted to convict or acquit, Michael wanted answers to some very specific questions. How had they voted on the first ballot? How was the foreman selected? Were there any disagreements among the jurors? Was one juror more persuasive than another with his or her arguments? If so, which one? Had they liked the prosecutor? Had they disliked him? What one thing made them decide?

In this particular case, Borelli wanted to know what they thought about the bike.

"Don't forget the bike," Borelli now whispered to the group. The bike in question was a woman's ten-speed Schwinn that had sat on the back porch of a small home on Eighth Street in south Stockton that had been burglarized by one Albert Hayes.

Albert Hayes, the twenty-two-year-old defendant, had been tried by the jury for the last day and a half, accused of burglarizing the home of one Victor Flores. When Hayes allegedly broke in to steal the family silver, Flores, who happened to be home sick, and shot him with a .45 caliber Smith and Wesson that he kept on his night stand for just such purposes. Although the dining room was small, Flores first shot missed Hayes. The next two found their mark, while the final three shots destroyed the hutch. If it hadn't been for an ambulance in the area at the time of the emergency call, Hayes would have bled to death on the cheap linoleum floor. Normally, the fact that Hayes was unarmed and almost killed would have garnered sympathy from the DA to get a plea bargain. But Hayes' luck crapped out when it turned out that the victim had a cousin who worked as a dispatcher for the San Joaquin County Sheriff's office. The sheriff was very loyal to the people who were loyal to him, so after a telephone call to the DA, Hayes' file had NO DEALS written inside the cover.

Hayes' grandmother, Clara, seated in the front row with his two sisters and current girlfriend, would have hocked her big-hearted soul to get her heroin addict grandson a 'street lawyer' if he'd had more than a dead bang looser for a case. She believed in the common street misconception that a lawyer you paid was better than any public defender. Until Michael was assigned the case. She immediately recognized him from two years earlier, when he'd represented her granddaughter on a misdemeanor possession charge, and took the time to fully explain the proceedings to her and got the kid in a drug program that didn't take.

"Remain seated," the bailiff announced loudly, as a black robed Hollins entered the court.

"I understand that the jury has reached a verdict," the judge said, swiveling to face them.

"We have, your honor," a balding man replied, rising slowly from his seat.

"Are you the foreman, Mr. Schmidt?"

"I am, your honor."

"Have you filled in and signed the verdict form?"

"Yes, your honor."

"And is the verdict unanimous?

"Yes, your honor."

"Please read the verdict madam clerk," Hollins continued, as the form was handed over.

The clerk cleared her voice. "We the people in the above-entitled cause, find the defendant, Albert Hayes, NOT GUILTY."

The court erupted.

"Oh, Lawdy," Clara wailed. "Praise the Lord."

"I'll be a son-of-a-gun," Borelli whispered. "Eleven in a row."

After grinning at his grandmother and her entourage, Hayes turned to the arresting detective, Rudy Johnson. "I tol you I'd beat you," he said. "You can't beat me."

"Shut your stinkin' mouth, you useless piece of shit," Michael hissed. "Or so help me, I'll have the bailiff take you back to the holding cell, and give Johnson a few minutes with you. Do you believe me?" he added, only inches from Hayes' black features.

"You crazy," Hayes responded. "You stay away from

me. Or I'll tell the judge."

Michael laughed. "Go ahead. I'd pay to see that."

"Order in the court," Hollins bellowed, slamming down his gavel. "We're not finished, yet." He then turned to the jury. "Ladies and gentlemen, the court thanks you for your service. I know this wasn't easy, but it was necessary. You are now excused from jury service for the next year, at least, and you are now free to talk about the case. However," he added, "you don't have to. You are now excused. Everyone remain seated until the jury leaves the courtroom."

"The defendant is discharged from custody," Hollins continued to Hayes, as the jury filed out through a back door. "You can either be released now, or go back to jail where you can collect your things. Your choice."

Hayes stood. "I want to go now."

"Fine. Mr. Hunter, I'd like to see you in my chambers."

The courtroom made a mass exit, while a reporter from the Stockton Record attempted to get a statement from both Michael and the DA.

While Sanderson and Rothman tried to interview the foreman and anyone else who'd sat on the jury, Michael handed Borelli a wad of cash.

"Here's thirty bucks, AJ, that's it," he said.

"You coming?" Borelli asked.

"Nah, I got to see the judge. Then I promised Johnson here that I'd swing by Lamberts after."

"Jesus, Michael, you ought to show for a few minutes. It's your beer."

"Screw 'em," Michael replied. "Just because I buy, doesn't mean I have to drink with them. Talk to juror number four. She was the hold-out. Okay? I'll see you at your place around eight," he added over his shoulder, already heading for Hollins' chambers.

Borelli raced down the third floor hallway and caught Juror Number 4 just as the shapely brunette hit the button for the elevator.

"Excuse me", said Borelli. "I'm Anthony Borelli and I am a public defender, and I just wanted to ask you a couple of questions about how you voted ."

The juror eyed Borelli coldly as she calmly took a cigarette out of her purse and lit it blowing a large cloud of smoke into the air. Stepping into the elevator as the door opened, she turned back to Borelli and said, "Buzz off".

"Well, Michael my boy," Hollins said, now seated behind his large mahogany desk that had once belonged to his father. "It's after five, I believe."

"It is indeed," Michael replied, reaching for a bottle of gin and two paper cups in the hutch that held more than law books.

"To creative arguments," Hollins continued, raising his cup.

"To predictable juries," Michael replied.

"Rocha never saw that bike thing coming." Hollins added. Michael merely shrugged and took a long pull on his cup of gin.

"Well, you don't leave much out when you read that instruction, Judge. And I could see that the jury was taking a lot of cues from you. So I decided to agree with you and put us on the same side."

Hollins sized up the tall, blond Irishman. "What's troubling you, Mike?" he asked.

"Nothing more than usual, I guess," he replied. "I'm just getting tired of this crap."

"The thrill of victory no longer there?"

"Gone a long time ago. Don't get me wrong, the

greatest rush in the world are the words 'not guilty.' But it's not the same."

For someone who's not yet thirty, he sounds jaded, Hollins thought. "Time for a change," he asked.

Michael shrugged, finishing his drink. "Maybe. But it's all I know."

"I may have a little favor to ask of you, Michael."

"Anything, your honor. You know that."

"Not so fast. You don't know what it is yet."

"I don't care."

Hollins smiled. "Well, it may come to nothing. We'll see. Now get out of here. The boys will be expecting you."

———⊛———

Xochimilco's Restaurant, San Joaquin Street, Stockton, California
Early Evening Same Day

"I already told you," Borelli said. "Thirty bucks, that's it. Besides, in this joint that's sixty beers. If we each leave a tip."

By now, more than a dozen public defenders were seated at several tables in the Mexican restaurant, pronounced Zo-chi-milko's, two doors down from the office. The occasion was a long, time-honored tradition, where the winner of a jury trial bought his colleagues beer, known as "The Buy." It was held infrequently, until Michael and AJ came along.

Hawthorne normally stopped in to slap the winner on the back, and make a little speech about how these wins were hard to come by, and so important to the balance of justice. In his opinion, you had to keep the police and prosecution from running rough-shod over the indigent citizens, and these occasional wins went a long way toward doing that. His discourse never failed to bring cheers from the mass of inebriated public defenders, most of whom shared Hawthorne's opinion that it was them against the great prosecutorial machine, out to get their clients. When Michael won, none of this happened, and after Michael made the mistake of agreeing to pick up an open tab that got completely out-of-hand, no one could remember the last time Michael attended one of his own "Buys."

Sandwiched between Borelli and Sanderson in a red leather booth, Larsen was eyeing the velvet paintings of bullfighters, Mexican heroes, and even one of the flag being raised at Iwo Jima, when an argument broke out.

"I don't know how you can apologize for that arrogant asshole," Latchman spat from a nearby table. "He thinks he's too good to drink with us."

"Nobody put a gun to your back and made you drink the man's beer, Stanley," Sanderson responded quietly.

"Screw you, Sanderson," Latchman replied. "You're as bad as he is. You guys on the third floor think your shit doesn't stink. You have no respect for the office traditions."

"Some tradition," Sanderson continued. "Getting your ass kicked and playing backgammon all day and drinking the winner's beer."

"Besides, you know Michael hates this tradition," Borelli interrupted. "You're lucky he buys the beer, at all."

"He's not too good to drink with cops and the DA," Latchman said.

"Meaning?" Borelli asked.

"Some of us are wondering what he might be telling

the cops about our clients in exchange for a little help," Latchman continued. "Let's face it, nobody wins eleven in a row legit."

"Oh, boy. Here we go," Sanderson muttered to Larsen.

By now, Borelli was out of his seat and had grabbed Latchman by the front of his shirt. "Let's you and me go over to Lambert's, right now, Stanley," he snapped. "And you can say what you've just said to Michael's face. Then those nicotine stained little rat teeth of yours can be clattering on the ground like your precious backgammon dice."

Clearly shaken, Latchman was trying to back away, when the entire family who owned the restaurant, threw them all out.

—————◦«◉»◦—————

LAMBERT'S BAR, (FREMONT STREET) STOCKTON, CALIFORNIA
AROUND THE SAME TIME

The DA and cop bar had no dance floor, no fancy views, no band, and no public defender or defense attorney was made to feel welcome. Except for Michael, who was now at the dark, time-worn bar, sandwiched between Detective Rudy Johnson and Deputy District Attorney Jim Rocha.

"I hate juries, Jerry Brown appointees, small titted women, and you, Michael," Johnson said into his glass of Scotch.

Michael smiled. "Have another drink, Johnson," he replied. "Let's drink to Jerry Brown appointees."

"I ain't drinking to that. I'd sooner drink to Albert

Hayes. The little scum bucket."

"Okay. Then let's drink to Linda Ronstadt, Jerry Brown's girlfriend," Michael added.

Rocha raised his glass. "Now you're talking."

Johnson put down his glass and slowly shook his head. "Linda Ronstadt dating Jerry Brown. Isn't that one of life's sweet ironies. That, and how you keep kickin' Rocha's butt. When are you going to beat this guy, Rocha?" he asked. "This's getting embarrassing."

"I thought we had him this time," Rocha replied. "How did you pull that out of your ass Hunter?"

"Even a blind pig can find an acorn once in awhile." Michael smiled. "The crime photos were color. And besides showing Albert's blood all over the floor, there was the girl's red, ten-speed bike in the background on the porch. All we did was show that picture to Hayes and suggest that if his story was to hold any water, it might be important if he'd ever seen a bike like that before."

"Pretty lucky that he had a sister living two blocks away that owned a bike like that," Rocha said.

"Not really." Michael waived to the bartender for another round. "These types always have some BS story with a small grain of truth. It's a made up cover in case someone answers the door when they knock. If it hadn't been the bike, it would have been something else."

What Michael didn't say was that he'd set a trap for the prosecution. Had he emphasized the bike rather than just have Hayes mention it in his direct testimony, it wouldn't have been a powerful issue. What most DAs loved to do when they got a witness on the stand that they absolutely knew was lying, was to take them apart. Michael was counting on the fact that the bicycle would be the bait Rocha would seize upon in his cross examination. Set up by a question from Michael, Hayes mentioned that when he saw the bike on the back porch, he was sure it was the right house and that it was okay to go inside to find the money his grandmother was holding for him. That's why he was searching the hutch, and if he hadn't been drinking heavily, he would have realized he was in the wrong house. Rocha immediately jumped on the information. Before his cross-examination was over, Detective Johnson was dispatched to call a black and white to prove there was no such house, or identical bicycle. Michael let him pound away at Hayes without objection. It was during the re-direct that he got to the specifics of the house, Hayes' sister and the bicycle, making Rocha very uneasy. Then as a final step and pivotal part of the case, Michael called Detective Johnson to the stand. When the detective admitted that Hayes had been telling the truth that his sister did live two blocks away, Rocha realized he'd fallen into the trap.

JIMMY YEE'S ISLAND & LATITUDE 20 NIGHTCLUB, LINCOLN VILLAGE SHOPPING CENTER, STOCKTON, CALIFORNIA
SOMETIME AFTER 9:00 P.M. SAME DAY.

Borelli was still growling at Michael, when they entered the dark, Polynesian decorated landmark club. Trader Vic's in San Francisco had nothing on this place.

"Do you really think this is a good idea?" Borelli asked for the tenth time since Michael had picked him up at his one hundred dollar a month flat on Center Street.

"Yes." Michael waived at Frankie Fanelli, a local Italian crooner legend, singing in the background.

"Well, I sure as hell don't. I'm hungry and I can't afford this place," Borelli said as they made their way to the bar.

"Relax. We'll only be here fifteen minutes. Then we'll meet my brother for dinner at Arroyo's."

"How you doin', Mike?" the owner, Jimmy Yee asked before they reached the bar. "We haven't seen you in a while. Your ol' man said you're doing good. Although he'd like you to take a job with Metro," Yee added, pumping Michael's hand. "First drink's on me." He turned to Borelli. "Who's your friend?"

"My pal AJ Borelli from Vallejo," Michael replied.

"You friend of Mr. Mike, you friend of Jimmy Yee," he continued to Borelli. "I have Gem fix you up with my special Mai-Tais."

"Oh, Hell," Gem said as Michael took his seat.

Borelli immediately recognized Elizabeth Giamanti as juror number four.

"You two know each other?" Yee asked.

The barmaid sighed. "Not really."

"Better than she thinks," Michael added.

"I got no idea what's going on, and I don't care," Yee continued. "Gem. Michael is son of Big John Moretti. You know him. That make Michael special friend. You give him and his buddy special Mai-Tais. The good rum. I leave you boys in good hands. Have fun."

"I hear you already met AJ," Michael said as Yee walked away. She stood a little over five feet tall and had deep close set almond shaped piercing eyes that twinkled constantly, always alert. Her nose held a slight roman tilt at the end and fit perfectly with her full lips in her Mediterranean shaped face.

"We shared a special moment," Gem replied, mixing the drinks. "It was moving for me as well," Borelli said, looking at his watch.

Gem placed their drinks on the bar. "You've already wasted a day and a half of my time. Why do you have to come here and bust my chops?"

Michael took a sip of his drink. "To ask you a question. Jesus! What's in this? Grain alcohol?"

"What difference does it make? It's free isn't it?"

"I need to know if I was right. Why did you change your vote from guilty to not guilty?"

Gem ignored the question. "How could you be Big John's kid?" she asked instead.

"You know him?"

"Just that he sells booze to this place, and my Pop knows him."

"He raised me."

"For how long?"

"Ten years."

"What about the rest of time? Who raised you then?"

"Wolves," Michael replied. "Now answer the question."

While Borelli sucked on a large slice of pineapple, Gem wiped the bar. "You tell me. Maybe it was your boyish charm."

"In the end, I think you didn't give enough of a shit to be late for work," Michael said loudly, over Fanelli's raucous rendition of 'in the wee small hours of the morning.'

"Why don't you guys drink up and take a hike." Gem turned away and moved to the other end of the bar.

"Are we done?" Borelli asked.

Michael drained his glass. "Yep."

But before he could stand, an arm rested on his shoulder.

"Hi, Mike," Fanelli said. "It's good to see you."

Michael gave the singer a big hug and kiss on the cheek. "How you doin', Frankie?"

"You know how it is. Still trying to break into the big time. I'm opening for Jack Benny at the Lake next month. Can I buy you a drink?"

"Thanks anyway. Just leaving."

"You be sure to give my best to Big John," Fanelli continued.

"You know I will. By the way, no one does 'send in the clowns' like you, Frankie. See ya."

Arroyo's Restaurant, South Center Street, Stockton, California
Less than an hour later

The restaurant's Mexican style food could be found nowhere else in the Valley. A rough place in an even rougher part of town, it was owned and operated by a father and his sons, one of whom carried a .45 caliber automatic in a shoulder holster while he waited tables. With sparse furnishings and cement floors that could be hosed clean instead of sweeping, the food was great, and cops ate on the cuff after 10:00 p.m.

The place was full of undercover cops working narcotics as Michael and Borelli now waited in one of the green booths. A few minutes went by, before a huge bearded man, wearing a surplus army parka and a faded Cleveland Indians baseball cap, squeezed in next to Michael.

"What's up, Mikey?" he said, giving Michael a quick hug. "AJ," he nodded to Borelli.

"Not much, Paul," Michael replied. "You keepin' your head down and your hands off the merchandise?"

Paul Moretti grinned. "My head's always down. You know that. Let's eat."

"I hear you kicked Rocha's butt," he added after the food was served.

Michael shrugged, but didn't comment.

"When you goin' to decide to take that job in Metro? You know it won't be open long. And the lieutenant has it wired for you."

Borelli stopped chewing. "What job in Metro? What's this Metro job I keep hearing about tonight?"

"Metro wants its own lawyer, search warrants, criminal procedure advice. Shit like that," Moretti replied. "We have federal funding for it, and all the guys and the lieutenant want Mike. Hell, he got me and my partner through the sergeant's exam."

"When were you going to share this little bit of news?" Borelli asked Michael.

Michael shrugged. "It's just something that came up recently. I haven't made a decision yet."

"The boss will never allow it. You going over to the narcs. You know that," Borelli continued.

"What do you mean? That fag boss of his?" Moretti responded. "He's got no say in this. This's a federal one year grant."

"One year?" Borelli faced Michael. "What you going to do after that?"

"I thought you wanted to go to Vallejo?"

"You know, this could work," Borelli said, after a few minutes of eating in silence. "That crap could look great on a resume, when we go after that Vallejo Public Defender overflow contract I'm dreaming' up. One year, huh?"

"Well, the old man wants you in Metro," Moretti said. "And he wants you at the house for dinner tomorrow night. Capisce?"

"Capito," Michael replied.

Short for Metropolitan Narcotics Unit, Metro was an undercover drug unit comprised of both sheriffs and city police officers under the command of City Police Lieutenant, Jimmy Flanagan. Most of the unit were experienced detectives, working undercover and independently of any other law enforcement agency. They were fairly secretive in what they did and how they did it. Because the unit was mostly comprised of top case makers, their abilities to make arrests began to clash with the ever changing and expanding procedural rights being afforded the accused. Their skill in making arrests relied heavily on information from reliable confidential informants and "hunches" that all good cops operated on, and learned to trust.

Unfortunately, recent federal and state supreme court decisions no longer allowed veteran police officers to detain and search suspects on the basis of "hunches." Try as they might, the cops were always a beat behind the exploding case law coming out weekly, describing more and more circumstances under which police were taking unfair advantage of suspects. Even more troubling was maintaining the confidentiality of their "CRIs" or "snitches." The theory was that you let the "little fish" go if he gave up a bigger fish.

All of this was adding up to Metro needing their own trusted hotshot to handle the process. And who better than the brother of one of their own. Someone who had a reputation for kicking the crap out of them on a regular basis.

"When does the decision get made?" Borelli asked.

"Sooner the better," Moretti replied, watching a Mexican head from the bathroom, immediately followed by a nervous looking white guy.

"Mike has to turn in an application," he continued. "Which he has yet to do."

"Who makes this decision?"

"That's the best part. The sheriff and chief of police. And that's wired, because the chief will defer to the lieutenant. He already wants Mike."

"What about the sheriff?"

"What about him? Mike hasn't pissed him off. Have you, Mike?

"What about that little fracas in the holding cell, last summer?" Borelli asked before Michael could reply.

The all out brawl had been between eleven prisoners waiting to be arraigned on felony charges, and Michael, who was locked alone with them in the second floor holding cell. By the time the deputy sheriff eventually arrived, Michael had a swollen cut eye, that later took three stitches to close, torn clothes and cracked ribs. He had been very fortunate that four of the prisoners were tough east-siders who owed Hunter. The other prisoners faired even worse. Those who were still ambulatory, went to court, along with their bruised and battered public defender. The incident made the front page of the Stockton Record, and to make matters worse, Michael called Sheriff John Lonigan and took full blame, exonerating the absent deputy who should never have let Mike in the cell in the first place, let alone leave him alone, which made Hawthorne even madder. It was lucky for all concerned that no one sued.

"Naw, Lonigan loves a stand-up guy," Moretti said now. "Mike took the heat like a man. Case closed."

Suddenly, the men's room door flew open, and the

Mexican, who Moretti had watched earlier, came rushing out, screaming that he'd just been robbed. Hot on his heels, was the white guy, this time with a gun in his hand. Borelli could only think that trying to rob a guy in a bathroom with better bars than the county jail was his first mistake. His second was doing it in a restaurant full of cops. In an instant, the air was full of "freeze, asshole!" as a dozen hammers clicked on service revolvers. Easily wrestled to the floor, the perpetrator was kicked in the ribs for good measure by the waiter with the .45 who had to be restrained from shooting the man in the head.

As Borelli viewed the scene, he said, "I think we should call it a day."

"Make sure you put our names in the report," Michael told Moretti. "So we can conflict out when they arraign this asshole."

Moretti gave him a hug. "See you tomorrow. And bring AJ. I think the folks like him better than us."

Chapter 2

On his first official day at work Joe Larsen found himself perched on an old padded stool between Snake Sanderson and AJ Borelli in Emma's Coffee Shop across the street from the south entrance to the county courthouse after having been handed off by Hawthorne's secretary, a youthful blond named Alice Benson.

Emma's was the original hole-in-the-wall 1940s coffee shop with no tables and about 15 stools. It was also the gathering place before court each morning. Everyone but Hunter, whom he had just met, was dressed for court. Hunter was wearing a faded San Francisco Giants sweatshirt and Levis.

"You going to let 'New Guy' handle anything, Snake?" asked AJ Borelli over coffee.

"One or two," said Snake taking a bite of his dry toast.

"How can you eat that crap?" asked Hunter.

"Because I'm not a human garbage can like you. I swear those hot cakes of yours are floating in syrup."

"I bet you'd eat them if they were drenched in beer," replied Hunter.

"I wish they'd serve beer here. I could go for one about now," Snake said wistfully.

"At 8:30 in the morning?" asked Joe unable to suppress his surprise.

"What's wrong with that? Wait until you've been here a month or two. Besides, Hunter, I don't know what you're talkin' about. You'll be in the bailiff's room in another 20 minutes drinking that cheap apricot brandy." Snake was referring to the marshal's break room on the second floor of the courthouse. Thanks largely to AJ, he and Hunter kept a bottle of apricot brandy in a locker reserved for them.

Besides managing the office's city league softball team, AJ organized virtually every activity and debacle the boys on the third floor participated in willingly or not.

It was AJ who decided who was given which office on the third floor. More specifically, who was allowed on the third floor, ever. Not even Hawthorne violated this unwritten rule. Where his power came from, no one knew or even questioned. It was just always there from the first.

"Speaking of beer," said Snake Sanderson, "when are we going to get our refrigerator so we can start saving some money?"

"Today," said Hunter, not looking up from the newspaper he was reading. "Has anyone seen the article about the school teacher that's missing?"

"What school teacher?" asked AJ looking over his shoulder.

"Kindergarten teacher at Lincoln Elementary. Graduated 3 years after me, but I can't place her."

"What do you think?" asked AJ.

"Elementary teachers don't just turn up missing in this town, is what I think," said Hunter.

<hr>

Monday, November 13ᵗʰ, 3 p.m., Third Floor

To Joe Larsen, the day had flown by. Morning court had lasted an hour and a half where he and Snake had handled, and mostly continued, some 31 misdemeanor cases. Snake even let him continue a couple of cases after introducing him to the judge. His first impression was that they were representing 31 people who were no strangers to the court and guilty as charged.

Larsen thought most of them were stupid and anti-social, although certainly not all of them. The prostitutes were his immediate favorites and seemed generally smarter, with fairly decent senses of humor. Each had several charges pending, all either prostitution or drug related 'beefs' as Snake referred to them. Using a variety of excuses, Snake got them all continued to some Monday in the future. This particular court, one of the busiest, was held three days a week, manned by different public defenders. When cases were continued, they were continued to that public defender's day of the week for continuity. And that was Snake's philosophy Joe learned. Continuances. Snake believed in 'stacking' cases. Criminals were going to commit more crimes and unless they were snitches, they were going to get 'popped' again by law enforcement and new charges would be piled on. In the case of prostitutes, their pimps would bail them out to keep them working and charge loan shark rates for the bail money. They had to stay on the streets and keep doing business to pay for it all.

Snake Sanderson, partly because it fit his procrastinating personality, was the king of continuances. He continued everything until he got the right deal. In the case of the prostitutes, that meant "stacking" 5 or 10 cases together and finally pleading them out to six months county jail time or better yet, 90 days and a drug program when he caught a DA and a judge in the right mood.

Snake had become a courthouse legend for continuances with one particular armed robbery committed by three defendants where he had the "heavy," (the mastermind), and two appointed street counsel had the other two guys. This had happened two years before and one of the perps had immediately made a deal to testify and plead to a light state prison sentence and was already released having served his time. The other one had been tried and convicted and was serving a heavy prison sentence. That was a year and a half ago. Snake's guy had yet to be tried after seven continuances of the jury trial.

Larsen thought that the straight under the influence of heroin defendants were the worst. They had constantly tugged at Snake's sleeve while he tried to speak to the judge on their behalf.

"Check this out," one said. "They didn't read me my rights."

"You didn't confess, idiot," Snake snapped at them. "It doesn't matter."

"Hey man, I got rights."

One even yelled at the judge that he wanted Snake fired. The judge, bored and disgusted, replied, "You didn't hire him, so you can't fire him."

Joe Larsen wondered how he would ever learn to handle these people.

"Where they stickin' you tomorrow New Guy?" asked AJ sitting in the same seat as he had been the previous Friday when Joe had met him on the third floor.

"The library," replied Joe.

Snake was again sitting behind his desk, but this time

he was playing chess with Hunter.

"Checkmate," said Snake.

"Shit," said Hunter.

"How many in a row is that?" asked AJ, without looking up from the orange felony file he was reading.

Snake opened a drawer and made a mark on a pad and announced, "Let's see, carry the one, uh, 178."

"Jesus Hunter, do you even understand the basic concepts of that game?" asked AJ.

"Anybody meet 'New Girl'?" asked Hunter, ignoring AJ.

"Yeah, I met her," said AJ. "Strictly second floor material." Because AJ made up the floor assignments, it was already set in stone.

He was referring to Sybil Waxman, who'd made the rounds with Hawthorne that morning and had been started with Stanley Latchman in felony arraignments in the afternoon.

"What's she look like?" asked Hunter, who'd spent the early afternoon in "crazy court" right after lunch.

"She's not your type, Mike," answered AJ.

"Everyone's his type," said Snake, setting the chess pieces up again.

"Trust me," said AJ, "not this one."

And, just like that, she walked in, curly red hair, freckles, and all. "Hi, I'm Sybil Waxman," she said walking around the room shaking hands with everyone except AJ, whom she had already met.

"I graduated from Boalt Hall, Berkeley last June; sixth in my class, and I just passed the bar on my first try and this is my first job. I'm looking for Michael Hunter."

"Right there New Girl," AJ said, gesturing to Hunter.

"I don't appreciate being called New Girl," snapped

Waxman glaring at AJ.

"Michael," she said addressing Hunter, "can I call you Michael?"

"No," said Hunter, stopping her in her tracks.

"I thought that was your name?" she stated confused.

"No, you can't call me Michael. I don't like it when you say it. Hunter will do. What can I do for you?"

"Well, the word is that you're the big trial poo-bah around here and that's exactly what I want to be. The best damned trial lawyer in this place. So I thought, in my spare time, I could job shadow you."

"I don't even know what that means," said Hunter.

"What school did you go to?" asked Sybil, trying to recover the high ground in the conversation.

"Which time?" replied Hunter. "I was thrown out of two colleges and one law school."

"For what?" Waxman asked amazed.

"Mostly for not showing up," said AJ.

"I don't get it," she said more confused than ever.

"And you never will," said AJ. "Listen, New Girl. We have very few rules here. Don't urinate in the halls, don't rat anyone out, and don't come on the third floor unless you live here or are invited. We actually insist on that last one as opposed to the other two. So if you will excuse us, we have a little business we need to attend to," he said, getting up and walking her to the door.

When she left, AJ turned around and said, "Now boys, about that refrigerator."

Wednesday, November 15th, 2 p.m.

"How you doin' Beau," said Michael Hunter strolling into the law library two days later carrying an orange file.

Beaumont "Merlin" Henderson looked up from the stack of books in front him, grinned, and asked, "Slumming Hunter?"

"Just looking for loopholes," answered Hunter dropping the file in front of Merlin. "How's Joe working out?" he asked nodding towards Larsen sitting at one of the long tables working.

"He's still working on the motion I gave him yesterday. You know how it is."

Hunter did indeed know how it was. One of the very few things he did like about Bradley Hawthorne was how he made every new attorney do about six months in the law library. No matter which law school you came out of, you had learned nothing about high volume, pressure crunching, criminal procedure, motion, writ, and appellate work.

The San Joaquin County Public Defender's office was reportedly the only one in the State doing its own appellate and writ work to the District Court of Appeals and the California Supreme Court.

Hunter also knew that for the first month in the library, you were useless. It was like learning to speed read. At first you just couldn't do anything right. You were sure that you weren't cut out for this type of work. It would take you a week to write one motion when Merlin cranked one out about every couple of hours.

"What do you got?" Merlin asked, picking up the file. "Possession for sale."

"Take a look at the police report and search warrant for me and read my notes. Something stinks," said Michael.

"What's got you worked up Mike?"

"This crankster swears up and down that two narcs serving the warrant weren't even looking for drugs," said Michael.

"What were they looking for?"

"Stolen machine drawings, which he says they found and took. But there's no mention of them in the return of warrant; and he's not charged with stealing them."

The return of warrant had to list all items seized and was usually filled out by the officers doing the searching. "Why do you believe this guy?" asked Merlin knowing Hunter almost never believed anyone.

"Three things," said Michael. "First, I know this guy and he's a thief, a good one. He is a crankster, not a manufacturer."

Merlin nodded. He knew what Michael knew. Cranksters were meth-amphetamine abusers. In this area, they were mainly located in East Stockton and were considered poor-white trash. You could drive around the area in the middle of the night and tell who the cranksters were because they would be the ones working on their cars at 3 o'clock in the morning all speeded up. Also, crank was manufactured cheaply in crude labs that could be set up in the kitchen or bathroom of any house. The problem was that it stunk to high heaven with a peculiar smell that travelled a half mile when the wind was right. Any law enforcement officer with half a brain only had to follow his nose. Therefore, manufacturers and dealers usually operated way out in the country in rental farm shacks with no one around.

"Second," said Michael, "this guy's got nothing on his sheet that suggests dealing. Third," he continued, "there's no property listed on the return, just a user's amount of drugs. So the CRI is bogus."

"Interesting," said Merlin, thinking. "Only way around

this is the CRI, you know that." If he's bogus, they can't cough him up. They'll have to dismiss. I'll take a look."

"Thanks buddy," Hunter said. To Joe, he said, "Keep punching. It gets better. Besides, you won't be worth a damn around here unless you can issue spot." "Issue spotting" was the best by-product of working in the library. After a while, you could just smell a procedure issue in a police report, even the subtle ones.

Chapter 3

Emma's Coffee Shop had only been open a couple of minutes and the coffee wasn't ready yet as Hunter and Alice Benson sat down on side-by-side stools, their morning ritual. Alice was 25 and pleasant to look at with a round face and freckles. She was also quiet and generally stayed in the background. Popular and outwardly polite to everyone, she formed few observable attachments. But everyone knew that she was the one person in the office that knew where every skeleton was buried. What many did not know was that she was fanatically loyal to Hunter. On this morning, she was delivering a storm warning.

"We have a couple of little problems brewing," she said quietly.

"You worry too much," Hunter said, giving her arm a squeeze.

"That's my job," she smiled.

"Well, what's up?"

"That little stunt the boys pulled the other day, bringing that refrigerator into the office didn't go over so well."

"What's the big deal? They stuck it in Rothman's closet."

"You can't be serious," she said scowling at Hunter. "They were drunk and they stole a dolly from Goodwill where they bought the damn thing. Of course, they didn't ask anyone's permission to bring it into the office which they wouldn't have gotten in the first place."

"They were going to take the dolly back," said Hunter defensively. "And, it was pretty chicken-shit of Goodwill not to loan it to them in the first place, because they had to push it six blocks," he added.

"Well returning it wasn't the problem, was it?" she said. "Since the nice police officer brought it back in the trunk of his patrol car."

"Ah, that was just Nickerson. He wouldn't make any trouble."

"No, but Hawthorne's toady, Litchfield, saw the whole thing and ratted you guys out."

"Me?" Hunter said with exasperation. "I wasn't even there. I was out seeing an informant."

"You think that matters? Hawthorne's pinning it all on you. Anyway, there's an all hands meeting in the library at 3 today. Don't miss it."

"You're just a little ray of sunshine this morning," Hunter said, going behind the counter and pouring himself and Alice a cup of coffee. "Anything else?"

"As a matter of fact, yes. The County car. I can't keep covering for you on this."

"Sure you can," said Hunter, giving her a pat.

They were both referring to the Ford Galaxy that Hunter had been driving for the last two months. San Joaquin County had its own motor pool of cars, most of them with County emblems on the side, stabled in a County garage and available for daily check out to County employees on official County business. Most of the cars were small and featureless, and the check-out process was time consuming. Two months previous, Hunter had gotten his hands on a nice Ford Galaxy with no emblem and had never taken it back.

"You got to take it back. It needs servicing. They're actually asking for the boss now when they call," she said. "You have to take this seriously."

"Look Al," Hunter said, turning toward her on the stool, serious for a moment. "You know Hawthorne has given me every shit detail, including a full felony trial schedule. I've got 'crazy court,' Manteca, and morning juvie when I'm not in Manteca. You know Judge Adams wants me out in Manteca at 7:30 and the garage doesn't even open until 7. No way I can make it."

"It's your own fault, and you know it," Alice replied sternly. "Maggie Adams is drunk in a bar by 3 o'clock every afternoon and you've got her court running like a Swiss watch. She's done by 10, thanks to you."

"What can I do about it?" Hunter said, putting up his hands.

"Stop showing up at 7:30. You know the boss doesn't want you to do it. Court is supposed to start at 9. Half the people around here think you've got something going with her anyway."

"You, too?" he smiled.

"I don't know Mike. You're not the most discriminating person I've ever met when it comes to the ladies. And Judge Adams can't stand anyone other than you and AJ. Boss only sent you out there because he was sure she'd hate you. Now that's backfired on him and he's just lookin' for excuses to nail you. Why do you have to piss him off all the time?" she asked.

"Because he's a hack. He's never tried a case in his life. All he cares about is making the office bigger."

"Grow up Mike," Alice replied turning back to her coffee, clearly irritated.

Thursday, November 16ᵀᴴ, 1 p.m.

They were walking back to the office from the Catholic Church's gym on Washington Street, two blocks away from the office, after the noon basketball game. Snake and Hunter were having their usual political argument over government's role in the everyday lives of its citizens.

"How long have you and Hunter known each other?" Larsen asked AJ as they walked along.

"We started two weeks apart. Hunter first," answered AJ. "But he hated my guts at first."

"You're kidding. Why?" asked a surprised Larsen.

"Because he was a runt, that's why," Hunter butted into the conversation.

AJ went on to tell the story of their first meeting. The office had five new positions in 1970 and Hunter and Snake had just been hired and started in the law library. They had exacted a promise from Hawthorne that he would let them sit in on new attorney interviews, but it hadn't happened. Instead, Hawthorne came in one day, announced that he had just hired a nice Italian boy from Vallejo who would be starting the next day and when the guys asked what sports he played, Hawthorne said that he played the accordion. When he showed up the next day looking like "Buster Brown" in a corduroy suit, they naturally hated him. According to AJ, his only introduction to the law library was to be thrown a motion to write and placed at the other end of the table and routinely ignored. Snake and Hunter couldn't remember him saying two words or changing suits for over a week, until one morning when AJ asked them what a particular sound was. The sound was the bells on top of the Bank of Stockton which banged out a song on the hour and then the time.

After they told him what it was, AJ went over to the phone, pulled out the phone book underneath it, and began thumbing through the pages while Hunter watched him through the corner of his eye. Finding what he was looking for, AJ dialed a number. When someone answered, he said "Gimme the person in charge of the bells."

After a few minutes, someone came on the line and AJ asked, "Are you the bell lady?"

Getting an affirmative reply that she was indeed in charge of the bells, AJ asked, "Do you take requests? I'd like to hear the Theme from Exodus and, let's see, Wipe Out by the Surfaris."

From that second on, he and Hunter were best pals. Two weeks later the phone rang in the library and the caller asked for Mr. Borelli. It was the bell lady asking if he was listening. She was playing the theme from Exodus, but said she was sorry that she was unable to find "that Wipe Out song."

Back on the third floor, Snake told Larsen about how a month later, AJ secured them their basketball gym. By then, AJ had become the organizer. They were playing in pick up basketball games on Monday nights at the local community college and getting killed by the black guys. It wasn't ideal, but it was all they had until the City softball leagues started in a few months with AJ's dad in Vallejo, Big Pete, of Big Pete's Auto Wreckers, promising to be the sponsor so long as AJ and Hunter played on his summer league team in Vallejo. Fair trade.

That year, a week before Easter, Hawthorne came into the library followed by a robed priest, whom he introduced as Father Emil from the local parish down the street. It seemed that the good father was having trouble with Sheriff Lonigan, who wouldn't let him use real wine at communion at Good Friday and Easter Sunday Masses in the chapel at the county jail. Hawthorne, himself a Catholic, wanted the boys to take an emergency writ to the superior court and obtain a court order allowing Father Emil permission to use wine in the services.

"No problem, Father," said Snake, who personally enjoyed sticking it to anything he perceived to be the unreasonable abuse of authority.

Hawthorne beamed at that response from his minions and turned away to usher Father Emil out of the library when AJ, who had said nothing to this point, said "Not so fast Padre."

Everyone froze. Father Emil turned toward him with a dumbfounded look on his face and asked, "What??"

"You have a gym at that church, don't you?"

"Yes, we do," said the father unable to connect the dots.

"Basketball hoops?" asked AJ.

"Yes, I think so, but it's been closed and locked for some time. We don't have a school there anymore."

"That's OK with us," said AJ. "Here's the deal. All the writs you need and anything else legal, so long as we get the gym at lunchtime."

"It doesn't have hot water in the showers," said the priest.

"We'll make do."

Hawthorne looked deflated. Hunter just shook his head in disbelief at his new friend.

After the "Bell Lady," it would be impossible to say

without interviewing the players themselves, which one latched onto the other. For Michael Hunter's part, he would have said, if asked, that he considered AJ Borelli to be the friendliest, most imaginative and soft-hearted person he'd ever met. Also, he was never boring.

AJ Borelli, for his part, knew the genuine goods when he saw it. As flawed as he was, Michael Hunter was the goods in his estimation. Some Chinese philosopher called it ying and yang. Whatever, they were mirror images of each other.

From the day the two of them got together, AJ had their future mapped out. Short term and long term. Short term, it was to have as much fun as humanly possible while paying their dues, learning the ropes, and building up reputations. And fun they had. A weekend never passed without something cookin—a Giants game, 49er game, out of town women.

With school, Hunter had basically been gone for seven years. He knew very few unattached local women anymore. AJ was strictly an out-of-towner from Vallejo by way of San Francisco, where he went to law school, so they would take turns setting each other up in their former haunts. These were the free love, birth control pill seventies, but still old fashioned enough that a guy with a bar card was a prospect for most single women that couldn't be ignored. Never a dull moment. The courthouse was another matter.

From the first day AJ walked into muni court in an old sport coat, and mis-matched casual khakis, treating himself like he was a green as grass idiot and everyone else like they were special people who held the secrets of the holy grail, he had become the darling of the place. There was something about his style and ease with the clients and the judges that set him apart from most everyone else. So, it was only natural, that Dusty would let him into the bailiff's poker game.

Dusty was Mickey Rhodes, known as Dusty since the first grade. From the toughest part of the white Oakie eastside of Stockton, Dusty was one of the hardest cases that had come out of there to make something of himself. If the courthouse was quasi-military in its organizational structure, then Dusty was its top kick first sergeant.

There probably weren't ten guys from the eastside that ever held a golf club in their hands, except to use as a weapon, but Dusty was not only one of the ten, he was a 2 handicapper. With his buzz-cut Marine DI haircut, which was only natural because he had been a Marine Drill Instructor before becoming a bailiff, he was in charge of Judge Goodwin's courtroom and because the judge was a golf fanatic, Dusty kept his clubs in the trunk of the judge's Mercedes and the two were inseparable, and almost always on the golf course when they weren't in court.

If a poll had been taken, you couldn't have found more than a handful of attorneys who could recall a personal comment to them from Dusty. Lawyers to him were vermin, low notches on the food chain of the ecosystem he was in charge of to see that it remained in balance. And Dusty knew everything that went on in his area of the courthouse; how every courtroom worked, its idiosyncrasies, and how the various juries that were out were deliberating.

Prosecutors never even thought to ask Dusty or one of the other bailiffs which way the jury was leaning. They would have deemed that completely improper. Probably was. However, no harm, no foul AJ figured. Pals were pals and you always helped out a pal.

From day one, Dusty and AJ spoke the same language and became buddies. All Dusty had to hear was that AJ was a 49er fan and that his old man ran a wrecking yard in

Vallejo. Dusty was also a car bug.

Most lawyers are people who are keenly aware of where they fit on the social strata. Listen to any personal conversation between 2 or 3 of them and you would find they spend the entire time trying to one up each other. Tell a lawyer that you went to San Francisco, and saw a hot show, and he'd ask you where you sat and manage to slip into the conversation that he'd already seen it and had better seats. It was in the blood. They didn't even know that they were doing it. And if you were not a lawyer, as far as they were concerned, you were just talked down to. You were there to serve them. They were lawyers and you weren't.

AJ not only was not afflicted with that disease, he couldn't stand people who were. He even defined it. He once told Hunter that it was the "superior group syndrome." He looked down on no one that wasn't pompous and despised you if you were. But, it was even more than that. He was a natural empathizer. If you were hurting or sensitive to something, so was he. And it wasn't phony. It oozed out of his pores. Everyone was comfortable with him - blacks, homosexuals, Mexicans, Oakies, you name it.

The first time Hunter introduced him at a Moretti family dinner, he became a member of the family within the hour. By the end of the meal, he and the entire family were all agreeing that Michael Hunter was a cross that they all had to bear, but what were you gonna do? Before he left, AJ was loaded down with leftovers and invited to the daily men's lunch at Big John's sister, Carmel's house on Union Street, with or without Michael. Everyone was at ease around him. The room lit up when he walked in, because fun had finally arrived and he could get away with murder.

While some people are instigators of outrageous behavior and never actually get the blame themselves, AJ could dream it up, fire it up, and immerse himself in it, always slipping the consequences with the instinct of a skilled matador avoiding the horns of a half ton of charging bull at the last millisecond.

AJ knew something was going on behind the closed door to the bailiff's break room and the fact that no outsider had ever breached that sanctum was irresistible. He began pestering Dusty immediately to just let him see the inside. What was the harm? Dusty had never been asked for just a tour and so was thrown off his guard. AJ was an alright guy and so he took him inside for a look see.

The room itself, with its lockers surrounding three sides of its smokey confines, was nothing special. It was the green-felted, octagonal-shaped mahogany table sitting in the middle with its eight cushy red padded leather chairs that drew the attention. Stacks of money, cards, and ash trays were strewn on the table. Some in front of the four bailiffs currently playing and some in front of empty seats waiting for the return of the regulars presently occupied elsewhere.

"This table has to be regulation," said AJ, without a clue as to what he was talking about.

"Straight from Harold's Club in Reno," said Dusty Rhodes proudly. "A buddy of mine up there got it for me when me and the judge played in their pro-am last year."

"It's a beauty," said AJ admiringly.

"You play the game?"

"You bet," AJ responded lying through his teeth. "Of course, I can't get a game in this town."

"Too bad," said Dusty shaking his head.

"Of course, what it needs is an old hand painted naked lady chandelier hanging over the middle of it," said AJ. "The flourescent lighting in here stinks."

"That would be swell all right," said Dusty rubbing his

chin warily. "I wonder where a guy could get his hands on something like that?"

"In my old man's wrecking yard in Vallejo there's just what you need. Of course, it's been a fixture there for years."

"Uh, huh," muttered Dusty.

"But I don't know," said AJ scratching his head. "It sure was made for this place."

They stood there for a while lost in the idea.

"Say, don't you own that hot Camaro in the lot downstairs?" asked AJ.

"Yeah, that's mine. What about it?"

"Two-barrel, right?"

"Yeah," Dusty sighed.

"My old man just got in a wrecker that was impounded by the police and never claimed. He said it had a four-barrel carb on it. Same year Camaro as your's I think."

"Yeah?" said Dusty rising to the bait like some 20 pound Steelhead from the bottom of a deep hole in the river. "What's he want for it?"

"Gee, I don't know," said AJ rubbing the back of his curly black head. "I'd have to ask."

Moments passed where they both stood staring at the green felt table, Dusty picturing the only light in the room coming from the new chandelier hanging low above it.

"Maybe we could work something out," said AJ after a long pause.

"What do you got in mind?" asked Dusty without looking at him.

"Well, like I said," said AJ. "I'm looking for a game."

"I think we might be able to work something out. Of course, you'd have to keep it way down low."

"Of course. Goes without saying," said AJ.

"We got a deal then?" said Dusty sticking his hand out.

"Throw in a locker and we do," answered AJ.

"Done."

"Michael Hunter too?" asked AJ shaking hands.

"What?"

"We're partners."

"Jesus Christ," said Dusty pumping AJ's hand. "You're lucky I like you kid."

———— ◎ ————

They started winning muni court trials from the start, working on them together. Nights mostly. They had nothing better to do. Michael would script them, curving the facts to meet their needs with AJ trying more of the cases than him at first, loving being up there in front of the jury, them loving him more than they hated his client. From the outset, Michael complained that there was no budget in the office for expert witnesses and the fact that the office's investigators, except for Frankie Sanchez, were basically useless at even serving subpoenas.

It was AJ that came up with the idea of being each other's experts.

In one case, Michael was certain that the key witness in a drug possession couldn't possibly have gotten from the West Lane Bowling Alley to a park downtown to witness the drugs change hands in the time he said that he did.

"No problem," said AJ. "You're my expert. We'll have my old man certify that your speedometer is accurate and you can drive it and keep the time and I'll call you as my expert."

Thinking about it for a minute, Michael began to warm to the idea. "How we going to get your old man down here to testify that my speedometer is accurate?" he asked.

"Are you kiddin?" said AJ. "You think that new guy Rocha's going to object to my asking you if it's been certified? He's more confused than we are."

AJ won that trial. And so it went for a while. Hunter mostly working them up and AJ being the star of the show and refining the rough edges. He had an uncanny instinct on what regular jurors would buy and what they wouldn't. He didn't win very many, but more than his share. Then, for no particular reason, it bored him. Even Michael didn't notice it at first.

For his own part, Michael was growing daily, working on innovative trial techniques, like running his upcoming trials by the secretary pool and letting them critique his approaches and themes before actually picking a jury. When he couldn't find a witness or get an answer to a question, he started paying informants, which were nothing more than criminals who owed them for past acquittals and good deals. The money came out of his own pocket. But it wasn't much.

As for AJ, it wasn't that he lost complete interest in the job, he just refined it. He no longer cared about trying cases. What was the point? That wasn't his future. What he became was the best deal maker and fixer in the courthouse as far as criminal cases were concerned. He could work anything out and fast. He would get a new case to try and a week later it was dismissed or pled out. And no one could say he laid down. Most of his people got great deals. He just had too many irons in the fire to waste time. Deal makers make deals and that was 95 percent of lawyering anyway, he figured.

Chapter 4

All of the attorneys were seated or standing in the Public Defender's Law Library. Grouped according to floor, there had already been the usual banter between Latchman and David Rosen directed to AJ about the reason for them having to be there. They just glared at Hunter who stood at the back, nearest the door, with his arms folded looking bored. This went on for about ten minutes until Bradley Hawthorne rolled in followed by his second in command, Jack Fletcher, looking stern. It was immediately apparent that Hawthorne was barely in control of his emotions.

"Uh-oh," said James Harris out of the side of his mouth.

The Boss, flanked by his assistant, was just standing in front of the silenced room with his mouth clamped tight and his head nodding.

"Ladies and Gentlemen," he began scanning the room, "I have been the public defender for seven years. And, up until recently, I have always been very proud of this office. We have always been a team," he said, his voice beginning to crack.

This was clearly going to be a long lecture. Hawthorne raised his eyes and made eye contact with Michael Hunter, who had a slight trace of a smile on his lips as he leaned back against the door jamb.

"What we have now," he said raising his voice, "is a rift in this office." His voice broke as he gasped searching for a word that wouldn't come. He tried again, and when the words weren't there, he stormed out of the room with a startled Jack Fletcher in his wake.

"Rift?" asked Sybil Waxman. "What rift?"

"He meant the refrigerator," Litchtfield said to her annoyed at the brevity of the proceedings. He had been counting on Hawthorne laying the law down.

"I didn't know that was its name," Snake Sanderson said to AJ Borelli as they were getting up to leave.

The boys all headed for the third floor where they decided to hoist a few beers in case "rift" was to be evicted. Snake had taken the liberty of stocking up that morning with a couple of cases of Regal Select, his "call" beer, which was so cheap and obscure that it could only be found at Eddie's Liquor Store which boasted of carrying at least one of everything.

Everyone except Joe Larsen filed into Snake's office to work on their cases for the next day.

Joe had already left for the police department in hopes of meeting Sgt. Paul Moretti. Michael had set it up so that he would get a lesson on needle marks for a motion to suppress what he was working on. They were just getting comfortable, when in popped Sybil Waxman and demanded to know who was representing Paco and Sylvia Ramirez on their felony drug possession charges.

"Why?" asked Snake without looking up from the chess board.

"Because I was in court with them today when they were arraigned on possession of stolen property allegedly found in their car and I'm sure they are not guilty and are the victims of police harassment," she said tapping one foot nervously.

"I thought we went over the rules on third floor trespassing at our previous get together," said AJ without looking up from the file he was reading.

"Hold it, AJ," said Michael. "I'm always willing to be enlightened. It just so happens that I have those two unparalleled pieces of shit. What makes you so sure that they're not guilty this time?"

"Because they told me so, and also no one would be stupid enough to be in possession of stolen hand guns when they are out on bail and pending trial on possession charges," she said defiantly. "Besides, the "pigs" stopped them for no reason and searched them without a warrant or probable cause," she continued. "In fact, just what are you doing for these people, Mr. Hunter?" she finished almost spitting out the last words with her chin raised.

"You got all this at the arraignment?" Michael asked, ignoring the rudeness.

"No, they came in to see me like I told them to. They're downstairs right now and they're both so exhausted they can barely stay awake."

"Maybe you're right," said Hunter standing. "Maybe I haven't been paying enough attention to the Ramirezes. Let's check it out."

On the way down to the interview room where she had left the Ramirezes, Hunter asked over his shoulder, "were they in custody or out, when they were arraigned?"

"Out. Why?" asked Waxman feeling fairly smug with this second encounter with Hunter.

"Bail or OR?" he asked. (Hunter was referring to release on the defendants' own recognizance without having to post bail.)

"I don't know. Does it matter?"

He didn't answer, but walked into the first floor room where the Ramirezes were nodding off to sleep, a little drool coming out of the corner of Paco Ramirez's mouth as his chin bounced off of his chest. Hunter walked up to him and kicked one of his sprawled out legs. Paco jumped, startled at the force of the blow.

"What are you doing!" yelled Waxman. "Are you crazy?"

"Ah shit man," Ramirez said as he focused with half opened eyes on his attacker. "Shit Hunter, what you doin' here, man?" he drawled in accented English.

"You know better than to come in here like this Paco," Hunter said, ignoring Sybil Waxman completely while he moved close to Paco.

"You know how it is man," Paco said. "I'm just chipping."

"Bullshit. Let me see your arm," Hunter Said.

"Oh, come on man," Paco whined.

"Now Paco."

Reluctantly Paco slowly and clumsily rolled up his left sleeve. There were six fresh swollen elliptical marks and old railroad tracks all over lined veins on his inner elbow.

"What are we looking at here, Paco, $200 bucks a day?"

"We got to live man, but I'm cool right now," he mumbled.

"Are you kidding me?" said Michael. "Your pupils are in your pocket, dude," he said referring to Paco's fixed and pin-pointed pupils that were non-reactive to light and a major symptom that he was under the influence of heroin at that moment.

"Why'd you guys come over here and mess with this lady?" Hunter asked.

"She said she could help us. You ain't doing nothing. Metro's harassing us man."

"That's their job Paco. You bailed or OR'd on this new beef?"

"Bailed."

"How much?"

"20 each."

"Where'd you get it?"

"Syl's aunt. Put up her house," Paco said nodding to his wife who was now sound asleep.

"What's with the guns?" asked Michael. "You graduating?"

"No man, I'm still a burglar and a pimp, you know me. The guns were for a dude. He'd pay me double what the fence pays. He's robbing bars. Needs a new piece."

"You want to give him up?" asked Michael.

"For what?" asked Paco, now interested.

"It's time to package you and Sylvia up," said Hunter. "You're running out of options. Let me talk to Dewey Gunnart and my brother at Metro. Now get the hell out of here. I'll have Frankie drive you. I don't need you popped for DUI."

After they left, Sybil Waxman said, "I don't mean to be critical, but you didn't even ask them about the search issues."

Michael turned and stared at her for a minute before he spoke, trying to make up his mind whether to waste any time with her at all.

"First, the Ramirezes are searchable, with or without cause or warrant, as conditions of numerous probations on previous cases, so there are no search issues. Latchman should have told you that since you were in court with him and I guess he would have if you had asked him. Second, don't you ever again talk to a client about a case of mine without checking with me first. Third, don't call law enforcement officers 'pigs' anymore. It's rude, it makes you look stupider than you already are, and it will come back to haunt you big time if they hear about it. This isn't Spraoul Plaza, and you're not hanging out with Mario Savio and the rest of the free-speech movement. Are we done here?"

"I guess so," she said deflated. "You hate me, don't you?"

"Don't flatter yourself."

"Can I go with you when you talk to that guy for the Ramirezes?"

"Only if you keep your mouth completely shut."

"It's a deal," she said smiling.

———◦《●》◦———

Joe Larsen arrived at the offices set aside for the Metropolitan Narcotics Unit at the Stockton Police Department in Downtown Stockton. The room was empty except for a gray-haired middle-aged man sitting behind a large metal desk that looked as if someone had literally dumped several large trash bins of paper and periodicals on top of it in the recent past. Joe thought a body could be under all that junk and no one would know until it stunk. The man rose up and walked briskly around the desk towards him. He moved lightly on his feet and carried himself like a fighter. He was wearing a white long-sleeved shirt with the sleeves neatly rolled up to the elbows, his collar opened and gray tie pulled down until the knot hung about the middle of his chest.

He extended his hand and said, "You must be Joe Larsen."

"Yes sir," said Joe. "I'm here to see Sgt. Moretti."

"Call me Jimmy," said Lieutenant James "Jimmy" Flanagan smiling. "Paul's not here. They're all out doing something that came up rather suddenly," he added vaguely.

"Will I do?" Jimmy asked.

"Sure."

"Good," he said clapping his hands together. "Let's get started."

For the next hour, Jimmy Flanagan showed Joe numerous pictures of drug marks and tracks of arrested suspects. He carefully explained all the various places that an addict could inject himself. Inside the elbow, where everyone has blood drawn was, of course, the most popular and most obvious. Most addicts began there and kept it up until the veins literally collapsed. Between the toes was also a popular option and much less obvious. The lieutenant explained the symptoms of being under the influence of heroin with its tell-tale fixed and pinpointed pupils. But most of all, Joe learned about marks left by the needles after a user injected himself. He was told how the mark left by a professional drawing blood or giving an injection appeared small and perfectly round and red. However, the mark from the "dirty" needle, with no alcohol wipe beforehand, appeared swollen, elongated, and elliptical-shaped with an almost tear-dropped look to it. When you looked at the two marks up close, they looked nothing alike. Since injection paraphernalia did not carry new or clean needles and no alcohol wipes, an addict's arm always had the elliptical swollen marks that oozed a clear serum for a short time after the injection. You could almost date the marks by looking at them closely.

Joe took copious notes and thanked Jimmy profusely when the lecture ended. As he was about to leave, Jimmy stopped him and said, "You know, other than Michael Hunter, you're the only criminal defense attorney who has ever come over here. That shows me something, so I'm going to give you a little advice that you didn't ask for."

Joe stood there in the middle of Metro with its myriad of desks, file cabinets, gun lockers, maps, and charts on the walls wondering what was to come from this little complicated man.

"I've done a little checking," said Flanagan, not a man to overstate a case. "And, I know your situation in Frisco is complicated. And, I know that although you probably haven't thought it through yet, you figured on doing a little time here in this jerk-water town and then heading back to the big city and the bright lights. Am I right so far?" he asked Joe, who was basically standing there open-mouthed thinking *who is this guy*?

To Joe, Flanagan was a throw-back to an old Alan Ladd or Humphrey Bogart movie from the 30's or 40's. Joe just nodded.

"So here's the deal," said Flanagan. "It's five-to-one against any of that happening. You're gonna' learn your trade good if you keep your nose clean and your eyes open. You're already getting and taking some good advice or you wouldn't be standing here listening to me rap."

"This is a connection kind of town, you'll see," he continued. "After you've made your share and learned enough, this is where you'll stay and make your money."

"Now, here's the good part I want you to listen to," he said, poking a finger into Joe's arm for emphasis. "You see this desk? A mess, right? But I can find anything I want on it–or not. You understand?"

"Yes sir," Joe answered, not really understanding, but enough afraid of this little police lieutenant not to want to admit it.

"Someday when some real money or something else really important is on the line, you'll come to see ol' Jimmy and need something in the way of information. Now, if you've been good people, then like I say, I can find pretty much anything on this desk or in this town. But, if you've been an asshole, well, then it probably never will show up, whatever you need."

"We understand each other?"

"I think so."

"Good," he said slapping Joe on the back. "You ever need anything, call me. Thanks for stopping by," Flanagan said walking him to the door.

Chapter 5

Harriet Lumpkin was exhausted. Her little sister, Janet, had not come home the night before and because she hadn't gotten home until after 11 p.m. from her night job as a security guard at GEMCO, she had hardly any sleep. Being tired was nothing new with two brothers and her little sister living with her. Both of her parents had been dead for years and Harriet could not remember when she hadn't held down two jobs, even in law school, as well as looking after her brothers and sister. She walked into the jury room of the fairly new municipal courthouse in Manteca, a town about 15 minutes south of Stockton on Highway 99, to meet with Michael Hunter, which she did before court every Monday and Friday. As usual, she hadn't looked at a file yet.

She was on her second cup of coffee when Michael Hunter breezed in. Obviously, a morning person she thought, as she eyed him up and down appraisingly.

"Already got your coffee for you Mike," she said trying to sound light , chirpy, and blond, none of which she was, "three sugars, lots of cream."

"How you doin' Rett, baby," Michael said, going around behind her and starting to massage her neck, which felt delicious to her. "You look like no sleep again."

"Janet didn't come home again," Harriet sighed.

"Damn it!" said Michael. "Put her ass in the hall. Let her

63

have a taste."

Michael was referring to Mary Graham Hall, not juvenile hall. Mary Graham Hall was where the dependent kids were housed if their parents or guardians couldn't or wouldn't care for them, or if they were abused physically or sexually.

"I can't do that, Mike, you know that," she said staring at her coffee.

"I know that, Rett," Michael said finishing the neck rub. "That's why I love ya."

Harriet Lumpkin was the Deputy District Attorney assigned to the Manteca Court. As such, she was in charge of all traffic, misdemeanors, and felonies until they went through preliminary hearing and were sent to the Superior Court in Stockton.

"Here's the good news," said Michael picking up the court calendar, "no in-custodies, no felony arraignments, and only ten continuances."

"Have you read them all?" she asked, weariness creeping into her voice.

"Sure. I don't have three kids at home with one of them on the lam," he answered. "Here's what I think. The deuces," he said referring to the drunk driving charges, "one's a .14 breath and you give me a Wreckless on that," he said meaning that she should reduce the charge to wreckless driving which carried a very reduced fine and no alcohol program.

"The other one is a .19 blood, and I'm pleading him to that."

The numbers referred to the percentage of alcohol that the defendant had in his blood at the time of arrest, or to be more accurate, at the time the test was taken. State law said .10 or more blood alcohol was a rebuttable presumption that you were under the influence of alcohol at the time you were driving.

While normally the DA wouldn't reduce a .14 breath test to wreckless, Michael was a recognized expert at beating breath tests and, therefore, a .14 was within his wreckless range. Harriet didn't say a word.

"We have a misdemeanor battery. The victim's his common-law and won't testify. Nothing serious. Dump that one," said Michael, looking at the file.

"OK."

"This next one's a piece of crap Okie-hype up on 11550," said Michael, referring to 11550 of the Health and Safety Code, under the influence of drugs, in this case heroin. "Offer 90 days and a drug program," he continued. "She won't take it, so I'll set if for trial and she'll pick something else up and we can stack it later."

"Not a 647f?" asked Harriet, referring to Section 647f of the Penal Code, which was basically the drunk in public section that carried a maximum of six months in the county jail and no minimum sentence. Weak under the influence cases were often plea bargained down to "f's" to avoid the 90-day minimums in jail.

"Naw," answered Michael. "You got a good case here. No search issues. Fresh marks, fixed pupils, etc. Don't drop it down."

And so it went until they had discussed everything. They were done by 8 a.m. and ready to meet with Judge Margaret Adams, 42, single, and very complex.

"Good morning your honor," Michael said walking into Judge Adams' chambers dressed impeccably in a camel-colored sport coat, brown slacks, yellow shirt, and green and brown stripped tie.

"Very stylish, Michael," Judge Adams beamed. She was wearing a very nice knit suit that Michael was sure was foreign and expensive. Her chambers were done exquisitely with Victorian antiques. Michael knew she loved order and beautiful things. This was her comfort zone. The persona she presented to the world. The rest was chaos.

"What do you have for me today?" she asked sitting down behind the 150-year old desk, putting on her stylish glasses which matched the barrettes in her short swept back brown hair.

"We'll be finished by 9, your Honor. A brief recess, then traffic court and we're out by 9:45."

"Good," she said organizing the court files for their pre-trial conferences before court started. "I'd like you to stay after court if you don't mind. I want to talk to you about what we discussed on Monday."

"Certainly, your Honor," he said.

⸺⸺◆⸺⸺

FRIDAY, NOVEMBER 17TH, 1 P.M.

Michael pulled the Ford Galaxy into a doctor's parking space at the auditorium of the Stockton State Hospital on California Street. He had a half hour to interview six patients before "crazy court," which was always held on the stage in the auditorium. As he got out of the car, a young man, dressed in pajamas, was standing on the sidewalk in front of a bed of ivy that ran along the front of the building.

"Count me off!" the man yelled to Hunter.

"Sure Dave," Hunter said recognizing him. "Swimmers take your mark!" Michael said loudly.

Pajama man moved forward with his arms swept back

behind him.

"Get set!" yelled Michael. Dave leaned farther out.

"Go!"

Pajama man leaped into the ivy and began "swimming" through the bed of vines, throwing up leaves and debris as he pulled himself forward until he reached the other side. As he did so, a little red sports car pulled into a doctor's spot next to the Galaxy and a large man wearing a white coat and name tag climbed out. He had flaming red bushy hair and beard with a tie-dyed t-shirt under the coat tucked into faded Levis. He was wearing old Mexican sandals. He watched pajama man climb out of the ivy and shake himself as if he was trying to get rid of the excess water before toweling off.

"That may be your personal best, Dave," said the red-haired man.

"You think so Dr. Barnes?" Dave beamed.

"Absolutely," the doctor said as Michael walked by him.

"Doctor," Michael said.

"Doctor," Dr. Barnes said frowning at the Galaxy parked in the doctor's parking space.

Thirty minutes later, court convened on the stage in the auditorium with Judge Harold Strickland presiding. The auditorium had old theater-style seats descending down to an actual curtained stage upon which was placed a wooden table with six chairs around it. The judge, clerk, court reporter, and deputy sheriff, and Judge Strickland's bailiff were already seated, having just arrived in the bailiff's sheriff's car as they did every Monday, Wednesday, and Friday at that time. In the front two rows were seated doctors and social workers, with various patient's relatives spread throughout the rest of the room.

The occasion was the mandatory writ hearings required by the L.P.S. statutes governing mental health patients. Ever since the book *One Flew Over the Cuckoo's Nest*, where the hero J. P. McMurphy was given a lobotomy he didn't need, legislators and special interest groups had gotten all riled up about the mentally ill and retarded being unfairly confined in state hospitals against their will. One of the aspects of the L.P.S. Act (Lanterman-Petris-Short Act) was that every patient that asked any health care professional working in the hospital to let them leave, was, in fact, filing a verbal writ of habeas corpus and had to be brought before a superior court judge, with a lawyer, within three court days for a hearing. The one saving grace for all of this was that the hearings could be brought only once every 90-days for each patient, and occasionally it actually did some good. Since most of these folks were not in any shape to be wandering around the courthouse, the court, in the form of Judge Strickland, came to them.

Judge Strickland was 62 years old, single, and very ambitious to be appointed to the Third District Court of Appeals in Sacramento. He fashioned himself as a legal scholar and he considered the municipal court appeals to superior court and the L.P.S. hearings his personal domain. For more than a year, Michael had been sentenced to that court as an unstated punishment for attitude and conduct unbecoming Hawthorne's code of office cannons. Truth be known, Michael wouldn't have missed it for the world, a fact he knew he needed to keep to himself. For the most part, he could relax and do the right thing and even have a little fun. Most of the clients, Michael had soon learned, were really very nuts and right where they belonged. Since the legal standard was the ability to care for yourself and the safety of others, you had to be very crazy or very disabled not to make that.

Michael found that most of them knew who they were,

but were vague on a lot of the other normal details of life, such as where they were, or what year it was, or where they would go if they got out. Occasionally, some were down right dangerous. Most of the time when the presenting doctor got to the danger part, Judge Strickland would stop him and make a finding that the patient needed to stay put. Once in a while, out of boredom Michael thought, the good judge would go on tilt. There was the time that the Chinese guy, Ching, who had tried to kill two or three people in the hospital had wanted to get out. Even Michael didn't fool around with this guy. He had the homicidal white shark-looking expressionless eyes with no emotion. The doc went through his litany and got to the part where the patient heard voices coming from the TV set.

"What?" asked Judge Strickland giving Michael a look that said *'hey do your job here.'*

The doctor repeated it and Strickland said, "What's so weird about that? I hear voices from my TV set all the time."

"Your Honor," Michael had said uneasily not liking the direction that this was heading.

"Let me question your client for you Mr. Hunter," the judge had said with a rebuking condescending tone. "Now, Mr. Ching, do you hear voices from anywhere other than the TV set?"

"No your Honor," Ching answered.

"You see there," said Strickland. "If that's all you have doctor, I'm inclined to grant the writ. He obviously is well oriented and seems docile enough on his medication."

"Your Honor," said Michael quietly. "Ask him if the set is turned on when he hears the voices."

Ching turned to Michael, irritated and said, "Of course the set isn't turned on. How could I hear what the voices tell me to do if the set was making a lot of noise?"

On this day, five of the six clients were routine. The sixth was a developmentally disabled or retarded, rather than mentally ill patient of about 25 years old. The California L.P.S. Act, and other code sections, basically defined someone as developmentally disabled if their IQ was 70 or below. Average was considered to be 100. In order to be confined to a state hospital, you had to be profoundly disabled and generally were wearing a helmet so you didn't hurt yourself. Number six that day was a pleasant young man named Ralph, who Michael could see clearly had some problems, but wasn't wearing a helmet and was dressed neatly and appropriately enough.

Michael asked him if he had dressed himself that day and Ralph said yes. When Michael asked him why he wanted to leave the hospital, Ralph responded that he didn't like it there and that he wanted to get a good job. With the developmentally disabled, doctors played a much smaller roll at the hearings. IQ was IQ. Medication wasn't generally an issue unless there were mental health overtones which wasn't the case here. Ralph's case was presented by a small Asian social worker named Julie Chen, dressed in a black female business suit. She had a nervous quick-speaking manner about her, and to Michael, she seemed unpleasant and devoid of a sense of humor. She was also very full of herself and her opinions, which was obvious from the way she matter-of-factly presented the case of why Ralph should remain hospitalized. He had no immediate family to take care of him and obviously couldn't live unsupervised, and was unemployable. "He would just get into trouble," Julie Chen said.

"What does that mean?" Ralph asked Michael with respect to the word "unemployable," in a somewhat inappropriate loud voice.

"You can't work," Michael said leaning over and whispering the answer to Ralph.

"I can so too!" said Ralph in a loud and indignant voice.

"What's going on?" asked Judge Strickland, stirring from his day dreaming and annoyed with the interruptions of Miss Chen's monotone dissertation.

"Ralph is taking umbrage at Miss Chen's opinion of his employability," said Michael. It was immediately clear that Miss Chen did not enjoy being contradicted, especially by Ralph.

"He can't work," she stated emphatically to the judge.

"I work now!" said Ralph.

"No you don't," Julie Chen scolded him.

"I do so too," Ralph shot back at her. This was getting everyone's attention, even the bailiff who mostly dozed with his eyes half closed in these sessions.

"Where do you work Ralph?" asked Michael.

"Here," answered Ralph.

"No you don't," said Julie Chen, clearly agitated that the process was heading away from her presentation.

"How do you know?" Michael asked her.

"Because any employment would go through me," she said.

"Have you tried to get him a job?" asked Michael.

"He's unemployable due to his disabilities. Have you even read his file?" she asked condescendingly. "I'm sorry, who are you?" she asked Michael.

Instead of answering her, Michael turned to Ralph and said, "Tell us about your work, Ralph."

"I clean toilets."

"Here at the hospital, you say?" asked Strickland.

"Yes."

"How long has this been going on?" asked the judge.

"I don't know time, but a long time," answered Ralph.

"I thought the hospital had janitors," asked the judge to everyone at the table.

"Of course they have janitors," Miss Chen chimed in. "This is all ridiculous," she added for emphasis.

"Do you get paid?" asked Michael.

"I get a dollar," Ralph said proudly.

"Who gives you this dollar?" asked Strickland leaning forward, paying closer attention now.

"John," said Ralph.

"Who's John?" asked the judge.

Michael could see that the bit was now firmly lodged in Strickland's mouth so he let him take over.

"John cleans things," answered Ralph. "He's my friend."

"And you help John?" asked the judge.

"He lets me do all the toilets," answered Ralph proudly.

"When do you do this?"

"Every night. I work at night."

"And he gives you a dollar?" asked the judge.

"Every night. I buy cigarettes at the canteen."

"And you knew nothing about this?" Strickland asked Julie Chen.

"How would I know?" she asked defensively.

"When was the last time you spoke with this patient?" the judge asked her with a touch of ice in his tone.

"I don't know," she stammered. "Let me see," she said fumbling through her file.

"When did you see this lady last?" the judge asked Ralph.

"I don't know her," Ralph said.

"You've never seen her before?"

"I never see her," he said.

Everyone was now staring at Julie Chen.

"Why do you think you could get a job?" Strickland asked him.

"Because I know no one likes to clean toilets. But I do. I do it good. Ask John. There's lots of toilets I could clean," he said.

The judge's clerk took a tissue from her purse and dabbed her eye. No one said a word. Finally, Judge Strickland turned to Julie Chen and said in a tone that could have frozen molten lava, "Miss Chen, you have exactly two weeks to find this patient a suitable place to live and a job he likes. That is a court order. You will be back in this court in two weeks with your supervisor and a progress report on this patient. And, if he is not happy and employed, I will place you in the county jail for contempt of this court order. Do you understand me young lady?"

"Yes Your Honor," she said looking down.

"And another thing, you and your supervisor will bring your complete case list of clients that you have at this hospital or any other facility within my jurisdiction, and all of the contact dates listed as to when you last saw your clients. And that list better be accurate."

And then to Ralph he said, "Sir, you will be leaving here very soon. Your writ is granted. The very best of luck to you."

Within a month, Julie Chen was terminated from her position with the San Joaquin County Social Services Department, primarily as a result of the handling of this particular situation. But there were other reasons.

Chapter 6

Sheriff detectives Clarence Williams and Elwood Carnes were Sheriff Lonigan's best and hand-picked men to head up the investigation of his missing niece, Elizabeth Van Houten, who had disappeared mysteriously in early November more than a week before.

Clarence Williams was a methodical black man, impeccably and conservatively dressed at all times and the only son of a school teacher mother and a retired Army sergeant. A graduate of San Jose State College with a degree in police science, he was a born homicide investigator, meticulous and thorough. His partner, since he'd hit plain clothes, had been the gregarious Southern Baptist, Elwood Carnes, from the east side. Elwood was from the school of hard knocks, who had risen through the ranks of the department through hard work and results rather than native talent. He knew everybody in town it seemed to Clarence, and there was no name or address he couldn't pull out of the massive rolodex that sat on his desk at the sheriff's department.

Lonigan had made it perfectly clear to both men that he wanted his niece found and that they were reporting directly to him. So far, they were stymied. The girl had vanished into thin air. At first, Clarence had likened the fiancé, Jerald Vanderland, a farm kid from the Lodi area, for foul play, but they had already interviewed him three times. Unless he was the world's best liar, he was genuinely distraught over the girl's disappearance, and besides, he had passed the polygraph that he had readily agreed to take.

Elwood figured her for a runaway, although he kept that theory to himself and Clarence. She vaguely fit the pattern. Too good for the fiancé and bored with the rut she was stuck in as a kindergarten teacher at Lincoln Elementary. But so far, not a single lead from other law enforcement agencies, including Mexico, had turned anything up. Also pointing away from that theory, was the fact that there had been no usage of her gas card or other credit cards since that weekend or any activity on her bank account.

When the call came in, both Clarence and Elwood were already resigned to the fact that she was probably dead. The call was from a pay phone near Lockeford, a town about ten miles east of Lodi and North of Stockton, still in San Joaquin County, near the Mokelumne River.

It was from a diving school instructor who had taken some students floating on the Mokelumne River in wetsuits as part of their training. At a bend in the river, the instructor had dove down into a deep hole to take a quick look at the big fish he knew usually held there, and had run smack dab into a Volkswagen with a body floating in it.

Carnes and Williams were in their unmarked car in less than a minute, heading for the scene, along with assorted sheriff's patrol vehicles, sheriff's divers, an ambulance, and a tow truck.

By noon, the vehicle had been fished out and pulled up on the bank for inspection. The doors were opened and water gushed out onto the ground along with the partially clad, badly decomposed body of an unrecognizable female, with what looked like a bullet hole in her head.

One look at the license plate and the detectives knew

the identity of the victim. They took a look around trying not to touch too much, although with that much time in the water, it wouldn't really matter. Carnes found the purse in the back seat, but no wallet or identification in it or anywhere else.

"Impound the car and have the evidence guys go over it with a fine tooth comb," Clarence Williams told the uniformed officer heading up the towing of the vehicle.

"Look at this," said Carnes to his partner. "It's been in an accident. I don't remember anything about the VW being smashed up."

"No, and look at the paint transfers. Have a piece sent to the Department of Justice (or DOJ for short), for analysis," said Williams."

"You better radio in and let Lonigan know," said Carnes. "Someone's going to have to tell the family and it's his call. But we need info on the accident angle."

"Make sure the coroner does a vaginal smear," Williams said to the officer loading the body into the bag.

"You think she was raped?" the officer asked him.

"She didn't have any damned pants on. What do you think? And whatever you think, all of you," he said loudly to everyone at the scene, "keep your mouths completely shut. I better not hear or read anything about this that we don't put out there."

A moment later, Carlo DeBennedetti drove up in a white pickup and was stopped by a uniformed sheriff's deputy from approaching the scene.

"This is my land you're on," he said loudly. "I can go where I please on my own land."

Clarence Williams walked down the bank to where the farmer had been detained and said, "It's OK, let him through."

When DeBennedetti approached him, Clarence Williams stuck out his hand and said, "Detective Williams. Can I help you?"

"You could tell me what's going on," said the farmer looking past Williams at the vehicle that was about to be towed and the body bag on the ambulance guerney.

"This your land?" asked Williams, ignoring Carlo's question.

"Yeah, I'm Carlo DeBennedetti. I own all of this land for 80 acres."

"You ever see this car before?" asked the detective.

"As a matter of fact, I have," said DeBennedetti.

"Elwood," Clarence Williams yelled over his shoulder. "Can I see you over here?"

Elwood Carnes could tell by his partner's voice that he was on to something, so he stopped what he was doing and ambled over to where they were standing.

"This is Mr. DeBennedetti," said Clarence by way of introduction. "Mr. DeBennedetti, this is my partner Detective Carnes." And then to Elwood, "Mr. DeBennedetti was about to tell me where he'd seen this car before."

"I saw it driving down my road here," he said pointing to the old dirt road between the two walnut orchards that led from the river to the county road.

"A couple of Fridays ago," he continued.

"You wouldn't remember the date would you?" asked Elwood.

"Sure," said DeBennedetti. "It was November 10th, the day my cousin Enzio got married in Lodi."

The two detectives shot glances at each other. That was close to when Elizabeth Van Houten was reported missing.

"You remember the time?" asked Williams.

"Right around 3 o'clock. I was pulling a dead tree out of

my orchard over there," he said pointing behind him. "And I was afraid I wouldn't have time to finish the job before I had to get cleaned up, when I saw this car here pull onto the road and head down this way toward the river."

"Did you see the driver?" asked Carnes, taking notes.

"Yeah, I saw him, but not real good. Skinny Italian looking guy."

"Had you ever seen him before?"

"No, I don't think so. But like I said, I wasn't that close and didn't get that good of a look."

"How do you know it was this car?" asked Williams pointing at the VW bug now being hoisted up by its rear-end, water still dripping out of it.

"How many blue VW bugs with wrecked fenders do you think drive down this road?" said Carlo.

"Good point," said Carnes.

"Do you think you could look at some photos and maybe pick the guy out if you saw him?" asked Williams.

"I don't know," said Carlo. "It could have been a million guys. I was only looking at him to see if I knew him, because people know I don't want them driving on my road."

"How come?" said Carnes.

"They dump shit; drive in my orchards; make messes. I hate that," he answered.

"Where'd you say your cousin got married?" asked Williams.

"In Lodi. Somebody's house next to Lodi Lake. Enzio's been married before, so no church. Who gets married at 5 o'clock on a Friday? It's inconvenient as hell," said Carlo.

"Listen Mr. DeBennedetti, I'm going to want to confirm the time of the wedding, so if you've got an invitation or something," said Williams.

"My wife saves all that shit," he said. "Stop by the house.

It's a quarter mile up the main road on the left."

"And for now, we want you to keep quiet about seeing someone driving the car down here on the tenth."

"Sure, sure," said Carlo.

Just then, a Chevy Camaro drove slowly down the oiled road toward them.

"Uh-oh," said Carnes. "The *Stockton Record.*"

"We have to give them something," said Williams. "I'll talk to them."

———=»((•))«=———

SATURDAY, NOVEMBER 18TH, 2 P.M.

Back at their office with the unpleasant task of informing the sheriff of his niece's death behind them, Williams and Carnes were busy writing up their reports.

"At least we didn't have to tell her parents. I hate that," said Carnes.

"All he said was 'find this guy'," said Williams referring to their brief talk with Lonigan. "So we better find him."

"Well, we gave the *Record* the part about the car wreck. Maybe somebody saw it," said Carnes.

"The perp will read the article," said Williams, leaning back. "We need some quick help on the paint transfer. It looks red to me."

"We can drive it up later today to DOJ. Let's call ahead. I know a guy there that can come in on his day off," said Carnes.

"Good, do that. And let's start checking body shops. The

best ones first."

"You're right. Whoever she got in a wreck with will fix their car. Probably has already taken it in," said Carnes. "We need to find out from the vic's parents who the insurance agent was. Maybe she called it in."

"OK, but I don't think so," said Williams. "The farmer's dead right about Friday the tenth. That's when she disappeared. If her car wasn't wrecked before and Lonigan's checking that out, then I'm thinking the driver of the vehicle she hit was probably our perp."

"Makes sense."

"We got to find that car," said Williams.

"I'm thinking," said Carnes, pouring more coffee for both of them from the pot on the hot plate, "that the perp thought he was getting rid of the car and her by dumping her in the river. Up til now, he thinks he's clear of this. Maybe he's taking it in to get it fixed. The body shops are our lead."

"We can narrow it down some if we had an idea of what kind of car uses this kind of paint," Williams said, holding up a plastic evidence bag with a paint scrapping in it that he'd taken off of the damaged fender of the VW at the scene.

"I'm going to make some calls," said Carnes.

Chapter 7

B ig John Moretti and his wife, Rose, lived in a modest three bedroom ranch style home a block off Lincoln Road in North Stockton. Paul and Michael had shared a bedroom from the time they were 15 until they both went off to college. That was eleven years ago.

After all of those years, there were a number of things you could still set your watch by at Big John's house. Two of them were Saturday night dinner of steak with diced potatoes and Sunday breakfast after 8 o'clock mass. Like the dinner the night before, breakfast was always the same. A huge omelet of leftover steak and potatoes with a steaming pot of hot chocolate.

Big John did the cooking on an old electric frying pan that had one leg missing. He used a brick to prop up the corner. Michael had bought him a new one for Christmas two years before, but it remained in its box in the hall closet until the older one was officially declared dead. The cooking in the electric frying pan was next to a gas range and oven that Big John refused to use unless absolutely necessary. "Why get it dirty," and "I don't have stock in PG&E," were his standard excuses for not using the appliances. Michael called it 'Dago cheap' referring not just to Big John, but to all Italians in general. However, Big John took cheap to an art form. Except with food and drink. "Life's too short to eat bad food or drink bad booze," he always said.

This Sunday morning was no exception. As Michael dropped into a kitchen table chair in front of steaming platters and pots, he could tell that Big John was distraught as he plowed through the Sunday paper spread on one end of the large kitchen table.

"What's up Big?" Michael asked reaching for a thick slice of buttered toast.

"This town's going to hell is what's up," he answered still reading. He held the edges of the paper spread before his massive 260 pound-plus frame with chubby, hairy fingers. The hair grew thicker as it proceeded up the massive forearms exposed beneath the short-sleeved white shirt he'd worn to mass that morning. Over the shirt he wore a very old apron probably worn by his now dead, sainted mother while she cooked endlessly for her husband and six children, never speaking a word of English in the old ram-shackled two-story house across from the railroad tracks on Union Street.

Big John looked fat, and was, but he was also a very powerful man. Michael and Paul still talked about the time that they and their high school buddies could not budge the "painted-over" lug nuts on the flat tire of Michael's first car as it sat in the family driveway. Big John came outside, grabbed the tire iron, lowered his massive girth to the wheel, and spun the nut loose with a flick of his wrist. His large head was covered in curly black and gray receding hair with thick eyebrows. The darker skinned big nostrils of his nose and thick lips were from the southern most part of Italy where he was born. He had spent most of his life in Stockton as had his entire family, which numbered more than thirty.

Just then, the front door opened and Paul walked in to have breakfast.

"You reading about the Van Houten girl?" he asked his

father as he sat down.

"Yeah," his father answered, still reading. "Her old man works at the Bank of America in the Center. You guys know her? You went to school with her."

"I remember her," said Paul. "You knew her didn't you Mike?"

"I don't even know what the hell you guys are talkin' about," said Michael.

"The Van Houten girl," Big John said looking up. "Don't you read the paper?"

"I don't get the paper."

"Well, someone killed her and put her in the river," said Big John with disgust. "What do you know about this?" he asked Paul.

"It's a sheriff's case," said Paul. "And she's the sheriff's niece."

"I see that."

"There'll be hell to pay," said Paul.

Big John nodded gravely and looked up at both of them. "You both stay out of this, capice?"

Rose, a gregarious loud, middle-aged Italian woman, and wife for thirty-one years to Big John, glided into the room and up to where Michael was seated and put her arms around him and kissed him on the cheek and asked, "Are you packed yet?"

"We don't leave for two weeks," Michael said patting her round light-skinned arm.

Rose was from Northern Italy, near the Swiss border and her tastes and manners were far more French than Southern Italian, with its heavy spices and Mediterranean preferences. It was mostly for that reason that Big John had done most of the cooking.

"I don't know why you and Anthony want to go to Mexico

anyway," she said.

"For the putanas, knowing him," said Big John good naturedly. "You don't be bringing back underwear full of Mexican clap for your mother to wash. You hear me?"

"Jesus Big," said Michael. "We're going because it costs $250 bucks a piece for the week, including air fare. You know AJ's almost as cheap as you are."

"You heard me," said Big John, poking his sausage shaped index finger at him. "And another thing, when you goin' to work for Metro?"

"I turned in the application Friday," said Michael to the group in general.

"You better not be shitin' me?" said Big John. "You need to get some better work."

After everyone turned their attentions to other issues, Michael said to Paul while they ate, "I need to talk to you about the Ramirezes."

"I saw Paco pimping Sylvia on Wilson Way last night," said Paul between mouthfuls of eggs and steak.

"They caught a new case," said Michael. "496 guns," he continued referring to section 496 of the Penal Code, possession of stolen property.

"I heard."

"I want to talk to Dewey about a package if they work off the beef," he said.

"What have they got?" asked Paul.

"They'll roll on the guy they were fencing the guns to."

"They won't roll on a fence," said Paul skeptically.

"Not the fence. The guy. He's a shooter," said Michael.

Paul ate for a while and pulled the piece of the paper over that had the article about the girl. After a while he said, "Talk to Dewey, then we'll see."

Chapter 8

Sheriff's detectives Clarence Williams and Elwood Carnes were seated in the small living room of the modestly fashioned wood-sided farmhouse with flaking paint, which was located northeast of Stockton. They sat surrounded by the Barnes and Fox families in a house furnished to the Barnes by the owner of the peach and walnut ranch that Jake Barnes managed.

The phone call to the sheriff's department had come just an hour before from Mrs. Barnes, the mother of Tommy, who had said they might have some information about the girl who had been found in the river.

Already at their desks on Sunday morning, Williams and Carnes were in an unmarked Chevy Impala within five minutes time, beside themselves with the excitement of a possible early break in the case.

Mrs. Barnes had explained that the family had been talking at breakfast about the front page article in the *Stockton Record* which had featured the sheriff's niece being pulled out of the river in a blue Volkswagen and that her son, Tommy, had blurted out that he thought he had seen that car a couple of weeks back when it was in a wreck. Tommy had admitted that he had been with his friend Jimmy Fox bird hunting. She went on to explain that Tommy sometimes exaggerated, so she had called the Fox home and spoke with Jimmy's mother, a family friend, and sure enough, after a little coaxing, Jimmy had confirmed what Tommy had said. Detective Clarence Williams told her to stop all questioning of the boys until they could get there and Mrs. Barnes said she would try to get the Foxes over to her house for a meeting.

And so they were now sitting in the living room on mismatched naugahide furniture sipping steaming coffee from mugs while a football game blared on the old black and white Zenith console.

"We would like to speak to Tommy first, alone, if you don't mind," said Clarence Williams to the assembled families.

"That's probably a good idea," said Tommy's father Jake without taking his eyes off the screen. "Since he's afraid his mama's going to be whipping him for disobeying her about that gun."

Mrs. Barnes ushered the detectives into the tiny bedroom with sports pennants plastered on the cheap imitation wood-paneled wall, and a San Francisco Giants' logo blanket atop a single twin bed where Tommy and the two detectives sat scrunched together.

"Why is your mama going to whip you Tommy?" asked Elwood Carnes opening his notepad and clicking his ballpoint pen.

"Cause we were shootin' birds and we wasn't suppose to," Tommy answered barely above a whisper.

"Where was that?" asked Clarence Williams.

"Over in the oaks where we seen the wreck."

"Tell us when that was," said Williams.

"Two weeks ago," answered Tommy rubbing his feet together that didn't quite touch the floor.

"On a Friday?" asked Carnes.

"Yeah, we was there on a Friday," said Tommy.

"So not last Friday, but the one before that," said Carnes barely able to keep the excitement out of his voice.

"Yeah, me and Jimmy."

"What time was that?" asked Williams.

"In the morning," Tommy answered.

"How come you two weren't in school on a Friday?" asked Carnes.

"Our school was closed for the day cause of a gas pipe break," said Tommy.

"Check it," said Williams to Carnes, making eye contact. Carnes made a note and nodded.

"What exactly did you see, Tommy?" asked Carnes.

"I saw this blue VW bug crash into this real cool red Corvette," he answered.

The detective stopped him and made him start over in minute detail explaining everything he saw from the crash to the two cars driving away. After they were positive that they understood his story and they had him describe both drivers as best as he could, they showed him a photo of Elizabeth Van Houten taken at her school earlier that year. Tommy stared at it a long time and said that it looked something like the lady that got out of the Volkswagen. He said the man in the Corvette was about his father's size and had dark hair and was Italian looking.

At that point, Elwood Carnes excused himself and went out to their car and radioed for a sketch artist to be sent out to the house. When informed that one was not available, he swore at the dispatcher and ordered her to get one from off-duty and get them out there on Lonigan's orders.

After they were finished, they brought in Jimmy Fox who seemed afraid and a little timid. It took 15 minutes for Elwood, who was normally great with kids, to warm him up.

Jimmy explained that he and Tommy had snuck out to the oaks two weeks before and spent Friday morning shooting blackbirds and blue-jays out of the trees. Responding to a question from Clarence Williams, he said he saw a blue car and a red car run into each other. He said the blue car was a bug and that Tommy had told him that the other one was a Corvette. Tommy knew cars better than he did.

"So when exactly did all of this happen?" asked Elwood Carnes.

"Two weeks ago," said Jimmy.

"On Friday?" asked Carnes.

"I don't know," said Jimmy. "Could have been Thursday or Friday."

"Tommy said Friday," Williams answered.

"Tommy remembers stuff better than me. It was probably Friday."

They questioned the boy about the details of the accident and showed him the picture of the Van Houten girl. He answered all of their questions and said the picture sure looked like her.

Clarence Williams thought Jimmy's answers were more confused and tentative than the Barnes boy, and put it down to immaturity. What he was sure about was the time and the fact that the right front fender of the blue VW had been damaged and that the car had been driven away along with a late model red Corvette following close behind. It fit perfectly with the date and time that the farmer, Carlo DeBennedetti, had given them with the car being put into the river on Friday the 10th at around 3 p.m. They were sure that Elizabeth Van Houten had been killed between the late morning and 3 p.m. on that day and every instinct that Carnes and Williams possessed, and those were considerable, told them that the driver of the Vette was the killer.

By the time they were finished interviewing the boys and their parents, the sketch artist had arrived and began working with both boys on a "sketch" of the Corvette's driver. The boys, by their own account, had been within 100 feet of him and they were pretty sure that they had remained undetected in the woods. After the sketch artist finished her job, the boys hopped into the back of an unmarked sheriff's car and took the detectives to the scene of the accident and walked them around the woods where they had been hunting when the wreck occurred.

It was after 3 p.m. when the two detectives admonished both families to remain quiet about the case and headed back to Stockton. Their day was just beginning.

"You think the Vette's been fixed yet?" Carnes asked his partner as they drove.

"Probably," sighed Williams.

"That Barnes kid is sure sharper than the other one," said Carnes. "You think he's right that the Vette's only a couple of years old at most?"

"You see those car mags on the coffee table?" said Williams. "His ol' man's a car buff. I'd say he's close on the age of the Vette."

"Let's go to Chase," said Carnes, referring to Chase Chevrolet in Stockton, the only local place anyone would buy a Corvette.

"Just what I was thinking partner," said Williams.

Carnes knew the sales manager personally and, for that matter, the service manager. So within 30 minutes, they had him pouring through old sales records looking for Corvette purchases.

Carnes had the service manager, who was at home, on the phone asking his opinion on where a two-year old Corvette would get repair work done in that area. The service manager told him that the first place would be right there at the dealership, but that no one had come in recently for body work on a Corvette, let alone a red one. He went on to say that there were only a half dozen body shops in the area even capable of doing a decent job on that type of vehicle.

After 45 minutes of digging, the sales manager found records of five purchases of red Corvettes in the last three years. One in particular stood out because the owner paid cash in hundred dollar bills and gave an impoverished downtown apartment for an address, both of which seemed highly unusual at the time. The guy's name was Eddie Reno and he'd given virtually no information about himself.

"What did he look like?" asked Carnes.

"Medium height and build, strong, tough looking guy with dark hair, said the sales manager.

"Italian?" asked Williams.

"Yeah, I think you could say that. Talked like he was from back East. Said he wasn't from here and didn't say much else. Kind of an asshole."

"What do you mean?" asked Carnes.

"I remember asking him what he did for a living and he said he minded his own business," said the sales manager.

"You got an address?" asked Williams.

"Funny, I don't," he said looking surprised.

Back at the office, Clarence Williams telephoned Lonigan at home and briefed him on the days' progress. Carnes busied himself trying to get a rap sheet on one Eddie Reno as well as a local address and the addresses of the local body shops the service manager at Chase had named. To be on the safe side, he called some law enforcement contacts in Modesto, a city 30 miles to the south of Stockton, and Sacramento, 50 miles to the north, to see where someone would take a relatively new Vette to get body work done.

"Well, looky here now," said Carnes dropping the tele-type DOJ rap sheet of Eddie Reno on Clarence's desk. "Our boy's no stranger to the courts."

Clarence Williams scanned the sheet and whistled. "Aggravated assault and loan sharking in New Jersey. Did hard time. And three arrests locally in the last two years, but I don't see any charges filed on those."

"We need a local address on this guy and a mug shot," said Williams.

"I'm on it."

"Let's get the mug shot out to that farmer pronto."

<hr />

MONDAY, NOVEMBER 20TH, 7:30 A.M.

Working into the previous evening, the two detectives had managed to get a booking photo from New Jersey tele-typed to them and had awoken a surly Carlo DeBennedetti to show it to him. Mr. DeBennedetti said that it could be the guy that was driving the VW down his dirt road on Friday the 10th.

They decided to start calling the local body shops on their list at 7:45 a.m., figuring someone would be opening up by then to accommodate people on their way to work on a Monday morning.

Ten minutes into it, they found the car. Red Vette dropped off over a week ago by Eddie Reno who had told the owner of Eric's Foreign Auto Body on Wilson Way "to *spare no expense. Get the job done right."* Eric said over the phone that he had ordered a new quarter panel, bumper, and headlights and was waiting on them. Fifteen minutes later, Williams and Carnes were walking through the front door and tapping the bell on the counter of Eric's Foreign Auto Body. There was the red Vette sitting in the corner of the shop, the bumper and right front fender laying on the floor in front of it. Williams immediately called for two other plain clothes detectives to meet them at the body shop and ordered the owner to not allow any employees to leave or make any telephone calls.

Leaving the other two officers to watch the shop, Williams and Carnes headed for Lonigan's office where a DA would be waiting for them to help them with a search warrant. Williams had decided that anything and everything they did at the shop would be second guessed by some scummy defense lawyer and so they had better have a warrant before they touched or looked at anything. Thanks to Lonigan's connections, they were able to set personal bests for obtaining a search warrant and were back at the body shop by 10 a.m. All had remained quiet, with no sign of the suspect. There had been no calls out.

Once the owner, Eric, had been furnished a copy of the search warrant, the detectives and eight members of the sheriff's department's forensic evidence squad, approached the Corvette like it was a sleeping cobra. Everything was photographed and fingerprinted and the removed fender, bumper, and headlight were carefully examined for the blue paint from the victim's VW.

Clarence Williams gave a deep sigh of relief when he saw the paint on the damaged fender, plain as day. Paint scrapings were carefully taken and placed into evidence envelopes while other members of the team began going over the interior for evidence.

Williams and Carnes were walking toward Big John Lonigan who had just come through the front door with his second in command, when a stunned evidence technician walked up to them with his hand stretched out as if he were holding a beating heart. Clutched in his gloved hand was a feminine-looking green woman's wallet.

"We just found this in the glove compartment behind some papers," said the technician. "We've already photoed it in place and I'm going to dust it now for latents."

The sheriff's officers were stunned. It wasn't possible. This couldn't be the victim's wallet. Barely breathing, Williams, Carnes, and the sheriff watched mesmerized as the wallet was carefully dusted and several latents were lifted from the smooth vinyl sides.

"Open it," said Williams in a hushed voice after the technician finished with the prints.

The technician carefully opened the wallet and lifted the driver's license of Elizabeth Van Houten from a card sleeve.

"That son-of-a-bitch!" spat out Lonigan as he turned and stormed out of the building.

Chapter 9

Monday, November 20th, 9 a.m.

AJ was in a hurry as he pushed through the double doors of Department 5 of the Superior Court on the third floor of the county courthouse with a big stack of files under his arm. He had pleas and sentencings in several courts that morning as he busily tried to clear his caseload for the upcoming Mexico trip in a couple of weeks. One week at the El Cid Hotel across from the beach in Mazatlán, $249 per person, double occupancy. Hell, they could barely fly for that and all they had to do was attend one lousy condominium presentation for a few hours. AJ knew he hadn't exactly broken that news to Michael yet.

This morning he had to get rid of a felony burglary set for pre-trial conference in front of the locally raised judge, Nicholas Chinchiolo, who was notoriously hard on residential burglaries. The client was an in-custody named Ricky Jones, an Eastsider he had never met, and all AJ knew about him was that from the police report and preliminary hearing transcript, the kid was cold and had already been to prison once. In fact, he had only been out two months when he caught this case.

All of the in-custodies were seated in the jury box in the courtroom wearing their jail-orange jumpsuits when AJ walked in and asked who Ricky Jones was.

"I'm Ricky," said a good looking baby-faced inmate

with slicked back black hair that shined under the recessed flourescent lighting.

AJ must have looked surprised because Ricky Jones said, "Yeah, I know, I don't look like a burglar. Look, here's the deal. I'm going to make this easy for you. I want to plead guilty today to state prison. I'm not waiving time for sentencing. I want to be sentenced this morning. You got that?"

"You need a probation report," said AJ somewhat stunned by the exchange.

"No I don't. Are you listening to me? I'm not waiving time," hissed an agitated Ricky Jones. "I know the law. They have to sentence me within six hours of my guilty plea if I want."

After a moment, AJ said, "OK partner. You got it." He was a little pissed off at being barked at by his client. He turned away and sat down in a chair across the courtroom, waiting to be called into chambers and passed the time making detailed notes in the file regarding the conversation so that when Jones decided that he'd made a mistake, there would be a record of his demands in the file.

Screw him, AJ thought as he waited. A few minutes later he was sitting across the desk from Judge Nicholas Chinchiolo and next to Deputy DA Joe Rocha, not believing what he was hearing out of the Judge's mouth. He had no more than gotten the words out that Ricky Jones was pleading cold to a felony burglary than Chinchiolo had started in on a story about how his father knew Ricky's father and what hard times they all had during the Depression and how Ricky's dad was the best auto mechanic on the Eastside.

"And never overcharged you a cent," the Judge continued. "I know they are sick about this kid. Fell in with the wrong crowd, that's all. Listen Rocha, I'm giving this kid a local. Let him clean up. Detox, you know. Then he can work for his old man in the shop on work furlough. He keeps his nose clean and I'll modify him in six months. Go out and give him the good news Borelli." The Judge waived Borelli out of his chambers. "Send in the next victim," he said jovially to his bailiff.

AJ was shocked and delighted. Now he wasn't going to have to talk this guy into anything. And, he was getting a fabulous deal. One year in the county jail, out in six months. A great start to the morning.

"This is your lucky day asshole," he said to Ricky Jones, as he walked up beside him in the box. "Felony local, a year, out in six months maybe. Don't thank me. Just doing my job."

"Are you out of your stinking mind?" Jones yelled at him. "Can't you do anything right? I'm not spending a year in that shit box of a jail. Now get your ass back in there and do what I told you."

AJ just stood and stared at him with his mouth open. The in-custody deputy began wandering over at the disturbance. "Everything OK AJ?" he asked Borelli as he moved between AJ and Ricky Jones.

"I'll give you 50 bucks for your gun," said AJ staring daggers at Ricky. "Listen Jones," he said leaning forward so that his face was a foot from Ricky's. "You tell me what's going on right now or I'll tell the judge you're insane. I'm not kidding," he added for emphasis, referring to Penal Code Section 1368 to declare the defendant mentally incompetent.

Ricky thought it over for a minute and then said to the deputy who had his hand resting on the butt of his .357 magnum revolver, "Can we have a little privacy here please?"

After the deputy had moved away, he said to AJ, "Listen, here's the deal. I've got it wired at Vacaville with a trustee to send me to CMC West this week. If I get there by Friday,

I get my lifeguard job back. I have to get sentenced to the joint today," he pleaded.

Ricky went on to fill in the details about the California Men's Colony West that AJ did not know. First of all, you couldn't get there unless you were a non-violent felon, which Ricky Jones was. It had no gun tower, no walls, only a chain-link fence, and dormitories with single rooms with locks on the doors from the inside, like a college dorm room. It had baseball diamonds, a swimming pool, tennis courts, and a rec room with ping-pong tables and a canteen where you could buy things. In short, it was summer camp for cons.

Ricky apparently knew a guy at the California Medical Facility in Vacaville, California, where everyone sentenced to state prison was sent for a 90-day evaluation to determine which state prison in the big State of California that they would be best suited to do their time. The evaluations were performed by social workers, psychiatrists, and prison personnel and it was an inexact science at best. The most important decisions that needed to be got right were gang affiliations. The hardcore big league prisons in California were San Quentin, Folsom, Soledad and DVI.

San Quentin was run by the Aryan Brotherhood with some help from the Black Guerilla Family. Folsom was mainly for serious older cons who just wanted to do their time. There was a mixture of whites and blacks with a few Mexicans. Soledad was, by and large, where the Mexican Mafia was housed with some Aryans and BGFs. Never a Nuestra Familia, the other Mexican gang. A mistake there and the guy's life span was less than a Monarch butterfly's. Duel Vocational Institute or DVI was primarily for the Nuestra Familia. Since no gang member would ever admit his gang affiliation, it was very important to tell who was

Patrick Riddle

who with the two Mexican gangs. This was done with captured lists that law enforcement confiscated surreptitiously
from time to time.

Vacaville itself was no picnic, housing the likes of Sirhan
Sirhan and Charlie Manson, each doing hard time, life. In
fact, when Sirhan Sirhan was occasionally moved about the
facility, the halls were completely cleared and a heavy guard
accompanied him for his own protection. A guy could get
killed at Vacaville if he didn't watch out for himself.

Ricky Jones had an insider. A trustee who owed his family
and who could get him immediately processed out to CMC
West. Since all prisons worked on paper, and at Vacaville
no one knew who anyone was, it was as easy as ginning up
some documents. But if Ricky wanted that cushy 3 hour-a-
day lifeguard job, he had to act fast.

So AJ did his job. With everyone raising their eyebrows,
and Chinchiolo painstakingly advising Ricky of his rights and
what he was giving up, AJ pled him out so that he could be
sentenced to CMC West summer camp for probably a year
and half, more or less, via Vacaville, for 48 hours or so.

Sybil Waxman was beaming with perceived prestige
and pride as she was introduced to Dewey Gunnart by
Michael Hunter in the DA's offices on the second floor of
the courthouse later that day. Dewey's office was cluttered
with memorabilia from the second World War and law enforcement. Sybil glanced about for any artifacts chronicling
Gunnart's legal career and curiously could find none. She
did, however, notice a large pistol in some sort of holster
hanging from a wooden coat rack behind Dewey's gray,

county issued metal desk. In many of the photos were people she didn't recognize and was sure that she wouldn't care about, except one small one on top of a waist-high antique oak bookcase which depicted a man vaguely familiar to her with his arm around a youthful Dewey Gunnart. She thought that the office itself was small and unimpressive and that the man himself was the same. Her pride came from the fact that Michael had come to her office and asked her to accompany him.

"Is he in?" Michael asked the attractive brunette wearing a phone headset when they first arrived. She gave him a big smile and waived them through the door. Halfway down the hall, Michael walked through an open office door, rapping his knuckles on it twice as he went through.

"Oh shit. Look what the cat dragged in," said the slightly built 50-year-old man with a full head of gray hair and a non-filtered cigarette dangling from the corner of his mouth, Bogey-style.

"What's the matter, the Owl Club closed this morning?" he said to Michael standing and reaching a gnarly and many times broken hand across the desk to shake hands with Sybil. "Who's your friend?"

"Sybil Waxman," replied Michael grabbing an ordinary steel-backed chair for himself and one for Waxman. She just stared. "Sybil, meet Dewey Gunnart the Assistant District Attorney."

Dewey caught Sybil's unimpressed gaze around his office and her fixed stare on the gun behind him hanging from the shoulder holster.

"Old habit," he said to her.

"Why would a lawyer need a gun?" she asked.

"You are new. What's up Mike?"

"Sylvia and Paco Ramirez," answered Michael. "I want

a deal."

"People in hell want ice water too," said Gunnart. "How many times have I told you, you can't keep going over the heads of my deputies and running in here all of the time. It upsets the system and order I try to maintain. Besides, they don't learn anything."

"Can't this time," said Michael. "Narcs won't deal unless you OK it personally."

"What do you got?" sighed Dewey lighting another Pall Mall.

"I don't suppose that you've read the surgeon general's warnings about those things?" asked Sybil waiving the smoke away from her head.

"Been ignoring warnings all my life Missy," said Dewey.

"I thought we talked about your not talking," Michael shot at her.

"Sorry," she replied trying to sound sorry.

"The Ramirezes just caught a cold 496 on a gun," Michael began. He went on to explain the situation in detail on what he thought Paco could do for the narcs to get a warrant to take this guy out and why the trade was so good for Dewey.

"You say he's the guy on those bar robberies out east?" asked Dewey.

"Yep."

"How do we protect Paco so the perp won't know who rolled over on him?"

"That's the good part," said Michael leaning forward. "Paco says he's dealing too. Paco's your CRI. Personal knowledge because he's bought from the guy."

"What do you want?" asked Dewey interested now.

"Well, you got to make it look good. So felony local on the 496; kick everything else; honor farm; out in six months," answered Michael.

"No good. They had too much cooking and they're cold on all of it. A bullet," said Dewey meaning he wanted them to do an entire year.

Michael sat back and put his hands behind his head, tipping his chair back so it rested on its back legs precariously. After a minute, he said, "From what I hear the shooter discharged his weapon twice in the robberies. Just a matter of time Dewey. You get a dealer and clear six 211s," he continued, referring to Penal Code Section 211 for armed robbery, "and probably save a life."

"I'm trading ten in the joint for Paco and six for Sylvia, don't push it," said Dewey.

"Out in six I can sell," said Michael not moving.

"You can sell a bullet."

"Can't do it."

"You're wasting my time," said Dewey opening his desk drawer. "Shall we settle this in the usual way?"

"Why not," said Michael letting his chair come forward and sitting up straight.

"Call it," said Dewey flipping a quarter in the air that he pulled from the drawer.

As it spun through the air, Michael said, "Heads." The quarter landed clattering on the stained blotter on Dewey's desk before coming to rest on some papers 'heads up.'

"Six it is," said Dewey. "Now take a hike. I'll clear it with Metro."

"Oh my God!" yelled Sybil leaping to her feet. "You just flipped a coin to decide someone's liberty. That's not legal."

"It's not a question of legal young lady," said Dewey. "It's a question of honor. Nice to meet you."

As they walked out of the DA's office, Waxman grabbed Michael's arm and stopped him. "What would you have done if it had come up tails?" she asked him still gripping his arm.

"Pled them to a year of course. A deal's a deal," said Michael smiling and continuing down the hallway to the elevator.

"Have you done this before?" she asked trotting along side Michael, trying to keep up.

"Lots of times. Mostly drunk drivings," he answered pressing the elevator button.

"Does anyone else do this?" she asked incredulous.

"Not to my knowledge. Just me and Dewey."

"How can you justify this? You can't flip coins to decide cases."

"I just did," he said.

A few minutes later they were walking down San Joaquin Street back to the office. A few drops of rain began to moisten the sidewalk.

Sybil stopped and looked at him thinking hard, trying to understand. How Dewey Gunnart, with his sad little office and his rolled up long sleeve white shirt with cigarette burns on the front, could be the Assistant District Attorney of San Joaquin County was beyond her. She had no intention of winding up like this, flipping coins for the amount of time her clients would do. She could see no relationship between where she was and where she was going back to, which was on the outskirts of Beverly Hills, living in her mother's penthouse on Wilshire Boulevard, practicing law at one of the better firms. She had come here because, frankly, the first half dozen interviews hadn't panned out and she had talked herself into it using the excuse that she would get some immediate jury trial experience which she could cash in on in LA. Down there, people didn't get to jury trial much and it was a valued commodity. She had thought hitching her star to Michael Hunter would help her get to trial faster and now, after seeing him in action, she wasn't so sure she had made the right decision. But, she was nothing if not practical and pragmatic. Course correcting was in her nature.

"Other than how to breach the cannons of legal ethics, is there anything else you wanted me to learn today?" she asked.

"Yeah, a couple of things," said Michael. "Get your ass into the library and do everything Merlin tells you."

She raised a hand and opened her mouth to protest, but Michael shut her up.

"You're not smart enough or good enough to skip what you can learn there. You will never be any good if you don't do it. No excuses. The next thing--" he paused, "cut out the Helen Reddy 'I am woman' bullshit. No one cares. Quit parking down past the chicken factory. You'll get hurt some night. People are noticing."

"Who?" she said trying to not sound too alarmed or upset.

"Never mind. If I noticed, they noticed. Stop it. You're a woman. Act like it. Use it. It could work for you."

"What do you mean?"

"You know what I mean," he said ending the conversation and heading off down the street.

Chapter 10

Detectives Carnes and Williams were seated across from each other at their desks which were back to back in the detectives' office of the San Joaquin County Sheriff's Office located in the basement of the San Joaquin County Courthouse. Williams was busy scribbling a hand-written affidavit for an arrest warrant for Eddie Reno. Carnes had a phone glued to his ear while he wrote down additional information regarding the address for Reno's apartment on California Street and as much off-the-record information he could obtain regarding Reno from his Stockton Police Department contacts, who wished to remain anonymous. For whatever reason, there was little or no information regarding the three arrests of Eddie Reno by the Stockton Police Department in the previous two years, but the contact was able to get the living address for Reno and the fact that he was unemployed at the present time as far as anyone knew and would likely be at that address during the day.

As Williams handed his hand-written affidavit to the Deputy District Attorney sitting next to him, for his final corrections, Carnes got up and walked around to face him.

"How many guys you want to take on this?" Carnes asked his partner.

Clarence Williams leaned back in his swivel desk chair

and thought for a moment. "Four," he said. "Two to cover the back door and two to go in with us."

"We getting a search warrant as well?"

"You bet my man. One stop shopping," said Williams.

At exactly 2:30 p.m., Eddie Reno opened the front door to his first floor apartment on California Street and froze as Elwood Carnes' .357 magnum was stuck in his face. He was spun around and slammed face first into the opposite wall and held there while both of his arms were jerked behind him and handcuffs were roughly and tightly snapped into place on his wrists. He was quickly patted down and when Clarence Williams was satisfied that he and the rest of the apartment were secure, he informed Eddie Reno of his *Miranda* rights against self-incrimination and right to counsel. Carnes made a mental note that Reno listened with a sneer on his face, while his partner read him his rights from a laminated 3x5 card.

As Williams finished, he said, "Do you understand your rights Mr. Reno and do you have any questions?"

"Yeah, just one," snarled Eddie Reno. "How's a spook like you get a white man's job like this?"

Carnes buried his right fist into the hard belly of Eddie Reno, causing him to double over.

"That all you got you nigger lovin' cracker piece of shit?" Reno gasped.

"Leave him alone Elwood," Williams said calmly as he stepped in front of his partner before he could meet out further damage to the suspect. "This piece of shit is through."

"What is it you assholes think I've done?" said Reno straightening up.

"You popped the sheriff's niece is what you've done," said Carnes. "And there's no thinking about it."

For just an instant, Reno's eyes flickered, then he

regained his attitude. "Screw you," he said.

"That your statement?" asked Williams. "Or you got more to say?"

"I got nothing to say," said Reno.

The search of the apartment took several hours and turned up nothing of interest except several guns with no serial numbers.

As for Eddie Reno, he never said another word, no matter how many questions were put to him or how long he sat in the interrogation room, which was hours in the basement of the courthouse.

⸺ ((◑)) ⸺

Monday, November 20ᵀᴴ, 2:30 p.m.

Jacob 'Snake' Sanderson was popping the top of a Regal Select with an orange file spread out in front of him at his desk when Michael walked into the room and plopped into the old cracked leather easy chair across from him.

"What are you reading?" he asked.

"The file on that DVI shanker. Set for trial in 30 days. They say no more continuances. So, I figured I better read the file," Snake said looking up.

"What's your hurry?" Michael asked sarcastically looking for a magazine to read.

"You know what my guy's name is?"

"Who cares," shrugged Michael.

"D. R. Johnny."

"D. R. Johnny? What's the D R stand for?"

"Death Row. The guy was on death row with an execution date next year when they overturned the death penalty last June," Snake said referring to the U.S. Supreme Court case of *Furman v. Georgia* decided the previous June overturning the death penalty in all states.

"You're kidding?" said Michael.

"Nope. All the guys on the row were sent to various other prisons. Pretty fast, huh? The word is that no matter what, they are never getting out even though they are all commuted to life sentences, which as you know, means 7 to life and most of those guys have been there long enough to be eligible for parole."

"That's scary," said Michael putting the magazine down.

"According to the crime report, they all have the moniker "DR" if they were on the row and it's the coolest thing you can have in the joint right now. The theory on D.R. Johnny is that he's got nothing to lose since he's never getting out, so he has turned assassin at DVI. Will kill you for 3 packs of 'cigis'."

"What's his story?" asked Michael curious now.

"The usual 'soddi' defense," answered Snake referring to the classic line in half the crime reports, and public defender investigator's interview notes. Soddi for "some other dude did it."

"Who's got the other guy?" asked Michael remembering the fight he'd had months before with the two inmates in the holding cell when they were arraigned.

"Stagnaro," answered Snake referring to Robert Stagnaro a fair to middling courthouse lawyer who had an office across the street in the California Building and took whatever came along. Nice guy.

"Is DR the heavy?" asked Michael.

"They'd like to make him out to be, but that's the funny

part. Stagnaro's guy won't roll over on him and he's been offered everything, including an early out."

"What are the facts on that mess?"

Snake leafed through the inch thick reports and said, "Exercise yard, guards looking down, see a rugby scrum of guys all massed around something, pushing and shoving. They yell at them to disburse and everyone pulls away except for these two bending over the victim who's got more pricks in him than a pin cushion, 22 to be exact."

"Blood?"

"Blood all over our guys, no one else. One shank, no prints. Black taped handle, standard DVI issue," Snake answered.

"Which guy's got the most blood?" asked Michael.

"Good question," Snake said. "It doesn't say."

"Curious. Well, you got plenty of time."

"The worst part is that I'm going to have to go out there," said Snake meaning to DVI.

"Not by yourself you're not," Michael said alarm creeping into his voice. "I'm serious."

"Thanks, I accept your invitation to join me," said Snake smiling.

"Checkmate again," said Michael. "This job's really starting to suck."

In reality, in the few months since the Supreme Court's decision to overturn the death penalty, state prisons had become the most dangerous places on earth. Life there had always been cheap, now it had virtually no value at all. There were numerous people in prison who thoroughly believed they would never get out, yet they were allowed to mill around with the local prison population, going to showers, jobs, rec rooms, meals, and the yard. Not even counting the gang affiliations and the usual gripes they had with everyone else that wasn't a member, in the big heavier prisons where they kept the violent criminals, everyone now had to watch themselves at all times. It used to be kind of fun to go see a client at DVI and now no one wanted to go there for any reason. Especially if you had to investigate the scene of a crime.

———◆———

Stanley Latchman walked into Sybil Waxman's second floor office carrying two cups of coffee. Sybil was busy writing on a legal pad.

Latchman set one cup on her county issued desk and said, "I don't know how you like it, so I threw in cream and sugar."

"Thanks anyway Stanley. I don't drink coffee, only tea," she said putting her pen down.

"What are you working on?" he asked gesturing at the pad.

"Just some notes on a meeting at the DA's office I was at this morning."

"I heard you were with Hunter," he said.

"Yes, we were meeting with Dewey somebody about the Ramirez case."

"You mean our Ramirez case, the one we just arraigned the other day? What was Hunter doing with our case?" he asked with annoyance.

"He thinks it's his. And he just settled it with the flip of a coin," she said glad to get it off her chest to someone she was sure would understand her discomfiture.

"What? He flipped a coin? What are you talking about?"

And with no further prompting, she spilled every detail

agreeing with Stanley on the unprofessional, improper, and, yes, unethical manner in which Michael Hunter had disposed of the Ramirezes' cases. When Sybil interjected that the Ramirezes technically knew that Michael was going to see Gunnart, Latchman quickly reassured her that they knew nothing about the coin flipping and deserved to be told. He went behind her chair and leaned over her shoulder to watch as she finished her handwritten memo of the incident.

"So, what do you think about your stand on the death penalty now that you and D.R. Johnny are going to be buddies?" asked Michael moving his bishop to take Snake's knight.

"I'm still against it. Nothing's changed. There are no statistics to support that it's ever been a deterrent to murder."

"Yeah, well if they had zapped DR within the first 90 days, then some other scum bucket would have 22 fewer holes in him right now," Michael retorted. "Come to think about it, DR may have performed a public service," he added.

"There you go," said Snake taking Michael's bishop with the queen he hadn't noticed. "How can you be so bad at this game," he added.

"Because I don't sit and think about every possible little diabolical move 56 times like you do. I just move," answered Michael.

"You don't think at all. You just react," said Snake popping another beer.

"I know this much," said Michael as he moved his rook away from Snake's queen. "I wouldn't have lived with no heat in my house for two months in the winter time."

"It's only been six weeks and it's not winter yet," said Snake defensively.

"Then why are your kids sleeping on the couch in front of the fireplace and your wife is wearing a parka around the house?"

"You can't rush these things," Snake sighed.

"Like the broken refrigerator last summer," said Michael.

"We got a new one," whined Snake.

"Sure, in September. It broke in July and you kept putting blocks of ice in it every other day until your ol' lady stormed into the gym at lunchtime and hauled your ass to Sears."

"I was checking *Consumer Reports*. I wanted just the right one. Checkmate," said Snake grinning maniacally.

"Don't worry about DR. No way anybody will ever make you try that case before someone shanks him or he dies of old age. Let's hit the Owl Club so I can kick your ass at pool."

—————=◉=—————

Directly across the street from the Public Defender's Office was The Owl Club, a small bar with one pool table that took quarters. The bartender, Ernie, a large dark haired man who served a variety of derelicts and transients who were mostly regulars, loved it when the third floor boys came in, which was at least three times a week in the late afternoon.

The bar itself was horseshoe in shape and made of an aged kind of wood that defied description because of the infinite number of nicks, stains, and cigarette burns from decades of use and abuse by mostly very serious drunks.

A dozen or so wooden stools, now covered with aged red naugahide, surrounded the bar that Snake had discovered because of the long-necked bottles of Budweiser served there.

"The only way to drink Bud," Snake said.

When Michael pushed through the double doors and entered the almost dark room, Ernie broke into a big grin and clapped his mitts twice and yelled, "OK you bums, clear the table we have working men on board."

This usual display of respect always embarrassed Michael and Snake, but since Ernie delighted in it and the derelicts acted as if they were being invaded by royalty as they cleared the table with its stained glass shaded light casting a pale glare on the scarred and worn green felted table, they endured it stoically.

Two iced cold bottles of Bud were slammed down on the bar, their necks dripping condensation, no payment required until the end when the bets were settled.

The game was "8 Ball" with conversation and kibitzing the order of the day. The regulars, who, by this time had been given nicknames such as "Covers" or "Covs," short for seat covers because Hunter said the old tweed sport coat Covers always wore, winter and summer, reminded him of the seat covers on the '56 Buick he had as a kid, and "Sage" which was short for Osage because he was a proud member of that tribe, joined the conversations when the compulsions seized them. The only light in the bar was the single bulb over the pool table with its ornate rose-patterned heavy stained glass shade that had survived many a bash from a cue stick during a disturbance. The "Owl" was not a place for light. Night or day, the atmosphere of smoke and stale beer was the same.

"So you wouldn't execute Charlie Manson?" said Hunter

lining up a shot.

"For the thousandth time, no. But I wouldn't parole him either."

"But you would execute Hitler?"

"No, I said I would have personally killed Hitler," Snake corrected him.

"You don't see the contradiction there?" Hunter asked moving around the table.

"Ah, Hitler wasn't so bad," said Covs from his stool.

"Shut up Covs," said Michael over his shoulder. "I always suspected you were a Nazi."

"Take that back," said a drunken Covers. "I was honorably discharged from the First Marine Battalion."

"Impressive," said Michael standing and turning. "I take it back."

"I wouldn't have executed him," said Snake. "I would have personally murdered him."

"So you don't believe in the death penalty, but you do believe in murder?" asked Michael seeking clarification.

"Exactly."

"You drive me crazy."

This was ground the two of them had plowed many times. Snake believed in big liberal government. He had come from no money in rural Montana and was the son of a hard drinking, hard working, telephone pole installer, who himself had been scarred by the Depression and believed that the only politician that would help the little man was a Democrat. All others were in the pockets of big business. Although they had never been to New York in their lives and never heard a game except for the World Series, father and son were hard-core Brooklyn Dodgers fans, "the Bums" as they were known. The ultimate Eliza Doolittles of baseball. Outsiders and overachievers.

To that day, Snake tried to never miss a night game radio broadcast from Los Angeles, the Dodgers' home since 1958, and used all kinds of radio gadgetry to get reception. His heros were Winston Churchill, Franklin Roosevelt, and Sandy Kofax. He and Michael had discovered early in their relationship that they both shared a passion for World War II history. Actually, passion was overstating Jacob Sanderson's emotion because he wasn't possessed with too many highs and lows that elevated to the level of passion. Michael, on the other hand, was truly passionate on the subject. He had, for many years, read everything he could get his hands on regarding the war and reached the conclusion that he had missed his time and war. Snake did not feel that he had missed anything, but was rather troubled and amazed by various aspects of it, such as the bombing of Pearl Harbor, which he more than once said was Japan's equivalent of kicking a hibernating grizzly in the nuts. Suicide. They would discuss Hitler and extermination of the European Jews for hours. Snake, from the perspective of how Hitler and his cronies could do such a thing, and Michael focusing on how the Jews and the rest of humanity just sat there and let it happen. They passed books on the subject back and forth and largely kept the discussions to themselves.

While observers understood the friendship between Michael and AJ, everyone missed the depth of Hunter and Sanderson's relationship. Michael considered Snake to be the finest cross-examiner he had seen or heard in a courtroom. The case of Boots Bixby solidified that opinion.

Boots had been arrested for drunk driving and been given a urine test that showed a .22 blood alcohol, more than twice the legal limit. To make matters worse, he had proudly told the officers that he had drunk over two cases of beer. Boots was a real cowboy who worked on a cattle ranch in the northeast part of the county and came to town on Saturday night to drink and sometimes fight.

The case was finally going to trial because Snake could not get Boots to plead guilty and the court ran out of patience. In a last ditch effort to avoid trial, Snake talked Michael into "good cop/bad cop" him in an interview room. Boots was as honest with them as he was with the arresting officers. He hadn't done anything wrong. He could drink two cases of beer and drive a NASCAR race. He had a well-earned high tolerance for alcoholic beverages and he wasn't drunk or anything close to it. When Michael, the bad cop, pointed out the field sobriety test where he fell over twice trying to walk a straight line, Boots said it was the worn rounded heels on his cowboy boots and the uneven pavement that caused that. Michael then grilled him about not being able to recite the alphabet past the letter 'f' and Boots retorted that he was a cowboy and not a speller and that was passing marks for a guy of his occupation. Try as they might, Boots wasn't pleading to anything and was looking forward to explaining this to a jury of his peers. Michael pointed out that he'd have to go to some shit-kicking county in rural Texas to get a jury of his peers, but Boots was dogmatic in his resolve to have his day in court.

So, Snake and Boots went to trial with no more preparation than that interview and a police report.

Hunter had decided to catch Boots' testimony and arrived when the DA was putting on his last witness, a Department of Justice expert to testify on how the urine test meant that Boots had a .22 blood alcohol when he was arrested. Snake never even looked up from his legal pad where he scribbled furiously during the DA's direct examination of the expert. The expert smiled at the jury and made knowing eye contact. Michael squirmed in his seat and wanted to bounce a shoe off of Snake's back to get him to pay attention to the lovefest going on in front of him and to make an objection or two to break it up.

And then it was Snake's turn to cross-examine. For two hours he took the expert through the process of how a person's pee could tell how much alcohol was actually in his blood at that time. Michael became convinced that, if he or any other lawyer he knew, or had ever known, tried that, the jury and everyone else in the courtroom would have been asleep from boredom in half an hour and the judge would have called a halt to the proceedings. But you would have thought they were watching the courtroom scenes from *To Kill a Mockingbird* where Atticus Finch was taking apart the alleged rape victim. Everyone was spellbound, including the DA. At the end, the disheartened and thoroughly defeated DOJ man, who had never been asked any of these questions before, had to admit that what they wound up actually testing was the equivalent of nothing larger than a grain of sand after they distilled the pee down. That was all it took. Nobody was going to jail in San Joaquin County on that shoddy evidence. The jury acquitted Boots in 20 minutes.

From that minute forward, Snake and Michael had a relationship born of mutual respect for each other's minds and abilities. While AJ was the leader of the Michael Hunter Fan Club and vice-a-versa, Snake was probably Michael's biggest professional fan and vice-a-versa.

After the trial, Michael congratulated Snake on that cross-examination and acknowledged that he could not have done it, which Snake took as the finest compliment he had ever been given. For his part, Snake confessed to Michael that he did not possess Michael's other skills. He went on to elaborate on them in great detail. Out of this sincere and genuine admiration, and appraisal of each other's skills and abilities, came a realization that they were mirror images of each other in the courtroom and they developed together numerous experimental protocols on how to conduct a jury trial or any trial for that matter.

They soon agreed that the office investigators were completely useless to them. Helen Keller could have found witnesses quicker, let alone serve a subpoena on them. So they did all of their own investigations, usually in the evenings. Because of Michael's high profile reputation amongst practioners of illegal activities, the criminal underbelly and their venues were continually available to them. That was where the real information was to be found and it wasn't open for business until after dark. Working under the theory that you had to fish where the fish were, their investigations and subpoena serving took them to some very creepy places where white civilians never ventured.

The black Elks Club was such a place. Situated in the black part of South Stockton, it was the scene of many violent black-on-black crimes when the "members" were revved up, which was mostly on weekends after dark. Certain pimps, drug dealers, and fences could be counted on to be there at various times. The trick was getting inside without incident and finding someone to vouch for you before the violence started. And then there was knowing who to talk to. You couldn't be there looking for information on a case when the client was hated by people in the room, so you had to ease into it; sit for a while, order a drink or two, maybe eat something, all the while giving free legal advice and feeling people out. There was always someone who Hunter could talk to as long as the wrong people weren't listening. When the mood was right, after awhile the witness that no one had been able to find, might come walking magically through the door. All of this was done as insurance for future times when Hunter, Snake, or AJ might be the difference in easy time, no time, or hard time.

While Michael considered this part of the job, Snake truly loved it. On any weekend night at the black Elks there were people in the room that could either kill you or get you killed without losing a night's sleep over it.

The weird part about it was that in this environment a lot of these guys were interesting. While there wasn't much formal education in the room, there was a great deal of native intelligence and street smarts. Snake could, and would, talk baseball endlessly with some of the guys who knew their ball. Also, in two years, they hadn't paid for a drink or a plate of food. It was always picked up. Even for Hunter though, there was danger in the room. Young muscle with that extra "x" chromosome, who were always pissed off, did not like them in their place of business and leisure and would glare malevolently at them muttering threats under their breath. This was greeted by harsh words and shoves from the older established men who took it as a sign of respect that Hunter and Snake came to their turf to ask for favors. Still, it was like walking through a cave of semi-hibernating rattlesnakes.

Every place wasn't so menacing as the black Elks Club. Some were down right interesting. Like the cock fights. If you wanted information from a Philippine national, the guy to see was the one in charge of the cock fights out in the islands to the West in one or another of the asparagus packing sheds. The DA, Douglas James, and Sheriff Lonigan let it go for the most part since it was a national sport in Manila and the Filipinos were an integral part of the asparagus industry, but it was an unpopular blood-sport in the U.S., so they raided one every six months or so to keep the voters happy.

Michael and Snake came within five minutes of being caught in such a raid, but were tipped just in time by the event organizer, who also tipped them to the name of a certain asparagus picker, who was the dead ringer for a tall Filipino with almond-shaped green eyes, Michael was defending on a robbery of a drive-in and who had been picked out of a photo line up as the perpetrator. Michael needed to find the look alike and subpoena him to court to create confusion amongst the three female Mexican hamburger flippers who had picked his guy's picture out of a mug book. Thanks to the cock fight impresario, Michael was able to lay paper on his guy's double and get two of the three witnesses to admit they had been scared to death by the big gun pointing in their faces and were no longer sure who it was that had robbed them.

On the whole though, the hookers were his best sources. They loved Hunter and would tell him anything. Find out things for him. Take risks for him. The reasons were simple. He got them off more times than not and he didn't look down on them and make them feel inferior. Prostitutes were important to the economic well-being of the county. The San Joaquin Valley could not get its crops grown, harvested, or to market without Mexican and Filipino labor and that labor was mostly a long way from home and in need of the professional services of Michael's fallen angels.

One of Michael's favorites was Ronnie Jean Simms, a former homecoming princess from Stagg High School, and someone who had become addicted with the very first shot of heroin her louse of a boyfriend had talked her into taking one hot summer night after graduation. She had mostly kept her fabulous blonde looks even though her liver and kidneys were about shot after five hard years on the junk. She turned heads one day as she strutted down the crowded second floor hallway in the courthouse to meet Michael for further arraignment on a prostitution and marijuana possession beef.

Ten minutes later, Michael had her case dismissed on a technicality and a grateful Ronnie reached up and kissed him on the cheek and whispered, "Come on Mike, let me give you something to show my appreciation."

"What have you got in mind, Ronnie?" asked an amused Michael.

"What I got for you has nothing to do with my mind. Let's hit the men's room."

"Don't you think it's just a little crowded in there right now?"

"Those stalls got doors don't they?" she said.

"I love the thought kid, but I'll take a rain check," he said.

"You'd have loved more than that, baby," she said giving his hand a squeeze as she turned to leave. "And you can use that rain check anytime," she said over her shoulder.

Another time Hunter was taking a female police officer he saw from time to time at her house, mostly after her evening shift was over, to one of Hawthorne's cocktail parties at his large home on Lake Lincoln. He had talked the decked-to-the-nines red headed bombshell in her low-cut cocktail dress into stopping at a bar on the Miracle Mile for a quick drink before the party. Already late and nervous about meeting his co-workers, the shapely Sharon Rogers was none too pleased, but what the hell, "just a short one." Five minutes later, seated at the bar smoking a cigarette, she realized Michael was there to interview the bartender, a chief prosecution witness in a bank robbery. To make matters worse, it was a police case and she was a cop. Not much of a start for their first actual date.

Michael called the bartender over and said he was an

attorney and had a few questions about the case. The way he said it, even Sharon thought he was a DA. After a few minutes, the bartender started to catch the drift since Michael's line of questioning was distinctly defensive in nature.

"Which office did you say you were with?" he asked.

"I didn't say," answered Michael.

"Maybe I should call the police before answering any more questions," said the bartender.

Completely fed up with the proceedings, Sharon's one remaining nerve snapped.

"I am the damned police," she yelled ripping her badge from her delicate sequined handbag and slamming it down on the bar. "Now answer his damn questions before I run you in."

Later, in the car on the way to the party, Michael said, "I think you might be hearing a little something about this."

"Screw it," she said, blowing smoke out the passenger's window. "I was thinking of getting my real estate license anyway."

Tuesday, November 21ᵀᴴ, 7 a.m.

"I better order breakfast," said Michael as he and Alice sat side-by-side at Emma's.

"Why don't you make it easy on Martha and just order the left side of the menu," said Alice stirring her coffee.

"I can't listen to you bitch at me on an empty stomach," he replied.

"Martha," he said to the waitress, "get me my usual."

"Speaking of bitches," began Alice. "What were you thinking with when you took 'Little Miss Boalt Hall' over with you to Dewey's?"

"Just seeing if a little of the behind the scenes education might re-channel some of that misplaced enthusiasm," he said.

"You confuse enthusiasm with ambition," said Alice.

"What's the problem?" he asked.

"Word is Latchman's talking her into reporting you to the Bar Association."

"You're kidding?"

"Nope. Somebody needs to straighten her out."

"Forget it."

"It's not that I mind the part-time job of watching your back, but you're turning it into a career and I could use a little cooperation," she said exasperated.

"Speaking of which, what's this I hear about you counseling her Honor?" she asked raising an eyebrow.

Hunter was truly stunned. He put down his coffee cup and turned to face her. "You really belong with the CIA," he said. "Where do you get your information?"

"Never mind. Answer the question," she snapped.

"Judge Adams has a little situation," he began. He decided to confide in Alice about the judge's personal problem that he had literally stumbled upon when he barged into her chambers one early morning before court and caught her draped over her desk with her skirt up and her married Mexican bailiff, Jessie Ortiz, on top of her. Up to that point, Michael had believed the rumors that she was a heavy boozer, if for no other reason than the way she looked every morning with her blood-shot eyes, aging and reddening facial features, and shaky hands.

After court that day, the judge had called Michael into chambers and tearfully confessed her lifestyle. Burdened from childhood with chronic disc abnormalities in her back, she had become a heavy abuser of prescription medication and, in recent years, alcohol. Never married, she had entered into a relationship with her young athletic looking legal secretary, whom she now lived with and passed off as her roommate, which she had been for many years. Recently, in the last year, she had grown closer to her bailiff, Jesse Ortiz, who had personally battled and licked similar problems when he had been on the local police force. It was during one of those counseling sessions that Judge Maggie Adams decided that she had been playing for the wrong team. Now, she was desperately in love with a man for the first time in her life and she and Jesse couldn't keep their hands off each other. She was now juggling three secrets like so many balls frantically trying to keep them all in the air.

"Are you kidding?" said Alice. "Just because she and her roommate go out to dinner once a week with a couple of rump ranger hairdressers doesn't fool anybody in town about their arrangement."

"Oh she thinks it's a big secret," said Michael.

"Listen, I was born and raised in that town," said Alice. "And the big secret will be that she's not a dyke."

Just then, AJ Borelli strolled in wearing Michael's sport coat.

"You dress in the dark AJ?" asked Alice.

"Where's your coat man?" asked Michael.

"Cleaners," said AJ sitting down.

"You took your coat to the cleaners and didn't have a spare?" asked Alice.

"I was following a girl that works there," he said. "And, I

couldn't catch up with her before she went inside, so what was I going to do?"

"There's a whole lot of things you could have done," said Michael. "Giving her your coat isn't top ten on my list."

"To clean," he answered flustered.

"Well, you better roll up the sleeves on that thing," said Alice.

"I've got it covered," said AJ pulling two large rubber bands out of the coat pocket.

"You can't be long, because I've got to see Judge Hollins after his morning calendar and that's my only jacket," said Michael.

"Either of you guys read the paper this morning?" asked Alice.

"No, what's up?" said AJ.

"They made an arrest in the sheriff's niece's murder," she answered.

"No kidding," said AJ peering over her shoulder at the headlines.

"Who was it?" asked Michael.

"Some guy named Eddie Reno," she said.

"Never heard of him," said AJ.

"We've never had him in the office before," said Alice.

Wondering how she already knew that little fact at 7 in the morning, Michael asked, "He got a lawyer yet?"

"Didn't say," she answered. "We'll find out at the arraignment. Looks open and shut though. They found her wallet and crap in his car."

"Perfect time to be leaving town for a while," said AJ getting up and slapping his friend on the back. "I'll get the coat back in an hour."

Chapter 11

"Got anything for me Beau?" Michael Hunter asked as he came into the law library.

Beaumont "Merlin" Henderson was seated at his usual spot, flanked by his interns along with Joe Larsen, looking up with a big grin, and Sybil Waxman, refusing to make eye contact with Hunter.

"I think so, Mike," said Merlin. "It depends on busting the warrant."

"What do you need?" asked Hunter.

"More than I got right now," Merlin answered. "But I know that it's out there."

He went on to explain to Michael that he needed some testimony on the fact that the narcs were really there looking for stolen mechanical drawings, not drugs. He also needed some evidence that said the drawings existed other than the client's testimony which no judge would believe.

"Let me see what I can do," said Michael.

As he turned to leave, Joe Larsen said, "Hey Mike, I got my first trial. Can I run it by you?"

"What kind of case is it?"

"Possession of marijuana," answered Joe.

"Come see me," said Michael.

Sybil Waxman glared at Joe as Michael walked out of the room without a word to her.

TUESDAY, NOVEMBER 21ST, 2 P.M.

Department 3 of the Superior Court of San Joaquin County was locked and dark so Michael went down to the clerk's office and found Agnes Brown, Judge Wallace Hollins' clerk, who greeted him warmly and accompanied him to the courtroom where she let him in the side chamber door with her passkey. Once in, he knocked on the door to the judge's chambers and waited until he was ushered in by the booming voice of the judge.

"Thanks for coming over, Mike. Sorry I couldn't see you earlier, but something came up," said Hollins.

"No problem your Honor. What can I do for you?" said Michael.

"Why don't you pour us a drink first," said the Judge.

Michael could see that his face was weary and drawn. He looked as though he'd missed sleep. He noticed, as he handed the Judge his paper cup of gin, that Hollins' hand trembled slightly. The Judge motioned for him to take a seat, which he did after placing the bottle on the desk.

"That favor I mentioned a week or so ago that I hoped I wouldn't need," began Hollins gravely. "Well, I need it."

"Whatever you need," said Michael. "I told you that."

"And, I told you that you'd better hear me out first."

"I'm listening."

"You know that I have a profoundly retarded daughter," Hollins began. Michael nodded.

He had found out about that fact during the Justin Rose

case. Justin Rose was an 18-year old mildly retarded boy from a poor family who coaxed a two-year-old neighbor girl into his back yard when no one was looking and strangled her to death with a length of electrical cord and then hid her body in a garbage can in the alley behind his parents' house. He then went off calmly bike riding as if nothing had happened. He even joined the search for her after her frantic mother couldn't find her and roused the neighborhood and called the police. With more than 50 people looking, her body was discovered in the Roses' garbage can before nightfall. The police immediately questioned the Rose family, who by now were home, and within 15 minutes Justin cheerfully confessed everything without the slightest bit of remorse or emotion. He was immediately charged with first degree murder and after a preliminary hearing, Hunter was assigned the case which happened to be in Judge Hollins' courtroom. Because of the press, and the sensational nature of the case, the DA, Douglas James, put Reggie Hind, his chief trial deputy, who reportedly had never lost a jury trial, on the case.

Before the first appearance in Superior Court, Michael had gone to the county jail to see Justin personally and was shocked at what he found. Not sure what he was expecting, he took one look at the baby-faced dimwitted Rose and knew that something was very odd. Rose looked no older than 14 or 15 sitting there in the jail interview room in a dingy white t-shirt. He acted as if he were at summer camp receiving an unannounced visitor from home. He smiled and politely answered all of Michael's questions and told him how much he liked the little neighbor girl who unsuspectingly went with him into the backyard where he threw a long electrical cord over the limb of an apple tree, tied it to her neck, and hung her. When Michael asked him what he did next, he said he went into the house and got a Pepsi. Justin told him that he then went back to the little girl, took her down and put her in the garbage can. When asked why the garbage can, he said if his father came home from work and found a mess, he would give him a good whipping and he didn't want another whipping.

Justin said all of that without showing the least bit of remorse, sorrow, or concern. When Michael asked him why he did it, Justin gave him a sweet smile and said he did it because he didn't want to look after her anymore. Michael asked him what he meant. Justin told him that his father made him work and one of his jobs was to look after this little girl when her mother asked him to and when she did, he couldn't go bike riding with the "older" kids which was his favorite thing. So he got rid of her.

After a night of fitful sleep, Hunter appeared the next morning with Justin Rose in front of Judge Hollins and entered a plea of not guilty by reason of insanity and requested that Rose be evaluated under Sections 1368 and 1370 of the California Penal Code. Deputy District Attorney Reggie Hind stood up and objected to the referral.

"Grounds, Mr. Hind?" asked Judge Hollins.

"I don't believe it is proper to enter a plea for a defendant and refer him for a psychiatric exam that says he can't cooperate with counsel," said Hind.

"Overruled" said the Judge. "Counsel was not pleading his client guilty and, therefore, he can enter this plea on his behalf. It is not inconsistent with the referral."

"Then I object to the referral under both 1368 and 1370," said Hind.

"Why?" asked Judge Hollins drumming his fingers.

"Because 1370 is a code section referring to mental retardation and 1368 is for mental illness. They are inconsistent."

"Why?" asked Hollins leaning forward.

"Because mentally retarded people can't be mentally ill within the meaning of that code section, they are one or the other. Mr. Hunter should pick one," answered Hind.

The judge reached up and pushed his glasses down to the end of his bulbous nose before speaking, "Mr. Hind, your ignorance in this area is colossal. First of all, you keep calling Mr. Rose 'retarded' on the record. The proper term is 'developmentally disabled.' Next, you obviously know nothing of the disability or you would never make the statement that they can't also be suffering from a mental illness. I'm appointing three doctors for each code section. Any suggestions, Mr. Hunter?" he asked turning his attention to Michael.

"I'd like to see the child psychologist, Dr. Arthur Rosenberg, on the 1370 panel, and child psychiatrist, Dr. Rita Sawyer, on the 1368," said Michael.

"Excellent choices," said the judge. "The court will appoint the other four from the approved list."

"Wait a minute," said an agitated Hind. "The people would like some say in this."

"I think the court has heard all it wants from the 'people' today," said Judge Hollins. "Give them a date in about 30 days and call the next case," he said turning to his clerk, Agnes Brown.

Up until that moment, Hunter had all but made up his mind to get rid of Hollins. He hadn't spent much time in front of him, but knew him by reputation and didn't think he would be much of a judge for technical defenses or in any way inclined to think outside the box on a criminal case. But now, he wasn't so sure. Whatever was going on between the judge and Reggie Hind, he was presently the beneficiary, so he decided to ride along for a while.

Within a short time, Michael met the mother, father, and sister of Justin Rose and found out that they were all at most in the "dull/normal" range when it came to intelligence. The father was an abusive sort and the mother took her occasional beatings stoically and expected the kids to do the same. On a hunch, he obtained the police and incident reports for the family and pieced together a strange mosaic of family behavior. Apparently, little Justin had been involved in some violent behavior before and that it had been dismissed because he was slow and sweet by nature. A few years back, he had shot his younger sister with a bow and arrow while she was up in the same apple tree that he hung the little girl from and put her in the hospital. Ruled an accident by the investigating officer who hadn't interviewed Justin, just the father. Last year, he set fire to the house; ruled an accident. Again, no one talked to Justin.

Hunter decided to make sure he was present when Doctors Rosenberg and Sawyer and Frank Hurley went together to do their interview with Justin, which was his right. Rosenberg had already given Justin an IQ test and scored him at 73, just over the 70 limit Michael was hoping for.

They had to put some extra chairs in the attorney interview room at the county jail in order for the three doctors to conduct their interview with Justin Rose.

Michael Hunter sat over in the corner of the room, taking a few notes and watching with mild interest as the angelic Justin, dressed once again in his orange jail pants and white t-shirt, answered the questions put to him by one doctor or another. He thought Justin was answering as any dull/normal/borderline developmentally disabled young man would and was doing his best to be cheerful and honest in his answers. In other words, Michael became quickly convinced that all of this was going to be a waste of time.

Justin clearly was understanding what was going on, was able to comprehend right from wrong as far as the questions were concerned, and was well oriented to place and time. The fact that he showed absolutely no remorse was a bit troubling, but Michael knew well that under California law, while there were a lot of parameters to the rules, basically you had to be so nuts that you couldn't comprehend that your actions were wrong or that you were unaware and disoriented with your surroundings at the time you took your actions to be not guilty by reason of insanity.

Clearly Justin knew he killed the little girl and he'd wanted to do it. Michael did not think the doctors were going to be impressed with the fact that the reasons didn't make sense or that he didn't have any remorse.

After a little while, Michael got bored and began leafing through the police report and his notes thinking about other ideas for handling the case. He was not looking in the direction of Justin when the question was asked. Rather, he was pre-occupied with his reading, keeping half a brain cell available to monitor the proceedings.

It was Dr. Rita Sawyer, the child psychiatrist that asked Justin, "Why did you put the little girl in the garbage can after you killed her?"

What happened next was one of those things that everyone in the room would later comment to themselves and to each other, that they were sure they would never forget the moment as long as they lived.

Upon later reflection, over lots of alcohol and lost sleep, Michael was sure that it was the voice rather than the words that made the hair on the back of his neck stick straight up and his head jerk around while he leaped out of his chair and slammed his back up against the wall of the interview room so hard that his back hurt for weeks afterward.

"TO HIDE HER REPLICATION OF COURSE!" said the voice coming from a person that was no longer Justin Rose.

Dr. Sawyer let out a gasp and put her hand over her mouth. Arthur Rosenberg, the child psychologist, tipped over backwards in his chair, sprawling his bulky frame on the floor, breaking his glasses. Dr. Frank Hurley, also a psychiatrist, sat frozen with his mouth open and his eyes bugging out in absolute terror.

Before them, sat the beast. The face was not that of Justin Rose. It was swollen and contorted and had a maniacal evil expression on it. It laughed a booming laugh and then it disappeared. And just that suddenly, Justin Rose was back.

The room was pure chaos. Michael grabbed the receiver on the wall phone and hit the emergency button. Within seconds, armed deputies were at the door unlocking it demanding to know what had happened. No one said a word. What was there to say. They were all grown adults who were absolutely terrified of this little 18-year-old boy who didn't look tough enough to lick his sister.

Days went by before Michael told anybody about the incident. When he did, he only told Snake who tried to pass it off as some split personality or psychotic episode which Michael knew was all bullshit.

He finally called each of the doctors and asked for a joint meeting, which they readily agreed upon. They met for lunch at a quiet downtown restaurant, taking a back booth. Michael could see that everyone was extremely nervous at what they had witnessed and found out that none of them had as yet written their reports. When he asked Dr. Sawyer why not, she said she didn't know how.

So after they ordered, Michael asked the question they had all been thinking about. "So what was that?"

Everybody shook their heads. The psychologist, Dr. Rosenberg, normally an affable gregarious wild man, simply muttered, "I have absolutely no explanation for this and I'm way out of my league."

Dr. Sawyer said, "I know what you're looking for Michael and I just can't do it."

"What do you think I'm looking for, Doc?" Michael asked her. "You think I'm trying to get you to write your report one particular way or another. Well, normally I probably would be, but not in this case. I just want to know what the hell that was."

Dr. Hurley, taking a sip of his water, looked up and said meekly, "All I know is that was the killer."

"I don't know about the rest of you, but I'm finding him insane," said Dr. Sawyer.

Rosenberg chimed in and said, "I believe that his developmental disability is such that he is susceptible to certain kinds of mental illness and strain that render him incapable of cooperating effectively with counsel and that's what I'm going to say."

Hurley added, "He's totally insane and should never be outside of an institution. He is the most dangerous person I have ever met."

Michael then told them what he knew about the family history and the other incidents. Nobody said much the remainder of lunch and they just paid their checks and left.

The other three doctors on the panel interviewed Justin Rose a few days later without Michael present. He had told each and every one of them to be very careful and that it would be a good idea to have a deputy sheriff in the room with them. They almost laughed at him on the phone and told him that it would not be necessary. Michael made them promise to do it and they assured him that they would if he wanted them to, but these attorney theatrics of his weren't helping his case any.

The reports on Justin came in all over the place except for Doctors Sawyer, Rosenberg, and Hurley who were all adamant that this young man was insane, deeply disturbed, and developmentally disabled. While Rosenberg felt that he couldn't cooperate with counsel, the other doctors said that he could, but that he was insane now, and at the time of the commission of these crimes. However, they would not give a medical basis for his insanity in their reports.

At the next court date, Michael and Reggie Hind went into chambers where Reggie immediately made a big deal out of the fact that the only doctors who knew what they were doing in this case were obviously the ones that the judge picked from the panel and not the ones suggested by Michael and that all of this was basically ridiculous.

By this time, Hind was up on his procedure and his knowledge with respect to developmental disability and the 1368 and 1370 code sections. He was itching to quote chapter and verse when Michael stopped him and told both he and the judge what had transpired in the jail interview room two weeks before.

Reggie Hind was once again very agitated and said, "Your Honor, you're not going to listen to this are you?"

Judge Hollins held up his hand to quiet Hind and said to Michael, "Tell me the story again and don't leave anything out."

Michael repeated the story again, including every detail he could remember. The judge just stared at him the whole time. When he finished, Judge Hollins took off his glasses and said, "I noticed you were walking a little funny when you came in today. Did you hurt yourself?"

Michael told him that he'd hurt his back when he

slammed into the wall in the interview room. Hollins just stared at him for a while and said, "Ought to get that looked at."

Then it was Hind's turn. "I don't know what's going on here, but if anybody in this room thinks that the district attorney's office is going to lay down and let some slick talking public defender walk this child murderer out the back of the courtroom, they're crazy. Crazier than Hunter thinks Justin Rose is."

Judge Hollins looked at Reggie Hind, like he was some yapping poodle, and said, "I don't think that's what Mr. Hunter wants to do here, am I right Mr. Hunter?"

Michael nodded his head.

"Well, I don't care what he wants to do," said Hind. "This guy's going to prison for the rest of his life."

Judge Hollins decided to ignore Hind at this point. The way he ignored him was with obvious purpose and no one, least of all Hind, missed the purpose. With a mere glance at him as one would give a buzzing fly when your attention is tuned elsewhere, in this case on Michael, he reduced him to an irrelevancy in the proceeding.

"What haven't you told me about this, Mr. Hunter? Now would be a good time."

Michael then made one of those choices that have to be made instantaneously and upon instinct rather than on reasoned thought. In that second, he decided to violate attorney/client privileges and confidences in front of the judge and the prosecutor and without his client's permission. He told Hollins about the previous incidents of family violence where, in his opinion, his client had attempted to kill first his sister and then his entire family when he set fire to the house.

"How do you know for sure he did those things?" asked Hollins.

"Because the beast told me," Michael answered, elaborating that after the incident with the doctors he had gone back by himself a week later and questioned Justin regarding the previous incidents until the 'beast', as Michael called him, returned.

"Oh come on," said a thoroughly annoyed Reggie Hind, painfully aware that he wasn't a part of the proceeding.

"Is the beast disabled?" asked the judge.

"If you mean slow like Rose, no. He's pure evil, but not slow."

"What do you want?" asked the judge.

Michael squirmed in his chair thinking about how to phrase it. "Your Honor, I have no idea what we are dealing with here and neither do the doctors. I know my job is to defend this guy, but there are no rules for this," he paused before continuing. "If a jury finds him guilty or not guilty by reason of insanity, it's irrelevant. Either way, someone is going to get killed again. Worse than that, if I put the three doctors on the stand and cross-examine them about what they saw, they will look like fools and their careers will possibly be severely damaged," he said pausing again, thinking as he talked. "What I think is best, is that you hold the 1368 and 1370 hearings in chambers with my permission so that the doctors can speak freely. And you find what you find."

"And if I find him incompetent to stand trial?" the judge asked. "What then?"

"Then you craft an order sending him to a state facility that is not an unpleasant place to be, but where they are capable enough to see that he doesn't hurt anyone else," said Michael.

"For how long?" asked the judge.

"For the rest of his life, your Honor. Justin Rose must never be released, in my opinion."

There was a long silence in the room, finally broken by the commanding voice of Judge Wallace Hollins, "I think that's the best we can do. Between now and then Mr. Hunter, you are ordered to select someone from mental health or from the regional center for developmentally disabled persons, or both, and together find the best location for this poor soul. You will do this at county expense."

And that was what happened. Hunter did as he was ordered and reported back to Judge Hollins, meeting him in his chambers where they got to know each other. It was during this that the judge confided that he had an adult daughter who was severely retarded and had recently become both very sexual and physically aggressive and his wife, Madge, could no longer handle her at home. She was in the state hospital now, a fact that deeply saddened the judge.

Now, here he was again in front of an obviously troubled Wallace Hollins, dredging up old memories.

The judge continued his explanation of his problem. It had come to his attention from one of the staff members at the hospital that a certain cab driver was picking up a couple of the retarded patients that were not too unpleasant to look at, taking them off the hospital grounds with phony passes, and then driving them out to the labor camps and prostituting them to the workers. His daughter had been treated for gonorrhea and a staff member had pieced the story together and called the police who sent over an officer from vice to investigate. Apparently the cab driver knew his business because he had picked women who were too disabled to give any usable information. Hollins had done a little discreet checking and confirmed what he had been told.

Michael listened intently to the story, anger rising through him with every word the judge spoke.

"I tried to keep Madge from finding out about this, but she was told about the VD and began asking questions," said the pained judge. "You know Madge, Mike," he said. "She's not a crier, but now she cries all the time."

Michael did indeed know Madge Hollins. He had been to dinner at their house several times. Their other children were all back in Georgia and they enjoyed having Michael over especially the hard-drinking, chain-smoking, no nonsense Madge who loved "putting on the dog" as she called it when Michael came by to visit.

Because Hollins was himself a very private person and recognized that trait in Michael, they didn't socialize very much. Hollins' passion was the law, and of late, the law had begun to disappoint him with what he considered to be unwarranted and unnecessary changes, especially the liberalization of the criminal justice system and the "no fault" divorce system recently adopted in California. When justice was either delayed or denied, then it was only a matter of time until the system completely broke down. These were the after dinner discussions he and Michael would have until late in the evening.

As Michael watched the obvious pain in the man he so admired, he realized it was a case of denied justice that they were going to speak about.

"I can't live with this Mike," said Judge Hollins.

Michael nodded and waited.

"I know that I shouldn't be asking you for this, but I can't think of anything else," he added.

"You want me to take care of this," said Michael. "No problem your Honor."

"I don't want anything bad to happen. I just want him gone," said the judge.

Michael stood up, drained his drink, and walked around

the huge desk and put an arm around the big man who was doing his best to fight back tears. He leaned down and whispered in the judge's ear, "Consider it done. My best to Madge."

Michael then walked out of the chambers and closed the door quietly.

Chapter 12

Alice Benson climbed the two flights of stairs to the third floor and walked into Snake Sanderson's office and said, "We need to have a little talk."

"What about?" said Snake looking up from the "weekly line" he was trying to figure out.

"Sybil Waxman," she said closing the door.

<hr>

TUESDAY, NOVEMBER 21ST, 3:05 P.M.

"Michael, my good man," said Merlin as Michael strolled into the library. "What can I do you for?"

"I think I got an angle on the 1538.5 on the guy with the mechanical drawings," said Michael in response to Merlin's question.

"Tell me about it," said Merlin.

"I want a 1538.5 on the warrant and I want an evidentiary hearing," said Michael.

"You want the usual boiler plate stuff about the prosecution having the burden of proof to prove that the warrant had probable cause?" said Merlin.

"Absolutely," said Michael.

"It's a dead bang looser unless you have a witness."

"I'm not going to need a witness in this case," said Michael.

"I may go over to watch that myself," replied Merlin.

———◄◉►———

Tuesday, November 21ˢᵗ, 3:20 p.m.

The library lit up when Sidney Grossman walked in and for good reason. He went right over to Beaumont "Merlin" Henderson with a huge smile on his face, slapped him on the back, and shook his hand. When Merlin pulled his hand away, there were two $100 bills folded into it.

"What do you need, Sidney?" said a smiling and pleased Merlin.

"Whatever you can do for me, Beau," said the almost bald Grossman using his rapid manic style of speaking, dropping a file on Merlin's desk. "Whatever you can do, buddy. Might have a little search issue here. Just take a look, see what you can do. How you doin' fellas?" he said shaking the interns' hands.

Grossman was an institution. A personal friend of Bradley Hawthorne's, he was the only private lawyer that was afforded the privilege of using the law library staff. A privilege he always paid for in cash to Beaumont Henderson who personally wrote the various motions that Grossman needed. The irony was that Grossman was all bark and no bite when it came to the practice of law. One of the highest paid attorneys in the county, he was a one-man office that took virtually every case that came in through the door, quoting high fees that he insisted on collecting in advance. His top flight legal secretary handled all of the law and motion civil practice with the help of three typists that she kept burning up the keys on their IBM Selectric typewriters. On the criminal side of things, Grossman knew enough to spot an issue when he saw it, but not enough to handle it himself and that was where Merlin came in. For a couple of hundred in off-the-books cash, he would scare up a motion that made Sid look good and, more importantly, could charge a grand or two for himself. Odd as it was, no one seemed to mind or resent the intrusion, mostly because Big Sid was one of the most affable people you would want to meet and knew everyone in town worth knowing.

Taking it all in was Sybil Waxman sitting at one of the long tables picking over a motion that she didn't want to write. She was preoccupied with the promise she had made Stanley Latchman to report Michael Hunter to the bar association for unethical conduct over the Ramirez case. She thought Sidney Grossman, who had just extended his pink sweaty hand to her, was the kind of glad handing Jew who gave other Jews, such as herself, a bad name. She sized him up as a big con artist who was nothing more than the legal equivalent of a rug merchant. Watching him mince around the room fawning over the interns for God sake, she made up her mind to not get caught up in this side show masquerading as a law office and to get the hell out of there as soon as possible.

"How you doin'? How you doin?" asked Grossman smiling. "Great place to work, isn't it? You couldn't ask for better experience."

"I didn't realize we would get the chance to work on private cases," said Sybil cooly.

Letting the insult bounce off his pear shaped frame, Sidney pressed on with his good cheer, "Aw, you know how it is. You go to the best if you want the best and this place is the best. Am I right fellas?" he said around the room. The interns nodded like grinning bobble-head dolls. They obviously enjoyed Sidney.

The exchange was not lost on Beaumont however. He didn't want Sidney to get his feelings hurt, so he said, "I'll read it tonight Sid, and if there's anything I'll write something up and drop it by your office at lunchtime tomorrow."

Sidney took the cue and began backing out of the room saying good-bye to everyone and great to meet you to an unsmiling Sybil Waxman.

"I hate people like him," she said after he left and drew only silence from the others in the room.

The smell of Sidney Grossman's Old Spice aftershave was still in the air when Jacob Sanderson walked through the door.

"In the immortal words of Marvin Gaye, Snake, 'what's going on?'" said Merlin delighted with all of the recent company to his stronghold.

"I need to learn a little more about aiding and abetting," Snake answered nodding hello to everyone in the room.

"What do you got?" asked Merlin dropping into his resident law genius persona.

"Two suspects found over a body in a crowd. One stabbed him; one didn't," said Snake.

"One knife?"

"One knife."

"Interesting," said Merlin. "Get me the crime report. In the meantime, grab *AMJUR* over there. It's in the index.

Cut here

You need a big overview. That'll give you everything on it nationally."

"Thanks. I'll send the CR down," said Snake grabbing the *AMJUR* index and selecting the correct volume, taking a seat next to Sybil Waxman.

"How's it going?" he said sitting down.

"You graduated from Boalt Hall didn't you?" she asked in response.

"How'd you know that?" asked Snake raising one bushy eyebrow.

"I checked you out," she responded.

"Why?"

She ignored the question and instead asked one of her own, "What was your class standing?"

"What difference does it make?"

"There are studies on this you know," she began. "How your class standing correlates to your job and how fast you advance," she continued. "I was sixth in my class," she added with emphasis.

"I remember you mentioning that," he said. "You mind a little advice?"

"No," she answered warily. You could have heard a pin drop in the room. Merlin and interns were all as still as Bernini sculptures.

"Don't mention that anymore. It's like wearing your high school letterman's sweater in college. Nobody cares and it makes you look stupid."

"Not everyone in this place agrees with you," she said defensively.

"That's another thing," said Snake. "Latchman and that group of second floor bozos are steering you wrong. None of 'em are good enough to carry Hunter's briefcase and that's why they can't stand him. He shows them up."

"Well, I'm sorry, but I think you're wrong. Stanley Latchman is very professional and an excellent attorney," she said sticking her nose in the air.

One of the interns snorted involuntarily and Merlin blurted out, "How would you know?"

Everyone turned and looked at him and Merlin said, "Sorry. I was just wondering if this was a private fight or could anyone join in."

Snake just shook his head in disgust and got up and left the room. Sybil looked around at the three young men staring at her. "What?" she asked.

Chapter 13

The Moretti family home on Union Street across from the railroad tracks was within walking distance of old downtown Stockton and everything an old Italian housewife could need. It was a single story, cheaply built for the times, turn of the century box with a basement which had only been partially finished on purpose. *You have to have the right dirt on the floor to cure the sausage and the salami.* Situated on a half acre lot, as were all of the old houses in the area, there was room for a large year-round garden, fruit trees, a pigeon coop and a brick bread oven. The place had been home to Big John Moretti and his five brothers and sisters since they arrived in this country as small children.

The house was now occupied by the unmarried and oldest of the children, Carmel, a thick, dark saint of a woman with swollen ankles and legs, road-mapped with varicose veins from thirty years of standing at a wood sorting belt at the pencil factory. She had sacrificed any chance of a personal life to stay home and take care of her ailing and now dead mother and her father, who was in his 80s and senile. She was the gatekeeper of all family recipes and lore and preferred the traditional methods and Italian tongue of her mother. There was a "new" 20-year old Sears gas range and oven in the upstairs kitchen, never used. Instead, all of the cooking was done in the basement on an ancient wooden stove and oven where large and small feasts were prepared. In the room with the oven, was a sink and cupboards and a bolted down table with bolted down wooden benches around which all of the Morettis had dined until they left home.

In the next room, was a long wooden table that could seat over 20, which it did every holiday. Off of that room, was a little 4 x 8 foot "bedroom" with a single bed and large crucifix on the wall with an old painting of the Virgin Mary where Carmel slept each night. In another room was the un-finished part of the basement where all the canned goods and jams were stored along with the curing meats in season and a variety of cooking apparatus that by now you'd have to go to Italy to replace.

Carmel's life was now taking care of her father and cook-ing lunch daily for the men in the family who ate there ev-ery day when they could. Ever since Michael had teamed up with AJ and brought him to his first family dinner, he had been welcomed as well. In addition, Carmel canned all of the family's sauces, jams, condiments, and fruit and made Thanksgiving and Easter dinners for the lot. The menu had changed only once in decades. That was when Michael had been taken in by Big John almost literally off the streets when he was 15. Instantly, all of the women in the family wrapped him in a protective cocoon of motherly love and doting which manifested itself in many ways, not the least of which was an unprecedented menu change at the next big family dinner. The normal menu had been antipasto, turkey, ham, ravioli, Italian salad, and yams. Because Michael had never had real Italian food before and had been raised on a bland Mid-Western diet, where the only steak he'd ever had until he was 9 was chicken-fried, they added mashed potatoes, gravy, and dressing just for him. "What's this shit?" asked the mostly blind and senile Giovanni, Big John's father, the first time he found some of it on his plate.

Now, eleven years later, Michael sat next to AJ at the long table eating Thanksgiving dinner. There were a half dozen loud conversations going on at the same time overlapping each other. Typically, everyone felt privileged to butt in with an opinion or comment on anyone's business being discussed. To the ordinarily private Michael, this was the only area in his life where he suspended the rules and gave in and allowed these people to pry and prod him for personal information. From the first day he'd met them all at a gathering, he'd been accepted by them because of Big John's status in the family's hierarchy. And, in short order, he'd gained his own status. First as an athlete and then for his brains and charisma. Now, he was the *consigliore*. A word that didn't translate well into English. It was not lost on AJ, at his first Moretti family dinner, that Michael was treated with a different form of respect than the rest of the men in the family, including Big John. A fair argument would be that you would have had to have been raised in a large first generation Italian family to appreciate the hierarchy, but AJ knew that it was more than that. It was extraordinary that this 24-year old Irishman would be accorded, with the obvious blessing of Big John, this type of respect. Teased incessantly, yes. But always with a note of respect. And, how first one, then another, would wait until the right moment and ask for a word with him outside.

And so, it took AJ completely by surprise when Rose Moretti turned to him during dinner and asked him to help her with her car accident case. Flattered, he stammered, "What about Mike?"

"Oh, he's too busy for that," she said matter-of-factly,

as if that was understood, and then reaching out and putting her hand on his arm, she added, "besides, you're better with money and I know you'll get me what's right."

"Absolutely," he said flattered by her trust. He had no intention of mentioning that it was strictly a firing offense to take a private civil case when employed by the county and that he had no idea how to handle her case in the first place.

Across the table, AJ could hear Paul say to his father, "I hear it's open and shut. They found her wallet in his car and are sure that DOJ will match the paint transfer."

"They get a confession?" asked Big John.

"No, he ain't talking."

"Then it's not open and shut," said his father. "You give your notice yet?" he asked Michael seated across from him.

"Not until it's official," said Michael.

"I thought it was a done deal," Big John said to his son.

"All but," answered Paul. "The chief's approved it and it's just waiting on the sheriff to bless it any day now."

"Jesus, pop's eating his Toscano cigar again," said Big John pushing his chair back. "He'll be puking in a minute."

"When are you and Anthony going to find some good girls?" a female cousin named Marie yelled from down the table. "You's not going queer on us are you?"

"AJ's got a new girl. At the dry cleaners," Michael yelled back.

"I bet he's got something for her to clean," shouted Marie to a roar of laughter.

"Is she Italian, Anthony?" asked Rose.

"I haven't exactly talked to her," said AJ sheepishly.

"Bring her to the house," said Rose. "I'll fix something nice."

"Did you miss the point where he said he hadn't met her

yet?" asked Michael.

"Meet, shmeet," scoffed Rose. "She's not going to turn down a nice professional boy like Anthony."

"Make sure she's not a putana looking for your money," said Big John from the head of the table where he was giving Giovanni an empty Folger's coffee can to spit up in, if necessary.

"I can't meet anybody until I get back from Mexico," said AJ trying to change the subject.

"Make sure you take plenty of rubbers," said Big John's brother Jimmy to shrieks of laughter and hoots.

"Jimmy!" said Rose trying to suppress a smile. And that was how they all whiled away the last carefree afternoon they would have for some time.

Chapter 14

The second Hunter walked through the doors to Emma's Coffee Shop and saw the look on Alice Benson's face, he knew there was big trouble. What could it possibly be the morning after Thanksgiving was his only thought as he took the stool next to hers. One tip off was that she was smoking. He thought that she'd quit.

"Morning sunshine," he said smiling.

"They're arraigning the guy that killed the Van Houten girl this morning," she said grimly.

"So?"

"So, the word is that unless someone shows up to represent him, we're getting it and the boss is immediately putting AJ on it," she said.

The news completely blind-sided Hunter. None of it made any sense. First of all, not that it mattered, but why was he being arraigned in the morning and not in the afternoon with the rest of the felonies? Second, why give the case to somebody before the prelim? There was no death penalty and, most important, why AJ?

"Where the hell do you get your information," Hunter asked her incredulously.

"Never mind," she said. "It's good. And you know what this means?" she asked, sadness in her voice.

"What?" he asked warily.

"AJ's Mexico trip is off," she answered. "I'm sorry Mike."
"Oh no!" yelled Hunter jumping off the stool. "No way. You can't cancel a guy's vacation. This is bullshit." Martha and Emma both stopped what they were doing as he hopped around in a rage. "AJ's not even up," he said pointing a finger at Alice. "It's one of those second floor bums' turn," he added slamming his fist down hard on the formica counter, hard enough to rattle a few dishes.

"Easy there stallion," said Martha bringing over his coffee cautiously as if she were approaching a wild animal.

"I don't know why he just didn't give it to me if he wanted to screw me out of my vacation. This is the lousiest thing he's ever pulled," steamed Michael referring to Bradley Hawthorne.

"It's not about you Mike," Alice said calmly.

"Oh, bullshit Al," he stormed at her. "You'd cover for Hitler if you worked for him."

"That's not fair Mike. You take that back right now. I mean it," she shouted, her eyes beginning to mist.

"Hey," Martha interjected, "You guys take it outside or get a room, whichever. I don't need you scaring away paying customers."

"Stuff it Martha," said Alice.

"I'm sorry Al," Michael said remorsefully. "I didn't mean it."

"I know Mike," she said patting his arm. "I don't know what's going on. But it's not about you. It's like the boss doesn't want to look like he's rolling over on this thing if we get it. But, he doesn't want to look too good either. You know what I mean?"

"Enlighten me," Michael said calming down a little.

"I'm just throwing spit balls here," she mused, "but what I think is that this case is going to get a monster amount of attention and he wants it to go away with the least amount of fuss."

"AJ's your man for no fuss, all right," Michael said thinking out loud. "Nobody can get rid of more cases faster than AJ Borelli. And, if there's any kind of a deal to be had, he'll find it and make it." Michael remembered the time they were chasing a couple of girls in Sacramento, an hour north of Stockton, and had to rush back the next morning so AJ could make his assigned court. Except, he left the files at some college girl's apartment. More than 30 of them. Realizing it too late, he eschewed Michael's advice to tell the judge, pay the contempt fine, put them all over a week, and live to fight another day. AJ wasn't about to pay the $100 fine. Hell, he didn't spend that much in two months on food. Instead, he pulled his chair at counsel table next to the DA's and looked over his shoulder at his files to refresh his memory and handled every one, pleading half of them. The third floor voted it the single best courtroom performance ever.

If Snake was the king of continuances, AJ was Monty Hall. Let's Make a Deal. Where Snake ground the DA down with excuse after excuse about why the case had to be continued until they were just finally glad to get rid of it, and Michael made them afraid that he had dug up some theory that would walk his client out of the back door of the courtroom at trial, thus embarrassing them yet again, AJ combined two attributes that in Michael's mind made him the best dealmaker there ever was or ever would be.

AJ had an uncanny knack of seeing a weakness somewhere in cases, and not just with the evidence, and he could instinctively tell if the judge or DA liked his client or if there was some attribute in the background that would sway someone's thinking.

He once had a client that had so many drunk driving convictions that he was never getting his license back. Drinking was no longer a problem for Lester-Chester "Buddy" McNatt. He'd gotten religion, married, and quit drinking. He just couldn't stop driving. He loved to drive. His wife had to work and while she was working, he'd take the two kids to the park. Nothing stopped him from driving, including 5 tickets for driving with a revoked and suspended license. A serious charge.

Lester had been sternly admonished by Judge Howard Stock not two months before that a repeat of that same offense meant six months in the county jail and no maybes. But, there he was again, caught red-handed and set to appear with AJ in front of Judge Stock. Even Lester figured he'd better get his affairs in order for a lengthy stay on the honor farm, because the DA wasn't about to reduce the charge again and Stock hated drunk drivers who wouldn't stop driving.

But AJ knew a couple of more things. No matter what Stock said about hating drunk drivers and defendants that didn't heed his admonitions, he had a soft spot for reformed drunks. AJ knew from the bailiff that Stock's former law partner had virtually lost everything after becoming an alcoholic, but had fought back and now had been sober for ten years.

The other thing AJ knew from Stock's clerk was that he loved kids. He'd been a doting father of two girls and was now a babysitter to his grandchildren on a couple of evenings a week. There were pictures all over his chambers of the grandchildren.

So on the day AJ was to plead Lester-Chester, he had him bring the year-old twins to court in a tandem stroller by himself, without his wife.

"Sorry about the kids, your honor," said AJ as Lester wheeled them up all dressed up, plump and neat looking.

Judge Stock peered down from the bench and muttered, "Nice looking kids."

"Aren't they though," said AJ letting out a little line. "Lester has to watch them days while his wife works and then he goes to his janitor's job nights."

"Wife works huh?" said Stock.

"Oh sure," said AJ. "You remember Helen, don't you Judge? I think you married them in chambers a couple of years ago when Lester quit drinking. That's right isn't it Lester? That was when you quit drinking?"

"That's right Mr. Anthony," said Lester referring to AJ's first name, but with the respectful "Mr." in front of the full first name that you would hear in the South. "She wouldn't marry me unless I quit drinkin."

Stock stared down at the family scene in front of him, sighed, and said, "Counsel, approach the bench."

Ten minutes later, Lester and kids were headed home, granted one more chance on the promise that he'd quit driving.

"He's going to go nuts when Hawthorne tells him, you know that," Hunter said to Alice.

"I'm sorry about Mexico, Mike," she said, truly sorry.

"What the hell," he said philosophically. "I got Mexico here everyday. I'll eat at Xochi's for a week."

"That's my big boy," she said smiling.

Friday, November 24th, 10 a.m.

AJ Borelli did go nuts when Hawthorne walked into his office and laid the Eddie Reno file on his desk and gave him the bad news about the vacation. "Some other time," he said. "Can't be helped. I need one of my best on this thing."

Still, Alice said you could hear AJ yelling all the way to the lobby. AJ stormed into Michael's office the second he returned from Manteca Court.

"I guess you've heard that we're not going to Mexico?" he said as he slumped into the old easy chair covered with faded brown soft corduroy, deflated from his morning of tantrums. "And, I suppose you've heard why?" he added.

"Can you get our money back?" asked Michael.

"I dunno," he answered. "Hawthorne said that he'd make it up to me."

"What else did he say?" Michael inquired calmly.

"What do you mean?" asked AJ. "Just that I have the school teacher murder. Why?"

"Did he say why he was wrecking our vacation and taking you out of rotation for a serious case?" Michael continued to probe.

"He said he needed one of his best on it," answered AJ starting to get agitated. "What? Why shouldn't he give it to me?"

"No reason, except he could have given it to Snake," said Michael.

"What you really mean is that he could have given it to you. Isn't that right Mr. Big Shot?" snapped AJ.

"No he couldn't. I'm leaving, remember?" said Michael soothingly. "It's just there's no upside in this thing for us AJ. Snake could just continue it forever until we're long gone."

"You're right Mike," said AJ. "I got no business getting

this thing now. No one's going to want to deal it. Not with it being Lonigan's niece. What're we going to do?"

"You're going to do that thing you do and get rid of this thing as fast as possible."

"But, you're not going to be here to help me."

"Snake will help you. Besides, you wrote the book on dumping cases. Call in some favors," Michael said unconvincingly.

"Boss said he would reassign my calendar day and I can just work on this if I need to," said AJ.

"You need to," said Michael emphatically.

"Do me one favor," said AJ.

"What?" asked Michael.

"Go out to see him with me later," he pleaded.

Hunter groaned. He hated the jail and didn't want to get his fingerprints on this case. He knew AJ. Give him an inch and he'd take a mile. "OK, but that's it. One time."

"One time, that's it," nodded AJ Borelli without the slightest conviction.

Chapter 15

Michael had just returned from crazy court and was thinking about grabbing Jacob Sanderson for an Owl Club run when Bradley Hawthorne walked into his office and closed the door. Michael could instantly tell that this was no social call. Hawthorne threw a piece of paper with a lot of writing on it and a big red circle around a number at the bottom down on the desk in front of Hunter and said disgustedly, "Take a look at this."

"What is it?" asked Michael guardedly.

"This, Mr. Hunter," Hawthorne spit out tapping the paper twice with his index finger, "is an invoice for over $2,500."

"For what?" asked Michael taken aback by the boss' manner.

"For what!" yelled Hawthorne. "For the damn county car you've kept without permission for over two months. That's what!"

"What's the problem?" asked Michael trying to calm the situation. "I'll just take it back."

"It's a little late now," said Hawthorne, his voice dripping with patronization. "Your little stunt is coming out of my budget. They charge you by the day if you keep the car overnight," he added.

"Oh," said Michael quietly.

"Yeah, oh!" said Hawthorne not about to lose the high

ground in the conversation. "And that's not the half of it," he went on. "I now have to file some bullshit report as to why we kept the car. Not you. Me!"

"I'm sorry," said Michael meaning it.

"Well, be sorry for one of the interns in the library. They're the ones who are going to pay for this little stunt ultimately."

"What do you mean?" Michael asked with apprehension.

"This budget hit means I can't keep both of them. When I leave here, I'm going down there to give one of them the bad news."

"Which one?" asked Michael crestfallen at the circumstances he had created.

"Maybe I should let you decide," letting that thought sink in for a moment. "But, no, those aren't the kinds of decisions you like to make, are they Mike?" he added.

Michael didn't answer. He just sat shaking his head staring out the window at the darkening late fall sky. After a moment, he turned, looked Hawthorne in the eye and said, "What can you cut that I can make up to you?"

"I don't know. Probably nothing," said Hawthorne calming down at the sight of Michael's obvious contrition.

"Take it out of my salary."

"I can't do that Mike. The county wouldn't permit it," he said. "Thank you for the offer."

They sat there for a long moment not saying anything. Finally, Hawthorne said, "I know you think I don't get it; what you do. That I'm no trial lawyer and on the last score, you're right. I only had but a couple of court trials and I was no good at those. So what? That's not my job." He went on, "That doesn't mean that I don't understand you and what makes you tick. I don't show it because you're always rubbing my nose in it."

"Wait a minute," Michael said defensively.

"No, you just wait a minute. Let me finish," Hawthorne interjected. He had a head of steam and he knew this talk was long overdue. "Every time you go out and win a jury trial, you make my job more difficult," he said.

Michael looked as if someone had just cold-cocked him with a sucker punch.

"Didn't know that, did you?" he said and went on to explain. "When you win again and word gets around to the judges, the DA, the board of supervisors, and the county administrator, they all think my budget should get cut."

Michael was now hanging on every word.

"You see," continued Hawthorne, "they don't want us winning cases. They expect us to lose. They want us to lose. We're only here because the Supreme Court said we had to be here. Do you get it?"

Michael nodded slowly.

"We're the Washington Generals," Hawthorne said referring to the team that played against Meadowlark Lemon and the rest of the Harlem Globetrotters that barnstormed from city to city playing to packed houses, doing their basketball wizardry night after night against the hapless Generals who lost every night to the delight of the crowd.

"We're just the guys the Globetrotters kick the crap out of every night," he said. "When we lose, I can cry poor. But when you win ten in a row and make the courts run smoothly and become father confessor to some drunk lesbian judge, keeping the county car out to do it, well then, they want to give my budget a haircut."

Michael just sat there feeling about as low as he had felt in a very long time. "Why haven't you put the brakes on me?" asked Michael looking up from his desk.

"You mean why have I put up with you basically setting

your own rules, violating all of mine, and pretty much doing whatever pleases you?" asked Hawthorne arching his right eyebrow.

"Yeah, I guess that's it," said Michael.

"Because, first I always wanted your talent and charisma and never had a tenth of it," Hawthorne answered him. "Second, with the exception of Jacob and Anthony, all of the other attorneys in this place combined don't care about doing their job right as much as you do."

"I don't know what to say," said a thoroughly chastened Michael Hunter.

"You don't have to say anything Mike, because you see, I'm going to let you go. I have approved your leaving for Metro with my endorsement," he said.

"Your endorsement?" said an astonished Hunter.

"Yep, it's time for you to go. You're burnt out here and you'll burn out there if you stay too long. So, Mike, don't stay too long. You can leave as soon as the county approves you, which could be any day now."

"Thanks," was all Michael could muster. He knew there was much more to say, but right now he just was too conflicted to say it.

"Don't mention it," said Hawthorne rising. "Maybe I can get some peace and quiet around here now. And don't worry about the interns. I'll think of something."

Sticking his hand out to shake Hunter's, he said, "Oh, one more thing. And this is serious. When it comes time to steal Alice from me, I want at least three months' notice. Deal?"

"Deal," said Michael shaking the boss' hand firmly.

Chapter 16

The phone rang in the law library and Merlin picked it up and after a few seconds said, "Sure boss." He then turned to Sybil Waxman and said, "Boss wants to see you in his office right away."

Waxman could not help a slight surge of pride at the summons to the boss' office regarding an assignment no doubt. With a smug glance at her co-workers, she picked up her purse and walked downstairs to Hawthorne's office.

"Come in Sybil," said Hawthorne seated behind his desk. "Close the door and have a seat."

Sybil did as she was told and smiling she waited with some anticipation for Hawthorne to begin.

After a long moment of reading some papers in front of him, Hawthorne looked up and said somewhat sternly, "I understand that you have a problem with how Mr. Hunter handled one of his cases."

Taken aback, Sybil Waxman said, "Actually, it was one of my cases," she corrected him.

"No Sybil, it wasn't. You don't have any cases that aren't directly assigned to you by Jack Fletcher or myself."

"Well, I don't think he was very professional," she said.

"Your vast legal experience led you to this conclusion?" asked Hawthorne sarcastically.

"He flipped a coin," she moaned.

"So what did Jack Fletcher say when you brought this fact to his attention, because I sure as hell know you didn't bring it to mine?" he snapped.

"I didn't talk to him about it," she said.

"No you didn't, did you?" Hawthorne responded. After a moment, he added, "Do you know why I hired you when you were turned down by so many other places?"

"I wasn't really turned down," Sybil said quickly, a raw nerve clearly having been tweaked.

"Yes you were, Sybil," interjected Hawthorne. "The only reason I took a chance on you is because you are part of a federal affirmative action grant program because you are a woman. You don't count against my budget. I get you for free. And, now you're making me regret that decision."

Sybil Waxman was experiencing the common feelings of inferiority that she fought so hard to mask. It came across as indignation. "I thought you would be proud to hire someone of my scholastic standing," she fought back.

"Oh please Sybil," said Hawthorne. "Look around you. Where do you think you are? Nobody here cares. Least of all me. Listen, I'm going to make this simple. No one here, and I mean no one, reports anyone to the bar association unless I say so. Do you understand?" he added with emphasis.

"Yes, I suppose so," she sniffed.

"And you better start making an effort to fit in around here, or you're gone. Now go see Jack Fletcher. He's assigning you a trial," he said standing to dismiss her.

FRIDAY, NOVEMBER 24TH, 4 P.M.

As they walked through the glass door of the county jail, Michael and AJ were greeted with the usual pungent odors of urine, sweat, and smoke as well as the zombie attitudes of the sheriff jail personnel behind the glass. Dressed in coats and ties, they stuck out from the 15 or 20 wives, mothers, and girlfriends waiting to be acknowledged and let into the visiting area. After 15 minutes of being actively ignored, AJ went to the pay phone and dialed a number he had memorized. A couple of seconds later, Michael could hear the faint ringing of the phone behind the bulletproof glass. A few rings and a sullen woman dressed in a sheriff's matron's uniform picked it up.

"Hi, I'm one of the two attorneys you have been ignoring for the past 15 minutes," said AJ.

She looked up confused.

"Turn to your left," he said.

She did as instructed and saw AJ at the pay phone waiving at her. "Do you think you could send up Eddie Reno and buzz us in?" he asked syrup voiced.

Another ten minutes and Eddie Reno shuffled into the interview room wearing shackles on his ankles. AJ stood up and reached out to shake Reno's hand and said, "I'm Anthony Borelli and I've been assigned to represent you. This here's Michael Hunter, who is assisting me today."

"I know that name," said Reno sitting down on the other side of the small metal table. "Didn't I read that you just got some spook off that got shot in a burglary?"

Hunter just sat impassively staring back at Reno without comment.

"I thought that I would come out and introduce myself and go over a few ground rules on what's going to be happening," AJ went on. "On Monday or Tuesday, when the crime reports come in, an investigator from our office will be out to take your statement and go over it with you. Then we have a court appearance on Tuesday– ."

"Let's cut to the chase here," Reno said interrupting. "I'm not waiving time. I'm waiving the preliminary hearing and all I want from you is the police reports delivered to me as fast as you can get them. In fact, get working on a discovery motion."

"Anything else?" said Michael sarcastically. "Since we're running your errands, how about a cheeseburger?"

"Smart guy, huh," said Reno smiling a mirthless smile. "As a matter of fact, yeah, there is something else. I want to pick my own lawyer and I pick you," he said to Michael.

"Not how it works, pal," said Michael. "You get who we give you and you're lucky to get Mr. Borelli here."

"Are you shitting me?" said Reno. "This little fat toad couldn't beat a parking ticket."

"Watch your mouth pal," snapped Michael, his eyes beginning to narrow.

"So, you also think you're a tough guy too, huh," said Reno. "Maybe I should find out how tough you really are."

"Take your best shot asshole," said Michael. "And when I'm done kicking the shit out of you, then we can conflict out of your shitty case."

"Wait a minute guys," said AJ trying to referee.

"Stay out of this AJ," said Michael. "You don't have to take any lip from this puke."

Eddie Reno just sat there staring at him. "Another time, you and I can dance," he said to Michael.

"No time like the present," said Michael in an equally calm voice. "I don't like looking over my shoulder."

"Like I said," smiled Reno, "another time." And to AJ, he

said, "Forget the investigator or anyone else. I got nothing to say. Just get me those reports and remember what I said about the prelim."

Outside in the cool air, AJ said to Michael, "What in God's name was going on in there with this guy?"

"Do what the man says. Get him the CRs. Send them out with Frankie," he said referring to the investigator, Frankie Sanchez. "Maybe he'll talk to him."

"I don't mean him," said AJ. "Well, I do mean him, but what I'm really asking about is you."

"What?" asked Michael.

"You tried to goad the guy into a fight. Why?"

"Because he's a mouthy little punk who thinks he can push you around. Besides, it would have gotten you off his case."

"And how would that have looked in the paper?"

"Who cares?"

"I think your brother's right. You do need a change of scenery," said AJ.

"I got a bad feeling about this one, Age," said Michael.

"What do you mean?"

"You're not going to be able to handle this guy."

"You don't think I'm up to it?"

"No," Michael said stopping and turning towards his friend. "No I don't. I don't think anyone can handle him."

"Not even you?" asked AJ.

"Not even me," sighed Michael. "I just have a real bad feeling about this thing. Do me a favor. Let's haul ass back to the courthouse and catch Dewey before he leaves and get all the CRs he's got so you can read them over the week-end," said Michael getting into his car.

"Can't it wait? I've had a long day," AJ pleaded.

"No it can't. This guy's not acting like someone who's

just had a dead girl's wallet found in his car and been arrested for her murder. And, you better figure out why," he said slamming the car door and firing up the engine.

=====(O)=====

Friday, November 24ᵀᴴ, 5:15 p.m.

"We got work to do tonight," Michael said poking his head into Snake's office.

"Pick me up after dinner," Snake said looking up from the D.R. Johnny file that was now definitely headed for trial in less than three weeks.

"What happened to 30 days?" Michael asked Snake as they climbed into Michael's car to go find his client in the drug bust case where the mechanical drawings were seized. Michael was referring to Snake's upcoming trial in less than three weeks on the D.R. Johnny shanking murder.

"What difference does it make? I wouldn't be ready to go in the next two months," Snake sighed.

"Lucky for you Hawthorne has pulled all of my assignments and is letting me float until I leave," said Michael.

"Well, you're floating with me out to DVI on Monday morning to look at the crime scene and try to scare up a witness or two."

"Swell."

They found their guy at the El Dorado Bowl in Downtown Stockton. He was sitting at a back table in the darkened bar with two white rat-faced men who disappeared as soon as Michael and Snake walked up. Snake immediately signaled the cocktail waitress to bring them a couple of Coors.

"Hey Larry, what's cookin?" said Michael taking a seat at the table.

"What's happening Mr. Hunter?" said an obviously surprised Larry Walker.

"Want to ask you a few questions about your case."

"Shoot man," said Walker very impressed that the two lawyers had taken the time to look him up on a Friday night.

"I need the dude's name that you stole the drawings from."

Larry Walker's eyes began to dart back and forth in apprehension. "Oh man, I don't know," he said. "How's that going to help."

"Listen asshole," said Hunter annoyed with the question, "I don't tell you how to do crime and you don't tell me how to do my job. Now answer the question."

Snake arrived with the beer and took down on a notepad the name and directions to the North Stockton home that Walker had burglarized, taking the plans that were in a briefcase he didn't bother to open, along with numerous other items.

"Look, Mr. Hunter, the guy never reported the burg and I don't need another beef right now," he wailed.

"Don't worry about it. He isn't going to say anything. Trust me."

From there, they went to the North Stockton residence in the old Park Woods neighborhood populated now by young working families on their way up and retired working class people who enjoyed the peaceful, generally crime-free, environment of wide tree-lined streets and homes built in the early 1950s.

The door to the white wood sided house was answered by a man about Michael's age, who when he was informed who they were, would not let them in, but instead directed them to contact his lawyer, the one and only Archibald Cox.

"What do you think?" asked Snake as they got back into the car.

"I think we just met the narcs' CRI," answered Michael.

"What are you doing?" Snake asked as he watched Michael filling out a subpoena that he had brought with him.

"I'm going back up there and invite this guy to Larry's 1538.5 hearing."

Michael got out of the car and walked back up to the house and rung the doorbell again. The young man came to the door, this time agitated and was about to say something when Michael handed him the subpoena and said, "Tell Archie Cox to give me a call. My number's on the card clipped to the subpoena. Have a nice evening."

"Where we going now?" Snake asked Michael as he got back in the car after serving the subpoena on Archie Cox's client.

"Let's go over to Metro and see if we can get someone to let us in the police evidence locker," said Michael.

"On a Friday night?" said Snake.

"What, think they don't log in evidence on a Friday night?" said Michael.

As luck would have it when they walked in to the Metropolitan Narcotics Unit, Paul was sitting at his desk doing some paperwork. Looking up, he grinned and said, "Let me guess. You's bums brought me some Chinese take out?"

"No such luck," said Michael. "But, I will buy you dinner if you do me a favor."

"What's the favor?" asked Paul warily.

"We need to look at the evidence log on a particular case.

"I'm absolutely sure that you have no written authorization from the district attorney's office for me to do this," said Paul.

"I can get it and you know it. Why waste the time?" said Michael.

Paul sighed, got up and said, "OK fine. What's the difference. It's just the log. What's the case?"

"The Larry Walker methamphetamine possession case."

"Hey, I had nothing to do with that one Mike," said Paul.

"Why you nervous then?" said Michael looking his brother straight in the eye.

"I'm not nervous. It's just not my case."

"But you know something about it."

"You want to see the evidence log or not?"

"Show it to me."

Michael and Snake scanned the evidence log without saying a word until Paul walked back to his desk to answer his phone at which time Snake whispered to Michael, "No mechanical drawings logged in."

"Nope," said Michael. Then to Paul, "Come on bro, let's eat."

Chapter 17

SATURDAY, NOVEMBER 25TH, 10:30 A.M.

Anthony Borelli sat staring at the copier that spit out sheet after sheet of copied crime reports on the Elizabeth Van Houten murder. Dewey Gunnart had stayed late the previous evening as a favor to get him the inch and a half thick preliminary CRs; and from what he'd already read, Eddie Reno was as dead in the water as the Van Houten girl. There were eye witnesses to a car wreck occurring on the day of the murder between the victim and Reno; an eye witness to someone matching Reno's description being seen driving the victim's car a few hours' later down a country road where it was later found to have been either driven or pushed into the river; the victim's wallet in Reno's car; and no search and seizure or other technical issues to wreck an otherwise open and shut case. And if all of that wasn't bad enough, the two best detectives in the sheriff's department were on the case.

Hunter was right. He needed to get rid of this case as quickly as possible. But how? So far, it looked about as simple as climbing straight up a glass wall. There didn't appear to be any cracks to gain a perch from which to cling. What DA or judge was going to make him a deal on a case like this–a brutal murder, maybe a rape, and the sheriff's niece? On top of all of that, Eddie Reno made him for a flunky, an errand boy. An errand boy that was afraid to be alone with his client. The fact was that Eddie Reno frightened Borelli and Reno knew it.

———— ⫸⫷(◉)⫸⫷ ————

Monday, November 27ᵗʰ, 8:30 a.m.

"All I'm saying," said Michael Hunter riding in the passenger seat of Jacob Sanderson's 1964 Ford Fairlaine, which may at one time had been blue in color, but with years of neglect and no maintenance, who could tell, "Is that if you hung these asswipes in Hunter's Square within 90 days of their sentencing, then the death penalty would be an effective deterrent."

"How are they going to do an appeal in that time?" argued Snake.

"You video tape the whole thing and assign a magistrate with the State Supreme Court to review it. You assign appellate counsel the day after the sentencing and get the whole thing done in 60 days."

"I couldn't do it in 60 days."

"You couldn't take a dump in 60 days. I'm not talking about you."

"I like my island theory better," said Snake.

The island theory was a combination of compromises by both Michael and Snake and was included as a part of their model penal system. It was born from a mutual realization that the present prison system was totally useless. First, it was too expensive. At $40 per day or whatever it cost, why, Michael argued, should the taxpayer pay anything to house prisoners. Under his penal system, a profit would be earned. You don't work, you don't eat. And no plush conditions either. Snake, a big tax and spend liberal, even agreed with this theory, because he thought tax dollars should go to better causes than housing scumbags in prisons with law libraries, TVs, and stereos in the cells and numerous other conveniences that seemed to be increasing daily with no responsibility placed on the convicted prisoner to pay his or her way; or, for that matter, do much of anything but sit there and soak it up. These were the times when prisons were supposed to rehabilitate rather than punish. This meant education, training, counseling, and understanding for the prisoners, all of which cost money. The emerging prison reform racing around the country was that rehabilitation and training would lead to much lower recidivist rates and thus, ultimately, a lower crime rate.

This was the popular theory of the times. Everyday, a new government sponsored program for drug addicts, sex addicts, alcoholics, gambleholics, and you-name-it-aholics sprouted up claiming a wonderful new method to cure people of their urges because, after all, it wasn't their fault, they were ill. They were victims of sickness which caused their particular compulsion and lack of self control.

In their few years of public defender service, one thing that both Snake Sanderson and Michael Hunter could agree on was that all of these theories and programs were basically a crock of shit with ginned up statistics to keep the grant funding pouring in the door. Every program kept its own success statistics to justify its reason for existence and the boys had noticed that curiously all claimed success or cures at a rate of between 30 and 35 percent. Upon closer examination, and you really had to dig for this, "cure" was defined by a self-standard that varied from program to program. For example, one program pronounced heroin addicts cured at a 30 percent rate, but "cure" meant that they weren't arrested for a heroin related offense within six months after leaving the program. Six months and one day, not our problem, we cured you.

Consequently, in the boys' mythical model penal system, there were no programs paid for by society. There was, however, one free bite of the apple for most crimes—probation. On serious felonies, except for murder, rape, and other heinous crimes there was probation if you agreed to sterilization. The boys had noticed that crimes seemed to run in the family and those families drained endless tax dollars in welfare, investigation, arrest, detention, supervision, and healthcare. Nuts and ovaries in a jar at least put a halt to some of that.

Snake's most ingenious idea, at least from Michael's perspective, was the "island theory." Returning serious felons who had proved that they couldn't stay crime-free were sentenced to a self-sufficient island for the remainder of their days. And this island cost the taxpayers nothing. It turned a tidy profit. Alcatraz was a great idea in the boys' estimation, except that it was too expensive. They discussed and argued endlessly on what life on this island would be like and how infractions there would be addressed. One thing that Michael was very keen on, and Snake had warmed to, was how local prisons would be run. They had to make a profit, even if only $1 and you learned a trade. You might start out on the business end of a shovel, but by the time you left, you probably would be sitting on top of a piece of heavy equipment thoroughly trained to do something useful on the outside. These discussions had wiled away many hours and cases of beer. This day, it was eating up the drive time to DVI.

"How much do you figure the Jones family has cost San Joaquin County and the State of California in say the last ten years?" asked Michael.

Snake thought about it for a while and said, "Well, I figure at least $2 million."

"How do you figure?"

"There's at least 25 of them on welfare and they're breeding at the rate of one generation every 13 years, so just do the math on the welfare alone. That's free healthcare by the way."

"Do you know even one Jones without a rap sheet?" asked Michael.

"Nope," said Snake.

The Jones family was somewhat legendary, but not completely atypical with the public defender's office. They were a revolving door of three generations of criminals. One of the most remarkable aspects of the Jones family was the fact that they seemed to take great pride in getting any Jones that wasn't already hooked on heroin, hooked. They would go to ingenious lengths to see that if you weren't doing drugs, you started doing drugs. This was a family trademark. All of the Jones' girls seemed to be prostitutes and all the boys were pimps, drug dealers, burglars, and murderers. Although they bred like rats, mother nature would step in and kill off a Jones at the rate of about one every few months from either an overdose, violent crime, or some other means. Sort of nature's population control. However, nature was losing the battle because the Joneses were increasing exponentially in number.

When the boys discussed their nuts and ovaries in a jar theory, they were always thinking of the Joneses.

It took almost an hour and half to get from the reception center at the prison to the courtyard where the murder took place. Accompanied by four guards, Michael and Snake moved around the courtyard to the approving and admiring glances of numerous inmates. It was quickly apparent to both that the guards were unnecessary. D.R. Johnny had a big fan club and the shanking had been popular. Nothing was going to happen to D.R. Johnny's lawyers, at least while this group of Nuestra Familia soldiers were in attendance.

After looking around a bit and taking a few pictures, which had taken the better part of an hour to get authorized, Snake announced loudly, "I need a witness or two here." No one immediately stepped forward.

However, within a few minutes, using slight of hand that a card sharp would have been proud of, small slips of paper were slipped into the boys' hands by passing inmates with names on them.

Back in the car, Snake asked Michael how he thought he should deal with these names and Michael, after some thought, said, "Just subpoena them. They have to bring them in if you subpoena them. Send Frankie out to lay the paper on them and subpoena them for the first day of the trial, that way you can interview them at the county jail, which is where they'll keep them and that's where they'll stay until you use them, if you do."

"By the way, you got a theory for this thing?" asked Michael looking at Snake as they drove back.

Snake kept staring straight ahead at the road and said, "I think I'm going to go with the aiding and abetting thing."

"Interesting."

The law relating aiding and abetting in California, as with most states, said that you didn't have to be the person who actually pulled the trigger in a murder to be guilty of it. You could be guilty of aiding or abetting that person by committing a variety of acts in concert with that person and, if that was proved, then you were just as guilty as the person who pulled the trigger. Same with the wheel man in a bank robbery. Maybe he didn't go inside, but he was just as guilty for everything that took place in that bank, including a murder if that took place even if the guy driving the car had no desire to have anyone shot or even thought anyone might get shot. That was aiding and abetting in a nutshell, but there were endless cases on the subject.

What Snake was working on was to either prove that D.R. Johnny did not shank the guy and did not aid and abet the other guy who did it. Easier said than done when you were the last two guys standing over a dead guy in front of half a dozen or so prison guards. But, you had to go with something.

When they arrived back at the public defender's office just in time for the noon basketball game, Alice Benson grabbed Michael as he came in and said, "Archibald Cox has called twice for you. What's going on?"

"Gimme his number," Michael said. "I'll call him before I head out for round ball."

Upstairs, Michael quickly changed into his basketball clothes and dialed Cox's phone number at the same time. In a minute he was put through and a booming voice echoed in his ear saying, "Michael Hunter. Archie Cox here."

"What can I do for you, Mr. Cox?" said Michael.

"Don't be coy, Michael. It doesn't become you. Let's have lunch tomorrow."

"I'd love to Mr. Cox. Where shall I meet you?" asked Michael.

"Let's meet out at the Stockton Country Club."

Chapter 18

Joe Larsen fidgeted nervously in his chair in front of the rail in Department C on the second floor waiting for his first court trial to be called. Joe took out for the third time the statement of his client regarding the citizen's arrests citation for speeding he had received a month ago. The city police officer that took the report would be testifying and as Joe looked around the courtroom and saw several uniformed Stockton Police Department officers, he wondered which one it was. He had not bothered to speak with the officer prior to the trial. Joe's client sat directly behind him and Joe had interviewed him three times already.

The facts were simple. According to Joe's client, he was driving down a city street, minding his own business, when a citizen threw a can of beer through his open passenger's window, striking him on the right shoulder and causing him to swerve his vehicle up on a lawn and hit a tree. The person whose tree it was called the police who arrived a short time later and ultimately cited Joe's client with speeding on the basis of the statement of the citizen who threw the beer can. Joe's client had pled not guilty and asked for a court trial and to be represented by the public defender's office. A week before the trial, Joe was handed the file by Stanley Latchman to prepare and try. Joe had researched everything he could on the speeding citation and the facts and felt ready.

178

Five minutes later, Judge Joseph Heinz called Joe's case. Joe and his client took a seat at counsel table and the DA called the police officer to the stand and elicited the facts that he had been called to the scene and been told by the reporting party about the speeding and the accident.

Joe leaped to his feet at that point and objected to the officer's relating to what he had been told because it was hearsay. His objection was immediately overruled, but Joe continued to argue with the judge that it had to be hearsay. After the judge had overruled him for the third time, he told Joe to sit down and not to mention it again.

The officer then pointed to Joe's client as to the one who had been issued the citizen's arrest citation and then it was Joe's turn.

Joe had two pages of questions for the officer beginning with how long he had been on the force and where he had received his training. The DA started smiling and stood up and objected that all of this was irrelevant to the case, which the judge immediately sustained. When Joe kept up the same line of questioning, the judge snapped at him that the objection had already been sustained and that he was wasting the court's time.

Joe could feel himself sweating through his sport coat now as he fumbled with his list of questions. It seemed that the court was not only not going to let him ask any of them, but wasn't interested. In a panic, he blurted out, "So you have absolutely no idea how fast my client was driving, do you officer?"

"I wasn't even there, counsel," the officer said in a bored voice.

"Then how could you possibly cite him for speeding?"

"I didn't. The complaining party did. I only took the report and had your client sign the citizen's arrest form and citation."

"Oh," Joe said mortified.

"Can we move on now Mr. Larsen?" asked Judge Heinz referring to his notes for Joe's name.

"Yes, your Honor."

The DA then called the complaining witness to testify that there were little children playing on the sidewalks and in the yards on this Sunday afternoon when he heard the roar of a car engine and saw Joe's client speeding down the residential street at what he estimated was over 60 miles per hour. On reflex, he threw the beer can he was holding at the car to get it to slow down. Then it was Joe's turn for cross-examination which he had practiced in a mirror for over an hour the night before.

He lit into the witness with a vengeance, hammering him about the throwing of a can of beer through the window of a car, causing it to veer across the road and smash into a tree, trying vainly to get him to admit that this was eminently more dangerous of an act than speeding down a street. After 15 minutes of this, everyone was exhausted and Judge Heinz finally called a halt to the proceedings with, "I think you've made your point counsel."

The DA rested and Joe put his client on the stand and had him tell how the beer can hit his arm, causing him to lose control of his car, striking a tree, and how dangerous it was. Joe then rested and the case was submitted.

Judge Heinz immediately found Joe's client guilty of speeding and fined him $100, plus $20 court costs.

As a shocked Joe just stood there, his client said, "I should have paid the $35 ticket. Thanks for nothing." He turned and walked out of the courtroom.

Outside the courtroom, a dazed Joe was tapped on the shoulder by the officer that had just been on the stand. "First trial son?" he asked.

"That obvious, huh?" said Larsen.

"No, not really. But sometimes you can kinda tell. Want some advice?"

"Sure, why not," sighed a dejected Joe.

"You tried the wrong case."

"What do you mean?"

"You tried me and the complaining witness, the beer can thrower. The can thrower wasn't on trial. What's his throwin' a can got to do with your guy speeding? You didn't ask a single question about the speeding."

Joe thought about that. He hadn't. Not a question. He just let the complaining witness estimate his guy's speed at 60 miles per hour and never challenged it at all.

"Worse yet, you made him sympathetic by beating up on him."

"What should I have done?" asked Joe.

"The tree and the beer," said the cop. "How many beers had the guy been drinking to impair his judgment so that he would throw a beer through an open car window. And for me, you should have asked if I had any experience with a car hitting a tree at 60."

"Have you?"

"Sure, every cop has that's been around a while."

"How fast did the car hit the tree?" asked Joe.

"Well, there were no skid marks on the street, so no braking. So I figure he hit it at about 20 miles per hour based on the damage."

"You never mentioned it," said Joe.

"You never asked me counsel," said the officer turning to walk away.

"Thanks," Joe said to the retreating officer.

"Don't mention it," he said over his shoulder.

Chapter 19

The offices of Allstate Insurance Company were more cramped than AJ would have thought as he sat there waiting for adjustor Ronald Lay to get off the phone. On a whim, he had called the number on the letter Rose Moretti had received from the insurance company of the owner of the car that ran a stop sign on Hunter Street, smashing into the Moretti's Chevy Impala, injuring Rose's neck. Ronald Lay answered and invited AJ down to his office to 'work things out.' Then he left him sitting there for five minutes while he told some other poor soul why he wasn't getting any dough. "They don't call me No-Pay-Lay for nothing," he laughed hanging up the phone. "Thanks for stopping by counsel," he said shaking hands with AJ.

"No problem Mr. Lay," said AJ.

"Call me Ron."

"OK Ron. I thought we might handle this quickly."

"What have you got in mind counsel."

AJ had the accident report that Paul had obtained for Rose and, which according to him, had personally been written as one-sided as possible as a favor to Rose. AJ handed it to Ron Lay who studied it shaking his head.

"Doesn't look too bad to me," he said. "Just a little front end damage. You know those Chevys are built like battleships. GM's got impact studies on those things. Ever see 'em?"

"No," said AJ fidgeting.

"She couldn't have been very injured, if at all. Nuisance value really," said Ron Lay, looking at some pictures he had in his file showing the crumpled-in left front fender, bumper, and wheel and the hood all bent back with the engine exposed.

"Didn't even bend the 'A' frame, I bet. You know studies show that if you don't bend the 'A' frame, things aren't so bad. What office did you say you were from?"

"Her doctor's an osteopath and she's had twelve adjustments on her neck," said AJ.

"You know that's another thing," said Lay. "I don't go along with raising these osteopaths to the level of M.D.s. What was the medical association thinking of on that one, huh? Far as I'm concerned, they're glorified chiropractors. And you know we don't pay nothing hardly on chiropractors. So I'm not terribly impressed with twelve adjustments counsel."

"Well, what do you think it's worth, Ron?" asked AJ, now pretty sure of himself that a bunch of neck adjustments weren't worth very much and that he was being backed into a corner by a real professional.

Ron Lay studied the file for a minute, looked back at the pictures of the car, scratched his head and said, "I don't know. Maybe $1,500. That's about the best I can do. She miss any work?"

"Naw, she's just a housewife. Well, if that's the best you can do, Mr. Lay, I'll take it. Can we get the check today?" said AJ.

Ron Lay looked at him quizzically and said, "Rose Moretti. What's her husband do?"

"I think he sells liquor," answered AJ.

"Big John Moretti is her husband?" said Ron Lay sitting up straight in his chair.

"Yeah, why?" asked AJ.

"Jesus, kid. You know anything?" he asked. "First, you didn't tell me this is Big John Moretti's wife Rose and next, you take the first offer I throw out on the table. That's not how it works."

"How does it work?"

"How it works is, I say $1,500, you act insulted and threaten to leave, get up, walk towards the door, and then I say, 'aw, come back here', sit down and we talk some more. That's how it works."

"Then what?" asked AJ.

"Then we go back and forth awhile and we wind up on a case like this with Big John Moretti's wife Rose, some major front end damage, and endless visits to a qualified physician, at, say $5,000. You hem and haw around; finally take the deal; I don't look so bad to the boss and you look real sharp to your client who's happy and more important, her husband's happy."

"I'll take the deal," said AJ.

"Wise decision. I'll prepare a release right now and a check and you get Mrs. Moretti to sign it and bring the release back to me. Nice doing business with you counsel," said No-Pay-Lay.

<hr />

MONDAY, NOVEMBER 27ᵀᴴ, 1:30 P.M.

Michael was all set to meet his brother at Metro when Alice buzzed him and told him that Hawthorne wanted him to handle a problem in Judge Goodwin's courtroom right away. Throwing on a coat and tie, he headed over wondering *what now?* He thought Stanley Latchman was in charge of most of the matters in front of Judge Goodwin, but Michael was the floater until he left to work for Metro.

Afternoon felony arraignments had not yet begun so the clerk waived him on through to chambers as if he was expected.

"What's up, your Honor?" he asked walking in and seeing Judge Adam Goodwin in a white short-sleeved shirt sitting behind his desk writing.

"Oh, hi Mike," said the Judge putting his pen down. "Hawthorne send you over?"

"Yeah. What's the problem?"

"It's Sybil Waxman. She's not cutting it. I want her replaced in my court."

"It's tough to mess up an arraignment," Michael said inquisically.

"Actually, I would have thought so too, before I met her," he said. "She's awful. She takes forever to get bail and OR information, then she argues endlessly. It's like she takes it personally if I don't OR them. But, then there was the prelim this morning."

"She did a prelim?"

"Nothing big. Just an open and shut burglary. Should have been 15 minutes tops."

"What happened?" asked Michael shaking his head. "Wasn't someone with her?"

"Nope. I'm not blaming Latchman. I don't like the little putz, but I'm not blaming him. He's had her sit and watch him three times. How tough is it?"

"So what happened?"

"Well, like I said, she is supposed to be representing this

guy on a burglary. I call the case and the defendant is sitting there already at counsel table. That's OK. The DA puts on one witness. The investigating officer. Found the guy's fingerprints everywhere. You know, just enough to hold him to answer. She cross-examines for 20 minutes. I can't shut her up. Where'd you go to school. Blah, blah, blah. But that's not the kicker."

"What's the kicker?" asked Michael.

"She puts her client on the stand!"

"No. Not at the prelim?" said Michael astonished. No one ever did that except in extraordinary circumstances and these weren't those. A preliminary examination was a hearing where the DA put on just enough evidence to show that a crime was committed and the defendant may have committed it. It's not a trial. The defense gets what it can, tests the evidence, so to speak, from any witness that was called by the DA, but never revealed their case, and never put the client on the stand, subjecting the client to a cross-examination, and waiving his right against self incrimination. Michael knew she had to have been told that by Latchman.

"But that's not it," said the judge savoring it.

"What?"

"She had the wrong client," said the judge.

Michael sat there not fully processing what he had just been told. "The wrong client? How . . ."

"Yes, sir," said Judge Goodwin. "She says, 'I call the defendant Juan Rodriguez to the stand.' The guy just sits there. 'Take the stand Mr. Rodriguez,' she says. He sits there like a stump. 'What's the matter?' she says. 'I'm not Juan Rodriguez,' he says. 'I'm Jose Rodriguez.'"

"No!" said Michael.

"You want the best part?" said Goodwin relishing the story that would soon become courthouse legend.

"There's more?"

"You bet. She says, 'take the stand whatever your name is.' That's when I put a stop to it. This dumb broad was going to put a guy, who she knew was not her client, on the stand to testify in a burglary he knows nothing about."

Michael just sat there. What was there to say. By tomorrow she would be the laughing stock of a place where it didn't pay to be laughed at.

"She's got no feel at all Mike," said Goodwin. "She's learning nothing. I've had people in here that stink before, don't get me wrong. But she's the stinkee. She's got to go."

MONDAY, NOVEMBER 27ᵀᴴ, 1:50 P.M.

Michael's head was spinning as he pushed through the double glass doors that led into the Metropolitan Narcotics Unit at the Stockton Police Department on Center Street in Downtown Stockton. He knew how unhappy the news about Waxman would make Bradley Hawthorne and while a week ago that would have amused him, today he got no pleasure from it. He figured he'd tell Stanley Latchman and let the little prick deal with it.

Lieutenant Flanagan saw him walk in and yelled, "Here to pick out your office, Mikey?"

"A little premature for that Jimmy. I'll be breaking your balls tomorrow on a case."

"What's new?" said Flanagan smiling. "All's fair."

"Paul here?"

"Yeah, he's in the back. What's up?"

"We need to talk," Michael said dead serious.

Flanagan caught the mood and said, "Sure Mike. Let's go in the back."

When Paul, Flanagan, and a couple of the other narcs Michael knew well were gathered around, he said, "Judge Hollins' daughter has a problem. This isn't coming from the judge and he's never to know about it. It's coming from me. The favor's to me. Not him. Got it?"

"Sure Mike, whatever you say," said Paul.

"I just don't want this getting back to him or anyone thinking he's beholding, because he's not. OK?"

They all nodded. Michael told them the story about the cab driver and Hollins' retarded daughter. He asked them to find out who it was and then to get back to him and they'd go from there.

"Just get me the info. Nothing more. OK?"

"Sure Mike," said Paul. "Jesus, it's like you're already workin' here."

<hr />

Monday, November 27th, 3 p.m.

Michael walked into Stanley Latchman's office on the second floor and closed the door. "You got a little problem, Stan," he said.

"Now, what could that possibly be, Hunter?" asked Latchman in his usual snide manner.

"Judge Goodwin just 86'd Waxman from Department B."

"You're kidding? How do you know?"

"Because he sent for someone and Hawthorne sent me. You've obviously heard about her preliming the wrong guy today."

"Yes, I've heard," said Latchman, his shoulders sagging. "I thought she was ready."

"Listen Stanley, I don't give a rat's ass one way or the other. I'm just delivering the message. Handle it any way you want to."

"Jack Fletcher's given her a misdemeanor jury trial. It goes in two weeks. Who's going to help her with that?" asked Latchman.

"You're the one who's been advising her, Stanley. So, I imagine it's your problem too. Good luck," Hunter said walking out of Latchman's door smiling.

As Hunter walked into his office to change clothes and head to the Owl Club, he found AJ sitting in his easy chair reading the Reno crime report. "What's doing Age?"

"Just reading the ever expanding crime report on the Reno case."

"Anything good?" Hunter asked, meaning had AJ found any weakness in the prosecution's case.

"Nothing that I can see."

"Maybe you're not looking hard enough. Did Frankie interview your guy?"

"He wouldn't talk to him. Just wanted the CR dropped off."

"That's weird."

"Hey, I settled Rose's case today."

"You're kidding," said Hunter impressed. "What'd you get?"

"$5 grand."

"Oh, man, you're in the family forever."

"I've already called her. She loves me more than you. By the way, we're both invited for dinner. She's making something special. I've got to give her the check and have her sign the release. Why don't you pick me up at my place and we'll go together?"

"No problem, but I got some drinking to do first. Let's go to the Owl Club."

"Naw. I got to keep reading this crap. You got to help me with it."

"Don't think so," said Hunter changing into his Levis, t-shirt, and sweater.

"Guess who shows up in this thing?" said AJ referring to the crime report.

"Who?"

"Juror Number 4."

"Aren't you full of surprises?" Hunter said tying his tennis shoes, looking up at AJ.

"Turns out she was the victim's teacher's aid."

"Why don't you come over to the Owl for a beer and we'll talk about it."

<hr />

MONDAY, NOVEMBER 27TH, 3:30 P.M.

Before they could get out the door, in stormed Sybil Waxman.

"And the hits just keep on comin," said Hunter.

"Again, with the trespassing violation," said AJ.

"You got me kicked out of Judge Goodwin's court," she

yelled at Hunter. "You hate me because I'm a woman. I think you're both a couple of queers."

"I thought homosexuals liked women," AJ said to her, amused for the first time that day.

"Oh shut up. You know what I mean. You're all threatened by a woman attorney. You've made it clear that you don't want me around and now you've gone over to see Goodwin and I'm not welcome back there anymore," she said sitting down in the chair AJ had just vacated.

"Have a seat," he said sardonically.

"Well, I've got to hand it to Stanley. He sure as hell knew how to handle this situation," said Hunter.

"Will somebody tell me what's going on?" said AJ.

"Goodwin kicked her out of Department B for impersonating a lawyer," said Hunter, "badly."

"He hates women too. I can tell," she yelled.

"I didn't know he was a queer," AJ said to Hunter.

"You know what I mean," she wailed.

"Listen Waxman," said Hunter. "As far as you being a woman, I don't care if you want to be a long-haul trucker so long as you can handle your own rig. Right now, you're not doing that. Someone's going to have to fill your slot and that probably will be me. And that I don't like. Got it? So, go home and figure out if you've got the chops for this job. If not, get out. If so, change your attitude. Either way, I don't care. Right now, me and Age got some drinkin' and thinkin' to do. Hit the lights on your way out," he said walking out the door.

Ten minutes later Snake and Michael were shooting a game of eight ball and AJ was sitting at the bar next to Covers who had already been warned twice by Ernie the bartender to quit butting in on the boys' conversation.

"I can't figure out why he won't talk to us," said AJ facing the table with his back to the bar. "Maybe he didn't do it."

"No good," said Snake moving around the table to line up his next shot. "If he didn't do it, he'd be singing like the Mormon Tabernacle Choir on Christmas morning."

"Snake's right," said Hunter. "He did it all right."

"How the hell do you know? You haven't read a word of the CR."

"Don't have to," answered Michael taking a long pull from the frosty Bud. "I met him."

"I don't know," said AJ shaking his head.

"Anyone want to know what I think?" slurred Covers.

"Shut up Covs," they all said at once.

"He knows something though, that's for sure," said Michael.

"Damn straight," said Snake sinking his third ball in a row, almost a personal best.

"What the hell does he know?" moaned AJ.

"That's what you have to find out," said Hunter. "How's Juror Number 4 figure into this?"

Elizabeth "Gem" Giamatti had been questioned recently by Elwood Carnes regarding the victim's relationships and habits.

"We could find out after dinner tonight," offered AJ. "I bet she'll be at the Islander."

Chapter 20

Michael could remember Rose saying at least six times during dinner what a genius AJ was. She had been overwhelmed with the $5,000 check. It was obvious that Big John was also impressed, but had to say that if they would have paid $5,000 so fast, maybe they should have held out for more. But even his *cheap dago persona heart*, as Michael called it, wasn't in the rebuke and he slapped a basking AJ on the back several times and admonished Michael to start following suit with his career.

The Islander was quiet even for a Monday night. There was no live entertainment and Jimmy Yee had the night off. Gem Giamatti was working the bar alone when Hunter and AJ Borelli walked up and sat down. Michael thought that she was one of those women who looked good in anything, including the Islander's black pants, long sleeved white shirt, red vest, and bow tie.

"Well, well, if it isn't the Bobbsey twins," she said as they perched themselves on the bar stools. "Let me guess. This isn't a social call."

"Not exactly," said AJ.

"How about one of your famous Mai-Tais with the good rum," said Hunter.

"Nothing but the best for a friend of Frankie's and Mr. Yee's," said Gem reaching behind the bar for the 151 Rum.

Michael found himself wondering just how good a friend she was to Frankie Fanelli.

"I wanted to talk to you about Elizabeth Van Houten," said AJ.

"Of course you do. And what makes you think I want to talk to you."

"Because we're alike," said Hunter quietly. "And because that's a rare thing."

AJ sat staring at them back and forth in the silence. He didn't have a clue what Hunter was talking about, not that it was anything new. "And because I'm Italian," he said laughing, trying to break the tension.

"Oh, please," Gem said returning his smile. "What do you want to know?"

That was the problem, AJ didn't know what they wanted to know, so he just turned to Hunter who said, "For starters, tell us about her."

"That will take longer than one Mai-Tai," she said.

"Keep'em comin," said Hunter.

"Well, for one thing, there was a lot more to her than they are saying in the newspapers," she said wiping the bar with a damp towel.

"What are they saying?" asked Hunter. "I don't read the papers."

"You're a lawyer and you don't read the newspaper?" she smiled. "You're a very strange man."

"You've no idea," said AJ. "You should see what he does with his mail."

"What's he do?" she asked staring at Michael.

"He has a post office box and he only goes there once a month to collect his mail."

"Can't you get your mail where you live?" she laughed.

"Sure, but then I'd have to get it everyday."

"And?" she said coaxing. "That would be bad because . . .?"

"I figure it this way," said Hunter. "Mail's very rarely good news. Most of it's bills; people trying to sell you something, or just down right stuff you'd rather not read. Now, I have a theory that says that if you don't look at your mail, except once a month, then 90 percent of it is irrelevant by the time you see it and you don't have to deal with it at all."

"And the newspaper?" she asked.

"Same thing. Most of it stinks," he replied.

"So you don't read about yourself in the *Stockton Record*?"

"Never," said AJ. "And, none of us can mention it to him."

"So you read no news at all?" she said.

"I didn't say that. We get the *Wall Street Journal* at the office and there's the *San Francisco Chronicle* sports page. Those are all you need."

"Well, you and Liz would have gotten along," she said. "Liz was an outside the boxer, same as you."

"How do you mean?" Michael asked sliding the second Mai-Tai she had just set down closer to him.

"I knew her before she started teaching. I never would have become an aid if I couldn't have worked with Liz," she said setting another drink down for AJ. "The kids loved her. She was, how can I put it, exciting."

AJ was scribbling furiously on a legal pad he had brought with him. This was how he processed. He wrote down every word because at the time they were spoken, he couldn't decide what was important, so he wrote it all down and sorted it out later. This drove Hunter up a wall because it was time consuming and distracting. He was about to rebuke AJ, but he stopped himself remembering that it wasn't his case.

"An exciting kindergarten teacher," said Michael.

"Well, yes," said Gem leaning on the bar, tapping her lower lip with her index finger staring vacantly, remembering, searching for the right words to memorialize her dead friend. "Inspiring and exciting. She wanted so much out of life. It was infectious. Even to five-year olds."

"What was she like away from school?" asked Michael.

"Full of conflict, like the rest of us. Well, at least some of us," she laughed. It was one of those laughs from the chest, full and unreserved, coming from a person who liked to laugh even at themselves.

"You know that her grandparents and uncles are dairy people from the Lodi area," she said referring to the small farming community some 10 miles north of Stockton.

Numerous Dutch, German, and Portuguese dairymen farmers had settled in that area and prospered. The Van Houtens were one of them. Their son, Henry, had gotten away from the business and married a city girl he met at the University of California at Davis, and settled into the banking business, becoming Vice President of the local bank in Lincoln Center in Stockton. All of this added up to the fact that the Van Houtens were an old conservative San Joaquin Valley family with old money. It made the tragedy all the more shocking.

In the next thirty minutes, Gem told them things, sometimes tearfully, about her friend and the fact that she was of two worlds, not sure which way she wanted to go. Elizabeth Van Houten was known as "Beth" to most of her friends, family, and her farmer boyfriend, and "Liz" to Gem and a few others. Gem said that Elizabeth preferred Liz, like Liz Taylor, whom she admired. On the one hand, Liz loved the kids and teaching, but hated the life she was being forced into, that of a farmer's wife. Her boyfriend, off and on since high school, was a Dutch dairyman's son, who never went to college, but instead had worked 12-hour days at every job there was at a dairy and the supporting alfalfa and corn crop land. His family owned more than 1,000 acres of rich peat land west of Lodi. Her boyfriend, Jerald Vanderlands, had a two-year old pickup, a little spending money in his pocket, the promise of a patch of land and a house to be built when he married, and an inheritance to be split among a brother and two sisters when the time came. It was a life that promised security and boredom as far as Liz was concerned. And she was being pressured by everyone in her family and Jerald's family to commit to it. But she stalled. She wanted what Liz Taylor had, or what she thought she had. Not some sap like Eddie Fisher, hopelessly puppy-dogged in love with her. She wanted a Richard Burton. The bad boy—hard drinking, full of life, passionate guy, someone with whom you never really knew where you stood. The fact that Richard Burtons didn't live in Stockton, only made her more desperate. So she would talk Gem and sometimes a couple of others into sneaking downtown to the Brick Works for drinks, dancing, and flirting with the kind of men that were, well, different from Jerald by a long shot.

As AJ listened, writing feverishly, he knew Gem was right. The papers didn't have this story. But, so what? Maybe there was a negotiating angle in it somewhere.

"Is that where she met Eddie Reno?" asked Michael quietly.

"I don't know," she snapped on guard now. "I never heard that name before. What makes you think she knew him.?"

Michael shrugged.

"Why are you trying to get this guy off? Do you think he didn't do it?"

"First of all, I'm not trying to get him off. AJ's his lawyer, not me. In fact, I'm out of the office in a few more weeks. Second, I am sure he did it."

Just then, Paul walked up to the bar. "Pop said you'd be here," he said nodding to Gem.

"You want a drink?" asked Michael.

"Naw. I ain't dressed for this place." And he wasn't. He looked like some burnt out white trashed druggie dressed in overalls and a faded cotton work shirt and dirty baseball cap. "Can I see you outside for a second?" he asked.

"Sure," Michael said getting up and introducing Gem to Paul before walking out of the restaurant into a chilly light rain.

"So," said AJ trying to make conversation. "Do you have a boyfriend or someone you're seeing?"

"Not any more," she said lighting a cigarette.

"Oh, sorry," he said. "Is that a recent development?"

"About 20 minutes," said Gem exhaling a big cloud of smoke.

Outside, next to Paul's unmarked "narc" car, the two stood shuffling their feet and trying to get some protection from the wind and cold.

"What's up?" asked Hunter blowing into this hands.

"We found the cab driver."

"That was quick."

"Took 30 minutes. One of my pimp informants knew all about him," said Paul. "Some Arkansas puke named Johnny Jacks."

"What've you got on him?"

"Nothing here, yet. But he was run out of Little Rock for pimping and lewd and lascivious acts with a minor. He's a piece of shit," pronounced Paul.

Michael nodded thinking.

"How do you wanna play it?" asked Paul.

"I'll come by tomorrow about 3:30," said Michael. "Ask Alex Fraser and Joe Garza to be there."

"What about me?"

"You take a hike," said Michael. "Pop wouldn't like it if I got you mixed up in this."

"Pop wouldn't like it if he knew you were mixed up in it."

"That's true enough," said Michael slapping his brother on the arm. "Keep your head down and your hand out of the till."

"Always," he answered ritually. "Hey, which one of you two is hitting on Nick Giamatti's kid in there?"

"Neither. She's mentioned in the CR in the Reno case."

"Hey, you're not getting mixed up in that are ya? Pop really would be pissed at that."

"No, I'm just gettin AJ pointed in the right direction."

Back inside, Michael could see that Gem and AJ were hitting it off. That was good. He was still scribbling notes on the now half full yellow legal pad.

"Drink up buddy," said Michael. "It's time to hit the road."

"What'd your brother want?" asked AJ.

"Just some family business," answered Hunter, putting a $20 bill down on the bar. "That cover it?" he asked Gem.

"More than," she said turning to the register to make change.

"Keep it," said Michael.

"Then you keep this," she said sliding a business card across to him. "Call me when you want to talk about something besides this case."

"I'll do that," he said meeting her gaze.

Chapter 21

"Don't take it so hard," said AJ to Joe Larsen as they sat at the counter eating breakfast. "Everyone gets their ass kicked at first."

"I felt stupid listening to that cop lecture me on what I did wrong," said Joe.

"The point is you listened," said Hunter who was sitting on the stool on the other side of him. "Most of the people in the office would have told him to buzz off."

"Well, I only have two weeks to get a whole lot smarter before my first jury trial. God, this was bad enough," he moaned. "Now, twelve people will be staring at me while I make a fool of myself."

"Oh, quit whining," said Hunter. "And tell us about this thing."

Larsen went on to tell them about the 19-year old North Stockton boy who had been driving his friend's car too fast and had been stopped by a young uniformed police officer in a radar trap and subsequently arrested and booked for possession of a baggy of marijuana found under the driver's seat.

AJ and Hunter glanced at each other and then peppered Joe with questions, some of which he couldn't answer. What did the CR say about what got the officer to get the defendant out of the car? What was the probable cause for the search?

Apparently, it all came down to seeds. The officer saw what he thought were marijuana seeds on the floor board of the car and therefore, seized the seeds which were in plain sight and gave him probable cause to look under the seat and arrest the defendant for possession.

AJ and Hunter became visibly animated about the case and how Joe should prepare it. Talking back and forth between themselves, leaving Joe out of the conversation, they discussed the best way to handle what they considered was total bullshit that the cop knew what marijuana seeds looked like. It was decided by the boys that they had to get their hands on some of the actual evidence. In order to do that, they had to get a hold of the baggy that had been booked into evidence. Then they discussed how to snatch some of the evidence and get that snatch into evidence without the snatchor getting popped for possession himself. This stymied them for a few minutes until it hit AJ. "Usable quantity!" he shouted. If you didn't possess a usable quantity of the drug, you couldn't be convicted under California law with possession. The trick was to steal, without getting caught, an unusable quantity of seeds from the baggy. All of this flew over Joe's head at the height of a Boeing 707 until they let him in on it. Michael agreed to meet Joe at 2 p.m. Joe was to arrange with the DA to look at the evidence which he had a right to do and to have the DA call over to the police department and clear it.

"Just play dumb," said Hunter. "Tell them you don't know what the stuff looks like and that you want to examine the baggy for age. That ought to throw them off."

AJ and Michael then argued for the privilege of going with Joe to steal some of the evidence, but in the end, Hunter won the argument that he was leaving soon and that Dewey would protect him if he got caught. Joe, for his part, was swept along in the enthusiasm for his little misdemeanor jury trial.

———⫷(◐)⫸———

Tuesday, November 28th, 11:55 a.m.

Michael Hunter walked into the front hallway of the Stockton Golf and Country Club and was greeted by a lovely middle-aged woman standing behind a podium in the entrance to a beautiful high ceiling private restaurant. He answered her request to help him by saying he was the guest of Archibald Cox.

"Mr. Cox phoned and said he would be here a few minutes late and asked if you wouldn't mind waiting for him at the bar in the Men's Grill," she said while ushering him through plush doors into a private area of card tables, wooden lunch tables with comfortable chairs, and a bar with windows overlooking the golf course. *Some place* thought Michael. Michael took a seat at the bar and ordered a beer and when he tried to pay for it, he was informed that his money was no good there and he just needed to give the bartender the member's name. The place was full of mostly middle aged men eating, drinking, and playing cards. A lot of cards. It seemed like half the place was engaged in games of gin. There was a lot of old money in the room.

Just then, an extremely fit and dapper man in his 40's walked into the grill and directly up to Hunter.

"Mike," said Archie Cox with a big smile and his hand

stuck out. "Thanks for coming. Grab your drink and let's take a seat at a table."

As they walked to a table, Cox greeted at least a half dozen other members declining gin game offers. He was dressed in gray slacks and a cashmere charcoal sport coat that Hunter was positive cost more than his entire wardrobe. As they sat down, Cox ordered an iced tea from a veteran waitress that suddenly appeared.

"Not drinking?" asked Michael.

"I never drink during the day," said Cox, but not in a patronizing way.

"Why not?"

"Because everyone else does," Cox smiled. "Gives me an edge in the afternoon."

Archie Cox was the complete package, at least in this town. He headed up a five-man firm which was big by San Joaquin County standards, and handled nothing but the best clients paying the biggest fees. He was also the best gin player in town and could get a bet down on a game when he wanted to, which he often did. He was what was known as an unlimited resources attorney; in that if you had Archie, you better have unlimited resources because he would spend what it took to win.

All of these things Hunter knew as he sat across from Archie at his club, nursing his beer. He also knew that he had Archie's client by the balls, if not Archie himself. So, he just sat there waiting for Cox to make his play, which came as lunch was half finished. Until then, it was sports, golf, and letting Michael know that Archie knew a good deal about him, including that he was up for the Metro job. *Here it comes,* thought Michael.

"You know, I'm not going to let my guy answer a single question you ask him at the 1538.5 hearing," said Cox out of the blue.

"I figured as much," said Michael.

"Then why call him as a witness?" asked Archie.

Michael could see that his left heel was tapping up and down on the floor rapidly, involuntarily. *Got to lay off the caffeine Archie,* Michael thought. "Because, when I'm done asking questions that he takes the fifth on, I figure he will be just about finished with his present career," said Michael.

"How's that?" asked Cox already knowing the answer.

"I don't think IBM wants some druggie that got unpatented proto-type drawings stolen, working for them any longer."

"And you'd see that they found out," said Archie.

"In a New York minute," said Hunter staring straight at Cox without the trace of a smile or a blink.

"You sure that's a good career move, Mike?"

"You mean do I think you have the juice to see that I don't get the Metro job? Yeah, probably. But if you move your checker to that square, there will be consequences."

"Such as?"

"Well, I have the Metro job wired I'm told. So, if I don't get it, and if I even think that it is the result of this case, then I'm going to sue your client, IBM, and anyone else I think was involved. Since I'm a county employee, then any cross-complaints back against me will have to name them as well. Don't you get a bunch of business from the County?"

Archibald Cox's eyes narrowed to almost slits as he sat staring at Michael Hunter. You could hear the tinkling of glass at the nearby tables and shuffling of cards. It was as if he was figuring the odds. After awhile, he put his napkin down on the table, cleared his throat, and said, "What do you want?"

"I want the narcs to lay down on the 1538.5."

"What makes you think I can deliver that?"

"Oh come now Archie," said Michael smiling. "Who's being coy now?"

Archie smiled back and said, "What assurances do I have that IBM will never hear about this?"

"Because I say so," said Michael.

"What about your client?" asked Archie. "What's his word worth?"

"My client doesn't know anything about this and never will."

"Your client's a little mutt that hooks people on drugs and then steals their goods," said Archie with rising emotion.

"You think you're riding a white horse and wearing a white hat, paying off some cops to recover those goods on a bogus search warrant?" asked Michael with an edge in his voice.

"You don't see the difference?"

"Damned if I do," answered Hunter.

"You know kid, you've got a set of stones, I'll give you that," said Archie Cox. "But I don't know if you've got the stomach to play in this league."

"You may be right."

"You play gin Mike?"

"A little."

"How's about you and me playing a little gin?"

"I think we just did Archie," said Michael grinning.

"Damned if we didn't," said Archie.

Tuesday, November 28th, 1 p.m.

AJ Borelli sat fidgeting in the jail attorney conference room with public defender investigator Frankie Sanchez waiting on Eddie Reno.

"I'm telling you AJ that this is a waste of time," said a grumpy Sanchez. He had already spent the better part of the morning at the jail interviewing in-custodies, the most hated part of the job, and he just wanted to sit in his cubicle in the office basement and write up his interviews in peace.

"Maybe he'll talk to us," said AJ.

"Talk to you, maybe. I don't see why I have to be here."

AJ couldn't tell him that he needed a witness to be in the same room to whatever craziness Reno might come up with today. Just then Reno walked into the room and said, "Did ya bring anymore reports?"

"No," AJ said and added quickly, "I'll have them at the court appearance in the morning."

"Then what are you wasting my time for," sneered Reno turning to leave.

"I thought we could talk about tomorrow."

"Nothing to talk about. Where's the other guy, Hunter?"

"This isn't Hunter's case," volunteered Frankie.

"Butt out beaner," snarled Reno. "If I want a taco, I'll ask you."

Sanchez started to get up, gripping the table in front of him with both hands and then stopped himself. He wasn't going to let this Anglo misfit suck him into a career mistake. He'd eaten too much crap to get this far. He glanced at AJ to see what he'd say and saw that AJ just wanted him to calm down.

After an uncomfortable minute, Reno hit the buzzer on the intercom to let himself back into the main jail and said,

"Jesus, what a bunch of pussies."

==========«(0)»==========

Tuesday, November 28th, 1:30 p.m.

"How was lunch?" yelled Alice from behind the glass in the waiting room when Hunter came hustling through the front door.

"Profitable," he yelled back, hitting the stairs up to his office.

"The meeting's been changed," she yelled after him.

Stopping and coming back down the first flight of stairs, he said, "to where and when, and how do you know?"

"That's my job," she grinned. "And, it's changed to the DA's office."

"Swell," said Hunter. "That makes it tougher."

Joe Larsen explained that the DA Helena Vorakais said that she'd have the evidence sent over and they could all meet in her office on the second floor at two. Hunter didn't know any Helena Vorakais. As they walked over, Joe had explained that she just recently joined the DA's office after passing the bar on her fourth try. She'd worked as a legal secretary for about ten years, putting herself through the local night law school at Humphreys College. When they were led into her office, a strikingly handsome Greek woman in her mid-thirties stood up to greet them. Joe introduced her to Michael and he got a big smile.

"I've heard so much about you," she said shaking hands.

"Whatever you've heard, it wasn't me," said Hunter

smiling in return.

"You're not trying this case are you?" she asked.

"No, I'm just working with Joe on the prep for it."

"Well, I don't know how much there is to prep for this one. It's pretty open and shut," she said. "He really should take the sweet deal we offered him."

"You know how it goes. Some people just are hardheaded," said Hunter. "How long have you been with the office?"

"About three months. This is my fourth trial."

"I haven't seen you around."

"I've been right here. I'm a friend of Harriet Lumpkin's. She just loves you," she beamed.

"She's good people," said Michael.

Helena pulled a tagged evidence bag out of her desk and handed it to Joe. "Here you go," she said. "If you're going to open it, I suppose we should enter into some kind of a stipulation," she said looking at Hunter for help.

"We will stipulate to the chain of custody so that when we open the baggy, it doesn't have to be resealed. In fact, you've been so nice, maybe we will stipulate that it's marijuana so that you don't need a witness on that subject."

"Aren't you nice," she smiled.

Hunter reached for the bag and pulled off the evidence tape and opened it, reaching inside and taking some of the product out and smelling it. "Yes sir, this is the real McCoy alright. Take a good look at the bag Joe. Looks fairly new to me."

Joe took the bag and made a pretense of examining it before handing it back to Helena.

"Well, I guess that's it," said Michael. "Thanks for everything, Helena," he said standing up.

"I hear you're going to Metro," said Helena. "Harriet told me."

"We'll see," he said.

"Well, don't be a stranger if you do," she said smiling.

As they walked out to the elevator, Michael pulled an envelope from his pants pocket with his right hand and placed three marijuana seeds into it with his left. He had palmed the seeds from the evidence bag when he pulled some of the marijuana out of it. He then licked and sealed the envelope and wrote his name across the seal with a pen and put it back into this pocket.

"What's that for?" asked Joe.

"Chain of custody," answered Hunter. He could tell that Joe was confused with the concept, so he explained. In order to get the marijuana seeds into evidence and claim that it was marijuana that had come from the baggy, there needed to be evidence presented in the form of testimony from a witness that had taken the marijuana seeds from the baggy and had been in custody of the seeds without them being tampered with until that time they were placed into evidence. In this case, Hunter had taken the evidence from the bag and placed it into the envelope, sealed it and written his name across the seal, and would be able to testify that the seal remained untampered with until he opened it at a later date in court.

"So you're going to testify in my case?" asked Joe.

"I am if you'll have me," said Michael as they walked back down San Joaquin Street. "Hey, I've got to get over to Metro for a few minutes, so I'm going to take off," said Michael. "Meet me after your court tomorrow for a field trip."

"Where are we going?"

"Lockhart Seed on Wilson Way."

Chapter 22

Joe Garza and Alex Fraser were waiting for Michael when he walked in.

"Hey Mike, Paul said you wanted to see us," said Garza. "We wanted to talk to you anyway."

Hunter had been expecting this. "Let's get it out of the way," he said.

"We called Joe Rocha over at the DA's office and told him that he should dismiss the Larry Walker case," said Fraser unhappily.

"That's good," said Michael. "I'll take care of it on the day of the 1538.5 hearing. Consider your subpoenas cancelled."

"You know, we could have cleaned up a lot of cases with that punk going down," said Garza.

Hunter realized that the call had already come in from Archie Cox, who was keeping his end of the bargain and that the two Metro guys were not happy about it.

"Next time," said Hunter staring back at them. There was obvious tension in the room. "We going to have a problem with this fellas?" he asked the two narcs.

"Naw," said Garza. "It's cool. You're just doing your job, man. That's why we're stealing you."

"Yeah, we're OK," said Fraser smiling.

"Good," said Hunter. "Now, let's get to something that could get all of our asses in the same sling."

Hunter went on to brief them about how he wanted the cab driver situation handled. The guy was working nights now and he owned his own gypsy cab, so there was no company dispatcher to deal with, just a service that acted as a dispatcher rotating the incoming call requests for a taxi through the various gypsy cabs using the service. So no one would miss the guy if he wasn't taking calls. The guy parked out in front of Day & Night Drug on Weber Street most of the time. Michael wanted him followed when he went on a run and stopped in an isolated area when he was coming back after dropping off his fare.

"That's when you give me a call," said Michael. "I'll be at the Owl Club."

They agreed sooner was better so that night was it. On the way out, Michael checked with Jimmy Flanagan on his appointment to Metro and Jimmy said the sheriff was the only hold up and that it should be any day.

━━━━●《◉》●━━━━

TUESDAY, NOVEMBER 28TH, 4:45 P.M.

"Jesus, Age. Don't you have your own office?" Michael asked AJ as he walked back into his office and found him once again sitting in the easy chair reading a file.

"I need you to go out to the jail with me to talk to Reno," said AJ.

"Not gonna happen," said Michael starting to change clothes into Levis and a sweatshirt.

"C'mon Mike," said AJ. "He won't talk to me. He wants you."

"If I go out there, you know me and this guy are going to get into a beef and I can't have that right now. Besides, I have plans for tonight."

"What are you doing?"

"I've got some personal business."

"Yeah, with the bartender at the Islander. That can wait. See her later."

"That's not it. Besides, I'm not going out there. There's just going to be trouble."

"I don't care," said AJ.

"Look, just go see Goodwin before court and tell him what's going on and let him handle it."

"The guy's goin' to make an ass out of me in open court, in front of everybody," said AJ.

"What's the rap sheet on this guy?" asked Michael trying to change the subject.

AJ leafed through the now inch and a half file he had on the case, looking for the paper that had Reno's prior record printed on it. Finding it, he turned the file so that Hunter could look at the entries. "Nothing recent," said AJ.

Michael looked at the two pages, studying the entries and then looked up and said, "You don't think this is a little weird?"

"What?"

"The guy's been taken into custody three times locally in the last two years. Twice for battery and once for strong armed robbery and there never was a complaint filed. He was just released."

"What's so weird about that?" asked AJ.

"Well, it looks like he did time for loan sharking and aggravated assault a number of years ago in New Jersey."

"So?"

"So, a guy with his record for violence gets released three

times in this county with no complaints filed. That's what's weird."

"Maybe they were lousy cases."

"Maybe," said Michael. "But, generally if they were good enough to take him in, they were good enough to file on. Once maybe not, but three times?"

"That's weird," said AJ scanning the rap sheet as if he was seeing it for the first time.

"Who arraigned him for us?"

AJ flipped to the beginning of the file to the complaint and handwritten notes on it. "Latchman," he said.

"What did the guy give him for bail and OR info?"

AJ studied the notes and responded, "No job, been here a couple of years, lives in an apartment downtown. No local contacts."

"When did he get out on that loan sharking beef?" asked Michael.

AJ read the rap sheet, "Uh—looks like a couple of years ago.

"Then he came here. No job, no local contacts," said Michael deep in thought.

"What kind of a car was he driving that they found the victim's wallet in?"

"70 Vette."

"Registered to who?"

"Him, I think," said AJ flipping pages in the crime report.

"Is it paid for?"

"Looks like it," said AJ. "Who is this guy?"

Tuesday, November 28ᵗʰ, 9:15 p.m.

The call came into Michael at the Owl Club at 9:15 from Joe Garza. Michael had been playing Covers endless games of pool waiting. Ten minutes later, Michael got out of his car at the far end of Union Street, next to the darkened railroad tracks. There were just empty buildings and no street lights. Garza and Fraser were standing between their unmarked car and an abandoned railroad building with a frightened Johnny Jacks who had a handkerchief up to his bleeding nose. Michael glanced at Joe when he walked up and Joe just shrugged.

"The son-of-a-bitch just broke my nose and my ribs," wailed Jacks.

"You'll live," said Michael. "At least if you do exactly what I tell ya."

"What's going on, man? What'd I do to you guys?"

"One of the girls you were pimping from the state hospital is the sister of an undercover officer," said Michael.

"Oh, man, you got the wrong—."

"Shut up asshole!" snapped Michael digging his right fist into Jacks' gut who promptly fell to his knees and started puking.

Michael grabbed him by his long stringy hair raising his face, "I hear another word out of your mouth besides yes or no and it's the last thing you'll say for a while. Do you understand?"

Jacks nodded, beginning to cry. "You're gonna kill me, aren't you?"

"I want to," said Michael. "And, I'd like to for what you've done to those girls, but if you do exactly what I say, then maybe I won't."

Michael reached in his pocket and pulled out a Greyhound bus ticket for Little Rock, Arkansas, and handed it to Jacks.

"The bus leaves at 11:15. The ticket will take you to Little Rock. I don't give a shit where you end up, so long as you never, ever come back here. You got it?"

Jacks nodded.

"Say it," said Michael kicking him in the ribs, making him scream in agony and roll over on his side.

"Got it!" he yelped.

"OK, these nice men are going to take you to that flop house you call a hotel and let you pack a few things. You have ten minutes," said Michael.

Johnny Jacks said nothing. Michael looked at him trying to make up his mind knowing that he couldn't trust Jacks to stay away.

"Gimme your piece," he said to Joe Garza. Garza looked at his partner Alex Fraser. "Don't look at him," snapped Michael. "Give it to me!"

Garza reluctantly pulled his snub-nosed .38 from his ankle holster and handed it to Michael. Jacks stiffened as he heard the hammer click back into the cocked position. Michael grabbed him again by the hair and shoved the barrel into his mouth. Jacks' every muscle stiffened and his eyes went wide with terror.

"You have to make me believe you aren't ever coming back here, or I'm going to have to pop you right here," he hissed at Jacks. "You see the thing is, Johnny, I want to pop you. I can't really put this thing you did to those girls out of my mind, and I don't trust that you'll stay gone."

Jacks shook his head back and forth, staring at Michael.

"Jesus, he's pissed himself," said Fraser looking down at the stain growing on Jacks' faded Levis.

Seeing it, Michael pulled the barrel out of his mouth and said, "Get him out of here."

Chapter 23

"What's cooking today that I absolutely have to know about?" asked Michael Hunter as he sat down next to Alice Benson for their morning ritual.

"You have felony arraignments in B this afternoon. And no basketball today. Boss wants some of you to take a prospective attorney to lunch."

"I'm sure he didn't mean me."

"He specifically asked for you."

"Who's the victim?"

"Reginald Jones. And before you start with sarcasm about his first name, he was a college basketball player."

"Well, looky here now," said Hunter delighted. "Now we're talking."

"I thought you'd be pleased with mommy's good news. Now, you boys play nice at lunch."

Just then, AJ walked into the coffee shop wearing his one good suit. He took one look at Hunter and said, "Where's your coat and tie? You didn't forget your promise?"

"No, I didn't forget, but court doesn't start for a couple of hours."

"What promise?" asked Alice on guard.

"Ah, I promised I'd go with him to see Goodwin before court so he can whine about Reno," said Michael.

"Why can't you handle it?" she asked AJ with an unmistakable edge in her voice.

"You know AJ—," began Hunter.

"I didn't ask you, I asked him," she said not taking her glaring eyes off of Borelli.

"Hey, what's your problem?" asked AJ. "It's none of your business."

"Don't talk to her like that, man."

"I'm making it my business. Boss won't want both of you in there."

"How do you know?" asked AJ angry now at being challenged by Alice Benson, the eyes and ears if not the heart and soul of the office.

"Let's ask him when he gets in," she snapped.

"Enough!" said Hunter. "Look Alice, I'll be in and out in 5 minutes, OK?"

⟞⟝⟞⟝◉⟞⟝⟞⟝

WEDNESDAY, NOVEMBER 29TH, 8:29 A.M.

"What the hell's the matter with you talking to Alice that way?" asked Hunter as they walked down San Joaquin Street to the courthouse.

"She thinks she runs the place and you," answered AJ in a foul mood ever since his confrontation at the coffee shop.

"She does."

"I'm just on edge. This case makes no sense. The guy looks guilty as hell and should be scared to death. Only he's not and I can't figure out why."

"So what's the mission today?" Michael asked his friend, trying to lighten his mood.

"Get rid of this thing for lack of cooperation," answered AJ.

As they entered the courthouse, Hunter had grave reservations about the strategy, but then again, AJ was a magician at working things out and Goodwin loved him. There were already reporters from several newspapers in the courtroom and one TV camera setting up in the hallway. Hunter now realized why they had arraigned Reno at an off hour. They wanted to avoid the circus. Not anymore. The clerk buzzed them right in to Goodwin's chambers.

Goodwin was clearly edgy about all of the media attention. "Sit down," he said somewhat formally, "let's wait for the DA."

"Your honor," began AJ. "I just wanted to go over a little personal problem I'm having with my client."

"Let's wait for the DA, AJ," said Goodwin.

Uh-oh thought Michael.

Just then Reggie Hind was let into chambers and took one look at Michael Hunter and smiled, "Well Mr. Hunter. Here to make it two against one?" he said exuberantly.

"Tone it down Reggie," said Goodwin. "What do we need to talk about gentlemen?"

Hunter could see that AJ was clearly off balance now with having to plead his problem in front of Reggie Hind. But, what else was there to do? So, AJ began, "Your Honor, my client wouldn't talk to me or my investigator when we tried to interview him."

"What do you mean he won't talk to you?" asked Goodwin looking amazed back and forth to AJ and Hunter.

"Just that," said AJ. "He won't talk to me."

"So what do you want me to do about it?" asked

Goodwin exasperated that this might become some spectacle that he might see on TV that night.

"I want you to relieve me and appoint private counsel," said AJ. There was silence in the room. For once, Reggie Hind didn't comment.

"Do you know what that would cost the taxpayers of this county?" Goodwin asked. "You're going to have to come up with something better than he won't talk to you before I'm going to relieve your office."

"He doesn't want me, he wants Hunter," AJ blurted out.

"Is that what you're doing here?" Goodwin asked Michael.

"No, judge. Look, I'm just a short timer here. You know Hawthorne has a strict policy against letting people dictate which attorney they get."

"Since when did you start worrying about your office policy?" asked Goodwin unimpressed.

"Look," stammered Hunter. "I just came over to give AJ some moral support. Let's not get carried away here."

"I think it's an excellent idea to appoint Mr. Hunter," said Reggie Hind. "That way the press won't think we're railroading poor Mr. Reno."

"For once in my life I agree with Hind," said Goodwin.

"Oh no," said Hunter standing up to leave.

"Save it Hunter," said Goodwin. "I order you to appear with the defendant and Mr. Borelli. You can take a hike when you leave the office. Now get your asses out there. I'll give you five minutes with your client in the holding cell area before I call the case."

As they walked out of chambers, Michael hissed out of the side of his mouth, "Look asshole, this isn't . . ."

"You heard Goodwin. You can take a hike when you get the metro job. Right now, just help me keep this guy from nutting up in open court."

Two minutes later they were in the holding cell with Eddie Reno.

"Let me get this straight," said Reno. "I get both of you."

"That's right," said AJ.

"What are you going to do, asshole? Carry this guy's briefcase?" Reno asked AJ.

"Wait a minute punk," said Michael. "I'm just helping him out temporarily. I'm not your lawyer, get it?"

"You know I don't like that word 'punk'," said Reno. "It's got a bad connotation where I come from."

"I know it does," said Michael. "It means you're a prison queen and that's the way I meant it."

"Look asshole, this isn't getting us anywhere. I don't give a shit if you want me or not. You're stuck with me. Keep screwing around and you'll find yourself hanging from a cross and I'll look like the Apostle John. All I want to know is if you're waiving prelim or not?" AJ hissed at him, fed up.

"No," said Reno cooly. "I'm not. But I'm not waiving time either."

"What's going on?" asked Michael.

"You're a bright boy. You figure it out," said Reno.

Two minutes later, the three of them were standing in front of Judge Adam Goodwin. "For the record, the court is appointing Deputy Public Defender Michael Hunter to assist Mr. Borelli. Mr. Borelli, what is the defendant's pleasure?"

"Uh, your Honor, my client wants a preliminary examination set and he is not waiving time," said AJ.

"Very well," said Goodwin. "The court sets the preliminary examination for 9 a.m., ten days from now."

Eddie Reno was ushered out of the courtroom in handcuffs and chains by two uniformed sheriff's deputies.

On the way back to the office, AJ raced to keep up with

Michael who was not speaking to him.

"Come on Mike," said AJ panting. "You can't blame me for this."

They had been able to escape the courthouse quickly without being swarmed by reporters because Reggie Hind was all too happy to hog the air and print time. Michael had stormed down the back stairs that led to Main Street with AJ in his wake. As Michael pushed through the glass doors of the public defender's office, he was greeted by Alice.

"What the hell happened?" she demanded.

"You're scary," said Hunter amazed that she already knew.

"And you," she yelled at AJ. "How could you?"

"What did I do?"

"You know damned well what you did. If you didn't have the balls for this case, why didn't you just tell the boss when he gave it to you?"

"Drop dead Alice," said AJ belligerently.

"I'm on to you AJ. You and I are quits," she said. Turning to Hunter, she added, "and you're an idiot."

Fifteen minutes later, Hunter was sitting in his office staring out the window gearing up mentally to meet Joe Larsen for the Lockhart Seed run, when Bradley Hawthorne strolled in.

"Go ahead and say it," said Michael already worn out from the day.

"Alice filled me in," said Hawthorne. "It's okay, Mike. It's not your fault. It's actually probably better for the office. Avoids the embarrassment of getting kicked off a case by the defendant. But, I'm sorry for you. I know you need this like a case of hemorrhoids."

"You were right Brad," said Michael. "I'm burnt out."

"Mike, I'm not asking you, I'm telling you. I want you to

take the rest of the week off. I know you're going to help Joe and that's fine. But that's it. I don't want to see you around here until Monday. OK?"

"OK."

Chapter 24

Wilson Way was on the east side of Downtown Stockton and had been at one time a major thoroughfare. It still had Risso's, a popular Italian restaurant for aging Italians, and the Hoosier Inn, which was still the best breakfast place in town, but it was now also the best place to pick up a hooker. Some things in life seem to resist change and hold on with a white-knuckled grip to a better, slower past. Lockhart Seed was such a place. The floors were wooden planked and the cabinetry were now themselves antiques. Behind the general store-style counter were endless small wooden boxes built into the shelving, each carefully labeled with the particular seeds they contained. This was still a place, Hunter knew, where the service was almost as historic as its surroundings and very knowledgable. Perfect for the task at hand.

As he walked through the front door, Joe had the feeling he was back at Molinari's Grocery in North Beach. It was like walking back into another century. The smells. Whatever millions of seeds smelled like, this was it. There was also the smell of fertilizer and soil. They walked up to the counter, which, at this time of year, had only one person, an older man with white hair, working it.

"Can I help you fellas?" he asked cheerfully as they came up to the counter.

Michael pulled the evidence envelope, that he had placed the seeds into, out of his Levi's front pocket and opened it. He carefully took out one of the seeds and put the other two in an envelope he had brought with him for the occasion and repeated the sealing ritual he had gone through outside the DA's office a day before.

The man behind the counter watched all of this with interest.

"We're looking for some seeds that look just like this one."

"What is it?"

"What difference does it make?" asked Michael definitely not in the mood for any more crap from anyone.

"Well, it's just that I have hundreds of seeds here and if you told me what it was, I could maybe narrow it down."

"You could do that?" asked Joe.

"Maybe."

"OK, it's a marijuana seed," said Michael.

"Raddish," said the man with conviction.

"What?" asked Joe.

"Raddish or marijuana seed—looks like a raddish seed. Here, let me show you," he said turning away and opening one of the tiny labeled drawers in the cabinet behind him.

For the next hour, the three of them examined endless seeds, many of which were indigenous to the area, and Michael taped 27 of them to various 3 x 5 cards, having the man label and sign the opposite side of each card. When they were ready to leave, Michael pulled a subpoena from his pocket and asked the man for his name, filled it in, and handed it to him.

"I hate to do this to you, but it may be necessary for you to testify to which seed is which, since you labeled them," said Michael.

"I don't mind," said the man eagerly. "I'd actually enjoy that."

As they walked out after thanking the clerk profusely, Joe said to Michael, "I don't know how to thank you. I'd have never thought of this."

"Not yet, maybe, but you'll get there.

———=⇒«(◦)»⇐=———

Wednesday, November 29th, 11:50 a.m.

"So, where is he?" AJ asked Snake as they were walking a few doors down from the office to Xochimilco's restaurant where they were taking the prospective attorney, Reginald Jones, who turned out not only to have been a college basketball player, but a large black man from Oakland.

"How do I know?" said Snake. "I heard that Hawthorne kicked him out for the rest of the week."

Jones was walking between Jim Harris and Peter Rothman with Snake and AJ trailing behind. They were busy selling Jones their basketball at lunch program for all it was worth. Normally, AJ would have been leading the sports discussion, touting the softball team, Jim Harris' informal betting book on virtually everything, and the fact that he could guarantee a third floor office. But today his heart was just not in it.

"So why wouldn't he come to lunch at least?" AJ asked in a loud whisper.

"He took off around 10 with Joe and no one's seen him since," answered Snake.

"You don't think Boss fired him, do ya?"

"Hell no, what for?"

"I don't know. It's just all turning to shit."

"What is?" asked Snake at a loss to understand what was troubling AJ.

"Everything."

Lunch was awkward. Everyone was going through the motions of courting Reggie Jones who was showing little interest. He finally said to them towards the end, "Look, you seem like okay guys to me, so I'm just gonna level with ya. I'm a young black lawyer. Do you know what that means in 1972? Man, I'm hotter than Miss America. I can get a job anywhere in the state because the federal government is gonna pay my salary. God bless affirmative action. For a change baby, we're at the head of the line. What in God's name would I want to come to this cracker town for when tomorrow I'm interviewing in San Diego."

And that was it. Who could blame him? The entire thing had been a waste of time.

"So why'd you even come to the interview?" asked Jim Harris, saying what everyone was thinking.

"My mama. She made me do it. Hell, Oakland's only an hour away."

"Why not work there?" asked Rothman.

"My mama said she worked too damn hard to see me wind up in the place she spent her whole life trying to get me out of," Jones said.

So they wished him good luck, divided up the check, and went back and gave Hawthorne the bad news.

WEDNESDAY, NOVEMBER 29TH, 12:15 P.M.

Judge Wallace Hollins was sitting alone at his usual table in the darkened eating portion of the bar area of Lambert's, nursing a double gin on the rocks when Michael sat down across from him.

"Have some lunch," said Hollins.

"I can't stay, but I wanted you to give Madge a message for me."

"And what would that be?" asked the Judge picking up his glass.

"Tell her that her daughter will never be bothered again. The man has moved away."

"Thanks Mike," said the Judge, relief and concern showing on his face at the same time.

"Don't have to thank me at all, your Honor. I had nothing to do with it. Turns out, for whatever reason, he'd already left the state. Apparently, he ran into a little trouble here and had to leave. Won't be back I'm told. So, all's well that ends well," said Hunter smiling.

"That's a relief," sighed Hollins. "I'd hate to think I got you and me mixed up in something like this after all these years."

"Well, stop worrying judge. Your record is spotless and your conscience is clear."

"And your conscience, Mike? Is it clear?"

"I'm afraid that ship sailed a long time ago, your Honor."

"Have you heard about your appointment yet?

"Not yet."

"I heard you got appointed to the Reno case today, speaking of appointments. How'd Hawthorne take it?"

"Better than I thought he would. He just wants me to take the rest of the week off."

"I think that's a good idea. Call me tomorrow about dinner this weekend. You know Madge will want that."

"Ask her if I can bring a date," said Michael.

"I don't have to ask her. She'll love it. You know she worries about you in that department."

"Her and my Ma."

"Let's just figure on Saturday night," said Hollins.

"You got it," said Michael getting up to leave.

———————((●))———————

WEDNESDAY, NOVEMBER 29TH, 3 P.M.

Stanley Latchman and Sybil Waxman walked into the California Rehabilitation Center Parole Office in Downtown Stockton, a block from the courthouse, and walked up to the sliding glass window reception counter.

"Stuart Larson, please. I believe he's expecting me. Deputy Public Defender Stanley Latchman," Stanley said to the receptionist in his superior voice.

Stuart Larson was a CRC parole officer in his late 40's. CRC was doper prison. If you were a certified narcotics addict and had committed a prison drug-related felony, you could be sentenced to CRC for incarceration and rehabilitation instead of prison. In reality, it was just another prison disguised as a program and when you were paroled, you were given someone like Stuart Larson as a parole officer to report to. It turned out to be a thankless job.

Narcotic addicts had a few things in common with regular prison parolees who were not addicted. Three of those things were the inability to work a regular job, not being able to show up for appointments and court appearances, and the inability not to get back into crime.

A fourth problem for this group was the inability to stay clean. Contrary to popular enlightened thinking of the day, there was such a thing as a bad boy. Somehow, caught up in all of the mistrust for government, institutions, religion, traditions, and historic culture was the manner in which criminals were viewed and treated. They had leaped from bring perpetrators to victims of a thoughtless society that had not met its responsibilities to keep the poor souls from anti-social behavior by providing them with a proper education, job training, and treatment for the dreaded addiction they so longed to kick. All of these theories sounded so good when you were sipping expensive white wine at high-brow cocktail parties or during testimony in front of some legislative task force considering judicial reform, but ask any veteran cop, parole officer, or public defender that knew the score, and they would tell you the same thing. What these people couldn't deal with was showing up. That was it. Most of us didn't think about that. We just did it. We showed up. Fifty weeks a year, 8 hours a day, 5 days a week, a lot of times when we didn't feel good. And because we didn't think about it, it didn't really occur to us that anyone would have a problem with that. We thought they would have loved to show up to work. They just needed a good job. They needed better self-esteem. They needed training. They just needed a chance. Every good public defender and most every DA came to the truth of this the hard way.

One of Assistant DA Dewer Gunnart's favorite stories was about Roscoe Cane, a legendary hype that had been in and out of jail for most of his adult life for heroin related offenses. Gunnart was a relatively new DA at the time and was in court with Roscoe, who was pleading to a year in the county jail for some offense or another. Now, strung out or not, Roscoe was a personable guy with an engaging personality, when he wasn't on the "nod".

As they were standing at the rail waiting for the judge to pronounce sentence, Roscoe turned to Gunnart and said, "You know Dewey, I'm through with this shit. I'm gonna clean up inside and get a straight job when I get out."

As Dewey would tell it, maybe it was the way the stars were aligned that day, because for some reason, he was touched by Roscoe's sincerity. As a gesture, he said, "You know Roscoe, if you're serious, look me up when you get out. I'll get you a job."

And that's what happened. At the end of his time, Roscoe got out and showed up at the DA's office and asked to see Dewey. After being reminded of his promise, Dewey set about, not just to find Roscoe Cane a job, but a good one. Pulling a few strings, he was able to land Roscoe employment at the Downtown Sears & Roebuck as an appliance delivery man. He even met Roscoe at the store on his first day. Cane was wearing his issued work clothes with his name sewn on over his heart. After thanking Dewey for the umpteenth time, he climbed into the delivery truck with Sears & Roebuck painted on the side and drove out of the yard waiving to Dewey, who proudly waived back. *There's nothing like going the extra mile and giving a guy a second chance*, thought Dewey proudly as he watched Roscoe drive away. Cane had promised to call Dewey at home that night and tell him all about his day.

Dewey received a call, but not from Roscoe. It was from the manager of the store asking him if he'd seen Roscoe. It turned out no one had. Roscoe Cane drove away from Sears that day with a panel truck loaded with new appliances. He never delivered a single one of them. Well, that wasn't exactly true. He actually delivered all of them to a fence in San Jose, where he not only fenced the appliances, but also the truck and his uniform with Roscoe stenciled on the chest.

Six months later, the money ran out and Roscoe was arrested in the Cavour Club on Union Street in Stockton for a bar fight, being under the influence, and the outstanding warrant for grand theft from Sears. He did a three-year stretch in Folsom for that and Dewey broke his "good deed for a hype" cherry.

Stanley Latchman was cut from another social bolt of cloth from Dewey, Michael Hunter, Snake and others who had wised up to the truth about habitual criminals, especially addicts. His pet theory that he had been relating to Sybil Waxman on the way over to see Stuart Larson on one of his cases for violation of CRC parole, was that if drugs were legalized, then addicts wouldn't have to commit crime. After all, he pontificated, drug abuse itself was a victimless crime. It was the other crimes that addicts had to commit to afford the drugs that were the problem to society. It made perfect sense to Sybil the way Stanley told it.

Stuart Larson was a heavyset black man in his mid-forties battling his weight, high blood pressure, and the onset of adult diabetes, as well as a swollen case load of CRC parolees. A graduate of Edison High School, a largely black populated school in South Stockton, and later the University of California, at Davis, he had devoted his adult life to raising his family and the management of criminals either on probation or on parole. He had been raised to believe by his parents that hard work and perseverance were the keys to achieving earthly rewards and the overcoming of racial prejudice, not handouts, from well meaning white people or the black poverty pimps that pandered for them.

As they were seated in front of Stuart Larson's messy desk, in his cramped little office with a picture of his wife and kids on the bookcase, Latchman was eager to show off for his protege with a little verbal sparring with a duffus like Larson.

"I'm here to see you about Rufus Washington, regarding his parole violation," said Stanley after introducing Sybil.

"What about it Mr. Latchman?"

"Well, I think you're only violating him for use of narcotics if I'm not mistaken," said Latchman looking at his file.

"That's right, counsel. He was found under the influence when I ran into him."

"What do you mean, you ran into him?"

"When he didn't report to me here when he was supposed to, I went looking for him and found him at the Black Elk's Club, loaded."

"How do you know he was loaded?" asked Stanley.

"The usual. Fixed, non-reactive pupils, fresh marks on his arms."

"How did you see the marks on his arms?" asked Sybil Waxman. "They wouldn't have been in plain sight this time of year."

"They weren't. I asked him to roll up his sleeves."

"What was your probable cause to search his arms?" asked Waxman getting excited about a possible illegal search.

"I don't need probable cause Miss Waxman. All parolees are searchable without warrant or probable cause."

"Why would you violate his parole and send him back to CRC just for being under the influence?" asked Stanley picking up the baton dropped by Sybil.

"Because there is a condition of Rufus' parole that he not use narcotics," explained Larson.

"You think that's fair?"

"I don't understand, Mr. Latchman. What's unfair about it?"

"Have you ever considered that being under the influence isn't really a crime, because there's no victim?" asked Latchman.

"Really," said Larson.

"Yes, if society would just wake up to the fact that legalization of drugs would actually prevent most, if not all, drug-related crimes, I dare say you'd be out of a job," said Latchman.

Wow, thought Sybil staring at Stanley with growing admiration. He was really attractive in an odd sort of way when he was aroused, she thought.

"Really," said Stu Larson still listening to Latchman.

"Yes, really," said Stanley. "Sooner or later, and I personally believe sooner, the legislature will get the courage to decriminalize drug use and possession and stop all drug-related crime. Think of it. No drug smuggling because it's legal. No turf wars for the right to deal the stuff. No burglaries, robberies, or prostitution to get the money. No murders of informants, because no need for informants. Hell, I might even be out of a job," he beamed.

"Really," said Larson.

"Sure, so in my view, my client is really only a victim and if all you've got is under the influence, why not cut him loose on the day of the hearing for time served and I'll get him into a walk-in drug therapy group to provide him with some support for his addiction."

"How well do you know Rufus?" Larson asked, tapping his pen on his desk blotter rhythmically.

I know that song, thought Sybil.

"I really have never met him," said Latchman somewhat proudly.

"You've never met him?" added Larson, a touch of

amazement in his voice.

"No, it's not necessary. My point is more philosophical. It covers all of the Rufuses that are merely being persecuted for their victimless crime."

"Well, counsel," said Larson. "You make an argument that I can see you are serious about, so I will address it seriously."

"Thank you," said Latchman, his chest puffing out slightly.

"First of all, at the core of your argument is the legalization of drugs. But all that would do is to make them more affordable. So, let's take your argument a step further. Let's provide them to the addicts *gratis*," Larson said pausing to let that thought sink in. "That way, you would also avoid several other problems that plague the addict and by implication the rest of society that has to pay for those problems. For example, dirty needles, which pass hepatitis around, along with other diseases; impure and improperly cut drugs which cause overdoses, which are usually fatal or at least cause long and expensive hospitalization; and then, of course, there's the risk of poisoning from drugs cut with the wrong substances."

"How would that work?" asked an interested Waxman.

"Good question Miss Waxman," answered Larson pulling a drawer to his desk open and after a little fishing, he pulled out a manila folder which he dropped on the top of his desk.

Sybil and Stanley sat staring at the folder.

"Have you ever heard of the Harrison Act, Mr. Latchman?"

"I'm not sure," said Latchman warily. "Please enlighten me."

"The Harrison Act was passed in 1914 and was a piece of federal legislation that regulated the dispensing of narcotics in the United States and effectively ended a physician's right to prescribe any amount of narcotics to an addict he wanted to feed his or her addiction," said Larson. "This ushered in a period of time where government sponsored clinics, established between the years of 1919 and 1922, handed out drugs to addicts to control their behavior and maintain them from withdrawal. These clinics were universally a failure."

Larson went on to explain to Latchman and Waxman that the clinics were designed to maintain addicts, not to give them unfettered access to as much heroin as they wanted. By 1925, the last of the clinics were pronounced a failure and closed. The reformists, who believed that providing heroin under such clinical conditions would at long last solve the problem of addiction, did not take into account the addicts continued desire for anti-social behavior, street life, and a state of euphoria that being stoned on heroin as much as they wanted, provided them. They didn't want maintenance, they wanted the street life that they had and that life was completely contrary to the norms of society.

"So you see Mr. Latchman, I need to know which type of reformer you are," said Larson. "Do you want the addict maintained with enough drugs to keep him or her from withdrawals, or are you a true Libertarian?"

"A true what?" asked Waxman.

"Libertarian," said Larson. "Which are you Mr. Latchman?"

"I'm not sure," answered Latchman.

"Well, let's examine the Libertarian point of view and then you can decide," said Larson.

He explained that Libertarians did not think medical clinics were the answer. In fact, Libertarians believed addicts should be allowed to purchase narcotics just the way people purchase alcohol. That it was a matter of personal liberty. Any person should be allowed to choose their own road to hell.

"I suppose that is what I favor," said Latchman.

"Well, unfortunately Mr. Latchman, there has never been a serious push for that position in this country and all evidence tends to support the theory that where it has been tried, the drug addict is likely to continue his criminal behavior despite being provided legal drugs."

"What about the fact that other countries have legalized drugs?" said Latchman. "It's working there isn't it?" he added defiantly.

"Sadly, that's a myth," said Larson. "China's legalization of opium earlier this century resulted in 90 million addicts being created and it took 50 years for them to repair the damage. Addiction soared in Egypt, Iran, and Thailand with free access to opium. In Amsterdam, where marijuana is sold over the counter, and cocaine and heroin users are rarely arrested, the addicts are blamed for 80 percent of the property crime. I could go on and on."

"You see Mr. Latchman, there's more to it than meets the eye," said Larson.

"Well, I don't know," said Latchman trying to recover his composure. "These are different times. The variables may be different and it still doesn't change the fact that using is a victimless crime."

Stu Larson shook his head and reached for Rufus Washington's file on his desk, opening it. "Let me tell you something about Mr. Washington," he began. "Rufus has been a known addict since he was 15. He's 28 now. When he's not incarcerated, which isn't very often anymore, he works as a leg breaker for a local dealer. His specialty is hurting prostitutes if they're late on the loan shark payments, which they often are. You see, Rufus likes hurting people.

Maybe more than he likes the heroin. Ask some of your clients if they're unhappy to see me violate Rufus. Victimless criminal? No Mr. Latchman, I think not."

"I would think that you, of all people, could relate to Rufus Washington and his problems," said Latchman.

"Why, because we're both black?" said Larson coldly putting the file down on his desk.

"Well, yes," said Latchman. "I would think you would be more understanding of the black situation."

"You think because he's black, he should get some special consideration?"

"Well, yes, in a way," said Latchman fumbling. "It can't be as easy for him, or you for that matter, as it is for whites to get ahead in this racist society."

"There's nothing you could say to me that is more insulting than that," said Larson. "It presumes that you, as a white person, are superior and that because I'm black and Rufus Washington is black, we are inferior and in need of a hand up."

"That's unfair!" flared Latchman. "I never suggested that you were inferior. You're twisting my words," he said visibly upset.

"Have I?" asked Larson with a trace smile beginning to form.

"Yes you have," continued Latchman. "I was a big supporter of Martin Luther King and civil rights. I still am."

"How noble of you," said Larson. "How familiar are you with Frederick Douglass?"

"Not very," said Latchman taken off guard by the inquiry.

"Mr. Douglas was the great Negro abolitionist born into slavery in 1817 or thereabouts," said Larson. "He was self-educated, became a free man, and was arguably the Martin Luther King of his day."

"Oh yeah," said Latchman. "I recall something about him. He knew Lincoln pretty well, didn't he?"

"Yes he did. And he hounded him about delivering the Emancipation Proclamation freeing the slaves, which Lincoln finally did," said Larson. "He spent his life first seeking emancipation for blacks from slavery and then the right to vote," Larson continued. "But do you know what he said about what whites should do for black people?"

"No, what?" asked Latchman.

"Nothing," said Larson. "Do nothing. He said that the white man's 'doing' had already caused enough mischief. If the apples will not remain on the tree, then let them fall. And if the Negro cannot stand on his own two legs, then let him fall. So you see, Mr. Latchman, you insult me when you suggest that Rufus Washington deserves a break because he's black."

As they walked to the public defender's office, Sybil could see that Stanley's spirits were low.

"I think you made as good a presentation as anyone could have Stanley," said Waxman. "And that was a good point about these being different times."

"I thought so too," said Stanley cheering up at her praise.

"And it's not your fault you didn't know all about Rufus what's-his-name's past. That's not your job to dig into that," she added.

"You're right. I'll just put Washington on the stand and let him tell his story. Whatever happens, happens. Not my fault that the law is the way it is," said Stanley rounding back into good form.

"Stanley," she said. "Do you think you'd have time to help me get ready for my trial? It starts Monday."

"You mean the 484?" he asked referring to Section 484 of the Penal Code for petty theft. "Sure, tell me the facts."

As they walked, she told him about how Jerome Leach, age 23, had been arrested for allegedly putting on a pair of new gaberdine slacks under his Levis and walking out of Berg's Men's Clothing store during a Saturday sale. He had been detained by the store owner and a clerk until a uniformed officer arrived and took Jerome into the fitting room and made him undress, finding the new slacks, with the tags still on them. Jerome had refused to plead guilty to an indicated judgment of a $250 fine and a year's probation and demanded a jury trial.

"What's his story?" asked Latchman.

"He says he's not guilty and will prove it when he takes the stand," said Waxman.

"What's he going to say on the stand?"

"He wants it to be a surprise."

"Well, sure," said Stanley. "I can help you with picking a jury, cross-examination, and the jury instructions. How about after work tonight? Can you stay late?"

"I've got nothing else to do," beamed Sybil. "I'm new in town."

Chapter 25

M ichael had gone home earlier and taken the phone off the hook and laid down on the couch in the flat he rented on Commerce Street, intending to watch a little daytime television and rest his brain, but within five minutes he was sound asleep and didn't wake up until after 5. He felt drugged from napping too long. He didn't feel like talking to anyone and because there wasn't much on TV at that hour besides news, he decided to indulge himself in one of his secret favorite pastimes, the public library. Besides, he needed to return some books anyway. Michael thought that a library card was about the best investment anyone could make. The librarians at the Downtown Stockton library knew him by his first name and stashed away copies of new arrivals of books he called in about, saving them just for him. He loved to browse the stacks and stacks of their many thousands of books that smelled musty and moldy and contained any information that he might be interested in. He never saw anyone he knew at the library and was never bothered. It was a place of total escape. An avid reader since before kindergarten, he was never without a book.

After a couple of hours of browsing and checking out two new novels that he'd been waiting for, he was in much better spirits, so he decided to take a chance. Pulling a card out of his wallet, he stuck a dime in a pay phone and dialed the number Gem had given him. After five rings, he hung up and went to his car, a 62 convertible red Caddy that he'd bought off of his Uncle Jimmy. He fired it up and headed it to North Stockton.

When he walked into the Islander, Jimmy Yee walked up to him quickly and said, "Where you been? Everybody looking for you."

"Who's been looking for me?"

"You brother. You friend. They both been in. You suppose to call them."

"Jesus," said Michael catching Gem's eye behind the bar. "Thanks Jimmy. I'll check in."

Whatever it was could wait he thought as he headed to the bar and sat down in front of her.

"Mr. Popular," she said smiling. "You'd think you were making book out of here. What'll you have?"

"Just a Coke and some conversation," he answered.

"The Coke I got," she said. "The conversation depends on the topic. I hear you been put on Liz's murder case. You want to talk about that, forget it."

"That's the last thing I want to talk about."

"Good, then what's on your mind?" she said leaning across the bar. God, she was Italian he thought staring at her oval shaped face, almond eyes, with her Mediterranean coloring.

"You full blooded?" he asked.

"Are you kidding? With this face? The map of Italy?" she laughed.

"What part?"

"Southern. Almost Sicily."

"That figures."

"What?"

"Nothin. It's just your temperament. Matches the location," he said.

"You think?" she said. "So your brother didn't look too thrilled when he was here. You been looking for trouble again?"

"Sister, I don't have to look for trouble. It knows right where I live."

"Speak of the devil," she said looking in the direction of the entrance.

Hunter turned to see Paul walking towards him. Gem was right. He didn't look pleased. As he approached close enough to be heard, he said, "Where the hell have you been? We gotta talk. Come outside."

"Christ, Paul, I don't need this shit right now," Hunter snapped at his brother.

"Hey man, this ain't a social call. Now get your ass outside."

In the parking lot standing by Michael's car, Paul gave him the bad news. "Lonigan's unbelievably pissed that you're on the Reno case. And there's rumors around about how you may have roughed up some cab driver. It looks like you won't get the Metro job after all."

"If he wants me off the Reno case, all he's got to do is okay my appointment and I'm off it," said Michael exasperated.

"That's what I heard Jimmy screaming over the phone to one of Lonigan's lackeys. But it's not that simple Mikey. Lonigan's apparently taking all this personally. He thinks it was piss poor judgment to get yourself appointed to the Reno case and a slap in his face," said Paul shifting from one foot to another in the chilly breeze. "Jesus, man, what were you thinking?"

"Doing a favor for a friend," sighed Michael. "It blew up in my face."

"I'll say. And Pop is ballistic. You better go see him right now."

"Christ."

"Tonight Mike. You want me to go with you?"

"No, I'll take care of it," said Michael shaking his head.

After Paul got back into his car, Michael went back into the Islander.

"What happened? Somebody shoot your dog?" asked Gem looking at him as he came back.

"Worse," he said sitting down on the stool and removing the logo coaster she had placed on top of his Coke, which was the customary bar sign that the patron had only temporarily abandoned his drink and location at the bar. Gem had made it clear that the seat was saved.

"Something to do with Liz's case?" she asked.

"Bad career move," he nodded staring at his glass of Coke.

"The Metro job?"

"How'd you—," he began.

"My Pop works at the jail," she shrugged knowing that didn't really explain her nosing around about him.

"Well, apparently the Sheriff's got no sense of humor."

"Lonigan? That asshole," she said spitting out the words.

"Not a big fan, huh?"

"Hardly. He stuck my Pop out at the jail for the last eleven years."

"How come?"

"Long story."

"Well, I wish I had time to hear it, but right now, I have to go get my ass kicked by my Pop," he said swallowing the rest of his Coke and reaching for his wallet to pay up.

"On the house," she said.

"Thanks. Look, I did come in for a reason. Are you

working Saturday night?"

"Why?"

"I'm going to dinner at Judge Holllins' place. I thought you might like to come along."

"You don't think that's weird?"

"What's weird?"

"Two weeks ago, I am a juror in a case you win in Judge Hollins' courtroom and now you want to take me to dinner at his house."

"So?" asked Michael.

"Seems incestuous."

"You wanna go or not?" he asked getting up.

"Let's get something straight first," she said looking serious.

"What's that?" he asked figuring he better sit back down.

"I don't want to play the dating game," she said. "Oh, I know I told you to call me, so it's my fault for what you're thinking."

"What am I thinking?"

"Take me out on an impressive first date, nail me on the second, probably after a movie, then blah, blah, blah. Been there, done that, hate it."

"So what's cookin?"

"That's just it," she said. "Nothing's cookin. You're not getting into my pants, you don't need to take me out Saturday. Just come over and bring a six pack," she said leaning across the bar close enough so that he could smell her breath. "I'm not lookin for a relationship, Mike. I've got one of those. And, it stinks. What I want from you is a little intelligent conversation, whatever else comes with it, and no strings attached."

"Is that a no to dinner?" he asked getting up again.

She stared at him for a moment and said, "What time?"
"I'll call you."

Ten dreaded minutes later, he walked through the front door of Big John's house. Rose greeted him at the door with a hug and concern on her face. "He's in there," she said gesturing to the small add-on family room off of the kitchen. "Let him yell a little, you know," she trailed off and went into the bathroom where she could still hear everything that was said.

As Michael rounded the kitchen corner, Big John said, "Sit down, stupid" without looking up from the TV. He was sitting in his boxers and white tank top undershirt that was at least two sizes too small, but still had some useful life in it so he'd wear it. Michael sat down in the easy chair and waited. He didn't have to wait long.

"You think when I tell you not to do something that I'm just making a suggestion?" Big John said still not looking at Michael, who knew better than to answer him. "Do you think I just like the sound of my own damned voice?" he said louder, but again rhetorically. "You've really screwed the pooch this time buddy."

They sat in silence watching a little of Archie Bunker yelling at his son-in-law. *How ironic* Michael thought.

"What were you thinkin?" he asked slamming his meathook hand down on the armrest of the sofa.

"I was just doing a little favor for a friend," Michael answered.

"Ah, bullshit!" shouted Big John. "Friends don't ask those kinds of favors when they know the score and smart guys don't do them. You're a smart guy, so what's goin on Mike? You disobeyed me and you better have a better explanation than you were doing a favor for a friend!"

Michael noticed that the big artery on the side of Big John's neck was bulging. He decided to tell him about his first meeting with Reno. How he was humiliating AJ and treating him like dirt; sizing him up without even knowing him; sensing his weakness; belittling him.

"So you had to rescue him? You have a weakness there Mike. Always have. Remember the times with your brother?" He was referring to the boys' high school years when Paul would lip off to a group of guys from some other school and the trouble would start, and out of no where would come Mike wading into them, usually with anything that he could pick up to swing; turning what should have been a little dust-up into something where medical attention and the intervention of Police Lieutenant Albert Puccinelli, who lived down the block, was called for before it was settled out.

"Now you listen to me good this time mister," he said turning his face to Michael. "I want you low-keying this, standing in the background. Don't be selling Lonigan short. He can make your life real miserable if he wants to. Let it go. Don't disrespect him."

Michael sat there taking it all in, not responding. There really wasn't anything to say. He knew Big John was disappointed in him and he was disappointed with himself.

"Has anyone else's name turned up in this thing?" Big John asked.

"Not that I know of. What do ya mean?" said Michael wondering where this was coming from.

"Nothing, just asking. If something does come up, you'll tell me right away?"

"What's goin on Big?" asked Michael, his antennae twitching for all they were worth.

"This is just a bad deal, Mike, and it needs to go away.

You just do what I tell you this time. Things will work out."

That was it. No more conversation. When Big John wanted to talk, you talked. When he was done, he turned off like a light switch. They finished watching All in the Family together and Mike kissed Rose and left.

=•((•))•=

Wednesday, November 29th, 8:30 p.m.

AJ Borelli was living the ultimate schizophrenic day of his life. He'd gone from the pit of despair, which at one point had left him sure that his best friend had been fired because of him and by implication had left him utterly alone with Eddie Reno, to where he was right now, which was sitting across a table from the auburn haired goddess of dry cleaning, Abby Howell, at Sambo's Restaurant on Center Street. Also, he'd found out that not only had Michael not been fired, the boss wasn't even mad at him, and Michael was still on the Reno case.

It was funny, he thought, how the worst days could be turned around by the tiniest of decisions. In this case, it had been to pick up his one good sport coat from the Hi-Grade Dry Cleaners on his way back from lunch. He actually wasn't even thinking about seeing her as he walked in off the street, lost in his problems. As he opened the door—he was hit in the face with the warm air loaded with that unmistakable dry cleaner smell, the bell ringing above his head. The sound caused dry cleaner girl, who was standing behind the counter next to a rack of used ties that had never been claimed by their owners, and all of which were for sale at under a dollar each, to look up and break into a huge grin. AJ involuntarily glanced behind him to see if someone else had slipped in when he opened the door.

"Mr. Borelli," she beamed. "I hoped you'd come in today."

"You did?" said AJ certain he was about to wake up.

"I saw you on the news at lunch on Channel 3. They said you were the lead attorney on the Van Houten murder case and you're getting national attention. You looked so professional," she said gushing.

They talked for 15 minutes and he left on cloud nine with a promise that they could get together that evening and here they were. AJ had picked Sambo's because it was a good non-threatening pre-date kind of place where you could get breakfast, lunch, or dinner, or even just coffee, 24 hours a day. They had been there talking for an hour and a half. Before that he had tried to reach Hunter, even going to the Islander before meeting Abby Howell at the restaurant, but he had never found him. Snake had confirmed, because AJ had put the bug in his ear, that Michael was only taking a few days off.

Now, staring at the freckle-faced Abby with her adorable wire-rimmed granny glasses and huge breasts, talking about the things they had in common, he had all but forgotten the earlier problems of the day. They would keep. For now, he was amazed at how they liked the same movies, music, or at least he mostly thought he liked whatever it was she said she liked. But more than anything, she was interested in the Reno case.

"It's the biggest case to hit this town forever. The Van Houtens, the sheriff's niece. My God Anthony, do you know how much attention that's going to get by the time it goes to trial? And you're the head attorney."

"Well, the boss wanted it handled right."

"So he gave it to the best attorney in the office," she added.

"Well, I don't know about that," AJ said trying for modesty and just missing.

"You'll be famous around here by the time this is over. You know you should bring that suit in tomorrow and I'll take care of it for you, no charge."

"Oh, you don't have to do that," he said thrilled that she had asked.

"No, no," she said. "My father would want it that way. He says these TV people will be using us all the time. We're the only cleaner in the area and they're always getting spots removed. You're good for business," she added. "But that's not why I offered."

AJ couldn't get over how she filled out the gray wool sweater she was wearing. They stayed another half hour and made a date for the movies Saturday night. AJ had drank so much coffee that he didn't get to sleep until 3 o'clock in the morning, but he didn't care. He just kept playing the evening over and over in his mind.

Chapter 26

"I'm so sorry," said Alice as Michael walked into Emma's.

"Don't worry about it. It's my own damned fault," said Hunter going behind the counter to pour their coffee.

"Your fault? It's that little shit Borelli's fault. That's whose fault it is," said Alice her temper beginning to flair again.

"I'm a big boy," said Hunter.

"That'll be the day."

"Although, there's no way that anything could have been decided yet, why don't you tell me what's in store for me at the office now that I'm staying for awhile."

"Juvie in the mornings, helping Borelli in the afternoon," she said without hesitation, lighting another cigarette.

"I guess quitting is no longer an option."

"Who can quit with you around," she said blowing smoke deliberately in his face. "What're you going to do for the next couple of days?"

"Going surfing. Santa Cruz. I leave after breakfast."

"I forgot that you used to be a beach bum in your former life."

"I didn't know that you knew."

"Oh, please."

"Did you bring them?" he asked her.

"Of course," she said reaching over to the empty stool next to her and removing a thick file from the enormous briefcase and handing it to him.

"Is this all of them?"

"All we got," she answered. "Although it really chaps my butt that you're reading them at all."

"Calm down," he said leafing through the reports. "Do me a favor. Call Dewey today and run down why this guy was released three times locally without a complaint. And then find out if they got the fluids back from DOJ."

"Anything else?" she asked smirking.

"I'll call you if I think of anything. Hey, Martha, hurry up with those cakes. I got a date with a wave."

"Keep your shirt on buster," Martha yelled out from the kitchen. "I ain't your mother. She's your mother."

Alice sat looking at him scouring the reports, amazed that he was completely oblivious of his gifts. That's why she loved him. "You don't even need glasses in this dim light with all the reading you do."

"No, why?" Hunter asked looking up.

"How did you get to be 4-F with the Army?"

Stunned, he put the file down and stared at her. "How in the hell did you find that out?"

"You're kidding, right? That was an easy finagle."

"The CIA has really missed the boat with you, you know," he said with awe.

"What makes you think they missed the boat?" she smiled back.

———⊙———

Saturday, December 2ND,

Any local will tell you the best surfing waves are in November in Santa Cruz and Aptos, two small Northern California towns south of San Francisco. Two days of wearing a wet suit to protect him from the bone-chilling water, and getting tossed around by those monster sets, had made Michael Hunter a new man. That, and catching up with old friends and being treated like a regular by guys who generally hated outsiders on their stretch of beach, had helped him recharge his batteries. The best part was that he hadn't thought much about Eddie Reno. That was back there in one of the five levels his brain always operated on, but never at the forefront. He had spent his time pondering the subtle crossroads of life and how things would be quite different if he'd turned left back there instead of right.

The guys he'd spent the last couple of days with were mostly guys he'd met when he was 13 years old, the year his grandmother, who had raised him, died suddenly and left him to an alcoholic uncle and his equally drunken wife. They had decided they could use the little bit of the money left him, so agreed to take him into their rented shack of a house in Santa Cruz. That was the year he learned to surf and made friends with some locals that taught him the ropes.

And those were tough ropes. Unlike Southern California, with the endless miles of churning, foaming surf, Santa Cruz with its rocky coast line had only a few places that had waves suitable for big board surfing. A stretch of water has only just so much room for surf boards to maneuver and in Santa Cruz, there had always been a number of unwritten rules and pecking orders regarding that water's use and who got to patrol it. After three or four fights with bigger kids, Michael earned his stripes. Many of these guys had turned left or didn't turn at all at the same crossroads and they were still there, eeking out an existence at the ocean, putting as much time on the water as they could fit in. As hard as the bonds were to form in the first place, that's how strong they still were when Michael showed up for a lost weekend of wave riding and beer.

Even when the drunken uncle was transferred to Stockton the summer Michael turned 15, he still kept in touch. Now, as the big red Caddy cruised back into Stockton late Saturday afternoon, he was ready to face the world again. He was picking up Gem at her apartment downtown at 6. He decided to pull into Eddie's Liquors for a bottle of gin. Madge and the judge didn't drink wine. Time for a quick shower and some fresh clothes.

Gem looked like a million bucks when she came to the door to greet him, which she did with a kiss. "Ready?" she said.

Not quite sure what she meant, he said, "Sure," and he turned to leave.

"Nice ride," she said smiling, getting into the Caddy. She was wearing a black shoulder strap dress that fit her slender figure and a white cardigan sweater against the cold.

Ten minutes later, they pulled into the Hollins' driveway at their ranch style home on the river near the Stockton Country Club. It was one of those homes that showed its age, but regally. The flowers and shrubs were manicured. Michael knew from experience that this was an obsession of Madge's. They were greeted at the door by a gray-haired woman in a beautiful green dress and a big strand of pearls around her neck. Michael thought she looked exactly like what Beaver Cleaver's mother, June Cleaver, would look like when she was a grandmother. She threw her arms around

Michael and pulled him to her and whispered, "Thank you." Before he could respond, she pushed him away and grabbed Gem and pulled her to her breast with a hug and said in a loud smoker's voice, "So who's this that gets this one to bring her to visit these two old farts?"

Gem broke into a big grin and hugged her back delighted. A second later, she was shaking hands with Wallace Hollins.

"I believe we've already met," said the judge.

"What're you drinking Gem?" Madge Hollins yelled from the bar.

"I'll take whatever you're having."

"Then you're drinking martinis."

"That'll do," said Gem walking over to the bar and taking a stool. "It's great to be on this side for a change."

"You tend bar?" asked Madge pouring a martini into a stemmed cocktail glass that was so dry that the gin was only shown a picture of a bottle of Vermouth.

"The Islander."

"I've been trying to get the judge there for years."

"You come by when I'm working and you'll have a night you'll never forget," Gem said raising her glass to toast Madge, who beamed back at her.

"Cent'anni," said Gem.

"What's it mean?" asked Madge.

"Well, literally it means 100 years. What it's suppose to mean is 100 years of health, life, and good luck," answered Gem.

"You mind if I smoke?" said Madge pulling a pack of Chesterfields from below the bar.

"Not at all," said Gem opening her purse.

Dinner had been a blur thought Michael as they were saying their goodbyes. He couldn't remember Madge or the judge in better spirits. And Gem. You could tell when people were being polite and when they were truly having a truly wonderful time. Madge and the judge didn't want the evening to be over or her to leave. This had been three perfect days thought Michael as he pulled the Caddy out of the driveway.

—————◦◉◦—————

Sunday, December 3ʳᵈ, 5 p.m.

The doorbell rang at Michael's flat annoying him. He was just in the middle of reading the Reno crime reports and taking notes.

After a great weekend, he had been out of sorts ever since he'd taken Gem home. He went to 8 o'clock mass at Presentation Parish, slipping into a pew next to Big John seeing Gem sitting up front next to a fairly good looking man with short dark hair who looked slightly familiar. The guy was sitting close to her and leaning over and whispering in a manner that suggested he'd done it plenty of times before.

Michael realized he was much more comfortable in the role of the one who left a woman after a wonderful evening, promising to call and then moving that promise down to about number 32 on his priority list. He had always felt slightly guilty about it and rationalized the behavior with the fact that he'd made no relationship promises. Of course, he would have behaved the same way if he had made a bunch of promises. But this was the first time he could remember that the tables had been turned on him.

255

He had spent the day thinking about that fact and that he should consider this a dream come true, a sexy woman, and absolutely no strings attached. In the end, he reached no conclusions and simply put it down to the fact of what Alice always said, *he was a Mick, and no Mick could tolerate good times for very long.* They didn't trust them. Besides, it would ruin a good excuse to drink.

In any case, he wasn't in the mood to open the door and see a grinning AJ standing next to dry cleaner girl.

"Hey buddy, where you been?" asked AJ walking through the partially opened door as if he'd been invited in.

"Out of town," said Michael staring at Abby Howell as she walked passed him. "Hi."

"Hi," she responded.

"Have you two met?" asked an obviously too exuberant AJ to suit Michael.

"Yeah, somewhere," said Michael, not sure that they had.

"You know where we've been today?" asked AJ changing the subject.

"I couldn't venture a guess."

"The Micke Grove Zoo."

"It's one of my favorite places," said Abby to Michael.

"Is the lion still alive?" asked Michael.

"I don't know. I didn't see any lion," answered AJ not wanting the subject to drift off to some lion when what he wanted to talk about was how his life was being opened up to even small beautiful things like the Micke Grove Zoo.

"I don't think he's alive anymore," said Abby.

"Figures," said Michael. "He looked like a lifer in that filthy cage doing two consecutive sentences waiting for the end to come."

"Well, I loved it," said AJ. "And the company was perfect," he smiled adoringly at Abby.

Michael wasn't sure of the purpose of the visit, so he just stood in the living room area of his flat awkwardly waiting for someone to make a point.

"So," said Abby breaking the silence. "How's it feel to be able to assist Anthony on such a big case. I bet you'll learn a lot," she said trying to sound encouraging. Out of her field of vision behind her, AJ had his hands folded in prayer, mouthing the word *"please"* to Michael.

Michael stared through her at AJ and said amused, "Oh, I already have."

"What do you do for him exactly?" she asked him making conversation. "I mean how does it work?"

"Well, I make sure that he has coffee and that everything is in his briefcase. And, I may even be the one picking up his dry cleaning. Things like that so he can concentrate."

"Well, I'm really looking forward to watching. It really is exciting. Can I use your bathroom?"

"Sure, it's down the hall."

After she disappeared, AJ said, "Thanks buddy. Look, I'm really sorry about the Metro thing. Are we okay?"

"Sure," said Michael.

AJ stared at him quizzically, not sure what, if anything, he was reading in the expression on Michael's face. Whatever it was, it made him uncomfortable.

"Look, the reason we stopped by was to make sure you were OK and I wanted you to meet Abby. I mean you just disappeared after court last week and we didn't have a chance to catch up. What do you think of her?"

"What do you think of her?"

"She's great. She's like a court groupie when it comes to the Reno case. She can't get enough of it. I've seen her every day since court last week. She saw me on TV."

"Well, that's great Age. Sounds like you'll be saving on dry cleaning."

"You too," he said cheerfully. "So how're things going with you? You seeing the bartender?"

"I've been over in Santa Cruz for a few days," Michael answered remaining obtuse.

"So what's our next move on Reno?"

"What'd you tell Miss Dry Cleaner?"

"Come on man. You're not gonna break my balls on that one are you? I'm just lettin her think whatever she wants to think. You know how it is."

"Look Age, I know the score. She thinks you're a big cheese, that's fine by me. I'm not going to rat you out. Besides, you are a big cheese."

"Thanks. Listen, you know I'm still concentrating on our future. I don't care what happens to this guy so long as it doesn't hurt us."

"It's gotten a little more complicated now," said Michael nodding at the closed bathroom door.

"Yeah, yeah, I know," said AJ. "Look, buddy, I never get to play this part. OK? Let me run with it a little while."

Michael stared at his friend for a moment. Everyone was trying to break out of the chains they thought life wrapped them up in. Why not AJ?

"OK buddy," he said. "Have your fun. Just remember, we've got a real problem here."

"I know. We'll think of something," AJ said with a smile of relief breaking out on his Mediterranean face as the bathroom door opened. "Where are we on this?" he asked quickly.

"I've got Alice getting stuff from Dewey, which I assume she has done. I'll pick it up in the morning. The first order of business is to figure out what that punk has in mind for a defense. Have you been reading all the reports?"

"Not really. I've been occupied the last few days," he said nodding towards the bathroom.

"Well, I'll meet with you tomorrow afternoon. I've got juvie in the morning."

"That sucks."

"It's okay. I don't mind juvie."

The bathroom door opened and Abby Howell cruised down the hall and picked the conversation up as if she had only been put on pause.

"So, do you have a girlfriend, Mike?" she asked.

"I guess I could scare up a date," he said.

"Well, that's not exactly what I asked. Let's approach it this way. Do you have a regular girl you take out on Saturday night?"

"You mean more than one Saturday in a row?"

"Yes. I mean like every Saturday," she said starting to get exasperated. "You know, like a regular date on Saturday night. Are these questions too tough for you?" she asked him thinking he was trying to be cute with her when all she was doing was trying to get to know him because Anthony had said he was his best friend.

"No, I don't have one of those," he said.

"What a surprise," she said picking up her purse from the living room chair.

Taking the signal that it was time to leave, AJ said, "Well, look, we gotta be going and get to dinner. You don't want to come, do you?" he asked in a manner that implied the answer.

"No, you kids go on. I think I'll just stay in and do a little self analysis over the fact that I don't have a regular date on Saturday nights," he said sarcastically.

As they walked to the car, Abby said, "I don't know how much help he's going to be on the Reno case. I don't think he's very bright."

"Mike's an acquired taste," said AJ taking her arm. "You'll like him when you get to know him."

"Well, he certainly has an odd sense of humor. No wonder he doesn't have a girlfriend. You should just use him for research and things like that. He can be your go-fer. You're the one in charge," she said giving the hand on her arm a pat. "You're the one on TV. Just keep him in the background."

"I'll keep my eye on him," AJ assured her.

After they left, Michael picked up the two inches of reports held together with a metal file compressor and turned to the return of the search warrant of Reno's apartment. He read again the list of four weapons and some twelve boxes of ammo found. None of the guns were registered to Reno and two had all of the identification numbers removed. Those were 22 pistols. There was also a 45 automatic and a 30 caliber military rifle with a scope. Plenty of ammo for each. Hunter tapped the Bic pen absentmindedly on his front teeth while he thought about the odd assortment of weapons. *Who is this guy?* he thought *and what's that got to do with anything?* He had forgotten to remind AJ that they were going to the Monday night football game in San Francisco. It was his turn to bring the brandy and Michael's turn to bring the thermos of hot chocolate, their traditional drink. Never missed a 49er home game if they could help it. And this was a big one. The Rams.

MONDAY, DECEMBER 4ᵀᴴ, 7 A.M.

"Welcome back Moondoggie," said Alice Benson referring to the surfer from the movie *Gidget*.

"Hey Al, what's new?" Michael said as he sat down next to her.

"Been quiet. You look great. I've brought the stuff. Took the liberty of reading it," she said handing him a manila folder of the requested material.

"Give me some of the Cliff notes," he said setting the folder on the counter without opening it.

"Well, each time he was arrested, he was kicked out after a few hours," she said referring to Eddie Reno's three local arrests. "Never got to the DA for evaluation."

"That's odd," said Michael.

"That's not the really funny part according to Dewey," she said pausing to let the suspense build.

"I'm waiting," he said looking at her.

"All of the actual reports are missing," she said referring to the officer's handwritten and typed arrest notes, police reports, and everything.

"How's that possible?" Michael asked no one in particular.

"Dewey says keep all of this under your hat and forget where you got it," she said.

"I know the rules Al," he said miffed at being lectured on the unwritten rules of not ratting out a confidential source.

"Don't kill the messenger," she sniffed.

"Hey, thanks for this. What about the fluids?"

"Not back yet."

"Well, I've got to get ready for juvie," he said.

Juvenile court was held in two locations in the courthouse. The juvenile court referee, who had to be stipulated to by both sides since he wasn't a fully fledged judge yet and, as such, had been given the nickname of "three-quarters" referring to the percentage of the full judge's pay that he received, was housed in the basement. The regular juvenile court judge, Ernie Sullivan, was on the third floor. That morning, Michael handled the referee's calendar in the basement. A juvenile court proceeding was not, by law, a criminal proceeding. Juveniles did not plead guilty or not guilty to charges or a complaint. Rather, they admitted or denied allegations of a petition. They were, however, afforded the right to counsel.

There were two schools of thought as to whether you had to represent the juvenile's desires in court or just the juvenile's best interests. Otherwise, the juvenile proceeding was just like any other criminal case, except you didn't have the right to a jury trial. The other difference was one favored by Michael Hunter which said you could do whatever was in the best interests of the little shit no matter how much he kicked and screamed. Every case filed and admitted or found true wound up with a juvenile probation officer making a dispositional recommendation as to what to do with the "Artful Dodger." The "trial" was known as a contested hearing and in most cases was an out-an-out waste of time. The dispositional was the thing.

Juvenile hall was kiddy jail and the first decision made in court was whether the kid was sent home or stayed in the hall pending the outcome of the proceedings. Generally, the hall was reserved for bad actors. The rest were sent home with a variety of restrictions and warnings, usually to the effect that they needed to stay away from the rest of the gang that they got into trouble with in the first place.

There was another side of juvenile court, a more tragic side. The dependency cases. These were the ones where the kids had basically drawn a bad hand in the poker game of life. They didn't have a fit parent or guardian who cared for them. In that case, they were removed from the home and placed in Stockton's version of an orphanage, Mary Graham Hall. Or, if one could be arranged quickly, a foster home. These were the sexual and physical abuse cases together with just out-an-out neglect. Sometimes parents just turned the kids in, saying they didn't want them anymore. All of these were seriously and quickly dealt with by everyone involved, acting as fast as possible, to get the kids back into some stable environment.

In San Joaquin County, this particular case load was growing almost exponentially and required smart people to keep it from hopelessly collapsing under its own weight. Michael Hunter, who was doing his second stint there, found it a great place to work, and a relief actually from the revolving door of adult court, where the mission in life was to get criminals back on the streets to commit crimes as quickly and efficiently as possible.

Within a few minutes of Michael's arrival, the bailiff brought a one year older, now 16, Bobby Samuels into the courtroom wearing a dirty red velvet suit, stained and wrinkled from being slept in, looking for all the world like some younger distorted version of the singer James Brown, whom he was obviously seeking to emulate. He didn't exactly walk into court either. He half strutted and half danced in.

Michael looked up, saw him, and couldn't keep from laughing. He said, "Bobby, Bobby, Bobby. You've got 15 minutes to get that outfit back to whatever circus you stole it from."

"Mr. Hunter," said Bobby rushing over to Michael like some Quasimodo seeking sanctuary. "Check dis out. Check dis out," he said rapid fire. "It's bogus man. I borrowed the car and the drugs weren't mine," he said still wired on whatever he'd taken.

"Calm down Bobby," said Michael trying to put a little space between them. "Let me see what they've charged you with," he said glancing at the report.

Ten minutes later Michael had connected the dots back to his former representation of Bobby Samuels who had a little bit of charisma, but little desire to make his way in life in any socially acceptable manner. He hated school, not because he couldn't handle the material, but because to him it got in the way of a fast buck. Bobby knew his "goes-inta's" and as far as he was concerned, school was out. He was an habitual truant from the age of 9. What he really enjoyed was the resale of anything he came by free or next to it. If there had been such a thing, he would have been sent to "fence" school. Since there wasn't, he settled for on-the-job training which had its pitfalls such as, arrest and time in the hall. On this occasion, Bobby had been arrested at an Exxon Station in Oakland when a motorist complained to the attendant that Bobby was trying to trade prescription medication for gas money for the 1960 Ford Edsel he had parked at the pump.

Bobby was trying to read over Michael's shoulder, hopping uncontrollably from one foot to the other.

"Check dis out, Mr. Hunter. You see those drugs weren't illegal man. They was PROscribed."

"Shut up Bobby," said Michael without looking up, finishing the report.

The small make shift add-on basement courtroom was packed with juvenile probation officers, court reporters, and other personnel and clerks readying themselves for the overflowing calendar of petition readings, custody hearings, admissions, settings, and dispositionals. It looked like the Holland Tunnel at rush hour. In charge of this mess was the special juvenile court's bailiff, Ernie Riles, a retired Army master sergeant familiar with chaos. Ernie's specialty in the Army for 30 odd years had been the establishment and setting up of obscure bases everywhere from Midway to Danang in Vietnam. Master sergeants ran the Army and lived by their own set of rules. Ernie was no exception. Generally, ignored as furniture by most DAs and public defenders, he was Michael's favorite county staff member. He had already logged endless hours of dead time grilling Ernie about his time in the service. His favorite stories were about how Ernie would establish remote posts in the middle of nowhere.

Because of Ernie's position in the Army, he had access to everything. The trick was in knowing who to call, as in some other master sergeant, and the endless trading of favors and goods. The first thing you did, Ernie said, and the trick to it, was in air shipping to the area huge commercial refrigerators and freezer units, with generators to operate them, and the best meat, booze, and beer you could lay your hands on. Feed 'em and water 'em and you could get 'em to build an airstrip in hell, he said. His new job, supplementing an Army retirement and investments he had squirreled away over the years, was in being the ultimate traffic cop and authority figure in juvenile court. Even the toughest young punks settled right down under Ernie's withering gaze. It was Ernie who had given Michael the high sign that Bobby Samuels needed to get in and out of court in a hurry.

Ernie could see that Bobby was still high and unstable and most likely wouldn't be going home with his grandmother Florie. Ernie and Florie were black people from the same era and understood each other.

Turning to Bobby with disgust, Michael said, "Check 'dis' out Bobby. It says here that the prescription you were trying to pawn off as codeine was your grandmother's heart medicine."

"So what?" said a thoroughly amped-upped Samuels. "It was PROscribed. Ain't no crime in that. Hey, you got to get me outta here."

"Who's your PO?" asked Michael referring to Bobby's probation officer.

"Miss Gretta," he answered looking in the direction of a tall shapely blonde with classic Nordic features who had emigrated from Germany a few years before and had been hired when she graduated from the University of the Pacific. She still spoke with a noticeable accent and reminded Hunter of a good-looking female version of Colonel Klink from Hogan's Heros.

"Stay here Bobby," Michael said getting up to go over to Gretta Beck, who was busy organizing her files on a table next to the clerk's desk where all of the probation officers were gathered. Hunter knew that unlike adult court, the DA had little authority in juvenile proceedings and any deals were done with the PO.

"What's cookin' Gretta?" asked Michael warily testing the water.

"Michael," Gretta greeted him somewhat cooly.

Uh-oh Michael thought. She was holding a grudge from that time last year when they ran into each other at the Hatchcover Bar and Restaurant and one thing led to another. He was trying to remember if he had called her and he couldn't.

"It's been too long," was all he could think of to say.

"Well, I don't think that was my fault," she said in her accented English.

"I love your accent," he said trying to thaw out the big floating iceberg standing in front of him.

"Obviously not enough to call," she answered stoically, although he could tell that a hunk of ice had fallen away.

"Well, we should fix that."

"I'm seeing someone now."

"Oh, I'm sorry to hear that. My loss."

"Yes it is. What can I do for you?" she said with just a hint of disappointment in her voice.

"It's Bobby Samuels. He says you've got him."

"I've got him all right. He's a mess."

"I can see that. Looks like he's still loaded. How can that be?"

"Let's see," she said leafing through the top pages in her file. "He was picked up yesterday at this time. He should be fine."

"Well, he's not. You got a psych on him?" Michael asked referring to a thorough psychiatric evaluation.

"I don't think one has been warranted. He's just your typical anti-social, uneducated ghetto kid, heading into bigger trouble. And, I must warn you Michael," she continued in a voice that made him think she was going to ask him for his "papers." "I'm going to want a residential program or CYA this time."

Gretta was referring to at least a residential placement, or at most, a dispositional that would put Bobby in the California Youth Authority, which most people thought of as reform school.

"I hear you Gretta," said Michael. "Listen, something's

going on with this kid. I'm thinkin' you want to move him into the psychiatric unit, get some blood work done, check him for drugs, and get an evaluation. What do you think?"

She stared at him, conflicted in her emotions; her logical side fighting with the other side, which wanted to plow Hunter into compost. "So you won't be arguing for his release today to that enabling grandmother of his?"

"Nope. You've got my word. But listen Gretta, two things. First, Florie is a favorite of Ernie's and you don't want to piss him off or you'll find yourself at the end of every calendar. Second, she's good people. She's worked hard all of her life and Bobby is all she's got left. Everyone else in her family has let her down."

"I don't understand these people," said Gretta, an honest statement of perspective from a different culture.

Michael gave Ernie the high sign that Bobby could act up and then went out to give Florie the bad news that he wouldn't be coming home.

"I got's to have my baby home Mr. Michael," Florie said tearing up. "He's all I got."

"I know Florie, but Bobby's in trouble," he said going on to explain his suspicions about the serious psychiatric problems the boy was experiencing.

"I don't have the money to get me more medicine for my heart," she said in despair.

A few minutes later, court convened and Bobby Samuel's case was called first. Gretta made her pitch for detention, glancing at Michael, and requested that the court order the minor to be evaluated in the psychiatric unit. Over Bobby's vehement jumping up and down objections, Michael concurred on his behalf with the recommendation for continued detention and the psych evaluation. He then stipulated to the evidence being the grandmother's heart medicine and requested that it be immediately returned to her along with her vehicle. The judge granted the request and Ernie firmly led Bobby away, his grandmother tearfully blowing him kisses while he yelled at her to hire him a real lawyer.

In another courtroom on the second floor of the same courthouse, a thoroughly exasperated Judge Joseph Heinz sat presiding over the jury selection in the misdemeanor petty theft jury trial of Jerome Leach.

Sybil Waxman sat at counsel table next to her client asking prospective jurors inane questions about their prejudices from the legal pad of notes in front of her, while Stanley Latchman, sitting on her other side, chattered in her ear, making suggestions that Heinz thought she couldn't possibly be taking.

"So Mr. Tungpollen, you say you are from the Philippines. Where did you go to high school?" asked Sybil not looking up from her notes as she read the question.

"Bot she mean?" Mr. Tungpollen asked looking at the judge. "I don't know," he answered in very broken English.

"Your honor," said Sybil standing. "I would like Mr. Tungpollen excused for cause."

"What grounds?" asked the judge for perhaps the fifth time over similar objections from Sybil.

"Well, because he obviously can't understand the simplest of my questions, so he's not competent to be a juror."

"Overruled Miss Waxman. The court is not sure that it can understand your questions either."

"May we take a recess, your honor," asked Stanley standing.

"Yes. Let's do that," said the judge. "I'd like to see counsel in chambers."

Once in chambers with the door closed, Judge Heinz sat down with his robes still on and said, "Look Miss Waxman,

I'm aware that this is your first jury trial and normally I'd be inclined to overlook over exuberance and mistakes, but this is starting to get ridiculous."

"I don't know what you mean, your honor," said Sybil defensively, knowing that she wasn't handling jury selection like she and Stanley had discussed last night at her apartment, but not knowing what the problem really was. After all, she thought, her objections were technically correct. The judge's rulings were appealable. She was fairly certain as she sat there under the unfair scrutiny, that this was what was really bothering Judge Heinz. He just didn't know the law. Besides, her client was clearly loving her questions and, yes, tenacious, zealous attitude; two observations that had been used to describe her by her father in a negative way. But not here. This is what lawyers were suppose to be. And Stanley hadn't been much help. Of course, last night in bed, she hadn't expected that much from him and didn't get it in any way. But today, he could be more supportive she thought.

"What I mean is that you are being argumentative with the jury and I can tell you that it's not winning you many points. They're not on trial. The object isn't to see how many of them you can get me to disqualify," said Judge Heinz, trying his best to remain calm and mentoring to the young, struggling attorney. He was well aware, as everyone else was, that she was the laughing stock of the courthouse with that stunt in "B" with the prelim. Now watching her in action, he could see how it could have happened just the way Goodwin had been telling it.

"My job in voir dire is to weed out the unfit jurors," she said thrusting her chin out combatively. "Your job is to rule fairly and competently on my proper objections."

Stanley Latchman's mouth dropped open and he stared

at her wide-eyed before the words had finished echoing off the walls. The judge's face turned to stone and his eyes hardened to flint as he stared back at her. The seconds passed and Latchman was certain that he could hear his heart beating, but still he just sat there saying nothing.

Finally, Judge Heinz said, "Miss Waxman, I'm going to let that go this one time because I can see you are in way over your head and under a great strain. But don't ever speak to me again in that manner."

Before she could dig her grave deeper, the judge continued, "Your job in selecting a jury in a case of petty theft is to ferret out those prospective jurors who are going to be inclined to convict your client simply because he's sitting here so charged. Now get your butt out there and do it and quit wasting my time. Stanley, I'm going to give you five minutes to talk to her. If this continues, I'm removing her and you'll finish up."

A badly shaken Sybil Waxman managed to get through the rest of the voir dire process and by 2 p.m., a jury was seated and the prosecution called its first witness.

The owner of Berg's Clothing testified how he and a clerk had seen the defendant looking suspicious as he went through a rack of expensive slacks, taking four pair into a dressing room only to emerge in a few minutes and walk very fast to the front door. Alerted by his behavior, the clerk ran into the dressing room and only found three pairs of pants. He and the owner ran after the defendant and detained him half way down the block, because he couldn't run that fast wearing two pairs of pants.

Sybil Waxman, still sitting next to Stanley Latchman, who had decided that he had better stay for the entire trial after all and not just for jury selection, objected at least ten times during the owner's testimony for everything from hearsay to prejudicial, which seemed to be her favorite. Every time the witness made a point, she would jump up and say, "Objection, prejudicial your honor."

After the seventh or eighth time, Judge Heinz said, "Miss Waxman. You have to stop doing that. Everything the DA is doing in this case from charging him to trying him is prejudicial to your client. That's his job."

The DA only called one other witness, partially because he could see that the jury hated Waxman and her client and partially out of boredom. He called Sergeant Alex Nickerson, who had taken the report and placed Jerome into custody after the citizen's arrest by the store owner. Nickerson testified that he had been dispatched to the scene and after listening to the store owner, he had asked the defendant to accompany him to a store dressing room where he watched him take off a pair of Levis only to find a pair of gabardine slacks with the store's tags still on them underneath. He testified that he read the defendant his rights and that the defendant declined to make a statement. He then took Jerome into custody for petty theft. Surprisingly to Judge Heinz, Waxman hadn't objected once during the sergeant's examination. It turned out that he had misread the signs of Hurricane Sybil.

When the prosecution finished with the five minute examination of Sergeant Nickerson, Judge Heinz said, "Your witness counsel," Sybil Waxman leaped to her feet and tore into the witness with all of the pent up snarling vengeance she had bottled up for weeks. She fairly shrieked at him with her questions, all of which implied that he was lying with every word he had testified to on direct examination.

"So you say you read the defendant his *Miranda* rights. IS THAT CORRECT OFFICER?" she shouted.

"Yes," Nickerson said more of a question than a

statement, staring at Waxman as if she was a rabid dog fixing to bite him.

"Keep your voice down counsel," said Judge Heinz realizing as he said it, Waxman wasn't listening.

"Suppose you tell us what you read him," she said pacing in front of the witness stand, the huntress.

Alex Nickerson pulled the laminated 3 by 5 card from his back pocket and read the standard issue *Miranda* warning, that pretty much everyone in the courtroom knew by heart. At least the beginning. "You have the right to remain silent. If you give up that right then anything you say can and will be used against you."

When he finished, he put the card down and looked at her.

"AND HOW DO WE KNOW THAT MY CLIENT UNDERSTOOD THOSE RIGHTS?" she shouted.

"I have no idea," said Nickerson.

"What?" she said.

"He never told me he understood counsel. And, he never made a statement of any kind."

The judge shook his head sadly and the jury sat there confused and uncomfortable. The DA was trying with the rest of the veteran courtroom personnel to not laugh out loud. It was like watching a child forget where they were in their first piano recital. They either sat there frozen unable to move, hoping everyone would just disappear, or worse yet, they would flail away endlessly at the keys searching for the right notes, hoping muscle memory would take over and guide them through. Waxman was a flailer. She next began to challenge Nickerson's credibility as to what he saw in the dressing room when he made Jerome remove his Levis.

"No one was with you in the dressing room when you

made my client disrobe, was there officer?" she challenged him.

"No, just Mr. Leach."

"So we only have your word for the fact that he was wearing two pairs of pants, don't we?"

"I showed the store owner and the clerk the pants and asked them to identify them, which they did."

"But no one but you saw my client allegedly wearing them. Isn't that right officer?"

"Yes that's right."

"So it's your word against his, isn't it?" she said defiantly.

"I don't know," said the sergeant.

"What do you mean you don't know?" she asked, her voice dripping with sarcasm and ridicule.

"I have no idea what he has to say about it, because he never told me."

"Have you ever been reported to internal affairs for citizen's complaints for dishonesty?"

Judge Heinz looked up at the DA on that one to see if he was going to object and received a slight shake of the head. The DA was content to let Waxman dig her grave to China.

"Not that I know of," answered Nickerson calmly.

Sybil had no where else to go. She had no questions relevant to her client's version of the facts because she didn't have the slightest idea of what his version was. She was aware that everyone was staring at her waiting for her to say something, but she couldn't think of anything to say.

"You have no personal knowledge that my client didn't pay for the pants, do you sergeant?" she asked, struck with a new thought.

"No, just what I was told by the store owner."

"Which is hearsay, which I object to your honor. And furthermore, I move that Sergeant Nickerson's entire testimony be stricken as irrelevant for lack of personal knowledge," she said triumphantly.

The DA started to rise, but Judge Heinz waived him back into his seat, "Overruled Miss Waxman," he said tiredly.

Stanley Latchman couldn't even look up from the scribbled circles he had made on the notepad in front of him.

With that, the DA rested and Sybil Waxman called her client to the stand. She could tell by his big smile, when he stood up, that he, at least, had appreciated her efforts. She only hoped the jury had caught her passion for her distrust for police authority. In Berkeley, no one she knew would take a cop's word over a citizen's without plenty of corroboration. After giving his name and address, the defendant was asked by Sybil to please tell, in his own words, what had happened on that Saturday he was arrested. Sybil hadn't thought to suggest to him what his attire should be and as she watched the jury stare at his lime-green polyester suit with the pink tie-dyed t-shirt underneath, accompanied by a large linked fake gold chain with a 4-inch round medallion with all of the signs of the Zodiac prominently displayed on it, she sensed their small town prejudice against his bold fashion statement. Even she had to admit that his outfit, along with his flame-red coarse curly hair sticking out 3 inches on the sides and back of his head while being completely bald on top, made him look like he was a red rubber-nose away from being a circus clown.

Jerome stared confidently down at Sybil as she finished her question, the question that he had been waiting patiently for weeks to answer. Swiveling in the witness chair to face the jury, he said solemnly, "I'm not guilty by reason of insanity."

The words hung in the air. Everyone just stared at him. Their expressions, which had been quizzical now, morphed into amazement. Most of them thought that if the carrot-topped freak wasn't insane, he was a short walk from it.

"What did you say?" asked Judge Heinz.

Jerome turned slowly back to face the judge and said, "I said that I'm not guilty by reason of insanity."

Waxman just sat there more taken aback than anyone. She had no questions prepared for not guilty by reason of insanity.

Heinz saw that she was gone. So he took over the questioning. "Perhaps you could tell us what you mean by insanity?"

As Jerome listened to the judge's question, he looked about the courtroom at the stunned faces. This was precisely the effect that he'd hoped for. His plan was working perfectly. "I would be happy to your honor," he said turning back to face the jury.

After pausing just a little too long, and smiling just a little too much, he began. "You see, I'm a strict vegetarian." He let that sink in before continuing. "As you have heard, Berg's was having a sale and as part of the promotion, they advertised 10 cent Pepsi and 10 cent hot dogs sold in the store. I have the ad right here. I saved it," he said fumbling with his jacket pocket and pulling out a rumpled piece of what appeared to be newspaper that he reached over and handed to Judge Heinz who took it and laid it before him staring at it.

"What does this have to do with you being not guilty by reason of insanity?" asked Heinz, the strangeness of the proceeding beginning to tell on his demeanor. Trials, in fact, all criminal proceedings, had a sameness about them. Most of them you could set your watch by. There was only a few times a judge was called upon to pay close attention. The best lawyers did very little objecting. Most of the time the judge could just mail it in. Not this case.

Heinz glanced out at Waxman at counsel table sitting there with the deer in the headlights look on her face and realized she was long gone. The prosecutor had wisely realized that the less said the better for his case. So it was up to the judge to bring this crippled ship of a case into port.

"As I said your honor, I am a strict vegetarian and when I saw and smelled the hot dogs, I blanked out. I remember nothing until Sergeant Nickerson put me in the police car," he said ready to be unshakeable in his insanity plea.

"How long have you suffered from these blackouts?" asked the judge.

"Oh, a long time. I can't be around meat."

"Have you sought treatment for this affliction?"

"Treatment?" he said caught a little off guard. He hadn't thought about this. "No, no treatment. I just avoid meat at all costs."

"So you went to Berg's for the sale."

"Yes."

"And this advertisement you just gave me a minute ago, is that what brought you?"

"Yes."

"What were you going there to buy?"

"I needed shirts. I went there to buy some shirts. Not pants. I don't even wear those kinds of pants," he said cementing the idea that he would never have stolen pants.

"You proffered this ad to show the court that Berg's was having a 10 cent hot dog promotion to get people to their sale. Is that correct?"

"Yes," he answered. "I think that is proof of that fact."

"Here's what I don't understand Mr. Leach. Why would you go shopping at a place you knew was serving hot dogs if you always have such a violent reaction to them?"

Uh-oh thought Jerome. He hadn't thought about that. Why hadn't he? He'd seen the black-out defense used in a movie with Jimmy Stewart. That hadn't come up. He just sat there staring at the judge wondering if he shouldn't black out again.

"Sergeant Nickerson," the judge said looking down from the bench at Nickerson sitting next to the prosecutor at counsel's table. "You're still under oath. From your seat, can you tell us how much money Mr. Leach had on him when he was booked into the county jail?"

Nickerson opened his file and leafed through it to the booking summary, "Ah, $5.32 your honor."

"Any checkbook or credit cards?" asked Heinz.

Nickerson looked again. "No your honor," he said looking up.

"Thank you officer," said the judge. "Any cross-examination or further direct examination of Mr. Leach or the sergeant?" he asked looking at the attorneys.

The DA shook his head and Latchman seeing that Waxman wasn't going to respond, said "No your honor."

"Does the defense rest Mr. Latchman?"

"Yes your honor."

"Very well. That concludes the testimony ladies and gentlemen of the jury," said the judge. "We'll take a very brief recess and then I will instruct you and you can begin deliberations."

The Leach case did not come close to beating the record of just under 10 minutes for a guilty verdict in a jury trial in San Joaquin County, but all courtroom personnel in attendance that day would have bet money that it would. Jim Harris was later upset that he didn't have a line on it because he would have cleaned up.

It took the jury almost 45 minutes to convict Jerome of

petty theft. Courtroom lore would later explain that there were actually two women jurors that voted not guilty on the first ballot, not because they thought the defendant was innocent, but because Sybil Waxman was so incompetent that they thought her client didn't get a fair run for his money. It was quickly pointed out by the other ten jurors that although they readily agreed with the assessment of Waxman, and would convict her of a waste of their time, if they could, Jesus himself couldn't have got this guy off. So they changed their vote on the next ballot to guilty.

All of this, plus the fact that Waxman locked herself in her office and wouldn't come out after the jury went into deliberations, and Stanley Latchman had to go over and take the guilty verdict by himself, was lost on Hunter and AJ who took off early for San Francisco for the 49er game. This had been a tradition since they became friends.

⸻ ◈ ⸻

Monday, December 4th, 2 p.m.

Michael had the two season tickets forever, back to Kezar Stadium, when the 49ers stunk and the owners practically drove the tickets to your house if you signed up for season tickets. Michael could still remember the cost per ticket, $7.50 at that time; and then he wondered where he would get the money and how to hide it from Big John and Rose. Big John thought listening to it on the radio and watching away games on TV was better than being there. Of course, it wasn't.

First of all, there was the parking at Kezar. There was no parking. Forty thousand fans, give or take, had to find their own parking. Michael had a little side street, a mile or so across Golden Gate Park, where he parked his car and then hiked to the stadium.

And the stadium. Who knows when that was built. As far as he could tell, there was one men's room and one women's room on each side of the stadium. That was it. If you took a date and she had to go to the can, she stood in line like some Russian waiting for bread. You wouldn't see her for two quarters. On the plus side, you could bring anything into the game you could carry. No restrictions. Michael's seats had been on the 35-yard line. Seats was the wrong word. It was a cement bench with chiseled numbers on it. The Roman Coliseum had that technology in marble.

One of the strangest things during the three seasons the 49ers played there when Michael had tickets, was the fact that his particular cement bench, like everyone else's, had 30 numbers. But for each of the seasons, there were 31 people sitting on that bench. Everyone had to sit slightly askew to accommodate the extra person. Arnie Moore was the unofficial policeman for the bench. Every season, at the first home game, he made the same announcement, "I don't care who the hell it is. You can stay. I just want to know which one of you 'sum bitches doesn't have a ticket. It's drivin' me crazy." There was never any answer. You just crammed yourself in and made the best of it. It was maybe the last time that Michael could remember that people just made the best of it.

The other strange thing about the seats was the fact that Bing Crosby had two seats in the row just in front of them. He would always bring his son Nathaniel. He actually introduced him. Bing had zero affectations about being

Bing. Always dressed nattily, as you would expect him to be, in a herringbone sport coat with patches on the sleeves and jaunty little hat, he was the consummate 49er fan; bleeding with every play, every game, every season. He had one annoying habit. Every time something exciting happened from the Niners' perspective, he would leap up. Arnie, because it was his job, would yell, "Dammit Bing. Sit down." Bing would turn around and say he was sorry, and sit down. This happened ten times a game at least.

There was no 49er fan alive today who had experienced that time that doesn't long for the days of Kezar. The 49ers moved to Candlestick Park in South San Francisco, the home of the San Francisco Giants' baseball team, in 1971. Michael's tickets on the 35-yard line turned into seats, real plastic seats on the 10-yard line. It wasn't the same.

As he and AJ left an extremely disappointing 26 to 16 loss to the hated LA Rams, they were dejected. The Niners' chances of making the playoffs had taken a tremendous torpedo amidships with that loss. As they shuffled out to the parking lot, Michael felt a tap on his shoulder. Turning around, he was staring in the face of a grinning Gem next to her father, Nick Giamatti, who wasn't smiling.

AJ was busy fake shadow-boxing on the guy in front of him like he was a heavy bag to the delight of the crowd around him. Michael kept a close eye on him because occasionally in this condition, under the influence of too much brandy and hot chocolate, he would hit the guy in front of him and Michael would have to step in and keep him from being beaten to a pulp.

"You boys having fun?" she asked staring at AJ.

"Niners lost," was Michael's reply. Enough said.

Wearing a John Brodie jersey, with Levis on, Gem introduced Michael to her father.

"Nice to meet you Sergeant," said Michael shaking hands with Sergeant Nick Giamatti of the San Joaquin County Sheriff's Department.

"Rank don't mean much at the jail," Giamatti said returning the handshake.

"Rank is hard earned and a man usually deserves more than he's got," said Michael staring him in the eye.

Just then AJ hit the man in front of him, who wheeled around to confront him. Because Michael was turned toward the Giamattis, he hadn't noticed, but Nick had.

"Excuse me," he said brushing past Michael and stepping between AJ and a large heavy set man in a bad mood after a Niner loss and who, up until that moment, had served as a perfect heavy bag for AJ.

"Take it easy pal," said Nick Giamatti to the burly man with the full beard who looked more comfortable on a Harley than at a football game.

"Screw you," said the big guy trying to step around Giamatti.

"No, no, you're not listening to me," said Nick quietly, the leaving crowd beginning to stop and stare. "Let's go over your two choices here. I'm a law enforcement officer here to watch this shit-bird game, same as you," he said looking the bearded man in the eye. "Now, if you go after this man, who is drunk and accidently tapped you, you're going to get hurt and go to jail. Who needs that? Am I right? Am I right!" he said over and over until the big man said, "You're right."

"Exactly," said Giamatti. "Choice number two, and the one I know you'll take, is that you can be the bigger man, shrug this off, and let the little guy live."

After a moment of reflection, the big guy said, "Screw it," and turned away.

"Excellent," said Giamatti, patting him on the shoulder

as he left. He then wheeled on AJ and hissed, "Are we done sparring Sugar Ray?"

"Yes sir," said AJ.

"I love this guy," said Michael staring at the entire scene.

"Me too," said Gem.

Nick turned back to Michael and said, "I hear you've been having a little trouble with Lonigan?"

"Just a smidge."

"Well, your father and brother are good people. I'm working days right now. Come by and see me after work. There's a few things you might need to know."

"Thanks. I'll do that." Turning to Gem he said, "I better get him out of here. We've got to stop meeting like this."

"Why?" she asked.

‒‒‒‒‒◈‒‒‒‒‒

Thursday, December 7th, 7 a.m.

The days had blurred with work. For a change, nothing had happened. Except Snake had the 'boat' towed again and Alice had to get it out of impound with no fine.

"I"m getting sick of this," said Alice stubbing out her cigarette in the ashtray sitting next to Michael at Emma's. "This is the third time I've had to get his car out of hock."

"You know Snake," Michael shrugged.

"Sure I know him. But what grown man has his car break down because he won't service it and just leaves it until the police tow it?" she asked exasperated. "I'm running a frat house here."

"What're you whining about? I've got to move him Saturday," said Michael sipping his coffee. They were both referring to Jacob Sanderson's legendary bent for procrastination. Alice's complaint was that when his car broke down, he just left it. He didn't mean to leave it. He just never got around to getting it. This was his life times a hundred. It drove his wife, an artist, nuts. She, herself, would never have been described as a detail person, but anything they had was a result of her making it happen, including the recent purchase of a house on five acres in the foothills east of town that had a barn that she envisioned would make a perfect studio. Saturday was moving day. The third floor tradition was that it was all hands on deck when a guy moved. Everybody was expected to show up. For AJ and Michael, a move would take less than two hours and a required pickup truck. This was to be there first big league, grown up, rent-a-truck move. They were showing up at 8, all of them, no exceptions, and Michael expected to be done by noon. He was hopeful because Snake was fairly excited about it and looking forward to driving the truck. Snake had once confessed to Michael that if he could have been anything in life that he wanted to be, it would have been a long-haul 18-wheel truck driver. Snake loved to drive. The longer the better. Taking a "rig" as he called it across the country, driving 12 hours a day, listening to the radio, was his version of heaven. The fact that his IQ was off the charts; that he wasn't strong enough to tie down a load; did not detour the dream.

"Did you hear about Waxman?" asked Alice.

"You mean her trial?"

"No, that's old news. I mean that she's banging Latchman?"

"Whoa!" said Michael. "How the hell do you know that?"

"Stupid bitch left a couple of files at the Eden Square Motel. The room was registered to one Stanley Latchman.

They called the office to see about returning them."

"Does she know that you know?" asked Michael.

"Nope. Just you, me, and the Boss, sweetheart," she said lighting up.

"You really don't like her, do you?"

"Not even a little bit," she said blowing out smoke.

"How come?"

"Because she tried to take you down," she said staring at him.

"Remind me never to get on your bad side," he said.

"Don't ever get on my bad side," she said.

"You're one scary broad Al," he said appraising her.

"You have no idea."

Chapter 27

Michael and AJ had spent the evening with Joe Larsen going over the list of prospective jurors and the cross-examination of the police officer. Michael concentrated on his specialties, picking the jury and putting on the defense case, and AJ stuck to picking holes in the prosecution's case.

They finally left at 1 a.m., when they felt that their protege was completely prepared.

"You can teach them to fly," AJ said. "But everyone has that first time when they have to take the plane up by themselves."

Joe had his notes that he had taken from Michael's lecture. "Kick everybody with a law enforcement affiliation. They will empathize with the cop you are attacking. Keep all truck drivers. They have all kinds of shit on their floorboards and don't want some cop scrutinizing it. Keep every woman, (except school teachers). They plant the gardens. Keep every queer or anyone you think may be queer. Kick school teachers. They constantly go through kids' lockers. They think it's their duty. Keep all good looking young women. They will like you better than the Greek woman DA. Kick everyone who lives north of Hammer Lane, because they will convict just because your guy is charged. Let the DA kick the young guys. Don't worry about it, they'd see right through your case anyway. Remember, you only have eight challenges. Phrase your questions so that you get your case out in front of the jury in voir dire. Skip that. That's a graduate course."

Sitting now in Dept. A, Judge Heinz's court with jury selection almost finished, Joe was settling down. He liked the jury. He had two truckers, four older women, and two young women, one who worked for the phone company and the other at a local bar known as The Graduate. The last two were young men who worked for PG&E and a bicycle repair shop. On instinct, he kept them. So far, he didn't think he'd pissed anyone off.

The young police officer began his direct examination at 11 a.m. He testified that he had made a routine traffic stop of the defendant for not coming to a complete stop at a stop sign. The vehicle was registered to another person. While the defendant was fumbling in the glove compartment looking for the registration, the officer testified that he leaned into the vehicle to see what was in the glove box for his own safety, and that was how he was in position to see the seeds on the floorboard on the driver's side of the car. Because he deemed it to be a usable quantity, he placed the defendant under arrest and searched under the driver's seat and found the baggie of marijuana.

And then it was Joe's turn to cross-examine. He looked at his watch and saw that it was 11:45 a.m. Snake had warned him that whatever he did, do not, in any case, begin a cross-examination and have it interrupted by the lunch break. It gave the DA at least an hour to re-coach their witness.

"Your witness Mr. Larsen," said Judge Heinz.

"Uh, your honor," Joe said standing. "I'm afraid I'm not quite ready to begin. In light of the officer's testimony, I'm going to need to refer to some material I have back at my office."

The DA, Helena Vorakais, stood up and said, "Your honor, I think we should begin and take a late lunch to save time."

Heinz repressed a slight smile and said, "I think we'll recess now and reconvene at 1 sharp."

During lunch, Michael and AJ were more nervous than Joe going over and over the cross-examination of a police officer. Joe told them every detail of the direct examination. The boys felt the trap had been laid. *Ease into it* they told him. *Don't, whatever you do, let the jury think you are picking on him.* By the time Joe walked back to the courthouse by himself, his head was spinning and he had a horrible case of acid indigestion. He had just enough time to stop at the corner store for some Tums.

Court reconvened on time and Officer Raul Rojas retook the stand. Joe stood up without notes and said, "Officer Rojas, how long have you been on the police force?"

"Eleven months."

"On how many occasions have you arrested people for offenses related to marijuana?"

"I can't remember."

"More than five times?"

"No, I don't think so."

"Five or less then?"

"Yes."

"Less than three times?"

"Objection, your honor," said Helen Vorakais. "He said he couldn't remember."

"Overruled Miss Vorakais," said Heinz. "Answer the question officer."

"Less than three."

"Have you ever before this time arrested anyone for

possession?"

"Once at least," said the officer starting to show discomfort in his seat.

"Can you remember the circumstances?" asked Joe trying to sound as pleasant and calm as possible.

"Not really. I think it was during a drunk driving arrest and we found it in the suspect's pocket."

"What did you find? A baggie?"

"No. I think just a hand-rolled cigarette."

"So it wasn't a situation like this one?"

"No, nothing like this one."

"I believe you testified earlier that when you were leaning in the car window, you saw what you believed was a usable quantity of marijuana seeds on the floorboard in front of my client?"

"Yes, that's right."

"What standard did you use to define a usable quantity?"

"Objection your honor. A usable quantity is a legal definition. It calls for a legal conclusion."

Judge Heinz took his time with that one. After thinking about it for a moment, he said, "Overruled. It is a legal standard, but when it serves as probable cause to make an arrest, it is also a factual one. I'll let him answer the question."

"Well, at the police academy, they told us that if the amount could make a half a joint, it was a usable quantity."

"So you saw what you thought were enough seeds to make a half a joint?" Joe asked.

"Yes, in my estimation there were enough."

"And were all of the seeds alike?"

"Yes."

"And you knew they were marijuana seeds?"

"Yes."

"Was it because marijuana seeds look different and distinct?"

"Yes. Exactly."

"And is that something you also were told at the police academy?"

"Yes."

"And did you get a chance to view marijuana seeds at the academy?"

"Yes. Well, not by themselves. They were mixed in with the leaves and stems."

"So you didn't have a class on seeds per se?"

"No. But I know what they look like."

Gotcha thought Joe. "Let's check that out," said Joe walking back to the counsel table and opening the big briefcase he'd borrowed from AJ and began pulling out several manila envelopes of the 3 x 5 cards that the seeds were taped to.

"What's going on your honor?" asked an agitated Helena Vorakais.

"I have no idea," said Heinz. "What is going on Mr. Larsen?"

Joe was busy trying to arrange over 50 cards on the counsel table and he realized he should have rehearsed that part because it was going to take a whole lot longer than he thought. In a slight panic, he looked over at the jury and made eye contact with a telephone operator named Smith. Without thinking, he said, "Mrs. Smith, would you mind giving me a hand here."

"Not at all," she said and began to climb over the rail.

"All right, HOLD IT!" yelled Judge Heinz. Mrs. Smith froze with one leg half over the jury box railing. "That's it. Bailiff clear the courtroom. You, Mr. Larsen, and you, Miss Vorakais, will stay."

Joe had no clue what he had done wrong, but he knew better than to move a muscle. After everyone, including the witness filed out into the hall, Judge Heinz looked down at Joe and said, "Just what in the hell do you think you're doing?"

"Who me?" said Joe. "I was just setting up an experiment."

"With a juror!" yelled Heinz.

"I can't do that?" asked Joe sheepishly.

"What are they teaching these people in law school?" he said to his clerk who just shook her head. "No, you can't do that. Mrs. Smith is going to have to eventually decide whether or not your client is guilty or not guilty," he lectured. "It would be somewhat helpful if she wasn't also a witness or an assistant in this very case. Sort of makes a mockery out of the impartial jury concept, don't ya think?"

"Oh," said Joe, a light going on.

"Okay. Here's what's going to happen. You're going to take five minutes and set up whatever you're setting up. And mister, this better be admissible. I don't want any mistrial here."

Five minutes later everyone was back in their places and the cards were all spread out on the defense counsel's table. Officer Rojas was eyeing them warily from the witness stand.

"Now Officer Rojas, I believe you testified that marijuana seeds are distinctive and that you know what they look like. I'd like you to come down here and pick out the marijuana seed."

"Objection your honor!" said Helena standing. "There's been no foundation laid for this experiment."

"Mr. Larsen?" said Judge Heinz raising an eyebrow.

Michael had carefully drilled the legal procedure for this

into Joe's head and made sure that it was memorized.

"Your honor. I'd like to make an offer of proof," said Joe practically holding his breathe.

"Go ahead."

"One of these seeds is from the bag of marijuana in evidence in this case. The rest of the seeds came from Lockhart's Seed. The defense will call one witness who will testify as to how the seed from the evidence bag got on the card and another will testify that the various other seeds, all 52 of them, are what they are represented to be."

"With that offer, I will overrule the objection so long as the testimony comes in later as represented," said Judge Heinz.

Officer Rojas stepped down and examined for the next ten minutes all of the cards and eventually settled on the raddish as being the marijuana seed.

Joe went on to carefully examine him regarding the fact that his client had offered the explanation that the car was borrowed and that the baggie was well underneath the front seat. He then called his young client to the stand who held up fairly well to a grueling cross-examination by Helena Vorakais. He then called Michael and the seed clerk who testified as to their part in the experiment. During his closing argument, Joe hammered the point that if a police officer couldn't tell marijuana from a raddish, then how could a 19-year old in a borrowed car. By 4:30 that afternoon, sitting at counsel table in Department A with Michael and AJ looking on like expectant fathers, along with the rest of the third floor rats and Alice, Joe Larsen heard the sweetest words a criminal defense lawyer can ever hear. *We the people in the above-entitled cause find the defendant not guilty.*

All agreed that the buy at Xochis that evening was one of the best that they had ever had. Even the second floor boys were less than their usual snotty selves. Michael and AJ even showed for a while and later remarked to each other that they were glad to see that Joe was subdued and taking the win in stride. Michael said that it was like the old Alabama football coach, Bear Bryant, use to say, "Son, when you finally get in the end zone, act like you've been there before."

Joe thanked them, of course, but privately, which was as he knew the way they would want it, and didn't say a word about the moment he'd had with Judge Heinz in chambers right after the verdict. The judge's bailiff said to Joe as the courtroom was clearing, that the judge wanted to see him for a moment. The judge had his robe off and was laying on his couch when the bailiff let Joe in to see him.

"If I live to be a hundred, I'll never forget that juror climbing over that rail to help you and neither should you son," he said. "You know why?"

"Why?"

"Because you had her. She was already rooting for you to win so bad she thought nothing about helping you out."

"I'm not sure I follow you," said Joe perplexed.

"You made her and, I'm sure, others root for you. They liked you. You made it interesting for them. You got them following you. I just wanted to tell you that. You may have what it takes after all. I was a little worried after your court trial. We'll see," said the judge.

Joe stood there dumbfounded. If you had taken all of the praise and compliments he had ever received in his life and stacked them on top of each other, this was bigger and more unexpected.

"I'm not saying you aren't green, because you are. You need to work on getting more of your case in when you're picking the jury. Watch how Hunter does it. Don't go getting the big head. Stick to what you're doing and maybe you'll make something of yourself," he said.

"Thanks your honor. I've never—well—thanks," he said. "And thanks for not kicking my ass in front of the jury," he laughed.

"Next time I will. But, hey, you gave me a story to tell. Getting a juror to help you put on your case," he said to himself, shaking his head, still smiling at the memory.

As Joe walked out of chambers, the courtroom was empty except for the bailiff and clerk. The bailiff said to him as he walked past, "I've seen worse." The chubby clerk nodded and mouthed, "Good job."

About an hour into the buy, AJ asked, "Where's Waxman? She still locked in her office?"

"Come to think of it, I haven't seen her in a couple of days," said Peter Rothman.

"Maybe she's in disguise," said Jim Harris. "I would be."

"Disguise or not, what court is the Boss going to stick her in now?" asked Rothman.

"She's going to be assisting in juvenile court when she gets back," said Alice leaning over from the next table.

"Back from where?" asked Harris.

"She requested a short leave of absence, and under the circumstances, Boss thought it was a good idea. She's visiting friends in Berkeley," said Alice.

"Friends?" said Rothman. "She's got friends?"

"Go figure," said Alice turning back to her table with AJ and Michael.

"Is Hawthorne crapping on Mike again, sticking Waxman in juvie?" AJ asked Alice between pulls on his Tecate.

"Nothing like that. It's her last chance. Waste of time if you ask me," she said fiddling with a tortilla chip from the basket in front of her.

"He'll probably talk to you personally," she said to Michael. "She doesn't cut it, he's going to want to know right away. None of your 'I can train any dog to hunt' crap."

"Yes mom," Hunter said taking the chip out of her hand and putting it in his mouth.

"I don't get it," said Rothman. "If she can't cut it in arraignment court, how could she possibly make it in juvie? Somebody tell me what the boss is thinking. I'm confused," he said shaking his head.

"Why?" said Harris. "You're always confused. Speaking of that, turn in your line. I need the money."

"I don't think the line is correct," sniffed Peter Rothman.

"Ah, we're not going to start that bullshit again, are we?" whined Harris. "I've told you a million times, the line is Monday's Vegas line. That's it."

"I just don't see why we can't negotiate it," said Rothman calmly. "Where's it written we can't negotiate?"

"Because there's no negotiating the spread!" said an exasperated Harris. "If you think the line is too much this way or that way," he said waiving his arms back and forth in an arc, "take the team you think has the best of it."

"But I want to bet on the Browns," said Rothman stubbornly. "They're my favorite team and I don't think I should have to give up 4 points."

"You're killin' me Rothman! You're killin' me," yelled Harris. "You've never been in Cleveland in your life!"

"I went to an Indians/A's game in Oakland two years ago. I love their uniforms."

"He loves their uniforms," said a completely agitated Jim Harris to Alice, AJ, and Hunter.

"You know Peter, this is why the world hates your people. I want to kill you myself."

"Not to change the subject," said AJ changing the subject. "Saturday is move day. 8 a.m. sharp."

"Nobody told me anything about it," said Rothman still hurt by Harris' invectives.

"Jesus Christ Prince. What planet do you live on?" snapped Harris. "You now have my personal invitation to be at Snake's house Saturday morning at 8 a.m. Bring the donuts."

"Donuts?" asked a ruffled Peter Rothman in all seriousness. "When did we start bringing donuts? How many donuts?"

"How did he get on the third floor?" Harris asked AJ. "Cause I know nobody asked me."

"Here's my line Jim," said Rothman taking a carefully folded piece of paper from the inside pocket of his sports coat and handing it to Harris.

"If you had it," spat Harris, "what was all that bullshit about negotiating?"

"Can't blame me for trying," smiled Rothman.

"God help me," said Alice. "I'm going to miss you guys when you're gone."

"Where we going?" asked Snake looking at the confused looks on the guys' faces.

"This is just grown up summer camp boys," she said stubbing out her cigarette and standing to leave. "This isn't reality. It can't last forever." And with that thought rattling disturbingly around the restaurant, she walked out the door.

FRIDAY, DECEMBER 8TH, 9 A.M.

The courtroom of Department B was absolutely packed for the Reno preliminary hearing. Much to the displeasure of the independent marshal's office, there were a half dozen sheriff's deputies providing extra security on Lonigan's orders. The Van Houten family had preferred seating in the front row just behind the rail. There were reporters from several newspapers, the usual court watchers, and other observers wanting to be part of the spectacle. In the hallway were several television crews from the local Sacramento NBC, ABC, and CBS affiliates set up and ready for breaking news.

AJ was in his cleaned and pressed suit feeling "throw up" nervous. He had sent for Reno to be placed into the small interview room near the holding cell. He was no longer dressed in jail orange, but rather in an all red jumpsuit with heavy leg and waist shackles befitting an axe murderer of an orphanage full of children.

When AJ was let in to see him, all Reno said was, "Get the hell outta here. Send in the other guy."

Of course, there was no "other guy." It hadn't occurred to AJ that Michael would not be with him at the prelim. He blamed himself for not locking that in because he had been spending every possible minute with Abby in the last ten days.

All of his life, up until now, he had been second fiddle to someone. His best friends in high school were good looking jocks who went on to great athletic careers. They had always gotten the girl. He was the funny, popular, confidant, big brother to all of these great looking cheerleaders that wouldn't give him a tumble. He was the most popular guy in school, receiving the most votes for student body president in the history of Vallejo High. In all of this, he had learned a hard lesson. Being king requires something more than being the most popular. There is a certain something that is recognized by others. A charisma. A certainty of purpose. The ability to tell a group something and that was it. Enough said. John Wayne characters had it. Maybe because John Wayne had it. He didn't know. He just knew it when he saw it. And he didn't have it. That was his curse. The worst part of the curse was that he knew better than the heros how to turn being a hero into a profitable advantage. That was the thing about heros. They didn't know how to make a profit from their status. They needed management and that was where he came in. Until Abby. To her, for whatever reason, that good looking, big breasted woman had cast him in the John Wayne role for the first time in his life and he wasn't about to let it go.

The preliminary hearing consisted of one of the investigating officers presenting the evidence from Elizabeth Van Houten's disappearance, to the discovery of her damaged car with her body in it, which led to the investigation of repair shops based on the information provided by two juveniles, Tommy Barnes and Jimmy Fox, who saw the Van Houten car collide with another vehicle.

AJ stood up to object to hearsay on what the kids said, when Eddie Reno hissed, "Sit down and shut up."

AJ sat back down and stared at him embarrassed, glancing at the bailiff and court reporter to see if they had heard.

"Just sit there Bozo," whispered Reno. "Don't talk unless I say so."

Right there, Anthony Borelli didn't know if he had ever hated anyone more than Eddie Reno.

Next to testify was the pathologist who performed the autopsy on Elizabeth Van Houten and fixed the cause and time of death in a general way. *A bullet to the head and dead about two weeks before she was taken out of the water.*

Then, although it wasn't necessary, the DA called one of the boys, Tommy Barnes, to the stand who testified to what he saw that Friday, the car wreck and the cars driving away. AJ could see that Eddie Reno was, for a change, riveted to this testimony. Why, he hadn't a clue.

By this time AJ was beyond humiliation. After each witness had finished testifying, Eddie Reno had hissed, *"No questions,"* in AJ's ear. "No questions, your honor," AJ would say standing. He could see reporters scribbling on their notepads every time he said it. He could only imagine what they were thinking and writing. He even tried to imagine what Hunter would do and couldn't.

He was about to do the same thing again when the boy finished direct examination, but was caught by Eddie Reno grabbing his arm in a vice grip and pulling him close. "Ask him if he was sure when all of this happened," he whispered.

AJ pulled away and stared at him like he was vermin. He stood and said, "Uh, Tommy, are you sure all of this happened on Friday around noon?"

"Yes, I'm sure," said Tommy Barnes looking around the room nervously.

"Thank you your honor. No further questions." *Some cross-exam*, he thought sitting back down in humiliation. What was he going to say to the reporters? He had to appear confident. He had to appear in charge because Abby would be watching the news.

"I like the part best when you said this was not the defense's time to put on a case. It made it seem like there was lots going on that you knew about that they didn't. You looked so confident," she said giving his arm a squeeze. "You were so important looking. You really have a good TV presence. Daddy thinks so too."

AJ had gone straight from court to the dry cleaners and found he'd already been on the air on one of the local stations. If anyone had been critical that he had no cross-examination of any of the prosecution's witnesses, except for Tommy Barnes, Abby hadn't heard it, so probably no one had said anything about it, he thought.

Reno had been held to answer to Superior Court for murder and once again, refusing to waive time, he was due to be arraigned there on Monday. What AJ didn't know, was whether any courthouse personnel had gotten wise as to how Reno was treating him. Also, the crime reports had doubled in the last week and he hadn't even looked at them. He hadn't finished the first ones for that matter. The Boss had asked him twice that week how things were going. He decided that he'd grab Hunter for a strategy session after he took Abby to lunch at the Gan Chy for Chinese, her favorite.

As they were walking back from lunch, she said, "Did you see the way those TV people waived at you at lunch? You're such a celebrity. Maybe we should go shopping this weekend for another suit for you. Something in a blue pinstripe would be nice I think."

"A new suit?" said AJ. "How much are new suits?"

"I don't know. You want to get a nice one. Maybe a $100," she said.

He was a guy who liked to spend no money. He would eat off of Hunter's plate at Shakey's Pizza Bunch-a-Lunch buffet to avoid paying; and here he was popping for lunches and dinners; and he was about to buy a suit he didn't want just so a woman he had the hots for could help him pick it out and tell him how great he looked in it. Go figure.

Back at the office he found himself once again

nose-to-nose with Alice.

"What do you mean he's at the beach? How can he be at the beach? He was just at the beach," he said with irritation.

"What's it to you?" said Alice. "He left after court. He'll see you at Sanderson's tomorrow morning for the move."

Oh shit, he thought.

"You forgot, didn't you?" she said accusingly.

"Hey, I'll be there," he said. "He didn't take any work with him did he?"

"He's only gone over night. Jesus, why don't you climb off his back and do your own work for a change."

"Why don't you get a real boyfriend and worry about him for a change?" That was telling her, he thought staring back at her.

Chapter 28

Michael's first thought when he pulled up to Snake's rental house was that he'd only had three hours sleep and had just driven two hours to get there and so he must be nuts. His second thought, where was the truck? The entire third floor was there already milling around out front, including AJ.

Michael knocked and opened the door without waiting for an invitation. What he saw stunned him. Nothing, absolutely nothing, had been packed. The two kids were sitting at the kitchen table in their feety jammies with Snake eating a breakfast of cold cereal.

"Hi fellas," Snake said as they all walked in and stared about the room disbelievingly. "You guys ready to work?"

"This is bullshit," said Jim Harris.

"Where's the moving truck, Snake?" asked Michael with an edge creeping into his tired voice.

"You know I was just about to make that decision. I'm thinking U-Haul," he said reaching for the phone book.

"You haven't reserved a moving truck?" asked an astonished Peter Rothman. "It's Saturday man. You can't get a truck on Saturday."

"Oh, I don't know," said Snake. "Let's make some calls."

"None of this shit's packed," said AJ, staring around

at a house that looked perfectly normal for a sleepy Saturday morning.

"There ain't even any boxes," said Harris looking around. "Have we got the right day?"

Snake's wife came out of the back bedroom yelling, "Mike, I've been hounding him for the last two weeks about this. But you know how he is."

"This may be a record Snake, even for you," Michael said. "OK guys, let's make the best of this."

"Yeah, let's get the hell out of here," said Harris.

"Snake and I will go get some kind of truck. The rest of you disconnect the washer and dryer and the refer."

When they were in the car headed for the nearest U-Haul, Michael said, "You realize that we are just going to have to pile everything loose into the truck if we find one."

"These things happen."

"Just to you Snake. Just to you. This may be your personal best."

Several large pizzas, two cases of beer, and ten hours later, they finished carrying a houseful of furniture and loose items into a large U-Haul paneled truck. At the end, they were just throwing things in. Harris made the over and under line to be 10 percent on the breakage, but everyone was too tired and pissed off to bet. To prevent a full-scale mutiny, Snake reduced everyone's duties down to just loading the truck. He would drive it up to the new house and unload it himself. When Harris heard this, he decided that he could book some serious action on when or if the U-Haul would ever be returned. The day was essentially shot by the time they drove away in different directions.

AJ was in a particularly foul mood. He'd called Abby several times from Snake's house during the day with updates. Clearly Saturday suit shopping was shot. But, Michael figured something was cooking the way AJ shot out of there. *The times they are a changing*, he thought. At least for now.

On an impulse, he used Snake's phone and called his brother in Metro to get Nick Giamatti's address and phone number.

"What do you need that for bro?" asked Paul over the phone. "Trying to make a few points with the old man? I thought you normally steered clear of fathers."

"A little business."

"What's up?" Paul asked with a note of concern.

"Tell you later."

"Pop wants to see you. Mass and breakfast tomorrow."

"What else is new?"

After apologizing profusely for the short notice and being assured he wasn't doing a damn thing anyway, Michael drove to the small house on the twisting street that backed up to the creek in Lincoln Village. The house was small, but impeccably maintained on a lot that had to be over an acre in size, filled with fruit and nut trees and rolling lawn. An oasis for the common man thought Michael as he drove in through the open gate, flanked by used brick pillars that looked liked they had been precision laid, brick by brick, a work of art rather than a masonry job. The circular gravel drive crunched under the big Caddy's wheels as Michael pulled up.

Sergeant Giamatti introduced Michael to his wife, Marie, a handsome shapely Italian woman, the spitting image of Gem, and ushered him into a high redwood ceilinged family room with a roaring fireplace that looked out on lawn, bordered in outdoor lights that dropped off to the creek. The place screamed pride of ownership.

"What're you drinkin' Mike?" Giamatti asked after they were seated in plush blue leather chairs.

Michael could see the Budweiser can on the lamp table next to Gem's father and said, "Beer would be fine."

A few minutes later, Gem's mother discreetly disappeared and her father turned to Michael and said, "So how you getting along with my kid?"

She may have gotten her looks from her mother, but her directness most certainly has come from her Pop, thought Michael drinking the beer. "I have no idea. I guess fine. I really haven't seen her since last weekend."

"She said you took her to Judge Hollins' house for dinner. She got a big kick out of that."

"They did too."

"I thought Hollins ate lawyers, not with them," said Giamatti.

"He can be tough," said Michael.

"But not to you?" Giamatti said lighting an unfiltered cigarette and staring at Michael.

Michael sat there not responding. He wasn't sure what Giamatti's point was, but he thought it best just to keep quiet and let him make it.

"You hear the rumor that's been floating around about some cab driver that got the shit scared out of him and was run out of town?"

"I might have heard something," Michael shrugged. "I don't know. There are a lot of rumors out there. Most of them turn out to be nothing."

"How do you feel about losing the Metro job?"

"Ten days ago, it drove me nuts. But I think it's behind me now."

"You're better off."

"Why?"

"Because if you worked for Metro, you really would have been working for Lonigan and that wouldn't have worked out," said Giamatti draining his beer.

"How come?" asked Michael.

"Because you don't strike me as a guy who can be controlled and Lonigan can't stand that," he said with bitterness.

"You sound like you speak from experience."

"You might say that."

"Is that what you wanted to tell me Sarge?" asked Michael quietly.

"No," he said taking a long drag. "I wanted to tell you this Reno deal doesn't add up and Lonigan's very nervous about it. You should get away from this thing. There's no upside."

"What's he nervous about?" asked Michael leaning forward.

"That's just it. I don't know. But I hear he is. The thing seems open and shut, but this Reno guy is a piece of work."

"What do you mean?"

"He's no cherry. He's been around, so he ought to know the score. He pops the sheriff's favorite niece and he should be scared shitless, but he acts like he's just killing time," said Giamatti swiveling around to face Michael. "And he never has made a phone call. Not one. Not one visitor either. He spends all his time reading and re-reading the crime reports. Guys that do that kind of crime are bugging their lawyers every two minutes. He hasn't said five words to anybody."

"Why you telling me all this?" asked Hunter.

"Because my kid likes you and I don't want her involved in this. She's been through enough with her friend getting killed."

"What makes you think she'd get involved?" asked Michael.

"Because I know her. If she's involved with you, she'll get involved with this. Which brings me back to my first question, which you managed to duck."

"Which was?"

"How you gettin' along with my kid?"

"Isn't she involved with somebody else?" asked Michael.

"You mean the sheriff's detective Mark DeLucca?"

"I don't know. The guy she goes to mass with."

"Yeah, that's him. I think that's over."

"I wouldn't be so sure about that and anyway, you've got nothing to worry about. There's nothing going on between her and me. Besides that, Anthony Borelli is going to try this thing and he's going to lose and everything's going to get back to normal," Hunter said. "And then in a short period of time I think I'll be leaving town."

"Leaving town?" asked Giamatti surprised at that revelation. "Where to?"

"Vallejo I think. But I'm not sure. I just know that if I stick around here that something bad's going to happen. It's time for a change. So you see Sergeant, you got nothing to worry about," he said standing to leave.

"I hate it when people tell me that. In my experience, that's just when you should start worrying," said Giamatti. "Listen kid, I don't know why, but I can see what Gem sees in you. You got moxie, I'll give you that. But moxie can get you in trouble. If you need any help on this, give me a call."

"Thanks Sergeant," Michael said turning to leave.

"Call me Nick," Giamatti said sticking his hand out. "And I've got one question."

"And what would that be?" Michael said taking his hand to shake it.

"Would you have pulled the trigger?" Nick Giamatti asked him gripping his hand tight and staring him in the eye for the answer.

Michael stared at him for a couple of seconds and then

let his eyes drift to the beautiful and peaceful estate of a backyard, admiring the world Nick Giamatti had created for himself away from the one he couldn't control. When he looked back, he said, "I think you already know the answer to that question Sergeant."

"Yeah, I do," said Giamatti letting his hand go.

———◆———

Sunday, December 10th, 7:50 a.m.

The air was clear and cold when Michael hustled up the steps of Presentation Parish Catholic Church on Benjamin Holt Drive to meet Big John, who he knew would already be seated in a back pew. Big was never late for anything and despised waiting, especially at restaurants. He always called ahead for a reservation and when he walked through the door, he expected to keep walking right to his table, no waiting. People that knew him, and almost everyone did, made it their business to see that he was accommodated.

As Michael sat down next to Big John, he glanced to the front to see if Gem was there. Detective Mark DeLucca was there, but no Gem.

"Where you been?" asked Big John, his standard greeting, giving Michael's knee a squeeze.

Michael was dressed for the game, but he was not now sure that he was going to attend. AJ had called him just before he left for church and said that he had to pass on the game to go suit shopping at Macy's later that day, breaking a standard tradition. This thing with the dry cleaner girl was getting out of hand as far as Hunter was concerned. The thing was, you could normally set your watch by AJ's habits. He was traditional and easy to read. Don't spend money for anything you don't have to. Go to ball games when you get a free ticket. Get back to Vallejo as soon as possible. Skipping a Sunday 49er game to go suit shopping at Macy's was totally out of character and disturbing. Michael didn't think you could get AJ in Macy's at gunpoint. All of these thoughts were rattling around in his head when he felt the hand on his shoulder.

He looked up into her face and she said, "Scoot over."

Michael motioned to Big John whose eyes went wide at the sight of Gem, but he quickly moved his bulk over to make room. Gem kneeled on the kneeler and crossed herself and prayed for a moment before setting beside him on the pew. She then reached across him and shook hands with Big John saying, "Nice to see you Mr. Moretti." Big John nodded with the same confused expression on his face that Michael had.

"You going to the game today?" she whispered.

"I don't know. AJ just bailed."

"That's weird. My pop says he isn't feeling so hot, so can I hitch a ride?" she asked out of the side of her mouth. "We can sit in our seats and scalp yours."

"Sure, I guess," he said.

"Don't guess. You're either in or out," she said.

"Sure," he replied.

Big John took it all in saying nothing.

During the communion part of the mass, Big John and Gem went forward. Michael noticed that Detective DeLucca said something to Gem as she walked past him on her way to communion down the middle aisle. She said something back and he looked in Michael's direction with a scowl clearly visible on his clean-cut face.

At the very end of the service when it was time for them to get a jump on the crowd, Big John rose up, as did Michael on cue, and as he slid past Gem to the aisle, he said, "Come over for breakfast. Mike will show ya."

"Happy to Mr. Moretti. Thanks," she beamed.

Jesus, thought Hunter. *Life is strange.*

Breakfast was even more strange. Gem acted like she had been in the Moretti house a hundred times and the weird part was that they acted the same way. She wound up serving the food and doing the dishes with Rose and smoking with Big John. They chattered about Italians and family and probably the strangest thing of all was when Big John hit upon his favorite pet peeve. The Catholic Church praying every week for the soul of Martin Luther King.

"I hate that shit," yelled Gem from the kitchen.

That spontaneous utterance was the key to Big John's heart. It was like lighting the fuse on the big finale at the Fourth of July firework's display. Big John had an ally on something that bugged the living crap out of him. That the Catholic Church would be praying for the soul of that stronzo, who he knew hated Catholics and Italians personally and, as he heard it from his other son Paul, J. Edgar Hoover himself, the little queer, knew King was doing stuff he shouldn't be doing. By Big John's personal unofficial count, the offerings had dropped by 30 percent since they'd started that shit.

He and Gem fed off of each other for ten minutes until Michael announced that if they were going to get to San Francisco by kick off, they had better hit the road. There were hugs all around and promises to return for a real meal before they could get out of there, with three Genova roll "sangwiches" as Big John called them because the food at the stadium was no good.

On the ride to San Francisco, Gem decided to set the tone for the conversation. "So tell me," she said, "how did you get into the family and don't give me any of that 'I was raised by wolves shit.'"

With that announcement, Michael felt he had little choice but to give it to her straight. She'd ferret it out anyway. He told her that it had begun almost the day he had come to Stockton. His uncle had been some big time jock before the war in the Midwest and thought that any male worth anything tried out for his high school football team. So Michael was to get his ass over to the Lincoln High School try-outs that were mentioned in the *Stockton Record* and discussed at the bar at the Shadows Restaurant where he drank.

Michael had spent every year from the time he was 4 until he was 13 on a farm with his grandmother, who had the good luck to get into a second marriage with a man with 180 acres outside of Hays, Kansas, loaded with oil. He promptly died, like Michael's real dirt-poor grandfather, leaving her money and two grown children who were in the Navy and Army respectively. Both children went to war. The stupider, braver one to the South Pacific, where he barely survived physically, but not mentally. Michael's father was smarter, much smarter than that. He was able to land himself cushy assignments far away from combat. An officer and a gentleman; part of the war, but not really. His mother, a want-to-be actress who spent more time on the casting couch than she did behind a camera, had been dumped by his father when he was a couple of months old. Michael just didn't fit into her future plans.

Her one son, was a no talent drunk, and the other, was a brilliant con artist with no conscience who would avoid gainful employment as much as possible for the remainder of his life. This one, Michael's father, had written a television show in the 1950s and sold it for squat, only to see it make millions. That was essentially his life's story. Except that he'd fathered a son by a good looking want-to-be actress who never made it, except in bed . Eight months after Michael was born, his father was long gone and his mother was moving on, angry and bitter that Michael's father hadn't let her douche the kid down the drain in some dive hotel in Kansas City, Missouri, where he was conceived. This piece of family lore was shared with Michael one night when he was 15 by his drunken uncle, who hated his father for the self-indulgent piece of crap that he was.

His grandmother, a strong woman by all accounts, had gone through extremely hard times after the love of her life, a hard scrabble Oklahoma farmer died of tuberculosis shortly after both son's birth. So hard that she had turned to bootlegging and prostitution. One of her clients fell in love with her and married her after he struck it rich in oil in Kansas.

Guilt is a terrible thing. It grips almost everybody at one time or another, and makes them do things that are contrary to good sense. Guilt made her over-indulge her boys. Spoil them. She even sent them to the Missouri Military Academy. It didn't take. The youngest became a fabulous jock that could barely make a complete sentence. The other was trying to figure out how to sell the place on the open market while breezing through any course they could throw at him.

In the meantime, Sally, as she was called, though her real name was Sarah, got religion. The real religion. The one where you bought it lock, stock, and barrel with humility because you knew that you were an undeserving piece of goo. She knew Jesus existed, but how could she ever make it up to him for being a hooker and a bootlegger. No matter, she was going to try. But, meanwhile, this husband died and left her flush with real estate and oil wells and two grown sons who weren't worth a damn. Sally just wasn't an aging ex-hooker when her first born fathered a son in August of 1945. She had been the favorite of important people from the Midwest to the West Coast. The secret of this died with her in 1958 when she had a sudden stroke, but Michael had seen the evidence of it. When they travelled to San Francisco by train from Kansas, she stayed at the Mark Hopkins Hotel at the top of Nobb Hill and waited in line for nobody at the best restaurants. Maitre d's and owners came out to give her a hug in her mink coat. Sally was somebody there. What that somebody was, Michael never found out. Sally agreed with Michael's mother when he was eight months old, to take Michael as her own if the mother would sign some legal papers that Sally's expensive lawyers drew up, which basically said that Michael was hers, no take backs. In those days you could do that.

Sally had been given one more chance by the good Lord in her view, to raise a kid proper and she wasn't about to blow it. In her view, she had spoiled and broken the spirit of both her sons, it never occurring to her that maybe they didn't have the right stuff in them in the first place. She just thought they hadn't been raised properly. Within a short time after the war, life patterns began to develop for both of her natural sons. The youngest got a job as a shoe clerk for a major chain, although his passions were drinking to excess and gambling. This cost money that she continued to funnel to him. Her oldest, Michael's father, was more ambitious. He was going from one big deal to the next, always needing large funding. Whatever his talents were, putting a big deal together to the pay off wasn't one of them.

As the years passed, Sally realized that the good Lord had blessed her. This grandson was special. He had brains and guts and needed protection from his father and mother. So she disappeared to Kansas to a piece of property the sons knew nothing about. 180 acres, 20 miles from Hays and 6 miles from Plainville. Two longs and a short was their telephone number on a party-line crank phone. Only a few people knew they were there.

Within a short period of time, an incident took place that would define Michael and forever scar his grandmother. There was a birthday party at the neighboring farm. Michael had just entered school. The school consisted of two rooms. First through fourth was taught in one room by one teacher and fifth through eighth in another. There was a pecking order. When Sally sent Michael off to the farm, less than a mile down the road, to the birthday party, riding his Shetland pony "Popcorn," she had high hopes. Three hours later, Michael came riding back crying and without his jacket. As he told it, a group of kids with a ring leader named Steven, two years older than Michael, had talked him into a game of hide and seek. One of the boys got him to hide in an animal crate, where Steven promptly put a lock on it and wouldn't let him out even after he became hysterical in the close confining quarters. Finally, the birthday girl's mother heard the yelling and released him. He promptly jumped on his pony and rode home as fast as he could.

Sally listened carefully to the tearful story, calming the upset Michael, and then very calmly asked, "Where's your jacket?"

Staring at her, Michael said, "What?" through his tears.

"Where's your jacket?" she asked again very calmly, although she was anything but calm.

"I don't know," he said getting control of himself and his

heavy breathing. "I must have left it there."

"Go get it," she said firmly.

"What?" he asked as if he hadn't heard her correctly. Surely she didn't want him to go back there after what had happened to him.

"Go get your jacket. Don't come home without it, or I'll give you worse than you got," she said turning away from him so that he wouldn't see the tears in her eyes.

Left alone with his pony and his orders, he was at a crossroad in his young life. Although he was way too young to see it for what it was, he chose the path that would direct his life. He went back.

An hour later, a pickup pulled into the long drive to Sally's two-story farm house on the Salinas River. It was the mother that threw the party and she had Michael in the front seat. She slammed her door and stormed up to the front porch with Michael in tow, who was proudly wearing his jacket.

"This boy of yours broke a boy's arm over being locked in a cage as a joke!" she yelled. "He's on his way right now to get it set at the hospital in Hays."

Sally nodded looking down at Michael. "Was his name Steven?" asked Sally.

"Yes it was. How'd you know that?"

"You tell his mama to send me the medical bill," she said.

"That's all you got to say Sally Hunter?" asked the woman exasperated.

"That's all, except I expect that boy won't be bullying mine no more."

A couple of years went by and life was good for a time until Michael's father found them. He showed up out of nowhere when Sally had forgot to tell a long distance operator not to let the person on the other end know where her call originated from. She had called his new wife to check on things and under the old rule that no good deed goes unpunished, Michael's father had found out where the call came from and one thing led to another, and there he was in the front yard of their Kansas farm demanding money. Michael was 7 and knew that his father was someone to be feared. His life, to that point, had been Kansas normal. He was accepted and well liked by everyone. He had a big quarter horse by then. The Shetland was long gone. He could ride and jump with any kid his age and some older. When you're 7 and things are good, you think it will last forever.

And there was his grandmother, his entire life, standing there scared to death, being hounded by a man calling himself his father. The gist of it was that if she didn't give him money, he was taking Michael and there was nothing she could do to stop him. Michael listened to this and her pleading for him not to do it and knew what he had to do. He went to the barn and saddled his horse and led him to the back porch and tied him to the porch rail. He slipped quietly into the house and went up the stairs to his room and into the closet and looked around until he found what he was looking for. A few minutes later, he was out the back and untying and leading the horse, Nightwind, around the side of the house half way. Dropping the reins on the ground, which was the horse's signal to stand there and not move, Michael prayed that Nightwind would remember the lesson this time. Michael walked around to the front of the house, where he could see his father on the steps of the front porch yelling at and still threatening his grandmother, who was now crying.

"Just give me a check for $10,000 and I'll go into Hays and cash it and you won't see me again," he said.

"Not til you run out I won't," she answered.

"Do it Mama, or I'll take the boy."

Seeing Michael come walking around the corner, he said, "Come over here to me son."

Michael just stood there.

"You hear me boy? Do what I say. I'm your father!" he yelled.

It was then that Michael raised the .22 rifle he had concealed behind his back.

"What're you doin boy?" his father said getting angry. "Put that down now or I'll give you a whipping you'll never forget."

Michael stood his ground and pulled the hammer back on the single shot .22.

"Boy, I'm not going to tell you again!" his father yelled taking a step toward him.

There was no more than 30 feet separating them. Michael knew that he would only get one shot off and that if he missed, his only chance was to get to his horse and get out of there before his father could kidnap him.

"Don't take one more step," he said in his bravest 7-year old voice.

His father hesitated for a moment staring at his eyes. There was something in those eyes, something cold. "Now, you're not going to shoot anybody," he said calmly. "I bet that thing ain't even loaded," he said starting to close the distance.

"MICHAEL DON'T!" yelled his grandmother seeing what was about to happen, knowing that there was no undoing what was about to be done.

Michael heard her, glanced at her quickly, and then sited back down the barrel. His father took a third step toward him and he fired, aiming at what he thought was the heart. The gun bucked just enough to raise his aim to an inch above his father's heart. His father fell backwards, not so much from impact, as from the surprise and the shock of being shot. Michael had taken two steps toward his horse, when he saw the man calling himself his father fall. He made the instant decision to finish it right there. Stopping, he pulled the bolt open, expelling the spent .22 cartridge. Fishing into his jeans for a fresh one that he had put there when he took the gun from his closet, he put it into the rifle and closed the bolt. He then ran to the downed man, who by this time was sitting up, looking at the blood smear growing on his left shoulder area.

Michael stopped about 6 feet in front of the man and said the words that would stay with his grandmother until her dying day, "If you don't leave right now Mister, I'll put the next one right between your eyes."

His father stared at the barrel of the .22 pointing at the middle of his forehead and again at the eyes of the boy and knew as certainly as anything that he'd ever known, that the boy would most certainly kill him, and this realization terrified him.

Every sane person fears certain death. Most never confront it in time to make a decision to avoid it. But for those that do, the choice is pretty much all the same. They choose to live.

And that is what Michael's coward of a father did. He got up and turned and limped, gripping his left shoulder, to the car that he had arrived in; got in and drove away. Michael never saw him again.

Michael never told anyone this story and to his knowledge neither had his grandmother. They never spoke of it after that day when she sat by his bed stroking him to sleep and being there for him when he woke fitfully as he did several times that night. After that, he seemed fine.

Life became normal, except for school where Michael was bored and restless. Everyone seemed to accept the fact that he was different intellectually, mainly because he was so likable in every other way. His grandmother had raised him to be a mannerly and polite young man who was by nature a natural leader and athlete, and this fit in perfectly with his peers in a rural Mid-Western environment that respected good manners and athletic ability.

It was at that time that life presented Michael with another drastic and unwanted crossroad. One Christmas morning when Michael was 13, his grandmother simply didn't wake up. Her great heart had finally given out.

Preparations had been made with her lawyers in Hays and in California, where she and Michael visited several times by train, for the boy's future. While most of her money went to a Lutheran church in Oakland, California, of all places, there should have been plenty of money to see Michael through college, except for the fact that the final mistake of her life was entrusting it to her second son, Michael's uncle, where Michael was sent to live. No matter your flaws, blood was thicker than water as far as his grandmother was concerned.

Amongst other things, the Trust money bought two new cars and a tract home, full of new furniture, in Stockton where the uncle was transferred the fifteenth summer of Michael's life. None of it was finding its way to Michael's care.

Michael had been in town two weeks and had met nobody when he found himself standing in line to take a physical before the football tryouts the next day at Lincoln High School, behind Paul Moretti, a gregarious popular young man, who was laughing and joking with those around him. Michael's sport was baseball and he had never played an organized moment of football in his life. Just a few pickup games with his buddies back in Kansas.

The next day at 7 a.m., they all reported back to the gym and tryouts began after equipment was issued. Again, Michael found himself standing next to Paul most of the day. They ran around blocking and tackling and generally did what they were told for three hours. The next day when they reported, Michael found his name on a list with others for the varsity, while his new buddy was with the junior varsity. Paul had conjectured all along the day before that they would both be sent to that team because they were only sophomores and that they would have a great time. Michael had met a couple of Paul's friends who were also sophomores and was thinking that the whole football thing might not be such a bad idea when, boom he's put on another team of mostly juniors and seniors with guys he didn't know.

The day after that, and for the next two grueling weeks, under the tutelage of the new head coach, Jack Long, Michael and the rest of the varsity beat the stuffing out of each other for three hours twice a day in the 100 degree August heat. At the end of it, there were 48 young men left on the team and Michael found himself the only sophomore starting on both offense and defense.

The head coach explained to them that they would have to wear coats and ties to school on game days and to the games. They were men and a team now and it was time to start dressing like it. Michael went home and told his aunt that he needed a sport coat and tie. She laughed and said there was no money for that shit. When his uncle came home late that night, he was slightly more understanding and went to his closet and found an old pair of pants and a very old sport coat and tie that he said Michael could borrow. When Michael tried them on, he knew that he looked ridiculous.

The low point came when he wore the outfit to school on Friday and had to see the kids staring at him in his shiny, almost silver, sport coat and gray wool slacks that may have been nightclub chic in the 40s, but not now. But he was on the varsity and starting that night. The game wasn't until 8 and they had to be at the gym by 6 and fed their dinner.

Michael's aunt was only 15 when she married Michael's uncle ten years before and had bred one not very bright girl. It had been obvious to Michael from the outset that his uncle had married for looks, not brains and personality, and whatever his reasons were, they had worn off long before he got there. She got the housework, such as it was, out of the way as quickly as possible, with everyone doing there assigned part, and then guzzled beer by the six-pack, chain smoking Pall Malls, and watching TV until she had to throw something together to eat for dinner, which was served at 6 sharp, no exceptions.

She was a lousy cook who hated to grocery shop, so on the one day a week she managed that chore, she merely walked up and down the aisles throwing things into the basket. She personally cared little about food and was much more interested in how many six-packs you could fit into a shopping cart and still pile on enough food to stretch it for another week. Her menus were as dull and tasteless as she was and leaned heavily toward mac and cheese and hot dogs. His uncle, when he did come home for dinner, which wasn't that often, expected much more and it always caused a fight that periodically got physical and at least involved a massive amount of yelling and door slamming.

She neither cared nor worried that Michael was a growing boy that needed about twice the caloric intake she was providing. It hadn't been too bad in Santa Cruz where they had lived before moving to the San Joaquin Valley, because Michael had worked at a surf shop, cleaning rented wetsuits after school and there were hamburgers he could fill up on with the money he made. But here, the closest places to eat were a couple of miles away and the only job he could scare up was a morning paper route that he tried to get through by 6 a.m. Since only a house here and there took the morning paper, the *San Francisco Examiner*, he had to pedal for miles to make his deliveries by bicycle.

In addition, his aunt had rigid rules that often made no sense to anyone but her. No going to the refrigerator ever between meals was one of them. "I ain't running no restaurant here, she'd slur.

The girl did the vacuuming, laundry, dusting, and cleaning the table. Michael washed the dishes, took out the garbage, and mowed the lawns every Saturday before doing anything else. The worst of all was the locking of the doors every day. They were locked out of the house from 10 a.m. to 5 p.m. "Find something to do outside where you can't dirty up my house."

So, it was on that happy note that Michael came home from school that Friday and knocked on the door and asked to be let in to get something to eat so he could walk back to school and be there by 6.

"Tough shit Mister," came the slurred sullen reply. "Dinner's at 6. You got other plans, that's your business. The dishes will be waiting for you when you get home." And that was it.

Michael played his first football game on an empty stomach. Paul and some of his classmates hung around after the JV game, which was played at 6, to watch Michael play and they were back at the gym waiting for him after the game. Because they were Catholic and didn't eat meat on Friday and it was 11:30 p.m. by this time, they were all getting rides to Straw Hat Pizza where they could get some "real" food after midnight and they asked him if he wanted to come. There was no way. He had no money and no ride, so he politely begged off.

As he walked away into the night for home, stiff and sore, wearing that ridiculous outfit that he'd had on since 6:30 that morning, Big John said to his son, who had just piled into the Chevy with a couple of teammates, "Ain't that the new kid that played in the varsity game?"

"Yeah, that's Mike Hunter," said Paul.

"How come you didn't ask him to come?"

"I did, Pop. He said he had to get home."

Big John thought that there was something forlorn looking about the way the kid was walking away into the night.

"Where's he live?"

"In those new places out by that new grammar school at the end of Meadow."

"Jesus Christ, that's a couple a miles. Don't he have no ride?" asked Big John.

Paul just shrugged, "Come on Pop, were starving."

The next morning, around 6, Big John was sitting on his front porch enjoying his first cup of coffee and the warm September air waiting for the morning paper so he could get the sports on his beloved Giants who were once again in a titanic struggle with the hated Dodgers. Septembers were always hot in Stockton, and this one was no exception. Just then the paperboy came whizzing around the corner and flung a perfect strike to within ten feet of the porch. He was pedaling fast and busy taking another paper from the front part of the canvas bag with the *Examiner* logo on it, wearing the bag like a poncho, folding and putting a rubber band on the paper without ever breaking stride.

I'll be damned thought Big John as he watched the kid already half way down the block throwing another paper. *That's the kid from last night. He's sure no time waster.*

It took only another week for Paul to wise up to what was going on. For one thing, Michael ate two lunches at school, but was still dropping weight. Losing weight was something even the coaches were noticing. Was he sick they asked? Paul wasn't shy and he and Michael had become pals. So little by little he pieced together a very disturbing picture that he shared around the Moretti dinner table one night.

Rose was, of course, appalled. "They're not feeding that poor boy enough," she wailed. "That's a disgrace. *Dio mio.*"

"You say he's locked out of the house and don't get no pre-game meal?" Big John asked his son.

"No, he don't even leave school anymore on Friday. He just hangs out in the library until they close," his son answered him.

"OK. It's a home game this week. You get him over here on Friday after school," said Big John getting up from the table.

"Where you going?" asked Rose.

"Down the street to the Puccinelli's to see Albert," he said. Albert Puccinelli was a cop.

That Friday, Paul did as he was told. He brought Michael home after school. It didn't take much convincing. Michael had nothing else to do.

"You a Catholic Mike?" asked Big John after the introductions were made.

"No sir."

"Well, Catholics don't eat no meat on Friday and Pauli's got to eat something now, so I made a platter of cheese enchiladas. I hope that's OK."

He sat smoking watching Michael inhale the food. It was clear that the boy was practically starving. No self respecting Italian could watch that.

"Why don't you stick around and watch a little TV Mike while I drive Pauli over to the gym," he said after they ate. Paul's game was at 6. "I'll come back and take you over when I go to the game."

Big John had a way of making suggestions that weren't really suggestions and besides it was Africa hot outside so Michael didn't mind. After Big John came back, he and Rose started getting ready to go to their son's football game. One of the things Big John did was make two big Genoa salami sandwiches on Genova french rolls. Genova was a local bakery that had been located on Sierra Nevada Street, downtown, three blocks from the family home since around 1918. It had been in operation since that time with its red brick ovens doing two bakes a day. There was no day of the year that the Moretti family didn't have Genova bread and rolls. It was like air and there was nothing like it anywhere.

As he was finishing making the sandwiches, wrapping them delicately in wax paper, standing at the pulled out bread board at the kitchen counter, a Camel cigarette dangling from his lips, he said, "Mike, I want you to do me a favor."

"Sure Mr. Moretti," said Hunter grateful for the enchiladas, the break from the heat, and having a place to be before the game besides the library.

"I want you should take these "sangwitches" with you and eat one for good luck before you get dressed for the game and the other one after the game. You'd be doing me a big favor. I hate to waste food and this bread is already two days' old," he lied. "And I don't want to throw it out.

Would you do that for me?"

"Sure, if it would help you out," Michael said more grateful than he could express.

"I want you to do me one more favor," he said.

"Name it," said Michael.

"Can you come to dinner tomorrow night? I bought too damned much meat. I thought my brother Jimmy was coming over, but he can't make it."

"I guess I could."

"Bene," he said. "That's good. Now, let's get you to the gym."

The sandwiches made it all of ten minutes after Michael was dropped off. He sat at his locker devouring them. The head coach, Jack Long, watched him from inside his office wolfing the food and knew there was a major problem with this kid.

Michael had a terrific game on a full belly and walked home in the dark in the cool evening air feeling better than he had in a very long time. It was short lived. He walked in on a dish-throwing, knock-down, drag out between his aunt and uncle. She was just in the act of hitting him in the head with an ashtray and calling him a faggot when Michael walked in on them in full combat mode. The ashtray hit his uncle above the eye, drawing blood. He became enraged and rushed her, punching her in the jaw and knocking her cold. Michael instinctively jumped between them and his uncle punched him in the face, knocking him over the coffee table and onto the living room sofa. It was a life changing moment for everyone involved. Michael came up attacking. Outweighed by 40 pounds, he still hit his uncle in the chest with his full weight knocking him over backwards. As they scrambled to their feet, Michael was up and leveraged and struck his uncle with a closed fist, knocking him back down.

Even drunk, his uncle was plenty full of fight and itching for one. Michael could see that and instinctively ripped a table lamp off of the end table and hit him over the head with it, dropping him like a steer in a slaughter house, sending shattered lamp and light bulb flying everywhere.

Standing there, he saw his young female cousin in the hallway, hysterical, and his aunt and uncle out cold on the living room floor. His uncle certainly needed stitches for the head wounds that were pumping blood onto the carpet with every beat of his heart.

An hour later, Michael was sitting on the Moretti front porch in the dark. He had no place else to go. Sitting there, he formulated a plan. The only one he could think of. He would rest for a while and then walk up to Lincoln Center and sit on the lawn until it got light and then he would walk around all day until it was time to go to the Moretti's for dinner. By then, maybe everything would have cooled down at home and he could go back. That's what he would do after resting for a few minutes. He was bone tired and the adrenaline had long worn off. He closed his eyes for just a few seconds.

In his dream, a big bear was shaking him, telling him to wake up, which he did to find Big John staring down at him as he lay on the front porch. It was barely light. He was stiff and cold and sore.

Big John took one look at the boy's discolored, bruised cheek and almost closed left eye, and the bile started to rise in his throat; he was so angry.

"What happened Mike?" he asked.

Michael couldn't think of a good lie or any lie for that matter, so he just told him the truth. He apologized for sleeping on the porch without asking and explained that he was supposed to be up at the Center by now, but that he'd fallen asleep.

"What about your paper route?" asked Big John.

"Oh my God," said Michael. He'd completely forgot about it.

He leaped up and was about to break into a full run for home when Big John grabbed him and said, "Hold it, hold it. Wait a minute damn-it. Let me think a minute."

He turned to go back inside and said, "I'll get my keys. What's your address?"

Michael told him and watched as he went to the phone and made a hasty call.

"Let's go," he said coming down the steps on tip-toes.

He was very light on his feet for such a big man thought Michael.

"Where're we going?" he asked following behind him into the garage.

"To deliver some papers."

On the drive over to his aunt and uncle's, Michael wanted to tell Big John Moretti what a bad idea it was to get involved with these people at this time, but he didn't. The look on Big John Moretti's face signaled that such conversation would be both meaningless and unwanted.

To Michael's surprise, when they got to the house, there were two police black and whites parked out front. As they pulled up, a Pontiac pulled up right behind them and out stepped a huge good looking Italian man in his mid-thirties who walked to the car and gave Big John a hug and asked, "This the boy?"

"Meet Sergeant Puccinelli," said Big John by way of introduction. "He's a neighbor and a friend."

"Good to meet you Mike," said the Sergeant. "I've heard very good things about you."

What could that be Michael wondered surreally.

"So let me tell you how this is going down. I'm going into the house with these uniformed officers and when we signal you, you're coming in and pack your stuff. I've already called your boss and he's willing to deliver your papers this morning. Tomorrow he'll drop them off at the Moretti's house."

Michael looked at Big John.

"You're going to stay with us for a little while, if it's okay with you," said Big John.

"I don't want to be any trouble," said Michael.

"Ain't he somethin' Al?" Big John said to Albert Puccinelli. "His face is all busted up and he wants to know if he's going to be any trouble."

"I love this kid already," said Puccinelli, patting Michael softly on the good side of his face. "Welcome to the neighborhood kid."

The cops knocked on the front door, which was answered by his cousin. They walked in past her and down to the bedroom where they found his aunt and uncle sleeping on bloody sheets. The uncle tried to be an irate tough guy, but that lasted less than five seconds. His aunt started screaming and was immediately told that the cuffs would be placed on her and she would be taken into custody if she didn't shut up.

As he was in his room hastily gathering up his meager belongings, he could hear Albert Puccinelli speaking to his uncle.

"OK asshole, it's your call. The bitch, who has been starving the kid to death, ain't his blood and has no say. But she ain't the one who busted his face up either. For that, I owe you. So give me any excuse at all and you and me are going to discuss this personally. Are we on the same page so far?"

His uncle must have agreed because Michael heard the Sergeant continue. "You're leaving town, the whole lot of you. You have 60 days. In the meantime, I'm going to bring some papers around next week for you to sign. An attorney friend of mine, Nick Chinchiolo, will prepare them and they will go something like this. You give up any rights to this boy and agree to stay away from him. If you don't sign them and leave town in 60 days, then me and mine are going to make your life unliveable which personally I'd do right now if it wasn't for Big John Moretti. Nod yes "pig shit" if you understand."

The officers helped carry all of Michael's stuff to Big John's Chevy and agreed to bring the bike over in their patrol car. Big John put his arm around Michael and walked him to his vehicle. They drove first to the office of Rose's brother, Theodore, a doctor that would examine Michael. Dr. Ted was waiting for them. He checked Michael out thoroughly, gave him a shot for his obvious vitamin deficiency and some pills for his swollen face, and welcomed him to the family. Then Big John drove him home. He never saw his aunt or uncle again. No Moretti ever missed one of his home games and Big John and Rose never missed any game ever, home or away.

Gem sat listening to a heavily edited version of the story and saw through Michael's down playing of the events for most of the two-hour drive to San Francisco without comment.

When it was over, she said, "That was some story."

"It isn't a published story," he said glancing at her.

"Nobody's going to hear it from me," she said lighting a cigarette. "But I got to tell you, there are various versions of it out there. One says you killed your uncle."

"That one's got to bother you a little," he chuckled.

"Nope," she said exhaling. "I'd have killed them both. Still would."

The game from the Giamatti seats was much better. She insisted on scalping Michael's tickets personally and split the double-the-face value she received for them with him. This delighted her almost as much as the Niners' 20-to-0 victory over the Atlanta Falcons. They decided to blow their scalping money on dinner at the Golden Spike in North Beach where they sat with a table full of local Italians who had also gone to the game. Michael couldn't help but notice that Gem was practically a member of their family by the time they left.

"My place or yours?" she asked as they drove into town a little after 9.

Chapter 29

Sybil Waxman had been keeping as low a profile as Hawthorne could allow one of his attorneys to keep, considering the courts that had to be covered. He thought better of juvenile court and had her working strictly out of the library doing two appeals to the Third Appellate District Court of Appeals under Merlin's watchful eye while handling a few traffic court arraignments and pleas in Department C on the second floor of the courthouse.

It was dark when she walked out of the Public Defender's Office on San Joaquin Street and locked the door behind her. She'd been working late because the opening brief on one of the appeals was due the next day. She had been almost clinically depressed since her jury trial a week before and had stayed as far away from people as she could. Of course, no one saw her side of it. How was she expected to know what the guy was going to say on the stand? If he hadn't wanted to tell her before court, what was she supposed to do about it? It hadn't helped any that Joe Larsen won his trial. But what would you expect with the great Michael Hunter and the equally great Anthony Borelli pulling the strings for their puppet. You couldn't even count it. All she had was Stanley Latchman who was making it very clear what he was really interested in. It was her briefs all right, but not her legal ones. She was lost in those thoughts as she walked down San Joaquin Street past the Catholic church where she'd parked her car for free. She didn't notice the two men coming out of the shadows of the church as she walked past.

Sergeant Alex Nickerson had just finished his dinner break at the Gan Chy where he was always "comped" by the owner and was turning his patrol car right onto Washington Street heading for Center, when he saw the Deputy Public Defender Sybil Waxman walking down San Joaquin Street, across Washington. He had warned those guys about this walking in that part of town at night, but you obviously couldn't tell this bitch anything, he thought.

Nickerson was only a block away when he saw them move in behind her. As he instinctively floored the patrol car, he saw the flash of steel from the knife in one of the guy's hands. There was only time to react. He yanked the wheel hard to the left, jumping the curb on the one-way street, sending the car hurtling across the bare ground.

Sybil was so lost in thought that she didn't hear anything, but two bone-crunching thumps behind her and then the screeching of brakes and the sound of a siren being activated. She sensed, rather than saw the bodies fly by her in the air. She heard them land with a thud some 20 feet away.

It was several seconds before she realized that Sergeant Nickerson, whom she had done her best to humiliate on the stand a week before, had just run over two people. He was out of his patrol car now screaming something at her, drawing his weapon. She thought he'd lost his mind until she heard him radioing in for back up and an ambulance for two robbery suspects.

Robbery suspects? she thought, her attention drawn to the two men writhing in agony on the ground. She was approaching to assist them when Nickerson grabbed her and pushed her away.

"What in the hell are you doing?" she spat. "You ran over these men."

"Yes I did, I surely did," he said staring down at them broken and bleeding on the ground.

Sirens were sounding from everywhere. Police lights could be seen coming from three directions.

"I want you to take a look at that knife laying on the ground over there," said Nickerson to Sybil. "Do you see it?"

"Yes, I see it," she said. "What's it for?"

"To cut your throat if you gave them trouble," he said. "You'll need to testify about this."

"You saved my life?" she asked surprised, the lights all finally coming on in her head. "Why'd you do that?"

"If you have to ask, you'd never understand it," said Sergeant Alex Nickerson patting each of the robbers down as they lay on the ground, both in need of a great deal of emergency treatment.

TUESDAY, DECEMBER 12ᵀᴴ, 7 A.M.

"How you doing with all this?" asked Alice Benson as Michael Hunter sat down on one of the old red vinyl stools.

"I'm fine Al," he said. "Joe's a good man. He deserves it."

"Life stinks if you ask me," she said bitterly.

"You know what I found out about life?"

"What?" she asked turning toward him knowing deep down he had to be hurting about it.

"When something bad happens and you think you've been given a lousy break, almost always something better comes along."

"Ain't you the philosopher," she said. "Sort of the Michael Hunter version of 'when one door closes, another one opens'."

"With a twist. I believe in trading upward from bad news."

"Well, I still think Joe Rocha getting your job at Metro stinks."

"I think it was probably for the best. I need a change of scenery."

"To where?" she asked.

"AJ wants to set something up in Vallejo."

"I like Vallejo."

"Pack a bag."

"I wouldn't be counting on AJ too much if I were you," she said pushing her cup up toward Martha for a refill. When Michael didn't say anything, she continued, "He's got his nose so far up that dry cleaner's butt he can't see straight anymore. The Reno trial's been set for a month and a half away and he just lets the file sit there collecting dust."

"What's bugging you so much about this AJ?" said Michael starting in on his breakfast.

"Because this looks like the Waxman trial all over again, except the grown-up version," she said. "Reno won't talk to him, he doesn't look at the file, he hasn't got a clue what to do, plus the whole thing is spooky if you ask me. It's going to blow up in all of our faces."

"I have to admit everything's been a little strange the last month. I suppose you heard about Waxman last night."

"Of course," she sniffed. "I can only imagine how that's going to get written up in the paper today."

"She's certainly a shit magnet all right."

"She's gotta go."

"Uh-oh," he said looking at her.

"Boss is looking hard," she said lighting up.

"Any luck?"

"There's one guy maybe, could have a little Mexican in him. That might qualify him for the Affirmative Action slot. We'll see."

"What's the problem?"

"His name's Brown. Whiter than you are from his picture," she said.

"Where's the Mexican come in?" he asked.

"Says he likes Mexican food on his resume. That's a start," she shrugged.

"I almost forgot to tell you," he said. "My Pop and I are taking a long lunch today. He's picking me up around 11:30 after juvie."

"What's up?"

"Beats me. But it's not optional."

⬤

TUESDAY, DECEMBER 12TH, 11:30 A.M.

Hunter barely had time to change from his court clothes when he was buzzed on the intercom by Alice.

"Better get down here or I'm going to lunch with him myself, the charming devil," she said.

"You made your usual big hit," Michael said sliding into the front seat of the Impala parked in the red zone in front of the office.

"You ain't the only one with great charm," Big John chuckled lighting a Camel.

"Where's lunch?"

"Lucca Orchards."

"Lucca Orchards," he said surprised. "Way out in Linden?"

"So what? You cleared the time didn't ya? You got no court this afternoon, right?"

"Sure, I cleared it. I just thought we'd be eating at Mellie's," he said referring to Big John's sister Carmel.

The drive east to the small farm town of Linden was the exact opposite of heading west into the islands. Toward Linden, the topography rose quietly as they headed towards the foothills. It was almost all pear, cherry, walnut, and peach orchards. Some of them were owned by people of Italian surnames who had originally been from Sicily by way of New York or Chicago. Big John knew them all. Lucca Orchards was such a place.

On the drive out they reminisced about Michael's time as a fruit and vegetable inspector during the summers he was in law school. He had been over every inch of this area handing out certificates so that the farmers could get their goods to market. Those were good long days where his car would always end up loaded with vine-ripened produce from grateful farmers. So much so, that Big John began making shopping lists for him and even took out the passenger seat of his VW bug so that he could fit more booty into it because, as Big John said, they had a big family. All of this was made completely legit because of an incident Michael had on his very first day.

USDA inspectors worked out of local offices. They were supposed to wear dark pants, white shirts, with their "shields" on the outside of their shirt pockets. The job consisted of going to locations and "grading" the ready-for-market produce and issuing a USDA certificate if it passed. The grade was the agreed upon standard that the markets, who were buying the goods, and the farmers that were selling, used to decide if the stuff was good enough to be shipped. A little training was involved on each commodity. The rich fertile area around Stockton had a record high of 32 different commodities that had to be graded.

Inspectors were dispatched each morning, early, to various locations where the inspections would take place. A lot of inspectors, and certainly the few that worked out of the Stockton office year-round, were frustrated wanna be cops who would have enjoyed giving traffic tickets and listening to people bitch. "Real small dicked guys" as Big John put it. Michael got the job after bugging the local boss every month for a year and was in it for the long summer hours with plenty of overtime. He was sent to an 80-acre onion field on his first day, with a wooden grading table, bungee corded to the back of his VW bug. The field was located on the outskirts of Linden and when he got there, the tractor pulled onion grader had already completed working a long row of onions.

An onion grader was nothing more than a large piece of equipment with a conveyor belt running down the middle of it on a raised platform that Mexican women stood on each side of picking out the bad onions. The good ones were dropped into 20 pound sacks with the logo of the supplier on it to be shipped by truck or rail directly to supermarket retailers. With any luck, they would be eaten within two weeks.

The training he had just received dictated that he would set up his grading table right there in the dirt, grab a finished sack of onions, dump it out onto the table, grade them, and re-bag them. Do that a few times a row, add up the score, and if they passed, issue a certificate. Easy-peasy-Japanesy. Except that it wasn't. A farmer made his nut on that certificate. No certificate, no sale. Without a certificate, they had to be pedaled in some other market at a fraction of the original contract price.

On this day, his first, Michael had just set up his table when a huge farm pickup truck rolled up and a large man with a heavy Italian accent climbed out, shook his hand, and introduced himself as the owner of the onions.

"New man," he said to Michael more as a comment than as a question.

Hunter told him that he had just started. The man stood there for a moment watching the grader now halfway down its second row, the morning air already in the 80s and said, looking at Michael squarely, "These good onions."

"I'm sure they are sir," said Michael. "We'll soon see."

"No, no boy. You no capice," he said in a voice that could and did make the hair on the back of Michael's neck stand up.

"These onions good, capice?"

"Yes sir," said Michael knowing very well what he meant.

The man climbed back into his truck and threw it into reverse, leaving Michael standing there in the fine dust kicked up by the big tires of the pickup. He grabbed a bag of onions and dumped them on the tray praying that they were perfect. They weren't. They were far from it. These onions had the one defect that there was little tolerance for; decay. The expression "one bad apple can spoil the bunch" was talking about decay. Decay spreads like bad cancer, only quicker. You put some decayed fruit in a boxcar in California and by the time it gets to New York, the fruit would be leaking out of the door like sewage.

These onions had way too much decay. Michael took another sample bag in the next row. Same thing. The last thing in the world he wanted to do was tell the old *Dago* that his onions weren't worth a shit. His next thought was that whomever was running the grading crew on the onion grader was an idiot. All they had to do was sort the decayed ones out. And then it hit him. He ran down the row in his nice pants and white shirt, getting dust all over himself and his feet pinching in new black Florsheims, yelling at the onion grader. He finally got it to stop. The next problem, no one spoke a word of English. Hand gesturing he made it stay put until he could get back to his car. Fishing around, he found a pair of cutoffs, a bandana, and some sandals. Stripping down to no shirt, he changed into the cutoffs and sandals and tied the bandana around his surfer length blond hair and climbed aboard the onion grader where he spent the remainder of the day making the crew take out the decay and other defects.

One time he saw the pickup sitting by his VW but didn't see the old man. Around 2, his boss came out and looked around, shading his eyes against the hot sun, and spied Michael working the grader. He trotted over and Michael explained what was going on. Finish up the boss told him and he'd see him at the office at 6:30 the next morning.

By 5 o'clock, they were all finished and the field workers were sitting around, waiting for their rides, drinking beer from an ice chest which they shared with Michael. Just then, the pickup pulled up and the old man got out and walked over. Michael got up and handed him the certificate with the "excellent" grade. The old man took it and stared at Michael looking him up and down. He was covered in grime, dust, and sweat and he had a horrible sunburn.

"Bene," he said. "Molto bene," and shook Michael's hand.

Michael finished his beer and thanked the crew as best he could and walked to his car on exhausted legs. When he got there, he saw something under the windshield wiper. It was a $100 bill. That night he told Big John the story. He asked Michael if he remembered the man's name. Michael repeated it from memory.

"Jesus Christ," said Big John almost in awe. "You did just the right thing kid. I'm proud of you."

Michael asked him about the money. He couldn't keep it could he?

"You didn't ask for it, did you?" he asked. Michael told him no. "Was the grade legit?" Yes Michael told him. "So what's the problem? Don't insult nobody and keep your mouth shut."

The next morning Michael met his boss who said they should get some coffee away from the office. Michael had been thinking he was getting fired. His boss, Lew, had no intention of firing him. To the contrary, he explained to Michael that he was just what he had been looking for, a guy who could make both sides happy. Make sure the produce passed inspection and don't flaunt it. What wasn't to like? In fact, he'd had four calls the day before requesting Michael in their onion fields. That's how fast the word had spread through the Italian farming community. He was going to have to work his ass off though; 18 hours a day; little sleep and just one favor. Every two weeks the big boss from Sacramento came around and wanted to see the men in action. He was a by-the-book guy who would not appreciate Michael's outfit or him riding an onion grader. So, they would pre-arrange a meeting place and Michael could put some clothes on for the occasion. The rest of the time he could go naked so long as there were no complaints. Within two weeks, Michael was inspecting everything that was ripe. Whatever it was, he would look in on the operation in the morning and tell them what they had to do to pass inspection and come back later and take another look and give them the certificate.

Michael's car would be filled with fresh produce, tortas, salami, copa, mortadella, you name it. Big John was in heaven. The word filtered back about his Mick kid and how Big John had raised him right. There could be no greater praise to the family. When Big John cut up the spoils among the rest of the family, they heard every word of it and they were proud. That is not to say that Michael didn't cut a few corners for these old Italian farmers. He did. There might have been a benefit here or there that wasn't quite kosher, but it was isolated and Michael rationalized that he wasn't doing any real harm.

These were the memories Big John and Michael shared while they were headed for lunch at Lucca Orchards. It was a big operation. Pears and walnuts mostly; hundreds of acres. It was named after a town in Northern Italy near Florence, where the owner's wife was from, along with about half the Italians in the area. Michael had never been down the long fenced and electronically gated drive past the main two-story house back to what looked like a series of three brick one-story buildings with numerous bedroom windows in them. Big John pulled the car up next to one of the buildings. They were surrounded by countless acres of walnuts. Unless you were right on top of the place, you wouldn't know it existed.

As they walked in, a small heavy set man came up and threw his arms around Big John and they embraced, "How you doing Sally?" asked Big John.

"I could complain, but who'd listen," said "Little Sally" Bonaconte. "And this must be your famous kid, Michael," he said coming over to shake Michael's hand with both of his. "We never met Mike, but I always appreciated how you kept our produce moving when it was inspected. I'm not sure we showed our appreciation adequately. Those pezzonovante they got now," he said waiving a hand in disgust, "sit down."

The table was 20-feet long at least, covered with a series of red-checkered tablecloths. They were in the middle of a brick dining room which was filling up with 20 to 30 year old Mediterranean men who were taking seats. Little Sally sat across from Michael who was seated next to Big John at the end of the table. An old fashioned barrel-shaped heavy water glass was filled to the brim with a dark Sicilian wine that Bonaconte said was from their personal stock, which was by far the strongest and best wine Michael had ever tasted. The meal consisted of gnocchi, salad, roast beef, and pachuco beans in olive oil, served after they first picked over platters of anti-pasta of homemade salami, foccacia, and fresh sliced tomatoes with fresh mozzarella cheese dribbled liberally with olive oil and balsamic vinegar.

Big John and Bonaconte made small talk that was hard for Michael to follow. Everyone else in the room was speaking a Sicilian dialect that Michael recognized, but didn't understand a word of. There were at least 15 of them and whoever they were, they weren't from here, thought Michael.

Michael's glass was filled again and Bonaconte turned his attention to him.

"I was sorry to hear you didn't get that Metro job. I told Lonigan personally that I thought he made a mistake. But, it was a family matter. What're you gonna do?" he said shrugging his shoulders. "It's better anyway." He didn't explain why it was better, he just segwayed into a related topic, Eddie Reno.

"How active are you on this Eddie Reno thing?" Little Sally asked.

"Not very. In fact, I haven't done shit," said Michael feeling the warm effects of the wine.

"Good. That's good," said Bonaconte, lighting a Toscano cigar after offering Big John and Michael one. "It was a terrible thing he done. I knew his father. He was always an embarrassment. He should have been dealt with a long time ago."

He let that thought float around in the air before continuing.

"He was sent out here to stay out of trouble, but he couldn't keep his nose clean. I hear you been asking around about that?" Now he was staring at Michael waiting for a response. How in the hell had he found out about that, thought Michael.

Michael finally said, "I just noticed that he'd been taken in three times and no complaints."

"Smart," said Little Sally gesturing to Big John. "Didn't I always tell you John that this kid was one smart Mick being raised right? Didn't I say that all the way back to when he was doing the fruit? Keepin' his nose clean, doing the right thing."

"Yeah you did Sally," said Big John quietly.

"Well that was us Mike; we intervened. Now looking back, we shouldn't have. It was a big mistake," he said taking a pull on the little foul smelling rope of a cigar. "I'll tell you this. We ain't interfering again. This little punk needs to take his fall like a man," he said.

He picked up his glass and said, "Cent'Anni." They all touched glasses and took a long pull.

"What I would appreciate Mike, is you let me know what this guy's saying, if you could. Not that he's got anything to say that would be negative mind you, but I'd like to hear about it ahead of time. I wouldn't want to read about it in the papers, capice?"

"I hear what you're saying," Michael said.

"So Mike, what are your plans? You can't keep walking blacks, spics, and low life speed-freaks out of the back of the courthouse forever."

"I'm not sure," said Michael not wanting to bring up anything he hadn't discussed with Big John first.

"Well, a guy like you could write his own ticket around here. Anything you want, you just have to ask," he said. Half drunk, a slight chill went down Michael's back.

On the ride back, Big John and Michael were unusually quiet, each lost in their own thoughts. There had been messages delivered and messages received. But what were they really? Clearly, this man expected Michael to keep him informed about Reno's plans for a defense. He wasn't interested in any attorney-client bullshit either. He expected to be told.

"What's going on Big?" asked Michael finally.

After a few minutes, Big John lit his third Camel on the drive back and said, "You remember Cadillac Johnny?"

"You mean the guy that owned that little drive-in out east that made the great burgers?" he asked referring to the Italian guy in his forties that owned the hamburger joint drive-in that looked like a Dairy Queen, but much better, in East Stockton. "What was his name?"

John Tossi. They called him Cadillac Johnny because he was always driving a brand new Cadillac. Big John would occasionally take Michael by the place and get him a burger and a great chocolate malt, the real old fashioned kind. The real McCoy. Always on the arm too. Michael always thought that Cadillac Johnny Tossi looked like the last guy to be owning a

drive-in in East Stockton or anywhere else for that matter.

"You remember he drowned duck hunting last year?" said Big John staring out at the road smoking.

Of course he remembered. He'd gone over to the house for Sunday breakfast and found Big John at the kitchen table with tears in his eyes. He was reading the small article in the *Stockton Record* that told the story of how one John Tossi had been found drowned in the Delta floating in a slough near the small boat with a 12 gauge shotgun in it fully loaded. It was presumed he had fallen overboard and drowned while duck hunting.

"Sure," said Michael.

"Cadillac Johnny couldn't swim," said Big John. "Never learned and was scared to death of water."

He didn't say another word and neither did Michael. The dots were there to connect. You just had to figure out how to do it.

When Michael walked into the office a little after 2:30, he made up his mind to get to the bottom of the mess and to stay out of it at the same time. He needed someone he could trust. What was bothering him was that the only people he had mentioned the Reno arrests with no charges being filed were to Alice and through her, Dewey. Was there anyone else? He couldn't remember anybody, so how did Little Sally Bonaconte find out he was asking?

So who could he trust?

He was so deep in thought, he barely heard Alice yell at him, "AJ's looking for you."

"Later," he yelled back and kept walking down the hall. He bumped into Sybil Waxman as she was coming out of Hawthorne's office with an angry look on her face.

"Well I hope you're satisfied," she said her jaw tightly set with her nose slightly tilted in the air in her usual defiant pose when things weren't going her way.

"I don't have much time for this right now, but I'll bite, what?"

"You and your pals have gotten rid of me. I've resigned," she said.

"Resigned, huh. Well, best of luck," he said starting to move around her.

"That's it!" she said grabbing him. "After all you've done to me, that's it? Best of luck?"

"OK, bon voyage then."

"I've never been given a chance by any of you. None of you have supported me," she said.

"Look Sybil, I don't begin to know what all of your problems are and frankly, you're so unlikeable it's hard for me to care."

"You say that just because I don't fit in around here. You and that idiot Dewey Gunnart flipping coins, playing at being lawyers. Do you think I want to be like him? Stuck in some shabby little office with stupid little photos all around me 25 years from now?" she snapped.

"Let me ask you a question, Sybil. Did you happen to notice that one little black and white photo on the wall, the little man with his arm around Dewey?" asked Michael.

"Yeah, I saw it, so what?"

"Do you know who the little man was?"

"No."

"That's Winston Churchill with his arm around Dewey. That shabby little man has seen more and accomplished more, and is better respected than you can be in twenty lifetimes." said Michael.

She stood there staring at him.

"I'm going to give you some parting advice that you're not going to take," said Michael. "You're in the wrong profession. Or at least the wrong end of it. You have no feel or gift for people. You don't even like people. You don't have a single instinct for right decisions and worse yet, you don't even know it. You simply don't belong in this business," he said.

"How can you say that when I went to Boalt Hall and graduated number six in my class?" she said. "How can you say I shouldn't be here?"

"Because all things being equal, you would never have been hired for this job if it wasn't for Affirmative Action programs, trying to fix something the government has decided was broken by doing the very wrong the government is seeking to redress. To hire somebody on the basis of anything else other than qualifications and merit. You were hired because you were a woman and the federal government will pay San Joaquin County for your salary. Nothing could be more wrong than that. Wrong for you and wrong for us. Someone should have told you a long time ago that this wasn't for you. If you had to get here on your own merit, you wouldn't be here. Now you're confused and hurt and I'm afraid you're irreparably damaged. So here's the advice part. Go home. Find out what you're good at in life. There must be something. Then do it."

Ten minutes later, he was knocking on Dewey's door jamb with a copy of the Reno file under his arm.

"Well, well, come on in. I should have you arrested for possession of marijuana for the dirty trick you pulled on Helena," said Dewey looking up from his desk.

"You can't have me arrested for possession," Michael said sitting down.

"Something else then. I know you're guilty of something. What d'ya want?"

"I want to know who ratted me out on the Reno prior arrest thing?"

"What the hell are you talking about?" asked Dewey getting serious.

"Some people that shouldn't know, know that I've made inquiries about Reno being released without complaint three times and as far as I know, you and Alice are the only ones that I told."

"Well now Cowboy, you're not accusing me are you?" he said raising his voice.

"I'm just saying. . ."

"Well, let's see. I had to make a few inquiries, at your request, I might add."

"Who'd you talk to?"

Dewey sat back and lit a cigarette and started to think. After a few moments, he said, "Are you ready for this?"

"What?"

"Lieutenant Albert Puccinelli"

Michael sat there stunned, trying to piece it all together. What was going on?

"You want to tell me what's going on Mike?"

"I don't know, but I've got a very bad feeling."

"Tell me about it."

Hunter told him about what Little Sally had said without letting him know who said it or that he was at lunch at Lucca Orchards. He told him that Reno was acting like the cat who ate the canary and couldn't wait for trial and that AJ was headed for a train wreck.

"First thing is to keep all of this between you and me," said Dewey. "Second thing is to find out about Reno without anyone getting wise."

"How can you pull that off?"

"I've got some connections in my old agencies. They can go down and dirty for us," said Dewey thinking.

"That still doesn't answer the question about what he's got up his sleeve," said Hunter.

"You've got to be very careful here Mike. If you haven't crossed the line, then your foot's right on the edge. This guy's your client. You could get into big trouble here."

"I know," said Michael thinking hard. "But I've got to smoke him out."

"How you going to do that?"

"Beats the shit out of me," said Michael.

They both sat there chewing on it, looking for angles.

"Listen, what's the best deal you can give us on this?" asked Michael.

"Murder one, baby. Parole eligibility in seven, you know that. It's Lonigan's niece!"

"How long you figure he'll last in the joint?" asked Michael.

"Honestly?" answered Dewey. "I make the over and under line to be one week."

"So what difference does it make if you offer me a second? He's just as dead."

"Because the boss would never OK it. There's no reason in the world to do it. The guy's ice cold. You tell me what he knows and then I can go to work on it. But, I can't imagine what it could be."

"Here's the deal," said Michael leaning forward. "Find

out what you can on what this guy has been doing here for the last couple of years, but, for Christ's sake, don't let a living soul that you wouldn't trust with both our lives know you're doing it."

"Can do," said Dewey. "Then what?"

"Then I'm going to confront him and tell him you're thinking about a manslaughter for some bullshit reason I haven't thought up yet. That will smoke him out, maybe."

"Maybe," said Dewey. "But then you got a problem."

"What?"

"Like what are you going to do with the intel if he gives it to you. He's your client and you can't tell anybody without his permission."

"I'll think of something by then."

"One more thing," said Dewey. "I'm real sorry about the Metro thing. Lonigan has his head up his ass on this one."

"Thanks Dewey."

On his way out, Michael stopped by Joe Rocha's office and popped his head in and congratulated him on landing Metro. On the walk back to the office, he thought about all of the slammed doors. The Albert Puccinelli angle closed off all of the Morettis, including his brother, anyone in law enforcement, with maybe the possible exception he would check out later. AJ was out because who knew who he was talking to now. Right now, he needed to talk with Merlin.

As he walked through the front door, Alice yelled, "Hey, Helen Keller. Did you hear me when I said AJ's looking for you?"

"Not now Al," he yelled back.

"For crying out loud, I'm not running an answering service here," she spat.

He took the stairs two at a time to the library. Once there, he could see copies of appellate briefs all over the place. "This looks like a bad time Merlin."

"I wish the boss would talk to me before he fires library staff," he said looking up. "This is Waxman's kiss goodbye to me. This has to be out by 5 p.m. and she didn't do half of what she was supposed to do."

"She was number six in her class though, remember?" said one of the interns.

"There is that," said Merlin. "You still remember your way around the library big shot?"

"Let me help you out," said Michael. "Then, when we're done, let's grab a beer."

"I never refuse beer when you buy," said Merlin.

At 4:30, the briefs had been dispatched with an intern to be filed and Merlin and Michael were sitting next to Covers at the Owl Club bar.

"So, what's up?" asked Merlin wrapping one of his big hands around his Budweiser.

"I need a favor that no one can know about," said Michael.

"My favorite kind."

"I need everything you can find out on a guy that was killed last year named John Tossi."

"What kind of stuff?"

"Criminal record, how he made his living, etc. There's just one catch."

"What's that?"

"You can't talk to anyone in law enforcement."

"Not a problem. This about the Reno case?"

"Yeah," Michael said ordering another round and one for Covers.

"What's the angle?"

"I'm trying to figure out Reno's angle, or what he thinks his angle is. Do me a favor, if you have time. Get Alice to give you a complete set of CR's on this and see if there is any technical motion that has some merit."

"What would help you the most?"

"If we could suppress the victim's wallet found in the asshole's car, then we got something to deal with," said Michael. "Oh, by the way, I've got a leak somewhere on this case, so not even AJ or the Boss are in this loop. Just you, me, and Al."

"I'll make time Mike," said Beaumont. "I haven't had any real fun since the selective enforcement deal on the B's."

Michael smiled remembering back to when he first started. It was about his third trial on some low-life, really stupid black prostitute charged with 646b misdemeanor, soliciting for an act of prostitution. He was in the library pissing and moaning about what an air-tight case the prosecution had since his client was a complete moron who would make a lousy witness. She had solicited an undercover vice officer in a downtown park late at night. That's when Merlin came up with his bright idea. He asked Mike if they ever arrested the "Johns" who drove by the prostitutes and asked them how much they charged. In reading various crime reports, it had occurred to Merlin that the majority of the Wilson Way and street corner deals were made by the guy driving up and rolling down the car window and calling the girl over.

"So what?" Michael asked.

"Selective prosecution, that's what," said Merlin. "It's an angle I've been thinking about for some time. You can't just prosecute the prostitutes."

They talked about it awhile and Michael checked with Paul to make sure Merlin was correct that there were occasionally some raids on high-end houses of prostitution where only the prostitutes were run in and charged. That was key.

Merlin cooked up a big discovery motion demanding the names of all the males mentioned in two years worth of crime reports and correspondingly the names on all complaints filed for prostitution in the last two years. The DA, at the insistence of law enforcement, put up a vigorous battle, but in the end Judge Heinz granted the motion and ordered the discovery. They were furnished the names on the charged complaints, all women, but law enforcement refused to give up the names of the men. Michael had counted on that, because rumor had it that occasionally some very prominent citizens showed up in those reports that never saw the light of day. For failure to comply with the court's discovery order, Judge Heinz dismissed the case. It was a year before any prostitutes were again charged with prostitution. It took law enforcement that long to purge their records and change the policy of not busting the "Johns" as well. In the meantime, Michael and Merlin were heros in the pimp and prostitute world, opening up a lot of free information as well as drinks and meals.

After leaving the Owl Club, Michael headed straight to the Islander where he hoped Gem was working. As he came through the door, he saw her down at the end of the bar restocking the liquor.

"Well look who turned up," she beamed as he sat down in front of her. "What'll you have big boy?"

"Coke," he said.

"Tough day?" she asked.

"Weird day, but yeah, tough. I need to talk to you about something," he said as she handed him his Coke.

"Shoot," she said eyeing him with concern.

"It's the Reno deal. I'm mixed up in it more than I want to be and I need to tell you what's going on."

"How come?" she asked guardedly.

"Because we're pals now and I know how you feel about this Van Houten business. I told you I was clear of it, but now I'm not. And besides, I may need your help and you probably won't want to give it," he said.

"Well, that's a mouthful. I guess you better say your peace," she said lighting a cigarette. He told her about his day and didn't leave out a single detail. She refilled his Coke, it took so long. At the end she just stared at him.

"What have I got myself into?" she asked him.

"Nothing you can't get out of," he said.

"It's not that simple anymore and you know it," she said, her eyes flashing.

"Well, I need someone in law enforcement I can trust and I'm down to your Pop on my list, but if he's connected in anyway it's out," he said.

"I don't know what to tell you Mike. He knows some of the same people as your pop."

"Has he said anything to you about Eddie Reno?"

"Only that he's a complete piece of shit."

"Do you know if he knew a dead guy named Cadillac Johnny?"

"He never mentioned it."

Michael sat shaking his head. This wasn't getting him anywhere. He needed to know what Reno knew and the only one who was going to give it to him was Reno and he had no reason to do it.

"What do you need Pop to do?" she asked.

"Tell me what Eddie Reno has been doing here the last two years."

"What do you need to know that for?" she asked.

"This asshole thinks he knows it all," said Michael. "I need to take him down a notch. I've got to get him to tell me what he's got up his sleeve. I can't let it just blow up in everyone's face at trial. It's probably shit, but just the same on the outside chance he actually has something, I can get him a deal and this goes away."

"You want to get this mother-fucker a deal?" she hissed loudly.

"Calm down for Christ's sake," he said looking around. "The last thing I need is for someone in this place to hear this."

"You told me you weren't trying to get this guy off!" she said totally upset but lowering her voice a notch.

"Nothing's changed Gem," he said reaching across the bar and taking her hand. "I have it on excellent authority that whether he pleads to murder one or anything else, he's history ten minutes after he hits the joint."

"You're sure?"

"Yep."

"OK, let me talk to Pop. I'll know if it's safe or not and I'll give you the hi-sign."

"You mean like this?" he said grinning and sticking his hand under his chin with his fingers hanging down, wiggling them.

She laughed and said, "You're a Little Rascals fan too, huh?"

"You bet. That was always Spanky's hi-sign."

"Now it's ours," she said laughing.

Chapter 30

"You've got to talk to him," she said referring to Snake. "You can't not return a moving van."

"What do you want me to do about it?" whined Hunter. "I got enough problems."

"Well, you just got another one. They're calling the office now looking for it. Why didn't you take it back yourself?"

"You've got to be kidding?" he said staring at her.

"You know, you'd think you two are married," said Martha setting Hunter's hot cakes and bacon in front of him. "My first marriage didn't last as long as your relationship. How's the sex?"

"We're not having sex Martha," Alice snapped in her direction.

"Just like my first marriage," said Martha walking back into the kitchen.

"You have a new assignment," said Alice lighting up. "I swear if you don't get out of this office soon, I'm going to die of lung cancer."

"What new assignment?" he said passing her an ashtray.

"Why don't you smoke for Christ's sake? You're like some damned typhoid Mary tobacco guy. You make everyone else smoke," she said taking a deep drag. "You're done with juvie. Boss wants you to work on Snake's case a little and AJ's case a lot."

"How come?"

"Cuz this Death Row Johnny guy is starting to get some real press, which you would know if you ever read a paper, and AJ doesn't live here anymore," she said.

"That's a little harsh," he grinned.

"Come on Mike, I'm not in the mood this morning. I'm cramping like my appendix burst and we've been together too long to start bullshitting each other now. You know he doesn't care about this. He hasn't read a report in two weeks or visited Reno."

"Speaking of Reno," said Michael ignoring her outburst, "I've got a leak somewhere that could cause me a lot of personal damage. It's just you and me and Merlin and Dewey on this, OK?"

"What leak?"

"Long story, but I can't even talk to my brother."

"Wow!" she said.

"If Dewey calls, take messages, but don't write them down and cover for Merlin when he's out of the office."

"What else is new?" she said.

An hour later Snake strolled into his office to find Hunter waiting for him. "What's up?" said Snake.

"You haven't taken the truck back," said Hunter.

"I will."

"When?"

"When I've finished unloading it," he said sitting down. "A little chess?"

"You're unbelievable. Do you know how much that's costing you a day?"

"I try not to think about it."

"Let's go," said Michael getting up.

"Where we going? I've got to work on my case."

"Your new place to get the truck. We'll work on it on

the way."

"Can we take beer?"

"Of course."

The D.R. Johnny case had been thoroughly researched by Jacob Sanderson. He had the law down cold on aiding and abetting, which was the only possible defense that had any chance. And the law stunk. As Snake explained it on the drive up to his place, almost anything helpful to the actual perpetrator could make you an aider and abetter. Encouraging him; obtaining the shank. Also, if D.R. Johnny took the stand it was going to be hard to keep the murders that put him on death row in the first place, out of evidence.

"How about too 'prejudicial?'" asked Michael under the somewhat insane legal premise that the evidence of the defendant's prior crimes would be so prejudicial to the jury that they couldn't give him a fair trial in this particular case. The evidence was, in fact, too relevant. *Go figure*, thought Michael.

"I'm working on it," said Snake. "Maybe I won't put him on the stand."

"Maybe, but I think you have to," said Michael. "If no guard saw him actually shanking the guy, then he's got to deny it. What kind of witness does he make?"

"Not bad, let's go see him after."

The moving van was parked in the front yard of what might have at one time been lawn. The house was unfinished inside. *Who buys an unfinished house?* thought Michael.

"We got a hell of a deal on it," said Snake. "I'm gonna finish it up in my spare time."

"Right," said Michael.

The inside of the two-story house didn't have walls. Only 2 by 4 framing for walls. The Sandersons had nailed up bed sheets where the wall boards would eventually, in some lifetime, go. The truck was only half empty. The extraordinary thing was that the stove, refrigerator, and washer and dryer were still on board. Snake explained that an ice chest had been working just fine.

"It's like camping. We are running out of clothes though."

Two hours later, everything was in the house and major appliances were plugged in and running and the moving van was on its way back home.

After an Arroyo's lunch, they were on their way to the county jail where D.R. Johnny was being housed now for the trial that was starting in a week. Snake explained to his client who Michael Hunter was and D.R. Johnny let it be known that no introductions were necessary. He had heard of Michael Hunter. After an hour of going over the problems of the case and the law, a theme to the case was decided upon. Johnny was the consummate professional. He wanted to know the good and the bad of it unemotionally and straight and he asked good questions. It also became clear that he didn't expect to win but that it would be nice to rub the guards' noses in it if he did. Michael's assessment was that he was a stoned killer and probably psychotic.

After they buzzed him back, Michael said, "You have to watch this guy Snake, he's crazy."

"I know, but it is refreshing not to have a guy whining at me for a change."

"The key is that one guard's testimony regarding the position of both defendants at the time the people cleared away, that and the fact that D.R. Johnny is left-handed."

"That was a nice catch there Mike," said Snake gratefully.

"You'd have thought of it."

"Hey, while we're here, you want to take AJ's guy's temperature?" Snake asked. Michael had briefed him a little over lunch. Snake had been aware that AJ hadn't been very active on the case.

They buzzed for Reno who only came up because he was told Michael Hunter wanted to see him. Walking through the door to the interview rooms, he took one look at Jacob and said, "Who's this asshole?"

"He's with me Reno," said Michael. "This is Jacob Sanderson, another attorney in the office."

"Looks like just as big a faggot as the other guy," he sneered.

"Actually, I'm not homosexual," said Snake very calmly in an almost bored voice. "Who I am is D.R. Johnny's lawyer."

They both saw Reno's eyes widen a little at that news, so Snake continued, "If you two haven't met, I could certainly arrange it. Would you like that Mr. Reno? Maybe he could explain to you that I'm not a homosexual."

The room was quiet for a few seconds while Reno and Snake stared at each other.

"What do you want?" Reno asked Michael.

"I want to know what you're going to say about Elizabeth Van Houten's wallet being found in your car," he said.

"I told you I'd let you know when the time comes."

"It's come."

"No it hasn't. Is that all?" he said making motions to have himself buzzed back.

"I know you knew the Van Houten girl," said Michael quietly.

Reno stopped and turned back, "That wasn't in any of the reports. Have you and that little twirp been holding back on me?"

"It's not in the reports," said Michael. "And I know about Cadillac Johnny."

Reno's expression changed to shock for just a second

before he regained his composure. "Never heard of him," he said.

"I'll never let you put on a defense," said Michael.

"You can't stop me."

"Sure I can. You can go now. Go on, buzz yourself out like you're a big man."

As Reno hit the buzzer and the security door clicked open, Snake said behind him, "I'll give D.R. Johnny your best wishes."

Reno stared back at him with ice in his eyes as he walked out.

"You are one scary dude when you want to be," Michael said to his friend in complete admiration.

"I don't want to know about any of this do I?" said Snake.

"Not yet, but maybe," said Michael.

Later that afternoon, Michael strolled into the Hi-Grade Drycleaners and asked the owner where Anthony was.

"He's in the office with my daughter."

Michael slipped around the counter to the office where he found AJ trying on a new pin-stripped dark suit.

"What do you think?" he asked Michael a little self-conscious.

"Clothes make the man they say," said Michael. "We need to talk. Owl Club in five minutes."

Ten minutes later, AJ came through the green double doors of the Owl Club and scowled at Michael who was sitting at the bar, "You could have been nicer you know. She doesn't think you like her."

"I don't even know her and I don't give two shits what she thinks. It's you I'm starting not to like," said Michael.

"What's your problem?" said AJ growing angry.

"You're my problem, you manipulative son-of-a-bitch," said Michael.

"Now wait a minute," said AJ.

"No you wait a minute. This conversation is overdue. You know I normally don't mind that you're the promoter. That's OK with me. Let's face it, we're playing basketball everyday because of you. I could probably go to Vallejo and make a good living because of you. But now you're going too far. You killed my Metro deal so you wouldn't have to deal with the Reno case by yourself. Now you're getting us both in a lot of hot water because you got your head up some court groupie's ass and you're headed for a cliff you don't even see coming, and once again I'm going over with you."

"I haven't the slightest idea what you're talking about," said AJ with indignation in his voice.

"Of course you don't, because you're not paying attention. When was the last time you read a report?"

AJ just sat there.

"When was the last time you did a damned thing?" said Michael bitterly.

"It hasn't been that long," AJ said unconvincingly, even to himself.

"Bullshit," said Hunter cutting him off. "And I know why. It's because you know that I'll do it. That I'll come up with something and in the end you can con me into making you look good for your new girlfriend. Alice is right about you. You're useless."

"I'm useless?" he said shaking his head looking down at the bar. "I've done everything since we've hooked up to make it easy so you could be you. Now I'm useless."

Taking a pull on his beer, he wiped the tears from his eyes and stared at Hunter.

"Sure, you're the star, now. The one with the talent, now. But what about the future? What about five years from now when you're a burned out drunk?"

Hunter merely stared back at him.

"What, nothing to say, big shot?" asked AJ working up a head of steam. "Let me make it easy for you. You don't think about it at all. You're a rat on a treadmill running as fast as you can, getting nowhere, except for me. I think about it. For both of us. All the time."

Now it was Michael's turn to stare down at the bar.

"You think I need you to be a success back home? Think again," said AJ. "I need you because you're the best friend I got and it wouldn't be as much fun without you. That and I know you've got nothing else."

They sat in silence for a minute listening to Hank Williams belt out *"Your Cheatin' Heart"* on the juke.

"Sure I'm sluffing off right now," said AJ. "I found a great looking woman who thinks I'm hot shit. So what? It's not like I haven't covered your sorry ass before."

"This time it's different Age," said Michael.

"How?" asked AJ. "How's it different this time? Because it's my turn to goof off?"

"No," Michael answered him quietly. "I don't care about you having fun. You're right. You're entitled. It's just that something very weird is going on with this Reno thing. And, unless I'm very wrong, this could be a career wrecker for both of us. You've got to start paying attention."

"Can't you handle it and just tell me what I've got to do?"

"I'm not sure this time. You need to get rid of this thing. Lonigan's no one to mess with. You know that."

"What difference does it make? I can't win this thing. That will make him happy," shrugged AJ.

"I don't think Reno knows that," said Michael.

"So what? Since when did you start worrying about what an asshole like that thinks? You worry too much Mike," said AJ draining his beer and getting up from his stool. "It's the Mick in you."

Two hours later, they had reports spread all over the floor of Michael's flat. AJ was reading a lot of it for the first time.

"Do you think there's anything here in the search of his car?" asked AJ.

"Forget it," said Michael spreading papers. "I've got Merlin on it. If there's anything there, he'll find it."

"What are we looking for then?" he asked.

"We're looking for the reason he didn't want you cross examining anybody at the prelim," said Michael.

"Why do you think he did that?"

"OK, let's go over what we know," said Michael. "It reads open and shut. Victim disappears. Body found in the car two weeks later with a bullet hole in her head; she'd been badly beaten and raped before she was shot. Farmer sees a guy matching Reno's description driving the victim's car down the road where the car was found in the river. Kids come forward as result of the newspaper article and say they see a car wreck between a car matching the victim's car and a new Corvette like the one Reno drives. This all happens a few hours earlier. The cars drive away. Cops find Reno's car being repaired because of the left front-end damage where there's a paint transfer that matches the paint off the victim's car. They match a paint transfer on the car they took out of the river and it has paint from Reno's car. They get a search warrant and they find the victim's wallet in Reno's Vette's glove box. They search his house and find weapons and ammo."

"That's it. He's cold."

"But we know more," said Michael.

"What?"

"We know he wouldn't waive time. What open and shut murder case defendant doesn't waive time? They always want to stave off the inevitable. It's psychological. They'd waive time until they died if they could."

"So what?" asked AJ playing devil's advocate.

"So there's more. He also wanted to waive the prelim. All he wanted was the crime reports. He had no visitors and he's made no phone calls."

"How do you know that?" asked AJ.

"Never mind, it's true," said Michael on a roll. "Then he changes his mind and wants a prelim, but doesn't let you ask any questions."

"There's one other thing," said AJ.

"What?"

"He told me in court Monday when I set the trial, time not waived, that he wants all the prelim transcripts put on rush and sent out to him."

"The key is in those transcripts," said Michael. "That's your job. Whatever you do, get them tomorrow."

"OK."

Just then, the phone rang. Michael answered it and Gem said, "Can you meet me at Pop's in an hour?"

"Sure, what's up?"

"You can trust him, but he has some questions for you."

"What kind of questions?"

"You coming out or not?"

"I'll be there," he said.

Two hours later, Michael swung the big Caddy through the gate at the Giamatti home. Gem's car was already there. Her mother let him in, nervously he thought, and there they were, father and daughter drinking beer together in the family room. Not exactly a Norman Rockwell painting.

"Thanks for coming over Mike. You want a beer?"

"Sure," said Michael sitting down on a leather couch.

After he handed Michael a beer, and opened a fresh one for himself, "My daughter has come to me Mike and made a very unusual request. And before I honor it, we got to discuss a few things."

"Such as?"

"I want to know some things about you. Gem filled in a few gaps, but it ends at high school and college. I want some more details. I want to know who I'm sticking my neck out for here."

"Fair enough. What do you want to know?" asked Michael.

"How come you ain't been in the service? There's a war on in case you didn't know," he said.

"That's kind of a long story."

"Give me the short version."

"I was going to be an airline pilot and my plan was to go into the air force after college and maybe med school, but that's another story, get my flight training and my hours and fly big jets for United."

"What happened?" asked Gem, getting a glance from her father that told her to butt out.

"I got drafted," he said.

"And?" said Nick Giamatti lighting a cigarette.

And Michael told them the story about how when he got his draft notice it was too late to enlist in the Air Force so he just went down to the Army recruiter's office and asked them if they had any planes in the Army. Only helicopters they said. By this time, he had found out that Vietnam had over 30 poisonous snakes. He'd looked it up. Michael hated snakes. He called United Airlines and they told him that 2,000 hours in helicopters would be just fine to qualify him to go through flight training, so he went back to the recruiter and said 'sign me up.' The recruiter just advised him that since he was going to the draft physical in a couple of weeks to do that and that he would stick out like a sore thumb in basic training. He could get into flight training just as fast that way.

"What happened?" Nick Giamatti asked.

"I flunked my draft physical. I'm 4F. They'd take Gem before they'd take me."

"Why?"

"How much do you believe that a life is a series of crossroads and the ones you take affect your entire destiny?" Michael asked.

"Way more than you think," said the Sergeant.

"Well, this was a crossroad, two 8-lane freeways," said Michael. Michael told him about how on the day of his draft physical at the induction center in Oakland, California, it was a complete madhouse. They were taking guys who couldn't even raise both their arms all the way over their head and he made a wrong decision to honestly answer a question on a form he was filling out. He had his knee repaired in college after it was torn up in a football game. Medical corpman told him he was a dumb son-of-a-bitch for checking that box because now x-rays would have to be taken and he would have to be examined by a doctor. Later, an angry orthopedist, probably pissed because he had been forced into the Army and had to sit there talking to some idiot like Michael, threw his x-ray up on the viewing screen, flipped on the light, took a look at it quickly, and told him the knee wasn't that bad and that the climate in Vietnam was warm and humid and his knee shouldn't bother him there at all. He stared at the x-ray for a minute more and asked Michael what he did for a living, and when he heard that Michael was in college, he turned and walked out of the room.

Three weeks later, Michael was 4F. Not 1Y, like most rejects, but 4F. Thus, effectively ending any chance of a military career, but also his airline pilot career as well. No 4Fs fly airliners.

"So you would've gone to war if your country had let you?" asked the Sergeant.

"Yes."

"Why?"

"Good question. It's just another one of those crossroads. And frankly, and I know this makes no sense, but somehow I think something got screwed up in the cosmos or heaven or where ever these decisions get made, when I got that 4F. I don't think it was supposed to happen. I think the whole thing's been a mistake."

"You were supposed to get drafted?" asked Gem.

"And fly helicopters in Vietnam," said Michael.

"You got any idea of what's happened to most of those pilots?" asked Sergeant Giamatti.

"Beats getting bit by a snake," said Michael.

"Let's change the subject," said Giamatti. "I thought I told you that I wanted my daughter left out of this."

"I know," said Michael looking at Gem. "Another one of those damn crossroads I guess."

"I don't want to embarrass anyone here, but in case you haven't noticed, my daughter ain't exactly like the rest of the girls. We couldn't have any more kids, Maria and me, and I probably raised her too much like a boy, so sometimes," he said looking at her, "she acts like a boy. A bit of a free spirit. Too much to suit me and her mother. And you, your reputation when it comes to women is shaky at best. So what I'm asking is what's going on here?"

Michael and Gem sat staring at each other. Nick Giamatti may not have wanted to embarrass anybody, but he sure as hell had.

"You're right Sergeant. I'm not good when it comes to women. If we're being honest here, I only like them for one thing and then I want to hit the road. I don't even want to stay around five minutes. But I think you hit the nail on the head here. Gem isn't a woman. She's really just a good lookin' guy."

"What's that make you?" she asked.

"Queer, I guess." And they all burst out laughing.

"Let me ask you a question Sergeant that's been on my mind," said Michael. "Why have you spent the last eleven years at the county jail?"

"And never got past sergeant?" Giamatti added.

"Yes."

"I wouldn't lay down on a vehicular manslaughter case," he answered.

"Who wanted you to lay down?"

"Lonigan. A friend of his had a son who hit and killed a kid after a football game. The son was drunk and 17 and ran this 15 year old St. Mary's sophomore down in a crosswalk who was walking home from the same game, and then he took off."

"Where do you figure in this?" asked Michael almost wishing he hadn't opened this painful can of worms.

"I was on patrol in that area and got the call. The 15-year old was DOA and I had to go tell his parents. I knew the parents and the boy. Nice people," he said lighting another cigarette. Michael could see his hands trembling a little when he did it.

"You never forget the faces of someone you tell that news to," he said. "You know one of the looks people get is hate. They hate you for telling them such an awful thing."

They sat there for a moment while Sergeant Giamatti

remembered.

"I nosed around a little and one of the residents in the area remembered a particular sounding car coming at a high rate of speed and the screech of tires and the impact. He hadn't seen it, but he heard it. The way he described the sound the car made, I was sure I had stopped that car a week or so before for exhibition of speed. I know cars, and the sound came from glass packs and a special 4-barrel carburetor that had been put on to make it loud and fast. Do you know cars?" he asked.

"Not really," said Michael.

"Well, if you did, you'd remember things. This particular one was cherried out, lowered in the front, a 50 Chevy with several coats of metallic maroon paint on it. Anyhow, I went through my ticket book and found the kid's name and address and went over there and knocked on the door. Same night, mind you, only it's after midnight. I ring the doorbell and a woman comes to the door. Been asleep. I ask to see her son," said Giamatti getting up and going to the refrigerator for more beer. Over his shoulder, he continued the story. "Kid says he's been home since a few minutes after the game. I ask to see the car and right away I knew he was dirty because he's still loaded. The boy's father is in it by this time, giving me attitude about if his son, who you can see is a spoiled piece of shit who's been given everything, says he was home, he was home, etcetera, etcetera. I go in the garage and there it is. Motor almost too hot to touch. Left front-end damaged, some fabric sticking to the modified grill along with some hair. After five minutes, the kid gives it up. I take a report and tell him not to leave the house," said the Sergeant lighting up again.

"That's when the fun began. Next day Lonigan has my captain take me aside and suggest we just let the car insurance people handle this, not file on it. I tell him he's nuts and then he lays it on me that the kid's old man is a personal friend of Lonigan's. I tell him I don't give a shit if he's the Pope's nephew. He's a spoiled little shit who just hit and run a kid to death while he'd been drinking and I'm going to the DA with it, which I do."

Michael can see that Gem wants to come over and put her arms around her father, but she knows better.

"Dewey Gunnart files on it in juvenile court and the next thing I know the judge gives this little maggot straight probation with the condition that he's got to go to church and pray for the victim a few times. Well, the judge ain't a judge anymore. Chinchiolo's got his spot, so that's something. But Lonigan's still the sheriff and I've been out at the jail ever since," he said finishing his beer.

"That's some story," said Michael.

"There's a moral to it," said the Sergeant.

"What is it?"

"Don't screw with Lonigan."

"I'd sure like not to, but I guess he already thinks I have."

"What you've got so far is a minor slap on the wrist Mike," said Giamatti leaning toward him. "Any more, it gets much worse."

"Thanks for the warning and the beer," said Michael.

"Here's what I got to tell you. Reno had some real juice behind him from out East. He's been given a pass on a few things, but nothing through our department. It's all PD. Lonigan's clean on it."

"Cadillac Johnny Tossi wouldn't be a PD case if he was found drowned in some slough," said Michael. "It would be a sheriff's case."

"You want to stay about 12 miles away from that," said Giamatti. "You don't want to mention that again. I'm serious. No good can come of it."

Michael nodded, thinking, "Can you let me know any calls in or out for Reno and if there are any visitors?"

"Yeah, I can do that. Now you two homos get out of here and do whatever it is you do. I wanna watch the news in peace."

After they left, they went to Lyon's Restaurant which stayed open late. Michael hadn't eaten anything since lunch. After they were seated, Michael asked Gem, "How can you keep working two jobs like this?"

"I'm quitting the teacher's aide thing after this semester. Friday's actually my last day. Christmas break."

"It doesn't feel much like Christmas," he said.

"Tell me about it," she said back to him, fiddling with her napkin. "You going to the big game Saturday?"

"Hell yes. It's the Vikings. The Niners can still make the playoffs."

"Pop says I can have both tickets again. Wanna go together?"

"Sure," he said. "I'll let AJ have mine. He can take his new girlfriend."

"Who's that?"

"Some girl works in the Hi-Grade Dry Cleaners across from the office."

"Abby Howell?" she said. "I know her. Been sniffing too much of that dry-cleaning fluid for my taste, but she's OK."

"How do you know her?"

"We all went to the same high school together, moron. Don't you pay attention to anything?"

"Not much."

"Hey, are you okay?" asked Michael taking her hand again.

"Sure why?" replied Gem nervously.

"Because your pop told me you weren't feeling up to snuff and that they were running some tests. Did the tests come back?"

"Not yet," she answered looking down. Then, with a strange smile she said, "I am fine really."

Chapter 31

Merlin popped his head in Michael's office and said, "Johnny Tossi was one strange dude."

"How so?" said Michael.

Closing the door and sitting down, Merlin said, "He was arrested several times over the years. Since I can't get his rap sheet without using law enforcement, I had to piece it together my way."

"Yeah?"

"Well, years ago he owned a whorehouse. A classy one. Then nothing shows up for a few years until he does two years for manslaughter that should have been a righteous murder one or two. Over money owed. I think he was loan-sharking out of a bar and card room he owned. Then he has this drive-in for the last ten years and nothing else," said Merlin reading from notes. "Oh yeah, don't you have an aunt lives on South Union Street?"

"Yeah, what about it?"

"That's were he was born. Same area."

"Thanks man."

"One other thing. I read the reports. No search issues at all. The wallet and the victim's ID come into evidence. That right there's enough to fry him. Hey, one thing though," he said getting up.

"What's that?"

"I don't see any labs back on the vaginal smears."

"So?"

"Well the autopsy report says semen found present with evidence of rape trauma. They had to send the semen out to be tested. Is your boy a secreter or non-secreter?"

"Good catch there Beau," said Michael. "I'll think about that one."

Just then the phone intercom buzzed and it was Alice, "Dewey wants to see you at Yasoo Yani's for coffee."

Yasoo Yani's was a new Greek restaurant just around the corner from the public defender's offices on Main Street. It had become a popular coffee and lunch spot for many of the upwardly mobile, but not the old-school crowd. When Michael walked in and saw Dewey sitting uncomfortably at a table for two waiting, he wondered if Dewey had ever gotten coffee outside the DA's office before, where they served it free, hot, and strong enough to melt a spoon.

"Let's get this over with," said Dewey after they'd ordered their coffee. "This place gives me hives."

"What's wrong with it?" asked Michael.

"First of all, it's Greek," he said. "Second, it smells like their burning sheep in here."

"I forgot your level of sophistication ends with a cheese burger."

"Nothing wrong with a good cheese burger, pal," he snorted. "Listen, I don't want us meeting in the office. That shit bird Reggie Hind is getting nervous about it. So here's what I got. Puccinelli is the guy that killed the three arrest reports. The reports are long gone. He probably tore them up himself. The arrest cards are still there though."

"Thanks Dew," said Michael.

"There's more," Dewey said lowering his voice even more. "I checked some records on a hunch. The Vette he was driving was bought locally. I know the manager over at the Chevy dealership where he got it, fully loaded. He paid cash for it, as in actual cash bills. You wanna hear the best part?"

"What?"

"No record of any insurance. He was paying cash to get the Vette fixed when he got popped. Spare no expense he told the body shop."

"Who doesn't insure a new Corvette?" asked Michael.

"A guy who doesn't want to provide an insurance company a lot of information about himself on the application, I'm guessing."

"How about your other agency contacts?"

"Nothing yet. Hey, call me at home from now on. I'm being watched a little."

"Are you sure this isn't your paranoia talking?" asked Michael.

"Listen asshole, just because you're paranoid doesn't mean they aren't chasing you."

"Thanks Dewey."

Walking back into the office, an all too familiar voice yelled out, "AJ's looking for you. Said to tell you he's in Snake's office."

AJ was perched in Snake's old easy chair with a transcript in his hands. "Prelim transcript," he said looking up.

Snake was busy using a two-hole punch on various different colored folders and papers; his usual last minute pre-trial ritual. It always amazed Hunter how the same person who was meticulously working on his files and trial prep could be such a disaster in his personal dealings.

"I may need your boy," said Michael to Snake as he walked in.

"Say the word," said Snake.

"What's going on?" asked AJ looking back and forth between them.

"Never mind. I'll let you know. So, you got it? How many copies?"

"Three, just like you asked. It was like pulling teeth. It's not due out for a week," said AJ.

"I've been giving this some thought. Here's what's weird. A guy has a new Vette, but has no insurance," said Michael.

"How do you know that?" AJ interrupted.

"Don't ask. He didn't. So the guy gets in a random car wreck, has a brief conversation, everybody drives away, and somehow he winds up killing her and dumping the car into the river. Then takes his car to a high-end repair shop and says 'money's no object'."

"Whose fault was the accident?" asked Snake.

"Good question," said Michael looking at AJ who merely shrugged. "Let's say her's," Michael said to Snake. "How's it add up chess boy?"

"They knew each other," said Snake after some prolonged thought.

"That's my take. You got the picture of this broad other than the autopsy photos?" Michael asked AJ.

"I don't think so."

"OK, I'll take care of that," said Michael. "Look Age, get the addresses of the two kids and the farmer. We'll go out there after 3 today."

"Why so late?" asked AJ.

"So they'll be home, after school."

"Is anybody interested in helping me?" asked Snake.

"You need any?" Hunter asked seriously.

"No, just a continuance, which I can't get. The DA thinks he can get this one on and off in three days," he sighed.

"Who'd you draw?"

"Joe Rocha," said Snake. "His last case before Metro. That's why no continuances."

Ten minutes later, Hunter drug Merlin out of the library and whispered, "I need a good photo of the victim by 3 today."

"You got it," said Beaumont Henderson.

"You up for a road trip this afternoon?"

"Love it."

"See you at 3 sharp."

THURSDAY, DECEMBER 14TH, 3 P.M.

They were all piled into Hunter's Caddy, Michael, AJ, and Merlin, driving down Eight Mile Road, east of Stockton.

"Where the hell is this place?" asked Michael.

"You're asking me?" said AJ.

"No, I'm asking Beau. He's got the map."

Three more turns and they were on it, driving past what must have been 20 acres of oak trees with a stop sign at the end. Michael slowed the car down.

"Okay Age, give it to me again."

"She was traveling north on this road. The kids were shooting BB guns over there," he said pointing to the oaks. "They hear the crash."

"Hear it or see it?" asked Michael cutting him off and pulling over to a stop about 100 feet in front of the stop sign.

"The report says here," said AJ.

"Beau?" said Michael looking at Merlin in the rear-view mirror reading the preliminary hearing transcript in the back seat.

"Kid testified 'here'," he answered.

"OK Beau, hop out and give me a picture of everything, especially where the kid says in the transcript he and the other kid were standing."

Beaumont Henderson climbed out of the back seat with the office Polaroid camera and spent the next 30 minutes snapping pictures.

The boys, Jimmy Fox and Tommy Barnes, ages 9 and 10 respectively, lived in modest farm houses within a half mile of the oak grove. Since Tommy had testified, they went to his house first. If getting witnesses to talk to you was an art, then AJ Borelli was Picasso. People just took to him so it was relatively simple for them to be seated in the simple and neat living room of the Barnes, talking to Tommy within five minutes of knocking on the front door. Michael did the questioning and Merlin and AJ took copious notes.

Tommy said that his mother didn't like him hunting birds with his BB gun because, like every mother, she was afraid that he'd put someone's eye out. So he and Jimmy, his best friend, would more or less sneak over to the grove on weekends where the bigger birds were. That's what they did that weekend for a couple of hours each day.

Tommy didn't see the Vette because of the trees, but he did see the Volkswagen coming down the road and paid no attention to it until he heard the tires screech and the cars hit. He said he and Jimmy ran to where they could see, but it was no big deal, so they went back to hunting. Tommy said he told his dad about it only after he overheard his parents talking about the blue Volkswagen being pulled out of the river and that it had been in a wreck. He wasn't sure that it meant anything, but he told them anyway and his dad called the sheriff and they came out and talked to him, a white guy and a black guy dressed in suits.

They thanked the Barnes and drove over to the Fox house and repeated the same thing. This time, Jimmy's mother was much more skittish and protective. She kept asking if they were sure it was alright to be talking to them and AJ kept reassuring her that it was not only alright, it was her civic duty while complimenting her home and the wonderful smells coming from the kitchen. Within 15 minutes, they were all eating cake in the living room talking to Jimmy who seemed much younger than his age and very shy. Michael could see why his mother was so protective. If she mentioned it once, she mentioned it ten times that she hoped her son wouldn't have to testify and could they see to it that he didn't. They assured her during mouthfuls of cake they would do all that they could. There was no question that she was sure they were from the DA's office, although they never actually said so. The phrase, "attorneys from the county" was what was actually used to gain admittance.

Jimmy had been much closer to the accident than either the transcript or the police report put him. Michael drew a crude map of the oak forest and had him place an "x" where he was standing. It turned out that he saw the accident and a man get out of the Corvette. He said that he actually thought he saw him get into the Volkswagen, but that couldn't be right because the drivers drove their cars away.

AJ asked if the two drivers were arguing and he said no they weren't. Michael asked him if he was close enough to recognize the woman and he said he didn't know. Merlin showed him the picture he had obtained from a friend at the *Stockton Record* earlier that day and Jimmy said he

thought that was the same "lady." They showed him a picture of Eddie Reno's booking photo and he said that he was
pretty sure that was the same man that was talking to the
lady. Michael then asked him some general questions about
his hunting practices and he looked very sheepish at his
mother who told him it was okay, he wasn't going to get in
any trouble, so answer the nice man's questions.

Jimmy said he told the police officers that they only
hunted that Friday, but really it was both days. He volunteered that it was hard to remember which day was which.

After they left, Michael said they were now headed over
to Acampo Road to the DeBenedetti Ranch to see if they
could talk to the farmer who testified. Driving up the drive
that the VW had been found, where it dead-ended into the
Mokelumne River, they saw a man sitting on a tractor in a
walnut orchard that bordered the dirt road on the east.

"That's him," said AJ.

Michael stopped the car and they climbed out and introduced themselves to Carlo DeBennedetti who asked them
just what the hell they were doing trespassing on his private property. AJ turned on the charm, but it was mostly a
no sale. DeBennedetti had already "wasted enough time"
talking to people and had nothing to add. He had chased
dozens of trespassers off who had driven onto his property
to get a glimpse of where the Van Houten girl's car went
into the river. They managed to get two things out of him.
He was 100 percent sure it was Friday around 3 because he
was late getting a dead tree pulled out with his tractor in
the middle of his orchard and he had to be at a wedding in
Lodi that day at 5 p.m.

The other thing was that he couldn't ID the driver of the
Volkswagen, except to say he thought the man driving had
dark hair. He took a quick look at Reno's booking photo and

said it could have been him and it could have been Hitler for all he knew.

On the ride back to town, Michael told the boys to get a secretary to type up the notes right away. Merlin said he did his own typing 'thank you very much.' AJ said to drive fast because he had a date. Michael assured him that he had a date alright, but with him and to cancel his other one. AJ could tell that Michael was in no mood for an argument on this point.

"What's got you all amped up?" he asked.

"I'm not sure," said Michael. "Something doesn't feel right."

"I don't get it," said AJ. "I didn't hear or see anything today that is inconsistent with the reports and the transcript. The guy killed her. That's it."

When they got back to town, Michael went into the office with Merlin. AJ heard him say, "OK Beau, here's what I need you to do," as they disappeared into the building.

AJ went directly across the street to break the news to Abby that their date was off.

"That's OK sweetie," she said. "I need to work late and get the books done anyway. You've got work to do. I understand."

AJ walked to his car feeling energized. This girl reminded him of his mother. Hardworking, cheerful, pushing him to be the best, yes, pushing. He needed a little pushing. Not that it was doing any good, but he was glad Michael was back pushing him to investigate something that was not a waste of time, like today or like tonight. At least no one could say later on that they didn't try.

On a hunch, Michael dialed Gem's home number. After a couple of rings, she picked up.

"Not working tonight?" he asked.

"Nope."

"Got any plans?"

"Laundry and cleaning my apartment."

"Well, how would you like to help me and Age do a little investigating," he said.

"OK, as long I have your word that at the end of this, Reno gets his," she said.

"Pick you up in an hour," he said hanging up.

On their way from AJ's place, where Michael picked him up, to Gem's, AJ growled, "I don't see why she gets to go and I can't bring Abby."

"Because your girl is baggage and this one's bait," said Michael pulling up at Gem's.

Thirty minutes later, they walked into the Brickworks bar in Downtown Stockton. The place was just starting to hop.

"You got the pictures?" Michael asked AJ as they sat down with Gem.

"Hey Gem, what's cookin'?" said the bartender pointing when he saw who it was sitting down.

"Hi George," she said, "not much."

Bingo thought Michael watching the exchange. They ordered drinks and Gem lit a cigarette.

AJ said, "Abby quit smoking. Now she hates to be around it."

"Isn't she the little princess," said Gem blowing smoke in his direction.

"How do you know this guy?" asked Michael referring to the bartender.

"He used to be here when we came in and he comes by the Islander once in awhile," she said.

"Good, here's the drill. You're going to get him over here and introduce us. Tell him we're county attorneys working on the Reno case and we need to ask a few questions. We'll take it from there," said Michael.

"I hate myself for liking this," she said. "Hey George, can I see you a sec?"

After the introductions, both AJ and Michael could see that George thought they were working for the prosecution so they skewed their questions that way. They were trying to connect Reno with the victim. Think hard, had he seen him talking to the victim? They showed him Reno's mug shot. Yeah, he'd seen him a bunch of times. He was a regular. Eddie something. Reno, sure that was it. He was always on the make. You could tell. Said he was from back East. George thought his line was way too edgy for these local girls. Probably would have gone over better back where he come from.

But Elizabeth Van Houten? Sure he knew her. "You were in here with her, weren't you Gem? But she came in more often than that looking for a little action, no disrespect to the dead, but Reno and her?"

He couldn't say yes and he couldn't say no. But one thing for sure, Reno had to be here when she was here, because he was always here.

They had a few drinks and a couple on the house and thanked George who said he'd see Gem at the Islander. She promised to take care of him when he came by.

Back in the car taking him back to his place, AJ said, "Can I say so what? What difference does it make that he knew her?"

"Just connecting the dots Age. Just connecting the dots," said Michael driving extra careful because of the booze.

⇒◦《❮》◦⇐

385

MONDAY, DECEMBER 18TH, 7 A.M.

"I see you finally got that little shit working," said Alice pouring their first cup of coffee.

"You know Age is the best Al," said Michael.

"I know he is. I'm just still pissed at him at how he got you into this."

"I know," he said.

"How's it going?"

"Let me ask you something. You're a woman," he said.

"Thanks a lot. I don't know whether to be insulted or to be flattered after all this time," she said.

Ignoring her, he said, "You dance a few times with a guy at the Brickworks; flirt a little, then find yourself running into him in your car in the country and it's your fault. What happens next?"

"You give him your insurance information and tell him to get an estimate and you call it into your agent. Maybe buy him a drink the next time you see him," she said.

"Suppose you don't want anyone to know you hit him?"

"Why?"

"I don't know. Suppose you got an old man who'd be pissed or a boyfriend who'll ask too many questions?" he said.

"Well, the boyfriend thing is an angle," she said lighting up. Thinking and smoking for a minute, she said stabbing her cigarette in the air, "I'd be open to working something out. Let's fix it fast and cheap before anyone finds out and pay cash."

"Suppose the guy's the one that makes the offer, say to be a nice guy. Get you out of a jam, say."

"I'm in then."

"Do you let him in your car?"

"Maybe," she said.

"Thanks Al. Maybe I'm getting somewhere here."

"Oh, before I forget. Judge Hollins wants to see you this morning before court," she said. "And Dewey called. Said call him at home."

A half hour later, Agnes, Judge Hollins' clerk, was letting Michael into the judge's chambers.

"I hear you have a girlfriend," she said.

"You been talking to Madge again."

She giggled and let him in. Hollins was sitting behind his desk reviewing the law and motion files he'd be ruling on that morning. He looked up and smiled.

"How's Gem?" he asked. "She made one hell of an impression on Madge. Dinner OK Friday?"

"Let me see if she's working," said Michael sitting down. "Is that why you wanted to see me?"

"I've arranged an interview for you at Muller, Jones, and O'Connell."

"The personal injury firm?" said Michael.

"Amongst other things. Danny O'Connell's a friend of mine, a Mick just like you. Well, not like you exactly. 4 o'clock this afternoon. Wear a suit."

"I don't know," said Michael.

"Do it Mike. It could be a great start for you. Do it for me and Madge."

"Sure," said Michael. "4 o'clock sharp."

As he walked into the public defender's office, Alice chirped, "I took your suit over to the cleaners. It will be ready at noon."

"Jesus H. Christ, Al. You really are starting to scare the shit out of me," said Michael going up the stairs.

Monday December 18th, 3 p.m.

"Whoa!" said Merlin as he eyed Michael up and down in his best suit as he came through the door. "Who died?"

"Me probably," said Michael. "Did you get out there?"

"Of course. And you were right. I've got the map and Polaroids right here," he said rummaging around his cluttered desk. Finding what he was looking for, he shoved it across to Michael.

"If Little Jimmy was correct, he saw the whole thing. Look at his vantage point. He couldn't have been more than 100 feet away."

"What about the Barnes kid?" asked Michael.

"That's the funny part. I put myself where he said he was when he went over after the accident and he's damn near 100 yards away from the intersection with trees in the way," said Merlin.

"His view looks pretty blocked to me," said Michael.

"I'm with AJ on this one Mike. You can add all of this up any way you want and you still wind up with a righteous paint transfer and the dead girl's wallet in Reno's car."

"Yeah, I know. He's the perp alright."

"So what are we doing here?" asked Beaumont.

"Looking for a little leverage."

Chapter 32

At 4 p.m. sharp, Michael Hunter walked into the offices of Muller, Jones, and O'Connell with its fabric wallpaper and expensive sconces and plush leather furniture in the waiting room. A woman dressed in a classy business suit introduced herself as Catherine, Mr. Muller's personal assistant, and ushered Michael into a library with floor to ceiling bookcases containing every volume of *California Reporter* and the California Appellate series and every research digest imaginable. Michael noticed that every book was lined up perfectly like it had never been moved. More decoration than reference.

A moment later, four men walked through another door and introduced themselves. Jim Muller, Arthur Jones, and Danny O'Connell, along with Chip Christopherson, their head trial attorney they said.

"How many you got?" asked Michael.

"Well, Mike, we're not a large firm. We have two more attorneys who are out taking depositions," said Jim Muller.

"But, let me tell you something. The insurance defense game is exploding," said Arthur Jones. "We've got the AAA contract and Farmers Insurance, and I think we'll land Allstate if they don't go in-house."

"We've heard fabulous things about you from Judge Hollins and, in fact, every judge gives you the highest marks," said Danny O'Connell, by far the most personable of the group.

"Normally, we would only consider applicants from Stanford or Boalt Hall or one of the prestigious back East schools," said Jones. "But in your case, with your reputation and endorsements, we feel that an exception can be made."

"What would the job be?" asked Michael.

The question took them aback. From the glances between them, it was clear to Michael that he had committed a social faux pas as far as they were concerned.

"Well," said Jim Muller clearing his throat, "you'd be the low man on the totem poll, so I guess you'd start out writing discovery requests and responses to discovery and work your way up to taking depositions. In awhile, you could second chair one of Chip's trials. But that wouldn't be for awhile."

"What's that?" asked Michael.

"What's what?" asked Arthur Jones.

"Second chair." said Michael. "What is that exactly?"

The glances between the men were more pronounced between them this time. Chip Christopherson had a smug preppy-boy smirk on his face that said, "I told you so."

"You sit next to Chip during his trials."

Michael caught Chip's look of condescension. He stared at him a moment and said, "When do you try cases? I haven't seen you around."

The look of condescension turned to anger in a heart beat. "I had a trial last January," he said. "In front of Judge Strickland. It was a vehicle death case."

"Did you win?" asked Michael.

"Well, we keep score a little differently," said Chip. "The plaintiff wanted a million dollars and only got $750,000. So yes, I won."

"You're right," said Michael. "You do keep score a little differently than I do."

Jim Muller tried to right the sinking ship. "Mike, we have excellent benefits and I'm confident that after five years or so a junior partnership would be in the offing."

Michael just sat there staring at them, feeling depressed and lost. Hollins had gone on the line for him.

"I don't think Mike's interested, are you Mike?" asked Danny O'Connell.

"No offense Mr. O'Connell, or to any of you. I thank you for even considering me," he said starting to get up.

"I told you this was a gigantic waste of time," said Chip unable to contain himself any longer after the perceived insult Michael had given him over his jury trial.

"Why is that?" asked Michael.

"Because with your academic record, you don't have the discipline or aptitude for a firm like ours. You're not even smart enough to know what a great opportunity you were offered. That's what I meant," he said lecturing the other three men in the firm, "when I said school and scholastic standing should be a prerequisite for consideration."

"Not smart enough," said Michael shaking his head. "Well, you're probably right," said Michael heading for the door. "My boss just fired an Affirmative Action hire that was number 6 in her class at Boalt Hall. I'll have her resume sent over to Chip and you can give her a call."

⸻

Stopping by his flat to change, Michael gave Dewey a call at home. His wife, Gladys, answered.

"How you doing Mike?" she said.

"Pretty good Gladys. How's things at the bowling alley?"

"Can't complain." Gladys managed the bar at the Pacific Avenue Bowling Alley. Had for years. She was one of those women who had to have been a show-stopper in the early 60's. She was at least 15 years younger than Dewey.

"Dewey there?" asked Michael.

"Just a sec sugar," she said to him.

Dewey came on the phone and said, "Heard from my contacts on your boy. He's bad people."

"Really? What a surprise."

"You want to hear this asshole?"

"Jesus, Mr. Sensitive."

"He was never a made man in New Jersey. But he did a lot of work. Got run out by the rest of the family for being crazy. Thought the scenery change would do him good. Shows you the kind of intellects we're dealing with," said Dewey who obviously was taking a break to light up. "Anyhow, he's being paid out here by some locals to take care of whatever needs to be taken care of."

"Can you be more specific?"

"Well, they like him for Cadillac Johnny Tossi, himself no pillar of the community, but it never went anywhere."

"So he knows things?"

"Probably knows a lot of things."

"Any trades there?" asked Michael.

"None that you would want to get in the middle of. But no. I think they're going to let him fall, then deal with him after that if he's still around," said Dewey.

"They'd better do it in the first 20 minutes."

"No shit."

"Listen Dewey. I've got a voluntary manslaughter angle on this to run by you."

"It's got to go to the boss."

"I know, but I'll run it by you first."

"When?"

"I'll have Alice call you tomorrow and set it up."

"I'll see you."

"Thanks again Dewey."

An hour later, he was on his favorite bar stool at the Islander with Jimmy Yee fawning all over him. Frankie Fanelli had walked by and gave him a hug and whispered in his ear, "Thanks for stealing my girl asshole."

"I did it for Mrs. Fanelli, Frankie," said Michael grinning.

"Aw you know I'm just kidding. How's Big John?"

"Actually, I'm stopping by after. I'll give him your best," said Michael.

"You eat?" asked Gem. "You're getting skinny."

"No, I'll get something later."

"No you won't. Jimmy? Get Mike something to eat at the bar."

"Can do," said Jimmy.

"Who works for who here?" asked Michael.

"I'm the only one he can trust."

"You working Friday night?"

"Yeah, why?"

"You made such a hit at the Hollins, they've asked for an encore," he said.

"I'll get someone to cover. I love those guys. What time?"

"Pick you up at 6."

After he ate, he went to the Moretti house for a visit.

"You keepin your nose clean?" asked Big John as they sat in the family room watching some mind-numbing show.

"Clean as I can."

"I hear you shit-canned another job today."

"Man, this town," said Michael mentally exhausted. "I can't take a crap here without everyone hearing me flush."

"Don't forget that either, Mister," said Big John.

They stared at the TV screen for a couple of minutes and then Michael asked, "Why'd they have Reno do Cadillac Johnny?"

"I don't know and I don't need to know. And neither do you. You hear me?" said Big John staring at him. "You listen to me now," he said turning his big bulk close to Michael on the couch. "The law you know can only take care of so much injustice. There's people outside that law. They got their own laws and their own justice. Capice?"

"Yeah I get it." .

"You're respected Mike, both sides of the street. You were a stand-up guy with the agricultural inspecting. People don't forget that. You don't owe nobody nothing. Keep it that way."

"I owe you," said Michael.

———

TUESDAY, DECEMBER 19TH, 7 A.M.

He had just finished telling Alice about the interview the day before. She'd already heard the results, of course.

"I could have told you that kind of deal would never work for you. Not in a million years," she said.

"How come?"

"Look pal," she said staring at him, "we're friends and I love you, so I'm going to give it to you straight."

Michael could see that she wasn't kidding around. You hold your breath a little when someone you respect and who respects you gives it to you straight because they probably know something you need to know, but may not want to hear.

"You're a brilliant misfit. Look at the guys you hang around with. Where're they going in this business? Nowhere. And why? Because they're misfits and law firms hate misfits," she said lighting up. "You know who most of the guys are that go into these firms?" she asked.

He shook his head listening. He really didn't have a clue who they were.

"They're guys who got the shit kicked out of them when they were about 13-years old or so on a regular basis and decided to get even this way," she said. "They're book smart, inside-the- box thinkers. They're like Latchman and Litchfield. They got a tenth of your problem-solving skills and a hundredth of your talent and they do what they're told. Mike, you did the right thing yesterday. Don't kid yourself," she said smoking away over a cup of coffee.

"Where am I going Al?' he asked her.

"I haven't got a clue sweety," she said.

Michael was headed to the third floor when Merlin grabbed him outside the library.

"The fluids come back yet?" he asked.

"I don't know. I'll check," said Hunter.

"You know they took blood from your guy before they charged him," said Merlin.

"I noticed. Why?"

"Why would he voluntarily do that when he'd been such an asshole about everything else?" asked Merlin.

Michael thought about it a minute and said, "Because he doesn't care."

"Exactly what I think."

"Good catch Beau," said Michael giving the head clerk's

arm a pat. Hunter poked his head into Jacob Sanderson's office and said, "Did you get a jury yet Snake?"

"Almost. My guy looks pretty good in his trial clothes. His family brought him some nice duds."

Ten minutes later, after grabbing AJ, they were in Michael's car headed for the county jail. AJ was none too happy. He despised all time spent with Eddie Reno.

"I don't see the point is all I'm saying," he whined from the passenger seat.

"The point is, if he knew her and for some crazy reason the whole sex thing was consensual, then there's a voluntary manslaughter argument to be made," said Michael looking at him.

"You think that's his angle?" asked AJ.

"You know these assholes," said Hunter. "The half that have an IQ above a tomato think they're jailhouse lawyers. Maybe this guy thinks he's got some kind of self-defense thing going here."

"That's stupid," said AJ.

"I've heard dumber. Look at Waxman's guy. Not guilty by reason of insanity because of a hot dog for Christ's sake."

"So what're we doing again?" asked AJ.

"We're confronting your boy with a few facts and seeing if we can't smoke him out and break him down."

"I swear to God we're going to Vallejo when this is over with," said AJ.

An hour later, they were in the interview rooms at the county jail. Getting in had taken forever. They had waited until the PD investigators were finished interviewing the in-custodies. They sent for Eddie Reno to be sent down.

"Sit down, Reno," Michael said not looking up on purpose from some notes he had on a legal pad.

Eddie Reno stood for a couple of seconds before

deciding whether he would do as Michael Hunter asked. He decided to play along and sat down. AJ, for his part, still had no real idea what Hunter's plan was, so he was content to keep as much distance between himself and the malevolent Reno as possible, and as such, had placed his chair in the far corner behind Michael. Michael knew it was not because AJ was a coward, far from it. To Michael's thinking, AJ was the pure definition of a brave man. A guy who was scared to death most of the time, but when the chips were finally down and he had to put himself on the line, Michael had absolutely no doubt that AJ would do it. It was an unspoken strong bond between them.

"Here's your transcript," said Michael tossing it across the grey metal table at Reno.

Reno picked it up without comment keeping his eyes on Hunter. *Boy would I like a piece of that guy*, he thought, but also thought better of it since that would get Hunter off the case and he'd just have to stay in this shit-hole of a jail that much longer.

"You might as well cut the crap, Reno," Michael said in an almost bored voice. "We know what you're up to."

We do? thought AJ staring at Michael.

"What's that?" said Reno trying to mimic the bored tone in Hunter's voice.

"The self-defense angle isn't going to work," said Michael.

"Self-defense?" asked Reno truly surprised, with the surprise showing on his face, a fact that was observed by Hunter before he went on.

"Yeah. You knew her. She let you in her car. One thing led to another. You guys had sex. She got mad at something, a fight breaks out and you shoot her. At best, that's a voluntary manslaughter," said Michael.

"What the hell are you talking about?" asked Reno with a totally surprised expression on his face. In that instant, Hunter knew that Reno had no intention of heading in that direction with his case.

"Look Reno, there's no way to keep the evidence of her wallet being found in your car out of evidence," Michael said fishing for what was going on.

"Who cares?" said Reno almost laughing.

"Look, we know who you are and how you've been making your living around here. When this thing's over, the feds will offer you a deal. Probably the witness protection program. Tell me what happened here and I'll get you a deal through a voluntary or murder two and you can make a deal with the feds after," said Michael.

"I ain't copping to so much as a parking ticket," said Reno.

"Why?"

"I told you, when the time comes, I'll let you know."

"We're done here," said Michael. "Buzz yourself out."

On the ride back to town, Michael was lost deep in thought.

"This guy's crazy," said AJ. "If he thinks he's not going down on this."

"He's not crazy," said Michael.

"Then what?"

"We've-I've been heading in the wrong direction," said Michael.

"What do you mean?"

"He thinks he can keep them from proving he killed her."

"How?" asked AJ perplexed.

"I don't have the slightest idea," said Michael staring at the road ahead.

As they walked through the office door, Alice yelled out,

"Snake's got a jury."

Michael made a mental note to check in with him at the lunch recess.

"Hey," said AJ looking through the information in his "in box." "The lab's come back on the Reno case."

"Good," said Michael. "Get them up to Merlin and let him play with them."

Chapter 33

Michael Hunter had slipped into the back row of Department 4 of the Superior Court where D.R. Johnny Gonzales and his co-defendant, Ricardo Sanchez, were on trial for the shanking murder of one Jason Rich at DVI prison. Deputy DA Joe Rocha was apparently finishing his opening statement to the jury of twelve men and women, plus two alternates. Michael felt a little guilty not helping Snake pick the jury, but they didn't look too bad he thought as he was seated in the back row waiting for the lunch recess.

They went to Xochi's for lunch and after they were seated, Michael asked Snake what Rocha had said about the prosecution's theory.

"He's going with the aiding and abetting thing. One shank, two shankers," said Jacob Sanderson ordering the same Mexican meal he'd ordered every single time since Michael had known him. Juevos rancheros–morning, noon, or night, it didn't matter–juevos rancheros. Eggs with hot sauce and beans over a cooked tortilla.

"That's good," said Michael. "It means he hasn't got an eye witness to the shanking."

"That's why I'm eating lunch and talking to you," said Snake dipping a chip into the free salsa. "One sentence opening–Ladies and Gentlemen of the jury, my client Mr.

Gonzales did not shank anybody or assist anybody who did."

"Perfect," said Michael. "Say it like you're Abraham Lincoln. Make them know you mean it."

"How's your deal going?"

"Dead end. We confronted him this morning. It isn't self-defense."

"What is it then?" asked Snake.

"I don't know. The guy's a stone killer. I don't get his lack of cooperation," said Michael.

"Maybe he doesn't trust you with the information," Sanderson said doctoring up his Huevos Rancheros with salsa.

"What do you mean?"

"Maybe he thinks that if he waits til the last minute, nothing can go wrong, otherwise you might queer his deal."

"I sure don't get it," said Michael shaking his head.

"Step back from it. Start over. Take another approach," said Snake.

After lunch, Michael stuck his head into the library and got Merlin's attention, and they stepped into the hall.

"What do the fluids look like?" asked Michael.

"Bad for your guy," said Henderson. "Semen was from a secreter, which means they could get a blood type from it."

"AB negative, same as Reno. Only 1 in about 150 has that blood type."

"I've hit a wall here Beau," said Michael.

"Face it Mike, he's the guy."

"Don't make any lunch plans tomorrow. We're eatin' together. I'm buying."

"You know me and free meals, but I hate to miss basketball," he said.

"I need your brain," said Michael.

A few minutes later, he called Gem at home and invited

her to lunch the next day at Xochi's. He told her basically what he'd said to Merlin. He needed some fresh perspective from other minds. He told her to also check with her dad on Reno's calls in and out and any visitors.

"We still going to the Dallas game Saturday?" she asked. She was referring to the first play-off game against the Dallas Cowboys. The game was taking place Saturday at Candlestick Park by virtue of the thrilling 20 to 17 win over Minnesota the previous Saturday, which they had attended together. They had done everything the same, including the dinner at the Golden Spike. Most people like new experiences. To try new things. Not Michael and Gem. "If it ain't broke, don't fix it" could have been a shared motto. That was one reason that neither of them suggested to the other that they hook up with Abby and AJ, who used Michael's tickets for that game.

That night, Michael called Snake at home to see how many witnesses Rocha had called that day. Snake said that he'd called the coroner to the stand and the attorney for Ricardo Sanchez had spent an hour cross-examining him and the only thing to come out of it was that everyone completely understood that Jason Rich died of a great many puncture wounds and whoever did the deed, no one knew, except that it didn't matter. It was one of the two defendants. After that, two guards testified that a crowd formed around the victim and when they blew their whistles and disbursed them, the victim was on the ground and D.R. Johnny and Ricardo Sanchez were the last to unpile. Sanchez was covered in blood, and D.R. had some on his khakis.

"So everything's going according to plan," said Michael.

"More or less," said Snake.

"Keep me posted."

"Will do."

WEDNESDAY, DECEMBER 20TH, 12 NOON

Michael had requested a table in the back room of Xochimilco's Restaurant for the hand-picked group consisting of Gem, Merlin, AJ, and Michael. When they were all seated and ordered, Michael wanted to try to turn the conversation to the business at hand, but AJ obviously still miffed at Michael for not letting Abby come to lunch since Gem was coming, kept making small talk.

"Abby said you were the school's mascot in high school," said AJ.

"That's right," said Gem. "I was Tommy the Trojan. I had designed and made the costume and thought, what the hell, it looks better on me than some little twerp."

"She said it took a lot of guts to dress up in that Roman soldier's uniform," he said.

"Yeah, well," she said, waiving her hand dismissively.

"Was that how you got your love for football, being a mascot?" he said.

"Is that how you got your love for the law, watching Perry Mason?" she responded.

"I hate the law," he said.

"Bad analogy then. How did Abby like the game?"

"Oh, she loved going. She's not much of a football fan, but she liked being there."

"You going to the play-offs? Mike's got some extra tickets," she said.

"No, I think I'll just watch it on TV," he said.

"Scalping time!" she said to Michael. "With any luck at all, we can upgrade to Scoma's for dinner after."

Just then, Abby Howell walked into the back room.

"Hope I'm not late," she said giving AJ's arm a squeeze. "Couldn't miss the big pow-wow."

Hunter stared daggers at AJ who avoided eye contact.

"Hi Gem," Abby said as she was taking a seat next to AJ. "Isn't it great to be included?"

"Swell," said Gem.

Hunter was busy calculating how the meeting could be productive without providing information to Abby who would blab it all over town the second she left the room. He decided to keep it generic.

Turning to Merlin, he said, "What are all the defenses to a first degree murder?"

"SODDI, self-defense, and mitigation down to manslaughter because you can't prove pre-meditation or deliberation, and insanity or diminished capacity," he said. "That's about it."

"Scratch the insanity and the pre-meditation and deliberation and you're left with you didn't do it," said Hunter.

"How can you work with all that evidence, including the wallet in his car?" asked Merlin, pecking at the tortilla chips and salsa.

"That's what I can't figure out," said Michael.

"What's a SODDI?" asked Abby.

"Some other dude did it," AJ said to her.

"How do you go about proving somebody else did it?" asked Gem.

"Only two ways that I know of," said Merlin. "Alibi or you prove who the other dude was and it was more likely than not him that did it."

"What do you think sweetie?" asked Abby defensively

trying to draw AJ back into the conversation.

"I think this is all a gigantic waste of time and we should just enjoy the lunch Hunter's buying," he said.

"Alibi's out," said Merlin. "He's cold on the accident right around the time of death and her wallet's in the car."

"Then that only leaves some other dude did it," said Gem thoughtfully.

The food arrived and AJ and Abby dove into it like vultures. Michael sat rubbing his chin, staring into space. Merlin and Gem watched him, waiting.

"He's laying this off on someone else," Hunter said finally.

"What?" AJ said with a mouthful of enchilada.

"Don't make any plans for this afternoon. We're going visiting," said Michael. "You too, Merlin."

They sat eating lunch, Hunter miles away, and everyone except Abby in her own little world.

"I didn't see you at the reunion last year," she said to Gem.

"I"m not a big 'remember when' kind of person," answered Gem.

"Well, you missed a good time," she said. I can't believe how many people are married. Elizabeth Van Houten was there with her fianceé. You guys were good friends, right?"

"Yeah, we were good friends."

"She was so popular," Abby continued. "Wasn't she a cheerleader?"

"Yes."

"And you were the mascot. Funny," said Abby.

"What's funny about it?" asked Gem.

"Well, you know, you were friends with her, but none of the popular kids would hang around the mascot. It was considered so dorky. But you had a lot of guts and pulled it off," she said, her voice trailing off realizing she had dug a hole she wasn't going to be able to climb out of very easily.

Gem let it pass and went back to her lunch. Hunter and Merlin stared at her. Merlin made a mental note to see what was going on between Gem and Hunter, because if it was nothing, he was definitely asking this girl out.

"Are you still an artist?" asked Abby nervously, trying to take the subject to a higher ground.

"I still kick it around a little. Mostly for my own amusement," answered Gem.

"Elizabeth was a fabulous artist in high school. We all thought that she would be in Paris by now painting," said Abby laying it on a little thick.

"I hate Eddie Reno," said AJ to no one in particular.

"How come?" asked Abby. "Everyone's innocent until proven guilty. You have to give them the benefit of the doubt."

"That's bullshit," Merlin said to her. "You're either innocent or you're guilty. The presumption of innocence is a legal fiction created by the Fifth Amendment and the Supreme Court of the United States so that you provide an additional layer of protection for the accused. The idea is that the jury is instructed to disregard all of their instincts that the accused sitting there on trial is guilty as charged and to remember that the law requires the prosecution to prove beyond a reasonable doubt and to a moral certainty that they are guilty. They are to "presume" innocence. That doesn't make scumbags like Reno innocent."

"Doesn't the innocent until proven guilty trace back to Biblical times?" asked Abby being serious with her question.

"No, it doesn't. It's really a very modern invention," said Merlin. "Many countries, including France and Mexico had the Napoleonic Code which presumed you were guilty until you proved yourself innocent."

"Really?" said Abby.

"Really," said Merlin. "Mexico operates that way as does much of the world. If they have any presumptions at all."

"It's only European countries, Canada, and the United States and a few others that operate this way," said Hunter. "And all of that is within the last couple of hundred years."

"What it all means," said Merlin to Abby. "Is that we don't have to buy any of this bullshit that we're selling to the jury. We just have to sell it to them. Reno was guilty or innocent at the second that girl was killed and no presumptions are going to change that fact."

<hr />

Wednesday, December 20th, 3 p.m.

By 3 o'clock the boys were once again driving to the oak forest where Tommy Barnes and Jimmy Fox witnessed the car crash on the day of the murder.

"You got the pictures, Merlin?" asked Michael over his shoulder.

"Of course," said Merlin.

"And the map?"

"Yep."

"What're we doing?" asked AJ who had been in a snit since lunch. He felt that the conversation was pointless and that Abby had not been given the respect she deserved by anybody at the table. She had been treated as an unwanted outsider.

"Tryin' to figure out what your guy thinks he has," said Michael.

"Why don't we wait for him to tell us?" said AJ obviously bored and unhappy with the road trip.

"Because by that time it's going to be too late to protect our asses."

"This creep is unmanageable," said AJ as if it was the first time anyone had thought of it.

"Well, welcome back," replied Merlin.

"What's he know?" asked AJ.

"Beats the shit out of me," answered Michael.

"Turn right up here," said Merlin from the back.

The sun was still high enough in the sky to give good light to see what Jimmy Fox must have seen. Michael parked his car where Merlin directed him, simulating the Corvette after the accident. They then climbed out and trudged through the forest until Merlin said they were precisely where Jimmy Fox was standing after the accident. They stared back at the car.

"You can see everything from here," said Michael.

"Told you," said Merlin.

"I'm once again missing the point of this," said AJ.

"You may not be the only one," said Michael. "Let's go see the Fox kid."

They drove to Jimmy Fox's house hoping to catch him home. As they pulled into the driveway, they saw him playing in the front yard, kicking a football in the air and trying to catch it before it hit the ground. He was wearing a child's 49er jersey.

"Hey Jimmy," yelled Michael as he climbed out of the driver's seat of the Caddy. "You a Niner fan?"

"Yes sir," Jimmy said politely recognizing the three men from their first visit.

The kitchen door opened and Jimmy's mother stepped through it with a look of concern etched on her face. "Can I help you fellas?" she said.

"Mrs. Fox," said AJ walking up to her with his hand out-stretched, a beaming smile on his face. "We have just a couple of more questions for Jimmy and we thought we'd stop by since we were in the area."

"I don't know. My husband won't like it," she said nervously. "He wasn't happy the last time."

AJ was glancing at the family pickup and noticed the 49er logo decal on the back window. "Your husband a big 49er fan too?" he asked.

"You have no idea," she said wearily.

"He going to the play-offs on Saturday?" AJ asked casually.

"Oh no. He has no access to those kind of tickets," she said.

"I might know where he could get a couple," said AJ, glancing at Michael.

"Really?" she said interested. "Are they very expensive?"

"Face value," shrugged AJ.

"Face value? He's tried and had no luck at all."

"Well, this may be his lucky day. Here, let me come in and I will write my phone number down and he can call me if he's interested."

"Oh, of course," she said stepping aside so they could come into the kitchen. "Where are my manners."

"Is that cake I smell?" asked AJ walking inside.

"You seem to have a knack for getting here at the right time," she laughed. "I'll cut you boys a piece."

A few minutes later, they were all seated in the living room with Jimmy Fox, ready to take him through the story once again.

"Jimmy, I want you to think back to when the officers were first questioning you," said Michael. "What did you first tell them you thought you saw?"

Jimmy squirmed in his chair and looked uncomfortably at his mother.

"He doesn't want to say anything that Tommy's not saying," his mother tried to explain.

"I know," said Michael. "I know that he thinks he was wrong in what he first told the officers. I just want to know what he was wrong about."

"Tell them what you told me Jimmy," she said to her son.

"I thought I saw the man get into the car with the lady," he said in a tentative voice. "But that was wrong," he added.

"Why do you say it was wrong?" asked Michael.

"Because the black man told me that it had to be wrong cause Tommy saw something else and because both cars drove away."

"Couldn't the man have gone in the car and got back out of it and drove his car away?"

"I didn't see him get out," said Jimmy. "I made a mistake."

"How do you know you made a mistake?" asked AJ.

"Because the black man said so and Tommy said so. I get things wrong some times. I even got the day wrong. I get days mixed up a lot," he added.

"He does," his mother chimed in. "It happens all the time. That's why I don't want him testifying. I don't want him embarrassed."

Michael nodded sympathetically and turned his attention back to Jimmy, "Did you watch the whole time until both cars drove away?"

Jimmy nodded yes.

"Did Tommy?"

"I guess so. I couldn't see him."

"What door did the man use to get into the lady's car?"

"The one on the other side."

"Not the driver's door?"

"No," said Jimmy quietly.

"Well that's it for me," said Michael. "We won't be bothering you again. Here's my phone number Mrs. Fox. I'm the guy that can get you the tickets," he said glaring at AJ.

"Actually, I'd like to get them as a Christmas present for my husband and Jimmy," she said.

"Well, I've actually got them in the glove compartment of my car right now," said Michael.

"Really! Oh that's wonderful," she said. "You're going to the 49er game," she said to Jimmy beaming with pride.

"Wow!" he said ecstatically.

The first five minutes of the ride back to town, each of the men were lost in their own thoughts.

"Do me a favor, Merlin?" said Michael glancing at the back seat in his rear-view mirror. "Compare your notes on what the kid said today against your notes before and the crime reports."

"Working on it as we speak," said Merlin without looking up.

"You're not thinking of putting this kid on the stand are you?" asked AJ. "You could confuse him about his own name."

"Not in this lifetime," answered Michael.

"Then what are we doing here?"

"Figuring out who the other person is," said Merlin.

"Bingo," said Michael.

"What? What other person?" asked AJ. "You don't seriously think there's another person involved in this? The kid doesn't even know what day it was, much less what he saw."

"He saw the guy get in the car with the girl and both cars drive away. That adds up to three people, one of which is now dead," said Michael.

"Can we prove that?" asked AJ.

"Don't have to," said Michael. "But I do need to figure out who it is."

"Why?"

"So we can confront your boy with it."

"And just how are we going to find out who was in the car with him?" asked AJ.

"Leave that to me," said Michael staring out the windshield at the road ahead.

———

Pushing through the front door of the office, he yelled in Alice's direction, "Find my brother," as he headed up the stairs.

"Yes master," came the sarcastic reply from behind the glass enclosure.

Michael saw Snake behind his big desk as he walked by still in his coat and tie.

"Knock off early?"

"Rocha ran out of witnesses," he answered pulling his manila folders and note pads from his briefcase. Snake was a compulsive scribbler during the prosecution's portion of the case. He wrote down everything they did. It helped him think. It also gave the jury the illusion that he was plotting an answer for what was being said by the witness. In truth, he rarely referred to the notes he took.

"How's it going?" asked Michael, taking a chair.

"Strickland's not letting Rocha bring in the priors," said

Snake with a mischievous smile, referring to each of the defendants' prior convictions. "Too prejudicial. He says letting the jury know they were in prison is enough."

"You're kidding?" said Michael. "How the hell did you manage that?"

"Law library last night," answered Snake with a sly smile.

"You dawg!" said Michael in admiration. "The old law library trick."

Michael was referring to a stunt that they'd pulled the year before. Judge Howard Stickland had almost no life outside of the law and his ambition was to be an appellate court justice. He read the law the way a rail-bird reads the racing form—constantly. Michael had heard his clerk bitching about the fact that every morning she had to type up notes he'd taken the night before on the new cases or code sections he had been reviewing in the law library until all hours of the night. Apparently, that's where he was, by himself, on the third floor of the courthouse, late into the evening, reading the law and writing his decisions in long-hand for typing the next day. By that time, Hunter had decided that the only cases he would try in front of Strickland were ones where he had a technical legal defense. Strickland had the habit of taking over the examination of witnesses.

"The court would like to ask a few questions, if you don't mind counsel" was Strickland's favorite expression.

What were you going to say in front of the jury? Yes, I mind you dottering old fool. You're going to destroy the traps I've laid and the mood I've set.

In truth, Strickland meant no harm. He just couldn't help himself. Unlike most judges, he took an active part in the presentation of the evidence. He actually listened to the testimony and if all of the questions he wanted answers to hadn't been asked, he'd just jump in.

This drove Michael nuts. It was like having some other director sitting in the front row of the theater, watching your play, taking notes and leaping up on stage and handing the actors new pages of dialogue. Also, by the inflection in his voice when he asked questions, he gave clues to the jury which way he was leaning, which was usually in favor of the prosecution because after all, in reality, almost all of the defendants were guilty as hell.

Michael had inherited a first degree murder case, which had sat around uncharged for over four years. The cops had always liked the defendant for the assassination of a competing drug dealer, but had no eye witnesses or murder weapon. They had recently gotten lucky with an informant who had told them where to find the gun at the defendant's sister's house and got even more lucky when it turned out that the defendant's fingerprints were still on it. Ballistics matched the weapon to the slug taken out of the victim's car seat after it first passed through his brain.

For some unexplained reason, the DA put the case before the grand jury, who decided that they didn't care that much about black on black drug dealer revenge killings under a variation of the "no harm, no foul" rule, and didn't indict the defendant for first degree murder, just manslaughter.

Litchfield had the case and set it for trial, but a week before it was to go, he took a bad fall at lunch basketball and had to have knee surgery. Hawthorne gave the case to Hunter on short notice.

At the Owl Club over pool and beer, Michael was pissing and moaning over how the DA could file a four-year old homicide and how hard it was to come up with any helpful witnesses after all of that time, when Peter Rothman had pointed out there was no statute of limitations on murder and the DA could file it 40 years from now if they wanted to.

With that, the lights went on in Hunter's head. The case was to be tried in front of Judge Strickland in two days' time. The night before, Snake and Hunter let themselves into the county law library on the third floor of the courthouse around 7 p.m. Judge Strickland was already there in a small conference room with a plate glass window in the wall facing the stacks of law books and periodicals, busy on some case. He glanced up as they walked in and made their way to the far side of the library.

"Get the *Cal Jur* on limitation of actions," Hunter said to Snake. "And get it open to the right section."

Within half an hour, they had books open and two old cases sitting out like cheese in a rat trap. As the minutes ticked by, Hunter began to believe that Strickland wasn't going to take the bait. But just then, he came strolling around the corner and said, "What's got you two burning the midnight oil? How come you're not using your own library?"

That was the rehearsed opening Hunter had been waiting for. "The research tools are better here," he began. "We've got kind of an unusual legal point."

Catnip to a big calico alley cat. Irresistible. Strickland walked over to the open volume of *Cal Jur* sitting on the library table and picked it up after first carefully flipping down from his forehead, the wire rimmed thick-lensed glasses he always wore to read anything. "What're you looking up?" he asked casually.

"Statute of limitations on manslaughter," said Hunter just as casually.

"You mean the jury trial tomorrow?"

"Uh-huh."

"Wasn't it originally charged as murder?"

"Grand jury indicted on manslaughter," said Hunter almost holding his breath.

Strickland read the book for a minute and then put it down and picked up one of the case books which was open to the published appellate court decision that Hunter and Snake wanted him to see. He read it for five more minutes standing beside the table. Putting the book down, he said, "Well, have fun boys." He then turned and walked back to his conference room.

"What do you think?" whispered Snake after he left.

"I don't know."

"Should we stick around? I could use a beer."

"I don't know. If we leave, he might get wise."

"Has it crossed your mind that if the DA finds out about this little meeting, Strickland's disqualified and we're in trouble?" hissed Snake.

"Quit being such a crybaby."

"Talking to the trial judge ex-parte, without the other side, can get your ass in a sling is all I'm saying."

"What's rule number one?" whispered Hunter back to him.

"I know, rule number one, 'there are no rules'. But Jesus, Hunter."

Snake fiddled with looking up a few more cases on the subject of statute of limitations while Michael busied himself writing a quick motion to dismiss in long-hand that he would get typed first thing in the morning. In reality, they were waiting for the bobber to go under the water to let them know they had a fish on the line. A little over an hour later, they were rewarded. Judge Strickland came around the corner again with a case book containing a bookmark and sat it down.

"You might want to take a look at this," he said turning away and heading back where he came from.

All that Michael had to do was pick a jury, let the first

witness answer one question, and the trap would be sprung.

The next morning, Michael and Judge Strickland acted as if they hadn't seen each other the night before. The DA thought that Hunter was remarkably subdued to the point of being disinterested during jury selection. In fact, he exercised no challenges and the jury was seated within the first 45 minutes. The DA gave a short opening statement about how even though the defendant had committed a heinous murder, the grand jury had only indicted him for manslaughter, and therefore, the case was open and shut and the defendant had already been given a tremendous break and didn't need another one from the jury.

Michael waived his opening and even though it was 11:30 in the morning, Judge Strickland told the district attorney to call his first witness. Michael waited until the police detective was sworn in and stated his name, before standing and asking the judge if he could approach the bench.

"I move the case to be dismissed with prejudice on the grounds that the statute of limitations for manslaughter is three years and four years have already gone past before filing it," said Michael.

The DA hissed, "What are you talking about? Even if you're right, which I doubt you are, I'll just refile a first degree murder. There's no statute of limitations on that. Ask your client if he wants me to do that to him before you make this motion?"

"No you won't," said Strickland. "Jeopardy's already attached. You can't refile. Motion granted. Case dismissed."

The DA just stood there stunned, staring at Michael and at Strickland, knowing that he'd just been had, but not sure how. Michael and Snake had used the old law library scam, which they kept just between themselves every time they had a technical legal defense and could angle the case into

Strickland's court.

"Where's Rocha in his case?" asked Hunter, stretching his legs out as he relaxed in Snake's easy chair.

"He'll be finished tomorrow. How's it going with Reno?"

"Funny you ask," answered Hunter. "Turns out there was another guy at the scene." He filled Snake in on the afternoon's details and his deductions.

"You figure he's going to trial and dump it on this guy?" asked Snake, a skeptical look forming on his face. "That doesn't figure."

"I know," said Michael. "But, I think that's the way he's going. You know these idiots. They think they can make shit fly to New York that can't even get off the ground."

"How you going to play it?"

"Talk to him again," he said. "Listen, ask D.R. Johnny if Reno talks or confides in anybody in his cell or in the yard."

"I'll ask," said Snake.

"You need anything?"

"Nope."

Just then, the intercom rang on Snake's phone. It was Alice for Michael. His brother was on the line.

"What's up brother?" asked Michael in greeting.

"You called me," came the answer.

"You working tonight?"

"Naw, I'm off. Going to the folks for dinner, then out."

"I'll meet you there. We need to discuss a few things."

An hour later, Michael pulled Uncle Jimmy's Caddy into the Islander parking lot to have a pre-dinner drink with Gem, who was manning the bar on her usual shift.

"Hey buddy," she said grinning as he walked up and took a stool.

"All set for the Niner's game," he said referring to the 49er - Dallas playoff game set for Saturday at Candlestick Park.

"You bet. Want me to scalp your tickets? I can move them tonight."

"Already got rid of them."

He ordered a Mai-Tai and explained about Jimmy Fox. He figured she'd be upset since they were splitting the proceeds and using it for a fancy dinner. He figured wrong.

"I can eat at Scoma's anytime," she said when he finished. "That little kid will never forget this."

"I just did it to get into the house," said Michael. "Not so he could see a game."

"Sure you did, tough guy," she said smiling.

"Look, we have to talk," said Michael uncomfortably. "I'm not the guy you think I am."

"OK, I'll bite. Who are you?"

Michael looked around to see if anyone could overhear their conversation. Satisfied, he said, "I've done some things and know some people that don't exactly qualify me for sainthood."

"I know," she said quietly.

"No, I don't think you do," he said looking around and whispering. "I think I drink too much. I chase women just to see if I can catch them, and whenever I can, I manipulate the outcome of things," he said pausing, glad to get this off his chest with her. "And I can't shrug off an insult or play by the rules. And judging by my performance yesterday at my job interview, I got no real future in this business."

Gem lit a cigarette and let the smoke out slowly before responding. "You left out, that you went in the tank a few times as a fruit and vegetable inspector, but not for money, so who knows why, and you're afraid now that those old Dagos have got their hooks into you, that you can't stay here. Also, most recently, you'd have blown a cabdriver's head off if he hadn't pissed his pants."

Hunter just stared at her trying to read the expression on her face.

"That about covers it I think, or is there more?" she said.

"How'd you find all this out?"

"My dad and I are very close. He's afraid that you and I are going to be an item and he wants to make sure I know what's in the box before I buy," she said stubbing out her half finished cigarette. "Look Mike, I ain't no saint either. I don't trust people who pretend they are. And I don't judge the ones who aren't. Not so long as they got a heart and don't kid themselves. You're too hard on yourself."

"Well, I didn't want there to be any misunderstanding," said Michael getting up to leave. "This probably isn't going to end well, and at best, I'll be unemployed."

"Well, you can always eat and drink on the arm here until you get set up," she smiled.

"Say, I need to see your ol' man later, can you fix it?"

"I get off around 9. Meet me there around 9:30."

"Thanks," he said throwing $5 down on the bar.

She shoved it back at him saying, "Keep it, you may need it."

———◦《◦》◦———

Dinner was a treat. The distressed oak table from M. Corren & Sons, the only place Rose would buy furniture because Melvin came to the house personally to help her pick out the furnishings, always giving an extra 10 percent off, was laden with three days' worth of leftovers and tonight's fare, roast chicken. Except for Saturday night, steak night, this was always the way the Moretti's ate. Three or four meals overlapping. Minestrone soup of one kind or another, depending on Big John's mood and what was in season and what was on hand, was assembled by him every three days and consumed until it was gone. So, soup every night. Since more food was made than could possibly be eaten, there were leftovers to go along with whatever else was on the bill of fare that day. All of this found its way to the table each night. That and the transistor radio, which was off, unless a game was on, tuned to a San Francisco Giants' baseball game.

The Giants of San Francisco were more than a passion with Big John. They were the object of his unrequited love. Each year, Willie Mays and the rest of the bums by the Bay would promise him fulfillment in the Spring, only to leave him empty and bitter each October with a second place finish. Only once in 1962, did they make it all the way to the World Series, only to have the New York Yankee's Bobby Richardson's miracle leaping snag of Willie McCovey's line drive for the final out in game 7, keep them from being world champions and Big John having his just reward for faithful and fanatical support. Faithful, because every year, a week was set aside for a pilgrimage by the family to the City for a homestand involving the hated Los Angeles Dodgers. Fanatical, because Big John never, ever missed a game on the radio. Not any of the 162 games. The Pope could have been over for dinner and if the Giants were playing, the radio, that sat next to Big on the kitchen table, would be turned to the melodious tones of Russ Hodges and Lon Simmons painting word pictures of green grass and white lines.

And there were rituals that went with this. Foul language at errors and opposing home runs and rallies; disgusting threats of breaking off the relationship for good, accompanied heart-breaking losses. But perhaps the strangest, was

Big John's constant yelling into the black portable box that he'd won for selling more Early Times one month than anyone else, when the Giants had a runner on third. "Passed ball," he'd yell over and over again until the inning was over or the runner was no longer on third. And because the Giants were often offensive in more ways than one, usually several times a game there was a runner on third. Now a "passed ball" is a baseball term that refers to a catcher missing a well thrown pitch that allows a base runner to advance. Sort of a catcher's error. Big league catchers rarely did this. Even more rarely with a runner on third base. It might occur once or twice a year that a runner would score that way. Big John cared nothing about these statistics. Several hundred times a year, he would shut down all conversation in his general vicinity with his maniacal chanting of "passed" ball into the radio. Over the years, his annoying pleas had been greeted by ever increasing insults of every kind from Michael and Paul at the idiocy of the practice. These bounced off Big John like BBs off a rhino. He barely took notice. And God forbid that the boys were there the one or two times a year when the Giants' runner on third would actually score on a passed ball.

"That's mine, Rose, damn it that's mine!" Big John would leap up and bellow.

"You're right honey. That was yours," the long suffering and loyal Rose would respond.

The celebratory ribbing would last several days. But this was the off season. The radio was silent and the talk subdued. The food was, however, plentiful and delicious. Everyone ate heartily.

"You using your play-off seats?" asked Paul.

"Sold 'em," said Michael.

"To who? I wanted them," said Paul with a mouthful of chicken.

"A witness in the Reno case."

"What witness?" asked Big John, taking a sudden interest in the direction of the conversation.

"Little kid saw Reno's car wreck with the Van Houten girl's V-dub."

"What's going on?" asked Paul with interest.

"It brings me to a subject I wanted to talk to you guys about," said Michael looking over at Rose with concern.

"I'm finished anyway," she said getting up and leaving the room.

"What's up that you can't say it in front of your mother?" asked Big John getting annoyed.

"Before we talk about this, I've got to tell you that I'm crossing a line here and if it don't stay in this room, they could pull my ticket," Michael said referring to his state bar license to practice law.

"Goes without saying," said Big John.

"Puccinelli's been covering for Reno the last two years," he said watching their faces as he said it, letting it sink in deep before continuing.

"You know anything about this?" asked Big John to his blood son.

"I've been in Metro," answered Paul.

"Not what the hell I asked you," snapped Big John. "Do you know anything?"

"No," answered Paul sheepishly.

"There was another person at the scene of the accident in Reno's car," said Michael satisfied that the Puccinelli angle was cleared up.

"What are you talking about?" asked Paul. "He was alone."

"No he wasn't."

"Then who the hell was with him?" his brother asked.

"I don't know for sure." Then to Big John, "Does Bonaconte have a son?"

"Yeah, he does," said Big John, all the lights coming on. "About 30."

"What's he look like?"

"Dark haired, kind of skinny."

"Can you get me a rap on this guy?" Michael asked his brother.

"You mean with nobody knowing?"

"Absolutely."

"Get it through Dewey if you can," said Pauli. "Somebody might notice."

"Take too long. He's being watched," answered Michael.

"OK, let me try," said Little Pauli with concern.

"What're you doing here Mike?" asked Big John.

"Connecting the dots. Trying to get myself out of this."

"You can't bring Bonaconte's kid into this," said Big John.

"Unless I'm sadly mistaken, I think Reno's going to try to lay it off on him."

"How's that going to work?" asked Paul. "The broad's wallet was in Reno's car."

"I didn't say it would work," said Michael. "It's just what he's going to try to do, I think."

"Your ass is hanging out a mile and a half here boy," said Big John. "If you even think this can happen, we got to tell Sally."

"What's the end game here Mikey?" asked Paul.

"Reno pleads out to a lesser," said Michael.

"How's Pooch figure into this?" asked Big John.

"Wild card," said Michael.

"No," said Big John lighting a Camel. "He figures somewhere."

———=»《①》《=———

Two hours later Michael pulled into the now familiar graveled driveway of the Giamattis. The crunching gravel felt secure, familiar, and safe. Gem's mom answered the door and ushered him into the family room where Nick and Gem were watching TV.

"There he is," said Nick waving, but not getting up. "Everyone's favorite public defender. Take a load off."

Michael flopped into an easy chair and took the cold beer that Gem handed him.

"It's never just social with you counselor. So what's up?" asked Nick not taking his eyes off of his program.

"I think I know what Reno's up to, but I got to get him to cop to it," said Michael straight away.

"How can I help you?" Nick Giamatti said turning in his chair to face him.

"I need all the dope you got on him. Who he talks to. Who he eats with. Shit like that."

"He stays to himself pretty much. Real aloof. Like he's just passing through," said Nick. "He knows the score," he continued. "He knows guys are going to try and get close to him so they can say he told them shit about the murder and get themselves a deal."

"Anything in or out?" asked Michael referring to visits or telephone calls.

"Not yet."

"What do you know about Sally Bonaconte?" asked Michael.

"Little Sally?" said Nick. "Enough to stay away from him. Why?"

"You ever get his son in there?"

"Christopher?" said Nick taking a deep drag on his ciga-rette. "Yeah, a time or two. Drunk driving. Two times, I think. Your buddy Archie Cox represented him."

"Nothing else?" asked Michael.

"No, I'd remember," said Nick. "How's he figure?"

"I'm not sure."

"You see Gem's new painting?" he asked changing the subject.

"No," answered Michael looking in the direction of the wall where Nick was pointing. There it was, in oil, a painting of an old Italian man wearing a short brimmed hat pulled down to shade his eyes. His tanned, stubbled face contrast-ed against a rust background. The gray stubble of whiskers showing life-like. Michael thought it was magnificent.

"My father," said Nick proudly. "An exact likeness. Better actually. It captures his spirit. I don't know."

"It's unbelievable," said Michael alternately staring at the painting and at Gem, who was obviously self-conscious and uncomfortable with the attention and praise.

"How long have you been doing this?" he asked her.

"Since I was about 10," she said.

"I take it she didn't tell you anything about this aspect of her life either?" said Nick. "Marie and I always hoped she'd pursue her talent professionally."

"I can see why," said Michael staring at the image of Gem's grandfather on the wall. "When are you going to confront Reno?" Gem asked.

"Probably tomorrow."

"What happens if he doesn't tell you what you want to know?" she asked.

"Depends. One way or the other, I've got to figure out what's going on. It's like I'm missing something."

"We still on for the Hollins' Friday night?" she asked changing the subject again.

"Madge would kill me if I didn't bring you over," he said.

"She's sweet."

"That's not a term I'd use, but yeah, she's aces."

Chapter 34

"Lieutenant Puccinelli on line 2," said Alice. "Watch your ass."

Michael stared at the blinking light on his desk phone. *I'm going to kill Paul* was his first thought as he reached for the button.

"Pooch," he said. "What's cookin'?"

"Let's have a chat," said Albert Puccinelli on the other end. "Let me buy you an espresso at Gaia-Delucchi's. Fifteen minutes."

"See you there," said Michael. *What was going on? Gaia-Delucchi's was a very old Italian grocery six blocks away. Why there? Because Puccinelli didn't want any law enforcement or courthouse personnel seeing them, that's why.*

Pooch had always been in his corner up until now. He fixed every ticket Michael had ever had since he had started driving. There was no avoiding him now.

Ten minutes later, he walked through the double doors of Gaia-Delucchi's on American Street. There was Albert Puccinelli in rich tan slacks and an off-green herringbone wool sports coat with an emerald green silk tie, knotted perfectly. His classically handsome Roman features were covered in dark curly hair; your classic ladies' man. He smiled as Michael walked up, and rose to give him a hug.

So far, so good, thought Hunter.

Puccinelli motioned for Anthony Gotelli to get Michael an espresso from the ancient espresso maker imported years before from Italy. The smells of food cooking, fresh baked foccacia, and Italian cheeses made Michael's mouth water.

"You want a pastry?" asked Puccinelli.

"I could eat."

"Get him a pastry, Tony," Puccinelli yelled in the direction of the owner behind the counter. If any other English was being spoken in the store at the time, Michael couldn't hear it.

It was the perfect place for this meeting, he thought. Everyone had plausible deniability regarding the subject matter.

Puccinelli waited for Michael to finish his espresso before beginning. "Everybody that matters is starting to get nervous on this Reno thing," he said.

"Yeah?" said Michael non-committingly.

"An old buddy of mine at the sheriff's office says Lonigan is asking a lot of questions about what you're up to. He doesn't think you're rolling over on this."

"Really?"

"Yeah, really," said Puccinelli starting to get agitated at Michael's non-commital attitude. "Some of our friends in Linden too."

"That what my brother told you?" said Michael.

"What the hell are you talking about?" said Albert getting red in the face. "You're starting to piss me off here."

"Really?" said Michael walking dangerously close to the line with the volatile Puccinelli.

"Yeah, really," said Puccinelli heading for his boiling point. "And another thing," he said scooting his chair closer, "not very smart to be dating Detective Mark DeLucca's girl-friend. He's a favorite of Lonigan's and you're not helping Nick any by pissing everyone off with that."

"Ah, he can bite me," said Hunter.

"Don't sell him short. He'd love to."

"So what's your angle in all of this?" asked Michael draining his espresso and holding his delicate china cup up for another.

"Same as always kid since you was 15. Your ass."

"Nothing else?"

"What're you fishing around for?"

"Why'd you kill all of Reno's arrest reports before they got to complaint? And what did my brother tell you last night or today?"

Puccinelli sat staring at him. "First, I haven't talked to Paul in a week and he's told me nothing, although I don't like him holding out on me, whatever it is. Second, how'd you hear about Reno?"

"Little Sally."

"You talked to Sally?" Puccinelli asked incredulous.

"He talked to me 's more like it."

"Then you already know why."

"So what do you want to talk to me about?" asked Hunter.

"What I just said," answered a less upset and more frustrated Puccinelli. "You're pissing off the sheriff's office for no reason. Lonigan has a long memory. Why you want to mess yourself up for a piece of shit like Eddie Reno? Besides, he goes shootin' his mouth off, he can embarrass a lot of people."

"You mean Little Sally?"

"Ah, Sally can take care of himself. I mean the DA's office."

"What're you talking about, the DA's office?" asked Michael boring in on the new information.

"He's screwing someone there."

"You have got to be kidding me!" Michael hissed. "Screwing a DA. Who?"

"Never mind who," said Puccinelli keeping his voice low as they now were starting to attract attention from the two Gotellis, father and son.

"I bet it's that Greek bitch," said Michael. "But, how did that happen?"

"Never mind. That's not the point. The point is that this guy needs to take a quiet fall."

"I'm working on it," whined Michael.

"Well, maybe it would help if it looked like you were working on it," said Puccinelli. "Here's the deal. My buddy at the sheriff's office told me that Lonigan's not going to resist a deal so long as it doesn't cast the girl in a bad light."

Michael sat back and thought for a moment. "There are no search and seizure issues, so all of the evidence comes in. It's murder one or it's nothing."

"What happens if the DA roles over on the search issue?" Lieutenant Albert Puccinelli asked quietly.

"Fat chance getting Reggie Hind to do that," said Michael.

"Hind will do what he's told on that or that judgeship he so dearly wants will never happen."

So there it was. The way out. He was negotiating with the man whose mission it was to save his ass and everyone else's and his authority came all the way from the top. All he had to do was sell it to Reno. As he sat there thinking, Michael wondered if Albert Puccinelli knew about Christopher Bonaconte being in the car with Reno on the day of the murder. Probably not, judging from the conversation.

"Will this square it with Lonigan?" asked Michael.

"This will square it. Joe Rocha will go back to the DA's office with a big promotion and the Metro job will be yours," said Albert with authority.

"I guess I'd better go see Reno," said Michael.

"I guess you'd better," said Albert Puccinelli.

———➤«(●)»⟞———

Thursday, December 21ˢᵗ, 10:30 a.m.

"Find AJ," said Michael to Alice as he headed to the law library. He wanted all of the ammunition he could muster for a showdown with Eddie Reno.

"He's at the dry cleaners," came the reply from behind the glass enclosure.

"Well, get him back here."

"Yes master," Alice said in a sarcastic tone that she didn't mean. She sensed something big was up.

"What did you find?" Michael asked Merlin as he took a chair at the table in the library across from him.

"It all checks out," said Merlin. "They placed way too much emphasis on the Barnes' kid's story. No way he saw what Jimmy Fox saw. Two guys for sure, unless of course, it was a girl."

"No, it was a guy, and I know who," said Michael.

"Enlighten me," said Merlin raising his eyebrows.

"Best you stay in the dark on this one Merlin. I'll fill you in later."

"I'll hold you to it."

Just then AJ barged through the library door. "What

couldn't wait until after lunch?"

"We're meeting with your boy. Let's go."

In the car on the way to the jail, Michael briefed AJ on his plan to get Reno to take a deal, leaving out the details of his conversation with Albert Puccinelli. AJ was for once calm and resigned about meeting with his client, ready to get it over with.

"What are you getting Gem for Christmas?" he asked out of the blue, wanting to change the subject to something other than Eddie Reno.

"What?" Hunter asked jarred by the directional swerve in the conversation. "I don't know. I hadn't really thought about it."

"Better hurry up. It's next week. I got Abby a pearl necklace," he said proudly.

"How long have you known this girl," Michael asked glancing at him.

"You know how long I've known her. That's not the point. I think she could be the one and I want to get her something special. Besides, I got 60 percent off."

"Where did you get it?"

"That Japanese jeweler friend of your Pops. You know the guy. Remember, Big John helped me get those opal earrings for my mom on her birthday last year?"

"How much you spend?"

"Fifty bucks. Hell of a deal."

"Fifty, huh. You didn't spend fifty on lunch all last year."

"Times are changing pal," said AJ.

"You said a mouthful there brother," responded Hunter now thinking he had one more thing to worry about. Christmas presents.

The jail was unusually quiet that morning. Everything court related slowed down at Christmas time. Crime continued, but arrests and the unusual urgency surrounding them gave way to the power of the season. They were let into the interview rooms in what seemed to be record time. Reno arrived in his usual foul mood and demanded to know why they were wasting his time. He had been watching a game show from his cell on the hallway TV.

"We want to go over your defense," responded Michael.

"I told you I'd let you know. Why do we have to keep going over the same shit? Don't you have anything better to do? Go get laid, for Christ sake," said Reno.

"We've actually been busy working on your case since you've been no help," said Michael. "When were you going to tell us about Christopher Bonaconte?"

The mention of the name was like a slap across the mouth to Reno. His head jerked back and his eyes narrowed to slits as he stared at Michael. "Whoa!" he said. "You have been busy."

"He was in the car with you that day," continued Michael.

"So what," snapped Eddie Reno. "And you two better forget about this if you know what's good for you. Christopher's old man is nobody to be messing with."

Now it was Michael's turn to be jarred by the conversation. He hadn't expected Reno to warn them off of Christopher Bonaconte. *Was it a feint?* Reno didn't look that smart.

"When were you going to tell us about Bonaconte?" Michael pressed on.

"Never. I ain't stupid."

"That's a matter of opinion," said Michael.

"Why are you always trying to provoke me?" said Reno. "I ain't going for it asshole. If you want a piece of me, you can have it in spades the second I'm a free man."

"Face it Reno," said Michael. "That won't be for a few

years at least."

"Says you," he sneered.

"Yeah, says me," Michael snapped back. "There's no possible theory of this case that gets rid of the evidence that you killed her under some circumstance or other."

"That's where you're wrong," smiled Reno.

"Bullshit," said Michael. "Name a theory."

"No you don't. Not yet. I'll tell you during the trial."

"By then it will be too late," said Michael, his mind racing to try to stay ahead of the conversation.

"Okay, I'll bite," said Reno. "Why?"

"Because we won't help you put it on. We're going to start setting it up with the judge that you're completely uncooperative; maybe crazy," said Michael.

"You can't do that," said Reno, the veins on his neck beginning to bulge, his face getting red. "I'll have you disbarred if you try and pull that shit."

"You're way out of your league here pal," said AJ. "No one's going to believe you. Face it. You're acting very strange for a guy that's facing murder one and all of the evidence they have against you. Maybe a little time in the state hospital will do you some good."

"You're bluffing," said Reno staring daggers at Borelli.

"Try me," said AJ calmly, now beginning to feel in charge for the first time in a long while.

"I got a witness," said Reno finally.

"Who?" asked Michael. "Not Bonaconte?"

"Hell no," Reno said irritated. "I told you to forget about him."

"Then who is it? And what could they possibly say that gets rid of you driving away from an accident with the victim and her wallet ending up in your car? Oh, and by the way, I forgot to mention that they found semen in the victim that is from a very rare blood type that you just happen to match," said Michael.

This was new information to Eddie Reno. The blood type. Michael could see the wheels spinning in his head like the tumblers in a cheap Vegas slot machine.

"What do you mean blood type? I ain't seen anything about that."

"It's in the lab report. You have to know how to read them, which you obviously don't." He let Reno mull that over for a minute before continuing. "You could fall on that alone."

"I've got a witness I told you," said a clearly exasperated Eddie Reno.

"Yeah, you told us. But you didn't say who or tell us what they would testify to," said Michael.

Reno just sat there chewing on the new information. AJ figured they had pushed him far enough.

"And there's no way you're keeping Christopher Bonaconte out of this," said Michael walking all the way out on the limb.

"I told you I ain't naming him. So he's out of it," yelled Reno starting to get out of his chair.

Uh-oh, thought Borelli. *Here we go.*

"We've got to go interview him now that you've admitted that he was with you," said Michael. "He might have some exonerating evidence to offer."

"You can't do that!" screamed Eddie Reno standing straight up. "I won't let you."

"You can't stop us," said AJ very calmly, remaining in his seat.

"Damn you!" Reno shouted.

"What's it going to be Eddie? You going to answer our questions or are we going to have to go find out for ourselves and maybe have your sanity checked out at the same time?"

"I got a witness. I got a right to call a witness. You can't stop me." Eddie Reno said slumping back into his chair.

"Look Eddie," said Michael leaning forward and changing the tone of his voice. "No witness is going to get you out of this completely. Why don't you let me make you a sweet deal. Manslaughter. You're out in four."

"No deal," said Reno shaking his head back and forth stubbornly. "I'm walking out the back door."

"You think about it overnight. We're done for now," said Michael. "Buzz Eddie out Age."

"I ain't taking no deal. And if you know what's good for you, you'll stay away from Chris Bonaconte," Reno said walking back to the main jail through the metal interview room door.

Back in the car headed to the office, AJ asked Michael, who was transfixed in thought, "So who's the witness?"

"Makes no sense," answered Michael.

"Tell me about it," said AJ. "Maybe we should 1368 him after all."

"Maybe," said Michael.

Chapter 35

Michael was finishing a "comped" plate of won-tons and Chinese spareribs at the bar of the Islander, when the phone rang and Gem answered it. A second later, she handed the receiver to Michael.

"It's Pop," she said.

"Hey Nick," said Michael in greeting. "What's going on?"

"Your boy finally made a couple of calls," said Nick Giamatti.

"To who?" said Michael standing up. Gem watched him closely, drying a glass.

"The Bonaconte residence in Linden and the DA's office."

"Jesus Christ," said Michael.

"No kidding," said Nick.

"How long did he talk?"

"About 5 minutes to Chris Bonaconte and a minute to a woman at the DA's."

"What did he say?" asked Michael with excitement.

"You better stop by," Nick said. "We'll talk here."

Michael hung up and stared at Gem. "I gotta go," he said.

"I get off at 9," she said. "Come by."

"OK. What do you want for Christmas?" he asked her.

"Your ass out of this mess," she answered.

Ten minutes later, he was pulling into the driveway of the Giamatti residence. He had promised Snake that he

438

would stop by later. Tomorrow were the closing arguments in the D.R. Johnny shanking murder case. He still had time.

Maria Giamatti answered the door as usual, ushered him into the family room, and handed him a beer before discretely disappearing.

"Counselor," said Nick greeting Michael as he came into the spacious heavy-beamed vaulted ceiling with its tongue and grooved knotty-pine walls. A true man's room. "Have a seat."

Michael flopped down in one of the cushy leather easy chairs and took a big sip of the ice cold Coors. It struck him that Nick Giamatti took pride in his beer. It was ice cold, like the Owl Club. Most people didn't keep their refrigerators cooled down enough to keep beer that cold. The beer regular people served never tasted as good as it did at a good joint like the Owl Club or Nick Giamatti's; condensation in the form of large droplets rolling down the cans and bottles. Glancing about him once more, Michael had the impression that everything in the house stated the careful pride and purpose of its owner. He would bet a sawbuck that Nick's garage floors had a coat of shellac on them which made them glisten and that you could eat a sandwich off of them, they were so clean.

He took one more long pull and said, "Look Nick, before you say anything, I just want to tell you that I know I put you in one hell of a bad spot here."

Nick Giamatti waived him quiet. "I'm a big boy. I know the score. Besides, I was never getting out of the dog house anyway."

The air cleared, Michael asked, "So what have you got for me?"

"Couldn't hear both sides of the conversation, but with the listening device, I caught him using the pay phone by having another inmate doing the dialing."

"What did he say to Bonaconte?"

"That you figured it out somehow that Christopher was involved. All vague shit that could be taken a lot of ways, but the gist of it was that he wanted it known that he had said nothing and wanted Christopher left out of it."

"Was it friendly?"

"More or less, I guess. But I'd watch my ass if I were you, because he made it clear that you're the one that's bringing this to light," said Nick lighting up. "How's Christopher figure into this?"

"He was in the car when the accident happened with the Van Houten girl."

"Jesus. How'd you tumble to that?"

"One of the kids. I pieced it from that and the fact that Sally Bonaconte was sniffing around."

"This is big league shit here Mike," said Nick with a concerned frown on his face.

"What about the call to the DA's office?"

"That was a strange one," answered Nick leaning forward.

"How so?"

"He never asked for anyone. He just talked to the person who answered the phone."

"And?"

"He knew the person really well. Called them 'baby.' Asked if they'd missed him. Shit like that."

"What's the weird part?" asked Hunter.

"He never asked to be transferred from the receptionist. He just talked to her," said Nick.

"Maybe he dialed direct to another number," Michael said playing devil's advocate.

"No, I checked the number. It was the main number all

right," countered Nick.

"He's got something going with the receptionist?"

"No, I don't think so," said Nick.

"Why?"

"Because he told her to tell her friend to hold her mud; that he was going to keep his promise and everything would be over soon."

Michael sat back and thought. Nick got up to get more beer from the small fridge behind the mahogany bar in the corner of the room.

"The regular receptionist is Phyllis Jones," said Michael absently.

"The one dresses like a hooker?" asked Nick.

"That's the one."

"When those D-cups finally go south and the push-up bra she always wears quits working, it's not going to be a pretty sight," remarked Nick walking over and handing Michael another beer.

"She'll probably be dead from lung cancer before that."

"Assuming he was talking to Phyllis, and I'm guessing he was, you know who her best friend is don't you?"

"No," said Michael.

"Gladys Gunnert."

"Whoa!" said Michael. "Dewey's wife? How do you know that?"

"Common knowledge," said Nick. "Neither of those two gals is Julie Andrews, if you know what I mean."

"That still doesn't mean one of them was running around with Reno, and so what if it did?"

"That's why they pay you the big money counselor. It's your problem. I'm just the messenger."

"Something stinks," said Michael draining his second beer.

"No kidding," said Nick. "Say what're you doing for Christmas?"

"The folks, I guess."

"Well, we kind of make a big deal out of Christmas Eve around here. You're more than welcome."

"Thanks Nick."

"You know Marie and I only got the one kid," he said. "It wouldn't hurt our feelings any if we saw you around here some. Not that you haven't already been making a pest of yourself," he went on awkwardly and uncomfortable at the intimate nature of the subject. "I guess what I'm saying is, you're not the worst choice our kid's ever made. And no matter how things work out with all of this, you can always hang your hat here."

Michael was unexpectedly touched by the awkward gesture, as well as embarrassed. Neither of them were at all comfortable with displays of emotion.

"For what it's worth," said Nick, "it's obvious you two kids like each other."

"Gem's great," said Michael quickly.

"That's not what I'm talking about," said Nick. "I know you're hot for each other. Hell, half the world's hot for the other half. That lasts a few weeks at best. What I'm talking about is 'like.' You guys actually like each other. That's rare. I know, because Marie and I like each other. It's got me through most of this shit."

"Really?" said Michael thinking about it.

"Yeah, you guys are pals."

"I gotta go," said Michael. "I know what I'm getting her for Christmas and I gotta go get it before the store closes."

"Well, get out of here then," said Nick smiling.

"Thanks Nick."

"Forget it. Don't make me sorry. Figure this thing out fast."

"I'm trying," said Michael standing.

Twenty minutes later he walked out of the book store in Lincoln Center with the wrapped present under this arm. There were a million thoughts pounding through his head. Some good and some bad. He couldn't wait to see Gem, but first, he had to get to the office and help Snake with his closing argument.

Jacob Sanderson's office looked like the war room at the Pentagon. Large pieces of construction paper were Scotch-taped to the walls, each bearing notes from the testimony of important witnesses in the case. Snake himself was hunched over the desk writing on a legal-sized yellow pad.

"How's it going big guy?" Hunter asked as he walked through the door and began studying the notes on the wall.

"Where you been?" said Snake only glancing up momentarily from his work.

"Working."

"I'm stuck on this closing."

"You always say that. You're such a pessimist during trial. You always think you're losing," replied Hunter reading the wall. "Did you put him on?"

"Yeah, he testified, but I don't know how it went over."

"I should have been there man, I'm sorry," said Michael.

"That's okay. You got your hands full."

"Well, give it to me," said Michael sitting down in the worn easy chair and propping his legs up on the corner of the desk. "What did old DR have to say?"

"Pretty much what we thought," said Snake. "He didn't shank anybody. He didn't know the victim. Wouldn't say who did."

"Did you come on with that prison code they have about minding their own business and not ratting anyone out?" asked Michael.

"Yeah, I got all of that in," said Snake. "He actually did pretty good on that part. He enjoyed lecturing on prison infrastructure and gang affiliations and how and why you could get yourself popped and the various ways it happens."

"Did the jury eat it up?" asked Michael.

"Oh yeah. It was a walk on the wild side from a real life bad guy."

"Sounds like you got it all in."

"I don't know," whined Snake. "It never comes in like you want it. I wanted to take him through life at DVI and explain how things were without sounding like he was the ring leader and head assassin."

"So?"

"Well, that's exactly how it sounded. He's sitting next to this dufus, Ricardo Sanchez, who looks like an original thought has never gone through his head, and I've got DR lecturing the jury on the dangers of prison life, gangs, and how not to get shanked, but oh, by the way, he didn't do it and he doesn't know anything."

"I know what you mean," said Michael. "How'd he hold up on cross?"

"Not bad. Rocha could never make a dent on getting him as the shanker or tie him to the victim. But he did a good job on making it clear to the jury that D.R. Johnny is not your average inmate and clearly knew what was going on."

"You think the jury bought that?" asked Michael.

"Oh yeah. Nobody's getting shanked in D.R. Johnny's vicinity without him knowing about it."

"Did Stagnaro put his guy on the stand?" asked Michael.

"Nope."

"OK, here's where you go," said Michael standing up and beginning his pacing. "If DR's come off as a smart guy, then you make him real smart. He's too smart to be involved in a clumsy shanking like this. But he's no rat either. Prison life's different. It's about survival. It's about keeping your mouth shut and your head down," said Michael working up a head of steam, lost in thought.

Snake was scribbling furiously as he talked.

"Don't insult their intelligence. Agree with Rocha that DR knows who did it, but he can't say. It would be putting the bull's eye on his back if he did. Now here's the tricky part that you, and only you, can sell," said Michael stopping his pacing and making eye contact. "These people like you. You've got to lecture them on the fact that the other guy had every right not to take the stand and he's presumed innocent, blah, blah, blah." said Michael. "But, you got to do it so that they know that you know that he is guilty as hell and that's why he really didn't take the stand and profess his innocence. But you gotta be subtle. Very subtle."

Snake put his elbows on his desk and his tired head in his hands thinking. Looking up, he said, "DR took the stand to tell you he didn't do it and to let you know how things are in there. You've got to be smart enough to read between the lines because he said all he could say under the code."

"You got it," said Hunter. "Somebody's going down for shanking Jason Rich. Give them Ricardo Sanchez."

"You going to be there?" asked Snake. "We're starting at 9."

"Wouldn't miss it buddy."

An hour later, Michael was headed for Gem's place, bone tired, when a thought hit him and he headed the Caddy north to Lincoln Village. Ten minutes later he pulled up in front of the house on Burnside Way and walked up and rang the door bell. A moment later, a plump dark-haired Italian woman answered the door.

"Mikey!" she beamed. "I haven't seen you in so long,"

she said, giving him a big hug.

"How you doing Grace. Sorry to barge in so late. Is Albert home?"

"Sure, come in. You eat? Let me fix you something."

"No, I'm fine."

"You sure? Albert's in the family room. You want a beer?"

"No, I'm good. Thanks Grace."

Albert Puccinelli sat straight up in his easy chair in front of the RCA console television he was watching, when he saw Michael walk into the room.

"You get him to take the deal?" he asked after glancing over Michael's shoulder to make sure his wife wasn't within ear shot.

"Not yet," answered Michael, taking a seat on the family room's brown naugahyde leather sofa next to Lieutenant Puccinelli.

"What brings you by then?" Puccinelli asked him directly without the pretense of their usual friendly banter.

"After I left him, Reno made a couple of calls."

"So?"

"They're the first calls he's made and they were to Christopher Bonaconte and the receptionist at the DA's office."

"I won't even ask how you've come by this information, as if I didn't know," said Puccinelli shaking his head.

"You didn't ask me why he called Christopher," said Hunter staring his old friend in the eye.

Puccinelli just stared back at him.

"You know he was in the car with Reno, don't you?"

"What difference does it make?" said Puccinelli.

"Just how deep are you in with these guys?"

"Not as deep as you are buddy," replied Albert.

"Well, assuming you still have my best interests at heart, Sally Bonaconte now thinks that I'm going to "out" his son on this," said Michael.

"And why would he think that?" asked Puccinelli sitting all the way up in the recliner.

Michael told him the story of his meeting with Reno and his attempt to agitate him into telling him what he was up to. After he finished, Albert said, "Let me try and square it with Sally. Shouldn't be a problem. I'll drive out there tonight."

"Thanks, but I need something else," said Michael.

"When does it ever end with you?" Albert asked in agitation.

"How does Gladys Gunnart figure in this?"

Puccinelli sat back and stared at the TV vacantly, his mouth clamped shut and his head shaking side to side slightly.

"Gladys, Gladys, Gladys," he muttered. Then staring up at Michael, he asked, " What do you know and what have you guessed?"

"I'm guessing Phyllis and Gladys get around some and one or both of them know Eddie Reno better than they want Dewey or anyone else to hear about," said Michael.

"You were always a smart little twerp. I've always said so. You'd have made one hell of a cop," said Puccinelli.

Michael just stared back at him waiting.

"How'd you piece it together, about me?" Albert asked him.

"You let it slip that the DA would be embarrassed over this and you implied that it shouldn't happen. What you really meant was everything would come out about Gladys."

"I knew the second I said it that I'd made a mistake," said Puccinelli shaking his head again. "You want a drink?"

"No."

Puccinelli got up and went to the built-in liquor cabinet next to the TV and poured himself a stiff one.

"OK, here it is," he said sitting back down, looking first to make sure Grace was still down the hall in her bedroom. "Gladys ain't what she used to be, but she's still one of the hottest numbers around. I used to stop in at the bowling alley and one thing led to another," he said. "You know how it is. It didn't last long. Shit, she's Dewey's wife for Christ's sake."

"And?" said Michael.

"It lasted long enough so she feels she can call me for favors, which she has from time to time. Gladys likes bad boys. So does that putan, Phyllis she runs with; so it's only natural she hooks up with Eddie Reno when she's out on the town. "

"How long has this been going on?" asked Michael.

"Couple of years, off and on. Dewey ain't himself anymore. Gladys says he can't cut the mustard. The war took it out of him, I guess. Old before his time. She's bored."

"Dewey know any of this?"

"Shit no!" said Puccinelli with emphasis. "He thinks she's a damned saint. Trophy wife, for Christ's sake."

"You're kidding me," said Hunter.

"Got damned blinders on when it comes to that broad."

"So that was the other reason you pulled those arrest reports."

"Two for one," said Puccinelli. "Make Little Sally happy and got Gladys off my back," he said.

"How's she figure in this?"

"Damned if I know," said Puccinelli. "Honest Mike, she hasn't called me on this one."

"So why did you think it would all come out?" asked Hunter.

"Because if he doesn't plead, then there's a trial and who knows what gets said."

"Makes sense. You're still playing all the angles."

"Been doing it for years, kid. Look, I've got to go if I'm going to catch Sally before he hits the sack."

"Thanks Pooch. Keep me informed."

<hr />

When he walked through the door of Gem's flat with the present under his arm, Frank Sinatra was singing *Have Yourself a Merry Little Christmas* in the background. Gem greeted him with a full mouth kiss and a cold beer.

"What's this?" she said staring at the red-papered, silver-ribboned box under his arm.

"A little something for Christmas. You got a tree around here someplace to put it under?"

"Nope," she said grinning. "So let's open it now."

"Really?"

"Oh yeah, really," she said taking his arm and guiding him to the sofa. "Who knows what tomorrow will bring. Tonight's the night."

He watched her carefully remove the ribbon and paper, folding it carefully so it could be used again. Nothing was more Italian. The sight of it relaxed him with many memories of watching Rose Moretti do the same thing and scolding him when he didn't. When she opened the box and lifted the heavy large book entitled "The History of Florence Art" from it, she began to cry. She threw her arms around his neck and nuzzled his ear.

"Thank you, thank you," she murmured.

"I don't know," he answered quickly. "I'm a book store

rat and I remembered seeing it. I thought it was pretty good."

"Shhhh," she said putting a finger to his lips. "It's perfect."

"Then why are you crying?"

"That you could have thought of this with all you have going on," she said dreamily. "It's time for yours," she said getting up and heading for the bedroom.

"Now you're talking," said Michael starting to get up.

"Settle down big boy," she said retreating to her room. A minute later, she emerged with a large 24 by 36 inch rectangle with a beach towel draped over it.

"Excuse the wrapping," she said handing it to him.

He lifted the towel and couldn't believe his eyes. He was staring at an oil painting depicting the back of a football player with his helmet hanging by one hand down at his side, legs apart, staring through the darkened stone archway of what had to be the Roman Coliseum, with the faceless crowd in the filled interior bathed in bright sunlight. Michael could feel the crowd screaming for the player to enter and perform once more and at the same time, the resigned reluctance of the player to enter the arena to his fate, yet, at the same time, Gem had perfectly depicted the emotion that the player, who had been here too many times, but would reluctantly enter once more. It was exquisite in its detail and emotion. The contrast of light and shadows. And then he noticed it, the player was wearing his old number on his old jersey. The player, of course, was him. She had captured his soul, his essence, with the work. He clamped his jaw as tightly shut as he could and looked away.

"What do you think?" she asked anxiously.

He didn't dare attempt to speak. He just nodded his

head and squeezed her hand.

Michael had never slept well. He problem-solved in his sleep. It was common for him to awaken at 3 in the morning as he did that next day, sitting bolt upright in bed.

"I've figured it out," he said to himself.

Chapter 36

"Y ou eat breakfast?" asked Michael into the phone.
"I drink coffee," came the raspy reply.
"Meet me at Sambo's in an hour."

"Is this really necessary?"

"You have no idea," said Michael hanging up.

At five minutes to seven, Dewey Gunnart walked through the glass door of Sambo's restaurant on Center Street in Downtown Stockton and saw Michael sitting in a corner booth, eating a waffle.

"Thanks for waiting, asshole," Dewey said walking up.

"You said you only drank coffee."

"That's just an expression."

"Well, I don't think you're going to want to eat much when you hear me out," said Michael staring across the booth at his aging friend that had already lived more lives than ten normal people.

"Sounds serious."

"It is. Listen Dewey, I wish I could think of any other way of handling this, but I can't. So, here it is. I figured out what Reno's up to."

"OK, what is it?" asked Dewey wondering what all the drama was about, but at the same time, growing very uneasy. It was like looking across at your doctor who was about to go over the results of your blood tests from your routine physical and seeing the unmistakable look of dread on his face.

"Reno has an alibi," said Michael quietly, pushing his half finished waffle aside.

"How the hell can he have an alibi when he ran into the girl's car on the day of the murder in front of God and everybody and they found her wallet in his car?" asked Dewey.

"Because they have the wrong day," said Michael.

"What?" said Dewey.

"Al Williams and Ed Carnes interviewed the farmer that placed the car going into the river at around 3 p.m. on a Friday.

"Yeah," said Dewey. "Are you saying he was wrong?"

"No, he was right. He can time it almost to the minute and he went to a wedding that same day. That's when her car went in the river all right. That's just not when the girl was killed."

"Are you saying Reno didn't do it?"

"Oh no, he did it all right. Just not on Friday," said Michael.

"When then?"

"Thursday."

"How do you know this?" asked Dewey, skeptical, but weary, waiting for the punch line.

"When they interviewed the two kids, one of them was sharp as a tack and the other was immature for his age and unsure of himself. The sharp as a tack kid was an embellisher; didn't see as much as he said. Filled in the gaps. But it fit the profile of what Williams and Carnes wanted to hear. All they needed were eyewitnesses to a car wreck, which they had. The timid kid tried to give them the second guy with Reno and the fact that all of it happened on Thursday, but they figured it for confusion on his part and he backed right down, which is what he always does. So they built their entire case on a Friday, November 10th for the killing."

"What really happened?" asked Dewey quietly.

"Hell, I haven't worked all the wherefores and whereases out yet, but it goes something like this. Reno drives away in her car because they know each other from the Brickworks. Sally Bonaconte's kid, Christopher, who just happened to be with him in his car, drove the Vette away after the accident. Probably out to his place in Linden," said Michael waiving the waitress over for coffee for Dewey and a refill for himself. "Something goes very bad in the car and Reno ends up popping her, probably to shut her up. Now, we're not dealing with the deep end of the gene pool here when it comes to brains, so about the best he figures out is to get Christopher Bonaconte to get rid of her and the car and she never turns up."

"I'm still listening," said Dewey sipping the steaming hot, bitter chain restaurant brew.

"Either Reno or Christopher pick the spot on the river. Destined to fail when the river goes down, but they don't know it. Someone finds it sooner than later by accident. Up until then, Reno thinks he's in the clear. Just get his car fixed. He doesn't know anyone besides Chris that knows about the accident. He didn't see the kids. He's removed her ID from her car just in case. He thinks he's clear of this until the cops show up with a warrant. But then he gets the big break of his life. They picked the wrong day for the murder and builds a case on it," said Michael.

Dewey just stared back, piecing it all together for himself. It all fit.

"So," said Michael. "That's why he doesn't say anything to anybody and he doesn't want AJ cross-examining any of the prelim witnesses. He wants them all under oath, making it to be Friday. No take backs."

"And he's got an alibi for Friday," said Dewey.

"You got it," said Michael.

"Who?" asked Dewey.

"Your wife."

It was almost the lack of outward emotion that surprised Hunter the most. Dewey was a statue. He had just been hit with about the worst news he could receive and he took it like the professional man he was and always had been.

"And you know this how?" he asked Michael with ice in his voice.

"I confirmed it with him at about 5 o'clock this morning."

"How'd you get in the jail at that hour? Never mind, don't answer that," said Dewey.

Michael played it back in his mind how Reno had been unbelievably pissed at having been awakened and literally forced into the interview room to meet with him. And how he just sat there grinning as Michael laid it out for him.

"Congratulations asshole," is all he said, except for the fact that he'd done a little research and he could hire an investigator to serve Gladys with a subpoena, which he would if Hunter gave him any trouble and that the least of Hunter's and AJ's problems would be disbarment if they screwed this up for him.

"I'm sorry Dewey," was all Michael could think to say.

After a moment's reflection, Dewey said, "Not your fault partner. You didn't deal yourself this hand. You just played it. Brilliantly as always, I might add," he said, saluting Michael with two fingers.

Michael sat there stunned at the demeanor and composure of Dewey Gunnart. This was a man thought Michael. A real old school, put-your-ass on the line to save the world without so much as a backward glance, man. He was literally furious at himself for bringing Dewey this pain.

"We're crossing new ground here Mike," said Dewey. "Whether you've thought it out or not, by telling me this, you've committed enough offenses to for sure get your ass disbarred and probably wind up in jail."

"Yeah, I know," said Hunter.

"And I know this has gone against every predatory instinct you have," said Dewey. Michael just sat there.

"So here's the deal," said Dewey. "I'm in this all the way with you. I'm not going to use anything you just told me the way I'm supposed to. So, for sure, worst case scenario, we're cell mates."

"I can live with that," said Michael.

"Do me one favor."

"Name it."

"Does anyone else in the world know about this yet?" asked Dewey.

"No."

"Keep it to yourself for a few days until I tell you."

"You got it."

⸺ ❀ ⸺

Friday, December 22ᴺᴰ, 7:55 a.m.

"You're late," Alice chided him as he walked up and sat down. "And you look like you've been up all night. Probably alley catin' around."

"This and that," answered Hunter.

"More 'this' than 'that', my guess. You're making Jacob's

closing, aren't you?"

"Yes mom."

"Don't mom me," she said. "Boss wants a Reno update and Joe needs some help on a case he's pleading out, and Judge Maggie Adams wants to see you in her chambers this afternoon, but Boss says no."

"I see you've filled in my dance card."

"Vacation's over. Back to work," she said taking a drag on her fourth cigarette of the morning.

"Vacation? Did I miss a meeting?" asked Michael.

"We haven't seen you much, so you must have been lollygagging."

"OK, tell Joe to meet me at Snake's closing. Call the good judge and tell her I'll see her late this afternoon. Tell Boss I've got Reno under control and will brief him later. Got all that?"

"Boss won't be happy."

"He's never happy, but he'll live with it," said Michael getting up.

"Where you going?"

"I've got to change. Busy day."

━━━━●))●━━━━

Friday, December 22ⁿᵈ, 9:45 a.m.

Michael had to hand it to Joe Rocha. He didn't miss much. He painted the two defendants perfectly. Ricardo Sanchez as the shanker, no doubt about it. But D.R. Johnny was the real perpetrator. No way anyone was getting shanked in his immediate presence without his blessing. Good stuff.

It was Robert Stagnaro's turn. He was passionate. He pointed out that no eyewitness had seen his man shank Jason Rich and therefore there was reasonable doubt. Now he could have said all he had to say in five minutes, but he took an hour. The jury was bored. Snake asked for a lunch break and got it. Michael, sitting next to Joe Larsen in the back row, signaled Snake to meet at Xochi's for lunch.

"Let's go," Michael said to Joe, "we'll talk on the way."

It was cold now for Northern California. No one dressed in California for the weather, especially in Northern California. It was like the weather always caught them unaware. Even people that lived there all their lives thought it would be mild. Everyone else did too. It amused Bay Area people to see tourists walking around San Francisco in May in shorts and t-shirts, freezing their asses off in 55 degree weather and wind taking the temperature down another ten degrees. Now, on December 22nd it was cold, so Joe and Michael walked fast.

"Tell me your problem," Michael said.

"I'm not sure I have a problem. Alice thinks I do."

"Well Alice usually knows," Michael said glancing at Joe trying to size him up. New guys with talent can get out of hand quickly.

"I'm pleading this guy to an 11550 and stipulating to a violation of probation ," said Joe.

"And?" said Michael. 11550 was under the influence of narcotics and carried a mandatory 90-day jail sentence as a minimum.

"Well, he gets 90 days on the 11550, which is the minimum," said Joe.

"What's the deal on the stipulation?" asked Michael.

"What?" said Joe just a little irritated with the couple

of hours of wasted time he'd blown sitting around to have this stupid conversation. "No deal. He just stipulates to the violation. He gets 90 days."

"Who's the defendant?"

"Winston Jones."

"Ah, Winston," said Michael. "What's he on probation for?" he asked. "No, let me tell you. Car theft."

"You know Winston then," said Joe smiling.

"Oh yeah. Winnie and I go way back," said Hunter. "I was thinking of naming a bulldog Winston, if I ever got one. After Winston Churchill. But Winnie's ruined that idea for me. It would remind me of him instead."

"Look Mike, I shouldn't be wasting your time with this. If I hadn't been talking about the case in front of Alice, she wouldn't have made me promise to speak to you first."

"You mean waste your time, don't you?" Michael said giving Larsen a rueful glance. When Joe didn't answer, Michael said, "I had a similar situation once . . ." He went on to tell Joe the brief version of the Horst Schultz case.

It had happened a few months after Mike was in the office. He and Harriet Lumpkin were new to their offices and helping out in traffic court. Horst Schultz had been arrested for drunk driving after blowing .12 in the intoxilizer and flunking a field sobriety test. Even though he had a job, Judge Joseph Heinz gave him the public defender when he said he couldn't afford a lawyer. The DA had also filed a violation of probation on a year old wreckless driving where he had been given a $125 fine and six months in the county jail, suspended for three years on condition that he obey all laws and not commit the same or similar offense during the period of probation. Since Judge Heinz had been the judge on the previous case as well, he wanted to make sure Schultz was represented on this case. So Michael got it.

After several meetings with Harriet, the two of them agreed that since he had already spent the night in the county jail when he was arrested that she would reduce the charge to wreckless driving and Horst Schultz could plead guilty to that and admit the violation of probation and receive a $250 fine this time.

Unbeknownst to either Harriet or Michael, a storm of trouble was beginning to build as a result of their poorly worded deal. Horst Schultz was a particularly disagreeable piece of white-Oakie trash whose only claim to fame was that he was a fairly decent auto mechanic when he had a job and was sober and not beating his wife and kids.

Judge Heinz hated drunk drivers and the deals they got just because the DA couldn't afford to waste time giving all of the low lifes jury trials. Every judge had a hot button that veteran lawyers learned not to push. But Michael and Harriet were a long way from being veterans. So when the case was called, a grumbling Horst Schultz approached the rail wearing a greasy oil-stained gray mechanic's jumpsuit with his name stenciled on it. Judge Heinz scowled down from the bench and asked Michael if his client was prepared to enter a plea.

Harriet cleared her throat and stood up and said, "Uh, your honor, the people would agree to reduce the charge of drunk driving to 23103 of the Vehicle Code, wreckless driving, and agree that if the defendant entered a plea of guilty to that charge, he would receive a $250 fine.

"Plea bargains should be approved by the court in advance, Miss Lumpkin," said Judge Heinz.

"I'm sorry your honor. I will remember that," stammered a flustered Harriet Lumpkin.

"The court will agree to the disposition. What about the violation of probation?" asked the judge.

"We'll stipulate to the violation, your honor," Michael interjected, trying to take some of the heat off of Harriet.

"Very well then Mr. Hunter. How does your client plead to 23103 of the Vehicle Code?"

"Guilty, your honor."

"And does he stipulate to a violation of probation as alleged?"

"Yes, your honor."

"Has he signed the rights waiver form?"

"Yes, your honor."

"Hand it to the bailiff please."

Michael handed the signed rights waiver form that he'd hastily filled out for Schultz, indicating that his client understood all of his Constitutional rights and that he was waiving them by pleading guilty and stipulating to the violation of probation. Judge Heinz carefully looked over the form and then looked up at Schultz standing there in front of the rail, displaying as much of an insolent attitude as he could muster under the circumstances.

"Is this your plea Mr. Schultz?"

"Yeah."

"Not yeah, Mr. Schultz. Yes or no please," said the judge.

"Y-E-S-S," said Schultz.

"Very well. On the 23103, the court sentences you to six months in the county jail, suspended for three years on condition that you obey all laws and don't commit the same or similar offense and orders you to pay a $250 fine. How much time will you need to pay?"

"I can pay on Friday."

"Very well. That's the order."

Shultz and Michael began to turn to leave simultaneously when they were stopped in their tracks by the voice of Judge Heinz. "Just a minute gentlemen. We're not close to finished yet."

It was like hearing the rattle of a snake in the brush. You may have never heard it before, but the sound of it gripped you in terror. As it should.

"What's the problem, your honor?" asked Michael as he turned back to face the judge.

"No problem, Mr. Hunter. I just haven't finished sentencing your client yet," said the judge cheerfully, enjoying the moment.

"You haven't?" asked Michael. He glanced over at Harriet Lumpkin and saw from the dumbfounded look on her face that she was as much in the dark as he was.

"No, there's the little matter of the probation violation that he has stipulated to a moment ago."

"I'm lost," said Michael. "You fined him $250."

"That was on the wreckless driving. The probation violation was not made a part of the deal."

"It wasn't?" asked Michael.

"No. If you had wanted to do that, you should have seen me before court as I explained to Miss Lumpkin earlier. You pled your client to wreckless driving with an agreed indicated judgment of a $250 fine. The violation of probation was merely stipulated to and left open for me to decide the sentence, which I am now prepared to do."

"But your honor–," said Michael.

"Mr. Schultz," Judge Heinz said to Horst Schultz, ignoring Michael. "You are no stranger to this court. You drink too much and you drive when you drink. You remember what I told you the last time I saw you?"

Schultz stood still staring malevolently at Michael Hunter, knowing that he'd just been railroaded and tricked by somebody, if not everybody.

"I am ordering that you serve the six months in jail I had

suspended on your previous conviction. Bailiff, take him away."

Ted Bowen, the bailiff, had sensed trouble and discreetly called for some back up which had arrived and was immediately needed as Schultz lunged for Michael, grabbing his throat in a vice-like grip with both of his powerful hands. Hunter fell back over the railing into the lap of a large black woman sitting in the front row behind the rail, who immediately began swatting him in the face like he was a bee that had just landed in her lap. The three bailiffs grabbed Schultz before he could do more damage and led him away screaming at Hunter that he would kill him for this.

When he finished the story, Joe and Michael were standing just outside the entrance to the office on San Joaquin Street, the cold air funneling between the buildings, creating an uncomfortable wind chill.

"What finally happened?" asked Joe.

"Well, a couple of the older guys went over and persuaded Judge Heinz to cut me some slack and he let the asshole out in about three days. They explained to Schultz that he got a great deal because no way the judge would have ever agreed to just a fine and he let it drop."

"So the moral of the story is I'm not as smart as I think I am," said Joe Larsen.

"We never are," said Michael.

"Thanks Mike."

"Don't mention it. Say, listen, there's liable to be some changes around here real soon. I'm going to be gone and so is AJ. I want you to clear these kinds of things with Snake or Jim Harris and even Rothman in a pinch."

"What's going on Mike?"

"Summer camp's over kid," said Hunter walking through the office door.

463

Friday, December 22ND, 12:10 P.M.

Snake slid into the booth just the moment the waiter sat a plate of juevos rancheros in front of him.

"I took the liberty," said Michael raising his bottle of Dos Equis.

"Thanks, I'm starved," said Snake. "What'd you think?"

"Sanchez is cold. He's going down. You've got some work to do. Matador him," said Michael, referring to the technique where 150 pound matadors got charging 1200 pound killer bulls to take the cape as they charged past within an inch of their scrawny bodies.

"I'm taking them through D.R. Johnny's life at DVI first," said Snake.

"You're going to have to give him up as being a big fish aren't you?"

"Of course," said Snake, as if that were a given and didn't need to be discussed, but at the same time, grateful for his buddy's reassurance on the strategy.

"You're the man," said Michael.

"Nothing you couldn't do."

"No," said Michael seriously. "If it was my ass sitting in D.R. Johnny's seat right now, you're the one I'd want closing today. No one else, except maybe AJ."

"The party's about over, isn't it Mike?" said Snake.

"Yeah, buddy it is. This is our last one together, so I'll be there."

Neither had any idea how right they were as they

finished their lunches talking baseball, something that was extraordinarily unusual just before a closing argument in a murder case.

An hour later, in the back row of Judge Strickland's courtroom, Michael Hunter, Joe Larsen, and Alice Benson sat mesmerized by the magnificent closing argument of Jacob Sanderson. He normally looked at his notes constantly when he argued, but not this time. He never lost eye contact with the jury, who stayed with him for the entire two hour ride through D.R. Johnny's life at DVI and its dangers. He laid it in there that the victim, Jason Rich, was not an innocent bystander in all of this and must have done something to bring about his own fate. But he did it ever so delicately, making his point without really making it. Careful to point out that murder was never justified, but that there were also circumstances where the rules about cooperating with the authorities made no sense and that it was up to the jury to see that and to take it into consideration when deciding whether or not to convict someone of murder.

He treated the murder itself perfunctorily as if it were a given that there was only one perpetrator and that D.R. Johnny was not that guy. The aiding and abetting was a treatise on the law, dumbed down for layman without it seeming to have been dumbed down. All-in-all, Michael Hunter considered the performance to be Snake's tour-de-force.

Chapter 37

"How long they been out?" Merlin asked Hunter who just walked through the law library door.

"Little over an hour," answered Michael referring to the jury who was now deliberating the fate of the two defendants.

"What do you need Mike?" Merlin asked.

"Nothing. Party's over," said Michael.

"You figured it out?" asked Merlin.

"Yep, I figured it out and it stinks like hot pig shit."

"Tell me."

"Soon. Not yet. Listen Merlin. This thing's not going to end well. You're taking the bar next year. I want you out of this."

"That bad, huh."

"You have no idea. You forget you ever heard of this case," he said walking back towards the door.

"Where you heading?" asked Merlin.

"Back to see the asshole. I got one more card to play."

"How long you think Strickland will keep them out tonight?" asked Merlin referring to the jury.

"Depends. You know Strickland. He's got nothing else to do, so he thinks no one else does either."

As he walked past the receptionist area, the all too familiar voice of Alice Benson rang out. "Your pop called and so did Lieutenant Puccinelli. They both said it's urgent."

"They'll keep."

"Michael!" she yelled. "Michael Hunter, you come back here!" But she said it to the closing front door.

———✺———

Friday, December 22ND, 5:15 P.M.

Eddie Reno walked through the interview room door and saw Michael Hunter sitting behind the metal table with no file or notes. He was immediately on guard.

"What now?" he asked. "You know all there is to know and there's nothing to talk about."

"You left out a detail," said Michael.

"What's that?" said Reno warily. That had always been his problem. All his life he had been leaving out details.

"You need a murderer and it can't be Christopher Bonaconte."

"That's for sure," said Reno. "Why do I need anything besides Gladys?"

"How'd the wallet get in your car?" asked Michael.

"The murderer left it there," said Reno smiling.

"How'd he get your car asshole?" asked Michael, a bitter biting edge to his tone.

"I don't know," stammered Reno, confused. "What difference does it make?"

"Because the jury might not buy your alibi if it doesn't all add up."

"Oh they'll buy it all right," said Reno feeling more confident.

"Why?"

"Because we were at the Stockton Inn and I know the bartender there and Gladys paid for the drinks with a check, asshole," said Reno sarcastically reveling in the moment and the look on Hunter's face. "As far as the rest of it's concerned, you figure it out. You're the great Michael Hunter. Should be easy. Now don't bother me again, ass wipe," he said getting up and slamming the palm of his hand on the exit buzzer.

Checkmate, thought Hunter.

⸻ ((◦)) ⸻

Friday, December 22ND, 6:15 P.M.

As Hunter pulled the Caddy up in front of the office and parked it in a yellow zone, he saw Alice, Merlin, and Joe pouring through the front door.

"They're back," yelled Alice.

"The jury?" asked Michael.

"They've got a verdict," said Joe.

This was either very good or very bad news thought Hunter as he fell in with them and headed for the courthouse. On a Friday night, after six, there wasn't a soul on the third floor of the San Joaquin County Courthouse, except for inside Judge Harold Strickland's courtroom. The clerk was already seated in her spot to the right of the bench, between the jury box and the judge's bench. Counsel and defendants were seated at counsel table, D.R. Johnny closest to the jury, Snake beside him, Sanchez, and then his attorney Stagnaro. At the next table was Joe Rocha and the investigating DVI officer. There were a few family members of each defendant present scattered around the room. In the back were four burly, well-armed DVI guards and the public defender's crew.

"Make sure everyone gets talked to," Michael said to Joe and Merlin. "Lots to be learned here."

They nodded just as the door to the hallway that led to the deliberation room opened and the jury began filing in, grim-faced. Michael watched their every move, thinking that their look, plus a three-hour verdict on a double defendant homicide with lots to talk about, didn't look good. A moment later, the door to the judge's chambers opened and the black-robed judge emerged and took his seat at the bench. He asked the foreman if they had reached a verdict and was informed that they had and he had his clerk read it.

Standing and clearing her throat self-consciously, she said speaking to D.R. Johnny by his real name, "With respect to count one of the complaint, a violation of 187 of the Penal Code, to wit, murder in the first degree, we the people in the above-entitled cause, find the defendant, Juan Gonzalez, not guilty."

There was a gasp in the court and Jacob Sanderson swivelled his chair around and made eye contact with Michael Hunter, who gave him a slight nod. The investigating officer sat shaking his head in disbelief. D.R. Johnny swivelled his chair and beamed a smile at his family as if to say, "Well, I'll be damned."

The clerk continued, "With respect to count one of the complaint, a violation of section 187 of the Penal Code, to wit, murder in the first degree, we the people in the above-entitled cause find the defendant, Ricardo Sanchez, guilty.

Again a gasp and a wail of "NO" from another part of the courtroom. Robert Stagnaro leaned over to say something to his client who was hunched over reaching for something in front of him. Michael sensed it before he saw it and started to yell, but Ricardo Sanchez beat him to it.

"You son-of-a-bitch. You sold me out," he yelled, half rising.

Everyone in the courtroom seemed to freeze for a half a beat. Snake half turned back to the man yelling next to him, not realizing in time that it was him that he was yelling at. Michael saw the glint of the blade arcing through the air as he screamed, "SNAKE!" Whether snake heard him or not, it was way too late. The blade struck him in the throat before he ever saw it. Blood spurting immediately three feet in the air. Sanchez's arm went back for another strike, but two things happened simultaneously to prevent it. First, a shot rang out as the bailiff fired his .357 magnum in the direction of Sanchez, missing him and fortunately everyone else. The second, was D.R. Johnny throwing himself on top of Snake reflexively protecting him from further harm. The combination of the two caused Sanchez to hesitate just enough to be swarmed by the investigating officer and the four DVI guards. And then total chaos. Women screaming; men yelling; Michael running to the aid of his fallen friend who was now on the floor, already unconscious, a great amount of his life's blood spilled out in a sticky mess in front of him.

Michael covered the pumping wound with his fingers, knowing that the damage was deep and critical. "Get some help!" he screamed.

Friday, December 22nd, 8 p.m. - St. Joseph's Hospital

There, in fact, had been no time for an ambulance and Jacob Sanderson had been transported to the nearest hospital by a sheriff's car where an emergency team was waiting for him and began operating on him immediately.

Snake's wife arrived and collapsed into Michael Hunter's arms, who himself, was still covered in his friend's blood. The boss and everyone else in the office that had gotten the word had arrived at St. Joseph's Hospital and were sitting around in stunned silence waiting for word. The place was swarming in law enforcement personnel, including Stockton Police Department detectives who were taking jurisdiction of the investigation.

Albert Puccinelli came up to Michael and whispered, "We'll need a statement."

"I know," Michael said. "Later."

"Tomorrow will do. I'll call you," said Puccinelli.

"Did you see it Mike?" said Dewey Gunnart who had walked up behind him.

"Yeah, I saw it."

"OK, we'll talk later. Puccinelli and I are going out to the jail to see Sanderson's client before they take him back to DVI."

The surgeon came into the waiting room and asked to speak to Jacob's wife, who grabbed Michael's arm and drug him with her. The doctor was still dressed in his scrub greens with his mask dangling about his neck. He had the grim look of a man about to give bad news.

"Mrs. Sanderson, I'm Dr. Greenberg. I've been operating on your husband. We closed his wounds, but I'm afraid the news is not good." He let that sink in before continuing. "Your husband had his jugular vein nicked by the puncture and he lost way too much blood before we could help him. He's in a deep coma and on a respirator, but I don't expect him to last the night. I'm sorry," he said reaching out to pat her arm.

"Michael," she said tightening her grip on Hunter's arm and staring him in the eye. "Do something."

"Doc, is there anything?" asked Michael.

"Nothing more than we've done. I'm sorry. If it were me, I'd let him go," said the doctor.

"Listen to me doc!" said Michael pushing past Snake's wife to get right in front of the doctor. "Nobody's pulling any plugs around here unless I say so, and I ain't saying so. Not yet. You want something to worry about, you worry about me. I better think everything was done that could have been done or you'll wish it had been. You think I'm kidding, ask around."

"And who might you be?" asked the shaken doctor.

"Your worst freakin' nightmare."

Driving to his flat, Michael suddenly remembered he had a date for dinner at the Hollins'. He was two hours late picking Gem up and he was a bloody mess and an emotional wreck. All hell had broken loose after he had threatened the doctor and the fact that he walked out of the hospital not in custody probably scared Dr. Greenberg more than anything.

He dialed Gem's number the second he walked in.

"I heard Mike. Pop called. You okay? No, of course your not okay," she said. "I called Judge Hollins. He wants you to stop by. He said that he didn't care what time it was."

"I've got to go see my old man," Michael said.

"You want me to come?"

"Why not. We got no unshared secrets anymore. I'll pick you up in half an hour. I got to take a shower."

Forty-five minutes later, they sat down in the Moretti family room. Rose couldn't keep her hands off of Michael.

"You could have been killed!" she wailed. "Those animals. They're not human."

"You can say that again," said Gem.

"Gem," said Big John calmly. "You and Rose get Mike some food."

Gem took the hint and guided Rose into the kitchen where food had been kept warm for hours.

"You okay kid?" asked Big John lighting a Camel. "It's square with Little Sally so long as Chris stays out of it."

"No problem there," answered a weary Michael.

"How's this going down?" asked Big John in a very low voice.

"Real bad," said Michael. He gave his dad the *Reader's Digest* version of what he knew, leaving out names.

"You gonna walk this guy then?"

"He's gonna walk himself."

"They'll blame you."

"Oh, yeah."

"Screw em!" said Big John raising his voice. "Lonigan wants trouble, he'll get trouble."

Michael looked at the old man with new admiration, but he didn't have time to respond because at that moment Paul came barging through the front door with AJ Borelli right behind him. At first, Michael thought they were to-gether for some reason, but, in fact, they pulled up at the same time, both looking for Hunter for different reasons.

Paul took one look at Gem filling the plate in the kitchen and smiled and said, "The Moretti family of the future, I expect."

"Hush," said Rose, hiding a little smile. "Your brother's in with your father. Go pester them."

Paul walked into the family room . "Jesus Christ Mikey, you threatened the life of the best surgeon in town," he said to his brother. "Not your personal best for inappropriate be-havior, but right up there. Oh well, that'll blow over. It's an ill wind that doesn't blow some good. Eddie Reno's dead."

"What?" asked Michael in disbelief.

"You're kidding," said AJ.

"Praise the blessed virgin," said Rose.

"Amen to that, good riddance," said Gem bringing the plate in and setting it on the table in front of Hunter.

"How'd it happen?" asked Michael in a quiet voice.

"Well, it's one for the books," said Paul picking a piece of rigatoni off of Michael's plate. "Your buddy Sanderson's client, D.R. Johnny, cut his throat. It's going down as self-defense. Apparently, Reno attacked him with a shank and Johnny took it away from him and stuck him with it. DOA at county hospital twenty minutes ago."

"Who saw it?" asked Michael.

"Dewey Gunnart and Pooch of all people," said Paul, and looking at Gem, he added, "Oh yeah. I think your old man was there too."

Gem locked eyes with Michael and he stared back at her.

AJ caught it and asked, "What's going on?"

Ignoring him, Michael asked, "How'd they all get in the same place?"

"What difference does it make?" asked AJ. "He's dead and everybody's off the hook the way I see it."

Looking back and forth between AJ and Michael, Paul said, " Gem's Pop was moving Reno somewhere in the jail and Dewey and Pooch had D.R. Johnny in the hallway interviewing him about Sanderson's shanking, and as Reno passed them, he jumped Johnny, but he missed. It was apparently over in two seconds. With Pooch and Dewey calling it, that's the end of it. I'm with Gem. Good riddance."

"Let it go boy," Big John said to Michael. "Eat your dinner before it gets cold."

———— ((•)) ————

FRIDAY, DECEMBER 22ND, 10:30 P.M.

Michael and Gem knocked on the Hollins' door at a little after 10:30 that night. Madge threw her arms around Michael and bear hugged him until he thought a rib would break. She then discarded him in favor of Gem who she took into the bar area, leaving Michael alone with the judge.

"Any word on Jacob?" asked Hollins after they were seated in the kitchen at the breakfast table. Hollins was still wearing the white shirt he had on at work that day, the sleeves buttoned. Michael believed that he did yard work in it.

"The same. They say he is virtually brain dead. We'll see," said Michael.

"Well, at least the rest of this mess is over with," said Hollins.

"Is it?"

"It is if you'll let it be. The death of Reno ends it."

"So you've heard about that?"

"Of course," said the judge pouring them both a cup of coffee.

A little late thought Michael, but so what.

"You hear how it was supposed to have gone down?" asked Hunter.

Hollins nodded as he stirred sugar into the china cup.

"You know it didn't happen that way," said Michael.

"I know that justice was served tonight and that I've been around long enough to have learned not to always question the instrument that dispenses it."

"Maybe your right," said Michael. "I know I broke all of my oaths on this thing."

"You're way too hard on yourself young man," said the judge. "A lot of what happened tonight was done to spare you from what you would have had to do or would have done. And trust me, the world is not out of balance because Eddie Reno is gone."

"Where do I go from here?" asked Michael looking up from his coffee.

Judge Wallace Hollins reached into his suit pants pocket and pulled out a thick envelope and put it on the table in front of Michael.

"You're going to resign from your job and go over tomorrow and clear out your office. I've already called Hawthorne and told him and he agrees. You need some time off Mike. At least six months, maybe a year. Madge and I have put a little Christmas present in here for you and it will tide you over. When you've got things sorted out, you call me and I'll get you started up again."

Chapter 38

Later that night, lying on the couch at Gem's place, both of them unable to sleep, Michael said, "I gave the hospital this number. Is that okay?"

"Of course," she said rolling over and putting her arm across his chest. "Do you believe in God?"

"Yes," he said, "I think I actually do."

"Just like that?"

"Yes. I thought it through a long time ago. No way those eleven guys would have ratted out Jesus that night he was captured, not even knowing his name, and then three days later they decide to spend the rest of their lives preaching the gospel until they're all executed, except for one, unless they saw him alive again. End of story."

"Me too."

Michael could see the money spread out on the end table—one hundred - $100 dollar bills. The Judge and Madge would not hear any arguments about it, so he took the money. It would last him a long time.

"Are you going to Florence with me?" Gem asked him quietly, trying to see his eyes.

"You know I always wanted to see that part of the world. Normandy, D-Day. I want to stand where those pill boxes were at Omaha Beach where our guys came

477

up out of the water. That should have been my time. That's where I should have been. I've always known that."

"Me too."

THE END

Coming Soon:

THE PRIDE

In the second book of Patrick Riddle's Michael Hunter Series, THE PRIDE, Michael Hunter has left the Public Defender's Office behind him and is on his way to Florence, Italy where he hopes to clear his head from the tragic deaths of his best friend and his first real love. He also is there to research his promised second novel after becoming a best selling author regarding the unusual events in his last year at the Public Defender's Office. He doesn't realize that he is being looked after by some very important and somewhat questionable people who introduce him to one of the strangest groups of friends anyone could meet.

There for a rest, Hunter can't help but be drawn into the intrigue of a Mafia Don's family and the wrath of a jealous fiancé. What happens next surprises not only Hunter, but everyone he knows.

CPSIA information can be obtained
at www.ICGtesting.com
Printed in the USA
LVHW030348160721
692784LV00001B/23

9 781977 238115

I dedicate this story to my family and friends, who always cared enough to ask how I was doing on "the book", or whether I'd heard anything yet? They kept the dream alive over all these years. They are my biggest fans, and I thank each and every one of them.

I give special thanks to Christopher McCoy, Ralph "Butch" Keasling, and author, James Alexander Thom for their endless time in making this book a reality.

And lastly, thanks to my loving wife, Colleen. She truly helped me make the final push. Without her support and confidence, my dream would still be just that ...

PROLOGUE

▼

He ran like never before. To where, he didn't know. His eyes searched in all directions. For what, he wasn't sure. Different scenes raced through his mind, an image here, an image there, none remaining more than a brief instant. His heart pounded with fear and his eyes streamed with tears, but why?

The confusing thoughts passed. One of them slowly settled, finally making sense. He crossed a broad expanse of grass and slowed. At last he saw what he was looking for. He was almost there.

He trembled as he approached and fell to his knees, a terrible moan escaping his lips. Gently, he lifted a small, motionless body and hugged it to his chest, crying in anguish. He held the little girl tightly, his face pressed against hers. Instinctively, he rocked back and forth, desperately trying to comfort her.

Through his tears, he saw the dress he'd put on her just that morning. It was one of the presents given to her for her eighth birthday, just yesterday. Her beautiful long hair was pulled back and bundled in the ponytail he'd combed out less than an hour before.

He held her, cradling her head in one hand. Frowning in confusion, he noticed bright speckles of red on her dark skin. They shouldn't have been there. He touched them with his fingertips, smearing the redness across her face. Her eyes were closed. She didn't move. She didn't breathe. He closed his eyes, finally realizing that he was too late. Tears streamed down his face, his mouth voicing a silent scream.

Suddenly, he felt something! He held his breath, motionless ... waiting. The frail body he held took a long shuddering breath. She was alive! His heart exploded with hope as the tiny eyelids fluttered open. Her mouth smiled slightly with recognition, but he noticed only hurt in her eyes. As he watched, tears began to form in them. She looked into his eyes and her tender voice broke the silence. "Daddy, I'm scared. I don't wanna die ..."

He found it hard to speak. His throat tightened. "Its okay honey ... you're gonna be okay ..."

She lifted her tiny arms and hugged him. "I love you, Daddy ..." she said weakly. She was so sweet ... so fragile.

He sputtered, nearly crazy with relief. "I love you too, baby doll ..." He smiled back with the joy that only a father could feel. He cried harder, loving her more than he ever had.

As he stood to carry her, the arms that hugged him so tightly, suddenly fell away. He looked at her precious face again. Her beautiful brown eyes had closed. Her mouth had fallen open and her breath blew upon his face in a long, final sigh. He watched and waited, but another didn't follow. He placed his ear to her chest and for the first time noticed the red wetness there. Desperately, he held his breath again, listening. He heard nothing.

His body jerked as the image disappeared. He took a long, moaning breath, vividly recalling what he had just gone through. It had been the most horrible nightmare he had ever had. He waited for the dream to fade away, as most do, but knowing that it would not. He'd had it far too often. Tears began to form again, where others had just passed. He choked them back, remembering, and wishing that a nightmare were all it had ever been.

Realization set in. He was awake, but when he tried to open his eyes, or move his head ... he could not. His eyes darted about behind closed eyelids, seeing light invading from somewhere. Slowly, he noticed his other senses returning. An immense cold crept into his being, causing him to shiver uncontrollably. Still, hard as he tried, he could not move. Concentrating, determined, he finally managed to force his eyes open. The light was blue, its intensity nearly unbearable. Features around him were blurred. Nothing was sure but the color.

Like a whirlwind, his confusion faded. Everything came rushing back, where he was ... what was happening ... what he was feeling. Through his chattering teeth, he released a sigh of relief. The cold would pass. He knew that now.

Heat began to envelope him. Within minutes, came the grateful pain of sensation, returning to muscles and joints that had been so cold and motionless for so long. How long? It didn't matter. He was alive. The air he took into his lungs was fresh and warm. The shivering would stop. His vision would clear. Everything would be all right.

CHAPTER 1

▼

The golden craft shone brightly under the three small moons of Belaquin. It sped without a sound through the streets of the city of Bentar. As late as it was, there was little or no traffic on the roads. The driver, shadowed by the overhead street lamps, maneuvered the hovercraft with precision. Its gyros whined in protest as he rounded each corner. The car approached the base of a massive building and came to a stop before a large alcove door. Punching in a code on a small dash panel, he watched as the door opened. A moment later, he steered the car into an elevator leading to the parking garage above.

Gary Kusan closed his weary eyes as the elevator rose. Recalling the days' events, a smile, impossible to suppress, spread over his face. He thought of the packet lying on the seat beside him. It contained a treasure; golden emblems he had dreamed of for so long. After months of impossible training and undaunted determination, he had attained his ultimate personal goal. He was now a member of Belaquin's Fighter Force. He was to be assigned to a gold raider squadron, designating him as one of the top of his class. It was the most prestigious position possible for any pilot. Although only an Ensign, his gold status demanded respect, even by higher officers.

He sighed in disgust at the slowness of the lift. He was anxious to speak to one person in particular, his closest friend, Kahn Bengal. Kahn, twenty-seven years old, was also a low level officer, carrying the rank of first lieutenant. He had gone through the same training five years earlier, and more than anyone, would appreciate Gary's accomplishments, and of course, would take full credit for it. Kusan knew he would never have flown a raider if it had not been for his friend's interminable urging and perseverance. Others played a part as well; his parents, friends, and once he enrolled, the Republic's Fleet Commander himself. Many of the instructors at the Academy bragged that he was one of the finest battle navigators they had ever seen. He remembered the words his own unit commander had said to him earlier that day. "You may be the youngest to ever graduate from this academy, but you are one of the best. Your skill is extraordinary. You should be a great asset. We are proud and privileged to have you in this service." The words had repeated a dozen times since his graduation, now only a few hours behind him.

His Commander's words were accurate, as well as warranted. Gary was young. Most of his fellow cadets were at least two years older than he. The maturity he may have lacked in age was made up for with his natural ability. His unnatural knack of solving problems in the simulation crafts had caught the instructor's attention, encouraging them even more to try and catch him off guard. They seldom succeeded. This, in turn, only strengthened his confidence and desire to be the best.

The successful culmination of his efforts, brought forth by this self-confidence, was not a common occurrence in his life. The confidence had not always been there. His adolescent years had been ruled by insecurity. In the tougher times, he often relied on the short-term solution of running away; at least in his mind. He had no siblings to confide in. His parents were always there for him, but they couldn't fathom the monumental challenges of a young mans life. They didn't have all the answers. Looking back now, he understood. It was his first time as a kid, and their first time as parents. Their solution to each of his problems was that he would grow out of them in time. It took forever, but they proved to be right. He finally passed through the incurable sickness of puberty. His father was hard nosed, demanding, and precise in his ways. By the time his only son joined the academy, he would be no stranger to discipline.

Gary, at twenty years old, stood an inch shy of six feet. He had a stocky, muscular frame and a kind, sociable demeanor. His cool blue eyes reflected the soul of a man, where a fragile, frightened boy had once existed. As an influential young man, he had been a perfect candidate for the Republic. He joined the academy at Bentar, the capital city of Belaquin, the most populated planet in the system. It held the reputation of being the toughest school. It had been a dream he thought would never offer him an opportunity, let alone come true.

Training had been long and agonizing. On the outside, he kept his composure, while his psychological and physical aspects were tested far beyond the limits he thought he could endure. Unconsciously making the right moves and decisions had given him strength, but more than that, the admiration he received from the other pilots in training, proved to be enough.

He closed his eyes as the elevator continued upward, imagining battles not yet fought. He could see himself flying through space, engaging the enemy. He felt the intense heat from his ship's blazing gun-ports. Explosions of light filled the void around his raider, rocking it from side to side as the enemy's fire creased the hull. A passing ship suddenly exploded directly above him, filling his cockpit with brilliant light as the vessel disintegrated. The vision faded, but the bright light remained. He opened his eyes. The elevator had stopped its ascent and the door had opened, revealing the well-lit parking garage. He was unsure of how long he had sat there daydreaming, but after a quick glance around, he saw no spectators. He steered the car clear of the elevator and moved down a ramp into another section. Soon after, he entered a parking module and switched off the engine. The craft settled gently to the floor as the magnetos reversed. With the low hum gone, the garage was completely silent. Exiting, he began walking, his footsteps echoing loudly. He entered a smaller elevator, which took him some twenty levels higher. Down another corridor, he arrived at his corner apartment, 3535.

"Open up, Jana. I'm back," he said quietly. The door slid aside. As he entered the dark room, the lights automatically came on at a low level.

"Well, you seem pretty happy. Tell me about it?" The voice emanated from all around him. It was feminine, friendly, and soothing.

Gary couldn't help but smile. "I got it. I can't believe it, but I got gold."

The voice that responded seemed filled with genuine excitement. "That's great! Congratulations! Do you want to celebrate?"

"Why not," he answered. "How about the usual?"

"You got it." The feminine voice belonged to one of the most sophisticated home computer systems available. Jana could perform various duties, ranging from complicated meal preparation to casual conversation. The owners, at their own discretion, could add a variety of character traits, accents, and other more personal attributes. Gary was lucky enough to receive the deluxe package free with his monthly rent. He had made only a few modifications to the system. Apparently, he and the previous owner had shared the same lifestyles.

Gary touched a switch, opening the window panels outside his living room. The view was spectacular. From his lofty vantage point, he could see nearly the entire city. There were eleven other structures identical to the one he lived in. The complexes were situated to form a huge circle, enclosing much of the city within their boundaries. The interior of the circle was over six miles across. In its center was the Interplanetary Space Port, one of the busiest transportation hubs in the Belaquin system. The port, easily visible from where he stood, appeared bathed in sunlight.

"Jana, can you get a hold of Kahn for me, please?" As he watched the traffic at the port, he thought ahead to the morning. The new graduates from the academy were to meet there. It would be the starting point of their first tour of duty. The planet Touchen would be their destination. On it was housed one of many military bases in the Belaquin system. From there, they would travel to and board the star cruiser, Aquillon. She was the largest ship ever built by human hands, and housed the most sophisticated advancements in technology. The Aquillon, a Searson Cruiser, was named after the man who blueprinted her. She was to be the first of many. The engineers had begun work nearly twelve years ago, and had just recently completed construction. It was truly sad that the man who had dreamt the dream had died two years before. The ship designs and capabilities were unparalleled, but it existed for only one purpose; it was a ship of war.

Warships had been common throughout human history, but not one such as this. The Aquillon represented a new breed of vessel. A new breed needed as a deterrent against new opposition. In the last fifty years, only one force had threatened, but it threatened the future of the entire race. They called them Thalosians, an alien race from a planet far away from their own. In the past, human enemies had been predictable, but this enemy was far from human. Neither they, nor their actions, had been anticipated. The ill preparedness of the Belaquins at the first meeting proved nothing short of disastrous.

Gary's gaze moved from the familiar view below, upward to the blackness of space. The coming trip there would not be his first, but he looked forward to this one more than any other. To actually serve as a pilot on the Aquillon was a great honor. Thus far he had seen only photos of the ship. To see it first hand would be incredible.

"Here's your drink." Jana informed him.

He took the glass from the wall dispenser, marveling at the blue liquid within it for a second and downed it in one gulp. He closed his eyes as he savored the taste. It was non-alcoholic, but it instilled an addictive lift, a strange rush that the advertisements had trouble describing. "I'll take another one of those if you don't mind."

"No problem. I've contacted Kahn for you." she answered. "He was asleep."

Gary chuckled to himself. They had met each other long before the academy. Kahn was eight years older and he considered him as the brother he never had. He used to follow him to Republic recruiting seminars, and was envious, as well as saddened when his older friend finally signed. At the time he was much too young to follow him, but finally, the day came, and he didn't hesitate. He didn't know it, but leaving home proved to be the hardest thing he had ever done.

Upon review of Gary's scores on the entry exams, Kahn, then an assistant instructor was authorized to approach him about pilot training. The school had always had a standing minimum age requirement, but Kahn had acquired some high connections. He had become an outstanding pilot in his time at the academy. His skill in the raiders was frightening. He knew most of the instructors well, and was especially close to the Fleet Commander, Leon Haute, who gave the final consent. The exception was made, and could continue to be made in the future, if the situation warranted. Kahn took Gary under his wing during the first several months, and no doubt, made a huge difference. The way of life at the academy demanded self-discipline and sacrifice. He prepared his younger friend for that, but during that time, had taught him much more than protocol and procedure. Kahn used the opportunity to give direction for real life. During that crucial period, Gary did a lot of growing up. The boy matured into a man. He owed his friend everything.

Gary was ecstatic when the powers that be saw fit to station him in Kahn's untested squadron. His friend had more than four years experience as a pilot, but had never seen actual combat. Few active duty pilots had.

Kahn was easy-going. Nothing bothered him. He respected authority for the most part, but his fun loving habits and over zealous mouth often got him into undesirable situations. Though standing an imposing six feet, four inches and weighing two hundred twenty pounds, at times, even that wasn't enough. He was good-looking man; blond haired and blue eyed, but had never been married. He had few admirable skills, but luckily, he had found his given strengths in the pilot's seat. His past was colorful, if not troublesome, but lately his behavior had calmed considerably. Pressure from his younger protégé had brought much of the change about. They had given each other a great deal more than friendship.

As Gary reached for the second glass, a viewing screen on the table came to life. After a few seconds of unrecognizable sounds, he was rewarded with the sight of his friend's unshaven face. Kahn's voice was gruff. "This better be good. You know I need my beauty sleep."

"I think it's a little late for that." Gary commented.

"So what happened?"

"I'm supposed to report with you to the space port at zero nine-hundred hours tomorrow morning."

"I told you, didn't I?" His voice was obviously pleased. "Damn, why do they want us there so early?" He suddenly became more awake, rubbing his eyes and whining in realization. "Wait a minute! I'm not due back til tomorrow night! What the hell?"

"Oh ... well, you're gonna love this. The last twelve hours of your shore leave has been canceled per orders of Commander Haute." Gary said, smiling.

"Aw dammit ..." Kahn growled. "This is the last break I'm going to get for a while. I had plans." He hesitated. "You know, you could just tell them you couldn't find me."

"Yeah right, I don't think they're doing it just for the hell of it. Something's up. They're re-calling all pilots off leave."

Kahn sighed. There was no use ignoring the message, they'd find him one-way or the other. Besides, if there was a possibility of real action coming, he definitely wanted to be a part of it. He'd waited for it too long already. "So, you didn't show your ass today?"

Gary shook his head, remembering the tests. "It was a bitch. I think I emptied a gallon of sweat out of my suit."

"Are you sure it was sweat, with the entire commission breathing down you neck?" Kahn asked. "I wish I could have been there to see you squirm, but you know the rules."

"You could have got in; you were just too hung over. One thing pissed me off though. Lankford scored the highest in the simulator, and no one said anything to him except me." Gary related.

"You know he was just lucky and so did they. Every dog has his day." Kahn knew his friend felt sorry for the other pilots. "Besides," he added, "Hearing a compliment from you was a good thing for him. I'm sure he appreciated it."

For a moment, nothing was said. Gary just stared into the monitor, his thoughts elsewhere. Kahn spoke again. "Well shit ... what time are you picking me up in the morning?"

"I'm picking you up? Since when?" Gary stammered.

"Well, a police drone got me last night on the Dermatt freeway. Bastard took my last credit. I won't be driving anywhere for the next six months." he whined.

Gary found this latest turn of events amusing, no credits, and no car. His friend and mentor might be an expert in a raider, but on the ground he was a maniac. "I told you, man ..." he started. "It's gonna cost you a little bit this time, isn't it?"

Kahn shrugged. "Maybe my wallet, but the only thing we'll be in for the next few months will be a raider, and I sure as hell don't need credits for that."

"You're damn lucky he didn't take you in to be tested ..." He hesitated, knowing his advice was futile. "All right man, I'll pick you up around eight. I'm going to bed. See you in the morning."

The screen went blank.

Gary fell onto the couch, elevating it so he could again watch the city below. He thought of his home and family, hoping to fill his dreams with both. Jana dimmed the lights as he closed his eyes and drifted off.

It was seven twenty-eight when he again opened his eyes. He rose and grimaced from a twinge of pain in his neck and head. He must have slept wrong. It wasn't any way to start this day. Fumbling in the bathroom drawer, he found a bottle and took a couple of the pills. The brand was cheap and he hated the bitter taste, but it worked as good as the expensive stuff he had tried. A cold shower left him refreshed. By the time he dressed, his pain was gone.

The city was alive with Belaquins rushing to their duties. The city's population doubled every workday about the same time, which unfortunately, was at that moment. He didn't drive carelessly as he had the night before. The police drones were out in force during the day. Lawbreakers always had a credit or two taken from them, if stopped. There were no warnings issued, no arguments listened to, and no bribes accepted. Kahn could attest to that.

He wished Kahn had been a little more careful, even though he had never been before. Why start now? Still, if his mentor wasn't so irresponsible, he could have maybe slept a little longer this morning.

Kahn resided in a small duplex near the spaceport. He was the sole occupant of the building at that time. The property had potential to be nice if taken care of, but its aesthetic effect had much to be desired.

As he pulled up to the front drive, he had to dodge a crumpled trashcan, left over from one of Kahn's late night or early morning arrivals. Other litter lay scattered across the unkept lawn. Gary recognized the same debris that he had seen last week. Shaking his head, he walked to the door. As he rang the bell, he hoped it would not prove to be Kahn's wake up call, as it so often was. He heard the door unlock and he pushed it open. The house was dark. "Are you awake?" Gary called.

"I'm up. Awake is debatable," answered a grumpy voice.

Gary stepped down into the main room. The mess was incredible. Clothes were strewn everywhere, even under the rug. "Do you ever do laundry, Chief?"

"If I run out ..."

Gary warily entered the kitchen. Dirty dishes were stacked a foot high. He had a whim and opened one of the cabinets. A couple of glasses and a plate were there. He nodded in understanding.

"Guess what time our bank opens?" Kahn's voice, clearer this time, came from the bathroom.

"Nine, I think." Gary guessed.

"Wrong!" Kahn yelled. "They open at seven. Some son of a bitch called me this morning, telling me I had to drop off a payment today. It was one of those … or else calls."

"What'd you tell him?"

"I said no problem. He said the tellers open at nine."

"We have to be at the port by nine!" reminded Gary.

"Well, he doesn't know that, and by the time he figures it out, where will we be?"

Gary shook his head, knowing it would catch up to him eventually. "Are you gonna eat anything?" He asked. He opened the refrigerator. What he saw inside answered his own question. "On second thought, maybe not," he mumbled under his breath.

Kahn entered the room, fully dressed in a Republic uniform. "No. Go ahead if you want to."

"No, that's okay." Gary was shockingly impressed. "Damn man, are we having an inspection?" Kahn, for once, really looked first-rate. The clothing he wore had definitely not come from the floor.

"You want a beer?" Kahn asked.

Gary visibly winced. He knew the inquiry was serious. "You don't have any," he answered.

"Yeah, I do. They're under the sink."

"Hot beer … you've gotta be kidding?" Gary had no desire to see what he had eaten the night before.

"You wimp," Kahn mused, "You ready?"

They drove to the spaceport, arriving a few minutes after eight-thirty. As they walked through the terminal, Kahn silently rehearsed what he would say to the new pilots. He had received official notification of his new orders the night before, after talking to Gary. He was to escort a group of men to the military base on Touchen. En-route, he was to brief them on what to expect once they reached their destination. The procedures were routine, but needed explained nevertheless. Some seemed trivial; after all, the pilots he would be addressing weren't kids. Each was between twenty-one and thirty years old, with the exception of Gary.

As of this year, with the new retirements there would be no veteran combat pilots on active duty. The hands on experience, gained from past decades when confrontations were common, would no longer be within the raider cockpits.

Each year, ten pilots were selected from each academy to fill top positions in the Republic Fighter Squadrons. One man from each of those ten earned a seat in a gold raider. The gold pilots were the best of the best. When needed, they would be the first to see action.

The other nine graduates from Bentar's school were found waiting patiently. Within minutes the men boarded the transport ship and were strapped in for take off. It lifted off quickly and smoothly. After a few moments, the safety belt sign went off.

Kahn took an uneasy breath and rose from his seat to face the others. He had not made a speech in a long time. He recognized each of the men before him, but he was still uncomfortable. "Okay guys, listen up. I'm not good at this kind of shit, so bear with me. My directions are to brief you on your first assignment. We're headed for Touchen. This you already know. Some of you may even know why. It's not as big a secret as it's supposed to be." He noticed some nods from the group. "We'll land at a place called the ice box, Touchen's main merchant trading center. It's not the greatest place around. I'm sure you've heard about it."

There was a chuckle or two from the listeners. "As I was saying, on the surface it's a simple merchant town. People live and work there. Traders come from everywhere to do business. The bars and sex shops never close. My advice is not to go there. Whatever you can think of, they thought of it a long time ago. No matter how bad ass you think you are, they're badder."

The men listened, each knowing where he was heading next. The information was to secret, but they'd heard about it in the academy. "Beneath the ice box is where were going. Deep enough to stay undetected by sensors is our main military station. It's not our largest base, but probably our most vital. All of our other stations connect there in one way or another. Almost all of our conventional weaponry is manufactured there, as well as the new prototypes. Some civilian companies we have contracts with are set up to manufacture their products there. You will no doubt have contact with some of these civilian counterparts. As always, you will share no military oriented information with non-military personnel. Common sense stuff, right?" Kahn felt that he had made that point clear enough for the men. "There are many entrances and exits in the ice box and the surrounding countryside. You will learn where some of them are, but not all. The locations and codes you will be issued are strictly classified. You will only be able to use the specific codes assigned to you. Codes will be encoded into your wristbands, and you better encode them into your brains as well. If anyone else is caught using your code, you will lose your pilot status." He paused, hoping his words were being paid attention to. The admonition was warranted. The Republic was stringent with their security. They had no choice. At the start of the Thalosian War, security had been negligible at best. Critical areas succumbed under minimal pressure. The Thalosians were intelligent, methodical, and thorough. Mistakes had been made. They would not be made again.

Kahn continued, "When we arrive at the base, you will receive your standard issue kit; a lot of crap you'll never use. After initial briefings, we'll go the hanger level, where you will be joined in holy matrimony to your assigned ships. Later, you'll be transferring them to the Aquillon. Landing procedures are similar to the ones you learned at the academy, so there shouldn't be any problems, right?" He didn't really expect an answer. "I know none of you have ever been aboard the Aquillon. You may have seen photos or film of the construction phase, but they can't do her justice. I'm fortunate enough to have been there and I've never seen anything like her. She's unbelievable. Imagine walking for a week and not seeing every room on the ship." Open mouths and raised eyebrows followed the remark. "There are four-thousand separate compartments. Even with a major breach of the main control deck, the ship can still maintain operational status. With one-hundred percent hull integrity, even damage from a direct strike would be minimal."

Moving at one-tenth the speed of light, the transport ship moved quickly through space. Soon it approached a region filled with what looked like white gleaming clouds. The clouds consisted of ice and dust particles thought to be remnants from an ancient comet. They filled the space and atmosphere around Touchen, maintaining a thick shield, blocking out nearly all sunlight. It left the planet a gloomy, inhospitable place. On the surface, ice storms were frequent, and nighttime temperatures, dropping at times to three digit negatives, made the globe virtually uninhabitable. Temperatures on a warm day seldom reached zero. Vegetation was nonexistent, offering no color whatsoever to its desolate landscape. The abundance of unique ore and mineral deposits needed by the Republic had initially been the only positive aspect the planet had to offer.

As the cloud was entered, the starry view was interrupted. Finally the curve of an enormous sphere became visible through the blinding shroud. Kahn confirmed it to be Touchen. As the men watched, another object materialized from the miasma, silhouetted against the dirty white background below. All were speechless as they recognized the object as their new duty station.

Gary stared silently, unable to grasp the enormity of the ship. A thousand pin-points of life escaped the hull, marking the decks and decks of life within.

Aquillon was indeed one of a kind. Nothing like her had ever existed before. The discovery of unlimited sources of the needed resources on Touchen had made the ships construction site elementary. The countless parts to the ship had been manufactured on the planet surface and assembled in space. After incalculable man-hours, the ship finally became the magnificent sight they now looked upon.

The Aquillon did not initially give the impression of a warship. With her sleek lines, she resembled a passenger vessel. Her appearance was misleading. The ship generated enough firepower to obliterate the planet it orbited. Hundreds of more personal weapons were also at her disposal, namely the raiders, whose collective power was considerable as well.

Gary stood in admiration as he marveled every line. He felt drawn to the vessel. Floating only a few kilometers away, he felt as though he could reach out and touch the smooth shimmering hull.

Kahn's voice broke the extended silence. "She is eleven-hundred meters in length and has seventy-one levels. Ship's complement is fifteen hundred, without the air wing. She can reach light speed in less than a minute, and can sustain it for five years without reconfiguration."

Time was a factor, so the preliminary tour was short. Soon after entering the planets atmosphere, they caught sporadic glimpses of light beneath them. It was their first look at the merchant town, the icebox. It was hard to discern anything due to the snowstorm outside, but they could tell the range of the settlement was considerable.

Gary felt a cold chill, even though he knew there was no chance that the icy air outside could enter the airtight shuttle. He wondered what true cold felt like.

The shuttle landed without incident. The storm they had just passed through was miraculously gone, leaving the air crisp and clear. Heavy coats and headgear were lent to each man before exiting. When the transports doors opened, a sharp bite of freezing air caught them full in the face. The cold was deep and would have brought down any unprotected man in seconds.

Kahn hastily ushered them towards the nearest building, a hundred steps away. Even before they could complete the short walk, another ice storm had descended. As they entered the shelter, the relative warmth embraced them. Even though they had only been exposed for seconds, the men shook uncontrollably, shocked at the hostile conditions they had just witnessed. A thin sheet of ice covered each of them.

Kahn removed his hood, shaking his head in amusement, even though in mild distress as well. "That's a good day guys. Most arrivals have to go through this. Departures leave from below, through secret exits."

After shedding the extra clothing, they made their way to another section of the arrival station. Kahn led them down a dead end corridor and at no particular place, stopped and removed an object from his vest. It appeared to be shaped like a pen, long, cylindrical, plain looking. He held it up, explaining. "Remember what I said about personal codes and entrances? Well, this is one of mine." He faced the wall and inserted the cylinder into a small half-inch diameter port. Within seconds, a section of the wall slid aside to reveal an elevator. "All officers and pilots carry these. They're used in a variety of security sections here and aboard the Aquillon. If you try to use it somewhere you shouldn't, you'll lose it. Once your briefings are over, you'll get your own."

The group was soon on their way beneath the icebox.

The reverberation of machinery, tools, and hundreds of human voices joined together to greet the new arrivals. The men seemed to go unnoticed as they ambled into the vast underground room. Kahn had to shout above the din. "We're five-hundred feet down. This is one of the production areas. They can manufacture everything we need here. Some of the Aquillon was built in this room."

The Aquillon was massive, but the last statement was totally plausible. Gary looked about the man-made cavern. The opposite wall stood two hundred meters away, with the ceiling a hundred or more feet high. Despite the excitement around him, he managed to notice a familiar face in the crowd approaching them. He nudged Kahn and gestured toward the future Commanding Officer of the Aquillon.

Leon Minden Haute had spotted the group of pilots and headed in their direction. He'd fully expected a late arrival, but Lieutenant Bengal had surprised him, at least on this occasion.

Haute, now in his mid fifties, was handsome and exceptionally fit for a man his age. His hair held more salt than pepper, but as long as it stayed, he didn't care what color it was. He had earned much respect during his thirty years in the Republic. He had been a distinguished pilot during the Thalosian War, a terrible time in Belaquin history. In this time he had nothing to prove and nothing to answer for. His heroism had done both long ago.

As he approached, he noted their youthful, uneasy faces. "Scared to death." he chuckled, just as he had been. He still knew the feeling well. It was a constant companion. He returned Kahn's salute, and then grasped his hand. "Good to have you back, Lieutenant? How was your leave?"

"Brief, Commander … very brief."

"Well, maybe when this is over, you can take the rest of it." Haute turned to the younger man beside him. "Gary Kusan, congratulations. It's nice to finally see you in a Republic uniform."

"Thank you, Commander. I hope I can fill the shoes too."

"I have no doubt that you will."

Kahn introduced the remaining men to their superior, a somewhat discomfited task due to the fact that he barely knew some of them himself. They talked on for a few moments and then, at Haute's bidding, a deck officer directed them to the fitting room. Once there, the men were measured for their new flight suits. Upon completion, a walking tour of the subterranean base began, led by a very captivating pair of tour guides. Gary, instead, embarked on a personal tour with Kahn.

He witnessed an incredible array of industrial, as well as scientific breakthroughs in machinery, each more astonishing than the last. Kahn assured him that he had seen nothing yet. To him, the tour went by in the blink of an eye. In reality, it had taken over an hour.

The time to depart grew near. The men met in the raider docking area, where for the first time, they saw their raiders. The ships were large, roughly thirty-five feet long by twenty wide and eight tall. Wide gold striping lined the shiny black exterior as designation. There were equipped with four ports of lasers, two on each wing. Power to the weaponry was inexhaustible, regenerated by the engines themselves. Although not standard, each ship could be fitted with eight Telanaar warheads to take care of larger needs.

The name given Kahn's raider, Gold Raider One, or GR1, began the numbering of the new squadron. Gary's was GR2, and so on down through the remaining ships. A total of thirty gold raider pilots would serve aboard the Aquillon, making up three separate squadrons. These pilots constituted fifteen percent of the compliment on board.

Kahn, assisted by a technician, strapped in. While he waited for the other pilots, he went through a routine systems check. When finished, he switched on his helmet intercom and spoke to the others. "This is GR1. You should have your checks nearly done. We're just waiting for clearance to lift off. Listen up. I don't care how good you think you are, keep an eye on your auto scanner and flight indicators. If you run into any trouble, shut down your main thrusters and head for open space. Establish and maintain visual with your wing man. Stay in contact with him as long as you're out. Don't crowd up. There's plenty of room, so take advantage of it. Just keep your heads on straight." Even as he said it, Kahn shook his head at his own hypocrisy, recalling his own driving record.

Finally, they received a green light. Great bay doors at the end of the hanger deck opened. It revealed a huge corridor, inclining upward and disappearing into darkness. It measured fifty meters in width, plenty large enough for two raiders to launch side by side. Tow vehicles pulled the first two ships to their launch positions. One by one, the raiders entered the tunnel.

Kahn and Gary emerged first from the planet's surface into a horrendous blizzard. Flying blind, they gained altitude rapidly, and a moment later, passed through the atmosphere into open space. Other ships followed close behind.

GR One broke the radio silence. "If everything's okay, you guys can break formation." An afterthought followed. "Believe it or not, some dumb shits have run into each other up here, so please don't add to the list …"

The ships spread out into clear space and soon were lost against the backdrop of stars. Gary stayed beside Kahn, who asked him to switch to a different channel to escape the other pilot's chatter. "How do you read, Chief?" asked Gary.

"Just fine number two, how's she handling?"

"Great. She feels good." Gary tried a well-practiced spiral. "Better than the trainers I've been stuck in."

"Well, get used to it. You may be strapped in there a lot the next few months. It'll get old, I promise you."

Gary couldn't even imagine it. "It won't be that bad." He paused. "Did Haute say anything about what's going on?"

"Well, not really, but someone else said something about trouble on some outpost."

"What kind of trouble?" Gary asked.

"Don't know. If we end up going, I know one thing. It's way the hell out there. It'll be a two or three week trip," remarked Kahn.

Gary whistled. "Jesus, that's pretty damn far out."

"No shit … too far! We don't have many long-range teams out right now. If it's the one I'm thinking of, it's not too far from the Thalosian system. If it's them, we could be in a real shit storm when we get there."

Gary frowned with trepidation. He recalled the battles he had imagined; remembered the anticipation of firing at an actual enemy. At the academy he had tried to treat the simulations as seriously as possible, but the emotion had never been there. There had never been any risk, and that fact, above all, was foremost in his mind. This would be the real thing … real battles … actual life and death.

Would he be able to handle it? For the first time in his life, he began to feel something he had never felt before.

CHAPTER 2

▼

Commander Haute's private shuttle left Touchen earlier than the raiders. Now on the Aquillon's main control deck, he watched as his new pilots arrived one by one. He listened intently to hangar bay traffic as they systematically went through docking procedures.

"Bay door opening."

"Bring up pressure in number fourteen vent."

"Blue Nine, turn starboard point seven degrees, and get your nose up a little. Okay, that's good. Five seconds, four, three, two, one, locking and holding."

One voice, recognized by Haute, came over the air. "Red Three, Blue Four and Blue Ten are on board. Close bay one door. All remaining ships redirect to bay area two. Repeat ... all ships report to bay area two."

Realizing something was awry, Haute spoke into the intercom. "What's the problem down there, Lemane?"

"It's not serious, Commander. There's a loss of pressure in one of the locking anchors. We'll check it out, but we don't think it's strong enough to support a ship right now."

Haute switched off the noisy channel without answering and turned to the navigation station. "When all pilots are on board, log in the preplanned course and initiate." Turning to leave, he had an afterthought. Switching communications again to hanger bay two, he left instructions for Gary Kusan and Kahn Bengal to report to his cabin as soon as they arrived.

Haute welcomed the stillness of his cabin. Removing his uniform jacket, he sighed deeply and laid back on his bed. His eyes wandered the room and finally rested upon the solitary picture above him. The frame held a photo of a young woman. Looking into her eyes, his thoughts filled with warm memories from one of the happiest time of his life. She had been his wife. They had spent seven wonderful years together.

He'd lost Sarah long ago, but not enough to allow him to forget the pain that had engulfed him. His thoughts settled on one terrible day ... her last day. He had been on duty on Touchen when it had begun. The Thalosians arrived undetected on Belaquin before dawn, while most of their unsuspecting prey still slept. Their plan was flawless. They struck the larger cities at the same time, taking out communication satellites, spaceports, and visible military bases, rendering the planet nearly defenseless.

It was late morning before any help from Touchen could arrive, and it proved all too late. Devastation lay everywhere, fires burned unchecked within the cities. Thousands of persons had been killed, but the horror didn't end there. Thousands of survivors were taken prisoner and were gone. Some of the smaller alien ships were still near enough for the Republic forces to overtake. The Thalosian attackers were far less skillful than the human pilots, but they were much more numerous. That difference proved too much to overcome. The list of human dead grew even longer.

Haute, then in his early twenties, did not participate in the initial retaliatory strike on the invaders. His first and most important duty was to his wife. He was not a religious man at that point in his life, but he uttered many prayers during the unmercifully long trip from Touchen to Belaquin.

Soon after his arrival in Bentar, he found that his prayers had been in vain. Sarah was missing. His home was a smoldering mass of rubble, but he had no idea if she had been there at the time of the attack. He had one wish ... a simple hope that he would just find her. His greatest fear was that she had been taken captive, as many others had been.

He searched for what seemed forever, finding only disappointment and frustration. He received the call on his third sleepless night. It summoned him to one of the many recovery buildings. He had wondered if knowing could be half as bad as not knowing. At least in the latter, there had still been a glimmer of hope. Once there, he was directed to a small still form, lying on a cot in a room filled with a hundred more. With trembling hands, and tears in his eyes, he hesitantly turned down the sheet.

His search was over. His question was answered.

He stayed alone with her for an hour. He held her, his cheek against hers, the warmth of his heart and his soul falling onto the skin that he had not felt for so long, and would never feel again. He spoke softly, telling her everything he had hoped to over their life together, over the many years they had dreamed of. Lastly, he told her how much he loved her, how much he would miss her, and how very sorry he was that he wasn't there. Finally, he tore himself away, kissing the eyes and lips he wished would see and speak just one more time.

His life was at an end. There was no understandable reason to prolong it after she died, but something he had promised long ago forced him to fight above the incredible grief. He had to live for both of them, to keep her alive inside of him … forever. As long as she was in his heart, she would never truly be gone. He had only one hope to hold on to … a belief that they would be together again someday. His love for her in life had been so strong that it would not die. He would live for her. It was enough.

Even after so long, he still had trouble quelling the loneliness. Sometimes the tears came, but after so much time, they didn't come as often. Guilt haunted him as well … the thought that if he had been with her, then she might still be alive. He had even more trouble putting that thought behind him.

His gaze fell from the portrait. Rising from the bed, he walked to a table and switched on a small viewing screen. He studied it for several minutes before the door buzzer upset him.

Gary and Kahn had arrived, attired in their standard ship uniforms. The two of them entered. There was no salute necessary, not as long as the ship was underway. Haute smiled at the younger of the two and asked, "Do the shoes fit?"

Gary laughed, remembering.

"Have a seat, gentlemen." His smile quickly faded. He turned the viewing screen toward the wall and transferred its images to it. A star chart appeared, filled with hundreds of points of light. One stood out from the others. "I know you're wondering what's going on." He pointed to the more prominent light. "An outpost was established on this planet a few months ago. It's just a small mining facility, home to sixteen families, a total of forty-four people. We've received regular maintenance and progress reports until now. The last one we got was a little different. The specifics weren't clear, but they were enough to imply they'd been attacked." He sat down at the table with the two men. "We haven't heard anything since that call." He paused and then added, "They're in the Delseyis system."

Kahn narrowed his eyes. "If I remember right, that's close to the Thalosian border. There can't be much doubt as to who it is."

"That's what I thought, but according to the data they recorded, the ships matched no known Thalosian type. It's been a long time since we had contact with them, so it's possible that they've reworked their ships, but we can't jump to conclusions. We need a first hand look. Unfounded assumption can be dangerous." Haute's face looked genuinely grim. "I don't like the way things are adding up. We could run into a lot of trouble, and we're going to be a long way from home."

"Are we ready for an all out war ... if it comes to that?" Gary asked.

Haute hated to hear the word, but he had already considered the likelihood. "I'll be disappointed if we're not after all these years. I don't relish the thought of losing all we have in the first battle."

Gary thought the statement to be somewhat amusing, but he answered with seriousness. "Excuse me sir, but I don't think there's a chance in hell of that happening."

The Commanders' reply was solemn. "Son, I've heard that before. I probably said it myself at one time or another. I admit you're a great pilot, and I have no doubt you're confident with what you're doing, but out there, you may have to depend on others to survive. Some of them aren't as talented as you. War is a far cry from the simulators. When it's over ... it's over. You don't get a second chance. Eventually, you will feel the fear ... I guarantee it."

Gary's smile drained to a cold-sober stare. He nodded with understanding and respect.

Kahn stood when Haute said nothing else. "When do we leave?"

Haute raised his eyebrows, smiling. "We already have." He received astonished looks in return. He continued. "Kahn, show Gary around. Teach him what he needs to know. Gary, don't be afraid to ask questions. It's the best way to learn. You don't have to do it right now, but he needs to be up to speed before we reach the outpost. I expect my officers to know this ship." The discussion was ended.

Later in the day, Kahn did as he was told. The tour began. Gary's questions were endless. His new classroom was mesmerizing and he had the finest teachers in the Republic ... the crew of the Aquillon. Everything was explained to him professionally and efficiently. After a few hours, he realized his new home to be a virtual city in space. Their last stop was the main control room. They noticed Commander Haute as they entered, but they didn't approach the busy man. Another officer took on the task of explaining the various stations and their functions to the pair. Gary couldn't help but notice the main view screen, which was more than a prominent fixture in the room. It nearly filled one wall. Beyond it beckoned a thousand stars.

They spent quite a while watching the goings on, when Kahn suggested a break. He was parched. He had just showed his friend an officer's lounge nearby, and decided to return to it. He coaxed his sidekick to join him, but his invitation was declined. Gary, intrigued with it all, wished to remain where he was. This confused his older, less enchanted friend, but the issue wasn't pushed. Kahn left an open invite as they parted.

The room was bustling with activity, each person enthralled in their personal duties. Within minutes, Gary noted the monotony that Kahn had been keen to. He decided to rejoin his friend in the lounge; if he could remember where it was.

Kahn entered the said lounge about the time Gary was being enlightened. The room was a far cry from the stark walls and corridors normally seen throughout the ship. He had spent time there only once before. It had still been under construction then, but was still a working bar, frequented by workers, some of whom would spend weeks at a time without leaving the ship.

The room was animated, filled with off duty men and women. It was darkened, except for the sporadic flashes of lights and strobes. Loud music filled the air, the vibrations touching him with every beat. His eyes gradually adjusted, and he finally found who he was looking for.

Slowly, he moved behind her and reached out, tenderly caressing her neck with his fingers. Her hand came up to cover his as she turned towards him. Bending down, Kahn hugged her, smothering her lips with his.

The blonde women stopped the kiss after a moment to catch her breath. "I thought you were going to call me?"

Kahn wished to answer, but was cut short as she continued the welcome. A moment later they sat together at the table.

The woman moved close and placed her arms around him. He still had not begun to answer her first question. "When did you get here?" She asked.

Kahn couldn't help but beam. He'd missed her terribly over the past week. The woman was his latest and most serious relationship to date. Her name was Deanna Wilkens and she held an officers rank of Ensign. Her supervisory position on the ship was in the Botany Department. She had also cross-trained as a security officer and pulled shifts as needed.

They had first met while attending the same high school. She was a few years younger than he, but had chased him anyway. Due to the age difference, they had never been childhood sweethearts, but had become good friends instead. The two of them had spent much of their lives together, but only in the last year or so had they become intimately involved.

Deanna was twenty-four years old; a trim, five foot seven, blonde-haired, brown-eyed picture of perfection, according to her beau. Her temperament was mature and likeable, and her beauty had coaxed many men to vie for her attentions. She and Kahn seemed to be, so far, a capable couple, and the bond between them was growing. The topic of marriage had only been mentioned by teasing friends and acquaintances thus far. Deanna had hopes, but was patient. She thought she sensed hesitation on Kahn's part and did not want to pressure him into that type of relationship. She considered him worth waiting for. She also knew his history with women. His closer friends had dubbed him a player. She had vowed to tame him.

Kahn finally answered. "We got here just this morning. I really haven't had time to get a hold of you. I had orders to show Gary around the ship."

Deanna's eyes brightened. "Oh my God, where is he? I haven't seen him forever."

"He wanted to look around a little more … you know, first time on board."

"Well, I told Colleen about him," she smiled.

"Aren't you the little matchmaker?"

"Whatever. She asked first. She asked if I knew any guys that weren't assholes." She paused as Kahn frowned. "I didn't lie. I told her all of them were. Some just aren't as big as others."

"That's great. The male population appreciates your candidness, myself included." Kahn countered, "Do I know her?"

"Yeah … at the activities center a couple of months ago, the girl I got a ride with … black hair …"

"Oh yeah, I remember." He did indeed, and would not easily forget again. From what he could remember, neither would Gary, when and if he got to meet her.

"I really think they will like each other." Deanna stated confidently.

"And why do you think that?"

"Because I got into the personnel files and found his picture for her. She liked what she saw."

"Well how do you know he'll like her?" The question sounded ludicrous even to him.

"He is a man … right? I don't think we have to worry about that."

Kahn leaned forward and drew close enough to whisper above the music. "What about us? I missed you. We need to go catch up on some things?" One of his hands slipped under the table and over her thigh.

An expression of sorrow mixed with playfulness came over her face. "Sorry babe, I've got a workout in a few minutes. I'll call you later tonight though, okay?"

He faked a sob. "You promise you won't forget?"

"Yeah, I'm not like you." She gave him a long kiss. "I gotta go …" She rose and promptly disappeared into the crowd.

Kahn sighed deeply, watching her go. Frustrated, he emptied the contents of Deanna's drink and caught sight of Gary waltzing through the door. The music stopped, seemingly timed for his grand entrance.

Gary spotted his friend, alone with a drink in his hand. As he drew close, he spoke. "What are you smiling about? You can't drink. We go on duty pretty soon."

"Don't I know it." answered Kahn. "There wasn't any alcohol in it anyway. Hey, sit down; I've got some news for you."

"Good or bad?"

"Oh … it's good … really good."

"The mission's been scrubbed? We're staying home?" Gary guessed half-heartedly.

"It's not that good. You just missed Deanna."

"She was here?" He whined. At once, he was sorry he had not joined his friend in the first place. He had always enjoyed her company, not to mention the fact that he had always thought her to be hotter than hell. Hesitantly, he asked, "That wasn't the good news, was it?"

"No … well, good for me maybe …" He didn't follow up the half answer.

"Okay … so what's the news?" Gary asked impatiently, his curiosity at its peak.

"De's got a friend she wants you to meet."

Gary groaned aloud. "Oh man …"

"I don't want to hear it … like you've got a lot of options. When's the last time a girl knocked on your door?"

"Well …" He felt he had to be honest with himself. "It's been a few months."

"Exactly, so shut up and listen. You've gotta meet this girl. I saw her a couple of months ago. I'm not kidding … she's a doll." He noticed his friend still appeared unconvinced.

"So how's this supposed to happen?" Gary sighed.

"Well, easy, I guess. She already likes you. I'm not kidding, this woman is gorgeous! Obviously, she's disturbed, but …"

Gary was confused. "When the hell did she see me?"

"Who knows?"

Gary shook his head. He detested blind dates and he had seen far too many of Kahn's "dolls", but he remained suspicious, if not somewhat interested. He couldn't help wondering how sober Kahn had been the first time he saw her. His voice was less than enthusiastic. "When do I meet her?"

"I don't know for sure, maybe tomorrow. I'll ask De to set it up. Jesus, man, don't sound so excited." He said sarcastically.

"What do you expect? I remember the last date you set me up on."

"Oh, she wasn't that bad." Kahn chuckled.

"Wasn't that bad ... are you shittin me?" Gary exclaimed. "You wouldn't have dated her."

"You got her in the sack didn't you?" Kahn defended. "Isn't that what you wanted?"

"Not in her parent's bed, two minutes after walking in her door! Shit, she damn near killed me ... and we got caught by her Mom!"

"Hey, some people like that kind of thing, the thrill ... the danger ..." Kahn joked.

"Oh, it was plenty thrilling, believe me!"

Kahn smiled, remembering the whole situation. It hadn't been that long ago and he'd received plenty of chastisement since. He glanced at his watch. It was getting late. "Well, I promise you this time ... you won't be disappointed."

"You know, I don't know why, but I believe you ... again." Gary admitted.

Kahn yawned. "Hey, I'm beat. I hear my pillow calling. I'll see you tomorrow. You do remember how to get to your cabin, right?"

Gary frowned.

Kahn shook his head. "Damn kids, can't ever find their way around. Come on." The music started again as they rose from the table. "Besides, there ain't nothing worse than sitting in a bar and not drinking."

Kahn left Gary at his cabin and arrived at his own a few moments later. He entered it for the first time in over a month. The lights were set low and as he reached for the dial, a soft voice came from his bedroom, startling him. "Leave them off."

He turned to see a feminine form, silhouetted by a light in the bedroom. The body shimmered beneath a shear garment. "I thought you said you had a work-out?" Kahn asked.

"Oh, I'm gonna work out all right. I just needed time to get things ready." She turned and walked out of sight, the garment dropping to the floor behind her.

Kahn followed without hesitation.

Gary woke early. By eight o'clock he had finally found Kahn's cabin and rang the buzzer. To his surprise, a female voice was heard from within. There was little doubt as to whom it belonged. "Who is it?"

"Uh … it's Gary. Are you guys up yet?"

"Yeah, just a second."

Deanna, fully dressed, greeted Gary with a hug as the door opened. "God, it's been forever since I saw you. How have you been?"

"Just perfect. You look like you're doing good." Gary said, admiring the view. "You look great."

Deanna patted him on the cheek. "Aw … you've always been a sweetie."

Gary grimaced. Oh God, he thought, the fatal name given to those guys who are nice, but don't stand a chance. He tried to avert his gaze, but couldn't help looking at her as she went into the bedroom. He had to admit that so far, he hadn't seen a better fitting uniform on anyone. He could hear her telling Kahn to get up, and his following groans of disdain. He looked about the room as he waited. As expected, it resembled his cabin and probably every other on the ship.

Deanna shortly returned. "Well, he's half awake. I'm gonna be late at the lab. You two come down when you get the chance … okay?" She was out the door before he could even speak. He had hoped to ask about the upcoming meeting with her friend, but evidently, she'd forgotten about it anyway.

Kahn shuffled from his room to the kitchenette to get a drink. He looked worse than usual. "Hey …" He offered a short wave.

"Hey," Gary answered. "Did you sleep at all last night?"

"Not very damn much." He couldn't hide the smile as he recollected.

"She didn't look too tired." Gary chided,

"Well, she shouldn't. I did most of the work." He chuckled, knowing she would argue the fact.

Gary smiled. "Did she say anything about that girl?" he asked, "I was going to ask her, but she got out of here pretty quick."

"Yeah, right …" Kahn joked. "No, she didn't say anything. We didn't do much talking though."

Gary had thought about the meeting the night before and had reached the point where he was actually looking forward to it, but Kahn's answer caused his anticipation to drop a notch. Obviously, the girl had not been as interested in him as Kahn had let on, but then again, he did have a record of over exaggeration.

Kahn studied his friends face, seeing genuine disappointment. No, he couldn't do this to him. He spilled it. "Deanna didn't say anything, but her friend called twice last night asking about you."

Gary despised it when Kahn pulled that crap, yet he looked at him and smiled, shaking his head. "Just remember, man, paybacks are a bitch."

At that point, the ship's intercom blared deafeningly, making both men wince. "ATTENTION ALL PILOTS, GOLD SQUADRON THREE, REPORT TO LEVEL FORTY-SEVEN, SECTION EIGHTY-ONE, ROOM TWENTY-THREE, AT ZERO EIGHT FORTY-FIVE."

"Damn man, you left that on last night?" Gary asked.

"Hell no! She must have turned it up before she left."

"Do you know where that room is?" Gary asked, looking for something to write on.

"I don't know, maybe. I won't know for sure til we get there," answered Kahn. "Why do they always do that? Fifty numbers at once? Do they think we've got every deck memorized?"

He hurriedly dressed, and twenty minutes later, they found a conference room matching their unsure numbers. There, they waited for the person or persons who had prompted the meeting. Over the next few moments, eight more pilots arrived and took seats. The last persons through the door were Leon Haute and two other officers. Their faces appeared grim.

One of the officers began with no introductions. "We've just picked up a signal from Outpost Thirty-three. It was short and broken, but it was an obvious distress call. They've been attacked several times since last word. They have severe casualties. Life support is failing and they request immediate evacuation."

Haute entered the discussion. "At our present speed, we don't think we'll be able to reach them in enough time to help. It's been determined that we should launch the scout ship. She won't be ready until fourteen hundred hours. I've chosen a crew of fifty from duty section six to make the trip. Two of you will be going. You're ships are being loaded as we speak. The rest of you are being moved up." He spoke to one pilot in particular. "McClure ... you will be acting squad leader during Bengal's absence. Kusan, get your gear together. Aquillon Two, with the new accelerators, will get you there a couple of days ahead of us." He looked directly at Gary and gave a nod of support. "All of you need to be ready. Remember, fourteen hundred hours. Dismissed!" He and the other officers left the room.

The words hit Gary like a slap in the face. Suddenly, he understood what the Commander had said to him just yesterday. He glanced at Kahn, who stared wordlessly ahead. Was he scared too? Finally, Kahn gave a return look, answering his unvoiced question.

Kahn saw the concern behind his friend's gaze and wished to say something encouraging, but the words weren't there. He wanted to tell him that combat wasn't as dangerous as he thought, but he could not, because he did not know. Yes, he considered himself a great pilot. Yes, he held some of the highest scores ever recorded in the academy, but did that really mean anything? He'd never seen an enemy ship, except on the simulator screens, the same ones that Gary had trained on. He felt something building inside him, but it wasn't fear. He preferred to think of it as justifiable apprehension.

The pilots remained behind for several moments, talking to one another. Some wished to go on the trip, but most were relieved to be staying behind. Each knew that their time would come. One by one, they filtered out, each lost in their own thoughts.

Kahn and Gary traveled several decks below to the Botany Department. Gary momentarily forgot his uncertainties as he realized where they were heading. He knew that Deanna and her friend would probably be there.

Eventually, they entered what had to be one of the most impressive rooms on the ship. A sweet aroma met them as the door opened. The room overflowed with thousands of plants, ranging from tiny flowers, to trees reaching thirty or more feet in height. It was truly a garden of exceptional beauty, generating a soothing, peaceful atmosphere. For a moment at least, it seemed they were in paradise.

They made their way through the forest until they found Deanna. Her back was to them. Kahn could see other women further down the path. None had heard them come up. He stopped short and pointed one of the women out to Gary. She stood with her back to them as well, but he was sure it was the girl Deanna had talked about. "There she is," he whispered. "Come on, we'll break the bad news after while." He moved closer and called Deanna's name.

Colleen Sluder heard someone call her friend's name and turned to see two men approaching. She recognized them as pilots by their uniforms. The tall one she knew right away, even though she had only seen him a couple of times. She smiled inside. The shorter man had to be Gary Kusan. He looked just like his picture. He was exactly as Deanna had described him, nice body … handsome as hell. And his perfect beard was an incredible turn-on. She could not, of course, see his backside yet. She'd have to take Deanna's word on that. She wanted to go to them, but her feet seemed as rooted to the ground as the plants around her.

As she stared, his eyes met hers for the briefest of seconds, and then he looked away. Her pulse quickened. An unfamiliar feeling rose inside of her, one she had not felt since she was a teenager. It was the uncomfortable anxiety one feels when confronted by a moment feared, but longed for. As she watched, Deanna laughed. She could not hear their conversation, but after a moment they all turned and walked toward her. Suddenly, she felt as though someone had changed the temperature in the room; too high, too hot.

Kahn grinned his little boy grin as they drew closer. "How are you, Colleen?"

"Fine Kahn, how are you?" She felt better. Somehow, the simple words had lifted the heavy air of the moment.

Deanna wasted no time. "Colleen, this is Gary Kusan, from Bentar. Gary, this is my best friend, Colleen Sluder," she said happily.

Their eyes met again as Gary spoke. "Hey, I'm happy to meet you."

Colleen took his extended hand and could feel the cold stickiness. Was it hers or his? "Me too, De's told me a lot about you."

Gary began to wonder what secrets might have been told, when Kahn spoke, a more serious tone in his voice. "Hey, can you guys take a break yet?"

Colleen turned to the other two girls. "Can you take care of those on your own?"

"No problem," was their quick response.

Walking through the corridor, Gary glanced at the woman beside him every chance he could. For once, Kahn had not exaggerated. She was adorable. Colleen had long black hair, reaching the middle of her back. Her brown eyes were captivating. He watched every move she made, looking away each time she turned toward him. He complimented himself with each successful evasion, but he had to look. Her attractiveness enchanted him, demanded his attention.

They made their way to an empty recreation room and chose a couch in the back. Kahn sighed heavily. "We just got out of a meeting. The conditions at the out post we're heading for have become more serious. Haute wants to send out the scout ship to get there quicker. Fifty people from section six are going, including Gary and me."

Deanna became instantly disenchanted with the turn of events. "I don't believe this," she complained, shaking her head in disparity.

Colleen, equally disappointed, looked at Gary. "When do you have to leave?"

Gary glanced at his watch. "In about five hours."

Deanna was fuming, knowing she had no choice but to accept it. She understood the Republic way, the militaristic demands. She knew that the reasons were good ones. Lives might depend on his actions. It was the job they chose. She understood ... but she didn't have to like it.

Kahn could see the hurt in her eyes. "I'm sorry babe, but it's not my decision. We'll only be a couple of days ahead of you."

Deanna nodded. "I know ... it's just hard."

"It'll be alright. I guess this is the price we pay to be the best." Kahn said jokingly, waiting for her to voice her agreement.

Deanna frowned, "Asshole."

Pressing duties forced the foursome to split, but they came together again at lunchtime. Gary and Colleen, mutually stimulated by the few moments they'd spent together to that point, sat and talked. Gary found himself absorbed with her personality, wit and intelligence. He had all but forgotten the mission. Much was discovered, one from the other, in the short time. Each remained open and honest about their likes, dislikes, past experiences and future dreams.

Gary learned that Colleen had French ancestry from her father's side. Her father was full blooded, and had planned to continue the lineage, but Colleen's mother had a diversity of ancestry, including English, German, and Dutch. With their union, the long chain of pure heritage had finally been broken.

Gary knew little of French customs, but was familiar with some of their art, architecture, language and food. Proud tradition had been preserved over the years by generations of families that had never seen their home country.

They talked without pause or want of anything else. With each moment together, they grew closer, neither sorry that their meeting had taken place. Kahn and Deanna sat nearby; spending what little time there was left.

Suddenly, the loudspeaker blared. "ATTENTION DUTY SECTION SIX. ALL SUPERVISORS REPORT TO OPERATIONS DEPARTMENTS. ALL DUTY PERSONNEL REPORT TO THEIR STATIONS IMMEDIATELY."

Deanna sighed, "That's us." She gave Kahn a long kiss. "I'll see you before you leave. Okie?"

Kahn forced a smile, "Dokie."

A moment passed in silence. Kahn looked at his friend, who seemed to be lost in thought. "So ... what do you think of her?"

Gary shook his head. "You need to ask?"

"I told you ..." Kahn said mockingly. He rose, slapping Gary across the back "C'mon, we need to get our shit together. No sense waiting til the last minute."

Over the next hour, the two men gathered their equipment and made final preparations to go. The time for departure was nearing. They made their way to the docking bay to deliver their gear to the Aquillon Two. The corridors leading to and from the hanger bay were bustling.

Gary had seen the scout ship on his initial tour and had stood in awe at his first view of it. He felt it again as they approached it. They stood on a walkway, directly in front of the ship.

The Aquillon Two filled the colossal docking bay, but still was diminutive compared to the mother ship she rested within. She was a shade over one hundred twenty meters in width and matched closely, the outer design of the Aquillon One. All exterior doors and hatches were open, including two larger openings, one on each frontal wing. Within these openings rested gold raiders one and two, positioned for immediate launching if necessary. Men and women could be seen inside the ship, scurrying about like tiny bees in a hive. Workmen, with the aid of anti-gravity units, loaded an endless array of supplies into the ship. One would have thought the coming trip would span years, instead of days.

Only fifty feet away, unseen by the two men, an elevator-car approached. Colleen Sluder stepped quickly clear of it, seemingly pressed for time. Deanna was with her, but still in the vehicle. She handed the former several small cases, but didn't get out. She spoke while Colleen tried to balance many of the items. "You go find the guys while I go back and get the other stuff. I'll be back in a few minutes." The car whisked off.

Colleen nearly walked past the two men, as she headed toward the scout ship, but Kahn, surprised and puzzled by her unexpected appearance, stopped her. "Colleen, what are you doing up here?"

"Oh, God, you scared me, I didn't see you," she exclaimed.

Kahn asked again. "What are you doing?"

"Well, when we left you guys, De had to go to the supervisor's meeting. When she got back, she had our new orders?"

Kahn sensed what was coming next. "Your new orders?"

"She volunteered us as back up security. We're going with you. De's right behind me." Colleen was bursting with enthusiasm and noticed that Gary, at least, seemed equally delighted. Kahn proved more difficult to read, but he wasn't smiling.

Deanna soon arrived and the group made their way to the boarding elevator. They checked in with their assigned duty officers, and began familiarizing themselves with the smaller vessel. The minutes dragged as they waited for lift off, giving the four shipmates time again to talk. The oldest of the group didn't participate to a great extent, however.

Kahn tried to stem his annoyance, but knew that he could not hide it. He knew that Deanna had noticed something was wrong. Sooner or later, her patience would be at an end and she would confront him. He had quelled numerous concerns about the mission after it had been announced. He knew that Gary was an excellent pilot and could no doubt hold his own, but wondered if it wise to put him into a combat situation so soon? There were other pilots with much more time in a raider seat than he. Any decision his commanding officer made would be respected, though he would have liked to discuss the matter with him. As he sat in thought, he recalled a story Haute had once told him. He had been told the tale only once, but had not forgotten.

It had taken place near the closing stages of the first war, almost twenty years ago. Kahn's father, Paul was one of the original gold raider pilots. He had become a legend, as had his best friend Captain Leon Haute, who served in the same squadron. They had grown into this status simply from being able to survive. There had been scores of attacks over the years, the Belaquin forces nearly always on the defensive. The recurrent skirmishes had nearly wiped out the limited number of raiders. In those early days, raiders were little more than prototypes with limited capabilities. They had huge disadvantages against the Thalosian fighters. The latter vastly outnumbered the former, and it was only an elementary matter of time. In Haute's vivid account of one battle, there were only three ships left out of their squadron, each under attack by superior numbers. Eventually, the Belaquin pilots became separated. Within minutes, one was destroyed, and Haute's ship was disabled. Paul Bengal circled back and tried to help. Six Thalosian vessels turned on his raider and he drew them away from his helpless friend. There was no hope against those odds, but the brave pilot had already known that. He died, leading certain death away from his helpless friend. He was the last raider pilot to die in combat. The Thalosians returned only once more after that day.

Haute, a Gold Squadron leader had no squadron left. He was mentally devastated, and never piloted again. A few years after the war, he was promoted to Fleet Commander. He and young Kahn became close afterwards, and when the boy came of age, Haute urged him to become a pilot. He prepared him for anything. He told him about the many pilots he had sent out that never returned. He hid nothing from him. Most of those brave men had been in their first year with the Republic. For some, their first mission was also their last. War was cruel, but it had to be met head on with the finest men possible, to insure their survival.

Kahn remembered his words. It was those same words that made him concerned for his friend. What about his own flight record? The fact that he had never fought in a battle hadn't entered his mind.

Now, the situation had worsened. He had two other close friends to fret about. If he had any influence, the girls would not be going on this voyage. Republic regulations state that married couples aren't sent into action on the same ship, but he and Deanna didn't fit the criteria. For a brief hypocritical second, he wished they did.

At a quarter til two, word spread that all equipment was on board. The last appropriations were being attended to and Haute had given the word to go. The mother ship had been stopped for the launch.

"Bay doors opened and locked. All pressure grids show green. Intra ship docking pads released." With the massive doors above the ship retracted, the ship became weightless. "Disengage." The scout ship floated independently.

"Aquillon Two, you are clear for elevation." The control officer sighed.

The scout ships commander acknowledged. "Roger, bay command." He turned to his navigator. "Engage vertical thrusters."

The ship rose slowly and effortlessly. Haute watched from the control room as the scout ship emerged from the bay. He had not been aboard during the shakedown cruise, so he was seeing the spectacle for the first time. It was a monumental, as well as a critical moment for all persons watching.

Haute kept his eyes on the launch, but his main concern was elsewhere. The last report from the stricken outpost had troubled him. He silently prayed for the men and women in the vessel before him, knowing his own could offer no assistance for some time.

In the scout ship's control room, Lieutenant Commander Kenneth Anson was giving the orders. "Give us full speed." There was no discernible movement as the main engines hummed to life, coaxing the ship forward.

In the mother ship's control room, the main screen was switched to allow forward viewing once again. The scout ship appeared from above, gliding slowly ahead of them. The five glowing engine ports brightened the room, their white light shrinking with each second. The glow finally disappeared as the vessel attained light speed. With the bay doors closed, the order given to resume course.

Haute nodded in satisfaction. He'd done everything he could for the outpost families. The scout ship's added speed gave some hope that it would arrive before their life support was gone. He spoke to the communications station. "Try to send word to the outpost. They might need some good news." He then headed for the silence of his quarters.

Aboard the scout ship, Kahn, Gary, and several other officers listened to a recorded transmission from the mining outpost. The message was garbled and at times impossible to comprehend, but they all agreed that the outpost's prognosis sounded grim. Commander Haute had also recorded further orders for the crew. They were simple and direct. "This is not an offensive-based mission. Your role is to get in, secure any survivors, and rendezvous with us as soon as possible."

Kahn was in full agreement. He had no desire to pick a fight. The situation before them was vague at best. Lack of information made it difficult to predict anything. If the Thalosians were involved, there was a good chance that this trip would be for recovery instead of rescue.

The briefing lasted half an hour. The Aquillon Two, by the end of that time, was millions of miles ahead of the mother ship. Each passing minute put the smaller ship nearly twenty seconds further ahead.

Kahn went to his cabin and found a message left by Deanna. She and Colleen had gone to the security department. He shook his head. He still felt some irritation towards her decision, but he had to accept part of the blame himself. He had fully supported her cross training to the field, bolstering his support of women's rights in her eyes.

He considered meeting her in security, but met Gary instead and visited the port hanger room, where GR One was housed. They spent a long while talking about what might be awaiting them at the end of their journey. It was late evening when they finally left the bay and made their way to the control room.

Once there, Kahn frowned in bewilderment, studying the man in the command chair. He had the feeling that he knew him from somewhere, but couldn't place him. He would meet him later. Maybe that would ring the right bell.

The main view screen was filled with an endless sea of stars. He thought of the outpost families and wondered why anyone would wish to live so far away from civilization, so far from help. The mining business had to be lucrative to put women and children at so much risk.

Even at the late hour, the room was fully manned. There were six persons at their posts, the commander, navigator, communications officer, engine's officer, and two sensor technicians. Except for the latter, the stations appeared less than demanding. Sensory technicians had to be vigilant, constantly alert for rogue asteroids and above all for other ships. Vessels encountered this deep in space would more than likely be alien. The only known aliens had a straightforward policy of shooting first and asking no questions.

One of the technicians spoke, drawing the attention of all in the room. "Commander Anson, I have contact at one, four, three, mark seven."

Kahn's eyes narrowed and his pulse quickened, but only partially due to the new scanner contact. Upon hearing the commanding officers name, he finally placed the familiar face. He filled with disgust, but knew he had to repress it. He had only seen Anson a couple of times, but knew him by reputation and from stories from Deanna, who had dated him for a short time. Did she know he was on the ship? And if she did, why hadn't she told him? His dislike would not cause problems on this flight, unless of course, provoked.

Anson sat bolt upright in is chair. "What is it?"

"It has to be a ship. They've altered their approach." The technician rechecked his screen. "We're on a collision course."

"Burchard, try to contact them on all frequencies." Anson's voice was calm. "Slow us to sub light. Is the ship within visual yet?"

"Not yet."

The navigator had input. "They have just entered range for weapons."

Anson nodded. "Get a lock on them. Hold until I give the word to fire. Any luck, Burchard?"

"Negative, sir, everything is being bounced back."

One of the scanner techs spoke. "Their engine signature is not in any of our records."

Anson had no intention of simply walking up to their front door. "Change course, pass on their starboard quarter. Give them a wide berth." He knew that the ship could very well be an unclassified merchant vessel. It wasn't that uncommon.

A moment later, the turn was completed. "I've turned twelve degrees, sir, but they have followed. We're still heading right at them."

"There they are!" Shouted Burchard. An object appeared in the center of the main screen. It was still too far away to be distinguishable, but was approaching rapidly.

"How far away?" asked the Commander. He considered putting the ship on alert. If they were within weapons range, his ship may be in danger also.

"They've slowed down, two minutes to intercept."

"Sound emergency stations." He'd already waited too long, but in his own judgment, raising shields could be construed as a hostile, instead of a self-protective measure. They were still two days away from known hostilities, but he could not take a chance.

A bright red glow descended throughout the ship and a low alarm sounded. The Aquillon Two's shields were automatically activated. At the same moment, a brilliant flash appeared from the unidentified craft, growing in intensity as they watched.

"They've fired on us, sir!" yelled the navigator.

"Return fire. Turn hard to starboard!" Anson gripped his seat hard, his eyes wide with fear. "Sound collision!"

The engine officer hesitated for only an instant, entranced by the blinding white light filling the room. His hand never made it to the collision switch. The Aquillon's weapons fired.

Twin beams burst forth from the scout ship as she leaned hard to the right. The ship rocked violently as the white light was met. Darkness and silence filled the ship as she began to drift.

CHAPTER 3

▼

Ban-Sor was having the time of his life. He wanted for nothing, and the privacy of his temporary home was all he could ever wish for. He held his extraordinary powers in admiration, even though he could not explain them. He'd had them as far back as he could remember. Only over the last four hundred years, mostly through trial and error, had he effectively mastered their complexities and potential. He had just recently learned to be comfortable with them. He no longer concerned himself with how or why he was able to accomplish the things he did.

He was limited by nothing. He could assume any form, or travel to any time and place he wished. Anything he could imagine was a thought away. If desired, he might have no physical form at all, but that required great concentration. He found it easier to be, than not. He could create and experience anything, sometimes becoming befuddled as to what was real and what was not. His life consisted of living through his mind's eye, but such a life was not without drawbacks.

Others of his kind disapproved. There were rules in his social order which he had on occasion ignored. He did not choose to heed the advice of authority. Instead, he disregarded it as well. By doing so, he was punished; vanquished to an isolated section of the universe. This was done in hopes of straightening him out, or rather, changing him to be more like the stuffy, unimaginative, tiresome beings his elders were.

Regardless, he now found himself overseer of a rather lifeless span of space. Although he could spend forever exploring its vastness, it wasn't what he wanted. He wished to go home, but the hassle would be worse than the reward. He forced himself to endure the temporary alternative.

Things had grown rather stagnant until two short centuries ago. He noticed a disturbance on one of his planets. Extraordinary ships had landed there, and colonies had begun to be built. These strangers, though primitive, were quite interesting. They were humanoid, like much of the life in his realm, but still unique.

The strangers also brought puzzlement, a not so pleasant emotion one well worth experiencing. Inquisitiveness ruled Ban-Sor's actions from that point. Who were they? Where had they come from? If he could envision their beginnings, then he could go there, but he did not have that luxury. The lack of answers in his pursuit for knowledge was regrettably, a thorn in his side. Finally, an answer presented itself.

He discovered that their ships used a fuel that left an easily traceable path. At the end of the trail, he came upon a planet in a desolate system with nine planets and only one tiny star for a sun. The system was unfortunately, in an area deemed "out of bounds" by his elders. This fact, of course, delayed, but did not discourage his actions. The elders were there … he was here.

The stranger's long journey had originated from a beautiful planet; very similar to the one they had landed upon. Ban-Sor's initial question was why they had left this place? The answer, he found soon enough.

What he discovered on the surface of the globe shocked even his broad imagination. The devastation was nearly absolute. There was little left untouched by the terrible destructive forces. Death was everywhere, but some life remained also. The strangers had evidently foreseen the catastrophe and escaped. That they had started again in his territory was of no matter. Whatever they were capable of would have no effect on any of his concerns. The decision to leave them alone to begin again was simple.

Instead, he decided to explore his new found treasure. The old planet, although ruined and abandoned, was fascinating. He retraced time, traveling through thousands of years. He witnessed the planets entire life … right up to its near death. Billions of humans had perished over the millenniums, many for pointless reasons. Their species was brutal, sadistic, unmerciful, and self-destructive. It was their way however; their decisions, their lives. In their end, one miniscule difference, the color of skin, had caused the greatest loss of all, the loss of an entire world.

Since then, Ban-Sor, with unsuppressed indulgence, had entertained himself with many adventures and discoveries. One such discovery had prompted his latest diversion, one that would take the newcomers in his system on another journey. But controversy entered at this point. Operating in forbidden space was a minor offense. Now he was considering a more hazardous undertaking. He would be creating future history, not just playing in its past. He had been warned and punished for similar games before. If caught this time, the consequences would be severe. He decided, as usual, to ignore the danger. He had a plan, and no one was going to spoil it for him. He was going to help these strange new beings whether they liked it or not. Why he felt the need to do so was of no importance. He was creating adventure, which was reason enough, but he had to do it in a way that they would understand. It would be interesting to test their minds. How much could they grasp?

So far, his plan was working perfectly. Their new journey had begun. Whether it was right or wrong, time would tell. He would set the times and the places, but these "Belaquins" as they called themselves, had to be on their own. Whatever choices, good or bad, they made during the near future, they would be responsible for. He would observe them, but would not interfere unless absolutely necessary. The game would be exciting, to say the least.

CHAPTER 4

▼

On the scout ship Aquillon Two, communications officer Burchard was the first to awaken. His left arm was aching and numb from where he had fallen and lain upon it. "Son of a bitch," he muttered. "What the hell did they hit us with?"

No one answered. The impact had been enormous. For a moment he felt anxiety building. Was anyone else alive? Would they be boarded by the unknown attackers, or had they already? He shook his head to clear his mind, knowing that he needed all his senses if such a thing were about to happen. He remembered that he was in the control room when the ship was hit. The room was dark and the ship listed heavily, meaning that the automatic stabilizers were out. The ship was clearly adrift, but at least gravitation was still working.

As he looked about the room, muted features became visible. The view screen was still on. The starlight provided a familiar place to start. He located the necessary switches to bring on the auxiliary power, praying that there was some battery power left. A long second later, emergency lighting flickered and stayed on. Burchard released a heavy sigh of relief. Within another moment, he had corrected the ship to a level position. Groans met his ears as other crew members began to stir about the room. He went to help them.

Gary could see only darkness. Was he outside the ship? No … that wasn't possible. He was still breathing, but there was no sound. He actually felt peaceful, possibly more relaxed than ever before. He felt he could stay there forever, but the harmony was short lived. Abruptly there was light, and he felt like he was falling. He tried to take his next breath, but it wouldn't come. He felt an incredible cold. Straining and thrashing, he tried to rid himself of the terror ... and if it was a dream, to wake up.

He heard voices coming from somewhere. "Gary! Wake up! Open your eyes ... wake up!" He could hear words, but didn't understand. Then something shook him hard! At last, like a whirlwind, everything came rushing back. He awoke, startled ... relieved. He saw Kahn over him, still shaking ... still calling. The light hurt his eyes.

"What happened?" he stammered, trying with difficulty, to sit upright.

Kahn steadied him. "Jesus man, I didn't think you were gonna wake up." He sighed, "I'm not sure what's going on. We got hit hard. All of us were out for a while."

Gary closed his eyes. "My God, I feel like shit. I almost feel drunk"

Kahn answered. "No ... drunk would be fun. This isn't. Can you stand up?" He helped Gary to his feet, practically lifting him from the deck. They overheard a voice from somewhere in the room; reports of other crew members being injured in the attack.

Gary rapidly became fully coherent. "The girls!" They left the room and found them unhurt except for minor bumps and abrasions. Paying no attention to their own injuries, the girls were helping others with theirs, some of them serious.

Kahn looked directly into Deanna's eyes. In them, he saw fear, confusion, and relief. All came with good reason. Each wondered what would happen next.

With the girls' fine for the moment, the two pilots headed back to the control room. By the time they got there, the engineer had isolated much of the damage to the ship. The list was short, but serious. There was power from the back up generators, but not enough to even consider running the engines. The entire ship was operating off battery reserves, which would last a very limited time. All unnecessary sections and systems had already been shut down. Communication was also inoperable. The Aquillon Two had no way of contacting the mother ship.

Kahn read worry in the commander's face as the engineer finished filling him in. No crewmember had been seriously injured. There was no hull breach. The shields were down, with no possible way to regenerate them. Without them, if they were hit with another blast, they would not survive. There was another point reported that was not on any checklist, but nonetheless, received the attention of everyone in the room. The navigator explained. "We're being towed."

All stood still as the words sunk in. Commander Anson spoke first, looking to the view screen. "Forward view," he ordered.

The navigator checked. "We have forward view, sir."

"Then why can't we see it?" He referred to the alien vessel, which was not visible.

The navigator, puzzled for a moment, checked their position. "We're facing starboard."

"Try using the vapor ports. See if they'll turn us."

Slowly, the ship pivoted and the alien ship inched into view. Only the rear of the huge craft was visible. Four gigantic engine ports faced them, each dark and lifeless. Again, the room was silent.

Anson shook his stare from the ship. "All right, what have we got that works?"

Numerous voices came from around the room. Most systems were found to be usable to a limited extent. Oxygen reserve levels were full. Heat and light was available as long as the batteries held out. Intra ship communication, control room stations and scanners appeared to be fully operable.

"What's our speed and heading?" Anson asked.

"We're point four seven below light speed. Heading one … eight … three … three."

Anson did some quick calculating and realized they were far from their intended course. Would the Aquillon One discover their deviation in flight path? It was possible, but not probable. He opened a channel to the engine room, making a strong recommendation to find the problem with the engines and fix it if possible. "What do the sensors tell us about them?" he asked another man.

"Nothing sir; no life readings, no power readings, I can't even see their tractor beam. They might be jamming our scanners along with communications. I don't know." The man's frustration was obvious.

The atmosphere was stressed, the options limited. The Commander had already decided on the next move to be made. "Send out an emergency buoy, and launch a scanner probe. Let's get a closer look at that thing." Within minutes, both orders were complied with.

All eyes followed the probe as it sped towards the huge vessel before them. New readings began to come in immediately. The distance between the two ships was over three thousand feet, an impossible separation for any tractor beam Republic ships could generate. The device glided over the top of the craft, illuminating small sections of it and sending back close up footage through its onboard recorders. The ship matched no known configuration. It stretched over a half a mile in length and at least a quarter of that in width. There were no running lights or identification markings visible anywhere on the hull. Interior scanning attempts were bounced back, the hull impenetrable. The probe was brought back without incident, with very little useful information.

Anson was at a loss. They were being towed by an unknown ship, to an unknown place, for an unknown reason. One fact was clear. The ship had demonstrated obvious aggression. The outcome would no doubt, be hostile as well. He called all personnel in supervisory positions to the control room. He felt it prudent for everyone on board to know the exact situation. Soon, everyone was assembled.

Anson wasted no time. "Long range communication is out. Our engines and shields are down. We're operating on battery power only. At the present rate, we have sixteen hours of juice left. Oxygen reserves are full. We have enough to last five days, but if our power goes, it won't matter. It'll get pretty damn cold in here." His eyes moved about the room, leaving no face unseen.

Kahn, standing beside Deanna, grew perturbed with the Commanders lingering stare at her. Anson's gaze finally met his, recognition noticeable in his eyes also.

He continued after a brief hesitation. "We've dropped the emergency buoy. Hopefully, Aquillon One will pass close enough to pick up its signal. We estimate they'll be reaching the point of our attack in roughly two hours. We've been under tow for about an hour to hour and a half. We're not really sure when they started." He paused. "Any questions so far?"

"Where are they taking us?" Someone asked.

"We don't know. All we know is our course, and our speed. If that ship doesn't increase speed, and Haute follows us, he'll eventually catch up. Hopefully, our power will last that long." No one spoke as he paused again. "We sent out a probe, got some good pictures, but that was it." He raised his hands. "I'm open to any ideas, theories, guesses, anything." Quiet talking began among the group, but no one volunteered any suggestions. "Don't keep anything to yourself, people. The only bad idea is one unvoiced."

One man finally spoke. "I guess it wouldn't be feasible to try to disable their engines?"

"I would consider it, but it would severely drain our power reserves, and if they fired back ... well, we wouldn't like it very much. Besides, we're coasting right now. It wouldn't slow them down any."

The man nodded his understanding.

Another man raised his hand. "Well, it's obvious we have to get our engines going."

"I agree. That's the key. They're working on it, but there are no guarantees."

Kahn spoke next. "I, for one, would like to see the video from the probe, see what we can see."

"Be my guest." Anson replied. "It's all on disc."

The meeting went on as Kahn left to find Gary and review the film.

Within five minutes, Anson cleared up the briefing. As he watched everyone file out, he rose and followed one particular person, catching up with her down the corridor. "Ensign Wilkens, hold up."

Deanna stopped, not out of politeness, but out of recognition of higher rank.

Anson stopped next to her. "I don't suppose you signed up for this trip because I was commanding, did you?"

"No sir, I didn't. To tell the truth, I didn't even know you were on board." She did little to hide the animosity in her voice.

He smiled weakly. "Ease up Ensign. We didn't have that bad a time, did we?"

"No doubt you remember something I don't." she smirked.

"Oh, I remember a lot," he said. "I remember everything." She turned to walk away and he reached out, touching her shoulder. "Hey, that was a long time ago ... too long actually. Can't we can get past what happened?"

They were alone in the hallway at that point. Deanna glared with a direct, cold stare, but her voice was pleasant. "I'll tell you what Commander. Since my least favorite part of your body was your dick, which, by the way, you couldn't keep in your pants, I'll make a deal with you. I'll date you again as soon as it's no longer on your body." She continued down the hall and spoke again without turning. "If you want to take me up on that, sir, I know someone who would remove it at no charge."

Anson, amused, watched her go, staring at the wonderful swing of her hips. He had always loved her spunk. He unquestionably would like to spend some time with her again, but it wasn't going to be in the cards, at least not yet. He turned undiscouraged, back towards the control room. Minutes later, he flinched as he saw Bengal enter the room. Had she said anything to him? He waited with apprehension as he approached.

"Commander ... I've got an idea," the larger man said.

Relieved, Anson was all ears. The pilot held several photos showing different locations on the alien ships hull.

Kahn explained. "These hatches look similar to every airlock I've ever seen. They're scattered all around the hull; all the same. If we could somehow get aboard their ship, we might be able to at least slow them down."

"And how would you propose we do that, Lieutenant?"

Kahn shrugged. "I don't know for sure. You said you wanted all options."

Anson began to shake his head, wondering if the idea was a little extreme, or dangerous, or both. Their predicament wasn't an easy one however. "What if they're not air locks?"

"Then we can rule them out. I just think we need to take a closer look." Kahn pursued. "Let us go out, check it first hand."

"I don't know. I don't want to take the chance on …?" Anson balked.

"A few minutes … tops. We go out, take a look, come right back."

The Lieutenant Commander mulled for a moment, finally admitting that it may be worth a try. "One move from that ship and you're back here. Understand?"

Kahn's eyebrows lifted. "Guaranteed."

Twenty minutes later, he stood amidships with Gary, Colleen, and Deanna. The pilots were now dressed in full flight gear.

Deanna expressed her disapproval. "You know why he's sending you, don't you?"

"It's got nothing to do with that and you know it," Kahn answered. "We have to try something. We're the only ones who can do this." He paused. "It was my idea, anyway."

"Oh … well, I'm sure he loved that," she said sardonically, shaking her head. "I'm sorry; I just don't want anything to happen to you."

"And you think I do?" Kahn sputtered.

She nodded. "I really have to wonder sometimes. Just be careful."

"It's in the rules, babe." He hugged her tightly.

Gary talked with Colleen, but didn't feel a hug was anywhere close. He half-heartedly smiled; a poor attempt at hiding his true feelings.

Colleen smiled back. "Be careful."

He nodded and turned to Kahn. "You ready, Chief?"

Kahn was still in an embrace. "No … are you?"

"No …" His answer was the truth.

"Then we're ready." Kahn held his forearm upright, which Gary met in mid air with his own. "See you outside, junior."

Each went their separate ways down the corridor.

The raider bays were two hundred feet apart, on opposite sides of the ship. Gary found the walk to his ship much too short. Climbing in, he quickly went through a systems check. Afterwards, he saluted the launch technician, who promptly returned the gesture before exiting the bay. Gary closed his eyes, waiting for the words, unsure whether he felt exhilaration or dread.

Finally, the word came. "Bays are clear. Doors opening."

His ship shuddered as the outer doors cracked open. Air, dust, and any loose objects misplaced or lost, were instantly sucked outward into the void. In seconds, both bays were in a vacuum. As the doors fully retracted, both pilots gaped in trepidation at the sight before them. The alien vessel looked close enough to reach out and touch. The view they had from the control room had been deceiving, making it seem much further away than it actually was.

Kahn swallowed, his eyes wide, wondering what the hell he'd been thinking when he came up with this idea. With the push of a button, the dock locks fell away. His ship floated free within the bay. With a delicate touch, he inched forward.

Glancing to his right, he saw his partner's ship, also clearing its bay. Maneuvering towards him, he drew within fifty feet and gave instruction. "Stay on my wing. The section we need to check out is on the port side." He turned and went back the way he had come, angling towards the stern of the dark behemoth. He looked carefully, but could not detect the tractor beam. Normally, one would be discernible, but in this case there was nothing. He led well below where it should have been.

Gary couldn't help but stare at the tremendous vessel. It almost looked as if the Aquillon Two could fit into one of its engine ports. He was cautious to stay just behind Kahn, only a hundred feet ahead of him. The sweat in his suit began to build, just as it had only days ago at his graduation. He checked the cockpit temperature. It read seventy-two degrees, but it felt like ninety. Who could have guessed he would be in this kind of situation so soon. The steering rod felt damp in his hand. He told himself to stay calm, do the job and return to the ship. Piece of cake …

Much too soon, they reached the lower side of the ship. It looked dead, but they knew that it was not. They used only the docking thrusters to maneuver. The raider's main engines were in stand-by mode. There was no radio traffic, as if their words would alert the unknown occupants of their minuscule presence.

Within minutes, Kahn found what he was looking for. He illuminated an area of the vessel with powerful spotlights and nodded in approval. What he saw in the photograph and what he saw now were the same. It resembled an airlock, easily large enough to admit a man. Whether that was a possibility was another matter. He broke the stillness. "Aquillon Two, we've found the first door. In my estimation, it is an airlock. I can make out an outer control panel from here."

Anson listened. "We read you GR One. Do you think it's accessible?"

"Unknown. There's only one way to find out."

Anson knew what he meant. To open the door would require someone to suit up and do it manually. He wondered if one or both of the pilots would be up for that task. At least fifty lives may depend on what they did or didn't do. He then had an unsettling thought. For a short while, he had forgotten about their original mission. The families at the outpost would be running out of life support soon, if they were even still alive. Their fate was decidedly out of his hands, but what about Haute? Where would he place his priorities if he discovered the scout ship's trail?

Kahn glanced towards his wing man. "We found out what we needed. Are you ready, or do you want to look around some more?" He asked.

"Let's head back, I don't like this shit at all."

"No problem." Kahn concurred. He had seen enough for now, though his curiosity was far from appeased. He waited for Gary to come alongside and they began to move slowly aft-ward beneath the vessel.

Kahn suddenly slowed his ship. Something above and ahead of him had caught his attention.

The unexpected appearance of bright light against the black background was unmistakable. He held fascination, rather than alarm, as he glided closer. It soon became evident that a large hatch was opening above them. "We're not playing this game!" Kahn muttered. Without hesitation, he hit the switch to power up his dormant engines, knowing Gary would be doing the same. Only five more seconds …

From the control room aboard the scout ship, the opening hatch could not be seen. Anson frowned at the senior pilot's puzzling statement. He looked across the room where Deanna and her friend stood watching. They had entered soon after the raider launch.

He was about to question Bengal's last statement, but hesitated, his eyes frozen to what he now witnessed on the screen. From somewhere beneath the alien ship, a green light had appeared. It seemed gaseous, it's edges defined but not solid. It moved like a living thing, reaching downward towards the two tiny ships. His eyes grew wide in disbelief. Didn't they see it? Why weren't they moving away from it? He finally spoke excitedly. "Bengal, get the hell out of there!"

Without instruction, the navigator highlighted the two ships on his monitor and magnified the view on the main screen. They suddenly leapt closer, now seemingly only a hundred meters away. Countless fingers of light surrounded the raiders, which still did not or could not move.

"Gold Raider One, answer!" Anson's tone was urgent, but there was no reply. His thoughts scrambled for something to do.

The glowing light from the alien ship swirled and wrapped around the ships, completely enveloping the space between. It grew brighter with each passing second, the color changing to red, yellow, and finally to a white so intense that the raiders could no longer be seen.

Within the background noise of the room, a lone voice could be heard repeating the same words. "Gold One … do you read? Gold Two … come in!"

Deanna and Colleen stood in incredulity, unable to speak. They watched the blinding light for perhaps fifteen seconds. In the very next, it blinked out. To their horror, the raiders and pilots disappeared with it. Anson stood slowly.

Deanna moaned aloud. "Oh my God …" she began. "Oh my God …"

Colleen tried to sustain her friend as she began to crumble. She had no words that could possibly help. Like all witnesses in the room, she too believed the two men were dead.

Shouts of shock came from around the room, but Anson tried to keep a professional tone. "Scanners, center on their last position. Do you see anything … fuel residue … anything?"

A few seconds later, the answer came. "There's nothing sir." The scanner officer knew where the Commander was heading and voiced it. "If those cells ruptured, we would have seen it."

Anson nodded in agreement and moved towards Deanna, who had begun to sob uncontrollably. "Deanna! Deanna! Ensign Wilkens!" Slowly, with the last words, she looked up to acknowledge him. When she did, he continued. "I don't think they're dead."

Deanna listened, revived with the possibility, nodding in understanding.

Colleen sighed, hoping he was right. "What do we do now?"

Anson looked again to the ship on the screen. "We go get them."

Haute had slept for only an hour when the intercom in his room erupted with a message. "Control room to Commander Haute."

He stirred, not wishing to answer, but reached across the bed to hit the answer button. "Yes, what is it?" he mumbled.

"Sir, we need you up here as soon as possible." The youthful voice held urgency, as they always did.

He sighed, knowing that minor problems to him were seemingly catastrophic in the minds of some of the younger crewmembers. He decided to at least establish the cause of the interruption before getting up. "What's wrong?" he asked.

The officer in charge answered. "Commander, we've got another message from the outpost. I think you might want to address it personally."

"Can you send it down here?" Haute hoped.

"You'd better come up, sir."

Haute gave in. "All right, give me a minute." As he rose, he wondered what it could be. Obviously, it wasn't a major crisis, or else they wouldn't have been so vague.

Five minutes later, he entered the control room. As he sat down, several persons approached him. The first handed him a portable communications pad. He yawned as he read the message. "TO AQUILLON, EN-ROUTE THIS LOCATION. RECEIVED MESSAGE FROM TOUCHEN CONTROL … DATED 10-06241 … 0928 HOURS. RESPONSE AS FOLLOWS. REPORTS OF ATTACK ON THIS STATION ARE UNFOUNDED. ANY REPORTS OF CASUALTIES ARE IN ERROR. ALL MESSAGES RECEIVED AS OF 09-14245 UNJUSTIFIED. PLEASE RESPOND ASAP. GERARD HOBSON, COMMUNICATIONS SUPERVISOR, OUTPOST THREE-THREE."

Wrinkles formed on Haute's brow as he re-read the message. "What the hell is this?" He asked the people around him. There was irritation in his voice.

"We don't know, sir. We've contacted Touchen. They got a similar message after we left."

"All right … this is a stupid question, but is this from the right station?"

"Yes sir. The signal was traced and confirmed."

Haute shook his head as he noted the origination line. "The call letters on the original distress call matches Outpost 33's."

"So does this last message, sir. The messages are from the same station. There's no mistake."

Haute smirked. "Oh, there's been a mistake, and we're gonna find out who made it!" He had calmed somewhat, but still seethed. "Contact Aquillon Two and give them an update. Have them continue until we can corroborate all of this."

"What about us, sir?"

"Continue on course," he answered. He placed a finger on the screen, erasing the message. "I'll write a reply to send to the outpost and give it to you later." He was left alone at his chair.

Only a couple of moments passed before the communications officer spoke from across the room. "Commander … Aquillon Two is not answering our calls."

Haute closed his eyes in frustration. Finally, he rose from his seat, some of his annoyance replaced by concern. He stood next to the young man at the station, placing a hand on his shoulder. He spoke softly, so only he could hear. "I guess you know, son, if you're doing this wrong, I'll have to kill you."

"Yes sir …" He glanced upwards to his superior, wondering whether he was serious. "They're not answering. There is some distance delay, but only few seconds."

"Jesus …" Haute breathed, "What the hell else can go wrong today?" He paused. "Send an emergency message." He turned to the navigator. "How far ahead of us are they?"

"Unknown for sure, sir … four … four and a half hours estimated," he guessed. "They've been off our scanners for a while now."

"All right, maintain course. Keep trying on all emergency channels. Let me know if you hear or see anything. I'll be in my quarters." He left, not knowing what else could be done. Moments later, he was again welcomed by the quiet surroundings of his cabin. This time however, sleep was not an option.

Kahn opened his eyes to an unfamiliar sight. His head rested on a floor, a wall opposite his vision. For a moment, he lay still, confused, trying to focus, with no thoughts clear. Finally, he remembered. He had been in his raider, beneath the strange ship, but where the hell was he now? His surroundings were eerily quiet. He could even hear his own breath as it moved in and out. Apprehension filled him as he realized he was not back on the scout ship.

He sat up slowly … cautiously. He had lain on his left side and felt the soreness as he moved. He turned to sit, putting his right arm behind him for support, but before he could touch the floor, he touched something else, startling him. He turned to see Gary lying beside him, either sleeping or unconscious.

He turned his neck from side to side, trying to relieve the pain, but getting no reprieve. He shook Gary only slightly before he stirred. In an instant, he was awake. "Are you okay?" Kahn whispered.

"I don't know. What happened?" Gary answered with a question.

"Tell me and we'll both know." Kahn touched his mouth with his finger, a signal for Gary to keep his voice down. "I know we're not on the Aquillon."

"No shit …" Gary agreed, painfully rising to his feet. They stood in a darkened corridor, its beginning and end unseen. He touched his side, finding his laser and communicator still on his belt.

Kahn found the same. He looked at his watch and tapped it. "My watch is dead. It was twenty til twelve when we left the ship. How long have we been out?"

"I don't know, mine's dead too." Gary answered.

Kahn took out his communicator and triggered it. It seemed lifeless as well. He examined his sidearm, but whether it was operational was impossible to check without firing it. He replaced in its holster.

Gary began walking the corridor, studying its featureless walls. There was no hint of a doorway or anything else. The ceiling appeared transparent and dim light came from somewhere above. They kept their voices quiet as they moved. "I remember following you under the ship, and that's it." Gary recollected.

Kahn paused. He could remember the door opening above him. "I think I know where we are."

Gary nodded in understanding and agreement. "We're on their ship, but how?"

Kahn shook his head and continued on. As they approached one end of the hallway, an apparent hatchway became visible. Kahn redrew his weapon, functional or not. They had no idea what to expect, other than the fact that they had already witnessed the ships unprovoked hostility.

The hatch they approached rested partly open, but what was beyond could not be seen. Gary placed his hand on the cold metal and pushed it open. A loud creaking noise accompanied the first hint of movement. The sound echoed down the corridor. Gary, startled by the unexpected break in the stillness, froze in his movements, unwilling to push any further.

Kahn moved ahead nevertheless. "They already know we're here anyway." With a quick shove and another incredible scream from the hinges, the door was fully ajar. The small square room beyond presented another dilemma. On each of the three walls was a door. Choosing one, they resumed their exploration.

A brief meeting had just adjourned aboard the Aquillon Two. Lieutenant Commander Anson was having second thoughts about the decisions he had just made, or rather given in to. There was no guarantee that the Aquillon One would discover what had happened, thus no guarantee that there was help on the way. The engines remained useless. Engineers, working non-stop, had been unable to trace the problem. Battery reserves would sooner or later be gone and life support with it.

Immediate steps had to be taken. It was decided to continue with the original, though imprecise plan to get aboard their captor ship and somehow slow or stop it. Now, with the recent occurrences, there was an added task to retrieve two missing pilots, if indeed they had been taken aboard.

The decision he had reservations about was who would be taking on the challenge. He felt he had let his personal feelings override his professional judgment.

The ships head of security, Major James Pritchart, would lead a team of three. Ideally, the most experienced personnel would accompany him, but with limited staffing aboard, there were only four other persons to choose from. One of those individuals had been injured in the earlier attack, with a possible torn ligament in his right knee.

The remaining three had adequate training, but held only secondary security positions. Making the choice among those three was where his emotions played the part.

Deanna Wilkens had rank and seniority above all, a fact she made quite clear to him. The only concern he'd voiced was her connection with one of the pilots, and her potential lack of emotional control. It could detract from her ability to choose rationally if need be. She made an equally strong argument back, that he was being prejudicial in his decision, solely due to their irreparable past.

He had attempted to place part of the decision on Pritchart's shoulders, asking if he was comfortable with who was to go with him, but his answer only bolstered Deanna's request. He was equally trustworthy of any of the three. With that, Anson gave in. Colleen Sluder volunteered as well. Her feelings for the other pilot, although still unvoiced, demanded her to take part.

With the decision made, the photo records were gone over once again and the plan set into motion. Within half an hour, three figures clad in space suits and thruster cradles, floated freely out of an airlock. Each was connected to the other by lengths of cable, allowing for individual movement, but preventing accidental separation. The cradles had thrust time of two hours, allowing plenty of leeway to reach their destination and get back. Sightseeing would not be a consideration on the trip. Free space walking at the speed they were now moving had never been attempted. There were many unknowns, and there were no more cradles on board the Aquillon Two. There would be no second chance if anything went wrong.

Pritchard gave instruction through his helmet microphone. His voice sounded odd … diminished. "Okay, I'll use my thrusters to pull you two along. When we get there you'll have to slow yourselves down. I'll tell you when." He had already demonstrated how the mechanisms worked before they were fitted, but this trip would be their first, and problems were expected. He thrust forward slowly, tightening the cables one by one.

Nothing more was said. The living, breathing ship fell away, the dark ominous hulk growing more imposing with each minute. The silence was broken only sporadically by the sound of Pritchart's mini-thrusters as he made directional changes. Within ten minutes, they had reached the rear starboard side of the ship. Pritchard illuminated the interminable metal cliff face only ten feet away. The ship was clearly ancient, the sides rough and pockmarked from countless unknown encounters.

Colleen stared, eyes wide with fear, at the colossus beside her. She felt tiny ... helpless. Her respirations had become shallow and rapid. She knew what was coming, numbness in her hands and face, sharp pain in her chest. She closed her eyes, trying to stop it.

Pritchart heard the heavy sound of breathing, but couldn't tell who it was. He'd seen people lose control before. "Easy guys, concentrate on your breathing. Slow down, take a deep breath and count to three before you take another." His voice was calm. "We're almost there. Just a couple more minutes ..."

Deanna touched her starboard rotational thruster and turned enough to see her friend behind her. From only a few feet away, she could see Colleen's face shield starting to fog. The climate control within her suit was unable to dissipate the added moisture buildup. "Hey girl ..." she asked quietly. "You okay?" She tried to make light of the problem even though she'd seen her panic attacks before. The severe ones, luckily, were few and far between.

Colleens' eyes darted back and forth from the ship to Deanna, but it was becoming hard to see. She closed her eyes again and shut everything out, cursing herself for letting it go so far. She concentrated on her friend's voice.

"Come on, get a hold of it. You know you can control this. You've done it before." She didn't say anything for a long while, listening to her breaths. Thankfully, they became deeper and slower. "You've got it. Just keep it up," she coaxed.

Pritchart's voice came over once again. "Is she okay?"

Deanna knew she was doing better. "She will be."

Less than a minute later, the hiss of thrusters could again be heard. "Okay ... ease backward on your jets. It'll jerk a little, but we'll stop." Pritchart slowed, but nearly overshot his target. At the last second, he reached out and hooked a cable onto a vertical bar beside the airlock. Holding onto the cable slide, he gripped it tightly, slowing himself to a jerking stop. It took another moment, but the two girls were soon beside him, out of breath, but safe. Pritchart relayed their status. "Aquillon Two, we've reached position one."

Deanna looked into Colleen's eyes. Her face had calmed, and she managed a feeble smile. De smiled back in relief.

Pritchart studied the possible entryway in the hull. The hatch was circular with a yellow reflective band around it. In the center of the upper half of the circle was a triangular window. He moved his light up, but could see nothing inside. He then located the control panel seen in the photos. It too was circled in a reflective band. It contained two buttons, both white, but with no visible markings.

He checked the position of his two partners, making sure they weren't in front of the door and pushed the top most button. The response was immediate. The yellow bands around the panel and the door began glowing steadily. Also, lights flickered behind the window, finally remaining on. At that point, the second button glowed green. He spoke to the others. "Doesn't green mean go?" He didn't really expect an answer and received none. He touched the second button.

In the next second, the hatchway slid aside, revealing a small white-walled room. Another hatch awaited on the innermost wall. Pritchart sighed under his breath in relief. "Good call, Bengal." He moved into the airlock, which was easily large enough to permit each of them. Deanna and Colleen wasted no time in following.

Once inside, the next step was obvious. The team leader touched the first of two buttons on the inner wall. The outer door moved back into place, followed by the loud hiss of air rushing into the chamber. At the same time, the threesome settled to a grated floor beneath their feet. Within seconds, the full weight of the suits and thruster assemblies rested on their shoulders. The inner hatch opened.

Pritchart no longer held the spotlight in his hand. Instead, he held a hand laser. Quickly, he scanned, pointing the weapon everywhere his eyes moved. He stepped forward into the room before them. Several cabinets and lockers lined the walls, filled with equipment as unfamiliar as the ship around them.

Pritchart maintained his watchful stance. "Sluder, do your thing."

Colleen, now in better control, took hold of a device hanging from her side. Touching the keys on its panel was difficult with the bulky gloves, but she managed. Two beeps, followed by a steady tone signaled the completed scanner reading. "It says we're good," she said.

Deanna cracked the seal on her helmet, and began ridding herself of the suit and cradle. It was not meant to be worn for long in a gravity rich environment. Taking her first breath, she noted that it smelled old … stale.

Pritchart immediately tried his communicator, but got no answer from the scout ship or the pilots. He frowned with frustration. There was no way to signal either without it. Whatever was in the walls of the ship that prevented scanning was inhibiting communications as well. Pocketing the useless device, he led the others from the chamber.

Deanna, before following, took from her suit, a wax marker, normally used for writing in space. She would use it to mark the way back. A ship as capacious as this could have many twists and turns.

Pritchart entered a simple corridor appearing to lead forward and aft. "Well, which way?" He was open for suggestions.

Colleen shrugged. "Our control room would be up and forward. Maybe theirs is too."

Deanna agreed. "We have to make contact one way or the other. That would probably be our best bet. It's the only way we're gonna find our guys."

Pritchart nodded to her. "Just don't forget the bread crumbs along the way."

Forward it was.

Haute finished the reply message to the outpost and fired it ahead. They had no trouble communicating with Touchen control, so the difficulty with contacting the scout ship was still a mystery. All they could do was continue on the original course and catch up with them at the outpost. Time passed monotonously, but Haute had the feeling; the relative peace couldn't last long.

He again returned to the control room. According to the ships chronometer, it was early morning. The room was minimally staffed.

A scanner technician caught his attention as he walked past. "Sir, I've got something here I don't understand."

"What is it Bobby?" Haute asked.

"Some kind of gaseous cloud ... pretty considerable ... showed up on one of our secondary scopes."

"Gaseous cloud?"

"Yes sir. We got a sample of it as we passed through. I'm getting the clinical on it now."

Haute waited for the results. He was guessing it wouldn't be anything natural, but did not expect what came up on the screen. The cloud consisted of many basic elements ... the most of which was nitrogen. It was a substance used widely throughout the Republic. It was usually stored as a liquid gas and was commonly used as engine coolant on most ships. He thought hard for a moment, then said loudly and clearly, "Turn around!"

The woman at the navigation station was puzzled, but obeyed the order without question. As they made the turn, he ordered the scanner tech to provide her with the coordinates of the "cloud."

Within minutes, they again approached the location. Haute ordered a schematic of the area and saw what he feared. Highlighted on the map were a large cloud and a thin unbroken line leading off in a different direction. He nodded in understanding; letting those persons close enough hear his summation. "This nitrogen is from the scout ship."

No one spoke, each pondering the statement. Haute's mind raced. If he was right, and the scout ship had left this point under their own power, then they couldn't go far. With the amount of expelled coolant needed to produce a cloud this size, the engines would overheat soon. It was puzzling that they weren't still within scanner range. Why they turned off their previous course, as the trail suggested, was the main question.

"Send another message to control. Tell them we're following the trail, additional information to follow." He nodded toward the navigator. "Let's get going … maximum speed."

The two pilots had no idea how long they walked, but their legs grew weary. Initially, they had been edgy, ready for anything, but now, after seeing a hundred empty rooms and corridors, they strolled easily, having come to the baffling conclusion that the ship was unmanned. The assumption, of course, could not be accurate. Unmanned ships did not fire upon other vessels, did not put said vessels under tow, and did not abduct pilots and dump them on their own decks. The ship didn't appear lived in, but the crew had to be on board, hidden away by chance or by their own design.

Gary sighed, "We gotta try something else." He looked about. "How do we know we haven't been here already?"

Kahn had to agree. "We don't." His eyes burned with fatigue.

"So what do we do?"

Kahn considered their options, and then spoke. "The next door we come to that won't open … we open it." He took out his weapon. "It's time to see if this works."

The next such hatch was found at the end of another barren passage. Kahn took aim, but was stopped by his friend. "Wait a minute. We don't know what's behind that door, right?"

Kahn frowned. "Yeah … that's why I'm cutting through it."

"Well, what if it leads outside?"

Kahn was forced to mull over the possibility for a moment. Suddenly, his new idea didn't sound so good. "Damn it man! What the hell made you think of that?"

"Sorry … I don't know … maybe because I don't want to die!"

Kahn didn't hesitate long. "Well, it doesn't look like a pressure door … so … we try it." He aimed again and triggered the pistol.

In the next instant, two questions were answered. The first was whether the laser would fire. It did. The second was what lay beyond the door. The blast struck it squarely. There was no explosion, no melt down or punch through, but nonetheless, the door was gone; where to, the men had no clue.

Gary, pressed against one wall, looked at Kahn, somewhat relieved. "Good shot."

Kahn, shrugging, moved forward. The section of the ship they now entered was nothing like any part they'd seen thus far. It seemed brighter, which was a welcome change, but the added light was far from the most interesting difference they found.

Their mouths fell open and their minds searched for answers as they stepped through the doorway. They now stood on a walkway leading toward another door far in the distance. They couldn't move, their feet seemingly frozen in place. Their minds couldn't comprehend what they saw. Up, down, and around them, was nothing! There were no walls, no ceiling and no ship. Everything but the hatchway behind them, the walkway, and the doorway at its far end, had disappeared. They stood in the void, open to space, surrounded only by the stars. There was no glass, and no force field, at least none that they could see, separating them from space. Fear and astonishment inundated their senses. One fear was the thought that they might fall off the narrow walkway at any moment. If they were truly in space, they would fall nowhere. If they were truly in space, they would also be dead.

Gary was speechless, his breath cut short by the unforeseen occurrence. He finally inhaled, wondering how he could breathe at all. He shook his head in bewilderment. "I can't believe it," he muttered.

"Jesus Christ! What the hell?" Kahn's voice was filled with panic.

Gary turned to see him looking back the way they'd just come. The doorway they had stepped through only a moment before was gone. As they watched in horror, the end of the walkway they stood on began to disappear as well. Unconsciously, they stepped backwards, distancing themselves from the fading edge. The walkway continued to vanish, inch-by-inch, foot-by-foot, faster with each second. Soon, the men were running toward the opposite door, still a good distance away.

Gary led the way down the precarious path, but suddenly slowed to a stop. He was out of breath, but not from the short jaunt. He was scared.

Kahn slowed also, passing him on the narrow platform. "What are you doing?"

Gary, perplexed, fought the overwhelming urge to keep moving. He shook his head in defiance. "This isn't real, it can't be. It has to be a dream."

"What?" Kahn looked beyond his friend. The walkway was still growing shorter. "Are you crazy?" he yelled.

"Just listen to me for a minute! This can't be happening. You know and I know it's not possible."

Kahn narrowed his eyes, considering the possibility, but his gut instinct wouldn't allow it. "I don't give a shit what's real and what's not. If this is a dream, I'm waking up on the other side of that door."

Gary stood his ground, watching the edge creep to within fifty feet.

Kahn yelled more fervently. "If you don't come on, I'm gonna knock you on your ass and carry you! This ain't the time to screw around!"

The edge was thirty feet away. Gary, his determination waning, turned and moved away again. "Wake my ass up when we get to the end."

Kahn followed. "No problem."

Within a minute they reached the lone, oval hatchway. Kahn fired toward the metal panel and as before, it was magically gone. Another room could be seen within. He shook his head as he ran into it.

Once on the other side, the panel closed behind them. Both men stood with their hands on their hips, huffing, after the sprint. Their hearts thundered in their chests. As Gary looked over their new surroundings, he turned to Kahn, who promptly slapped him across the face.

The impact shocked him. "Damn it! What the hell was that for?"

"You told me to …" Kahn sucked in the much needed air "… wake you up when we got to the end."

Relieved to be at that end, Gary couldn't help but be somewhat laughing, even though his cheek hurt to a great extent. "What just happened out there?"

"I don't know. I don't understand any of this." Kahn studied the short corridor they now stood in. It led to still another closed door. He shook his head in aggravation. "I'm not doing that again."

Gary nodded without argument. Without hesitation, he strode to the new door and pushed hard against it. To his surprise, it swung easily inward. What he saw beyond it shocked him more than what he had seen behind the last one.

CHAPTER 5

▼

The navigator on board the Aquillon Two sipped his coffee carefully. He'd scalded his tongue the first time and wasn't about to do it again. His eyes burned as well. He'd stared at the view screen for too long. He saw the same fixed scene every time his eyes wandered its way. He had been without sleep for twenty straight hours and had made up his mind that in the next hour, he would seek rest, no matter what happened. The coffee he drank wouldn't make any difference at this point. He drank it only out of boredom. The security team had been gone exactly one hour. Their last message was received eighteen minutes after they had left. Nothing had been heard since. There was no more that could be done.

Some good news had come from engineering. They had found and repaired a large leak from the liquid nitrogen storage tanks, but there was still no word on why the engines were inoperable.

Only he and two others were in the control room. Most of the crew had retired. He had no doubt that Commander Anson was still in engineering, cracking the whip. Oh well, let him go without sleep, that's why he makes the big bucks.

He faced forward to set down his cup. As he let it go, his hand jerked, causing it to fall to the floor. No attention was paid to the mess. His eyes grew wide with confusion. The view screen was filled with stars and nothing else. Finding his senses, he touched a switch, changing the angle of view, but still saw nothing. He then realized all he had to do was check his scope. Unbelievably, he saw only his own ship. He moved hastily to the unmanned communications console. "Commander Anson to the control room immediately!" he yelled.

The other two men in the room, puzzled at first, finally noticed the screen, which no longer framed the rear of the ship. One of them mumbled, "Where is it?"

The same words were said again as Anson burst into the room.

"Sir, one second it was there, the next it wasn't." answered the navigator.

"Are we still moving?" asked Anson.

The navigator checked, the thought never crossing his mind. "Negative, sir, we've stopped."

Anson signaled a mandatory station recall, and within minutes, all consoles were re-manned. He walked to a scanner station. "Where are they?" he asked, expecting at least one solid answer.

"I don't have them anywhere. There's nothing, even on maximum range."

"That's impossible." He looked for himself, seeing the same. He left the station, shaking his head in disbelief.

A female officer across the room made a suggestion. "Commander, everything on that screen is recorded. Whatever happened should be on tape."

"You just got a raise, Ensign. Make it happen."

A moment later, the all too familiar engine ports were again on the screen. As they watched, the image suddenly was gone. Anson spoke. "Rewind and slow it down ... quarter speed."

This time, they saw what their eyes could not before. In slow motion, the ship lunged forward, accelerating to an unimaginable speed and disappearing.

"Can you plot their course?" Anson asked, knowing they would be following if possible.

"Affirmative ... same course, sir."

A number of peculiar events occurred almost simultaneously. Calls, directed to the control room, came in from all over the ship. It wasn't possible, but all previously non-working sections of the scout ship were abruptly back on line, including communications and engines.

Anson took urgent action, ordering messages sent to Touchen and their mother ship, which hopefully, wasn't far away. The reply from the Aquillon One was nearly instantaneous. Within minutes, Anson had given a rough report to the Fleet Commander and was given orders to wait where they were until he arrived. The order had to be obeyed. The scout ship was stranded until precious coolant could be replaced.

Anson thankfully ended his summation to his superior. He leaned back in his chair and closed his eyes for a gracious moment. His mind and body were exhausted, and he knew the other members of his crew felt the same. Aquillon

One was closing rapidly and would rendezvous at their position in an hour or less. For once, he saw no reason to leave his comfortable seat. He kept his eyes closed. Before drifting off, he had the afterthought to cancel emergency station status, allowing others to stand down. His last conscious thoughts were for his missing crewmembers. Were they still alive? Had he made the right decision in sending them out? They were questions that only time would answer.

Pritchart, Sluder, and Wilkens had walked for what seemed like miles through empty corridors and rooms, marking each turn as they went. Their weapons, having grown heavy in their hands, rested unused in their holsters. They had initially moved forward through the ship, but at this point in their exploration, they didn't know in which direction they faced. All they knew for sure was that they had not backtracked, and were on the same level, having found no way to leave it.

Pritchart stopped in a room typical of all the others, and sat down heavily in one of the chairs that were there. If there was one conclusion that could be deducted from their venture, it was that the unseen crew must be humanoid. The fixtures and furnishings on board seemed very similar to those of humans. He glanced at his watch, which he already knew was useless. "We've been here at least an hour."

"And we still don't know anything." added Colleen, sitting beside him. She had the urge to take her boots off. "Are we going to stay here for a while?" she asked.

Pritchart sighed with frustration. "Why not."

Colleen sighed as well. "Good." A few seconds later, her feet were free.

Deanna sat down, tired of the seemingly endless trek. "What are we gonna do now?"

"I don't know. I'm open for suggestions." Pritchart answered.

Since their arrival, Deanna hadn't had time to think. Maybe they hadn't found the missing pilots because they weren't there. She sat with closed eyes, lost in thought. With each empty chamber they found, hope that Kahn and Gary were on board shrank. For the first time since they had left the scout ship, the possibility of living without Kahn crept into her being. The feeling was unacceptable and she despised it. In the back of her mind she heard Colleen say something, but she wasn't paying attention. She turned to her, "What!" she asked.

Before Colleen could repeat herself, there was a dramatic change in the silence they had experienced thus far. A distant, but distinctive sound met their ears. It was short-lived and its pitch high, like a shriek.

Pritchart stood instantly, his gun in his hand. "That was laser fire!" he exclaimed.

Deanna jumped to her feet, her heart and hope re-energized. Even though laser fire usually meant trouble, she realized it could have only come from one source. She stepped toward Colleen's boots, kicking them to her.

It was impossible to tell which direction the sound had came from. They stood in perfect silence awaiting another. A minute passed, when suddenly, without warning, a door only ten feet away and yet untested, burst open.

Pritchart jumped, nearly firing his own weapon. The girls cried out in shock and fright. The two unwanted emotions gave way to relief and elation as the two missing pilots entered the room.

Pritchart couldn't help smiling, even though he was only one left un-hugged. "Glad you two could join us."

Gary, being hugged by Colleen, was equally glad. "Well, we didn't really have anything going on, so ..."

Deanna held Kahn tightly, her embrace telling him everything she couldn't say.

Pritchart chuckled in good humor. "Either of you got an extra pair of pants, I think I just pissed mine."

Several minutes of explanations were traded, followed by the question of where to go from the small confine. Deanna was ready to leave yesterday. "What's back that way?" she asked, indicating the direction Gary and Kahn had just come.

Both men spoke together, relaying, "We don't want to go that way." They promised to explain at a later time.

It was agreed to backtrack to the airlock and make plans from there. It was the only sure way off the ship, and also the only way to contact the Aquillon Two. There were only three space suits at their disposal, so a solution would have to be established.

Deanna's wax marks were easily distinguishable on the featureless walls and within minutes, they had followed them to their end. Once back at the entry room, the situation became even less desirable. Three of the five persons stood speechless, and the other two wondered why.

Pritchart's face held disgust. "What kind of bullshit is this?" he said heatedly.

Kahn stepped forward. "What's wrong?"

The angry man drew his laser once again. "Someone's fuckin with us. Our suits and cradles were right her!"

Deanna noted the red arrow pointing out of the room, right where she had drawn it before. Colleen moved closer to Gary, both realizing that they were no doubt being watched. It was no longer a surprise that they had not seen any of the crew. It was clearly just a game of cat and mouse.

"I don't like this shit, guys." Gary mumbled under his breath. Whoever was watching could probably hear them as well. It was an uncomfortable feeling.

Pritchart walked toward the airlock, striking an open locker door in the process. It slammed shut, making an exceptionally loud reverberation.

Kahn presented his thoughts. "All right, we're trapped here unless we find our ships. They're watching us. We know that now. They want us here for some reason. They want the Aquillon for some reason." He paused, pondering the possible repercussions of what he was considering. The crew of the Aquillon Two was still in danger. "We came over here to slow down or stop this ship. Our circumstances have changed, but our goal is still the same. Let's work on that first."

Colleen was confused. "How are we supposed to do that?"

"We keep opening doors until we find someone." Kahn suggested. He saw Gary's eyes grow wide, obviously remembering their last episode. "I said we'd open them. I didn't say we had to go through them." His friend nodded his approval. Kahn looked to Pritchart, who had calmed somewhat. "Major ... is that cool with you?"

The man nodded. "It sounds all right ..." he consented.

Kahn continued. "One of two things is gonna happen. We're going to find a way to stop this ship, or we're going to meet whoever is playing these games."

Gary thought of another possibility; that whoever was running the show thus far, would continue to do so, no matter what they did. He kept the opinion to himself.

Kahn left the room, his hand laser drawn, and walked to the first locked hatch. Taking aim, he squeezed the trigger. The short burst of energy struck the center of the panel, and as before, it was instantly gone, revealing a brightly lit room beyond. Each of the others drew their weapons as well, not knowing what waited for them next. Kahn warily stepped through the opening.

The room was much different than what they had found thus far. The walls were filled with view screens, and below were console tables with multitudes of controls. With vigil, Kahn began to explore. The others followed, eager to see.

Pritchart was the last to go through, and as he did, the door slid shut. The security officer, surprised, but calm, turned and aimed his own weapon, following Kahn's example. He fired center and watched as nothing happened. The laser burst was absorbed completely by the metal. There was no ricochet or burn.

Twice more he fired with the same results, then stepped forward and touched the metal, finding it cold and unblemished. Turning back to the others, he nodded his head. "I guess this is where they want us now."

Before anyone else could speak, the lights in the room dimmed until they stood in pitch blackness. Each dared not move. Colleen maintained a death grip on Gary's arm. The complete darkness only doubled the dread they all felt.

Suddenly, a cold rush of air wafted through the room. For a brief second, all had the awful feeling that the room had suddenly been opened to the outside, but the fact that they could take their next breath dispelled it. The cold air continued for only a few seconds and abruptly ceased.

Kahn blinked rapidly, trying to decide if light was again returning. Soon, he realized it was. Almost immediately, he noticed that their surroundings were somehow different. He half expected to see stars around them, as before, but was relieved only to see walls, ceiling and the like.

The five huddled together, each astonished at what they now witnessed. The room they had stood in a moment before was gone. It was difficult to tell what had happened, but the end result was undeniable. They now stood in a much larger chamber, resembling in no way where they had been when the lights went out.

Colleen was the first to speak, her voice shaky. "What the hell's going on?" No one answered.

They stood on an open balcony, the upper level of a much bigger room below them. From where they stood, only the far wall could be seen beyond the railing twenty feet away. Within seconds, the chamber was brightly lit, giving the group the confidence to move.

Gary walked to the railing with Colleen, who was not about to leave his side. Both now figured that nothing else on the vessel could surprise them. They soon saw that they were wrong. "My God!" exclaimed Gary.

Below them rested the first familiar sight they had seen. Two Republic raiders, side by side, rested on the floor of the lower room. The cockpits were open and at first glance, they seemed undamaged. A vertical ladder was quickly found along the railing allowed a rapid descent to the ships.

The pilots went directly to their ships. The raider's bows were positioned toward a huge door recessed into the bulkhead. Hopefully, it was a door leading out. Even as Gary climbed to the cockpit, he had second thoughts about everything that had just happened. He voiced one of them. "Something's not right here."

Kahn, already in his own ship, answered him. "Nothing's been right since we got here."

"Exactly, that's what I mean. Just hear me out." Everyone paused. "Isn't this all a little too convenient?"

Pritchart spoke first. "It's weird. I don't know about convenient."

"No. I mean look at it. We just happen to run into you guys on a ship as big as this? The lights go out and all of a sudden we're here? I feel like a rat in maze or something. I don't buy it."

Kahn considered it. "He's right. We didn't run into you by accident. Somebody or something has been pulling our strings since we got here."

Pritchart nodded his head. "I agree. We don't know who or why, but what difference does it make? What can we do about it?" He pointed to the huge door before them. "I say we discuss it after we get off this son of a bitch."

Gary nodded. "That's what I'm saying! They want us off. Look at this; it's just part of the game ... our ships just showing up out of nowhere? All of it!"

Deanna voiced her exasperation. "So what do you suggest, we don't try to get out of here just because they want us to?"

"I don't know what we should do. I'm just saying I don't think we should just blindly do what they want?" Gary answered.

Kahn looked over his control panel of his ship. "I don't give a shit what kind of game they're playing. There's room enough for all of us in these. We're leaving."

Gary moved aside so Colleen could climb in behind his seat. Once there, she took note of the space. "De was right; there's a lot of room in here." she commented.

Gary smiled half-heartedly. "If you want, I'll give you the grand tour." He paused and added. "If we live through this."

Colleen reached around the seat and squeezed his arm. "I may take you up on that ... if we live through this."

Her hand lingered. He reached over and laid his upon hers, hopefully to reassure.

Kahn donned his helmet, which he strangely found hanging just where it should have been. It was almost as if he'd parked the ship himself. Checking the comm, he switched it to the emergency frequency and hit the transmitter. "Aquillon Two ... Aquillon Two, this is GR One, how do you read?" As expected, there was only static. He switched the channel without trying again. "I guess you can't hear me either, can you?" he said, giving Gary a glance.

Gary heard the words through his headset. "Believe it or not ... yeah."

"Well damn ... everything's perfect." He smiled.

Within a minute, the canopies were closed and sealed. The engines flared, filling the chamber with a loud whine as they reached full power. Kahn looked about the room, expecting something to suddenly appear and try to stop them. Seeing nothing, he spoke. "Let's open these doors. Lasers first, full power spread on my mark. Three ... two ... one ... mark!"

Eight separate beams of bright white leaped from the ports, blinding them, but it was short lived. The massive door split on its center seam, buckling outward, but not completely open. The force of the air being sucked outward rocked the ships, threatening to pull them toward the narrow opening. Kahn quickly fired again. The second blast finished the job.

The doors ripped from their housings and went spinning out of sight. The glorious blackness of open space beckoned to them. The pressure within the closed chamber equalized within seconds, allowing the ships to float freely once again. No time was wasted in exiting the ship that had held them for so long.

Kahn led the way from the vessel, still afraid that she would somehow pull them back. Fifteen seconds out, he began a wide circle, not knowing where the Aquillon Two would be found. Even before the turn was completed, he had full view of the alien ship and instantly knew that something was very wrong.

The radio remained silent as the pilots took in the astonishing view. Below the huge ship was an immense planet, only a few hundred miles away. The ship appeared to be in a high orbit above it. More distressing than what they saw, was what they didn't see. The Aquillon Two was nowhere to be found.

Panic was not a common emotion to Kahn Bengal, but with what he and the others had been through the last few hours, combined with the lack of sleep, and now the disappearance of their ship, he had nearly nothing left but that. "Someone want to tell me where we are?"

Gary too, felt helpless and discouraged. The planet looked similar to some in the Belaquin system, but he knew that it was not one of them. Its surface was white with cloud cover, but patches of green and blue, suggestive of land and water, were visible. It looked inviting if nothing else. He checked his medium range scanners, but only the huge ship beside them was registering. Wherever the scout ship was, it wasn't close. He answered his friend. "I don't know, but we can't stay up here."

Kahn answered back. "I agree. We're out of choices."

There was no movement from the vessel they had just quitted as they steered below it. It fell rapidly behind them. In seconds they approached the planets atmosphere.

Kahn eased the stick to the left and pulled up slightly to correct his approach for entry, but suddenly, his raider wouldn't respond. "Gary, I may have a problem over here."

"What's up?" Gary began to ask, pulling up also. "What the hell?" he murmured.

"I don't have control!" Kahn advised.

"Same here … I've lost all manual." He'd never had a ship not do his bidding, and found it to be a disagreeable experience. Gary hurriedly flipped switches on the panel.

Colleen's voice came from behind him. It was filled with concern. "What's wrong?"

Gary moved the stick in every direction, but it was as if it was disconnected. "I don't know yet. I can't steer the ship. Nothing is working!"

"What's that mean? What do we do?" she continued.

"We're falling into the atmosphere, but if we don't hit it just right …"

"We burn up …" Colleen answered her own question.

Gary swallowed hard. "Exactly," He watched the level indicator change slightly, followed by a stronger descent toward the planet. Looking to GR One, he saw it seemingly turning as well, apparently changing to the same course. Suddenly, he felt that he understood. "Kahn, I'm gonna try something."

Kahn paused in his own frustrated efforts to steer his craft and waited.

Gary opened a clear covering over a switch and paused, weighing the consequences of what he was considering. He was about to perform an emergency shut down and re-start of his craft's systems. If the ship were on a controlled course, then interrupting power would allow the vessel to be taken over by the pull of gravity from the planet below. In essence, he would begin to fall out of control. Only one problem remained. If the engine did not restart, then it was over. The ship would plunge out of control into the atmosphere.

Gary smiled, confident that he knew precisely what would happen with the experiment. The odds of two ships, losing manual control at the same time, while all other systems remained operational was absurd. Throughout the last hours, he had seen things that defied rules that could not be changed. This was just another example. They may be free of the ship, but free was an exaggeration. They were still being manipulated; still in the game.

Without hesitation, he flipped off the switch. The lights on the control panel in front of him blinked, but stayed on. An alarm began sounding in the cockpit, followed by a computer voice. "EMERGENCY SYSTEMS SHUT DOWN HAS BEEN ACTIVATED. IF YOU WISH TO ABORT, YOU MUST

RE-ACTIVATE CONTROL WITHIN TEN SECONDS." He felt Colleen's hand squeeze his arm again.

At the count of ten, the controls went dark, signaling complete interruption of power. The alarm as well went silent. Seconds passed with no discernable change in course or attitude. Gary sighed with relief. He had been right. The raiders were under some control, just not their own.

Within another minute, the systems had been restarted. As power returned, he heard a voice begin halfway through a sentence, "... you hear me?"

"We're still here." answered Gary.

"What did you do?"

"Emergency shut down and re-start."

"What the hell for?"

Gary hesitated. "I needed to test a theory." When Kahn didn't respond, he voiced his idea. "Someone's bringing us down. I mean, look at our angle, it's perfect for entry."

"It doesn't look like an accident, does it?" Kahn agreed.

"Negative. I guess we'll just ride it out."

The view of the planet was breathtaking. It resembled Belaquin in many ways, but a much larger portion of rich blue was evident. As their home planet was, the one upper cap that could be seen appeared pure white, possibly covered with ice. The view became limited. They dropped quickly, the blackness of space disappearing as they entered the upper reaches of the atmosphere.

Kahn sat powerless as the outer hull temperature climbed. He prayed that the heat shield below him was sufficient. He had only taken a raider into a planets atmosphere a few times before. He turned in his seat, looking back past GR Two, trying to catch one last glimpse of the ship that had brought them there. Far behind them now, it seemed so small. It was no longer a threat, but what lay waiting below?

Within seconds, flames and smoke marked the paths of the two ships. The heat inside became nearly unbearable. The passengers closed their eyes and prayed.

Haute left the briefing room mildly unsatisfied. He had just finished a long meeting with the tired skipper of the Aquillon Two. He had reviewed the tapes, and listened to all related recordings. The alien ship was still a mystery, as well as a hindrance. It still carried their shipmates, whom he would make every effort to rescue.

His ship was at top speed, following the same heading last documented by the scout ship. How far they would have to go, and if it would make a difference was still unknown.

The meeting with Anson could have gone better. Review of the moments preceding the attack brought some question concerning Commander Anson's actions. It was standard procedure that any unidentified space vessel be deemed a potential danger, requiring immediate raising of shields and locking of weapons. Anson's order for shields however, came much too late in the situation. Computer records upon the Aquillon Two showed that shield deflective levels were only at fifty percent upon impact. Decisions surrounding the loss of five individuals and two gold raiders were briefly debated, but sanctioned by all attending. With all the unknowns facing the young commander, his actions were found prudent and adequate.

Haute made his way to the observation deck where he contemplated what was to come. Sitting down, he stared into the blackness, separated by glass so unblemished that it might as well not have been there. A myriad of indecisions berated him. How far would they have to go? How far should they go? Would the alien ship change course? That alone was an important query. If it did, then the five could be lost with absolutely no way to find them. What does he do if he does catch up? Should he fire on the ship, and possibly put their comrades in danger? Were any of them still alive, or were they on a body recovery mission?

It didn't matter; they were all shipmates and some more than that. He felt great responsibility to at least one of them. His best friend's last request could not be ignored. The words would echo in his mind for the rest of his life. Bengal's simple request before he died was for him to take care of his family. He had done his best to fill the impossible void left by his death. More heartache and responsibility fell upon him when Kahn's mother chose to take her own life. Without his help, Kahn was just another orphan.

He had no regrets with the crew chosen to go on this mission. It was his personal obligation to watch over Bengal, but the young man's father would understand his professional decision to provide the best man for the job.

He stared at the stars. The course they now followed was into uncharted space, but the star systems they approached were familiar. They were still close to home. Maybe some of his great greats had traveled here long ago. Perhaps this vastness had been charted at one time or another, either on paper or memory. He closed his eyes and leaned back, trying to dispel the soreness from his shoulders and neck. He should be in the control room, just in case, but his second in command was a good man. I'll stay just a few more minutes. They'll find me if they want me. Just a few more …

The freezing winds in the lower atmosphere rapidly cooled the raider's hull temperature, which had reached uncomfortable levels. Kahn, drenched with sweat, tried his stick again, but still found no control. He turned again to find his wing man still with him, and heard his voice at the same time. "I don't ever want to do that again." Gary said simply.

"I still got nothing." Kahn answered. "We're coming in too steep. My drop is ten thousand feet a minute." Gary read.

"We're still under power though. I'm showing forward thrust."

Gary nodded in agreement. He heard his friend asking his passengers if they were all right and he did the same. "Colleen …?"

"I'm here … slightly toasted," she answered.

"Yeah, I know. I'm sorry about that." He knew the ride had to be worse on her than him.

"I'll live. Where are we?"

"Don't know, we're still above cloud cover, but it's coming up fast. We won't be in it long. Can you see?"

She placed her face close to Gary's, but was unable to draw close due to the angle of the glass. She looked below, around, and ahead of them. The clouds seemed like a white and gray ocean, stretching as far as she could see. "It's beautiful," she said.

"Yeah, for about another minute …" Gary related.

"Good flying," she said gratefully.

"Well thanks, but you haven't seen any yet. We're still kind of falling right now. I still don't have control." Colleen didn't answer. "But don't worry. I think we're gonna get it back pretty soon. I don't know how, but everything that's happened has been for a reason. If we were really out of control, we'd already be dead."

Kahn's voice came over. "Boy, you're really inspiring confidence over here. I mean … falling … no control … dead. Those are words every pilot should give his passengers."

Gary didn't answer. Instead, he instinctively braced for entry into the cloud cover below, which they had reached sooner than expected. His scanner showed the planet surface to be several miles below, but he still hated flying blind. "Here we go," he finally said.

The ship was suddenly enveloped in white. Beads of moisture formed rivulets across the glass, but instantly were gone, replaced by others. Rushing wind could be felt buffeting the craft. The white veil was short lived. It soon began breaking up, revealing flashes of other colors. Suddenly they were clear. What lay below them was predictable, but also unexpected. The sparkling shine of blue and white lay on their right. Blinding rays reflected off an endless expanse of water. To their left was a purplish-green landmass that stretched to the horizon. Hundreds of small clouds floated above its surface, casting shadows, hiding details, although tiny spots and lines of blue could be seen, marking bays, lakes, and rivers. It would have been breathtaking in any other situation.

Gary looked at his altimeter. It read nine thousand meters and was falling rapidly. He swallowed hard as he pulled back once again on the stick, realizing that if he was wrong and he did not regain control, then he had perhaps two and a half minutes left in his short life.

To his horror, there was still no response. His thoughts raced … his eyes searched desperately for an answer, finally finding it on his control board before him. His only remaining option rested with a single switch located beneath two words. It read, "FULL EJECT"

He closed his eyes, knowing that the words represented his only chance to survive. He shook his head, knowing that the woman behind him had no such choice. If he triggered the switch, she would be dead in seconds. He reopened his eyes, glancing at Kahn's raider, ahead and below him. He knew already what his friend's decision would be if it came down to it. GR One's canopy would not be opening, no matter what. He loved Deanna too much to live without her.

Suddenly, he felt panic and liberation at the same time. He would not touch the switch, even as much as his being screamed at him to do so. He wouldn't be able to live with what he had done; knowing that his friend had the courage to do what he could not. He raised his left hand above his head, where Colleen grasped it and held on, squeezing hard. The other hand he kept on the stick, pulling backwards with all his might and will … waiting. The altimeter read six thousand five hundred meters. They were still over water, but the land was rushing closer. At their velocity, it wouldn't matter where they hit.

A voice came over the receiver; so quiet he could barely make out the words. It was Kahn. He said simply. "Don't do it …"

It took only a second to understand what he was asking. He whispered back. "I won't, Chief." He looked at his friend, seeing movement in his cockpit, but unable to tell what it was. His eyes moved again to the altimeter. The numbers dropped below four thousand. Thinking back to flight school, he remembered the numbers. At their rate of fall, if the number went below five hundred, he wouldn't be able to pull out in time.

His thoughts turned desperate. He had so many unanswered questions. At what point do you ask for help from above? He hadn't spoken to God since he was a child beside his bed, and even then, it had been due to his mothers bidding. If he spoke to him now, after all this time, would he even be heard? Did his heart really believe?

Three thousand …

It didn't matter. If he were going to die, he would just as soon be talking with God, or at least trying. He looked below, trying to find the right words. It was so beautiful. His thoughts grew confusing. Had God made this world as well?

They were over land now, moving nearly perpendicular to the coastline. He was low enough to make out thick green forest, broken only by rivers spilling into what had to be an ocean or sea.

A loud steady alarm filled the small cockpit, a proximity alert warning him to pull up. It was almost too late. With tears in his eyes, he squeezed Colleen's hand.

One thousand …

Gary closed his eyes tightly, thinking back to his childhood … his parents … family gatherings … good times, all of them. He'd never said goodbye before this trip. There hadn't been time. Tears of regret came with the thoughts … so many regrets.

Gary opened his mouth, salty tears trickling into its corners. He licked his lips. "Please God, please …" he pleaded.

The instant the words left him, he felt the nose of the craft move upward. The ship was responding! Within seconds, he and Colleen were pressed downward by an invisible force as the raider fought the incredible force. Colleen's hand released his, her cries of fear reaching over instead. The ship shuddered violently with the strain. The steering stick shook so badly; he could barely maintain his grip. Gary tried to look up to see the other ship, but could not lift his head. He could, however, see the altimeter still falling, dropping below four hundred meters. His neck and back felt as if it would snap. The alarm still blared.

Gradually, the pressure eased; the shuddering lessened. The trim indicator leveled. The raiders were under their control once again.

Kahn laughed over the radio. "Son of a bitch! What a rush!" His relief and exhilaration was obvious.

Gary laughed out loud as well. He couldn't contain it. Nor could he wipe the smile from his face, but did reach beneath his visor and wipe the tears from it. He checked the scanner, finding GR One about two hundred feet below and directly in front of him. His altimeter read only two hundred meters. Tipping his starboard wing, he could see the other ship easily against the dark trees beneath him. As he watched, Kahn yelled again and turned his ship into a full roll. Shouts of protest could be heard in the background as he completed it. "Colleen, you okay?" asked the elated younger pilot.

"God ... I don't know," she answered. "I think I'll take a rain check on the tour of this ... hole back here. I've seen enough of it already."

"I don't blame you." Gary chuckled.

Kahn moved skyward to meet up with GR Two. As he came within sight, he remarked. "I've got two passengers over here about ready to piss down their legs. We need to set down somewhere, figure out what we're gonna do. I'm hungry ... thirsty ... tired ..." He paused, "... and my watch is working again."

Gary glanced at his and shook his head. It was running as if nothing had happened. There was no way to tell what time it was, as if it made any difference. It was somewhat unsettling, not knowing. Every aspect of their lives revolved around time, but in this place, under these circumstances, it didn't matter.

Kahn led the way, staying inland of the sea to the right. His voice called in vain for an answer from the scout ship while they searched. It was hoped originally that they might land on a beach along the coast, but there was none within view. The forest reached to the water, and in some areas only rocky shoreline was accessible. Soon, he spotted a large, open region amidst the unbroken forest farther inland of their position. A small stream or river appeared to run through its middle, bordered by trees on either side. Tall grass, pushed by the wind, rippled like waves across the field. Within minutes, they had landed side by side in the meadow, the low whine of their engines dying away.

Gary welcomed the rush of cool air as the cockpit lifted away. His flight suit, soaked with sweat, would be shed as soon as possible. Moving the pilot's seat forward, he allowed his disheveled passenger to gratefully exit the tiny space. He hopped to the wing and helped her climb down, admiring the view as she backed into his waiting arms.

Colleen saw the look. She knew exactly where his eyes were resting. Once down, she turned and smiled. "Thanks ..." she said, "Did you like what you saw?" With any immediate danger gone for the moment, some of her more playful side peaked through.

Gary's mouth opened in embarrassment, realizing that he could have hidden his gaze better, but he was primed with an adequate comeback. "Couldn't see what I liked," he answered truthfully.

She gasped, surprised by his candor. Both were sidetracked by the other three adventurers walking toward them through deep yellow grass. Gary began to take off the bulky flight suit. As he slipped it from his shoulders, the breezy air met his damp uniform shirt, giving him a chill. He considered leaving it on, but knew he needed to dry first. Climbing up to the cockpit, he stowed the suit inside. He noticed the temperature gauge on the console. It read sixty-four degrees. He frowned, hoping it wasn't indicative of what was to continue. Closing the canopy, he climbed down to join the others. As he slid off the wing, his hands brushed against the upper tips of the grass. It felt cold and wet. He glanced at Kahn and the others, seeing that they were soaked from the belt down. It may have rained recently or it could be heavy morning dew if indeed it was morning.

It was determined they should take care of as many needs as they could. Sleep, food and water were necessities, but where and how they could be obtained was still to be figured out. The sun shone brightly with only a few clouds present, but if it were this chilly during the day, night would be very uncomfortable. Staying warm could be another problem.

One by one, each made their way to more private area's to take care of personal needs. After, they approached the line of woods in search of a streambed and hopefully, drinkable water. The former was found, but unfortunately, it was filled with only dirt, stones, and leaves. The downhill direction of its previous flow was obvious, and it's solid base easy to follow. It was a fact that all streams led to larger ones, so eventually, water would be found. The next step was discussed with mixed opinions.

Both girls recommended staying close to the ships. "What if we can't find our way back?" Deanna said.

"What if it gets dark?" added Colleen.

Both were excellent points that were countered by the men.

Pritchart had equally valid excuses for going. "Look, we've been without food or water for how long?" he began. "Food can wait, but we can't go much longer without something to drink."

Kahn added. "We're not going to get lost. Look at this …" He gestured toward the dry stream bed. "All we have to do is follow it down and then follow it back."

Gary voted to continue as well. "Come on, you have to go. We don't have any way to carry water back."

Kahn moved in a position to look at Deanna's eyes close up. His voice was calm and convincing. "Hey, we have to take care of ourselves until the Aquillon gets here."

"The emergency beacons are on. They'll see them and we'll be out of here." Gary added.

"The longer we wait the better chance it'll get dark on us." Pritchart said impatiently. "I, for one, don't want to be out here when it does." He turned and started down the stream, apparently tired of the debate.

Deanna licked her dry lips, nodded, and moved to Colleen's side, taking her arm in hers and following.

Gary stood for a moment with Kahn, looking about the meadow. Nothing could be seen except grass surrounded by forest. He spoke quietly to Kahn. "Do you really think they're coming?"

The older man looked towards the glow of the single sun and considered the question. What had become of the scout ship? If the worst had happened and it had been destroyed, then no one would even know they were missing. Finally, he shook his head. "I don't see how. They would have followed us if they could." He sighed heavily. "I think we're on our own."

Gary noticed the seriousness in the words. He nodded as his friend turned to follow the others, hoping for once that he was mistaken.

They walked a steady pace, passing many small, muddy areas, but no standing water. The damp soil was becoming more frequent however, and the knowledge that relief for their thirst was close, kept them moving.

At first, the explorers saw no life other than plant, but as they ventured past the edge of the meadow and entered the forest, they met many other types. The trees were filled with birds, their calls filling the shadowy confines. The forest was nothing like Belaquins. Great tree trunks, some fifteen feet in diameter, supported tons upon tons of branches and leaves above. Their canopies shut out the light, seemingly creating night from day.

Thus far, the trek had been easy, and the trail unmistakable. The sun was still high in the sky. More sunlight could be seen further ahead, beckoning with its sure warmth. There was no reason not to go on.

Pritchart, still leading, slowed as he approached another break in the trees, noticing a prominent change in the landscape. The stream continued forward, but the greenery that had surrounded it up to that point, did not. For the next several hundred yards, every surface of earth, wood, and rock, was bare, stripped of leaves, grass, bark, and moss. All that made the forest what it was, was gone. The five stood at the forests edge, baffled by the sight. Pritchart spoke first. "What the hell did this?"

"A fire?" suggested Gary.

"I don't think so. Something would have grown back." Colleen answered. "Nothing looks burned."

Deanna stepped forward into the sunlight, welcoming the heat. "Should we cross it?"

Kahn looked to the other side, perhaps a quarter of a mile away, where the forest resumed. The streambed led sharply downhill and disappeared into the trees. He studied the bizarre landscape, not comfortable, but not frightened by it either. Water had to be close. "Why not?"

With no explanation, Pritchart suddenly left the streambed, walking away through the dead timbers.

"You see something?" Kahn asked.

"Yeah ... I'll be right back. Go on ahead, I'll catch up." He answered without turning.

Kahn moved to the front and led the way.

Pritchart crossed the barren ground, winding his way through standing and fallen timber, toward what had drawn his attention. Perhaps a hundred and fifty yards from the stream, he had the first clear view of a large cone-shaped mound. It looked to be made of dried dirt or mud. Trees appeared to be growing from it, but the mound was simply wide enough at the bottom to encompass them. It was a curious sight and obviously out of place.

Even before he drew near the yellow brown mound, he could hear the sound. It was constant, barely perceptible, seemingly coming from everywhere. He searched his memory for recognition, but found none. He thought it sounded like the high-pitched buzzing of a locust, but it was difficult to tell.

He looked back toward his companions, but could not see them among the trees. He looked also to memorize the direction back. For a moment he felt a pang of uneasiness, but quelled it. To make sure, he found a large branch and stuck it into the side of the mound, pointing the direction to the streambed. Intrigued, he circled the strange pile, ignoring the sound, which now seemed different. Was it louder? No, he reasoned; he was just becoming used to hearing it. On the far side, the slope was decidedly less steep, providing a way to answer his next question. What was on top?

Within a minute, he had gained the twenty-foot high crest and found it to actually be the rim of a crater, some three feet in diameter. The hole went straight down into darkness. Instantly, he had a different outlook toward the mound. His fascination turned to apprehension as he realized the strange sound was coming from within the cone. It took only a second for him to decide where he wanted to be. Turning quickly, he sunk into the soft edge of the rim, nearly falling. Large clumps of dirt fell inside.

He stood and dusted himself off, cursing his clumsiness. Two things happened at once. The sound of the chirping grew much louder and in turn, increased the concern he already felt. He leapt down the hill, easily spanning half the distance to the forest floor. On the next jump, he landed just above it, but sank up to his knees in the loose soil. Unable to move his legs forward to stop himself, he fell forward, landing heavily on his right side. The ground, littered with rock and broken tree limbs, didn't welcome him well. He lay for only a moment; the breath knocked out of him, and then rose to his hands and knees. Sharp pain came from his right side. Forgetting what had caused his fall in the first place, he raised his torn shirt and found a jagged scratch running along one rib. It was slightly bleeding, but with the intensity of pain, he had expected much worse.

Slowly, he gained his feet and began circling the mound to find the branch he had stuck in it. Following the direction it pointed, he jogged away, wincing with each breath. He turned back, but saw nothing. Shaking his head in anger, he slowed his retreat, realizing he'd let his unwarranted fear make him lose control. Feeling foolish, he began fabricating a different story to tell the others.

He stopped after a few yards to check the aching wound. His shirt, damp with blood, stuck to it as he lifted. As he tenderly touched the edges of the injury, a new sound startled him from behind. He turned.

Terror filled his being as he watched the yellow brown dirt of the mound turn to a living, moving blackness. It took a long second, not of indecision, but rather absolute disbelief, for him to move his legs. The chirping sound was louder and clearer than ever.

Within seconds, the whole of the mound was completely covered. The blackness spread to the ground. Pritchart moved as fast as the terrain would allow; the pain in his side forgotten. He tried to concentrate, not wishing to fall again. At the same time, he dodged and weaved, ducking and jumping, trying to maintain the right direction. Looking back out of sheer fright, needing to know what was happening, he realized his worst fear.

The black mass was rapidly approaching, following his path of retreat. With incredulity he recognized what formed the dark wave rolling toward him. They appeared to be huge insects, each one a monster. By their actions, there was no doubt that they knew he was there.

He ran faster, no longer as careful as he had been. Direction no longer mattered. He took the easiest route, holding on to one thought ... simply to get away. His mind searched for options, but found none. The insects clearly had little problem negotiating the rocky, wooded path. With every second, it was evident that the gap was closing. Constantly looking back, Pritchart noticed that fact.

His side hurt again. Both sides hurt. His breaths came in short, painful gasps. He had run too far, too fast. His legs were heavy ... his steps uncertain. They smashed against fallen limbs. His shins would surely be bruised and torn after this was over. His hand laser banged against his hip. He desperately wished to use it against the onslaught, but couldn't bring himself to stop.

At first, he had no doubt that he would find safety, whatever form it may come in, but that safety, with every second, faded. He ran on, losing ground with each step. As realization set in, his thoughts became frantic. He had never felt panic before, but now he felt little else. Finally he could hold it inside no more. The sound from behind him was too much. Moans escaped between his tortured breaths. They turned to incomprehensible sounds, and finally to words, the only words in his terrified mind. "Help me! Help ... me ... Jesus Christ ... help me please!" He yelled. Tears flowed freely down his face ... tears of desperation ... of indescribable fear ... and tears from what might come. He repeated the same words as he stumbled along, nearly falling with each labored step.

Gary, walking in the streambed, stopped suddenly. He was sure he had heard someone's voice. It was faint, far away, and if he had truly heard it, could only be from one person. He called for the others to stop. "Hang on a minute. Don't talk. Listen?"

They had just re-entered the dark forest, but unlike before, it was strangely quiet. The birds were silent.

Kahn, far ahead, stopped and waited. He was sure of what he could see at the bottom of the hill ahead. It was water, sparkling in the sun. He looked back at the others. The girls stood quietly after Gary spoke. The latter stood twenty yards further back, his hand held in the air to keep them quiet.

Gary tried to catch the sound again. He heard something, but couldn't place it. Suddenly, he rapidly moved back the way they had just come, positive he had heard Pritchart's voice. "Something's wrong ..." he yelled to the others.

In the clearing, Pritchart's emotions had deteriorated to panicked numbness. He couldn't think ... he couldn't breathe ... his legs moved only with instinct to survive. Between breaths, he tried to yell, praying someone would hear him. Through teary eyes, he saw the dark forest only a few yards ahead. Somehow, he felt relief, imagining that if he could only reach that milestone, he would be all right. A smile spread over his face. He was going to make it.

Kahn saw Gary far ahead, climbing out of the streambed. He cut up at the same point when he reached it. They were out of the shadows again, in broad sunlight. He looked in the direction Gary was running, seeing nothing before him but broken timber. He stopped only for a moment, to try and catch a glimpse of whatever his friend saw. Then he heard the sounds. Climbing atop a fallen log, he found the source. It was Pritchart! He could see him running, stumbling, screaming ... and as he watched, falling. He jumped down and ran on as quickly as he could.

James Pritchart, thirty-nine years old, rolled to his back, half senseless. He hadn't seen the low branch that had caught him across his forehead, nearly knocking him unconscious. As he sat up, he noticed wetness on his face and lips. Water ... finally! He raised his hand to touch it. It felt warm and slippery. Wiping it from his eyes, he saw its bright red shine.

With his next thought, he regained his wits, realizing that he was on the ground, bleeding badly. Everything came rushing back ... too late. Quickly, he wiped his eyes again; only to see the first of a hundred insects close the last few feet between them.

The gigantic ant, a foot in length, crossed his first leg and sank its pincers into the pant leg of his second. Horrified, Pritchart knocked it away with a swat of his hand, his pants tearing where the monster had bitten. As he regained his feet, he drew his laser, a coarse scream coming from his lips. He tried to aim, but could not. The targets moved much too fast. He fired out of sheer hopelessness. As thick as the approaching horde was, he struck home with nearly every shot. He squeezed the trigger as quickly as he could, unable to think about escape any longer. The ants were all around him, leaving no place to run. Suddenly, three leapt onto him, followed by three more. He kept firing, turning and running ...

The second bite cut through his clothing, finally reaching flesh. The pain coursed through his body like a hot knife. He whimpered in agony, pulling the ant from his hip. Another took its place, biting, stinging, then another ... and another. The whimper increased to a steady wail, his body quivering with torture like he'd never imagined.

Gary slowed to a walk, not able to conceive what he was witnessing. Pritchart had stopped, ten feet short of the woods. He could barely be made out, flailing, kicking, and screaming in torment. His body was covered with black, writhing movement, separate from his own. Unintelligible words came from him. Gary winced in disbelief at the incredible scene, sickened by the pure horror he was experiencing.

Kahn, within seconds, stood at his friends' side, equally absorbed in repulsive fascination. Perhaps five insufferable seconds passed before he took action, cursing himself for waiting even that long.

Cries came from behind them as the Deanna and Colleen finally drew close enough to see. Gary turned toward them. "Stay back!" he yelled.

Kahn drew his laser, took deliberate aim, and fired a solid stream of cutting light into Pritchart, who somehow was still on his feet. His dreadful cries ceased as the beam struck him. His body collapsed. Only the sound of the unremitting chirping remained.

Gary watched as Kahn mercifully ended the man's suffering, and his life. For a moment, he was confused and shocked at the action, but suddenly realized why he had done it. He felt ashamed that it had never occurred to him to do the same.

Kahn's aim did more than end Pritchart's pain. The sound, the light, or their presence alone, drew attention to another source. Almost as one, the mass of mindless predators turned and scrambled toward them. Together, he and Gary fired their weapons, and like Pritchart, were unable to miss, but their aim had no visible effect.

Kahn yelled loudly. "De … Colleen, run back to the stream … don't stop!" As he followed, he yelled again. "Go back down the hill. There's water … get in the water!" Silently, he prayed that his eyes hadn't deceived him; that water was what he had seen.

Once the streambed was reached, Kahn stopped for the first time. They had distanced themselves somewhat from the pursuers, but they still came, following their every turn through the dead trees.

Gary, already descending the streambed, turned to see Kahn standing still. Ahead, Colleen and Deanna were nearing the base of the hill. They stopped for a moment, looking back. Then, in frustration, they turned and disappeared.

Kahn, fighting the urge to run, switched his laser to wide field to try and set fires between him and the ants. On wide field, the power in the hand weapon would be drained in seconds, but it was the only chance they had. After only a few shots, a large area of white smoke drifted upward. He'd seen enough. Running to join Gary, they continued their flight. The sound behind them was incessant.

At the bottom of the hill, their senses were filled with relief. A river, at least seventy-five feet wide, passed before them. The girls waited just past the edge in knee-deep salvation. It would be deep enough. The shrill sound was steady and growing closer. There was no time was waste.

"Oh shit! It's cold!" exclaimed Gary as he plunged in. Regardless, it was better than what waited behind them. Staying together, they moved downstream, the water reaching to their waists. They hadn't gone ten yards when the riverbank behind them turned from green and brown to shiny black. Thousands of insects covered every inch of ground to the water's edge. The insect forerunners had stopped, confronted with less than stable footing, but the advancing horde behind forced hundreds of them into the water. Shouts of alarm came from their prey, which immediately moved toward the center of the stream. The water soon reached the height of the girls necks, but no deeper. Kahn, standing a head taller, helped them keep their footing in the current.

The sight mesmerized Gary. The ants blanketed everything with their uncountable numbers. As the ground filled, they spread upward. The trees were soon inundated as well, every branch bending with the clinging weight. It was that observation that distressed him the most. Maybe fifty feet ahead of them, and fifteen feet above the water, were long branches, nearly spanning the river. Even as he watched, they bowed deeply as the weight increased. If it reached the water, they would have trouble getting around it.

Numerous ants drifted toward them, some drawing far too close. Gary splashed violently as one came near, pushing it away. A blood-chilling scream erupted from beside him. He turned to see a single ant, clinging to Colleen's long hair. She flailed at it, wrapping it further into her black strands. Ignoring his loathsome dread of the creature, Gary grabbed it with both hands and tore it in half, flinging one part far away. The other half, after a few seconds of untangling, soon followed. "It's gone! It's dead!" he yelled to the still panicked girl.

Kahn began pulling Deanna toward the opposite shore, which appeared devoid of any life other than plant. Looking above, he noted that fortunately, no branches from the opposite banks met in the middle, offering no bridge for the demons to cross. Finding good footing, he forced a sharp angle to the nearby shore. "Deanna ... lock arms with them. We need to get to the other side." At his request, she reached out for Gary, who already was joined with Colleen.

The branch ahead, now only thirty feet away, sagged to the rivers surface, and soon reached below. As the current caught enough mass, the inevitable happened. With a mighty crack, the limb snapped, plunging into the water with a powerful splash. Ants were flung into the air with the limb's upward whiplash. Others continued to fall as the senseless forward flow continued.

A moment later, Kahn had reached knee deep water and helped the others to relative safety. Each sat on the dry bank … cold, wet, and shivering, trying to catch their breath, worried that somehow, the insects would find a way to cross.

Kahn watched as two ants somehow dragged their waterlogged bodies to his side of the water. With no mercy or remorse, he picked up a large boulder and smashed each one in turn.

The chirping across the waterway continued without interruption.

Colleen shuddered as she watched hundreds more float downstream. She touched her head, seemingly still able to feel the one that had met its end at Gary's hands.

Kahn knew they were met with a dilemma with many parts. What to do and where to go were just two of them. He was afraid to let the insects out of sight for fear of them catching up to them without warning. On the other hand, if the ants could see or sense them, they may remain constant in their labors to reach them. The raiders were a long ways off, but at least from where they now sat, they knew where. If they moved very far away, it may prove impossible to make it back. The decision was as clear. "We have to get out of sight."

Deanna felt the same, having no desire to stay anywhere within sight or sound of the terror still so close. "Where can we go?"

Kahn thought hard. The easiest thing to do was to wait until the ants left, and to sneak back up the streambed to the meadow, but neither he nor the others would knowingly go through the same situation again. "We'll go upstream, and try to find a place to cross back over. Maybe we can cut back to the ships that way."

Colleen listened in disbelief to the words. "Go back?" she cried. "My God … we can't go back there!"

Kahn, remaining as calm as he could, helped Deanna to her feet. "We have to get back to the ships."

Colleen looked to the seething madness less than a hundred feet away, remembering her last vision of Pritchart, not wanting to imagine what he must have felt. Had he known he was about to die in such a horrible way? She felt so sorry for him, and was upset that the same fate had nearly befallen her and the others. How many other unknowns were waiting to kill them? She finally nodded her head. Kahn was right. There were a hundred ways to die here, but only one way left to survive. She stood with Gary's help and turned, wrapping her arms tightly around him, voicing silent thanks. She then spoke to Kahn. "Come on then, we're wasting daylight."

"We'll get out of sight, but stay close to the river. As long as we can do that, we shouldn't lose track of where we are." He led the way into the shadows of the trees, each step guardedly taken. Soon, the sights and sounds of the black army were left behind.

After a while, they stole back to the waters edge. On the opposite bank, nothing moved. Only the sound of birds filled the air. It was a good sign. Indeed, if the insects were near, then no other living thing would be. That knowledge could help them to a great extent in finding their way back.

There was no accurate way to tell how far they had walked, or if the river had made any gradual turns. If it had, then a precise angled path to the streambed would be impossible. The shadows grew longer across the ground and water. It soon became evident that the sun was falling and the temperature with it. The foursome, still damp from the swim, shivered in the forest shade. It had been hoped that there would be something spanning the water on which they could cross, but the river had widened considerably. Some trees, fallen from weakened, uncovered roots along the edge still fell short. It seemed there was no way they could keep from getting wet again. Gary voiced his concerns. "It's gonna be dark soon. I don't think we've got enough time to make it back."

Kahn sighed, looking at the water. Spending the night away from the ships wasn't part of the original plan.

Deanna looked puzzled. "So what do we do … stay out here?" she asked, obviously dismayed at the prospect.

"We find a safe place to hole up until morning. Then we find the ships and get the hell out of here." Kahn answered. To where, he had no clue.

"We'll freeze …" shivered Deanna. "… we already are."

Gary had an answer. They had seen fire earlier in the day. There was no reason they couldn't see it again. He looked forward to the prospect of being warm. "We'll build a fire." There was little argument after that, each knowing how few their options were.

The sounds of the birds quieted with the coming dusk. Darkness descended much earlier within the forest, making it more difficult to see. Kahn found a monstrous tree.

Its thick, low hanging branches reached nearly to the ground. With their wet clothing, he knew the ground would suck the heat from their bodies, possibly causing hypothermia. Using dead branches, they constructed reasonably flat platforms between some of the lower limbs. Then, piles of leaves, which rested thickly on the forest floor, were gathered and situated atop, forming crude mattresses. Another pile of the driest wood served the purpose they longed for. A fire soon blazed, thanks to their durable firearms. Two of their immediate needs had been met; thirst and warmth ... with only two remaining, hunger and rest. None of them had slept since their last night on the Aquillon One, at least a day and night before. Even the hunger pangs they felt took a back seat to their exhaustion. The fire meant everything. They stood close and long enough to it to dry everything but their boots. It had grown so cold, that in its light they could see their breath. Reluctantly, one by one, they left the flames and climbed upon the makeshift beds, rough as they were. As best they could, they covered each other with a thin layer of dry leaves. Any movement shifted the branches below, threatening to collapse the platforms. Gary, although willing to fulfill his chivalrous duty by keeping Colleen warm, still felt awkward doing so. He lay on his right side, his head resting on one arm. His other, Colleen promptly pulled across her chest, cradling his hand in hers against her mouth. Her breath was warm. She pressed her back against him, touching him with all of her body that she could.

Before closing his eyes, he searched the black leafy canopy above, finally finding a small break in it. He could make out only three or four stars, but the sight of them seemed a comfort. His eyes burned from exhaustion and the smoke from the fire. He closed them thankfully, not noticing how uncomfortable the thin layer of leaves beneath him was. It was good enough just to be off the ground. Colleen's breathing soon grew heavy, signaling sleep. As tempting as his own bed on the ship might sound, he wondered if the choice was possible, whether he would rather be there alone or here with her. He sighed, burying his face in her hair. Her body felt wonderful, his awkwardness long gone. The leaves around them soon grew warm. The forest had grown nearly silent with the darkness and cold. The moment was serene. His breaths soon became deep as well. His last thought was that the choice was easy.

CHAPTER 6

▼

The hours passed slowly aboard the Aquillon, en-route to its unknown destination. Commander Haute had somehow found some rest, which he badly needed. He had awakened, but had not yet left the comfort of his bed, so when control room called, he was for once, uninterrupted. He rose and dressed quickly, not worrying with making himself presentable. A planet had been picked up on the scanners, directly in the path of their unwavering course. Minutes later, he stood on the control deck. "Give me the details, guys."

"Any sign of the alien ship?"

"Negative."

"How far out are we?"

"I should be able to pull it up in just a minute."

"I want full circle sensors. I don't want that ship sneaking up on us like it did the scout ship." The proper procedures for contact with unknown vessels were still fresh in his mind after the meeting with the Aquillon Two's commander. He had no wish to repeat the meeting with himself on the receiving end. He walked to the scanner station where he saw some of the estimated figures on the planet. It was slightly larger than Belaquin, but little else could be seen until drawing closer. The navigator placed the view screen on maximum magnification, where in the center, a bright globe had appeared. "Standard orbit when we get there." said Haute, gaining his seat.

Within minutes, the planet was in full view. The colors on the surface were magnificent, even from a great distance. Haute admitted to himself, there was no planet in the Belaquin system that could rival the one before him. The planet was blue for the most part, with large, green landmasses visible. White clouds completed the array of color, covering in small intermittent swirling patterns, the entire surface. As orbit was attained, more impressive land features became apparent. Shadows suggested tall mountain ranges, and great rivers could be seen crossing the surface.

The scanners came alive with information. A crewmember handed some of the findings to the Commander, who sat mesmerized by the view. Finally, he broke his stare to look at the numbers.

Diameter—12,756 kilometers

Equatorial Rotation speed—.48 kilometers per second

Rotational Period—23.93 hours

Surface Gravity—9.78

Atmospheric Composition—Nitrogen 78%, Oxygen 21%, Minor elements of Argon, Neon, Carbon Dioxide, and Hydrogen

Surface temperatures: -130 Degrees F to 140 Degrees F

Water surface—139 million square miles

Land surface—58 million square miles

He barely had time to read the list, much less understand it, when his attention was diverted.

An animated voice spoke. "Commander, I'm picking up two emergency beacons from the planet surface, both with raider signatures."

Haute's interest peaked. My God, he thought ... they're alive! Thank God we followed!

Another excitable voice came from a different station. "Commander, we have contact with a ship, orbiting this planet!"

"Raise shields. Take us out of orbit." He walked to the scanner tech that had discovered the contact. "Is it the one we've been following?"

"By the data I have ... yes sir."

It was all Haute needed to hear. "Sound emergency stations. Get weapons lock on it." The main screen changed views. The new image was of the ship itself, greatly magnified. It remained in steady orbit, offering no hint that whoever or whatever was on board had noticed the Aquillon.

Haute checked his own ship. The shields were at maximum strength. They had withdrawn to a safe distance, allowing time and room for evasive action if needed. "Anything on the scanners?" He knew the scout ship had previously been unsuccessful with scanner efforts.

"No power, no movement, no shields … nothing."

"Is its orbit deteriorating?"

"Negative … it's stable."

That fact alone revealed that it was under some power. With confusion and limited answers, Haute pondered his options. The raiders were on the surface below, suggesting that his pilots had flown them there. How could he be sure that some of the missing persons weren't still aboard the alien vessel? Silently, he reminded himself that his prime concern was to the fifteen hundred lives aboard his own ship. If fired upon, regardless of the consequences, he would have to retaliate.

He cursed the timing. If they could have picked up the beacons sooner, they could have gained an orbit above their position and attempted to establish contact. To do that now, the Aquillon would have to risk close quarters with the hostile vessel. There would be no room to maneuver and almost no time to react to an attack.

How far should he go? To what extent should he endanger his crew to rescue five individuals? Was it possible that the alien ship hadn't seen his vessel? He doubted it, but if so, it might be possible to take up an opposite orbit long enough to launch recovery ships. The only drawback with the plan was losing the ability to maintain visual or scanner contact with the strange ship. Were the lives of the persons below worth that risk? Haute nodded with his decision.

He gave order for a wide berth around the ship, and an approach to the planet from the opposite side. Then, matching the same direction and speed as the ship on the other side, they would gain orbit once again.

Minutes later, they again rested in orbit, sheathed in darkness. Below, the blackness of the planet was absolute.

Haute wasted no time. "Contact hangar bay one. Get a shuttle ready … three security men and a single raider escort. Ten minutes." With those words, he left the room.

Nine moments later, he entered bay one, wearing a work uniform, complete with all associated equipment. It was not unusual for the Commander of any ship to include his or her self on a mission, but this type of mission was far from typical.

He noticed the stares, but turned them to smiles with a non-chalant explanation. "Hey, this old man was doing this crap before you guys were born. This might be my last chance." He boarded the shuttle, finding a seat behind the pilots. He was soon lost in thought. Yes, there was risk with his actions, but Kahn was like his son. He had an unspoken duty to him. He had to find him, dead or alive. Besides, he'd sat on his ass and watched for too long.

A moment later, the bay door opened into darkness. Marker lights revealed the position of the waiting raider escort. Lining up, they dropped toward the atmosphere. Haute checked the graphics on the screen. According to it, the beacons location was still under the cover of night. By the time they arrived there, the sun should just be coming up. The timing would be perfect.

Kahn awoke before dawn, but did not rise. He was amazed at the stillness of the forest. He rationalized that the morning should be the coldest time of the day, and if insects were insects, they would not expose themselves to the frigid temperatures. Logically, it should be the safest time to search for the ships. He turned and looked to the fire. Faint reddish embers could be made out, with thin lines of smoke curling upwards. He hated to move, but the soreness of his body required it. How long had they slept? How long was a day and night in this place? How long until the sunrise?

Rolling over as carefully as he could, he sat up. Right away, he noted the near freezing air which had descended overnight. Grasping a branch above, he steadied himself and swung off the platform to the ground. Deanna moaned, but did not move. He rubbed his burning eyes, wondering if he'd truly slept at all. He recalled waking a hundred times, filled with paranoia of what lay around them.

As he stood, seemingly every muscle in his body screamed. The idea of sleeping on the ground had not been popular, but it would have at least been flat, and allowed a position change when needed. He frowned, finding that his boots were still saturated. He rubbed his arms vigorously, trying to create any warmth he could. Glancing again at the fire pit, he smiled in anticipation. An unused pile of wood rested nearby. He crouched beside it, thrusting smaller twigs beneath the charred ashes. In seconds, more smoke rose, signaling the coming flame. Towards the river, a faint glow could be seen in the sky.

By the time he roused the others, the fire had recovered most of the brilliance of the night before. Kahn considered using it to dry his boots, but then remembered that there was still a river to cross. For a while, the foursome huddled around the circle of heat. The sounds of waking birds filtered downward as the sunrays touched the tops of the trees.

Kahn finally voiced that it was time to move. He led the way toward the river. "We should just go ahead and cross, not get any further away." He received sour looks in return. "Look, I'm cold too. I don't want to get wet again, but we haven't found any place to cross. We may not. If the Aquillon comes, they'll go to where the beacons are." Reluctant to argue, he slid down the steep riverbank and splashed into the water. Immediately, he regretted his impatient decision. The others looked on, befogged at his loss of rational thought.

"Come on. It's really not that bad." Kahn lied, gritting his teeth. It took everything he had not to go back to the smoldering fire. The water was freezing; the pain from it overwhelming, but it was too late to turn back. The water had probably been the same temperature yesterday, but the adrenalin that had propelled their actions then, was now tucked deep inside.

Gary, knowing his friend was right, hesitantly slid down the same bank to the waters edge. He then turned to help the girls, who had no alternative but to follow.

Kahn, standing waist deep in the current, prayed they would hurry. His nerve was diminishing as fast as his legs were numbing. "Just jump in. It's the easiest way." he coaxed.

Gary closed his eyes, not believing that he was about to get back in the stream. Finally, he gathered his courage, held his breath, and jumped in. Shocked by the frigid water, his body forcibly released the air. Deanna and Colleen, held hands and followed. They too, were overwhelmed by the cold.

The distance was crossed in a moment's time. The water, to their relief, never reached above their waists.

Kahn didn't stop to dwell on the cold. Instead, he convinced his shivering companions to move ahead. It made sense to keep the muscles working to rebuild body heat. He continually looked to his left, shaking his head each time he considered veering away from the only familiar landmark they knew. The idea of returning to where Pritchart had died brought back the horrifying scene again and again. Which was the lesser of two evils, chancing the dry streambed again, or risk missing the clearing altogether? It was a decision that deserved to be made by everyone, but as ranking officer, the choice was ultimately his. If no one said anything, then he would keep the river in sight.

About forty-five minutes to an hour passed before they came upon the hills they had seen the day before. As they topped the first rise, Kahn stopped abruptly. Just below them was a streambed. He looked to the left once again. Far away, the leading edge of the dead wood could be seen. The others, one by one, realized where they were. The stern rebuke that he expected never came. Maybe, each of them had subconsciously known where they were being led. Kahn spoke just loud enough to be heard over the wildlife around them. His tone was serious. "We'll cut up the stream, as fast as we can ... no sound!" This time Kahn voiced his earlier beliefs, "They won't be out when it's this cold." All nodded in under-standing and agreement.

Gary turned to Colleen, reached out and took her hand. "Stay close to me." He led her down the hill.

Kahn took Deanna by the hand and turned toward the slope as well, but she pulled him back. As he turned in confusion, she embraced him tightly. "I love you ... just in case."

He held on and managed to smile, "I love you too, babe, and we won't need the just in case. Come on."

The command shuttle and its escort glided silently through the darkness. The raider pilot didn't report it, but during the fiery descent, he'd experienced a short of some kind in his electrical circuitry. His attention was aroused by a silent alarm and flickering control lights. The alarm suggested a possible fire, but soon after it began, it shut off. A quick systems check showed normal. He ignored it as a glitch set off by the excessive re-entry heat. No need to report it until they got back to the ship. Besides, he wouldn't miss this assignment for the world.

The two ships headed directly toward the rapidly brightening horizon. At an altitude of ten thousand meters, they would meet the sun's rays long before they touched the ground below. The shuttle pilot checked their course. "We've still got a ways to go; probably thirty minutes." The ship rocked as it met strong crosswinds. He turned to face the other crewmembers. "We better stay buckled in. There's a lot of turbulence up here."

"What's under us?" asked one of the security men.

"Good old terra firma, about five miles down." He studied the graphics on the horizon display. "I think our guys are on land too, but it's hard to tell from this far out." He directed a question to Haute "We're coming up on daylight pretty fast, Commander. You want to stay up here, or drop below cloud cover?"

"Let's drop down ... see what we can see," suggested Haute.

The pilot obliged the order and began the descent. "Sir, I'm not certain, but we may not have communication with the Aquillon when we land."

Haute nodded in acknowledgement. He figured as much, but it didn't change their mission. He had left standing orders regarding the rescue mission. One of them addressed the eventual loss of communication. Without satellite assistance, direct line of sight signal was all they had. To maintain contact with the Aquillon would require coming close to the mysterious ship. It would not be risked.

Brian Pierce sat staring at the dark screen. The bottom half was as pure a black as he had ever seen. The upper edge of the planet was easily discernible against the radiance of the nearest star, more than ninety million miles away.

He had to admit that he was surprised when the Fleet Commander included himself on the surface trip, automatically putting him in charge. He had commanded the Aquillon only once before for a few hours during her shakedown cruise. Haute hadn't even been aboard that day. There had been other occasions when the fleet boss was gone, but they had unfortunately fallen on his off duty days. He was only twenty-nine years old, but as a Lieutenant Commander, he relished the notion of his own ship someday. Only Anson and his seniority had stood between him and the scout ship mission.

He leaned back, his hands behind his head, staring at the ceiling. Truthfully, he wasn't really running the ship. Haute had left specific standing orders upon his departure. He was just one of the puppets fulfilling them.

"Commander?" someone called.

Pierce answered, somewhat disinterested. "Yes?"

"I've got a contact ..." said the scanner technician. "... conflicting readings, though."

"What do you mean?"

"It's bearing zero one eight, but it's changing ... shape ... speed ... everything."

Pierce at once gained interest, "Put it on the main screen." The schematic came up, revealing the contact. Its edges were unsteady ... fluctuating ... bits of it even separating from the whole and rejoining a second later. "What the hell is that?" asked Pierce.

"Nothing's coming in clear."

"Can you enhance?"

"I'll try. It's hard to lock on to." The tech answered.

The screen went blank for a moment, but came back on to show a greatly magnified, but blurred planet edge. A diminutive area of movement could be distinguished, but was impossible to make out. Pierce suggested other options. "Try different settings, heat differential, infra-red, anything." The screen went through a series of diverse scans, finally stopping on one. The unknown entity suddenly became very clear.

Pierce stood in stunned silence for only a second. "Take us out of orbit, Mr. Gallien. Resound emergency stations at level one!" As he said it, his heart began to race.

The view screen now showed quite well what was approaching. At least twenty-five or more separate contacts were now discernible, advancing close enough together to give the appearance of one entity. Their movements were steady and purposeful, their course ... directly for the Aquillon. There was little speculation on what they were or where they had come from.

Pierce checked the shields, finding their capacity at one hundred percent. Their ship was ready. "What do you see?" he asked several stations at once.

"Thirty ships sir, small erratic formation."

Another man spoke. "No power readings at all. Just like the other ship."

"Lock main banks on their center." Pierce had a consideration. "Do they match any known configuration? Are they Thalosian?"

"Unknown ..."

Pierce turned it over in his mind. What would Haute do? Would he fire on them without provocation? Was the earlier attack on the scout ship reason enough? He had always been a firm believer that a strong offense was better than a strong defense, but his orders stated not to fire unless fired upon. It seemed clear enough. "Send word to the surface team. Tell them what's going on."

"Lasers locked, range already minimal."

The answer to the young commander's dilemma came in the next instant. The weaving, unorthodox paths of the ships suddenly became much more controlled, as they formed a new rough circular pattern. Small pinpoints of energy appeared before each craft.

Pierce had expected it. "Fire all banks!" he said with assurance. As close as the small ships were to each other, it was probable that most would be taken out at once.

The beams spanned the gap in an instant, enveloping all of the unidentified crafts. Simultaneously, a beam of light shot back, erupting against the Aquillon's shields.

The immediate retaliation was unexpected. The shields deflected most of the impact, but the blow was felt throughout the entire ship. Pierce was shocked as he felt the tremor. Even the combined strength of thirty raiders, couldn't have generated enough punch to penetrate the shields. The voice from engineering reported the damage, "Shield integrity down six percent."

The Commander barked an order, "Hit them again ... repeated fire." His idea was to possibly stop a second shot from the crafts with successive follow-ups. The Aquillon's weapons lit the void again. The second burst hit the formation again, and oddly enough, an immediate blast returned again to strike the huge ship. The third burst ended with the same results, and a fourth, before Pierce ordered a cease-fire. His ship was rocked with each return volley.

The small ships were now easily within visual range, with no indication of damage. The Aquillon's own shields however, were down to eighty four percent.

Pierce pummeled his brain for answers, finally faced with a far-fetched possibility. It seemed as if they were shooting themselves. "What was the strength of our first shot?"

Bewildered stares proceeded the answer, "Over three hundred mega-joules, sir." The technician knew where the Commander was headed. He hurriedly punched figures into the terminal and turned to Pierce with the results. "It would take at least three hundred to drop our shields like that."

"Unbelievable!" Pierce said. Somehow, the crafts were deflecting all energy back to the source, like light beams off of a mirror.

As they drew near, the alien ships broke formation and surrounded the ship, firing their weapons at point blank range. The threat of the tiny vessels against the Aquillon was minimal, but each blast absorbed by the shields added up to a whole and the whole would have to be dealt with sooner or later.

Pierce mulled over his choices. The easiest solution to rid the ship of any further damage would be to simply leave, but they needed to remain. Eleven shipmates depended on it. To let them return to find the Aquillon gone, replaced by thirty alien fighters would be a death sentence.

Main weapons couldn't begin to track targets in such close proximity, and it wasn't reasonable to sit and draw fire for the duration. They had only one other defense against the attackers. "Any word from the command shuttle?" Pierce asked.

"Negative."

His orders were to return fire, if fired upon … simple … direct … and most importantly, standing. "Launch Gold Squadron one, Red one and Blue Squadrons one and two." He sighed. It was done. The decision was made. For the first time since the Thalosian war, Republic raiders were entering into combat … and by his order.

Minute's later forty-four pilots watched the hangar doors open. They listened as Pierce gave the order to drop shields. Eight ships at a time emerged from four bays, entering the fray. They were making history, whatever it may be. Within the first moment, five alien fighters were destroyed.

Pierce listened attentively to the fighter pilot's traffic, and watched some of the drama unfold. The alien ships, from the start were outnumbered and after a very short time, their numbers had become severely depleted. The remaining vessels were fully expected to retreat, but it quickly became apparent that they had no intention of doing so. The aliens were unrelenting in their attacks, but seemingly could not lock onto their targets. The Republic ships, however, with guidance and tracking systems, could not miss. In less than five and a half minutes, it was over.

Pierce knew the battle had gone well, but still dreaded the coming report. He had ordered the ships into combat, but in doing so, he had sent men out to die. "How many did we lose?" he asked hesitantly.

There was silence as the readings were counted. "I've got green boards on ... forty-four ships. Minor damage to twelve, but ... we didn't lose any!" a voice finally reported.

"You've got to be kidding?" Pierce asked again.

The man counted again. "I've got forty-four confirmed." Sounds of celebrated relief came from around the room.

The Commander stood stunned. "Thank God," he breathed.

A communications officer turned to Pierce with interesting news. "Commander, BR eight and nine report a disabled alien ship adrift. They are requesting orders."

Pierce contemplated the request. It would be prudent just to finish off the craft and its hapless pilot, but securing and bringing it aboard would be of great interest to scientific and military intelligence. Also, they would finally find out who or what they were dealing with.

The ship may be disabled, but was still potentially dangerous. If it was brought into one of the bays and it fired weapons or self-destructed, then harm to the Aquillon could be severe. Another idea presented itself. The craft could be stored in one of the smaller cargo bays until an investigation team could extricate it. If the ship became a problem in any way, then it could be quickly expelled into open space. The storage unit would also meet strict quarantine guidelines as long as it was kept sealed from the rest of the ship. "Get supply to open one of their empty bays and have it towed in. Have BR Eight and nine stand by until it's secure. If they see trouble they have permission to destroy it."

Minutes later, a towing vehicle delivered the powerless craft to its destination. The doors closed behind it.

Kahn, Gary, Deanna, and Colleen could barely contain their relief as they ran through the tall grass of the meadow. They had made it up the streambed with no sign of any insect. The two raiders sat where they had been left. The cloud cover that had partly masked the sun yesterday was gone, allowing the heat to raise the morning mist. The ground was still cool, the grass still wet, but the humidity could already be felt. This day's temperature would no doubt reach higher than yesterday. Ignoring the flight suits, the pilots assisted their passengers aboard. In minutes, they were airborne.

The shuttle pilot tinted the windshield as the sun's full force topped the horizon. They were cruising at three thousand meters. The variety of terrain that passed beneath them was incredible, forested hills and mountains stretched as far as they could see.

As much as Haute would like to have explored more thoroughly, he knew he could not. The mission they were on was not a sightseeing tour. They had one purpose, and hopefully, it would be realized soon.

The pilot checked his sensors. "Commander, the beacons are still stationary. We've got maybe seven minutes to intercept."

"Try the radio."

"Gold Raider one … Gold Raider one … this is Aquillon Command shuttle … come in please." There was no answer. He looked below and felt he knew why. With no satellites to assist, the signal had to be blocked somewhat by the terrain, "We'll have to try when we get closer." The final minutes passed.

From their lofty altitude, the pilot noticed a distinct change in the landscape ahead. The rolling hills dwindled in height to perfect flatness. "We've got water coming up, and a lot of it … and something else." He looked in confusion at the forward schematic. "Those aren't hills."

Haute rose and stood behind the two men, looking toward the far horizon off the port side. Shapes, unrecognizable from a distance of more than thirty miles, became more visible with each passing second. Haze hid any specific features, but one thing was dramatically clear. The area they approached was not naturally formed. Haute checked the reading on the beacon. "Is that where they are?"

Another glance at the scope was made. "Negative. They're further south. We'll pass close to whatever that is on the way."

"Any readings at all?" Haute asked, referring to the rapidly approaching skyline.

"Nothing," The pilot gazed ahead in fascination as the haze thinned and features became visible. He had dropped to five hundred meters in a gradual descent. What the men finally saw nearly made them forget what they were searching for.

Before them was a city, stretching out in all directions. Glistening water lay beyond, reaching to the horizon. Rows and rows of immense structures, hundreds of feet high, stair-stepped to the shoreline. Some were true giants, standing far above any others. One in particular, very near the water demanded all attention. It easily towered a thousand feet or more above the ground.

Nothing moved beneath the shuttle and raider, by sight or by sensor. Smaller structures rising from the unbroken tree cover were passed over. Occasionally, long open areas resembling streets could be made out. As they flew southward, they passed over a huge rectangular break in the stone and steel. It was filled with forest, appearing strangely out of place.

Haute and the others watched in wonder as the pilots drew close to the tallest buildings. The sight was breathtaking, but the destruction was appalling. Some great force had collapsed many of the buildings, which lay in unrecognizable piles. Forest growth hid a great majority of what rested below. If there was life in the city, it was hidden as well. As the shuttle drew within a stones throw of the tallest tower, the magnificence seen from afar, slowly gave way to the reality of crumbled stone and broken glass. The once richly painted walls had changed to dirty, rust-streaked brown. Inside each shattered floor was darkness. Below the visible levels were others, covered by encroaching plant growth. Enormous vines entwined and even spanned from some buildings to the others, forming living bridges. The design of all they could see seemed all too familiar.

An urgent voice blared loudly over the radio, bringing everyone back to their senses. It was the raider pilot, who thus far had been a silent companion. "Uh … Shuttle one; I'm having some trouble over here." Alarms could be heard in the transmissions background.

The shuttle's copilot answered. "What's going on, Tim?"

The raider pilot wrestled with his sluggish ship. He had watched warning lights come on one by one, followed by numerous alarms, many of which he had silenced. One he could not ignore was the same one that had caught his attention earlier, during the trip through the atmosphere. It again signaled a fire somewhere below his feet, but this time, other signs accompanied it. Many of his systems had lost electrical power, one of them vitally important. Manual control felt very wrong. The ship would move in the direction he wished, but only after a long delay. Then, when changed again, would lurch in the new direction. It was no way to fly. "I've got a possible fire, and I'm losing steering."

The shuttle banked and came up behind the raider, whose path of flight was obviously erratic. The raider's nose rose and fell, the ship weaving drastically from side to side, out of control. A thin line of white smoke escaped from somewhere beneath the crafts hull, marking its path. The shuttle pilot spoke quickly. "Tim, your fire is confirmed. Hit your dowsers!"

"I already have … twice."

"Keep it up … you should still have some left."

The fighter pilot hit the fire control switch again, listening to the hissing sound as the tubes emptied their contents. Genuinely worried, he made a decision. "I'm taking her down," he said nervously. He pushed gently forward on the stick. As expected, the raider tilted steeply downward. Instinctively, he pulled back, trying to gauge the delicate pressure needed. As he did so, the remainder of his cockpit lights flickered and went completely dark.

The shuttle stayed close. The raider belched white fire control gas each time the pilot triggered it. The ship began to smoke excessively; white mixed with black, suggesting possible structural, as well as electrical damage. Both ships turned to the only possible safe landing zone; the large wooded area now behind them.

Finally, over the trees, the raider pilot breathed easier. At least now, if he had to ditch, he would have a chance. The stick in his hand felt disconnected. Again, the ship dove sharply. For a moment, he considered ejecting, but wondered if that mechanism would function. Suddenly, the buildings and trees in his path disappeared, the blue sky above taking their place. The pilot cursed as his ship rolled upward, under no control. For an instant, its belly faced the sky.

At the shuttle pilot's request, the men had returned to their seats and belted in. Haute snapped the lock and looked up. He looked again for the raider, but it was gone. Loud yells suddenly filled the cabin. The next second held confusion, shock and dread like he had never felt.

The two gold raiders leveled out at five hundred feet, heading toward the coastline. The emergency beacons were still working properly, but whether anyone was there to see them was unknown.

Upon leaving the meadow, Gary dipped low over the area near where their shipmate had died, but saw nothing. It was just as well. His last image of the scene would be enough to last a lifetime.

No sooner had they gained the air, the radio exploded with activity. It was a man's voice, yelling, obviously distressed. The words were hurried and garbled, but the message was clear enough. "Mayday … Mayday! Shuttle one is going down!" Only silence followed.

Kahn switched to the frequency as the words ended. "Shuttle One … this is GR One, do you read?" There was no answer. He glanced at his wing man in frustration.

"I heard you fine. You're transmitting." Gary said. He keyed the microphone. "Shuttle One, this is GR Two, come in please." Still there was nothing.

"Shit! Where are they?" Kahn asked in confusion.

Gary switched to the emergency channel. "This is Gold Raider Two, emergency transmission, requesting response from any Republic vessel. Please acknowledge."

As Gary's voice went out over the airways, Kahn checked his limited range scanner, seeing nothing. "I'm going up and north."

"Okay, I'm heading back the way we came." Gary shook his head, figuring the search was a waste of time. The shuttle could be anywhere within a hundred miles. Ten minutes later, after looking visually and electronically, they had found nothing.

Kahn followed the coast and eventually began to see more than forest. Structures could be made out along the waterfront and further inland; true evidence of intelligence of some kind. Eventually, buildings stretched as far as he could see. A massive city could be made out to the northeast, buildings towering higher than any he'd ever seen. Beyond those towers, a line of black smoke rose. Smoke meant fire. There was little doubt of what had caused it. He called elatedly. "Do a one-eighty GR Two, I've got smoke"

Gary turned his ship. "I've got your position."

It took only moments to reach the area above the possible crash site, but only smoke could be seen through the treetops. After a quick search, an open area was found to set down near the buildings at the edge of the trees. After only a few precious moments in the air, the two ships were again grounded. They were an estimated two hundred meters from the source of the smoke.

Colleen exited the cockpit and stared in awe at the sheer stone walls before her. Some reached so high that the tops couldn't be seen. At their bases were familiar things, some of them easily recognizable; windows, doorways, streets, all covered by vegetation, but still retaining a hint of their original appearance. The plant life covered every possible piece of ground, sprouting from every crack and crevasse, climbing high on the buildings faces. A flower seemed to bloom on every branch. Even before her feet touched the ground, Colleen spotted species of plant she couldn't identify. As important as what was happening around her, she felt the urge to stop and explore. This place was a botanist's dream.

That dream lasted only seconds. Kahn and Gary entered the trees in the direction of the smoke, beckoning her and Deanna to follow. Whether they could find their way back to the ships was considered, but from the air, the boundaries of the central forest had been easily defined. Again, they passed enormous trees, undoubtedly rooted long before the city around them.

Soon, the two men's sense of direction was rewarded with the smell and sight of smoke. The cause was easily found. The fire still burned around the downed craft. It had tried to spread, but the lush growth around the perimeter would not support the flame. The ship rested on its side, the base nearly vertical. The side that had struck the ground was crumpled and partially imbedded in the soft earth. It leaned against a massive tree. The tons of falling metal had broken even the largest branches on the way down. Jagged, torn edges of the same metal had scraped along the trunk, shredding the thick bark like paper.

The ship was blackened by the fire, as was much of the area around it. The fuel tanks had no doubt been torn open, their contents spilling and scorching everything touched. Most of the flame had died as the fuel was used up, but smoke still choked the air. The foursome drew closer until the top of the ship and cockpit glass became visible.

Kahn, stopped short by the heat, took a hard look and spoke. "Jesus! This is a raider!" he exclaimed.

Gary came close, choking on a breath of smoke. "You're right," he managed.

Deanna noted the surprise in their tone. "So, didn't we already know that?"

Gary turned to her. "The mayday said shuttle one," he explained, confused by the situation.

Colleen, on the opposite side of the charred hull, yelled excitedly. "Hey … get over here!" She pointed as the others joined her.

A Republic shuttle, white as snow against the backdrop of dark green, rested on or near the ground, less than a hundred steps away. The group moved toward it, abandoning the fighter that could have held no one alive. The second ship had escaped the fire and rested moderately upright. Its once sleek hull, creased and broken, resembled a can, crumpled in some giants' hand.

They approached from the front. The ship was silent. Above the pilot compartment, the most forward section, the roof had been crushed, shattering the forward glass. It was compressed far enough that they could not see in. Gary, making his way to his left, or the starboard side of the craft, noticed immediately, that something was terribly wrong with the scene.

The damage to that side of the ship was less severe. The shuttle door had been opened, either by the occupants or the impact, and it remained that way.

Deanna gasped as she moved beside Gary, who stood silently, his laser now in his hand. He reached out and touched her arm, signaling her to be quiet. He did the same to Kahn and Colleen as they stepped near. All stood in shock as Gary knelt in the shuttle doorway.

He reached out and placed a trembling hand on the chest of a man, laying face up, his body halfway out of the hatchway. There was no movement, no breath passing in or out. In a crash as violent as this one had been, fatalities would be expected, but this man had obviously not died from the impact.

Kahn knelt beside the body as well, but looked to the trees and undergrowth around them instead. He also held his weapon. Finally, he turned his attention to the dead man. The man's clothing was soaked with blood. What had caused his death was easily evident. A crude wooden arrow, a foot and a half in length protruded from either side of his throat. It had torn through the major arteries and airway. Bright red blood had poured from his mouth, now turning dark and thick. His eyes were open, glazed with reddish film, staring sightlessly into the trees above. Kahn touched the feathered shaft, his heart pounding with fear. "What the hell is going on?"

Leaving the body, they entered the darkened shuttle. One of the pilots was still in his seat, crushed from above by the collapsed inner roof. Two other men were found. One was still strapped in his seat, which had broken from its floor fixtures and been thrown across the cabin. The other lay near him. Neither of them had any sign of life.

On one of the chairs still upright, more blood was found. It covered the seat cover and the floor beneath. Neither of the men on the floor had any open wounds. Blood seemed to be everywhere, but from whom? There were many unanswered questions, but the crash had claimed at least five lives, four in the shuttle, and one in the charred raider.

Kahn gestured toward the man outside. "He's a pilot ... I knew him from the academy."

Colleen, shaken by the death around her, spoke. "I don't understand ... who killed him?"

Kahn answered. "Whoever did it is still out there somewhere."

Deanna nodded. "What do we do now?"

"Well, the ship is looking for us already, and now these guys. We don't know if the beacons are working. Haute may not even know they've crashed." Gary suggested.

Colleen had a rational suggestion. "Well, the ship is up there somewhere. Why don't we just go up and find it?"

"I agree. They're all dead. We might be too if we stay." Deanna added. Her words made perfect sense.

The men nodded. There was nothing more that could be done for the unfortunate men. Kahn, weapon still in hand, exited the lifeless ship and turned. "Get their weapons ..." He paused, "... and their ID tags." He had thought about it before, when Pritchart had died, but knew that it wasn't possible.

While Gary collected the tags inside, Kahn took the necklace from the shuttle pilots' neck, wiping it, and reading the name. "Joseph Harlow." He hadn't remembered it before, but now did. Reaching down, he closed the eyelids. As the others exited the ship, he spoke. "Gary ... help me. I'm not leaving him out here." Together, they dragged him in, closing the door as best they could. It would at least keep any wildlife from getting to the bodies until they could be retrieved.

Colleen stayed near the ship, but kept her eyes and ears open for anything. Whoever had killed the pilot had apparently not lingered for long. Sounds from the forest grew louder, as birds, evidently driven away by the fire, returned. As she waited, something caught her eye. It was more blood, but there was no sign of another body. "Kahn?" she called.

He answered, still pushing hard on the shuttle door. "What?"

"There's more blood over here. Looks like quite a bit." As he joined her, she pointed to a line of droplets leading away.

The pilot narrowed his eyes, trying to see more clearly in the shady surroundings. The leaves on the ground following the path of the blood were disturbed. There was little doubt that someone, bleeding, had walked away from the crash.

Deanna and Gary came close. Kahn pointed out Colleen's discovery. "Someone else was on the shuttle. They're still alive."

Gary, examining the leaves and the ground, had to concur. "But why did they leave?"

"Maybe they were disoriented." Colleen suggested.

"Or running away from something." said Deanna. "We don't know if this is someone from the ship or not." she added. "It could be the one who killed the pilot."

Gary spoke again. "Whoever it is, they're hurt pretty good. I'd say they probably wouldn't be able to go very far."

Deanna wasn't swayed easily. It was easy to see where the conversation was leading. She still agreed with the original plan of returning to the ship and had no trouble voicing it. "Well, it doesn't matter; we need to get out of here."

Gary looked in the direction of the path. "No ... we need to find out if it's someone from this ship."

Deanna was astonished. "We're going to go look for them?"

"We have to!" Gary answered sharply.

Deanna could only envision the dead pilot. "Bullshit, we don't have to. We can go back to the ship and send down a rescue squad!"

"And what if whoever this is dies before they get here. They might not be able to even find this place?" Gary argued. "Jesus ... they came down here to get us. Some of them died coming down here. I don't know about you, but there's no way in hell I'm leaving before I find out for sure!"

Kahn stepped between them, unsure of which side made more sense. His voice was firm. "Look ... both of you are right, but we've gotta think about this." He hated being in the middle. "All right, I agree with you De ... a rescue team would be better equipped to handle this ..."

Deanna nodded in thanks.

"But, I think time means a lot here. We don't know who killed Harlow, or who this is, but we can't leave if one of our men lying a hundred feet from here bleeding to death." He spoke to Deanna specifically. "If it was me, wouldn't you want to know?"

Deanna nodded, not arguing with the decision. Within her, she had already realized that they really had no alternative. These poor men had come to help her and they deserved the same.

Kahn led the way, following the path of disrupted leaves more than the blood, which could also still be seen. They moved quickly and quietly with constant vigil, wanting no surprises. The vision of the wooden shaft jutting from Harlow's neck was on each of their minds as the leaves crunched beneath their feet.

The trail was easy to follow. It led to the edge of the woods where the city walls stood before them once again. The path of rustled leaves ended. The path direction led straight away from them, down a narrow street. Nothing moved as far as they could see. The unknown, possibly hidden in the trees behind them, now perhaps waited in the buildings above them.

Kahn looked in all directions. He pointed to the right. "The ships have to be that way. We just follow the street back."

Deanna voiced a concern. "Whoever this is ..." She pointed to the blood on the street. "They can't have much left."

In contrast to the forest floor, the flat gray of the street, though cluttered with debris, was an excellent background for the red spatters. They were unmistakable. As they continued, the view around them became eerily familiar. With every step, confusion mounted as new objects became visible. The buildings and streets were evidence that a culture frighteningly close to their own had flourished in this place. The vegetation gradually fell away, revealing other discoveries, impossible to understand.

Gary stopped, shaking his head at the surroundings. He bent down and picked up a rusted piece of metal, still flecked with yellow and black paint. It was only one of many similar examples around them. "What the hell is this place?" he thought aloud. The metal in his hand had words imprinted on it. Some of the letters were gone, but it read. "WILEY STATIONARY AND OFFICE SUPPLY ..." Gary dropped it, dumbfounded.

Colleen looked about incredulously, seeing words written in her own language on nearly every building, doorway, and even on the streets themselves. "How is this here?" she mumbled.

Deanna answered. "I don't know. Look at this ..." She touched a broken window painted with lettering. "Watch and camera repair, while you wait?" she read aloud. Every word made sense, if nothing else did.

Kahn followed the blood trail, absorbing other intriguing clues. He had an unvoiced theory, but felt it too ludicrous to express without proving it to himself first. As he negotiated piles of rubble and rusty metal, he found the proof he was searching for.

A great stone structure, rising fifty or more stories, stood silently before them. Above its doors, was the answer to all their mind wrenching questions. Kahn spoke, although in total disbelief. "My God, this isn't possible ..." The others joined his side, reading the words etched into the stone wall.

"New York City First Bank of ..." Colleens' words trailed off, as she grasped its meaning. "We're on Earth." she stuttered. The name she saw was known by every Belaquin alive. It had been the greatest city ever built on the ancient planet, and now, even in ruin, it still rivaled all others. This was their history.

"We're on Earth ..." repeated Gary, as if saying it would make it more real. "How?"

Nothing was said for a long uncomfortable moment. Kahn finally spoke. "It doesn't make any sense. How can we be here? I mean, my God, we aren't even three days from Belaquin. Someone would have found it by now."

Gary answered. "Maybe not. They would have had to come pretty close. They've just never come this way." He couldn't hold the exhilaration as he weighed the significance of the moment. The realization of being one of the first humans to return after so long was almost too much to fathom.

Deanna asked the obvious question. "What about the history books. They said all of it was destroyed."

Colleen summed it all up. "They were wrong," she said simply.

Kahn, had started to climb the stone steps, but turned to the street again. There was nothing he wished to do more than explore, but at least one life, maybe more, was possibly at stake. "Come on, we need to go, no matter where we are." He reacquired the trail.

They counted the streets they passed, committing them to memory for the way back. There was no sign of any living thing. Gradually, the trail of blood decreased as the bleeding slowed, but before it disappeared, it led off the street into a building. It was one of many bordering a large plaza. An elaborate fountain rested in the center, water within and around it, but forever still. A few trees, surrounded by tall grass, grew in the area, but it would be easily accessible for any airborne vehicles.

Kahn considered backtracking to the ships and relocating them there, but whoever or whatever was in the building would then be well aware of their presence. At least for now, with any luck, no one knew they were there. He looked back down the street they had followed. The forest was still visible at its end. Around them, some of the taller structures were still visible, but the largest tower, by far the most prominent contact point from the air, had been hidden since their landing.

Kahn cautiously approached the building's entrance, looking above to the large windows filled with multicolored glass. There were no markings on its front. The doors stood open. The interior was dark, but gradually, some identifiable shapes became visible. Upon entering they stood within a large room, at least sixty feet high in the center. It was easily evident that they had entered an ancient church. Rows of wooden pews lined the middle walkway before them. A portion of the roof had collapsed at the far end, hiding whatever had been on the raised stage. Rays of light poured in from the opening above. Marvelous carvings of wood could be seen around the room. Stone statues of persons unknown, peered mutely downward from their niches within the wall. The floor and pews were covered with pieces of plaster, which over the ages, had fallen from the ceiling. Two long centuries of dust covered every surface, obliterating any beauty that the room might have once had.

Deanna spoke. "Why would they come in here?" Her voice, though whispered, sounded frighteningly loud in the emptiness.

Kahn noticed where several persons had walked, leaving tracks through the dust. Each one had worn shoes.

Looking closely, Deanna made a humbling observation. Some of the prints were obviously from a Republic boot. "He's one of ours," she admitted.

"They went in there." Gary gestured to another doorway partially obscured by debris. As he investigated, weapon at the ready, he found a stairway leading downward into perfect darkness. "Shit," he muttered. Hesitating, he strained to see. There was no telling what lay at the bottom. If there were trouble, the narrow stairwell would be the ultimate disadvantage.

He spoke to Kahn, who startled him, literally staring over his shoulder. "What do we do?"

Kahn took a deep breath, looking back to the girls, who remained near the rear of the room. He wasn't sure.

Deanna whispered loudly. "Are you ready to get out of here yet?"

He ignored the enticement, and turned back to Gary. "I don't know ..." A multitude of ideas coursed through his mind. It was now apparent that whoever had killed the shuttle pilot had brought another shipmate here, for reasons still unknown. He measured what some of those reasons might be, and what they might be facing below. "All right ..." He turned back to Deanna and Colleen. "We're going down. You guy's stay here and ...!"

Deanna interrupted. "No way ... fuck that! We're not splitting up!"

Colleen joined the decision. "If you're going in, so are we."

Kahn considered arguing, but knew his rank meant nothing to them at that point. He gritted his teeth, saying nothing for a moment. "All right, I guess we'll all go." He conceded without a fight.

As he turned back toward the doorway, the younger pilot stepped aside, offering the point position to his friend. Kahn didn't smile, but there was humorous sarcasm in his sneer. "Thank you so much." He looked down the narrow alleyway, seeing nothing. If he drew fire from below, the narrow kill zone would be hard to escape. He turned to the three, no more humor in his tone. "Stay out of the doorway until I get all the way down."

Gary nodded his understanding.

Kahn took a long look into Deanna's eyes. No words were needed. Pointing the muzzle of his weapon into the darkness, he took the first step. His finger was taught, ready to pull if necessary. The air was cold and still. Creaks and cracks came from each wooden step as he made his slow descent. His heart raced with anxiety. By the time he had put ten steps behind him, his eyes had begun to adjust to the lack of light. The base of the stairs could be made out. There was nothing waiting for him, as he had so feared.

Once at the bottom, he breathed easier. A hallway ran to his left and right. To his left was total blackness, but to the right, less than twenty feet away, faint light could be made out. No tracks were visible, thus offering no clue as to which way the unknown persons had gone. Kahn called above, his voice barely above a whisper. "It's clear, come on."

The stairs creaked horribly as the rest descended. Kahn cringed, absolutely sure that they would be heard. He carefully led them further. At the end of the corridor, another door was found open, light coming from within. It led to another stairwell, this one wide and distinctly more visible as it went down. The light Kahn saw came from somewhere below, somewhere very well lit. He took the first step, knowing there would be no sound, for the stairway was concrete. Eight steps down was a landing where the stairs turned and descended again … another eight steps … and again … and again. By the time they completed the sixth flight, the source of the light became known.

Now at the bottom of the stairwell, they came upon something very out of place in the seemingly abandoned city. Another corridor waited, leading straight away. Its fluorescent lighting was so intense it almost hurt the eyes. The floor, walls, and ceiling were white with a glossy shine … and strangely clean. No dust had invaded this deep beneath the city streets. The white walls were polished ceramic or stone with no features of any kind. The corridor curved gently, splitting into two. Where they went from there couldn't be seen.

In stark contrast to the cleanliness of the hallway, were dirty footprints left by whoever had passed. Also evident once again, were intermittent drops of red. They followed and made a left turn at the intersection. As the foursome moved noiselessly ahead, they noticed that along with the light, there was welcome warm air blowing from various ceiling vents. Closed doorways appeared ahead. The first one passed read "STORAGE ROOM 5F" Many more were passed, as well as three intersecting corridors. It was up the third corridor that the droplets led, and where a startling change in the immaculate white surroundings was found. Along one wall, numerous tiles had been gouged out, the broken pieces lying on the floor. Ahead, there was much more.

Colleen gasped as she drew close enough to see. More broken tiles and large pools of blood covered the floor. Large spatter patterns at two separate places along the wall marked where someone or something had died. Blood on the wall had run downward, painting long narrow lines reaching the floor. Footprints were everywhere, all leading toward a stairwell. Wide trails marked where at least two bodies had been drug away.

Gary breathed quietly. "Jesus Christ … do you think …?"

"I hope not … but who else?" Kahn answered. He suspected the worst, but it was impossible to be sure. "Come on."

The girls flinched as they hesitantly followed, finding it impossible to step around the mess. The fresh blood was sickeningly slick beneath their feet.

The stairway was met and two flights were descended upon. A closed door waited at the bottom. Kahn pushed the lever and opened the wooden panel just enough to see out. Another short corridor waited, glass panels lining the walls, curtains hanging within from ceiling to floor. At the far end, some fifty feet away, was an open area, but nothing more could be made out. He listened intently, but heard nothing. Opening the door further, he looked the other direction, seeing only more of the same corridor. Stepping through, he had the forethought to reach around to the opposite door handle. It moved easily and hopefully would not lock behind them. A plaque on the wall was marked simply enough, "STAIRS." The others followed him into the hallway. There was some blood on the floor outside the door, but it ended there.

Deanna investigated the nearest glass wall and the small room on the other side. The inner curtain was open, allowing full view of the interior. "These are hospital rooms," she remarked.

Kahn turned. "How do you know that?" He looked inside as well.

"Because," she gestured. "They're hospital rooms."

Kahn frowned and nodded sheepishly. The room contained two beds and looked like every hospital room he'd ever seen.

"What now?" asked Colleen. Before anyone could answer, the sound of distant voices shocked them into silence.

Kahn's eyes grew wide as he realized the sounds were undoubtedly getting closer. He motioned toward the nearest curtained room. Crouched behind the beds in relative darkness, they waited. The voices grew more distinct as they grew louder. Another sound accompanied them, similar to a squeaking wheel. To their astonishment, they understood every word they heard.

There were at least two separate voices, both male. The conversation was short. "I just don't understand why we have to do it. It's got nothing to do with us."

"I know … let's just get it done and get back."

"I don't see what difference it makes. Nobody ever goes up there."

"Well they did today, so quit your bitching unless you're willing to go down and tell him to do it himself." The voice faded with the sound of a door slamming shut.

Gary looked at Colleen in bewilderment.

Kahn rose and found the corridor clear. He shook his head. "My God, they're just like us!" The notion was incredible, but plausible, considering where they were.

Deanna kept her voice low. "I don't care what they are … they shot down two of our ships, and killed at least five of our men … maybe more." Her tone was stern.

Kahn nodded. She was right. Alike or not, they could not drop their guard and just walk up and say "Hi." He thought hard for a moment about where they were and what they were doing. Was this the ideal situation? Of course it wasn't. The person or persons they had come to help may or may not be dead, but they had no clue what they might be facing. The persons they had heard in the corridor sounded like perfectly normal human beings. Wouldn't they be able to be reasoned with in any situation? There were a hundred unanswered questions with no answers. Kahn closed his eyes and made the decision. He turned right, following the glass wall, moving away from the stairwell door.

Walking to the open area, behind a four foot high counter, they found a doctor or nurses station. Two computer terminals, their screens blank, rested among stacks of paper. Countless more pages were strewn across the floor. The corridor made a right turn and continued on. Cautiously, they followed it.

Kahn stopped cold after advancing only thirty steps. He turned, pointed ahead with his weapon. Voiced could be heard once again.

Advancing against the wall, he paused at each open doorway he came to, checking inside before moving on. Deanna and Colleen with Gary behind followed closely, each with weapons drawn, ready to duck into one of the rooms at a seconds notice. The corridor ahead was unlit, but an intersection, some twenty meters up could be made out. Light came from a room to the left, shadows from within playing on the corridor floor. Kahn, now in the darkened section, cautiously approached the door.

The next voice they heard was loud and clear. It belonged to a man, and the tone was less than sociable. "Why are you lying? What point could it possibly serve?"

The return answer was from a man also. "I have no reason to lie! I'm telling you the truth!"

Kahn paused in recognition. He knew that voice. It belonged to a very familiar face.

The louder man spoke again, more calmly. "The Manna is on his way up. You will answer his questions."

Kahn watched the floor as one shadow became larger. Someone was approaching the doorway. Hurriedly, he looked about, finding no place to go. He braced himself and waited.

CHAPTER 7

─────────────── ▼ ───────────────

A man emerged from the doorway and turned toward him, coming face to face with the muzzle of a hand laser. Kahn pressed it onto the startled man's forehead. No one moved for several uncomfortable seconds. The man could easily be seen in the light of the room. The four Belaquins stood in disbelief.

He was indeed human, but much different than they may have pictured him the moment before. He was tall, taller than Kahn, and appeared normal in all respects, at least the normal of two centuries ago. The man's mouth gaped open in surprise, his white teeth standing out starkly against the dark brown skin of his face. Kahn knew him, or rather his race, from every history book in existence. He was known then as a black man ... a Negro ... a Kogran. There had been two opposing sides in the final war on the planet. To their Earthly ancestors, they had been the enemy.

Kahn, his wits tested nearly to its limit once again, maintained his composure. He didn't waver in the least. He knew he could not. Pushing the laser firmly insured that he had the man's full attention. Reaching to the man's side with his left hand, he removed what appeared to be a weapon of some kind ... metal, heavy, strange looking. He handed it to Gary, who now stood beside him.

"Go back!" ordered Kahn gruffly, pushing him backwards into the room. As they entered, they saw five other black men within the room, each of them dressed in strange colorful garments. The man who Kahn had grown so close to was different. He wore a hooded cloak over his clothing. Beneath it could be seen glimpses of truly exotic materials. Each man's head was completely shaved. At least two of them had facial hair. Only two carried weapons. The missing shuttle crewman was seated on a table. He wore a large bulky dressing around his lower leg.

Two of the startled Kograns moved immediately towards them, but were stopped by Kahn's words. "Don't even think about it!" he shouted. It was obvious that they understood every word. The caped man was pushed to join the others. Within another second, three more lasers held the men at bay.

Kahn turned his attention to the injured crewman on the table, whose face held total disbelief. His adrenaline raced, but he kept his voice calm and controlled. "Mr. Haute, it's time to go." He intentionally left out the man's title, even though he had no idea what had already been disclosed to the captors.

The Commander slid himself off the table, flinching as the injured leg touched the floor. "How in the hell did you get here?"

"It's a long story, believe me." answered the frightened pilot. He kept his laser steady, knowing how precarious their position was. He looked each of the black men in the eyes. Not one of them showed fear of any kind. "All of you lie down on the floor, face down. Put your hands out in front of you ..." None of them moved, other than to glance at the man in the cape. Seemingly, they waited for him to follow the command first. Kahn moved within five feet of him, leveling his laser once again at his head. "Tell them to do it now. It won't bother me a bit to take your head right off your shoulders. It's your choice." His voice was firm, as was his hand, but inside he wondered if he could truly do it. He had never killed a man before and had no wish to do it now. He stifled a sigh of relief as the man slowly knelt and laid down. The other men followed suit. "Colleen, get him out of here. De ... keep on them. Gary, get their weapons. We have to hurry."

Within seconds, Gary had tossed the curious weapons into an adjacent room and closed the door, locking it from the inside. He then joined Colleen in helping the Commander out the door. "Can you walk?" he asked, noticing blood seeping through the thick dressing. "You've lost a lot of blood."

"Yeah ... it's a pretty good gash, but my bones are still good."

Kahn waited until the three were well on their way to the stairwell and then spoke again. "De ... get going." She turned and left. Thankfully, none of the six men had moved. Backing to the door, Kahn aimed and fired several bolts upward into the ceiling, bringing down burning panels, bits of metal and showers of sparks from electrical wiring. Smoke and a sickening smell of burnt insulation filled the room. The lights flickered and went out as he turned and ran.

Loud shouting followed him up the corridor. Ahead, Gary, Colleen, and the Commander rounded the corner adjacent to the nurse's station, Deanna close behind. Sprinting to catch up, he didn't look back. More shouts met his ears as he neared the corner. Then came a new sound. A deafening, fast popping noise echoed down the hallway. At once, the glass walls, ceiling, and even the floor, exploded in a thousand different places around him. Broken shards of glass, wood, and metal flew about as he dove for the corner, landing heavily onto the floor. "God damn it!" he yelled, his words impossible to hear above the crescendo.

Ignoring the broken glass on the floor, he scrambled behind the counter top on his left, shaken by the frightening barrage. The Kogran weapons had gained his full measure of respect. He knew the sound of the crude weapons, and knew how deadly they were. The melee continued for only a second more, the partition offering cover until he could sit upright. Muffled shouts came, at least one from Deanna, who stood with the stairwell door open. His ears reverberated from the violent noise and he couldn't understand her words.

As he tried to get up, Gary was suddenly at his side, helping him. "Go!" he yelled.

At the same time, Gary stood; exposing himself to the direction the fire had come from. He fired a dozen shots down the corridor, directing them at targets he couldn't see. More shouts and firing from the Kogran guns came again. The open area erupted a second time, unseen projectiles striking and exploding everywhere. By the time it stopped again, the two men had entered the white corridor one floor above.

Once there, they encountered a strange sight. Far ahead, the Commander and Deanna ran on, but Colleen stood over two more black men, each face down in soapy, bloody water on the floor. Mops lay beside them. The conversation the Belaquins had overheard at the bottom of the stairwell, suddenly made sense.

Gary couldn't help but smile slightly at the woman holding her weapon on the two men. "Get out of here, Colleen." he said. She turned gladly and ran.

Kahn looked up the corridor, trying to gauge the distance to the intersection at the other end. There was no doubt that it would take several seconds to make the distance. The men pursuing them would be right where they now stood, before they could make it. He yelled at the two men on the floor. "Get up … hurry up!" They stood, soaked from head to toe. "Go … get back down the stairs!" In less than five seconds, the men were gone.

Gary had already started moving away. "Now what? They're gonna be here in a minute!"

"Just keep going … I'll catch up!" Kahn shouted.

Gary suddenly thought that his words sounded strangely familiar, and then remembered that the late Pritchart had said the same thing. "This ain't any time for hero bullshit, Kahn!" he shouted back, angry that his friend wasn't yet following.

Kahn heard the words, but went about his task. He took little time to aim, but his shots were effective. Firing around the corridor, he began cutting and collapsing the walls around and above the stairwell door. Soon, the opening was nearly gone. He nodded with satisfaction. The few seconds spent in the lone corridor would at least give them a chance. As he turned, gunfire came up the stairs, some actually reaching the corridor behind him. Broken tiles rained down.

As he arrived at the main stairwell, he found only Gary waiting at the top of the first flight. Heavy breathing, coughing and footsteps echoed from somewhere above. Kahn stopped, trying to catch his own breath. "I didn't see … anybody." he managed.

Gary thumbed toward the stairs. Go ahead … I'll get this one."

Kahn nodded, wiping a trickle of blood from his cheek, only then, noticing that the broken glass had not left him unscathed. He groaned as he mounted the first step, knowing there were many ahead. He laid a hand on his friends' shoulder as he passed. "Don't take all day."

Gary nodded and started firing, the doorway nearly collapsing in the first moment. The high-pitched scream of the laser echoed upwards, accompanied by the sound of crumbling, falling concrete. Choking dust filled the chamber, forcing him to stop earlier than he wished. The stairs grew dark as the light was smothered. As quickly as he could, he moved upwards. He took the steps carefully, barely able to see what was ahead. The sound of footsteps above him slowed, but continued. He heard Kahn's voice. "Deanna, wait for us at the top!" He shouted.

"I can't see anything," was the prompt reply, her voice holding understandable fear.

Gary shook his head. Neither he nor Kahn had considered the loss of light. No matter, the stairwell was easily negotiable. It only led to one place … out.

Within minutes, the five exhausted persons stood within the brighter confines of the church. No one waited there or outside in the plaza. Haute sat down heavily on one of the wooden pews, trying to recover from the impossible climb. He had to rest, no matter who was following. His heart was about to pound out of his chest. His legs felt like jelly, and his arms were sore also, from pulling himself along the banister. Every muscle in his body screamed. He winced as sharp pain shot through his ribs with each breath.

Kahn knelt beside him, also breathing heavily. He couldn't imagine how bad his superior must feel. "What's the matter old man? You gonna make it?"

Haute answered between grimaces. "I'll live. You don't look so ... good yourself."

"I bet." Kahn checked the bandage, which was now nearly soaked through. "You've lost a shit load of blood." He gestured outside. "That's how we followed you."

Haute shook his head, seemingly saddened. "That wasn't me. It was Hays."

Kahn frowned. "Hays?"

"One of the security men from the shuttle," He paused between sentences to breathe. "He was hurt really bad. He had a big ... gouge out of his shoulder ... bled all over the place." He almost couldn't continue. "There wasn't anything I could do."

Gary listened impatiently, guarding the doorway they had just exited, but his nerves were about to get the best of him. "Sirs ... don't you think we'd better move?"

Haute stood painfully, nodding toward the young pilot. "Close it up too," he ordered.

Deanna felt the need to ask, even though she knew it had to be done. "What about Hays?"

Haute, walking away, turned to face her. "He's dead. They killed him down there. I don't know what they did with him after that." The others were silent as they followed him out of the building.

Once they were gone, Gary triggered his weapon. Dust leapt from the corner where he concentrated the beams of light energy. Soon, fire appeared, spreading rapidly to the walls, igniting any dry wood it contacted. Soon, the heat became too great to remain. Exiting quickly, he looked back, watching one wooden statue as it caught fire. The form's arms were outspread, still welcoming all who wished to visit. The statue's features were familiar. The face and figure still adorned all churches in the Belaquin system. He wondered momentarily if there were any repercussions to burning a church, even one that was no longer used. He stood, surprised at how fast the flames spread. Black smoke billowed from the great hole in the roof, drifting upward, obliterating the sight of the buildings behind. Loud popping and crackling sounds came from ancient wooden boards splitting from the massive heat.

"They won't be following us through there," Gary thought, turning away. The sun was high in the sky. The impenetrable smoke, as it drifted through its rays, cast huge shadows across the plaza. He looked upwards at the thousands of windows overlooking him and the others, hoping all would remain empty as they made their escape.

They moved, as quickly as they could. Kahn was still shocked with the revelation of where they were, asked the Commander. "I know you saw the signs … this place. You know where we are?"

"I had an idea as soon as they took us out of the shuttle. All of this … it made sense then."

Colleen listened. "How could they have survived?"

Haute shrugged. "I'd say our ancestors were under the premature assumption that all this was gone." He looked at the buildings, still majestic, still whole. "Obviously it wasn't as bad as they thought it would be."

Gary caught up in time to here the conversation, "Unbelievable …" he muttered.

A hundred feet below the street, a man knelt to examine three bodies, lying side by side in a narrow dark corridor. Flaming torches provided enough light for him to recognize each one. He placed his hand over one man's still mouth, but no breath escaped the parted lips. Standing, he looked at the silent faces of the other men around him. His gaze met each of theirs. He felt like yelling, placing blame, but did not. He himself was as much to blame for this regrettable turn of events as anyone. None of his men looked away, either out of respect, or fear, or both.

Wordlessly, he stepped over the bodies, and into a still lighted room. Upon entering, he was handed a weapon by one of his men. It was unlike anything he had ever seen. He studied it momentarily and handed it back, uninterested. A more important matter held his concern.

On tables lay two more bodies, covered with white sheets stained with blood. He turned down the first, exposing still another of his men. The lifeless eyes stared, seeing nothing. He touched them lightly, closing them. The dark skin was still warm. Without turning, he spoke, his deep voice penetrating in the stillness of the room. "Take him and the others to some place appropriate."

With that, he approached the other body, hesitating before touching the sheet. He already knew what he would see. It had not seemingly been that long, but it would not lessen the initial shock. He pulled it down. His eyes narrowed as he sucked in a quivering breath. The pale white skin was indeed real. He held the breath for a long moment, staring, imagining what the events of the last hour would bring. He had believed for so long that it was over … truly ended. He had so many plans for his people. All of it was now at an end.

A man spoke from behind him. "Manna, what do you want done with him?"

Without turning, he replaced the bloody sheet, leaving the man's dead eyes open. "Burn him." He left the room, knowing that revenge for the dead and the living was at hand.

The hurried trek to the raiders was thankfully uneventful. Haute, throughout the walk, explained the circumstances of the disastrous rescue attempt. He described the fire in the raider, and the mid air collision, which killed the shuttle copilot outright. The surviving pilot had partial maneuvering, but the fall, all the same, was steep and fast. He could recall one of the security men being thrown around the interior of the ship as it pitched out of control. The time from collision to ground contact was perhaps ten seconds.

The crash, he remembered only vaguely. The impact was violent, but slowed by the trees. The shuttle disintegrated as it spun to the ground, the men helpless inside.

He didn't believe that he ever lost consciousness. What had caused the injury to his leg he had not seen, but the pain was intense. He sat stunned in his seat, which miraculously had remained in place, while others did not. Within seconds, he realized others were alive. The pilot, Harlow, was at his side in an instant, seemingly uninjured, but in the smoky dim light, it was difficult to tell. The acrid stench of burnt plastic brought the fear of toxic gases. It filled the compartment, prompting Harlow to kick open the partially sprung door and move outside.

Haute looked about the cabin, now that light was allowed in, his leg throbbing and wet with blood. Only one other man moved. At first he'd thought the man had possibly lost his arm, but with the limited light, the wound was deceiving. The man had a terrible gaping laceration that had poured out blood, soaking his uniform. He held a hand over the maw to try and slow the loss. Haute was tearing off another man's shirt to wrap it, when he heard Harlow in the hatchway. He didn't realize anything was wrong until he turned to speak to him. "Harlow, I need help in here." There was no answer.

Haute turned and what he saw made his blood run cold. The man was lying in the doorway, his legs kicking furiously as if having some sort of seizure. The thrashing ended quickly.

Unfamiliar sounds filled the air. It was deafening, an intermittent rapid chattering. He held his position beside the injured man, wondering what was happening outside. His hand crept to his side, finding his weapon. Perhaps thirty seconds passed before a shadow appeared in the doorway.

The Commander's first glimpse of the man was enough to shock him to his feet, but the forceful words and the weapon held in his face demanded his attention even more. The intruder screamed the order. "Move outside … now!"

Haute moved slowly, prodded forward as he moved. He felt his laser lifted from his holster. It was at that point, he saw Harlow, lying still, blood coming from his mouth and neck. His eyes stared blankly upward. Sickening, gurgling sounds came with each breath. He knelt beside him, but was quickly pulled back to his feet by another man.

"He's already dead," the stranger said in a calm voice. "They will kill you too if you stay." He pushed Haute roughly away from the shuttle to follow five other men, already disappearing into the trees. Looking back, he saw Hays being brought out of the ship, struggling, holding the shirt to his shoulder. A fire raged nearby, filling the forest with choking white smoke. By the time they made the long walk to the church, Haute was well aware of where they were and who their dark skinned captors were.

It was underground where Hays stupidly tried to overpower one of the black men, wrestling away his weapon. He and one of the other men were killed in the short exchange of gunfire. He was questioned for only a short time before the unexpected rescue.

Kahn, in turn, related some of their own adventures, in severely edited dialogue, describing the alien ship, the death of Pritchart, and how they came upon the shuttle.

Haute praised the four's bravery for risking everything to rescue himself and Hays, even though their identities had at that time, been unknown.

Crowded once again in the raiders, they gratefully put the city behind them. The plume of black smoke from the plaza was visible for miles. Climbing at high speed, they soon breached the atmosphere and entered the stillness of space. Once there, communication finally became possible.

An officer on the Aquillon acknowledged the initial call. "Gold Raider one and two … we have you on scope. We are at heading three … two … three, by two … two … one … from your current position."

The voice was a welcome one. Kahn changed his heading and answered. "Thank you Aquillon, return course verified." He felt it prudent to at least give some additional information. "Gold raider's one and two have five souls on board, including commanding officer, your vessel, ETA twelve minutes."

There was an expected pause. "Understood, sir, awaiting your arrival in twelve."

In fourteen minutes, both raiders rested in a pressurized bay aboard their mother ship. In the fifteenth minute, the Commander left the bay, en-route to the command deck, ignoring a warranted visit to medical. As he passed through hangar bay control, he stopped abruptly to answer the emergency stations alarm, audible in every part of the ship. He called the control room. "What's going on?" He guessed that the alien vessel was making an ill-timed move.

"Commander Haute, we've already been attacked once. We've got confirmed contacts approaching again." The excited voice belonged to Pierce.

"Are our shields up?"

"Yes sir, one hundred percent."

"How close are they? Do we have time to break orbit?"

"Negative. They're already supersonic."

Haute ground his teeth in frustration. "I'll be right there." He hobbled from the room to an elevator. As he whisked upward, he wondered what he would find. Confusion set in. What attack was Pierce talking about? Evidently, he had a lot to be updated on. He bent down to touch his tender leg, but the bandage was too thick. It would take time to heal. He thought of the men they left below. He had hated leaving them there, but the situation had forced it. An effort would be made to recover their bodies. The elevator stopped.

He had just cleared the open door when a second alarm sounded. He instantly recognized it as the collision alarm. Ignoring it, he moved on. The control room was only seconds away.

On his next step, the ship rocked violently, the deck dropping from beneath his feet. The ship shook as it attempted to right itself. Ceiling sections fell every-where, exposing electrical and ventilation conduits above. Haute first ended up against the wall, then on the unstable floor. Unhurt, he regained his feet, but the ship lurched again in the same violent manner. He found himself down again. This time, sparks flew from numerous places in the open ceiling, as well as water from an apparent ruptured pipe. The Commander remained still for some time after the second hit. The Aquillon was no doubt badly hurt. "Son of a bitch!" he yelled as he stood again. Numerous alarms still sounded, so many that he couldn't distinguish one from another. The entire ship still shuddered, listing badly, forcing him to actually walk uphill. Water ran down the corridor, soaking his lower legs as he sloshed through it.

The corridor ended at the main control room's door. No one saw him enter the room, so he stood, listening, trying to piece together what had happened. He found the room in total disarray. Some stations were dark from partial power loss. He saw at least four persons lying on the floor, no doubt injured. The moment was intense. He couldn't deny the adrenaline rush, regardless of the circumstances. He was agitated, as everyone was, but tried to maintain some semblance of order. Finally, he shouted above the din. "All right people … shut off some of these alarms!"

They stopped, one by one, until only voices filled the room. Halfway to his chair, Haute met the man he had placed in command when he left. He looked haggard and emotionally spent. "Sir … we're hit bad."

Haute waited before replying, expecting a little more than the explanation he had just received. "I felt it, Commander. Who hit us? What hit us?"

The younger man pulled himself together. "We don't know. Two contacts from the planet surface."

"From the surface?" he exclaimed, thoroughly shocked.

"Yes sir. We don't know what it was. Both hit our lower lateral port shield. The first blast was partially deflected … the second got through. The shield generator for that section is gone."

"Casualties?" Haute asked grimly.

The man sighed. "We have hull breaches in engineering maintenance and supply section four. There was total decompression in both. Six confirmed dead so far. More are missing. Only a few reports are in. There's gonna be more."

Haute spoke to the navigator. "Take us out of orbit as soon as possible."

"We're leaving?" Pierce asked hopefully.

"Not yet, just give us some room to run if we have to."

Pierce nodded, only then noticing the state of his commanding officer, the dirt, the blood, and the water running from his boots. "You're hurt?"

"Yeah … a lot happened down there … a lot of things we can't leave undone." He paused, wondering if those occurrences had just caused the deaths of more innocent lives. His mind was torn as to what to do. None of this had been planned. So many things were unclear. How had any of it happened? It was almost as if they had been led here, but why? God knows he hadn't wanted any of the misfortune that had plagued the last few hours. Nothing could change what had transpired. Only what happened in the next hours would make any difference.

One fact sat clearly in his mind. He would not, could not, continue the ancient war that had decimated the billions of persons who had once lived below, the same war that had spawned the Belaquin race. He would not contribute to that injustice. Even if the Kograns had sent the weapons against his ship, there would be no retaliatory strike. Puzzled, he spoke again to Pierce. "You mentioned being attacked before?"

"About thirty small fighters … I'm assuming from the alien ship. I sent out four squadrons to intercept." He paused, coming to the bright spot of his report. "We didn't lose a single ship. Our pilots took out every one of theirs. We even managed to capture one of them. It's quarantined down below."

Haute nodded, impressed and relieved with the report. The young man seemed to have held his own. He had to ask. "Are you still pissed off about the Aquillon Two mission?"

Pierce considered the question. He'd sweated the last hours, but felt as if for the first time in his career he'd been a part of something important. He'd wished for a history of his own for so long that it had snuck up on him without warning. "No sir … not in the least." His face revealed a hint of embarrassment. He had no idea that Haute had even known.

"You did well, Brian. I'm going below to get fixed. Keep me updated on the damage. I'll need a list of casualties … maintain battle readiness until I get back."

"Yes sir," He hesitated for a moment and as Haute turned, he asked. "Sir … what happened down there? Who hit us?"

"Do you know where we are, Commander?" "What do you mean?" Pierce was confused.

"The planet …"

"No … it's uncharted. This whole system's uncharted."

Haute looked at the view screen, where the entire planet could now be seen. It was beautiful, but so far … deadly. "A long time ago, they called it Earth." The younger officer stood speechless. "And if you know your history, son, you'll know who the Kograns were … and who they still are." He paused, letting the words sink in. "What happened is that we lost six men down there."

Pierce said nothing.

Haute changed the subject. "We've both got reports to log. Stay where we are. Get a fix on that other ship. If it makes a hostile move, destroy it. I'm going to call a department head meeting in a couple of hours. Have your report done by then." He turned and limped away.

Pierce gazed in wonderment at the planet on the screen. Was it possible? Could all that they knew be wrong? How did the Kograns survive? My God, he thought … Earth! The historical importance of this mission had suddenly become immeasurable. He shook his head, astounded at the possibilities.

The next two hours passed quickly. Haute's exhaustive report was ready to be sent to Touchen. Many other reports had been given to him over the last hour alone. The casualty list had grown considerably. The total number of crew lost in the recent attack on the ship had risen to twenty-six. They were the first Republic personnel to be killed in battle in over twenty years, and God willing, the last. Their names, as well as the names of the men still remaining on the planet surface were included in Touchen's report. In all, including security head Pritchart, thirty-three of his crew had lost their lives in the last few hours.

Another report drew concern to the damaged area of the ship. The shield that had been obliterated was still down and would be for some time. This created two immediate problems. One … if another strike was taken in that region of the vessel, the casualty figure would be compounded ten fold. Two … the absence of even minimal deflector protection prevented the possibility of high-speed space travel. With no such protection, even a small, undetectable asteroid with enough density and velocity, could pass completely through the vessel without even slowing. Such a scenario would be disastrous.

A third report, marked immediate, was handed to him. It reported that there was no trace of the alien vessel. Its whereabouts was unknown. Normally, this would have drawn great attention, but he took it as a good sign.

The auditorium was packed as he arrived. The meeting began with the sharing of the contents of the reports. He followed up with other facts, which he knew would bring about a majority of emotions. "The last two days have been filled with some questions we don't currently have answers for. Historic, as well as tragic events have occurred during this same time period. In the historical aspect … we have stumbled on incredible discovery. I think its significance surpasses any in the last two centuries. The circumstances leading up to these discoveries are confusing to say the least. The planet below us, through computer record verification and visual confirmation has been identified as Earth." He waited while many in the room became somewhat boisterous. Eventually, it became quiet once again, prompting him to continue. "We all know our history, however inaccurate it may prove to be. What happened here before and during the last two centuries is of no immediate concern at this time. What has happened today however is." He paused, uncertain of what to say. "For reasons unknown, I think we were led here. I don't know how or why, but I don't believe we were brought here to die, as so many have already. If that was the case, then the scout ship could easily have been destroyed earlier. We have been attacked twice since we arrived. The reasons for these attacks are also unknown. The unfortunate accident on the surface below, involving my shuttle and one raider was as I said, only an accident. It has led to many more startling revelations however."

"We have identified the intelligent life encountered below. They are human beings. They speak our language. They have the same mannerisms. They eat, they sleep, they feel pain, and they would die to protect each other, just as we would. They share some of the same history as our people." He paused, unsure how to say it. "Our ancestors knew them as the Kogran race," he said with finality.

There was some hesitation before the room erupted once again. Expressions of shock, disbelief, and confusion were seen. Unseen was anger, hate or hostility. The persons in the room could not feel those emotions, not based on the color of skin. The Kograns, ancestors of the people living below, may have once been the hated enemy, but not now ... not in the eyes of today. No hate could possibly span so many generations. He continued once again. "I have no intention of continuing hostilities with these people. Somehow, we have been given an incredible gift. We have been shown the way back to this special place. How we treat this gift, I think is most important. We can continue the senseless war, or we can stop it now. We can be better than the mistakes made before. We can do the right thing." He met as many eyes as possible and saw many nodding heads, evidently in support of the decision he'd already made. "I have prepared a report to the council outlining my intentions. It will be sent as soon as possible. This ship and crew is not completely out of danger. We are extremely vulnerable until repairs can be made. I plan to start peaceful negotiations as soon as that is done. We have an opportunity to set right a multitude of wrongs and that is what I intend to do."

"I have one thing left to say before adjourning. I would like to express my appreciation to all of you and your people for maintaining the integrity of this ship through a very demanding time. I would also like to personally thank four individuals who demonstrated the utmost in courage in effecting the rescue of myself and the attempted rescue of other members of this crew. This was done so with extreme danger to themselves. I would not be here without them." He named the four, though none of them happened to be in the room. The meeting ended.

Haute retired to his cabin, where he began editing the reports to the council. Tomorrow, he would begin the peace.

CHAPTER 8

▼

Ban-Sor was placidly pleased. He found the battle he had staged with the Republic Raiders to be quite rewarding in his constant quest for entertainment. Although he had lost all of his own ships, he had received immense delight out of piloting all of his ships at the same time. He discovered very early in the skirmish that the Belaquin people had rightfully prided their pilots. They were indeed excellent marksmen, while his skills had much to be desired. He tried to make his attack last as long as possible, but his opponents made short work of his fleet. He did compliment himself on one aspect; the fact that there was at least one rule he had not yet broken. It was forbidden to take life indiscriminately. It forced the diminutive battle to have only one outcome, but was fulfilling none the less.

He materialized into the main room of his massive citadel. The place he had chosen to temporarily reside was a small globe in the Beta Oxidillia galaxy. In that system of one hundred and twelve planets, he was the sole inhabitant of his kind. Many other species existed on other worlds, but none remotely like him. His elders estimated that he was safely hidden away from outsiders, but they couldn't be more wrong. Forms of life around him were too primitive to understand his existence and his contact with them was extremely limited. Blatant interference with their lives or natural development was strictly forbidden; therefore it was just a matter of time before Ban-Sor dabbled with it. Obviously, they had been too shortsighted to realize whom they were dealing with.

His mind was an endless whirlwind of dreams and adventures of discovery. It seemed that nothing was beyond his imagination or his reach. Only one question troubled him without end. Where had he come from? He had no inkling, and no memory of ever knowing. He could take himself to any place or anytime he could visualize, but when he tried to go to his beginning, he had no foundation and could go nowhere. Maybe it wasn't possible. Maybe his powers did have an end. After many exhausting attempts, he'd discovered only one thing ... the feeling of frustration.

He had lived, loved, and died a thousand different times in a thousand different places, only to end up feeling the same way. After each adventure, he would ultimately experience dissatisfaction ... stagnation ... boredom; at least until his imagination took him somewhere new.

He had just returned from his most recent outing and was again, exhausted. On this day he was in a generally humanoid form, large, somewhat construed as reptilian, with some rather unique conglomerations about the head, a true monster in most respects. His clothing was filthy, streaked with dull silver splotches. It hung on him, soaking wet, only adding to the weight of the metal body armor draped around him. The pieces clanged against each other as he walked. Ignoring the ghastly condition of his attire, he fell heavily onto an elaborate white couch and released a loud guttural sigh.

He smiled inside, recalling thoughts of the last few hours. He had just involved himself a clash between two warring parties on an unnamed water planet in the Austrinous system. This had been his third visit there during their war. The participants were extremely crude races living in harsh primitive settings. They had not climbed out of the spear, arrow, and sword age as of yet, and at the rate they were killing each other off, they would never do so. Ban-Sor already could see their bleak future. He knew this would be their last century.

He closed his eyes, vividly recalling the last adventure. Enormous iron clad ships, a hundred of them, rammed one another with limited speed, inflicting little or no damage, accomplishing only to knock off their feet, the crewmen thereon. Over and again they collided, one ship as strong as the next. As two ships would grind together, the crews would seemingly change places, and the most brutal fighting Ban-Sor had ever witnessed would commence. Swords and axes flashed; the decks soon running slick with silver blood. One aspect Ban-Sor had swiftly learned in these battles was not to go down under one of the swordsmen. They had the vicious habit of hacking away at the recently fallen, evidently assuring themselves that they were dead and would remain so.

For the life of him, as he fought, he could not tell one soldier from another, so he simply fought whoever attacked him. He had been killed on both previous visits, but today he had held his own. He admitted he had enough when he unceremoniously slipped on the iron planking and fell backwards into the waves. He sunk rapidly, his heavy armor sealing this day's fate. Was this a fate befitting a victor? He didn't believe so.

It was at that point he willed himself home, due a well-deserved rest. In all his travels and times, he had never found any being, including himself, which could go without food and sleep. He needed both now. His last waking thought was to try and do something really challenging; an adventure like never before. Now if he could only think of one.

Some time later he awoke. He had dreamed … or had he? The new adventure had arisen. He had a plan, or at least the beginnings of one. It would be precarious, but worth the risk. It was something he had never done before. He was toying with the idea of revealing his existence, his true existence, to the Belaquin people, or at least one of them. He knew what the future held for them and he felt the familiar temptation to intervene, not to break another rule, but to prevent a repeat of the tragedy that occurred two centuries before. He could give either side unlimited power, but would not. That would be a certain and destructive move.

Still draped in armor, he rose and readied himself. Concentrating, he began the change. The room filled with bright white light, emanating from the single being within it. When the light faded, the change was complete. The blood stained armor and clothing were gone.

He now stood in a human form. He was in male form, average height and average weight for the relatively small species. He chose common brown eyes and hair also, and might appear handsome to any other human who might see him. His body was young and strong, around twenty-five to thirty years old. Now draped over his noticeably slimmer shoulders was an officer's uniform, designated to the Republic of the Belaquin Star System. He looked himself over and was satisfied with the result. He smiled in anticipation. It was time to visit the Aquillon.

Commander Haute, during the long overnight hours, had finished his plan for peace. It would not be an easy task. It could be one of the most dangerous things he had ever tried to do. He knew only what history told him about these people. They were proud, powerful, irrepressible, and now in his own time, adamant survivors. Thinking about the coming day, he hoped for the miracle he knew he must have.

Two shuttles were planned to make the trip. Haute, five officers, and ten security men boarded the first. The second carried more security personnel and with them, special combat soldiers, all heavily armed in anticipation of hostile contact.

Five raiders would fly escort. Kahn and Gary requested of him to go along, but were denied. Haute reasoned that they had been through enough.

Approximate location of the Kogran base had been determined. It was already known that it lay beneath what used to be a part of New York City. Using ancient maps from computer files, the city was charted and the route planned. The first phase called for the ships to come down several hundred kilometers east of the city and fly in low over the water, hopefully undetected.

Haute wasn't looking forward to the trip. He'd had too much time to think about it and his apprehension was high. No one knew what awaited them. The Kograns had already proven that they still had control of sophisticated and powerful weaponry. Extremely high caution would be demanded on this mission. Without further delay, the shuttles launched. En-route, the raiders maneuvered around them. The Commander sat in silence, contemplating the coming events.

He looked out a window at the blue and green planet below him. It was so comparable to Belaquin. It held unparalleled intrigue and fascination in the fact that all human life had originated there.

Movement away from the planet caught his attention. Slightly above and behind was the second shuttle, and further away could be seen one of the raiders. He squinted, but didn't recognize the pilot. As he watched, the ship did a quarter roll and moved closer, coming within fifty meters. The pilot raised his hand in silent salute. Haute smiled, returned the gesture, laid his head back and closed his eyes. They still had at least a half hour flight left.

A strange sound interrupted the silence. It almost sounded like ice tinkling in a glass. Obviously he had dozed, but not more than a moment. He opened his eyes and noticed the raider beside him, but something seemed odd. He leaned and looked closer, wishing he had his glasses. The same pilot was still looking toward him and to his astonishment, still had his hand in the salute position!

"What ...?" Haute murmured. He waved to the pilot, but got no response.

He sat back, dumbfounded, and looked about the shuttle cabin. It took a few seconds, but eventually he saw that no one moved. No one spoke. No one even breathed.

Shaking his head, he stood up and heard the same strange sound from before. Startled, he whirled to face a man seated behind him. Even though dressed in uniform, Haute did not recognize him.

The man stood and offered one of two glasses filled with the tinkling ice. Haute stood still with confusion.

Again the unknown man gestured, "Take it. I think you might need a drink for this."

"What?" Haute stammered again. He again turned toward the men seated around him. Each person was still as stone. He glanced at the stranger, who casually took a sip from his own glass. Haute walked to the pilot's chair and studied its occupant. "Chambers?" His voice was almost a whisper.

The man at the controls did not respond. As Haute looked further, he noticed other impossibilities. The planet below them had ceased turning. Shaking his head in disbelief, he looked at the ship's chronometer. It was stopped as well. Everything he saw ... even time, had just ... stopped. His breath quickened as he tried to understand. He was startled when the man spoke again. "Are you about ready for this drink now, Commander?"

Slowly, he turned back toward the voice. He wasn't sure how he felt at this moment. He knew what was real and was entirely sure that this could not be. His mind blurred with possible explanations, but only one made sense; he was still asleep. He still did not speak to the man, who finished his glass and set it on the table. Haute searched his memory, and was sure he had never seen him before. The Republic uniform, complete with captains bars looked entirely ... normal. Finally, he did speak. "Who are you?" He had no anger or alarm in his voice. "What's going on?"

Ban-Sor extended his hand. "Easy enough questions to answer, Commander. Have a seat and I'll try to explain everything." He paused, politely adding, "Please."

Haute reluctantly shook the offered hand. The stranger seemed friendly enough, but his intentions might be far from the same. Were he and his men in danger? He reminded himself that there were hand lasers only a few feet away. He looked again to his men, silent, immobile and apparently oblivious to the conversation.

"Oh, they can't hear you." Ban-Sor related, reseating himself. The Commander did not, so he continued. "Please try to accept what I say, even though you may find it ... difficult." Without pause, he continued, "I've simply stopped time for a bit, so I could speak with you alone without upsetting the others of course. They wouldn't understand all of this, as you do not. The moments I spend with you will seem only a second to them."

Haute chuckled sarcastically. "You've stopped time?" Again approaching the shuttle pilot, he reached over and pressed a switch. "Aquillon, this is Command Shuttle One!" he said assertively.

No answer came, "Aquillon, this is fleet Commander Haute, emergency traffic!" The silence remained. He frowned in disappointment. After a few seconds of indecision, he approached and finally sat across from the visitor. Outside the view port, he saw the same raider. Nothing had changed. "All right, I'll listen for now." He felt he was beginning to understand. "So what did you do ... drug everyone, or just me?" The hand lasers were now three feet away.

Ban-Sor raised his eyebrows. "No, my good man, there are no hallucinations here, and you won't need any of those."

Haute's eyes narrowed in puzzlement. Were his intentions that obvious, or did this man know his thoughts? "Who are you?" He humored, "What are you?" As he spoke, he reached out, opened a panel and removed a hand laser, making no attempt to hide his actions.

"My name, as you would pronounce it, is Ban-Sor. As to what I am? Well, right now, I am what you see. I am a human being like you; a little older perhaps, maybe around fifteen hundred years or so."

Haute fingered the stun setting while he listened. The dream was getting better by the second. "You hide your age well," he answered.

"I live through my imagination. I do whatever I want, create whatever I want, and become whoever or whatever I want." Ban-Sor smiled broadly. "You don't believe a word I've said, do you?"

Haute brought the laser up and leveled it at the strangers' head. "No, I don't. It's easier to believe you just stowed away on my ship and pulled some kind of trick on my crew and me. Now, let's hear some truth. You weren't with us when we left, so how did you get here."

Ban-Sor didn't falter. "Rest assured sir, I did not stow away, as you put it. And this ..." He waved his hand around the cabin, "... this is quite what I said it was. It's no trick." Ban-Sor explained, surprised at how hostile and untrusting the human was.

"You haven't answered my question," pressed Haute.

"Very well ... how did I get on board? Like this ..." Before an incredulous host, Ban-Sor disappeared, only to reappear at another table on the other side of the cabin.

Haute was visibly startled. He felt flushed and nauseated as he finally realized that these were not simple tricks. He placed the laser on the table and watched as the man moved in the same matter back to his original seat. The Commander shook his head. "How ...?"

"You haven't been listening. I can do whatever I wish. I know what you are going to do before you do it."

"Then you know where I'm going now and that every moment I delay getting there could cost lives?"

"So easily you forget. Time is not moving. Yes ... I know very well that you are attempting to stop a war. That's why I am here."

Haute frowned. "Here from where? How do you know about all this?"

"I know everything about everything; about you, your people and your enemies." He continued, "Let's see ... when you were five years old, your father became head of your military fleet. At age seventeen you joined and distinguished yourself in battle, earning numerous commendations. At age twenty-one, your mother was killed in an unfortunate accident. Your wife was killed ...!"

"That information is all on record. You easily could have accessed it." Haute interrupted. He was impressed, but not convinced.

"You are right of course." Ban-Sor agreed, but continued. "Just two years ago, you had an affair with a close friend's wife. Just this morning you entertained the thought of seeing her again ... to remind her of your feelings toward her, but so far have thought it unwise. Show me that in one of your record files, Commander?"

Haute was again astonished. If he knew that, then he did indeed know everything. It wasn't possible, but his words and actions proved his boastings. He sat in silence, unsure of his next direction of thought.

Ban-Sor continued. "The reason I am here Mr. Haute, and believe me, I should not be here at all ... is to stop what was to happen and in doing so, save all of your lives." He motioned towards the planet below them. "If I were to let you land on Earth ...!"

"Earth!" Haute interrupted again. "You know about Earth?"

"Of course! Why do you think you are here? Quite a wonderful place. I thought perhaps your people would like to call it home again." He paused, noticing that his captive audience of one was beginning to piece it all together. "Anyway ... if I were to let you land in the city, you and all of your men would be killed before your first word of peace could be uttered. The Kogran warriors have prepared themselves and are awaiting your arrival as we speak. Instead, I've come to help ... or interfere, as some would say."

"Why are you ... interfering?"

"I feel this meeting could be important to the future of this planet and its entire people. Other than that, you could say that I have never been one to ... abide by the rules. My constituents would not approve, but they haven't approved of many things I've done." He shook his head, "No matter, we will have plenty of time to discuss my dilemmas, but for now, I'm sending this shuttle back to your ship. You and I will continue to the planet surface."

"You just said they were waiting to kill us."

"And they are, but we will be safe, I assure you."

Haute had to admit, the man was very convincing, but it was all too hard to believe. He shook his head. "I don't understand any of this. It's too much …"

Suddenly he felt a hand on his shoulder. Ban-Sor had moved behind him. He heard the sound of tinkling again. "Take this. It will help. This day will change forever the lives on this planet and yours."

Haute took the glass, still wary.

"You asked why, Commander? I guess I hate to see things go to waste … this planet … you … your people …" He paused, "… that drink."

Haute eyed the glass and downed the contents with one swallow. He watched as Ban-Sor took the seat across from him once again. Almost immediately, he began to feel weird and his eyes grew weary. His vision clouded, the shuttle interior fading completely. He closed his eyes, thinking that it was all just a dream.

Haute had no idea how much time passed before he awakened. Realizing his eyes were closed, he jerked them open, remembering. Right away, he knew he never should have closed them. The dream was not over.

He and Ban-Sor stood together on a deep red carpet. They were in a room with high cathedral ceilings, filled with some of the most ornate decorations he had ever seen. Statues, paintings, and colorful drapes adorned the walls. Torches burned, sending eerie shadows throughout. Gold seemed to glisten everywhere, reflecting the fires brilliance. At the far end of the room, the floor was elevated. Upon it rested what could only be described as a throne, incrusted with the glint of gold. Draped over and around it were fantastic blankets made from the skins of long lost animals. Haute had seen pictures of them. The names zebra … leopard … and tiger came to mind. The room could have been in a museum.

The lavish items befitted well the black man seated upon the majestic seat. To Haute, he looked like a king, as well he should. He did not know it, but he was in the presence of the very man he wished to speak with.

The surroundings were all taken in within a second, but his initial emotion was not awe; it was fear. His first thought was for his own protection, but the hand laser, which had been within his grasp a moment before was now far from it. He felt a hint of panic and looked to Ban-Sor who stood calmly with no visible emotion. Incredibly, even though they stood in plain sight, the Kogran king and the several men with him still seemed ignorant of their presence.

Haute's eyes were wide with uncertainty as he whispered. "My God … what the hell are we doing?"

His companion on the other hand, answered in a normal tone. "There's no need to restrict your voice. They can't see or hear us."

They stood quietly, watching and listening. The seated leader was addressing some twenty men. The man's voice was deep, distinguished, and demanded attention. "They will attack, or they will leave. It's that simple. We don't have the power to reach them now, so we have no choice but to wait."

Another man spoke. "How long, Manna?"

"I think they will come soon, but we will be ready."

"He thinks we're going to attack?" Haute asked, still whispering.

"Of course, that's precisely why I didn't let you land." Ban-Sor answered. "His actions are dictated by uncontrollable circumstances; his most recent memories and history. When they last saw your race, it was war. To them, you are both still at war."

Haute grew silent once again, pondering the words.

Second Lieutenant McTierney was following his preset heading when suddenly; the shuttle nearest him began an unexpected turn toward him. Repositioning well out of the way, he waited, puzzled. When the turn was finished, the white vessel had turned one hundred-eighty degrees about, returning, apparently to the Aquillon. The other shuttle remained on course.

He moved to where he could see the shuttle pilot, Captain Lisa Chambers, through the view port. He knew her as a seasoned pilot of at least ten years. "What's going on, Shuttle One?"

The Captain's voice hurriedly answered. "Stand by!" After a few seconds, "Uh, bay control, this is Command shuttle. We have lost manual." Chambers knew her voice was shaky. She had tried everything to regain control of her ship, but it would not respond. Strangely, the ship was not technically out of control. Normally, that problem alone would have been serious enough, but there was another that distressed her even more. Looking toward the rear of the cabin, she worriedly watched several persons moving about.

An officer appeared from a rear compartment. The man's facial expression said everything. His words only confirmed the impossible. "He's not here!"

Chambers turned back to her controls, staring at them helplessly. Her mind scrambled for answers, but found none that could explain what was happening. She considered looking for the Commander herself, but dismissed the notion. If he were still on board, they would have found him. She felt like screaming. Questioning her own sanity, she decided not to inform control of his disappearance as yet. She had a ship to land. In seconds, the Aquillon loomed in her path.

The shuttle bay commander's voice came through, "Shuttle one, this is bay control. Constitute emergency docking procedures. I am switching you to our control. Just relax and enjoy the ride."

"Over confident prick ..." said Chambers.

In bay control, a technician punched in a new heading for the shuttle. "Sir, the bypass conversion isn't responding."

Commander Lankford leaned over, "Try again."

"It's being rejected ... from their end. It says that manual is engaged. Someone has to be flying that shuttle."

Chambers heard the entire conversation over the open channel. Angrily she cut in. "I say again ... bay control, no one is flying this ship! All of our controls are unresponsive!"

Lankford answered. "All right, Captain, just stand by." He turned off the intercom and studied the screen. "Their approach pattern is right. They should come straight in. Get a tractor beam on them and slow them down." He reopened the channel. "Shuttle one, regain manual control if possible, but rig for collision just in case."

"Affirmative, control." answered Chambers. She noted the fading confidence in his voice.

An alarm claxon sounded in the bay area. "FIRE CONTROL PARTIES, BAY AREA SIX. SECURE FOR RE-ENTRY COLLISION."

Lankford watched as the holding beam locked onto the ship. Within seconds, he saw that it had no effect. The shuttle came on.

Chambers watched the Aquillon grow closer. She shook her head, totally baffled by what was happening. Her ship was perfectly on course back to the bay, apparently in some control, but whose? Nothing made sense at this point. She began docking procedures. "Docking retro in one minute ..."

She noticed a figure standing beside her and recognized him as the officer who had been searching for the Commander a moment before. He looked visibly shaken. Finally, he spoke in a low voice. "I don't understand. How can he not be on this ship? My God ... he was here. I saw him. We all saw him ..."

Chambers looked straight ahead, but said nothing to him. She already had enough on her mind. "Shuttle two and all raiders stay clear of bay six," she instructed.

The man stood silently, waiting for an answer or suggestion.

Chambers reached out and squeezed his arm. "Make sure everyone is strapped in. This could be rough," she said quietly.

The bay doors had opened. Glancing at the approach graphics, she saw that they were perfect. The docking beam had to have them, even though the computer said differently, but they were coming in too fast. She took a deep breath as the starry blackness faded, replaced by brightness of the bay.

A hundred eyes were on the sleek white ship as it entered the Aquillon. The ship slowed nearly to a stop. All witnesses breathed sighs of relief as the landing pads touched the deck. It went by the book. Over the next few moments, the second shuttle and the raider escorts followed. The pressure stabilized, the chamber oxygenated, and within seconds, numerous persons approached the recently departed ships.

The ludicrous rumor reporting Haute's absence raced through the ship. Ludicrous was the initial impression, but a more thorough search confirmed the impossible. Certain facts were undisputed. The man was on the shuttle when it departed. Exactly four minutes into the flight, shuttle one first reported the loss of control. Also about that time, the Commanders disappearance occurred.

The shuttle then returned to the Aquillon, minus one passenger. How and why these circumstances occurred was unknown. One fact that could not be argued was that there was no conceivable way for a person to have gotten off the shuttle while in flight. All aboard would have been killed by a hull breach of any kind. These simple scientific facts could not be disputed.

Security personnel poured over the ship with intricate scanners, checking each and every space. One by one they left the ship, shaking their heads, none of them able to offer any explanation. Chambers and the other crewmembers of the shuttle were questioned extensively, and each of them had the same answers. He was there, and then he was gone.

Wild theories followed, ranging from a conspiracy to kill the commanding officer, to mass, drug-induced hallucination and others even more far-fetched, all completely absurd … all easily dismissed.

The search raised more questions than answers. Puzzling clues were found near the Commanders chair. Two empty glasses and a hand laser lay upon the table. The containers had traces of an alcoholic beverage called Tiense, easily identified by its unique odor. The drink was stocked on the Aquillon, but not on board the shuttle. The shuttle did not carry glass containers either, leading to the assumption that they were carried aboard. All items were sent for analysis.

The Aquillon's intricate scanners searched outside the vessel, but found nothing. There was simply no trace. The Commander had been missing twice in the last two days, but this time there was no logical explanation. Word again spread through the ship. The compliment of the crew was staggered. They had run out of options. The unexplained, the impossible had happened.

Oblivious to the chaos aboard his ship, Commander Haute watched as the Kogran meeting ended. The leader rose and took one step before stopping and staring. Haute turned pale as he realized that the man was looking directly into his eyes. The room grew silent as the other men followed his gaze, but the immediate response was less than Haute expected.

The Manna sat back heavily in his chair, but did nothing more. He simply stared at the obvious illusion, knowing that it could be nothing more. The apparitions made no movement. He had seen similar conjurings before, but these seemed so real.

After a long moment, he became less than amused at the trick. He looked questionably at his men and broke the silence. "Who is doing this?" he demanded. There were no answers from his silent companions, who shook their heads in denial. Again he asked, this time with obvious annoyance in his tone. "Whose doing is this?"

"It's my doing!" Ban-Sor answered loudly.

Haute was visibly startled by the unexpected report. He thought he caught a hint of defiance in Ban-Sors voice, but why wouldn't there be?

The Manna was also shaken by the sudden outburst. The realization that the illusions could speak brought shocked confusion. Other feelings invaded as well, feelings impossible to suppress. As he sat in thought, one of his men moved to his side, stating that he recognized one of the intruders as the same man who had escaped from them earlier.

The Manna pondered the fact. This was not the time to make hasty decisions. His men were unarmed, and though twenty against two were acceptable odds, anyone who could enter a room as these two men had, must control power like he had never seen. They stood fearlessly, where no white men had stood for over two hundred years.

Apparently, the two strangers were not here for a fight. They did not appear to be armed. He decided that the best course of action under the conditions at hand was to hear them out. He asked the first question, "Who are you …" and the second, "… and how did you get in here?"

Ban-Sor took a step nearer the group of men and answered. "How we got here is of no importance." The Kograns were obviously distressed by his movement toward them. Haute joined him at his side. Ban-Sor continued, "Who we are and why we are here however, is most important."

Haute felt it was a good point to join the discussion. He spoke with no defiance in his voice. "My name is Leon Minden Haute, Commanding officer of the Star cruiser Aquillon." He saw no reaction of any kind from the Manna, whose eyes he looked straight into. He continued. "I'll get right to it. I have come to propose a peaceful mutual existence." He thought to himself how ridiculous the statement sounded, but this wasn't how he had initially planned the discussion.

The Manna directed his eyes to Haute's companion. "And you?"

"My name is Ban-Sor. I am ... an assisting friend!"

The black man answered quickly. "You say you want peace, but we have seen no peace from any of your people. You expect me to forget everything that's happened? How can there be peace, when none of our differences have been resolved!" His voice echoed loudly throughout the room.

Haute stayed calm in his return. "The differences you speak of are two hundred years old. Our culture has changed. We have learned from our ancestor's mistakes. We don't have room for useless insanity, such as racial prejudice. That time is over. All of the people that caused it are dead."

The Manna suddenly stood, his face contorted with rage. "You are wrong! We are far from dead! Our actions were not prompted by insanity. These offers of peace ... we've heard it all before. They came from men who lied with every breath they took. You killed millions of us with no mercy ... no remorse! We did the same, as we should have. We survived ..." He calmed suddenly, lowering his voice. "We survived, and we will continue to do so, no matter the cost."

Haute, though confused by the words, answered carefully. "Yes ... sir ... you will survive." He moved closer, stopping only a few feet from the throne. He wasn't sure how, but he knew he would not be harmed. "I know about the killings, the countless atrocities committed on your people. It makes me sick to think that human beings could do the things they did. That society is gone. I wish I could change what happened. I would, believe me. My people, we aren't the ones you speak of. I promise you, we want peace, nothing else ... no more fighting, no more killing."

"You have already killed four of my men." The black man said sharply.

Haute hadn't seen the statement coming, but immediately thought of his own losses. "And your attack killed twenty-seven of mine!" He said it firmly, but with no anger.

The Manna reseated himself, but did not speak.

Haute continued. "I came here for only one reason, to talk to you and your people. What happened down here a day ago was a mistake, an accident. We have so much to do, so many things we can learn about one another. Both our pasts have been plagued with mistakes, but what we do now could make up for them." Haute's hands rose from his sides, palms open. "I am completely unarmed. If you don't believe what I am saying, then kill me where I stand." He paused, hoping his invitation would not be acted upon. No one moved. "I know you love your people, as I love mine. Just give us this one chance … I beg you."

Ban-Sor stepped forward. Haute noticed a slight smile on his face. Obviously, he approved.

A different man spoke. His attire gave the impression of importance. "Where are your people?"

Haute smiled. "Not on this beautiful world, but on another, far away." The answer brought more puzzlement to the Kogran faces. Several of them whispered to one another.

The Manna thought over the words. This man seemed sincere, but to claim he lived on another world? Was it just a lie to protect his people here? What about the spaceship orbiting above? He had to consider some truth, but he had listened and believed so many times. He had hoped for truth from the white man, but had never received it. It had always been his wish to provide his people with a safe place, instead of a bloody battlefield. Maybe it was time to listen, instead of argue, but how could he be sure? Finally, he spoke. "You speak highly of your people, but how can you make promises for each and every one of them?" He didn't wait for an answer. "I don't know of any other world. I know of only one ship and a handful of men." Even as he said it, he knew that they were much, much more.

"You are right. My promises are based on the nature of the many. I cannot speak for all men. No one can. As commander of our armed forces, I can promise you that I will not continue this war." He used his most sincere tone. "I would not lie to a prospective friend just to make him one."

The Manna said nothing, pondering on the promises he had heard before. Misguided trust had proven costly in the past, but at this point, he still had some control of the situation. He looked at his men. He knew their minds and their hearts. They would fight to the death at his word, but they longed for peace, as he did. Each of them waited for his answer. Finally, he gave it. "I believe you speak the truth."

To Haute's surprise, the man's face softened with a slight smile. He could not help but return the gesture.

The Manna knew his face revealed a side rarely seen, but he felt a sense of pure honesty from this mans words, true or not. "For the good of my people, we will listen. For now, I will accept your proposal of peace."

Without hesitation or fear, the Commander stepped within three feet of the Manna. "Thank you, sir. You have made a choice you will not regret." He offered his hand in hopeful trust.

The Manna stared at the outstretched hand. He had never trusted a white man before, much less shook the hand of one in friendship. He had a premonition that he might be confronted with many such things in the future. He took the hand and held it tightly. The return grip was strong … sincere … binding.

Haute felt the same. He had always respected strength in a simple handshake. He felt great strength in this mans.

The Kogran king excused himself momentarily to speak to his men. Haute meanwhile, turned to Ban-Sor and offered his hand again. As the stranger took it, Haute gripped it tightly, still wondering many things. Who was this man? How did all of this happen? All he truly knew about him was his name. The short time he had spent with Ban-Sor thus far would require an in-depth explanation and one that he was incapable of providing at this time.

Regardless of the circumstances, without his help, the outcome could have been disastrous. How could he possibly explain this man and his actions to the crew of his ship, and more importantly, those higher up? They would think him insane. It was obvious that Ban-Sor would have to be seen and heard to be believed. At least he felt confident in one aspect. This was no dream.

Over the next several moments, numerous introductions were made by the Kogran leader, but Haute, throughout, looked for an opportunity to make a request. He felt it imperative that he contact his ship. He could only imagine the state of his crew. Upon his request, he could see the Manna's confusion, but the man asked for no explanation. They were led upwards through a maze of tunnels, finally emerging on the surface, where Haute succeeded in gaining signal. With the disappearance of the alien ship, the Aquillon had moved within range. He spent several uncomfortable moments trying to explain what had happened, an effort that only brought new questions. He decided to cut the inquiry short, not wishing to give their new friends the impression that he had absolutely no idea of how things had come about.

He couldn't blame the crew's curiosity. Their senior commanding officer disappears without a trace under impossible conditions. He then contacts them from the most unlikely location, giving what they are forced to view as ridiculous explanations. His control room personnel were justifiably cautious.

Haute requested a crew to be assembled and sent down upon his order. Meanwhile, his host offered a short tour of his age-old complex.

The Manna began the journey through cold, dark corridors. The way was lit only by torchlight, creating shadows and turning the ceilings black with soot. He explained that only a small part of the underground city was operational, due to electrical circuitry being damaged or destroyed in the past. Miraculously, the small section in which the Kogran's had been living remained operating at a low, but stable level. This fact intrigued the Commander, bringing forth questions that the Kogran leader answered the best he could.

The first was how they maintained that power within a city that had none. He told of a substance known only to those within the Kogran realm until now. "We don't know exactly what it is. The scientists who discovered it and built the generators died long ago. Its power must be limitless to last as long as it has."

Haute was incredulous, a power source of this magnitude existing virtually unknown? The thought was fascinating, but also unsettling.

The Manna continued. "We don't know how it works. All we know is that it is here, and we are alive because of it."

The knowledge of the power source answered many of the Commanders questions, but raised others. "This substance provided power, I understand that, but after the war, we know there was a nuclear winter. How did all your people survive down here with no food or water? Where are your women and children … your parents?"

The Manna's eyes widened with realization, only then seeing the obvious. If this man didn't know, then no one did … but how could they? Haute had not lied. The tragic events of yesterday had indeed been an accident. They hadn't known that he and his people were even here. They had no idea of the secrets the past held. He hesitated, not sure how to answer the man. He finally did. "Commander Haute … my mother and father died four-thousand miles from here, in the year 2034. I was thirty-six years old."

Haute stood speechless as he repeated the sentence in his mind. It took several seconds for the words to sink in. He frowned, shaking his head. "2034? That's not possible. That was before the start of the war …"

The Manna interrupted him. "I can see we have a lot more to talk about. We both have many unanswered questions. I think our next stop will answer most of yours."

A hundred questions berated Haute as they walked. At one point, he wished to include Ban-Sor in the conversation, but the strange man was suddenly gone. Soon, a man approached the Manna and spoke to him, handing him a piece of paper. The Manna glanced at it and gave it to Haute. "This was left for you."

Thoroughly puzzled, Haute read the handwritten message. "Thanks for the experience and your cooperation Commander. Perhaps we'll see each other again some day. Take care of things as I know you can." It was unsigned.

Haute smiled, muttering, "I'll be damned." He knew eventually he should explain everything to the puzzled black leader, but right now, he didn't know where to start. Instead, he urged him to continue.

As they walked, the black man talked on. "It was confusing for us at first. What happened to us was unforeseen ... unimagined." He paused, wondering where to begin. "My given name is William Thomas Vient. I was appointed leader of our cause at the start of the war. We were called Kograns some time later. You asked about our women and children ... my parents? Out of the millions that fought, we are all that's left; five-hundred of us locked away, sleeping beneath this city for two centuries."

"Sleeping?" exclaimed the shocked commander.

"I was born in 1998, Mr. Haute, here, in New York City, when the world was whole. I am two hundred and forty-three years old. The war wasn't fought by our ancestors. It was fought by us."

Haute shook his head in disbelief. "My God ..." He swallowed hard, finally grasping the incredible truth. He remembered the man's name. He'd heard it before, but until this moment, it had dwelled in his memory with Galileo, Washington, Einstein, Hitler, men long dead and gone.

"We awoke only a year ago to this new world and a new life. When we found out how long ... it was almost too much for us. It was hard to adjust in the beginning, but we rejoiced in the fact that our simple goal had been accomplished. That was all that mattered."

"Your goal?" Haute asked.

"To survive," the man answered. "In that horrible time, in this place ... when everyone one else was dead or dying around us, it's all we could have hoped for." The Manna's eyes looked beyond Haute, through the cold walls around them, remembering another time.

Haute was indeed mesmerized. It was inconceivable. These people had somehow managed two centuries before, what scientists today still couldn't conquer. Yes, he was intrigued and had many questions. "You say you slept for two hundred years? Were you frozen or ..." Still shaking his head, he paused. "This is difficult. Please excuse my ignorance."

The Manna stopped walking. "There's nothing to be excused for Commander. I don't know what they technically called it. It was a prolonged sleep. I was very skeptical at first. Many of us wanted to wait it out, no matter what, but it got too bad. We didn't have the supplies we needed, and couldn't get any more. Finally, we didn't have a choice. I'm no expert on it, but I know we weren't frozen. Some of my people will explain everything to you." At that point, they entered a stairwell leading downward into darkness.

The Commander studied the black man closely. He had misjudged him. In the first few moments with him, he had dubbed him a leader who ruled with fear, intimidation, and cruelty. Now, he found him to be a kind, compassionate man. It was hard to believe that anyone could be at odds against someone such as this, but he knew that there had been drastic, desperate issues at hand two centuries ago. Haute prayed that they would forever stay there. He listened further.

"A few years into the war, some of us had premonitions of what might happen. We didn't have the capability of escaping this planet, as the whites were rumored to have. No one actually thought it would come to that. So, we started preparations after we found this complex. It took a long time, even with the new generators working. After the last bombs fell, five hundred of our men and women were put into the chambers."

Haute interrupted. "You said men and women ... what about your children?" Even in the dim firelight, Haute could see sorrow in the Manna's eyes as he stopped his descent and turned toward him.

"Our children?" he said, "Most were taken at the beginning to try to make us give up. Many did. I could not make that decision for my people. To choose life and death for your children is not a choice. Thousands surrendered ... threatened with the murder of their children." He paused, remembering the rage he had felt. "All of them were killed." He studied his guest, who stood, mortified. "Would you give your life to save your child, Commander? Would you give your life to save someone else's?"

Haute could say nothing.

"Those were some of the terrible choices we were faced with. No parent ... no human being should have to make that kind of decision." He paused again in thought. "If you know your history, Mr. Haute, then you know who I am ... who I was. I am alive today, but my life ended on that first day. It was May 17th, 2031. My daughter, Jamie Lynn, was raped and stabbed by two white men on her way to school. I was holding her in my arms when she died. There was nothing I could do. She was so hurt ... so scared. She knew what was going to happen. She told me she loved me. That was the last thing she said. It was the day after her eighth birthday."

Haute's throat tightened with the words.

The man continued. "She was everything to me ..." He sighed deeply. "They arrested the two men the next day. The day after that, they were released. The judge said the word of the ten and eleven year old witnesses wasn't good enough. I couldn't take it. I found the two men and killed them in front of their wives and children. I had no conscience, no remorse. All I felt was hate." He lowered his head and shook it slowly. "I had no idea what the mistakes I made that day would do to the world. When I was arrested, it began, the riots, the killing. It went on and on. Towards the end, there were no prisoners taken. We were killed on sight." Vient swallowed hard. "You asked about our children? They were careful to make sure none of them survived. We were no different, we did the same. Kill the seeds ... make sure you will never have to fight the children of the parents you've killed."

Haute heard the pain in the man's voice and saw the regret in his face.

"The last days were worse than anyone could imagine. First the police turned against each other ... then the military ... then the governments ... black against white. Everything fell apart. We don't even know who sent the first bombs. Entire cities all over the world were wiped out. A large warhead landed close to here, but it somehow missed this part of the city. We heard it. We felt it. Luckily, we were ready."

"We still had contact with some survivors above, but we couldn't let them in. A couple of weeks later, the last missiles hit. We think they were biological. We lost all contact with the surface soon after that." His eyes met Haute's as he held out his hand, treating it as if it wasn't a part of him. "This hand sent some of those bombs. I was responsible for the deaths of hundreds of thousands of people, maybe some of my own family ... these men's families. My only consolation is the belief that they were already dead. There were so many innocents." He dropped his eyes. "It didn't matter then. This region was mostly under white control. To kill them, we had to accept the sacrifice of some of our own. Our hate blinded us. We didn't look at them as good or bad. Only the color mattered. We hated the white man for what he tried to do, and he hated us back. Even now, it's uncomfortable to stand here with you, though I know you weren't one of them. To your people, this is all just history written in books. To us, it all happened yesterday."

Haute nodded in agreement, fully understanding. He had seen war as well. "You did what you had to do. You're right; we can't know what it was like. I appreciate the trust you have shown me ... more than you know. I feel I know my people. I truly don't believe they hold the hatred you knew." The black man's face, as far as he could tell, held no expression. "Hopefully, some day, you can believe it too."

The Manna spoke, with a slight smile crowding through. "Please forgive me for rambling, Mr. Haute. I didn't mean to bore you with a history lesson. Let's continue." He was filled with eagerness. The arrival of the unexpected visitors and the strange events of the morning had delayed, but not changed this important day.

The stairway wound downward. The darkness and cold seemed deeper with each step. Suddenly, they could hear muffled shouts from below them. The Manna hurried towards the yelling. As he reached the bottom of the stairs, cold wetness shocked his senses. His smile had turned to a grim look of horror. "Oh my God!" He exclaimed. He splashed forward through knee-deep water into the darkness.

More torches were lit, shedding light on what Haute could not see before. They stood in a huge room, filled with rows and rows of coffin like containers, seemingly hundreds of them. He already knew what rested inside them. The entire room was filled with water at least two feet in depth. The Manna approached the stairwell, again speaking to his men. His voice was desperate. "We have to stop this now!"

"Are the chambers waterproof?" asked Haute.

Another man, out of breath, answered. "Yes, but the controls may not be. They could short out if the water reaches them."

The Manna stood near the first row of chambers. "My wife and all of our women are here. We left them asleep until we were sure we could survive. We were going to awaken them today." He checked the readings on the closest chamber, which appeared to be thus far unaffected by the water. He turned to his men, almost pleading. "Find out what happened and try to stop it. Our lives depend on it."

The Commander's mind raced as well, searching for ideas. "You can wake them up, right?"

The same man who spoke earlier, answered again. "We can, but the process takes at least two hours." He looked at his leader. "We may not have that much time."

Haute quipped in. "Then we have to hurry." He addressed the Manna. "Start the process. Get me back to the surface."

The Manna didn't argue. Instead, he removed his cape, heavy with water, and rushed up the stairwell.

The hurried climb to the top of the stairs was exhausting. Haute followed as quickly as he could, his leg aching with each step. They passed a hundred men on the way up, all descending to help.

Reaching the surface, Haute recalled his ship. As someone answered, he gave the orders. "No questions! I need four P-580 water pumps and the men to run them down here immediately. I want priority initiation on this. Cram the pumps and all the hose that can fit into five raiders, portable generators in five more and get them down here. Send them to the same coordinates as the original shuttle mission earlier. Expedite!'"

Within moments, raiders were powering up for the flight. A dozen damage control technicians had already boarded a shuttle and lifted off. Haute was notified that the ships were on their way. He in turn, informed them who and what to expect at the landing site. The Manna also addressed his men before sending them above to assist with the equipment and guide the shore party. With that done, they returned below.

Haute thought as they descended, how perfect the timing of Ban-Sor's disappearance had been, and how easily he might have taken care of this potentially disastrous situation, or had he already known it was to happen?

Minutes later they reached the flooded chamber. The water depth appeared the same, but they were told that it had risen an inch more and was now within a foot and a half of the chamber controls.

The Manna found a torch and went directly to one of the chambers. He stood over it, staring through the glass. He touched it, caressing the transparency as if it wasn't there. He said nothing, but it was easy to tell that whoever was within it was deeply missed.

A man approached, but stood silently until the Manna turned toward him. "William ... all the chambers are on revive mode."

"Good James. The water ...?"

"We've found the crack on the far wall, but the leak is behind it. It's hard to get to."

The Manna looked down again, nodding. "Have all the men standing by when the capsules unlock. We'll have to hurry."

The man nodded and left. The sound of splashing water came from all around them as unseen persons rushed about.

Haute moved closer and looked inside the chamber. A woman lay inside. Only the slight rise and fall of her chest revealed any sign of life. "She's beautiful."

"This is my wife, Commander." A smile pursed his lips. "Our two-hundred and tenth anniversary is growing near." He looked at the older man. "Are you so engaged?"

"Married? No, not anymore," He lowered his eyes in thought. "I still love her very much though," he remarked. He changed the subject. "Some of your men call you Manna?"

"Yeah, some still do. It's more of a title I guess ... one I'd rather forget. I was William before all this started. I would like to be William again."

"I know exactly what you mean. Commander is so impersonal."

Vient became distant as he spoke. "I know how this happened."

"What?" Haute was confused.

"The flooding ... it was from the missiles. The ones we fired at your ship." he said reluctantly. "We weren't sure where they were, or if they still worked. The silos were closer to us than we thought. The vibration from the launches shook the whole complex. Some of the sub floor must have ruptured." He looked about the room. "If they die because of my stupidity ..."

Haute laid his hand on his shoulder. "They won't, William ... not if I can help it." He turned and sloshed toward the stairwell. Thirty precious moments passed before the first group of Republic arrived from above, led by Haute. Two pumps and generators were carted into the chamber and hooked up. A hundred fifty feet of hose were run down from the surface through nearby elevator shafts. The portable generators were started. The normally quiet engines were uncomfortably loud in the vast chamber. Within minutes, two more pumps were set in motion. The wait began. The water level was only six inches below the lowest set of chamber controls. Fifteen minutes later, it remained the same. Haute breathed a sigh of relief as he spoke to the Manna. "It's working."

By the time the first conscious stirring of life appeared in the chambers, the water level had dropped nearly two inches. Joy and relief filled the Kograns as they thanked the men who had probably saved the two hundred fifty precious lives around them. The women were the lifeblood of their race. If they had been lost, then all would have been lost.

It was time for the Kogran leader to put his hand on Haute's shoulder. "I thank you Commander. We owe you all of our lives."

The Commander returned the man's smile. 'You owe us nothing, sir ... and please call me Leon." His request coaxed a chuckle from Vient. There was little doubt in his mind that peace between their peoples was at hand.

The hour passed. Haute stayed below and witnessed the unbridled joy of family and friends reunited. Years of unshed tears fell into the dispersing water on the floor. His own eyes grew moist as he watched, sadly remembering someone from long ago.

Stretchers, one by one, were filled and taken above. The women, as expected, were much too weak to make any major movements, such as sitting up or walking, but the men were prepared, having been through the same ordeal less than a year ago.

Portable mini-suns filled the room with light. The Belaquins stood in awe at the vaulted ceiling high above them. Up to that moment, they had no idea of the enormity of the underground room.

William Vient tenderly helped lift his wife to a stretcher. She had just begun to awaken. He placed his face close to hers and spoke softly. The young woman opened her eyes only slightly. Tears ran down her cheeks as she recognized the voice. She tried to speak, but her husband stopped her, assuring that everything was understood. The Manna looked up and smiled once again at the man who he now would call friend. Tears of joy traced his face as well.

Within the hour, the damage control techs had found and sealed the leak. The flooding became only a memory. More than half the former chamber occupants were well on their way to recovery. Haute's thoughts turned yet again to his ship. After giving instruction to maintain their efforts below, he left his men and again made his way up the stairwell, making a silent reminder to fix the elevators as soon as events allowed. His future intentions were to provide equipment and technicians to help bring the entire complex into working order. With the Manna's permission, the plan would be put in motion.

Halfway up the stairs, he saw a familiar face. It was Captain Chambers, the command shuttle pilot who had piloted his shuttle earlier.

She spoke as she drew close. "Looks like there was quite a mess down there, sir?"

"It could have been a lot worse, Captain," he answered. "Hey, as soon as this is finished, I'm gonna need a ride home. I've got something to do first, though."

"Yes sir. We should be ready in thirty ... forty-five minutes at the most."

"That's fine. I'll meet you topside." As Haute turned, he noticed hesitation on her part. "Was there something else, Captain?"

"Yes sir. I'm sorry, I ... don't understand. I mean, I'm really screwed up with this."

"Don't worry, you're not crazy. It's just complicated. As soon as I understand it ... you will too."

"Yes sir." She turned, mildly unsatisfied, and left.

The Commander went in search of the Kogran King, and after receiving directions, found him in one of many recovery rooms with his wife.

He was seated at her side and didn't notice as he walked up behind him. As he approached, he saw that the woman became somewhat surprised, her eyes growing wide.

William saw the sudden change in his wife's face and at the same time was startled by a hand on his back. He turned. "Commander Haute, I'm glad you're here. I'm sorry … I didn't mean to leave you alone down there."

"That's all right, I don't blame you."

With pride, he spoke. "Mr. Haute, this is my beautiful wife, Tangela." He then spoke to her. "This is the man I told you about."

Haute reached down and took the woman's hand in his. She felt incredibly cold to the touch, and her grip was very weak. "I'm very happy to meet you, Mrs. Vient. Welcome back."

His voice was pleasant. The anxiety lessened. With relief she realized all that her husband had told her was true. Everything would be all right. Finally, with difficulty, she managed to answer. "Thank you."

William stood, sensing a specific reason for the visit. "Did you need me for something Commander?"

"Yes … at your convenience. It won't take but a moment." The Manna joined him in the corridor where he explained. "I must return to my ship for a while, but I've set up communications between us. With your consent, I would like to bring down what we need to begin repairs on your complex. Also, I would be honored to have you, your wife, and others to visit the Aquillon … when you're ready of course. I think you would enjoy it."

"You have my consent, and I am honored by your invitation. I will call when we're ready. I have a lot of catching up to do down here first." He shook the white man's hand once again.

"I understand," Haute nodded.

"Again, from my people and my heart, I give you thanks. I promise I will see you soon."

Haute left, returning to the surface. He dreaded some of the items he needed to address, knowing how ridiculous his report would sound. How else could he explain what had transpired?

The sun blinded him as he left the building. He squinted, studying the surroundings. It was the plaza he had seen on the first day. The church, burned and collapsed, rested across the way. Smoke still drifted from its ruins. Several shuttles sat near the fountain in the center, waiting for their crews to return. It was muggy out in the open. He felt perspiration beading on his forehead. Finding a shady spot beneath a tree, he sat and waited also.

Out of the perfect stillness around him, a cool breeze reached his side. Leaves from above broke loose and fell around him. He closed his eyes and enjoyed the relaxing moment. It was almost familiar … but not in this place, not on this planet.

What else would they find here? What would the other survivors be like?

Taking in a deep breath, he held it as long as he could and listened. He could hear birds far away, and men talking, their words faint but getting louder.

Soon, many people moved about the plaza. Reluctantly, he opened his eyes. It was time to go. He rose and joined the others in the ship. Moments later, as the clouds slipped past, he closed his eyes again, wondering when he opened them if Ban-Sor would be there. Probably not, he reasoned. Truly, at this point, he had to wonder if he had ever been there at all.

CHAPTER 9

▼

Three long days passed before word was received from Earth. On the first day, the sad task of recovering the bodies of crewman still at the shuttle crash site was addressed. Haute's face was grim as he watched them placed in storage for the trip home. An effort was made to locate the unfortunate Pritchart, but the exact location was impossible to find. The body of the man killed in the Kogran complex had already been taken care of. Official notification of the families would have to be attended to as soon as possible.

On the second day, the Commander of the Aquillon prepared his official report to send to Belaquin. Nearly every sentence written was accompanied with a silent, though malice free, curse directed to the one man who could explain everything. Regardless, there was at least one other man who could back up some of his story. Hopefully, he would be on board very soon to do so.

Due to the circumstances, he had forced himself to be cooperative. The psychiatric tests he had so reluctantly agreed to were stressful, and redundant, but at least they had come back normal. As far as the physicians were concerned, he was the average middle age man with a slightly overactive imagination. They of course, found no explanation of their own.

His report was simple. The specifics of this mission had been planned, the ensuing events unplanned, and the outcome favorable. Perhaps the council wouldn't necessarily care how it was done ... only that it was.

He was occupied when the call came from the planet surface, but returned it as soon as he could. The Kogran visit was set for the next day.

The shuttles and the raider escort departed at eight a.m., New York City time. Haute joined the trip as a friendly face. A half hour later as they dropped below the cloud base, they encountered an early morning rain shower. The archaic city soon came into view.

The rain ended abruptly and the sun hit hard and bright, silhouetting the lone tower on the eastern horizon. Other buildings rose high around it, but none came close to its incredible height. The shuttle banked and Haute could see the forest below shrouded in foggy mist.

Gliding between the skyscrapers, they approached the plaza. Several persons greeted the Commander as he stepped off the ship. Also greeting him was a warm sprinkling of rain. It was refreshing, though inopportune. Wiping his eyes, Haute recognized one of the men as the Manna's top advisor. "Commander Haute, we welcome you. The Manna is anxious to see you."

Haute was led underground once again, this time to a different section of the complex. He noted that much of the way was well lit. Apparently, work was progressing as planned. The escort explained that they were heading for the Manna's personal spaces.

The latter appeared overjoyed to see his older friend, but seemed unmistakably nervous. He and his wife were in the main room, conversing with three men. The woman turned. Her smile showed that she didn't share her husband's agitation. Haute couldn't hide his astonishment at the sight of her. She had changed so much in the last few days. Her beauty was unparalleled. She strode toward him, her white gown flowing as if blown by a breeze. It was she who offered her hand this time. "Commander Haute, welcome back." This time it radiated warmth.

"Thank you. I'm glad to see the effects of the sleep have worn off."

"I'm glad to feel that they've worn off. I guess I wouldn't be feeling anything if it weren't for you, would I?"

"A lot of strange events came together to bring us together. I'm just glad I could help. I'm sure he wouldn't have let anything happen to you." He looked past her and asked. "Forgive me, but is everything alright?"

"Oh, you noticed too? He says it is. I guess I don't know him that well after ten years. I know he's nervous, this being his first trip to space and all."

"And you aren't?"

She spoke quietly, since the subject of the discussion was approaching within earshot. "Of course I am, but I'm not going to let him know that."

Haute smiled and nodded his approval, shaking hands with William as he joined them. "And how are you this morning?" He asked.

"I've been better thank you. I guess it's time?" Vient sounded less than enthusiastic.

Haute chuckled. "Well, I guess we're ready if you are."

"Ready ... I'm not sure, but we'll go anyway."

Reluctantly, the Manna, his wife, and six other delegates of the Kogran people finally boarded the command ship. Haute acted as steward, preparing them for the trip. "You'll find seat straps to either side of you. I think they're self-explanatory. We'll wear them only during take off and landing." He winked at the shuttle pilot. "We probably won't need them. Our flight survival rate is up to ninety-seven percent this month." He maintained the utmost seriousness to his voice. Out of the corner of his eye, he saw the black leaders eyes widen considerably. "That's the best this year, so don't worry." As he seated himself, he felt the ache in his leg, considering then that the joke was perhaps ill timed.

The pilot brought the shuttle nose up smoothly and headed east over the ocean. It took about ten minutes to climb into the lower atmosphere where the blueness of the sky started to fade. Finally, it dimmed to complete blackness.

Haute unstrapped himself and walked to the rear of the shuttle where the Kograns were seated. They leaned in their seats, trying to see as much as possible through the view ports. "It's okay, you can get up. We're through the rough stuff." Anxiously, one by one, they did so, each in awe at the slight weightlessness they were experiencing.

The Manna looked in puzzlement at his host. "Are we moving?"

"Of course, about seventeen thousand miles an hour, give or take a few. You see, there's no air in space, therefore no resistance; at least none that we can feel. Come up to the front."

Tangela Vient touched the back of her hand to the main frontal view port and drew it back quickly. "It's so cold," she exclaimed.

"Yes, space is very cold, about two hundred-fifty degrees below zero. Out there, you would freeze to death, if you didn't suffocate first. It would only take a few seconds."

Tangela visibly shuddered at the thought, remembering the terrible cold she had awakened to only a few days before.

The pilots made a slow ninety-degree turn, bringing the Earth into full view of everyone on board. "My God ... this is unbelievable," muttered the Kogran King. "I can't believe it."

"That's what she looks like from up here." Haute fully shared their admiration.

William turned and shook his head in disbelief.

Haute smiled broadly, "Welcome to the future."

"There's so much we don't know." Tangela said. "Too much ... it's frightening."

"Don't worry. We'll teach you more than you can imagine." Haute spoke directly to her. She smiled back, but it was half-hearted. He then directed his words to her husband. "In turn, we hope to learn from you."

"What could we possibly teach you?" Vient asked.

"History for one. We only know what our ancestors brought with them. Your people could help us fill in the gaps. Your sleep chambers, for instance. For our people, it doesn't exist. We've always had the dream of exploring the universe, but time has limited us. With a working system such as yours, the possibilities could be unlimited."

"You have explored?" asked another man.

"For decades ... but progress is slow."

Tangela Vient grew intrigued with the conversation. "Commander ..." she asked, "What about other life?"

"In my lifetime, the only life supporting system we have explored is our own, and now this one ..." Haute noticed a hint of disappointment in her eyes, but he continued. "There is other life however."

"Really?" She was again bright eyed.

"We call them Thalosians, humanoid, insect like, highly advanced. If we have an enemy, they're it. They've always been hostile. Any dealings we've had with them have cost lives. Needless to say, we avoid contact."

"So do you think there is life other than the Thalosians?"

"I have never believed that the people who left Earth just happened to stumble on the only system in this universe that can sustain life. It's absurd to think it. The Belaquin system has seven planets that our people live on. I believe there are a thousand different forms of life out there ... somewhere." Haute thought of Ban-Sor, but it wasn't time to include him. "With your technology, and ours ... we may be able to find them."

The Manna felt the Commanders' enthusiasm. "Your scientists are welcome to learn the process as soon as you wish." He reached out and touched the window as his wife had done, feeling the extreme cold. "Our lessons have already begun."

The pilot turned from the planet and began to circle it. The minutes passed and as the voyagers watched, an object, shining brighter than any star, came into view. Not recognizable at first, it grew in size quickly.

The Manna's eyes widened once again. "What is that?" he asked. He had his own suspicions, but wasn't sure.

"That … William … is our home away from home … the Aquillon." he answered proudly. They were still too far away for the Kograns to possibly appreciate her, but Haute knew that they would, soon enough.

A voice came through the pilot's station. "Shuttle One, we have you in sight and on the board, switching you over to bay control upon your cancellation."

"Switching over now. Bring us in easy; we've got several VIP's on aboard," The pilot rose and made his way rearward.

Haute offered the two pilot seats to the Manna and his wife, giving them the best possible view. The other six men crowded close behind to witness the incredible sight. Haute touched the transmit button. "Bay control, this is Haute … give us a three-sixty around the ship before you bring us in."

"Yes sir, will do."

He moved out of the way, allowing an unhindered view to the visitors. Within seconds, the ship took on shape, becoming more defined. Hundreds of view ports allowed light to escape from within, suggesting a living being, instead of a cold metal shell. No one uttered a sound as they came in on the starboard side of the massive ship. Each of them stared in silent appreciation.

"How many people are on your ship, Commander, two or three hundred?" guessed one of the men.

Haute laughed, "There's a few more than that. If I'm not mistaken, we have over two hundred persons in the engineering section alone. One thousand five hundred men and women are on this ship. Thousands more are serving on other ships throughout the fleet."

The Manna said nothing.

Returning his gaze to the ship, Haute continued. "The Aquillon is over a half a mile in width. It weighs over five-hundred thousand tons, and she can travel faster than the speed of light."

The Manna simply could not believe what he was seeing or hearing. A ship this large … and how fast was the speed of light? These thoughts were alien to him.

The shuttle, still under bay control, continued along the starboard side of the Aquillon, and made a slow right turn as they approached the stern, dropping below the five massive engine ports, oval caves in the mountain if metal. After the turn was finished, they continued forward and slightly below the port side.

Haute took a quick breath and held it, noticing the huge blackened areas below the left wing of his ship. The smooth sleek metal gave way to a scorched, misshapen mass. He hadn't seen the damage before and was shaken as they passed near the ruptured hull. He couldn't help but glance at the Kogran leader, who also saw the destruction, knowing full well what had caused it. The man lowered his eyes and shook his head. Haute knew his thoughts. He felt the same. They both were sorry that it had ever happened.

A moment later, the shuttle approached a docking bay and the Kogran party was asked to retake their seats. The landing was uneventful except for a remark from Tangela Vient as the shuttle sat down. It was a welcome voice in the uncomfortable silence. "I guess this ups your flight survival rate a couple of points, Commander?"

Haute smiled back, admiring her attractiveness and her sense of humor.

Haute led them off the shuttle and began a personal tour of his ship. He believed it to be the best way to satisfy their curiosity and answer their questions.

Two enjoyable hours later, he found that he had been right. His guests were amazed. Every aspect, no matter how diminutive, had impressed them.

As much as he hated to, the Commander eventually had to break from his role as tour guide and attend to other duties. He reluctantly excused himself and assigned another officer to take over where he had left off, promising to join up with them soon.

Arriving on the control deck, he got to work. There was much to do. Engineering shore parties had to be replenished and science and medical teams assembled to study the sleep chambers. There was so much to discover, and all with the Kogran King's blessings.

An hour later, Haute did as he promised and caught up with the Kogran party after their meal in the officer's lounge. With what they had been used to, all appeared to have enjoyed it immensely.

William asked a surprising question as they continued the tour. "Where is the man who was with you when we first met? I'm sorry, I don't remember his name?" He wished to ask many more questions regarding the strange meeting, but did not.

"Oh, his name is Ban-Sor ..." Haute answered. He hated to mislead the man any further, but wasn't prepared for the inquiry. "To tell you the truth, William, we have a lot to talk about concerning him. I know you have questions, but I may not have the right answers just yet." The Manna nodded in mild understanding. Haute knew the inquiry was coming.

The tour finally ended in the main control room. Filling one end of the room was an impressive view of the Earth. "This is the main control deck. Most of the ship is run from here. Engineering has a secondary control room, just in case. It's in one of the most protected parts of the hull." He started around the room, explaining various functions of the different stations.

Haute took William aside for a moment. "I've been thinking about something for a time, and I've decided to ask you."

The black man's eyebrows lifted. "It sounds serious."

"It's a huge step, believe me. I doubt that you've even thought about it, but it would do me a great honor if you and your wife would consider going back with us."

"Back with you?" he said in puzzled reply. "To where?"

"Back to our home," Haute answered. "Belaquin … it would be a extraordinary trip for you."

The Manna's face held no discernable expression as he pondered the question.

"I mean … I thought I would at least offer …" The Commander immediately felt uncomfortable. "I'm sorry. It's too much, too soon."

William interrupted. "Your invitation is tempting, of course, but …" His thoughts turned to the hundreds of persons who waited on the planet below. "I can't answer yet. As you said, it's a big step. We just need some time to adjust I think."

Haute nodded his head in understanding. The man was right. He didn't want to push and he couldn't shake the feeling that he might have already done so.

The tour had lasted several hours. The visit was pleasant and informative. The Kogran King did not wish to leave, but he knew where he was needed. The shuttle made one more trip to the planet surface.

Three days passed. Haute and his one time adversary spoke frequently and had accomplished much. Research operations were well under way. The sleep chambers and mysterious power source had the scientists drooling. Much of the complex below the ruined city had deteriorated to the point that restoring it with power and heat was not easy. It was a problem that would take weeks to remedy and many sections would have to be abandoned. Surprisingly, the Kograns had only occupied a small part, leaving much untouched and unexplored.

Early on the fourth day, Haute received an answer from William Vient concerning the earlier invitation. The black leader felt that his people were ready to step into the future. Preparations had already been planned in anticipation of the decision and he now set them in motion. Departure time was set for four o'clock the next evening, Earth time.

Time passed slowly for the Aquillon crew, but their spirits renewed as the departure time grew near. The Commander was no exception. He was anxious, as well as apprehensive about the trip home. He had some face-to-face explaining to do.

Haute assured that the Kogran party of ten men and women arrived safely and were settled comfortably in their quarters. He requested that the Manna and his wife join him in the control room for the departure, which they gladly did.

Before they arrived, he walked to the main communications station. "Contact the shore party."

"Contact established, Commander. Captain Clark is on."

"Captain, how's everything going down there?" Haute asked.

"Pretty good, sir. We've got the entire upper two levels working. Some of their old systems are still giving us trouble. We still have to figure out this twentieth century mess. We need some specialized equipment, but the ship doesn't have it."

"Just send us the list."

"Sounds great, sir, but it might be a long list."

"No problems then?" Haute asked hopefully.

"None whatsoever, sir. We'll be fine down here."

"Glad to hear it." He turned at that time to see that his guest had arrived. "We're heading out. I'll send back a high-speed interceptor with the things you need. It'll be here in a few days. Good luck, Captain." He switched off the frequency and approached William.

"Are you ready?"

The black man smiled and took his wife's hand in his. "I think so."

Haute turned to the navigator. "Let's go home."

Below, in Colleen Sluder's quarters, no one noticed the increasing throb of the engines. She, Gary, Kahn and Deanna sat around the room, playing a new combat game called Copernicus. Each player flew a ship through asteroid belts filled with derelict vessels, while at the same time attempting to destroy one another. Colleen won her third straight contest as Gary's ship disintegrated in a fiery explosion.

Gary was annoyed. "I don't believe this shit," he whined, "This is impossible." He handed her three of his last six chips.

"Believe it lover boy," she giggled, "It pays off watching older brothers do this twenty four seven."

"You're just lucky," retorted Deanna. "I've beaten your ass before."

"Maybe it's luck, maybe it's not. If it is, I want to put it to the test. Don't we have some shore leave to burn in the next week or so, Kahn?"

"By God, we'd better after what we've been through. Why, have you got plans already?"

"Yeah … I want to go to Shannate. My sister Kelsey lives there."

Gary was impressed. "What did she do, marry a millionaire?"

"Not hardly! She's a pleasure girl at one of the casinos; been there a few months now. I promised her I'd come and see her one of these days."

Kahn's eyebrows lifted at the thought. He'd seen pleasure girls before.

"I bet she makes more than all of us combined," guessed Deanna.

"She does pretty good and she has fun doing it. You have to make a lot to live on the richest planet in the system. The last time I talked to her, she'd just rented a suite in the Burgis Grand Casino."

Deanna shook her head. "You gotta be kidding?"

Gary dropped his play pack. "She sounds spoiled to me."

"What would you do if you made as much as she did? Wouldn't you have all the luxuries, live at the Burgis and do whatever you wanted?" Colleen defended.

Kahn interrupted before Gary could open his mouth to defend his meager lifestyle. "Hell yes, he would." He snapped his fingers, "In a heartbeat." He reached out and pinched Deanna in the ribs. "And so would she!"

"How would you know?" The blonde woman pushed him down on the couch and bit his neck, bringing forth a howl of pain.

"Dammit! I know that hurt!" He rolled her onto the floor and pinned her arms. "Girl, don't start anything you can't finish." He felt her strain against his grip, knowing she didn't have a chance. "You have me, and that's the best luxury of all."

Colleen, ignoring the fight on the floor, stood up. "Hey, I think I've got a picture of her somewhere." She went to the adjoining bedroom and could be heard rummaging around, returning a moment later with a long roll of paper. "I couldn't find a picture, but this is better." She unrolled what looked to be a poster, and turned it around to face the others. What they saw was a nearly life-size poster of a young woman even more beautiful than the one holding it.

Gary noted the strong resemblance in the eyes, the mouth, and other attributes, which he silently admired. The girl was barely dressed, wearing only a pair of white panties, which made her tan skin seem even darker. Her long blonde hair draped down in front of each shoulder, reaching low enough to hide the center of each of her breasts. She looked well suited to her occupation. She was a pleasure simply to look at.

Kahn, temporarily distracted, allowed Deanna to escape from beneath him. "Are there any job openings in the Burgis for bachelors who can pretend like their rich?" He asked.

"I didn't know you could pretend," said Colleen sarcastically.

"Only in bed," answered Deanna, eyes wide and playful. She wasn't finished with the snide remark. "He pretends he's a man, but he looks more like a little boy."

Colleen played along. "Really ... I thought you were only kidding about that."

Kahn narrowed his eyes and snarled. "Oh, that's funny. I'll tell you one thing; this little boy sure as hell can make you scream."

Gary watched them wrestle once again and chuckled to himself, catching one last glance at the poster as Colleen began to re-roll it. "Jesus ..." he thought to himself.

Kahn, watching the poster disappear, acted as if someone had taken his candy away.

"Hey, wait a minute. You wouldn't let me borrow that for a couple of days would you?"

Colleen didn't get it right away. "What for?" she asked innocently.

Gary burst into a laughing fit. Deanna screamed an obscenity and tried to hit him in a vulnerable spot, but repeatedly missed.

The afternoon hours gave way to the night. As Gary and Colleen expected, their two friends, having been in a boisterous mood most of the day, retired early. They, however, had other plans. For a time they stayed in the cabin and after changing into more appropriate attire, visited the ships main lounge. The lights were low and the music slow as they entered. It presented a seldom seen romantic atmosphere on the military vessel. It was just what the young couple needed; some quiet time alone together.

The lounge offered dinner and dance combined. They took advantage of both. After a delicious dinner, Gary led his beautiful partner to the dance floor, where the slow music set the rest of the evening in motion.

As they swayed, Gary pressed his mouth close to Colleen's ear. He could smell her perfume. Her hair touched his face for a second, reminding him of the night on Earth. He wanted to say so many things; things he had never said to anyone before. They'd spent nearly the entire last few days together, their relationship forged by the stressful adventure now behind them. They were no longer strangers to one another. Their first time had been unplanned, but wonderful. It seemed to him now, that they truly belonged with one another, and that there was no place he'd rather be than in her arms. Did she feel the same?

He held her as close as he could, his eyes closed; just letting his fingers caress her back. She was so soft, so sensual. He felt an emotional rush with her. It felt so content … so right. Those were some of the things he wished to say to her, but didn't know how.

As he opened his mouth to at least try, she placed a finger to his lips, stopping him. For a long moment, they just stared into each other's eyes.

Colleen knew that no words were needed, but she spoke anyway. "Je t'aime," she said softly.

Gary narrowed his eyes in question. He had no idea what she had said, but regardless, it sounded wonderful. "What did you say?"

Colleen smiled. "Je t'aime. It means … I love you."

Gary felt his throat tighten, his breath quickening. Her words were a surprise, but he knew that they summed up what he felt also. The simple words said all he couldn't. His mind raced. Do I really love her? And if I'm not sure, should I say it anyway? Kahn told him once, that if you cared enough to give your life for someone without a second thought, with no regrets, then it must be love. Gary knew that for her, there would be no hesitation. He had been willing to do it in their earlier fall to Earth and knew he would again. Was it that simple? He looked into her eyes, knowing that he had to say something. She has to be wondering. He'd hesitated too long already. He squeezed her tightly, and finally answered. "I love you too, Colleen."

As she heard the words, she closed her eyes, repeating them in her mind. She had waited, hoping he would say it. The tears came. She couldn't stop them. She'd heard the words before, but no man had ever sounded so sincere. This time it felt real. She sniffled, causing him to hold her away. She dropped her eyes to the floor.

Gary moved her hair, trying to see her face. She finally looked up, her eyes wet and glistening. He spoke softly. "Don't cry, babe? What's wrong?"

"Nothing … it's just everything we've been through. I can't believe we're even here." She paused. "Everything is right." She would remember this moment forever.

The music finally changed to something that didn't suit the mood, and they decided to sit for a while. They talked about one another, the past, the future, oblivious to all that was around them. The evening grew late. It was then that Gary made an entertaining suggestion. "You know what I'd like to do that I haven't done in a long time?"

Colleen looked at him seductively and reached below the table. "Yeah, but it hasn't been that long."

"Funny, but that's not it. I think I remember seeing a swimming pool some-where on this ship. How about it?"

Colleen, surprised, glanced at her watch. "Now?"

"Why not? We might have the place to ourselves."

She shook her head slightly. "I don't know, aren't there specific times for it? What if we get caught? It's pretty late."

He shrugged. "We'll get our hands slapped. Nobody told me anything about a curfew. There probably isn't one." He could tell she didn't share his enthusiasm. "C'mon … just for a little while?" He pleaded.

She thought for a moment. She wasn't tired yet; the lounge was dead, so finally, against her better judgment, she consented. "We better not get caught …"

"Don't worry, nothing's gonna happen, I promise." Shocked that she had given in, he wasn't about to waste any time. He led her into the empty corridor. "Okay … first I have to remember where it is." He paused. "It seems like we were on deck twenty-seven or deck seven, section twenty …!"

"I thought you had all this planned out? I guess we could fill a sink or some-thing."

He ignored the remark and walked to a computer panel on the wall. "This should tell us where it is." A keyboard was ready to receive his commands. He punched a total of four buttons, the letters L and O for layout, and the numeral's 27. Immediately, the entire diagram of the twenty-seventh level appeared on the small screen, the hundreds of rooms indistinguishable. Gary pecked at the board, typing in the words "SWIMMING POOL" and entered it.

Words appeared at the top of the screen. "LEVEL TWENTY SEVEN, REC-REATION DECK, SECTION J, ROOM ONE THREE ZERO." Below the words was a schematic of the section. Room 130 was a flashing black square, by far, the largest in that section.

"Modern ingenuity … let's get wet." Gary proudly said. They found an el-car and punched in the coordinates.

Moments later, they stood outside the pool. Gary was right when he said they might be alone. There wasn't anyone around. He opened the door and they entered. As the door closed behind them, he hit a switch on the door, locking it.

"Why did you do that?" asked Colleen. She watched him jog to the other side of the pool to a second set of doors, locking them as well. "So we won't be dis-turbed."

"Oh really?" She knew what he had in mind. While he watched, she kicked off her shoes and slipped out of her skirt.

Gary looked on approvingly, surprised at her boldness. The white slip she wore reached below her hips, just covering the tops of her thighs. He knew one thing above all; he had never seen a more desirable woman. He had always been a legman and found hers to be flawless. He sighed, shaking his head in marvel. This was the woman he had just confessed his love to. As she walked slowly towards him, she slipped the shear garment over her head and tossed it aside. She wore nothing beneath it. Brushing past him, she dove into the clear water.

When she came up, she noticed that her swimming partner had not yet begun to get undressed. He sat on the edge of the pool, watching ... smiling. She could only imagine the thoughts running through his mind. She made it to him in two easy strokes. "I thought you were going for a dip?"

Gary shrugged his shoulders, "I changed my mind."

Colleen's eyes flashed and she gritted her teeth in a wide smile. "Changed your mind my ass!" She lunged toward him.

Gary tried to get up, but wasn't fast enough. Grabbing a wrist, she braced her legs and easily pulled him off balance. He didn't even have time to plead before disappearing in a thunderous splash.

Coming up quickly, he sputtered, "I can't believe you did that!"

"I thought you said you changed your mind?" She smirked, splashing him.

"I just wanted to see you with all your clothes off," he answered, returning the splash.

Colleen began to swim away, giving him a wink. "Well, you didn't have to go to all this trouble, but I hope you enjoyed it. I know I did."

Gary slipped his shirt over his head and threw it out of the water. This was not exactly what he had planned. She was full of surprises and unpredictable at all times, but maybe that was one of the things he was attracted to in her. He swam slowly toward her, hoping to corner her eventually. He wasn't about to let her win round two.

Colleen had other plans. She baited him until he was within arms reach, seeming an easy catch, and in one quick move, reached out and dunked him. She quickly swam out of the way, anticipating an assured retaliation. What happened next however was not expected.

Gary came up, choking, flailing his arms, unable to get his breath.

Regret gripped her as she hurried toward him. Her trick had backfired. "Oh my God ... I'm sorry! Are you okay?" Even as she asked, she knew that he wasn't. His eyes were wide, and his breaths short and rapid. She felt terrible ... helpless. By the time she reached his side, he was starting to calm.

Gary, through blurred vision, saw her trying to help. He reached out for her, and before she had a clue, returned the dunking.

Colleen came up, rubbing her eyes and coughing between silent curses. They weren't for him, but for her lack of foresight, knowing that she had been fooled … completely. A second later, she managed to catch her own breath. "You've had it!"

Gary led her to the shallow end of the pool. As she came close, he grabbed her and pulled her struggling form to him, finding her mouth with his, kissing her deeply. Only when she stopped fighting, did he let her go. As he hoped, her hostility was gone, replaced by an almost sleepy look of surprise. "Even?" he asked.

"Maybe for now," she nodded. Their lips met once more.

CHAPTER 10

▼

Commander Haute stood in the control room and watched as they passed through cloudy sheets of ice and dust. Soon, the characteristic lines of white planet began to appear. He noted how inhospitable it appeared. This time however, Touchen seemed a very welcome sight.

Earth was days behind them, but the Kogran visitors didn't seem overly homesick. Instead, they were still very animated. Haute had spent a great deal of time alone with William Vient, speaking of events to come, listening to events long past. He felt he had started a great friendship with the interesting man.

William rested alone in his cabin. He felt comfortable and relished in the feeling. Since they had left Earth, he had actually been very contented. These people were everything Commander Haute said they were. He, his wife and the others had been treated with remarkable courtesy and had wanted for nothing. They had been baptized into a weird and wonderful world and were asked to trust the Belaquins completely with their lives, but even so, he felt truly safe.

There was so much to look forward to. His life was finally ridded of the burdens of war. In all his memories, he couldn't recall one waking moment that wasn't disturbed with worry of attack or plans of assault. He felt at ease for perhaps the first time in his adult life.

Still, he couldn't shake uneasiness amidst the contentment. The new technology he had witnessed was disturbing to say the least. If prejudice would somehow raise its ugly head again, his people would be helpless. These people, descendants of their most mortal enemies, with the advancements of the last two centuries, could crush them like eggshells. It was unsettling. Today's events would mean everything.

Haute had taken every precaution to ensure that his guests were treated with the highest respect, and their welcome comfortable. He had notified all who would be involved, so there would be no surprises. He was already aware that some of the media networks had picked up the story and with no concrete information were running on rumors. They would not have to deal with them until they arrived on Belaquin.

The Manna had made it a point to become well acquainted with the history and ways of the Republic. Haute, in turn, listened tirelessly to the fascinating man from the past.

The Kogran suspended animation process was a vast improvement on the failed methods experimented with before. A crude procedure that had been called cryogenics, required complete freezing of the subject, but none who participated in the process had ever been brought out alive. The Kogran scientists utilized a less drastic method, lowering body temperatures to slow the heart rate, but not stop it. That in turn, decreased brain function and cellular activity to nearly a standstill. The chambers automatically regulated intermittent turning of the occupant to prevent blood pooling and other associated problems. Their first chamber experiments had lasted only a few months, but proved successful. As William had explained, the timing couldn't have been more perfect. The Kogran specialists finalized tests just in time. They had time to build only five hundred chambers before the end. Their hard work in those last few months had solved the riddle of the ages. It would prove to save their lives and their race.

The Belaquin scientists would have a field day with the secrets Haute was bringing back for them. They would no longer be hampered by time in long space voyages, which so many had risked their minds, sanity, and lives to undertake. In the past, there had been only a handful of serious ventures into deep space, manned exclusively by volunteers, the last being a great many years ago. None of the missions had been deemed successful, and only one crew had ever returned intact. The science and space industry as well as the general public, finally agreed that the projects should be terminated.

Now, the program could be re-evaluated and possibly reopened. It was assumed that the failure of some previous missions was caused by human error, as opposed to mechanical. Original planning and supplies permitted trips of a safe maximum of only five years. If missions were permitted once again, the least the new explorers could look forward to was the chance of finding a fascinating new world waiting when they returned. Haute believed the idea had merit, as well as some exhilarating possibilities.

Aquillon locked into orbit and the larger passenger shuttles started back and forth to the planets icy surface, taking with them, nearly thirteen hundred weary travelers. The first ship held the most precious cargo. They carried the persons killed in the unfortunate incidents on and around Earth. Memorial services had been withheld until the return home.

Most of the crew had been granted several days off due to the intensity of the mission they had just quitted. Upon arrival on Touchen, they could inform the transport services where they wished to go on their shore leave. Commercial travel was free as long as space was available. Very few wished to stay at the military installation, even though accommodations were inviting.

The exception to the rule was of course, Commander Haute, who never seemed to want to leave it. After boarding his shuttle, accompanied by his guests, he informed Touchen control that they were en-route. VIP accommodations for the visitors had already been prepared.

Even though precautions prevented an embarrassing altercation or wrong word said, there was no hiding the expressions on some faces as Haute and the new visitors left the shuttle. He had expected as much. He explained to the Manna. "I apologize, William, for some of the reactions you might see, but our history has led us to believe that your people no longer existed. I hope you can forgive them."

"Don't worry yourself Leon, their actions are completely understandable. I saw the same chaos in my city when we discovered you and your shuttle after it crashed."

"I imagine you did." He smiled broadly. "While we're on the subject of chaos, there's a council meeting in about an hour, and the President of that council respectfully requests your presence."

"I guess I should fit that into my schedule?" William joked.

Stephen Sievers, the head chairman of the Belaquin Republic Council just happened to be a close acquaintance of Commander Haute. To say they were friends would have been pushing it, considering their past disagreements. He was an older gentleman, close to eighty-five years of age. Unlike Haute, he did not hide his age well. His wrinkled body, one of the most respected bodies in the Belaquin system, strained with every movement. He walked unsteadily around the table and nearly fell into his chair. Though his body was giving out, his mind was still fresh. His ideas and words were still as trusted and commanding as they had been thirty-five years earlier when he had been appointed. He was distinguished, hard nosed, and proud of the system he had helped to build.

The other council members filed into the small auditorium, each taking their place on either side of Sievers. Most were close to the same age as the head speaker, each with years of experience. Soon, the idle chitchat that always preceded the meetings commenced.

Sievers discussed this particular gathering with the member seated next to him. Even though there were few secrets between the men, he whispered. "I know I gave Leon the okay to bring them here, but I'm having second thoughts."

"Why? You heard what he said. Everything is fine."

"I know what he said, but I know what they were like. The Kograns were some of the most savage people in history."

"That was two hundred years ago, Steven. Generations have passed."

"For us, yes, but not for them! Nothing has passed. These are the same people that fought that war. They killed millions."

"I agree. That is not disputed, but we are not here to judge them for those acts. We are here to forget who they were and accept who they are now." The man shook his head after he spoke. He was used to Sievers' bullheadedness and knew it would be short lived. "Besides, there are only a few of them. Even if they did have ulterior motives, which I personally feel is absurd to even consider, they wouldn't stand much of a chance. Agreed?"

Sievers said nothing.

The man continued the discussion. "Whether time has passed for them or not, it did for us. The racial differences that caused the war don't exist any more."

Sievers finally spoke. "That's only because there hasn't been any racial difference!"

The man sighed. He knew no one had ever won an argument with the man, and no one ever would. "Look, I have no doubt that this is going to be awkward. These people aren't here to hash up old problems. Regardless of what they were like in the past, Haute says they are not what we expect and I for one believe him."

"I know, I know," Sievers conceded. "They're probably easier to get along with than I am right now." He frowned. "I'm just ... not sure."

The man beside him chuckled, knowing the minor dispute was over. "You'll be fine." He hoped the old man would not repeat any of what he had just vented during the coming meeting.

At that moment, the Commander of the Aquillon and his guest entered the room. The chitchat stopped.

Sievers didn't know why, but he felt the urge to stand and did so. The other council members stood as well. This man had been a King in his time ... a man to be respected, but he did not rise out of respect of status, at least he didn't feel as if it was. Something told him that it was the proper thing to do. The black man easily captivated the attention of everyone in the room.

Haute didn't need the silence. He was uneasy already. Not even the clearing of a throat was heard as he led the way to a center table. The room's mood would have been no different if he would have brought in a living breathing dinosaur. He knew that any apprehension he felt, had to be compounded ten fold in his companion. Able to take it no more, he broke the stillness. "President Sievers, members of the Belaquin council, I am honored to introduce this distinguished representative of the planet Earth, leader of the Kogran people, and my friend ... William Thomas Vient."

Sievers stated his greeting. To Haute, it sounded somewhat rehearsed. "On behalf of the Belaquin council and the members of the Republic, we welcome you and your people."

Unexpectedly, the black man stepped forward and stood directly in front of the obviously nervous white leader. He extended his hand.

Sievers took it, immediately impressed with the eagerness of the stranger. He gripped it tightly, but it felt pitifully weak compared to the return strength of the Kogran King.

The Manna spoke. "It is I who am honored, Mr. President. Thank you."

Other introductions were made and after a few minutes of chat, Sievers began to see the hypocrisy in his thoughts. He found this person, who history called a ruthless murderer, to be just what Haute said he was. He was finding him to be likable, well spoken and intelligent. It would be easy to befriend the King, no matter what his own great-great grandfather had said about him.

He held in the back of his mind however, the facts that were not disputable. All records could not have been wrong. This man, two centuries ago, had been one of the most sought after war criminals in history. Sievers had trouble believing he could be the same person.

Part of the long discussion included the planet that had spawned life for both their races. "Well, Mr. Vient ... did I pronounce it correctly?" asked Sievers, receiving a welcome nod. "It has been two hundred years."

"It is hard to believe," answered William.

"Extremely. From what Commander Haute has told us, your sleep chambers ... they are apparently flawless in their design?"

"They are indeed. I only wish the men who built them had survived to witness their success."

"What does it feel like to sleep for that long?" The older man was indeed curious.

"How does it feel for you to sleep overnight?" Vient shrugged his shoulders. "The sleep seemed short ... timeless. The only difference was the trouble we experienced after we awoke. Our muscles wouldn't function. We couldn't even walk until several hours afterwards."

Sievers chuckled. "Well," he surmised. "I know that feeling ... every morning." All within earshot laughed aloud. Sievers sat open mouthed. "No. I'm serious," he said. More laughter followed.

Another member of the council asked a question. "We have been told that the Earth has somehow rejuvenated itself. Is that true?"

"I can only speak for the small part of it I've seen, but yes, it is true. The planet is alive, but it has changed from what it was before."

Haute offered what he knew. "Survey of the planet shows overall radiation levels to be very low. There are still hot spots at some locations around the globe, but for the whole, very few. We don't really know how bad the original damage was, how much of the globe was affected."

Still another council member entered the conversation, directing his question to William. "What we are suggesting sir, is the possibility of repopulating the planet. Do you think it is feasible to do so?"

The room grew still as all eyes turned toward the youngest, yet oldest man in the room. Finally, William answered by giving a statement. "I think what you are suggesting may be a much larger venture than you think. As I said earlier, things have changed ... physically, as well as biologically. The land is wild. Commander Haute has witnessed some of its savagery. In our ventures outside the city, several of my men have been lost to someone or something we have not even seen. I think a great many, other than ourselves have survived, but they are not as we remember."

Haute interrupted at this point. "He is referring to the circumstances surrounding the death of Harlow on the initial shuttle mission to Earth. Whoever killed him used extremely primitive weapons."

"Primitive, but deadly," added the Manna.

Sievers nodded his head. "We did read about that in the report." Sievers changed the subject. "The underground complex where you are living now ... your people did not build it?"

"No, we did not. It was a secret military installation. A few of our men, officers in the army, knew about it. We took it over a few years before the end, constructed our chambers and were subsequently trapped there."

"Trapped?" asked someone.

"Yes sir. From the beginning, we controlled Manhattan and the surrounding boroughs, but eventually the white armies came back in strength. Fortunately, we were ready. We sealed ourselves in, rather than risk losing our chambers. We knew the end would be soon."

"How did you know it would come to that?" asked another member.

"We didn't know for certain, but we prepared for the worst. A few weeks before we went below, the first bombs were detonated in Africa. Once that line had been crossed, there was no going back. It was only a matter of time."

Sievers thought about the answer for a moment. "Did you not know that other people had made plans to leave the planet before the war?"

The Manna shook his head. "We had heard rumors, but didn't believe they had the capability." William hesitated, pondering the discussion. He was curious, as well as concerned with all of the inquiries, but did not feel the need to ask any return questions, at least not yet. "We did not know that anyone had escaped."

President Sievers and Commander Haute could see obvious uncertainty on the Kogran King's face. Sievers explained. "Please forgive us, sir. We don't mean to ask so much, but there are many things we don't know. I know you must have questions as well."

William nodded. Indeed he did, but there was plenty of time. For now, he still felt unthreatened. He spoke with respect. "Please ... ask me what you will."

As the meetings participants discussed the past as well as the future, Gary Kusan and Kahn Bengal made plans for a much more immediate future. They registered with the recall office in case of emergency, donned civilian attire and went looking for the girls.

Colleen and Deanna had gone in search of a privately owned ship to take them to Shannate. Finding private passage might cost substantially more, but it proved much faster than waiting for the free Republic transports or commercially owned flights. The latter procedure operated on a first come, first serve basis, and occasionally took days to obtain due to the thousands of persons they catered to. The hassle of waiting, combined with the reduced speed required by the passenger safety regulatory committee was too overwhelming. It was well worth the money to go the alternate route.

"If we can find him before someone else does, we can be there in a few hours." remarked Colleen. "I just hope he got my message."

They had entered a large bar, crowded with civilians as well as fellow military, but Colleen had little trouble spotting the man she was looking for. She led Deanna through the maze of bodies and approached a table with only one occupant.

Colleen whispered to her girlfriend as they drew closer. "Whatever you do, don't stare at him, it make him self conscious."

The man they approached had his back to them, but to Deanna, appeared to be a normal, white haired, older man. "Why would I stare? Is he deformed or something?" She was confused until the man, seemingly aware that they were there, turned toward them. She couldn't help but gasp as her eyes met his. She knew then, full well, what her friend had meant.

Colleen extended her arms as the man rose from the chair and embraced her. They both turned toward Deanna.

Colleen had to speak loudly over the music around them. "This is my best friend, Deanna Wilkins. Deanna, this is Avraham Coleridge."

The man offered his hand in greeting, which she took. "I'm glad to meet you," he yelled above the din.

Involuntarily, her eyes dropped to look at the hand that held hers. "I'm sorry … I've never seen a …"

"An albino?" The man laughed aloud. "Don't be sorry. I'm used to it. I consider it a blessing, actually. I'm usually the talk of the party."

Deanna was spellbound. The unique man had fantastic pink eyes, and his skin was deathly pale. It held no pigment at all. His hair, beard, and mustache were as white and pure as the snow outside. She had no doubt that what he said was true. He could not go unnoticed.

"Please, please, have a seat." Being the perfect gentleman, he pulled out the chairs. "Do you want something?"

"No thank you. I'm fine," answered Deanna. Colleen also declined.

"Okay, but I hate drinking alone." He picked up his glass and sipped the contents. "I had a really gorgeous redhead with me a minute ago … don't know where she went." He made a point of looked around the room, even though only one glass rested on the table.

Colleen smiled. "And just what is it we're drinking nowadays?"

"Milk actually. I've abstained from all beverages alcoholic in nature, and look what it's done to me." The girls were amused at the pun. "I'm hoping I'll get some color back, if I start drinking again. Any color will do."

"I guess you got my message?" asked Colleen hopefully.

"You don't think I live in here do you? Besides, it's hard to stand up a beautiful lady." He turned to Deanna, "Make that two. Do you know what kind of tempers French women have?"

"Yeah ... I do. How do you guys know each other so well?" Deanna asked.

"I've known her since she was a little girl. I'm a pretty good friend of her mother and father. Have you met them yet?"

"Yeah ... about a year ago." Deanna related.

"Well, then you know where her temper comes from," he smirked.

Colleen smiled, "I dare you to say that in front of her," referring to her mother.

"Not a chance in hell," he answered. "So where we going?"

"How would you like to see my sister?" Colleen asked.

"Kelsey! My God, I haven't seen her in four or five years ... still in school?"

Colleen explained, "Kind of ... she lives on Shannate."

"Shannate!" He exclaimed. "Is that where you want to go?"

"That's the place."

"Then what are we doing standing around here?"

The council meeting was winding down. Commander Leon Haute was attempting to explain the drastically confusing events leading up to the initial meeting between him and William Vient. He felt he was doing quite well until he got to the part about Ban-Sor.

The Manna sat with a subdued, but fascinated expression on his face as Haute related that he knew virtually nothing about the being, his intentions or his current whereabouts. At that time, Haute apologized to him for the details at their first meeting, but also assured him that it had been unplanned. Ban-Sor's connection to the Republic was indeed a deception, but the man's incredible powers were not. Haute assured the Manna, that he had not been in control of the certainly unique situation.

The Commander told the story, embellishing every detail he could remember. The council listened intently, and there were questions ... many of them. They consented that the story was incredible, but a second party, who had seen and spoken to the man, substantiated at least part of it. The occurrences could not be explained any other way. The mysterious exit from the shuttle and the entrance deep into the Kogran stronghold defied reason as well as the laws of physics.

Haute ended with his summation. "Gentlemen, I can't say this enough. I know how this sounds, but I've had plenty of time to think about it. I know in my heart and my mind that what I've told you was real. There are things in this universe that you and I cannot imagine. Things that go against everything we know. Life exists in places where it shouldn't ... at least in places we believe it shouldn't ... based on our opinions, based on our scientific brilliance."

"I don't know who this man was, but I saw him, I talked with him, I touched him and I witnessed what he could do." He made eye contact with each and every man as he spoke. "All of you have known me for years. I have never been a liar; I've never had wild hallucinations or anything like that. I know what happened seems impossible, but I don't have any choice but to accept it. I wish this man was here to explain himself, but he isn't. I've told you the truth, as crazy as it sounds. If any of you feel that I've lost it ... or that I'm not mentally fit to command ..." he paused, "Well, there isn't anything I can do about that, is there?" He stood quietly, wondering why he felt defensive. These men hadn't accused him of anything, but the mood of the room reminded him of a courtroom. It was as if he were seeking exoneration for some crime, with his words as his final argument.

Sievers did not rise to speak. His voice betrayed no emotion. "Thank you Commander. We will be in touch with you. Thank you Mr. Vient, we appreciate the time you have given us today. If no one has any more questions, we will adjourn." He then rose and left the room, followed by the eight other members. The room became silent.

Haute looked at his fellow questioned, who glanced back with raised eyebrows.

William spoke first. He humorously came straight to the point. "It did sound bad."

Haute shook his head, smiling. "Yeah, you'd think I could have made up something better, anything but the truth."

The Manna had to ask. "So this ... Ban-Sor, what is he, some kind of god?"

"I don't have a clue. The things he did ... I believe he's capable of whatever he wants. What he wanted with us, well ... like I told them, he said he was there to help ... that it was very important. Why ... I don't know."

"And it was important," William surmised.

"I agree." After the stressful meeting, Haute's throat was parched. "Do you feel like a drink?"

William stood. "I think I need something."

Haute led the way from the room, wondering where William's "God" was. If the power that Ban-Sor possessed was as real as it seemed, he knew that he would be found only at his willingness to do so.

Ban-Sor did have other plans at the time. He had quickly discovered that this Earth's history held endless avenues for adventure. He felt drawn to explore them. He had thus far found humans to be intelligent and stimulating. In the last few days, he had visited numerous times and places. Today, he had once again stepped back through time to an older Earth. The day he had chosen for his venture was a period filled with pirates and kings, a primitive time where law and order was not something to be troubled about.

He shriveled his nose at the sickening odor that met him as he materialized. He stood in an alleyway between two buildings. It was devoid of any other persons ... living ones at least. The unnerving smell permeated from a human body lying against a wall. The body's face was featureless, eyes gone, its gray skin sloughing from the bone. It was partially clothed, but some had been torn away, allowing something to feed on the putrid flesh. It wasn't possible to tell if it had been male or female. The unlucky soul was long dead and in the stifling heat of the season, the decaying body had grown quite ripe.

Quickly exiting the dark alley to escape the stench, he walked to a dockside street. It ran along a waterfront facing a bay. The water was full of various types of sailing ships, schooners, and warships. Each tugged at its anchor as the incoming tide tried to push them landward.

It was night. The full moon reflected off the incoming waves. He caught lightning flashes in the distant clouds. There were puddles at his feet, remnants of the rainstorm that must have just passed.

A row of sagging wooden structures lined the street facing the bay. He breathed in the musty smell of the rainwater. There was also a slight fishy odor from the bay. It wasn't pleasant, but still better than the alley.

He looked both ways down the street. There was no one as far as he could see, but he could hear laughter from a large sailing vessel a few hundred yards out. As he listened, the faint rumbling of thunder from the lightning rolled in. A far away bell rang three times. Stillness came again, broken only by the sound of dripping water.

A door slammed open from behind, startling him. A form, slouching heavily to one side, exited the building. The person was obviously not a prestigious entity in his world. He seemed to be dressed in rags. He carried a flaming torch and lifted it to light two others mounted on either side of the door. It took several seconds for the wetness to burn away.

As light fell on Ban-Sor, the man noticed him and smiled. With what little light there was, he could see that the man had no front teeth, and the ones he did have were stained brown. The man laughed, grunting something incomprehensible. The smell of sweat soaked clothing was overpowering.

Was this what this small part of the world had to offer as far as intelligent life? Looking past the man, he could make out more forms inside a dimly lit room. The slouching man turned and re-entered, leaving the door open for the potential new customer. Ban-Sor followed, closing the door behind him.

The room was lit only with candles and wreaked of something spoiled. Even if this proved to hold no adventure, the variety of odors he had experienced thus far was at least unique. He took in every aspect of the room in one long glance. There were nine other persons in it. The slouching man was obviously the proprietor. Four women, or at least they were dressed as such, and four men, all self proclaimed rulers in this pirates' world rounded out the rest. If there were trouble to be found tonight, it would be here.

The mood was boisterous, but there was a short pause as the tavern patrons stopped to observe the uninvited intruder. They noted the stranger to be well dressed, obviously well endowed with coin. They also noticed that he was armed with sword, short knife, one pistol, and possibly other weapons under his knee length coat. Most importantly, they took note that he was alone.

Ban-Sor walked toward the bar, followed by nine sets of eyes. He studied the four men as well, seeing that they were well armed. Ban-Sor knew their kind. Every form of life he had ever seen had produced beings with the same temperament. They were beings that made their ways by others sufferings, hardened by the lifestyle that had molded them.

One man was bald, but neatly bearded. While the others continued their party, he sat quietly … watching. His intelligence level was no doubt far and above his compatriots. Though small in stature, he seemed to Ban-Sor as probably the most dangerous of the four.

The other three were considerably larger, unshorn, with shoulder length hair and thick beards, making one indistinguishable from the next. The females were of no consequence, but he was relatively sure that they were armed as well.

He thought the trouble would have started as he walked past them, but was wrong. He was ignored as he approached the bar. He spoke to the man who had lit the torches. "What do you have to drink?"

He wasn't sure what the man answered, but it sounded like, "Rum."

Ban-Sor inquired further, "What kind of rum?"

The man turned and filled a silver mug, placing it and a pitcher before him. "Just rum," he grumbled.

With his "rum", Ban-Sor made his way to a table and purposely turned his back to his rowdy prey, which in fact, they would soon be. He thought as he waited, how his elders would feel about the games he was playing. Would they stand for them, even if he explained the harmless circumstances? Absolutely not.

He alone knew those circumstances. He knew that each of the four pirates behind him would die within the coming week. Two of them would finally be caught by the king's soldiers and subsequently beheaded, punishment for the countless crimes they had committed against their countrymen. The other two would sink with their ship in a battle off the shore of this very village.

The way he saw it, it didn't matter whether they died now or then. It might, in fact, save a few innocents lives if they met their demise tonight. The scenario made perfect sense, but he reminded himself that it was these exact kinds of situations that had gotten him in trouble in the first place.

After a few moments, the four men took a break from their drinking and started concentrating on other things, namely the aforementioned women. Two of the drunkards proceeded to carry one of them, kicking and pleading, outside to have their fun.

Ban-Sor thought sarcastically how considerate it was of them to take their business elsewhere. As the front door closed, he decided that it was time. He rose, tossed some coins on the table and began his carefully thought out plan. He chuckled in anticipation. Picking up the large pitcher of stinking rum, he proceeded toward the table where the remaining participants in his drama waited.

Pretending to push his way past one of the women, he accidentally spilled a small part of the contents onto the head of one of the men, where it wetted knots of greasy hair and thriving lice. The man yelled in anger and whirled to his feet, dumping the female seated on his lap to the floor. Ban-Sor was knocked stumbling to the side. The pirate was a huge, heavy man, a full foot and a half taller than his seemingly clumsy adversary. As he watched, the man drew his sword from its scabbard.

Ban-Sor produced a look of genuine terror as he took a step backward. He actually felt a brief second of trepidation, which excited him greatly. It was not something he was accustomed to. He then smiled his most sincere smile and replied calmly. "I'm terribly sorry, my good man."

The pirate was at first enraged, but the rage soon turned to amusement, as he took in the difference in size. He laughed aloud. "You'll be a lot sorrier when I'm done!" He raised the three-foot sword over his head, intent on cleaving his tiny opponent in half with one swipe.

"Wait!" yelled Ban-Sor, raising his hand. Surprisingly the man halted in mid swing, obviously puzzled by the little mans actions. Rum dripped from his beard. Still smiling, Ban-Sor took another step backward and flung the entire content of the pitcher into the bigger mans face, drenching him and several others. Yells of objection filled the room.

No one moved for several seconds. The room became deadly silent until Ban-Sor spoke. "You're wrong. I'm not any sorrier than I was before." Ignoring the pistol in his belt, he drew his own sword.

Wiping his stinging eyes, the pirate screamed and lunged at his intimidator. He swung his blade in a wide arc, parried easily by Ban-Sor. He had of course done this before. The fight ensued. For a few moments it was a good one, broken bottles, tables and the like, and more than once, the bigger man fell on his face. Eventually, Ban-Sor grew tired with the lop-sided contest and decided it was time to bring about a spectacular and unexpected end.

The man lunged one last time … frustrated … embarrassed, only remaining on his feet due to the absolute fury he felt. The small man had made a fool of him over and over again. His sword, heavy in his hand, thrust forward. His target didn't move aside, nor block the blow. The exhausted man received instantaneous satisfaction as his sword disappeared fully into his chest. Ban-Sor fell to his knees and "died."

The pirate strained to catch his breath and wrenched the bloody blade from the lifeless body. He wiped it off and re-holstered it, turning back toward his friends. "Now he's sorry." He wanted to laugh, but he was too tired.

The two men, who had left with the woman earlier returned alone at this time, saw what had transpired and joined in the celebration. The slouching man moved quickly to the tables with refilled pitchers. He knew better than to keep them waiting. His tavern had been wrecked before, and not always by fights. He looked at the body on the floor. He should catch a fair price for the clothing. The foursome of course, would absorb the weapons and money, if they remained sober long enough to collect.

The winner of the contest grabbed a tankard of ale and began to guzzle it. The others cheered him to finish it all. One was heard to say, "This runt makes five in one day!"

While he drank, the shouts of encouragement suddenly ceased. He sat the pitcher down, confused, then he heard a strangely familiar voice from behind him. "And you sir, are number six!"

The man turned, only to receive a slashing cut across his throat. In the last seconds before he lost consciousness, he recognized the face and the voice. They belonged to the man he had killed a moment before. There was a look of frozen disbelief on his face as he fell to the tabletop, his blood and his life ebbing away to mix with the spilled rum.

Cries of shock came as the witnesses realized what they had seen. With their own eyes, they had watched a dead man rise up and take revenge on his murderer. The room was cleared in seconds as Ban-Sor's laughter echoed through its emptiness.

After a moment, the shouts of witchcraft and devils died off in the distance. Only a rumble in the western sky could be heard, signaling another storm moving in. Ban-Sor went to a barrel behind the bar, found a reasonably clean mug from the shelf and filled it with the clear liquid. He sniffed it and snarled his nose in disgust. It can't taste worse than it smells, he surmised. He brought it cautiously to his lips and nearly gagged before his mouth touched it. He fought the urge and told himself that he had to try everything at least once. Finally, he took a sip. It was quite possibly the vilest taste he had ever experienced, but even though it turned his stomach, he managed to hold it down. He wondered what possessed these humans to satisfy themselves in such horrid ways. He threw the mug against the wall, knocking a rotted board out in the process.

He was suddenly startled by a sound behind him. Was the man not dead? He turned in time to see the recently deceased body slip to a heap on the floor. As he looked on, he saw three huge rodents approach the body. Hunger and the smell of fresh blood quelled whatever fear they might have had, for when Ban-Sor drew near, they stood their ground. One stopped from his meal to look at the man who towered above him. As it did so, Ban-Sor faded and vanished. If a rat was capable of feeling astonishment, it did at that moment.

As he whisked himself back to his home, he housed an ill feeling. Some, he thought, would have judged the last episode an unfair fight. He mulled it over carefully. The man did deserve to die. There was no telling how many innocent people he had needlessly butchered. On the other hand, did he reserve the right to make that decision and deliver punishment? No ... he could not leave things as they were. With that thought he set matters right, at least with his own conscience.

In the next instant, the fire-lit tavern was again filled with men and women. The slouching man was lighting the torches outside, wondering if he would eat on this night. The same four pirates were drinking their fill and creating new trouble. Everything was exactly the same as it had been a few moments before, with one exception. Ban-Sor was not there.

For the remainder of time before the departure to Shannate, Avraham Coleridge got to know his latest fares, and what better way than to let them help load his ship. Actually, he would let port personnel do the job, but he got surprised looks from his new friends when he first suggested it. The ship was loaded with the passenger's personal gear, food for the synthesizer, fuel and other items they would need on the weeklong shore leave.

Colleen and the others had convinced the private pilot to stay on the pleasure planet and to return them afterward. Finally, all was ready; a full three hours before the first Republic transport vessel was scheduled to lift off.

Coleridge led the way through the civilian complex to an exit near his ship outside. The enormous complex was a variety of shops, bars, living quarters and storage spaces; all protected from the inhospitable surface of Touchen. There were no enclosed hanger bays available to civilian ships. All private travelers wishing to do business had to brave the harsh elements to and from their ships to the post. Avraham and his passengers were no exceptions. He took them to a large window overlooking the landing platforms, pointing out the ship that waited for them.

Everything on the frozen surface was white, including many of the vessels visible through the ports. Snow quickly covered those not equipped with hull warmers, which were not standard and not cheap. Avraham's ship however, was far from cheap. No ice stuck to its heated surface. He chose his cargo and his passengers carefully. He was well known among the privateers. They often hovered near him, hoping to profit from passengers who found his fees too extravagant. People wondered whether or not he was rich from the beginning.

Whether he was well to do at the present, however, was not in dispute. His ship was one of the largest within sight. White was, of course, the pilot's favorite color, therefore, his vessel matched. Its sleek exterior was unblemished, while vessels around it seemed to attract filth. The covering of snow and ice actually improved the appearance of some of the competition by hiding their meager exteriors. People could be seen through the falling sleet and ice as they loaded individual ships.

Avraham could see that his was almost ready. The albino man led the foursome to a personal storage area and opened a large set of lockers. "You've got to put these on."

Gary and Kahn of course, recognized cold weather suits hanging inside.

Avraham continued. "Believe me; you don't want to go out there without them. You wouldn't get a hundred feet. The wind chill alone would kill you." He took one and began putting it on over his clothes. "I don't understand why anyone would want a post in a place like this. Sometimes it can really be a pain in the ass." As he complained he noticed a green light above the exit door. "Well that's it. As soon as we get suited up, we're outta here."

It took perhaps one minute for the five persons to walk the short distance to the vessel. The ship's exhaust had melted much of the icy area around the ship. An elevator platform dropped from beneath the ship as they approached, allowing them to climb aboard. As they moved upward, the lower hatch slid shut. Even though they were in the storm for that short time, their suits were completely iced over.

Due to the many trips to this particular planet, Coleridge had installed an interior hot air blower. The addition melted the ice and dried the suits quickly and efficiently.

The ship was named the Albino Albatross, attesting to the owner's sense of humor. The ship had a narrow bow, widening rearward in a long triangular shape. Engine ports dominated the rear of the craft. Its sleek design suggested speed. The craft was streamlined in every aspect of its unique construction, offering minimum resistance within an atmosphere or without.

The interior of the craft consisted of four main rooms. The largest by far was the main crew compartment, where passengers could relax in relative luxury. There was a rear storage room, the entry room, which the passengers saw first, and the control room, positioned lower than the main deck, in the bow. Below the main deck were specialized storage chambers where liquid or solid cargo could be transported.

The vessel had been over thirty years old when Coleridge had acquired it. He did so at an irresistible price. It was obvious to Avraham that major changes would have to be addressed, but he could envision the final product. At the time, the future Albatross had been in disrepair and the engines nearly useless. Fortunately, Avraham had been recently blessed with several large financial gifts, making his troubles no trouble at all.

First of all, he installed the newest, most powerful method of propulsion that money could buy. That bill alone amounted to more than he paid for the craft itself. After the worn structural elements were repaired or replaced, it became time for the maiden voyage.

He related to the others that the ship was much faster than he had anticipated. On the first flight, he nearly crashed into a tower that was under construction.

He counted his blessings that he had meticulously adjusted the maneuvering controls. With propulsion on line, he refinished the outer hull. He then moved onto his pride and joy, the interior. He alone designed and decorated it, spending a great deal of time and money for the finest furnishings. It was, upon finishing, fit for a king.

The entire rectangular shaped passenger compartment was carpeted ... floor, ceiling and walls. It housed a refreshment center and state of the art entertainment system equipped with the latest in music, movies, and games. There were no private sleeping quarters due to the short flight times normally involved.

After the short tour, it was time to depart. There was no flight officer on duty within the civilian complex at that time. This struck Avraham as odd due to the large amount of traffic. That being the case, there was no need to wait for clearance. Coleridge checked his flight board, waited for a cargo ship to pass overhead and smoothly lifted off. Visibility was zero, but the screen was clear. The sleek ship quickly left the atmosphere, the pilot, as well as the passengers eager to reach their destination.

With the ice storm behind him, Avraham relaxed. There was nothing he hated more than flying blind. He spoke to the others, "Hey, we've cleared the runway. Hard part's over. Have a drink if you like. I'll be back there in a minute." He made some adjustments, leaving no need to remain in the control room. Everything would be automatic until arrival in the Shannation quadrant, some four hours away.

In the lounge, the four passengers relaxed with the pilots blessing, anticipating the fun times ahead. Avraham joined them, becoming the professional host he was known to be. None of them knew it, but this shore leave would be longer and more exciting than they could have ever anticipated.

CHAPTER 11

▼

Leon Haute was elated. The Kogran peace discussions with the council had gone very well, and frighteningly enough, he was getting along with President Sievers better than he had in years. The reconnaissance ships were well on their way to Earth with supplies. On the return trip, they would hopefully be bringing another group of Kogran visitors. Last, but not least, his report on the Earth mission and the strange circumstances involved, had been closed. He was dubbed as … sane? Everything he could think of was running smoothly, but he had a premonition that it would not last long. His pessimism was based on experience.

Christopher Nichols was stuck with the late shift on the Touchen scanner station. As he watched over the surface traffic, he almost wished for something out of the ordinary to happen, good or bad. His job was to monitor, give advice or transfer communications throughout his range.

He had just come on duty and had already gotten the first of what he referred to as "idiot" calls. He had been in touch with a hysterical pilot landing at the port. The pilot was not surprisingly, a civilian who had reported having almost been run down by an enormous cargo cruiser. He said it was in the wrong approach pattern; wrong sector and illegally operating in restricted air space. He demanded that the ship be stopped so that he could press charges.

Nichols took down the preliminary information and assured the irate caller that everything would be taken care of. As he went off the air, he reminded himself how he hated being the middleman when this shit came down. He then located the exact position of the suspect ship and tried to contact it with no success. The cruiser was on his scanners and well within communications range. The

Captain either had radio failure, or realizing the screw up he had made, just refused to answer. Nevertheless, he was now out of Touchen's airspace, heading towards Belaquin.

"Okay, asshole, you want to go the hard way, we'll go the hard way." He alerted the underground. "This is surface control to command ... I need to speak to air traffic control."

An equally indifferent voice answered. "This is Captain Halter. What is it?"

"Sir, this is Lieutenant Nichols. I just received report of a rogue cargo cruiser in restricted air space. I guess he almost ran somebody down. The guy is really pissed off and wants to press charges. He didn't get any markings to identify her, but she's on my scanners ... won't answer any hailings."

"You know nothing ever happens to these guys. He'll just say his scanner was screwed up, or the storm was too bad." Halter said. "Did you try to talk to him, try to change his mind?"

"That would be a negative." Nichols answered, shaking his head. He thought to himself, wanting to say, "It's not my job, dumb ass!"

Halter rolled his eyes. It was just another bullshit run. He sighed in disgust. "All right ... just send out a couple of raiders to get him. I'll notify patrol."

Nichols acknowledged and got on the channel, calling the first two pilots on that nights list. Their names were Hennings and McCarter, two pilots whom he knew relatively well. They usually liked getting missions like this. It gave them a chance to fly, but this time they gave him some static. It was obvious they'd already gone to bed.

"Come on Chris, we're not even in overtime tonight," one of them related.

"Well, just look at it this way; you'll be even closer to it when you get back."

"Are you sure we're up?" complained the other, "I could've swore we weren't on until tomorrow morning."

"You know damn good and well you're on. Besides, it is tomorrow morning. You also know the longer you screw around, the farther you'll have to go. He's already on the way to Belaquin." There was no return reply from the two. "Halter picked you guys personally," he lied. "He said he could trust you guys to screw up a simple job like this."

Hennings knew better, "Of course he did. What an asshole!"

McCarter gave in, speaking to his roommate. "Let's go. We're not going to talk our way out of this one." He keyed the transmitter. "Just remember, Chris, paybacks are a bitch."

"I'll be waiting with open channels, boys."

The two pilots took off within ten minutes and soon found the large freighter, indeed on a direct course toward Belaquin. There were no identification markings anywhere, and most of the required marker lights were out. Attempted efforts to contact her brought forth no answer, and the two men pondered what to do next. They had never run into this kind of problem before. Usually, the arrival of the almighty security forces brought favorable results.

"I don't get this. They know who we are." said McCarter.

Hennings agreed. "I know. I wonder how old that damn thing is. It's been through hell. The radio's probably wasted."

"What do you think?" asked the younger, less experienced pilot.

"I don't know," was all Hennings could come up with.

"Well that's encouraging," remarked McCarter. "So much for seniority having all the answers." He thought for a moment. "Let's try cutting him off. He'll have to stop." There was no objection voiced.

They maneuvered their ships in front of the cruiser, allowing plenty of stopping distance, and stood their ground, waiting. It didn't take long for Hennings to note, "Jesus, he's not slowing down!"

They barely got out of the vessel's path. Once again they took up positions on either side of the huge ship.

McCarter was sweating. "Son of a bitch! Who the hell does he think he is? I don't believe this!"

Hennings was also feeling edgy. "What now?"

"I don't know about you … I mean, my God, he didn't give a shit about running us down. I'm ready to try something a little more forceful."

"Such as?"

McCarter got on the radio. "Air traffic control … this is Blue Raider six. We have been unsuccessful in all attempts to stop the suspect ship. He has already demonstrated blatant disregard to safety regulations. We request permission to fire across her bow." He switched off the transmitter and spoke to his wingman as he waited. "If that doesn't get his attention, we'll call in a tractor ship. We already know his brakes don't work."

"Permission granted Blue six." Halter answered, monitoring the three vessels on his scanners. As he watched, one of the smaller blips on his screen moved in front of the larger one.

Hennings watched as his friend moved toward the unidentified ships bow. Positioning slightly in front and parallel, McCarter fired a series of broad laser bursts into space as he passed. He had aimed carefully. The bolts of light went nowhere near the ship.

The warning shots brought forth an immediate change of circumstances. The cargo vessel, theoretically unarmed, as most are, returned fire of its own. Its aim however, was not meant as a warning to the raider pilot. It was meant to do much more. Blue raider six vaporized into a brilliant ball of fire!

Hennings mouth dropped open in horror as he tried to comprehend what had just happened. His expression turned to panic. His friend was gone! He could think of only one thing ... escape. He gunned his engines and took his raider directly beneath the front of the ship, turning toward its stern. Forgetting military professionalism, he screamed into the radio. "Chris ... God damn it ... they just killed him!"

Nichols started to answer, but even if he had, Hennings never would have heard him. Another blast from the stern of the hostile ship, also took its toll. He watched the second ship disappear from his screen, just as the first one had. Suddenly, there was only silence on the frequency.

The scanners aboard the Aquillon and Touchen noticed the two explosions right away. One of the many persons who noticed them was Leon Haute. "What is going on out there?" he demanded of Touchen control.

"We sent two raiders after a cargo ship operating in unauthorized space. We've had two explosions. The raiders are gone." Halters voice was shaky as he answered.

"What the hell happened?" Haute asked.

"All we know is that they tried to stop it and it fired on them. Now it's increased its speed considerably."

"What's its course?"

"It looks like it's headed for Belaquin."

A nervous voice came over the speakers. It was Nichols. "We need some help up here! We just lost two men!"

Haute couldn't begin to fathom what had happened, or why, but he was determined to find out. He fingered the transmitter. "I want that ship stopped. Use the destroyer interceptors. Tell them to blow out its engines and drag it back with a rope if they have to."

Four destroyer class ships, double shielded, quick and powerful, were sent to stop the rogue vessel. The ships were basically engines and guns with a pilot stuck in the middle. They were very intimidating crafts.

The cargo vessel had not changed course. As the interceptors caught up, they made it clear once more that it was to stop or be disabled. Again there was no response. Twenty minutes later, one cargo ship, its engines blown to bits, was being towed back to Touchen. Huge docking ships were dispatched to bring it down to the surface.

Haute ordered a security team to assemble in the main assembly hanger, the only space large enough to accommodate the size of ship being brought in. They were to remove the captain and crew of the ship using whatever measures necessary, and take them to the prison chambers to await legal proceedings.

Haute monitored the arrival of the ships from the control level. He felt more at ease when the seldom-used outer doors closed, sealing the bay. The security officers could handle the problem from there. He wished to see the person or persons responsible for the deaths of the two pilots, but that could wait until morning. They weren't going anywhere. It was very late. He left the control room and went to his cabin for some much needed rest.

Once there, he finally reached a point very close to sleep, but found that it wasn't meant to be. A claxon alarm went off and literally jerked him to his feet. Before he could even dress, his door buzzer rang. Opening it, he recognized one of the top officers from the security department.

Haute was puzzled with what he saw. The man was out of breath and obviously in distress. His left arm was injured somehow and hung flaccid at his side. Haute stared in shock, his eyes seeing, but his mind not comprehending. As the man tried to speak, he coughed and fell to his knees. His laser rifle, which he had been holding in his right hand, fell clattering to the floor in pieces. As Haute watched, countless droplets of blood followed, coming from his useless arm. His shirt and trousers were speckled with bright red.

The alarm suddenly stopped, and the bewildered Commander moved forward in an effort to help. The man began to speak, but a disturbance at the far end of the corridor drew their attention. A group of men and women ran toward and past them, their eyes and voices filled with panic. At least two of them yelled something as they stumbled past; their words indistinguishable.

Less than half a minute had passed since Haute had opened his door. Suddenly, the sound of laser fire filled the air, some shots distant, but others very near. The security officer immediately grew more agitated.

Haute looked at him for answers, but got none. "What happened?" he yelled.

The officer managed to stand, stared blankly at him and turned away, starting down the corridor as best he could, staggering with every step. Five steps away, he fell heavily against a wall and slid to a sitting position onto the floor, coughing uncontrollably. Haute could see from where he stood, the blood spurting from a hole in his side, previously hidden by his wounded arm. The bright red spattered the floor with each cough. It began to come from his mouth as well.

More movement came from the end of the corridor as another security man rounded the corner, his weapon drawn and ready. He turned back and shot at something Haute couldn't see. The exchange of fire didn't last long. A sweeping arc of light that cut into the bulkhead itself, coursed through the corridor. Haute stared in horror as the beam caught the man in mid-torso, instantaneously cutting him in half. The two parts fell twitching to the deck. Thick smoke filled the corridor with an acrid electrical stench. Haute looked again to the injured man beside him. He had fallen onto his face, blood flowing from his mouth. He had seen more than enough. He broke away and ran toward the elevator he had exited only moments before.

As he reached it, the loudspeakers blared, "ALL UNITS TO BATTLE STATIONS. THIS IS A CONDITION RED ALERT. INTRUDERS IN D SECTION. SECURITY PERSONNEL CONVERGE IN SECTIONS C AND E. ALL COMMAND PERSONNEL TO THE CONTROL CENTER IMMEDIATELY!" He was already on his way.

It took only a moment to reach it. Even as the door closed behind him, he noticed the chaos in the room. Not a soul was still. Each face held confusion and fear. He could not begin to imagine who had attacked the complex, but he didn't have to wonder long.

An officer caught his attention. "Thalosians, Commander. They've captured section D" The man paused for a second; obviously picturing deck plans in his mind. "They control hanger bays seven and eight, and everything in between."

"Thalosians?" Haute was stunned. "How did they get in here without us seeing them?"

"We did see them. They were on the unmarked cargo ship that was brought in by the tractors. The security team blew open the doors and were taken out. We had to seal off the section as soon as we could. We didn't have any choice. Some of our people didn't get out."

"You're sure they're sealed off?"

"So far. They're carrying hand-held weapons. They don't have a chance of getting through those doors with them." He silently hoped the bulkheads were as strong.

Haute felt his blood run cold. He had ordered that ship brought down. He said nothing.

The young man continued. "They did a good job of disguising themselves. Their ship is an old Republic supply tanker. That's how they got this far into our territory."

Haute found his wits. "Order the Aquillon and all outlying stations to be on full alert." He thought about what the man had told him. His own cabin was in D section. A sickening feeling filled him as he realized something else. "My God," he gasped. "The Kogran delegates are staying in that section!"

At that moment, the door opened and some of the group just mentioned entered briskly. Included were the Manna and his wife.

A sigh of relief came from Haute as he said, "Thank God you're safe. How did you get out?"

The man who had led them through the door, answered. "Luckily, sir, we were up late in the assemblage room when we heard."

The black leader spoke softly, but his voice stood out above the surrounding din. "Then it's true? You have been attacked by someone?"

"Yes, it's true, but not by someone ... by something. The Thalosians, we spoke of them earlier if you recall? They must have been planning this for some time. I'll explain everything after we get this cleared up." Haute counted quickly. At least six Kograns were not there. "William, some of your people may be trapped."

"I thought as much. What can we do?" The Manna fully trusted the man's judgment, but was still very worried for his missing friends.

"We've got them trapped in a specific area, but we can't get in there without them getting out. It creates a problem," explained Haute.

William agreed, but had a suggestion. "In the war, we used to flood captured buildings with gas."

"I don't know it would have any affect on them. They don't breathe as we do. Besides, we still have people down there that might be affected." Haute countered. He had never known the insects to ever show mercy or to negotiate. He knew the only way anyone was still alive in section D was if they hadn't been found.

They needed answers quickly. Every second of delay could mean more lost lives and increase the chance that the intruders would find a way to spread through the complex. Several possibilities raced through his mind and were dismissed for different reasons.

His gaze rested on one of the view screens at the far end of the room. On the screen was the Aquillon, in orbit far above them. The room grew nearly silent as he tried to shut out the distractions. Only a few bits of information reached his ears. Damage reports ... estimates of casualties. Three words from an Aquillon transmission pushed through the din and made him think. Someone had given a routine status report. They had said, "Gravitational levels … stable." Haute repeated the words in his mind.

Walking to a computer terminal, he punched in a series of questions, and waited. Soon his inquiries were answered. "GRAVITATIONAL ATMO-SPHERIC ADJUSTMENT IS AVAILABLE."

Haute turned and shared his thoughts. "We'll increase the gravitational pull until they're too heavy to move. Then we go in with anti-grav units and get our people out." He heard no argument. By all theories, it should work. It was at the least, worth a try. "Equip all teams with the AG units and have them stand by." As he spoke, the security men who had accompanied the Kograns to safety turned and left with their new orders.

He turned back to the console and made his instructions known to the officer who now manned the station. A series of buttons were punched and the computer provided readout of figures on a scale.

Haute watched the scale. "We'll increase the pull in five percent increments." Before doing so, he had one more question for the computer. "Will the increase harm human life on that level?"

"NEGATIVE, NO DISABLING INJURIES WILL RESULT."

Soon, the security teams were ready. Haute gave the signal to begin increase. After a few tense moments motion sensors in D section revealed no movement. The computer verified it. Its monotone voice gave the details. "ADJUSTMENT COMPLETED. GRAVITATIONAL LEVELS IN SECTION D, NOW ONE HUNDRED SIXTY PERCENT ABOVE NORMAL."

Haute gave the order to go in. The bulkheads opened and the men viewed corridors and rooms filled with bodies lying on the floor. Neither Republic nor Thalosian could move a muscle. Most of the men entering the section were too young to have ever seen a Thalosian in real life. They would never forget this day.

Even though the creatures walked upright, the Thalosians were not human by any means of description. Their size ranged from six to seven feet when standing and they weighed usually over one hundred kilos. Their large round multifaceted eyes and spindly appendages made them appear as man-sized insects. Most of them had four or more of these appendages, but some with six or more had been documented. The body was sectioned as head, thorax, and abdomen, again similar to an insect. The outer body shell was relatively hard, dark brown to black in color, shiny and smooth on the anterior, but ridged and rough posterior. In technology, they had to be highly skilled in all facets of construction. They had the capabilities to build ships, weapons, and no doubt great cities yet unseen.

Physically, they had extraordinary characteristics that made them … durable. They were survivors. There was no disputing that. Information gathered during the war years was sketchy, but the known facts would concern any commanding officer. It had been a long time since those facts had been discovered. No one dared guess what changes might have taken place since then. They were nearly indestructible without the involvement of firepower, and it took concentrated fire to bring them down. Ground soldiers were tireless, fighting even when severely injured or after the loss of numerous limbs. Hand to hand confrontations were decided before the fact. One on one, the strongest human was no match for a typical Thalosian. They had been witnessed to lift and throw a man thirty feet or more.

Scientific experimentation was performed in an effort to find any weaknesses, but their conclusions were disappointing. The creature's metabolism was remarkably flexible. In captivity, they shunned food, but needed water. They were not aquatic, but could remain submerged for long periods. Oxygen deprivation was unsuccessful; the creatures still able to function on less than a five percent mixture and simply going into hibernation if subjected to any lower. As for climactic changes, they seemed very similar to their frail human enemy. They burned and they froze.

Research found that they had only one fault that could be possibly used against them. Thalosians had a short life span. No creature had ever survived more than three months in captivity. It was unknown whether it was lack of water, food, or something else, but separately confined individuals expired nearly at the same time. There was no discernable illness involved and no deterioration of body structure. They still seemed as healthy and strong as the first day of capture. Scientists estimated that the creature's life span was from three to six months. It was unsure how the information could be used against them, but it was a possibility.

Language was another matter altogether. They seemed to have none, at least none that was audible. No person had ever witnessed them to utter a single sound. Upon examination, their anatomy produced no vocalizing parts at all. Scientists had an unsubstantiated theory that they must utilize a telepathic type of communication. If it were true, that type of skill would be an incredible advantage on the battlefield, wherever it may be.

The increased gravity harmed none of the human survivors, but proved quite fatal to the aliens. Their outer skeleton, although relatively strong, was not flexible enough to withstand the drastic change in pressure weight. Their bodies collapsed inward and were crushed.

Haute waited impatiently in the control section for any word. After only minutes, he received it. Everything was clear and gravity had been returned to normal. He immediately went to the section. He already knew what he would see.

Republic bodies were strewn throughout D section. It had been a massacre, especially in the hanger bay. At least twenty dead men and women lay scattered about the Thalosian ship. Against the unexpected intruders and their powerful firepower, the unprepared security staff hadn't stood a chance. The weapons they carried were only meant to disarm humans. Eighteen more bodies were found near the bay, killed as they tried to escape. Casualties could have been much more severe. There were nearly a hundred survivors located, those fortunate enough to remain out of sight. The missing Kogran delegates were among them, uninjured.

There were fifty or so Thalosians lying on the floor of the complex, and twenty more aboard the ship. Upon investigation of its interior, they found contents that raised interesting questions. Some rooms were stripped down to the metal walls, and others were filled with stockpiles of food and water. In still another, they found enough weaponry to equip a small army.

Haute was grim at the emergency council meeting. "Gentlemen, I have consulted with the senior fleet officers and advisors, and we believe that Thalosia is about to launch an attack on this system."

One of the members spoke quickly. "And what would you call what just happened here, Commander, a friendly visit?"

"I call this a minor incident sir, nothing compared to what might be coming. This disguised cargo ship was reported missing seven years ago. It carried only a small force. It was probably only a scout ship."

Sievers thought differently and disagreed as usual. "Commander, if they meant to attack later, why would this so called scout ship attack us now, with such a small force? Why would they tip their hand?"

"It was an accident. I don't think it was their intention to attack us here at all. We got a report of a ship in unauthorized airspace. Two raiders were sent to bring it in. When they attempted to stop the ship, they were destroyed. We originally thought the captain had illegal cargo or something. I don't think the Thalosians had any idea that this base existed. They were as surprised as we were when the hatch was opened."

"Well they know it exists now, don't they?" another man quipped.

Another member defended Haute, and his actions. "You seemed to handle the situation well enough Commander. I think it could have been much worse."

"Thank you. We were just lucky." He paused, taking a deep breath, drawing strength for his next statement. "I will to come straight to the point. Time is important. Do I have permission from the council to continue with my plans?"

"That's one thing we need to clear up," said Sievers. "We've read the preliminaries. Just what are your plans, exactly?"

Haute didn't hesitate. "We have to reinforce our boundary stations, at least for a while. They should be repositioned within minimum scanner range of one another and maintain contact at all times. Also, I suggest we increase defensive measures around Belaquin. If they attack, I think it will be their main target." He didn't feel the need to remind them of the past war. They remembered it well. "We should also check every vessel coming in and out of this system." He already knew the reaction the last staggering suggestion would bring.

One council member laughed. "Are you joking? That's impossible. We can't even begin to ..."

"It's not impossible ... it's just never been done before. We've got upwards of thirteen thousand people in service. There are only fifteen hundred on the Aquillon." He paused, knowing that most of those fifteen hundred were gone on shore leave. They, of course would have to be recalled immediately. "Those fifteen hundred and the two thousand here leaves almost ten thousand available for reassignment. It won't take a tenth of that for what we need."

"One thousand-five hundred of those people have already been reassigned. In one month, another ship like your own will be put into commission." Sievers was making another excuse, but appeared to somewhat agree with the scenario. "That leaves only eight thousand; just enough to run the facilities and protect Belaquin. We have other planets to protect. If the Thalosian army is anywhere near the size you think it is, and if you are correct in your assumptions ..." He did some silent figuring and then turned in his chair, studying the other faces in the room. "Then we could be in serious trouble."

Haute had one more thought for the council. "I suggest we get the recruiters busy taking names, and we need to light a fire under the construction company's asses to get that ship ready. We're gonna need her."

The Commander left the room soon after the final vote. He received a unanimous decision to do what he had to do. To manage with the limited resources would take careful planning and placement. It would take several days to complete the reorganization, and to put it into works. He prayed that they had that long.

Again, he thought about the one being in the universe that could put a stop to this mess? Ban-Sor's early assistance was now even more of a mystery. Why would bringing peace between the Belaquins and the Kograns make any difference, if he allowed the Thalosians to defeat the purpose? Maybe his actions weren't meant to be understood. Maybe his reasoning was beyond human understanding. Still, there was the same nagging possibility that he had always held in the back of his mind; that he had only been a figment of his imagination. He shook away the thought once again.

The passengers on the Albino Albatross knew nothing of what was going on behind them. Only what was ahead of them occupied their thoughts. What waited was a week's vacation on the most fabulous resort in the system; a week of dancing, gambling, and the rare luxury of sleeping in if they wished.

Soft music met Kahn's ears as he was awakened from his nap. Deanna informed him that they should be nearing Shannate. She had been asleep beside him until her alarm went off. He sat up as she again closed her eyes. Gary and Colleen relaxed on a doublewide recliner across the room, still asleep.

He stood, yawned and considered lying down again with Deanna, but instead walked the short distance to the control room. As he entered, he saw a planet looming before them. It was small, only two-thirds the size of Belaquin and it rested alone in a vast section of space. The climate was warm, the resorts privately owned and operated, and the entertainment endless, making it a popular corner of amusement for all travelers.

Avraham was seated in one of two seats. Evidently, piloting the ship had been a two-man operation at one time. Kahn was startled when the man spoke.

"Have you ever been here before?" asked the white-bodied man without turning around.

"No, I never had the chance, or the money." Kahn moved beside him. He couldn't help but study the man's uniqueness while he had the chance.

"It's unreal. They thought of everything when they built it. I've been here a dozen times, but I just can't get enough of it. If I ever settle down, this will be the place, believe me." Avraham smiled. He could feel Kahn's eyes on him, but didn't mind. He was used to it, and would probably do the same thing. "You've never seen anyone like me, have you?"

Kahn moved his glance to the planet, feeling somewhat foolish. Had he been that obvious? "I'm sorry ... no, I haven't." He heard nothing in return. "Were you born this way?"

"Yes, I was quite a sight I guess … forty-eight years ago. I imagine there's not too many of me around. I've never met one anyway."

"How long you been doing this?" asked Kahn, sitting down next to him.

"Seventeen long years," Avraham boasted.

"Still love it?"

"Yeah, it's all right. I make good money; get to see lots of places. You know … kinda like the military."

Kahn chuckled. "Yeah … right. Ever been to a place called Earth?" The question was needless.

"Oh … that's right. I heard about that on the news, and some from Colleen that wasn't on the news."

Kahn wasn't surprised. "Yeah, that's all that's been on."

Avraham laughed. "I guess you guys had a hell of a time there?"

"It got pretty hairy a couple of times." Kahn remembered.

"You guys will be kind of celebrities, right, after everything gets told?"

"Jesus, I hope not. To tell you the truth, all I care about right now is this shore leave. I need it"

"It's hard to believe … I mean the Kograns and everything. A lot of history books are gonna have to be rewritten."

"Yeah, it's going to play hell with a lot of school kids head," Kahn suggested. He knew what the experience had done to his own.

"So what's the deal anyway? All I've heard is what's on the tube. They sure as hell didn't say anything about this super being that supposedly came out of nowhere to save the day. Colleen was talking about some pretty weird shit … had to do with your supreme commander."

Kahn shook his head. "Believe me, all I know is what you know; what came through rumor central. I'll let you know when I know. That's a promise."

"Good enough. Just don't make me wait for the movie." Avraham checked his scanners. They were within communication range. "You want to hear a little of what we're getting ourselves into?"

"Sure." Kahn answered readily.

Coleridge reached forward into a maze of controls and flipped some switches. After a few seconds, he frowned, dark wrinkles standing out on his forehead.

"What's wrong?"

"Don't know for sure," He picked up a headset, listened, banged it on the console, and listened again.

"Is your radio out?"

"Nope." He handed a second pair of headphones to Kahn. Putting them on, he listened for a few seconds. "I don't hear anything."

"Exactly, that's what's wrong. This channel is the busiest station on Shannate broadcasting. It should be blowing us out of here." Avraham related. He reached up, slowly turning a dial, listening intently for a moment. After a few seconds, he switched to still another frequency. "Shannate control, this is the Albino Albatross, call numbers … 36994." No one answered. He repeated the call with the same results. He leaned back and switched the ship's control to manual.

Kahn could see that they were nearing the upper atmosphere. Avraham put the ship in an orbital pattern to stay out of it. It was obvious that the pilot was somewhat concerned.

Avraham was at a loss. "Something's not right; we should have heard something by now." He turned to Kahn. "I'm gonna try the emergency channel. If this one's dead, we've definitely got a problem. We can't land if we don't reach control."

"What if they answer? What are you going to tell them?" Kahn asked. He knew that using most emergency frequencies when there was none, carried huge fines.

"I'll tell them that Shannate control isn't answering." He switched on the transmitter, speaking loudly. "This is the Albino Albatross, call number … 36994. We are currently in quadrant fourteen, requesting approach. Please respond." The two men sat in silence. He tried again. "This is the Albino Albatross, 36994. We are declaring an emergency. Please respond and advise." Avraham looked at Kahn, whose eyes grew wide at what he had just heard, then added, "Hey, if I don't get down there, I'm going to have an emergency."

Kahn agreed and nodded. "No shit …"

"Our equipment checks out, transmitting, receiving … it all shows normal." He sighed with frustration. "I don't understand. It's like nobody's there. They should answer."

Kahn had a foreboding thought, but didn't know why. "Maybe they can't," he suggested. The two men exchanged sullen looks.

Avraham made a decision. "Well, we'll know in a few minutes."

"We're going down anyway?" Kahn was apprehensive, but this wasn't his ship and it wasn't his ass if it came down to it.

The two men were startled when a voice unexpectedly came over the speaker. Reception was poor and they could barely understand the words. The person on the other end spoke hurriedly. "Anyone who can hear me, this is Shannate control. We have been attacked … we are under attack!" The transmission became broken. It was obviously a low power unit being used. "Get word ... Republic ... has been taken ... my last trans ... they're cutting through ..." A loud crash resounded through the receiver on the white ship, followed by a yell and what sounded like laser fire. The radio went silent once again. The last words they had heard had been all to clear.

Kahn felt his blood run cold as he stared at the speaker. "Jesus Christ!"

"Whoever crashed the door crashed the transmitter too. The signal is gone," said Avraham. "Son of a bitch! I knew something was wrong! Go get everybody up."

Kahn got up and saw Avraham turn the ship into the atmosphere. "What are you doing?" he asked, confused. "You heard what he said! We should get the hell out of here!" Kahn was not one to run out on a fight, but he had been through enough to last him for quite a while.

"We can't, not just yet. We're already here. I want to see what's going on down there."

Kahn shook his head in disagreement, but turned, wondering if the ship had any armament. Being private, it no doubt did.

By the time he returned with the others, the ship was out of the lower atmosphere, slowly dropping through cloud cover. Finally, their sight was clear. They could see for a hundred miles in all directions.

Far on the horizon, huge plumes of black smoke could be seen reaching skyward. "That's Shannate City." Avraham said. He shook his head, knowing what they found would be bad.

At high speed, the miles turned to seconds. Night was approaching to that side of the planet and lights on the ground and in the taller buildings started to grow visible. The origin of much of the smoke grew visible as well.

Avraham alone recognized where they were. A solid fuel refinery on the far side of the city could be seen burning out of control. Many other fires could be made out in buildings and streets. It was not the Shannate City that he remembered. They were now well over the residential areas. They seemed to be untouched, appearing free of fire at least. The downtown and casino area looked as if it had been hardest hit by whatever was happening. "We'll go over the space port." He banked to the left. "It's on the other side of these towers. That's where Shannate control is."

Gary and the girls stood behind the pilot, looking ahead. As they cleared the buildings, the spaceport came into view. Gary spoke. "What the hell?"

One by one, the Albatross passengers saw what Gary had already noticed. At least ten enormous vessels had landed within the port boundaries. Some of them were no doubt of alien design. Crowds of persons surrounded the ships.

"Are those people? What are they doing?" Kahn asked.

Avraham answered each question in turn. "Some of them are. They're getting on those ships." He'd seen enough. "I don't know about you guys, but my curiosity has been satisfied. We're gonna do what you suggested earlier, Kahn. Colleen, get your friends strapped in."

With a twist of his wrist, he turned away from the city, gaining altitude rapidly. As they raced skyward, the ship entered a column of thick black smoke. When it exited, it came face to face with another alien ship. Only uncanny fate kept the two vessels from colliding. Avraham cursed the curiosity that got them here, "Damn it ... they know we're here now!"

Quick maneuvering succeeded in bringing them parallel to the huge vessel. With little choice, Avraham cut across the ship's bow. Seconds later, it became apparent that the alien ship's crew had indeed seen them.

As Avraham hit the throttle, laser bolts clipped his ship. The Albatross shuddered with the hits. He wrenched the steering bar backward, bringing his bow nearly straight up. Yells of protest came from the back. Kahn tried to move, but was pressed too tightly into the seat.

Far ahead of the alien ship, Avraham leveled out. A loud beeping gained his attention. He focused on the control panel where a red light glared. "Oh shit!" he said simply. "We didn't need that."

"What?" asked Kahn, "Don't tell me the engines have been hit?"

"Okay ... I won't," the pilot answered humorously, but concerned.

"How bad are we?"

"Your guess is as good as mine, but it doesn't feel good."

"Are we going to make it out of here?" asked Kahn, hoping his new friend would tell him that they would. He didn't.

Avraham kept a close eye on his scanners. As he expected, "They're following us."

Colleen, suddenly standing behind the two men, asked. "Who's following us?"

"We don't know who, but they don't like us too much." answered Kahn. "Should we go up or down, Avraham?"

Avraham glanced at the power level readout. "Well, I think they might have hit our generators, but we've got plenty of juice. We might be able to outrun these guys upstairs. That's our best chance," He forced himself to sound calm, but he voiced the alternative as well. "If we don't make it to space, we're gonna have a long way down."

The generators held out, allowing the white ship to make it through the atmosphere, but that was as far as it got. The power levels dropped rapidly and the main engine finally failed. Propulsion was gone. As they drifted, Avraham walked to the back of the craft. He was bombarded with questions.

Gary asked the first. "What did we hit?"

"We didn't hit anything. A laser blast hit us," explained the pilot. He went to a wall panel and removed a section of it, exposing a multitude of switches and circuitry. He began tracing wires and hitting buttons. All interior lighting suddenly went out, plunging the ship into darkness. Tracking lights located outside the ship went off as well. Emergency lights came on, dimly lighting the cabin. All systems eventually shut down, including gravity control. Everything on the ship not secured, began to float freely.

He explained his actions to the others. "I'm killing all systems, even life support. We're on the dark side right now. They might not find us if they're tracking by sight. If they do find us, they may read us as a dead ship and leave us alone. Other than that, we don't have any choices."

Deanna was bothered at the possible consequences. "What if we can't restart these systems?"

"Don't worry hon; we've got plenty of battery power for that. We just don't have enough to go anywhere."

"So we hope they don't find us … and if they don't, then what?" Colleen joined the conversation with a legitimate point.

"Then we have to hope someone else does." He knew his answer wasn't inspiring, but it was the truth.

Kahn was still strapped in his seat in the control room, bathed only in starlight. Shannate lay behind them in darkness. He waited, hoping Avraham's ruse would work.

In the next moment his pulse quickened. Stars began to disappear on the right side of his view. It was a ship! As it turned in front of him, his seat began to vibrate along with the rest of the ship. A loud hum penetrated the Albatross hull."

Kahn released a deep breath, not realizing that he had been holding it. He now sat in complete darkness. The ship was massive, passing so close that it blocked out everything else. Its outline was marked by dozens of lights. It was not sleek like the Albatross. It was ugly, unimpressive, except in its size. It was, in a word … alien.

His attention was suddenly diverted, as Avraham came out of nowhere to move himself into his seat. They watched together in silence. The ship stopped, directly in front of them, seemingly only a few meters away. Both men sat perfectly still, as if any movement would betray their presence.

The frightened passengers of the Albatross didn't know it, but a second ship had approached them from the left side, waiting out of view. Suddenly, a white light enveloped the ship. It emanated from a point somewhere in front of them, so bright that it was blinding.

Avraham had seen it before. "Tractor beam," he said simply.

Before anything else could be done, another laser blast, this one from the ship they had not seen, violently rocked them. The blast was directed once again toward the engines, ensuring their demise. It disabled the passengers as well.

The first ship moved above the stricken craft and utilizing the beam, pulled it close enough to allow external docking locks to engage, holding the stark white ship firmly against the hull. It joined at least four other small ships, similarly fastened to the alien cruiser. Seconds later, the same ship turned away from the planet. The engines flared and soon it was just another bright light among the stars. The second ship re-entered Shannate's atmosphere, evidently having unfinished business below.

The alien ship's destination was an incredible distance from Shannate. It was bound for Thalosia, home planet to the race of creatures named after it. The distance between the two planets was great, but not enough to discourage the Thalosians from accomplishing their goal. They were relentless, and like any race, would go to whatever lengths necessary to insure their survival. The reason for the attack was still unknown to anyone but them, but what had transpired in the past few hours on Shannate would stun every living person in the Belaquin system, and bring back haunting memories to many.

Dozens of ships had landed in the three major cities on Shannate. The heavily armed Thalosians met little or no resistance. The unsuspecting guests staying in the casinos and hotels were easy to control. City police and security personnel were taken out as soon as they were encountered. The people were rounded up like cattle. Any who resisted were killed outright, so resistance became minimal after the first slayings. The alien ships were systematically loaded with men and women alike. The children that were discovered were left untouched. As ruthless as the aliens seemed, this act of mercy seemed out of place. After many hours, one by one, the ships lifted off, their captives unknowing what their future held. Finally, five hours after the initial shots had been fired, the last ship left the planet, leaving behind burned out cities and many dead. Survivors, who had somehow remained hidden, milled about, lost, wondering what had happened, wondering where everyone had gone.

CHAPTER 12

▼

Colleen felt the first stirring of consciousness arrive in the form of pain. Her head pounded, but her neck hurt even worse. She turned it, trying to displace the throbbing tension, but it remained. She found herself lying supine on the floor, and noticed, strangely, that there was an absence of soft carpet. She opened her eyes, but could see nothing but darkness. With her senses returning, she became aware of other bodies around her. As her eyes adjusted, the surroundings became unfamiliar. She was definitely no longer within the comfortable cabin of the Albatross. This realization brought terror with her pain.

Some of the fear subsided as she recognized the person lying beside her. She moved close to him. The form did not move, but was breathing. Tears of worry filled her eyes. "Gary!" She shook him lightly. "Gary … are you okay? Wake up! Please wake up!" He did not respond. She gave up, knowing that if he could, he would. The tears ran down her face, as she tried to put some of her confusion together. Looking around again, but unable to see more than a few feet, she realized that Avraham, Deanna and Kahn were not with them.

In the darkness, she could barely make out anything, and couldn't really be sure of what she saw. The place was filled with seemingly hundreds of people, either lying or sitting on the floor. Only a few figures stood, dimly silhouetted in open doorways around the room. She squinted, but it was impossible to see them clearly. All she knew for sure was that they weren't human. They seemed to be standing guard over the people on the floor. Slowly, she pieced together the facts that she was sure of. At once she knew!

The alien ships on Shannate … the hundreds of persons around her were obviously from there. They were imprisoned! Where? Why? Was this a ship?

Questions and possibilities filled her thoughts. Desperately needing his reassurance, she tried repeatedly to wake Gary, but it was useless. He remained unresponsive. Finally, feeling alone and helpless, she cradled his head in her lap and waited.

The minutes turned to hours. Colleen watched and learned. Once in a while, a person would rise up a little too far, and would be struck down or threatened by the silent aliens. Her legs grew sore from the uncomfortable floor. There was almost no room to move or stretch out. If only she could stand up, it would make all the difference.

To pass the time, she examined Gary as best she could. His breathing seemed normal. She found a hard lump on the back of his head, but no open wound. A serious concussion had to be considered at the least. Her continual tries to awaken him did no good, but she tried to remain optimistic.

By talking to some of the people around her, she learned what had happened and exactly who the inhuman guards were. They told her that they were indeed on one of the ships, and that she and Gary had been added to their midst much later. They also related that they had not seen anyone else brought in with them. No one could make a guess about where they were going. Most people slept. It was the one and only way to escape the ship.

Colleen closed her eyes and thought about the past several days. How could so many things happen in such a short span of time? How could they take any more? The lack of information about her three friends was disheartening. Surely they would have all been put in the same place, unless they only took the living. She tried to erase the possibility. A cramping pain twisted her abdomen. The need for a bathroom, incredibly, overshadowed everything else.

As it started to grow cool in the room, she lay close to Gary's warm body. The floor was metal, damp and cold to the touch. She could feel the heat being drawn from her. Unable to take the cold, she sat up and pulled Gary to a slight sitting position to get his back off the frigid surface. At one point a guard walked rigidly past, close enough for her to make out its hideous black form. She closed her eyes from it, crying until she fell asleep.

Kahn, Deanna, and Avraham, even though they didn't know it, were on the same ship as their friends. They actually lay in same room, but the dark quiet conditions kept them apart. Kahn knew upon first sight who their captors were and had a relatively good idea where they were heading. The reason behind it was another matter. He explained it to the people around him, at least the ones within earshot of his low voice. "In the last twenty years, since we started cross quadrant traffic, hundreds of people have disappeared. The ships that were found were empty, but no bodies have ever been recovered. The Thalosians have always been suspected, but we've never had proof."

An elderly woman nearby listened to Kahn. From an earlier conversation, he had learned that she was a room cleaner at one of the casino hotels. She knew now of his position as an officer in the Republic. Neither her eyes nor her voice could hide the fear she had inside her. "You say none of those people had ever been found? What about us?"

Kahn, in a seldom seen comforting mood, took one of her hands in his. "Don't worry hon. They're not going to be able to hide this from the Republic, not something this big. They're probably already coming after us." His words sounded sincere. Inside, he hoped that he spoke the truth. He sat in silence, studying the surroundings.

They were situated near the edge of the crowd, where the creatures made their rounds. There were several armed guards in the room, but their number was minuscule compared to the number of captive people. It would be possible for several men to overpower a guard, but it seemed useless to do so, unless all were taken at once. Even if they did, there were too many unknowns. There could be a hundred more Thalosians in the next room. Kahn shook his head. There wasn't any way to set it up, not a sure way, but the need to do something nagged at him.

An hour later, he noted that the already poor interior lighting of the ship had seemed to have grown even fainter. Soon, it may be pitch in the room. Any opportunity would be gone.

He had come up with a preliminary plan, or at least the first step. Where it went from that point was yet to be seen. Against Deanna's wishes, he got to a crouching position for the second time in an attempt to get a weapon from a guard, the only one he could see, and hopefully, the only one who could possibly see him in the darkness. He knew the incredible strength attributed to the aliens, but the one nearest him looked so small, so frail. Decidedly there was really only one way to find out. Due partly to his military status, he felt some obligation to try. On this approach the Thalosian guard had its back turned. Kahn snuck to within ten feet of it.

He froze as the creature did a half turn toward him. Kahn watched, tensed, ready to move. The guard turned away. Kahn coaxed himself forward. Still slightly crouched, he moved. "Almost there," he breathed. Then it was over.

The intended prey turned at the last second and fired its rifle, point blank range. The short powerful blast caught its target fully in the chest. Blood exploded from the first sized wound, spraying everyone close by. The lifeless body was thrown backwards to fall among the other prisoners. Screams filled the room, one of them Deanna's.

Kahn saw it all in slow motion. The creature had turned just in time to see a different man lunging toward it. Kahn, concentrating so intensely on his own attack, had not even seen him. The unexpected action caused him to duck instinctively to his knees, where he remained.

The screams died away as more insects moved into the room. Kahn slowly moved away, his plan quickly discarded. The Thalosians were obviously determined to maintain control on this ship; taking whatever steps they needed to. The human lives around them were clearly expendable.

He slowly made his way back to Deanna and Abraham. He sat down beside her, putting a hand in hers. She was trembling. He put his arms around her, squeezing tightly. They and the other prisoners had no choice but to ride out the trip.

As far as Leon Haute knew, everything was progressing smoothly in the Belaquin system. No other Thalosian ships had entered scanner range since the alert of the lookout stations. The re-routing and re-manning of stations all over the system was well underway.

Only one thing puzzled him. He had issued an emergency recall for all off duty personnel, including the crew of his ship, some of them only hours into their shore leave. Nearly all of the Aquillon crew had either returned to the ship, or had acknowledged the recall and were en route, all except for thirty-nine persons. He understood that many people could be delayed with calling in, or be difficult to find, but understanding turned to suspicion when he learned that thirty of those persons had been destined to the same place, most on privately hired flights. More distressing was the fact that he knew many of the missing personally. Two of them happened to be members of his finest raider squadron.

Not long after he received these coincidental facts, he received other related information. His suspicions now turned to worry. No one on Shannate could be reached by any approaching ships or on any long-range frequency. Receivers on the planet showed to be operative, leading Haute to believe that there may be a problem with the satellites. His advisors called it a temporary communications breakdown, but he couldn't shake the feeling that it was something more. It couldn't be that simple. The only thing he could do was to investigate it using some other means. He ordered a transport vessel to go to the planet, find the problem, then locate and bring back the missing Aquillon crewmembers.

Three hours later, a transport ship made its final approach toward the planet. As the ship drew near, an unknown object that had been on their scanners for some time became visible. A small ship soon glowed in the spotlights of the transport. There were no power or life readings from the vessel. It was adrift, slowly falling to its fiery end in the atmosphere. As the transport moved close, the pilots knew exactly what they were seeing. The tell tale burns of laser fire creased the craft. A large hull rupture could be seen at the rear of the ship. The crew of the vessel had died quickly.

The transport left the ship to its fate. With no response from any communication attempt, they tracked and found the first Shannation satellite. It had been destroyed. What remained was an unrecognizable mass of metal, spinning out of control. The next two they found were the same, crushed by some unknown force. The first report was sent to Touchen.

Numerous power readings were still evident on the planet surface. It was decided to investigate there next. The pilot took his ship towards the capital city. It was night and the lights of the city's taller structures could easily be seen once below cloud cover. Much more easily seen was the massive fire on the near horizon. Seemingly hundreds of fire units could be seen battling the huge blaze. There was still no communication with anyone below, even though they were well within portable range. On the first pass over the city, it was noted that even though airborne traffic was non-existent, ground vehicles were still active in large numbers. The more the men saw, the more puzzled they became. The transport landed in an empty area close to the casino hotels. Cautiously, the crew opened the hatches.

The initial survey of the plaza and nearby streets found no one, at least no one alive. Dead bodies, hundreds of them, littered the streets like trash. A certain few of those bodies told the story. Even though none of the crew had ever seen a Thalosian in real life, they recognized them easily. There were far more human bodies than alien and evidence of a massive struggle. It appeared to have been one sided. The resort guests of course, would have had no weapons. Many of the dead were security and police who had been armed, but limited in numbers and strength.

Upon entry of the casinos, they found much of the same. In the first hour of searching, the shore party found survivors who had hidden themselves when they heard the transport setting down. From these survivors, they heard the incredible story.

The aliens had taken the city completely by surprise. Smaller ships came down in the streets, blocking escape routes, while the larger ones took over the spaceport. Herding the people to the spaceports, the aliens loaded their ships with as many as they could hold, and then tried to kill the rest.

The crew of the transport tried to restore some semblance of order, but it was impossible. There remained far too much fear. People began coming out of nowhere, some pleading, some demanding to be taken off the planet. Others asked for help to look for missing loved ones. Soon, it became overwhelming. Hundreds of angry frightened people watched, as the transport crew had no choice but return to the air. The mission captain radioed back to Touchen with the horrible news.

Haute was on top of the reassignments to the outposts and security beef-ups. He had assigned his own ship to orbit Belaquin and was en-route there when the urgent message from Shannate reached Touchen. On the control deck, Lieutenant Nichols intercepted and relayed it.

Haute listened intently as the lieutenant replayed the taped message. It said, "Shannate Recon Team to Touchen control … priority one emergency transmission. Shannate has been attacked by Thalosian forces … casualties are extreme … thousands have been taken hostage and there whereabouts unknown. Request all emergency services to implement disaster plans immediately. Security enforcement will be needed prior to E.M.S. arrival. Further transmissions will follow. Reconnaissance team out."

As the tape finished, the young lieutenant expected to hear an answer from Haute, but instead heard nothing. The man simply hung up. Nichols leaned back, incredulous, knowing full well that this incident would trigger a war. He felt sorry for the man he had just spoken to. He knew his past.

Haute strode heavily down the corridor, a thousand thoughts pummeling his troubled mind. He had never felt so old. Above anything else, he felt rage. It was inconceivable. How could this have happened? He already knew the answer. It could, and did happen … quite easily. The planet had no defense system in place, thanks to the four men who owned the global rights. They had decided that a military presence would be detrimental to the original concept of the resort, and would keep many families from visiting. This in turn would decrease revenues … personal ones, no doubt. He wondered how much fun those four individuals were having right now.

The Aquillon was ordered to return to Touchen, where matters advanced quickly. The emergency council meeting didn't last long. The adamant Fleet Commander had no trouble getting permission to go to Thalosia, undoubtedly the destination of the alien abductors. He had made up his mind even before attending, not to take no for an answer. Too many lives were at stake. There were stipulations made that he was not pleased with however. He had specific orders to wait an unspecified time period before leaving. An estimated six to seven days was the minimum time needed to bring Aquillon Three to combat readiness. Aquillon four and five were still years away from being finished. The shakedown exercises would have to be made during the trip to Thalosia. Haute didn't agree at first, but knew that it made sense. Even his own ship didn't have a full crew as yet, and with the task ahead, he would need all the help he could get. He and the Republic had to wait.

The following days passed unmercifully slow. Public outcry was tremendous over the decision to delay the rescue mission. Many believed that the imprisoned people would probably be dead by the time the Republic took action.

Haute, above all, was anxious to get his people back alive, but to go in ill-prepared against such a powerful force could mean many more deaths and possibly a total defeat.

The aliens had taken an estimated twenty thousand persons. An exact figure was impossible to ascertain due to the unmonitored amount of traffic to and from the planet. Whatever the correct number was, it was staggering.

Over that time, Haute recovered from his initial rage. He had not rested well, having to resort to sedatives to sleep at all. Without them, he would have eventually collapsed from shear fatigue. Even with forced sleep, he was exhausted.

Finally, nearly a week after the disaster, the Aquillon One's sister ship, a full crew complement, and one hundred seventy-five new raiders were ready. Haute anxiously gave the order to start toward Thalosia. To all who watched, the sight of the two massive vessels moving together was breathtaking. Within thirty minutes, they had cleared the outer markers and had entered light speed on their way to battle. Ten destroyer class interceptors followed them. Combined, they commanded enough firepower to annihilate, if necessary, the entire Thalosian system.

Haute sat in his command chair and watched the endless expanse of space pass by. Somewhere ahead was thousands of frightened people, their freedom viciously ripped away by an alien presence not felt in more than twenty years. The Thalosian race had never been challenged by the Belaquins. There had been no reason to do so. There had been little or no contact with them since the first war. The unwritten rule had been live and let live, but now that rule had changed. The Republic had reason and means.

He could partially envision what was to come. When they reached Thalosia, the battles would ensue, and with them, the inevitable loss of more lives. The aliens would be fully expecting them.

He put his head in his hands and stared at the floor, silently wishing for another way out, but knowing his wish was in vain. The Thalosians had started this, but with God as his witness and hopefully on his side, he would put an end to it, once and for all.

The trip to their destination took six long days, according to Gary's estimates. On the first day, he had finally awakened with Colleens coaxing, to the same dark world they were now in. His head hurt badly at first, but the pain had eventually subsided. He, Colleen, and the hundreds of people around them were cold, uncomfortable, and hungry. The anxiety and fear lessened as they all fell into their individual routines of eating, drinking and sleeping. The Thalosian rules were unspoken, but abundantly clear, as was the punishment for disobeying them. He didn't know what the immediate future held for them, but for now, he and the others seemed to be safe from harm. The aliens had plans for them, and evidently needed them alive. If that were not the case, they would have been dead already.

The prisoners had plenty enough water to sustain them, but the alien captors had misjudged either their food stores or the number of prisoners. The food was given often, but in meager amounts.

To temporarily escape the prison ship, he and Colleen tried to sleep most of the time, but the unforgiving floor, the cries and moans from other people, and their own cramping muscles made rest difficult if not impossible.

The worst torture by far, was the horrible stench of the confined spaces. The Thalosians had provided sustenance to keep them alive, but had neglected, either by ignorance, or lack of compassion, to provide the basics needed for bodily relief. The smell of urine and feces was sickening. There were those who forced themselves to wait, but eventually they gave out, usually while they slept. Some did not move about, simply to keep from being soiled by others. They remained still, sitting in their own and others filth, praying for a way out. For many, their prayers were answered. They slept, but never awoke.

On the sixth day or night, at one of the few times that he managed to doze off, Gary was awakened by an abrupt change in the smooth ride they had experienced thus far. It felt as if they were slowing down. He knew from experience that to feel it at all, one had to be an environment with gravity. The following bumping and jarring signaled a probable landing. Cries of fear and relief came from the surrounding crowd as they realized it as well. They had no clue as to where they were, but at that point, they didn't care. What could be worse than their current state?

With no warning, the lights came on, so intense that welcome heat could be felt. After six days of near darkness, it was impossible to see until their eyes could adjust. Gary locked arms with Colleen, determined not to let go. With the number of persons around them, if they were somehow separated, it might be permanently. He looked at her, forcing the blurring from his vision, and finally saw her clearly for the first time in a week. Her face was dirty; her cheeks streaked with tear paths, but just the sight of her in the light made his heart leap.

She finally could see his face as well. A weak smile crept through her suffering.

Above the quiet din of voices, a sound broke through. It sounded like giant metal doors creaking open. Gary sat up and through squinted eyes, saw at least a hundred new figures enter into the ship through the open ports.

Preceding those figures was an onrush of fresh, warm air, thankfully replacing the rank, sour air of the chamber. The breeze was welcomed by the sounds of hundreds, gulping down the long overdue relief. Some people began to stand, followed by many others. As far as they could tell, the creatures were trying to herd the half blind people out the doors. Sunlight poured through various open hatches. It felt fantastic to the two Republic crewmembers as they painfully stood and walked. Gary knew as he stretched upright, that he was too weak to resist even if he wanted to, but maybe that had been the alien's plan all along.

As they stumbled down a ramp, their vision became clearer, and for a moment, they thought they might have been back on Earth. The ship had landed in a huge clearing surrounded by forest. The green of vegetation covered everything around them. On some hillsides in the far distance, the trees seemed to grow in perfect rows, possibly cultivated. The sky was blue, uncluttered by even a single cloud. The temperature felt comfortably warm.

For several moments, they stood in one place. Then, a few at a time, they were forced in the direction of a line of hills. As they walked, Colleen held tightly to Gary and looked among the countless faces for any that looked familiar.

Gary nodded his head, feeling that he had some understanding of what had happened. He remembered the violent blast that had sent him and the others into unconsciousness, and also waking up in darkness and confusion. Somehow, they had been taken off the Albatross. How that had been accomplished was still a mystery.

There was no sign of Kahn, Deanna, or the albino pilot. If they had been taken aboard the ship at the same time, it seemed logical that they would have been placed near them in the crowd of persons. On the darker side, as Colleen suggested, they may have only removed those left alive. They had discussed it many times in the past days, and if they were alive, whether it would be possible to find them. Now, seeing the thousands of people filling the clearing, they realized how slim the chances were becoming.

The crowd of people approached an opening in the trees. A wide trail led into the forest and up the slope. Looking a little ahead in the line, Gary noticed a group of five persons who had broken away from the main line and ran toward a certain tree a few yards off of the trail. He could see its branches were laden with some sort of red fruit. Before they reached it, the air filled with high-pitched screams from the nearest Thalosians. The aliens also moved quickly toward the tree, apparently in an effort to cut the hungry people off. They were too late. Two young females reached the low hanging branches before the insects could stop them. Ravenous bites were quickly taken.

The Thalosian guards had stopped and beaten down an elderly man and woman, and then turned upon a fourth woman who had almost reached the tree.

Colleen thought she recognized the clothing of the two women eating the fruit. They were dressed similarly to Shannation pleasure girls. She right away thought again of her sister. She had wondered for days whether she had been taken.

The fourth woman had reached up to grasp one of the red bulbs, when she was struck down by one of the insect guards. It had swung its weapon in a full arc and caught her arm near the elbow. The girl fell to the ground with a scream. Colleen grimaced. As hard as she had been hit, it had to be broken.

The column of people steadily moved forward. Colleen and Gary drew within fifty feet of the scene.

Colleen squinted and looked hard at the injured girl on the ground. At one point, she saw her face very well. She looked at Gary in horror, her face pale. "Oh my God! That looks like Kelsey!" Without hesitation, she moved out of line toward her.

Gary grabbed her hard by the arm. "What are you doing?" His voice was stern.

"It's her, I know it!" she pleaded.

"It can't be her ... out of all these people?"

Colleen looked into his eyes in desperation, trying to wrench free her arm. She gritted her teeth, her voice angry. "I'm telling you ... it's her!"

Gary gave in. He remained calm, but didn't release her. "All right ... okay, I believe you, but you're not going out there! Just wait until we get closer. I'll get her." Still walking, they drew within twenty feet.

Colleen grew more anxious with each step. She was convinced as to the woman's identity.

Gary looked closely, but could not positively be sure that it was she. He'd only seen her once. The woman in question still lay beneath the tree, rocking, holding her arm.

Gary was puzzled as he took in the whole scene. The insect guards had pushed the elderly man and woman back into line, but strangely enough, had not touched the two younger women who had already started to eat. Those women sat on the ground, continuing to devour the fruits. The guards simply left them there, returning to watch the line.

It was perfect timing. The guard that had struck the woman down suddenly turned away from her. Gary painfully ran the few short steps to the injured woman, picked her up and carried her back to where Colleen waited. The insects screamed loudly at the action, but that was all.

As everyone passing watched, one of the women beneath the tree stopped eating and suddenly collapsed to the ground. Her body began shaking violently, red, foamy sputum coming from her mouth. The other girl dropped the fruit she held in her hand. She began to scream as she realized what possibly lay in store for her as well. Within seconds, she also collapsed, her screaming cut short with her unconsciousness. They eventually lay still. The endless crowd walked on, only then understanding the insect's earlier intervention.

Tears flowed heavily down Kelsey Sluder's cheeks as she recognized her sister. She shook uncontrollably, unable to speak, and clung to Colleen as if her life depended on it.

Gary couldn't help notice the girl's absence of clothing. She wore nearly nothing. He took off his light sweater and put it on her. As small as she was, it hung like a nightgown. She said nothing, but he could see the thanks in her eyes.

Colleen spoke to her. "Kelsey, you've got to walk! You have to walk!"

She nodded, forcing her legs to move. The Thalosians pushed them forward.

While they continued, Gary checked her arm, which had already started to swell and become discolored. Any movement brought pain. "Well, I'm not sure, but it might be broke."

Colleen had never seen her sister in such a state. She jumped at every sound and had an unfamiliar, wild look in her eyes. She looked as if she was losing her mind. All of them had been through hell the last few days, but something worse had to have happened to her. She hugged her close and spoke softly, trying to bring her some comfort. She couldn't bear to see her like this. Her own tears fell into her sister's hair as she helped her walk. She shook her head in disbelief. "I can't believe we found you," she whispered.

After several moments of walking, loud talking started through the mass of people, starting from the front and working its way back.

Gary saw what caused it, as they topped a short rise. They stood over a large valley. A breathtaking view was laid out before them. The valley extended to the left through a series of foothills and up to a line of small mountains several miles in the distance. Some of the hills were covered completely with rows of trees, similar to what they had seen earlier. Other hills, like the one they were on, were covered with wild growth. The sight of the orchard of trees seemed out of place, and even more so, the thought that they were managed by these horrid creatures. Gary had thoughts that he shared with the others. "At least they aren't meat eaters."

Colleen didn't completely agree with the statement, but kept her opinion to herself. She surmised that since they had been eating fruit for the past week, that maybe it was for them only.

To the right, the valley extended to the shoreline of a large body of water that reached past the horizon. Thriving forest was everywhere.

There was a scar on the perfect scene, however. In the center of the valley, at the end of the well-worn path they followed, was a wide clearing where the rich green of the forest gave way to the dull brown of dirt and rock. It continued across the valley floor, reaching the nearest foothills, where it sloped gently upwards and joined a series of small steep cliffs. On the cliff faces were a dozen large openings, passages to somewhere they couldn't see. On the right, the clearing stretched all the way to the water. Figures could be seen moving about the clearing, but were too far away to make out. Another unnatural addition could be seen as well. A huge wall surrounded the clearing on three sides. The remaining side was open to the water. Was the wall there to keep someone in, or to keep something out? The prisoners proceeded without pause down the steep path. It became evident that they would find out soon enough.

Kahn passed through the huge gate into the clearing, following the hundreds if not thousands of persons before him. The path had ended. Deanna was beside him, as well as Avraham, who had suffered with headaches and nausea throughout the last few days. It was hoped that he didn't have a concussion or worse.

As they entered the walled clearing, they noticed a sickly sweet aroma. The source of the smell soon became obvious. The famished people, some of them having no solid food for days, fought their way to the piles upon piles of fruit stacked within the compound. They proceeded to grab all they could carry, not knowing when they would eat again. Many persons, although starving, chose to bypass the crowd and sought out any private place to take care of more personal business.

Avraham stepped up to a pile and picked up some of the fruit, sharing it with Kahn and Deanna. Reluctantly, he took a bite and found it was the same food they'd eaten on the ship. He personally loathed the sickly sweet taste, but forced himself to chew and swallow it anyway. His nausea, which he'd had since awakening on the ship, grew worse with each day. Much of the time, what he ate came back up, but food was food, and in their case, food was life. He followed his friends to a tree near the wall and sat down, reclined against a half-rotted log. It actually felt good, its softness falling away beneath his weight. His head ached, but he was growing used to it. He closed his eyes, knowing that something was very wrong inside it. The only comforting thought regarding the pain was that relief would come eventually in one form or another.

Deanna looked into his eyes with sadness. She and Kahn had tried to make him as comfortable as they could on the Thalosian ship, but their kindness could do little. She knew that he must be seriously injured. A bruise, which they could not see in the darkness, covered his right temple. His right eye had turned dark red. Both discolorations stood out starkly against his white skin. Avraham needed help soon, or it may be too late.

She sat and watched the hundreds of persons scrambling over the dwindling food. Some of them, covered in filth and excrement didn't even look human any longer. She thought it incredible how civilized people could be reduced to such a condition in so little time. Did she look as bad as some of the animals she watched? She leaned against the wall under the limited shade of a tree, not knowing that her missing friends sat under another.

Gary studied their surroundings and shook his head, wondering how it all could have happened. His wandering gaze finally rested on the two women beside him. Seeing Colleen's sister made him think of how close she had come to not being with them. How with one innocent bite of the poisonous fruit, she could have been gone. Then it hit him, how real this was and how easy it could be to die here. The compound around them looked ancient. He wondered if the Belaquins taken in the first war had been here and how hopeless they must have felt. How long did they pray for the rescue that never came?

There had to be a way out, over the wall, through the water, or at night. They needed to be patient for now. With the limited number of Thalosians visible, though armed, it wouldn't be that difficult to overrun them, but it would take the cooperation of many to work. How could he or anyone possibly organize the thousands of persons around him, half of them elderly, the other half nearly paralyzed with fear? No, it would be better to wait.

His eyes wandered again to the wall. It was fully twenty-five feet tall and angled inward at the top, ruling out an easy climb. Some of the trees branches reached well above its top. Would it be possible to gain the crest that way?

As he looked toward the gate, Colleen noticed him. "Thinking of getting out of here?" she asked, taking a bite of fruit.

"Always," he answered.

"Even if we got out, where would we go?"

"I know. I think getting out would be the easy part."

Colleen changed the subject. "Do you think they know about us yet?" she asked.

"They know." Gary noted her less than optimistic expression. "They'll come after us, maybe in a few days. If not, we'll find Kahn and the others before we try anything."

"If they're still alive," Colleen added sadly.

Gary nodded in agreement. "If they're alive …" He withheld his notion that what happened on Shannate might have happened on Belaquin and other planets as well. It was possible that there was no one left to come to their rescue. The idea was hard to fathom, but had to be given some consideration.

In the following hour, Colleen and Gary talked in length to Kelsey and learned what had turned her into the frightened, paranoid state in which they had found her. She took her time and tried to tell the nightmare as best she could.

She had exited a casino elevator, ready to begin her shift for the night when the aliens first entered. Immediately, she saw people running and heard the screaming. Laser fire and explosions forced her to return to her apartment. Repeatedly, she tried to call someone on the main floor, but got no answer. The chaos visible in the streets below her seventeenth floor window proved that something very serious was going on. She activated the auto lock on her door when she heard trouble on her own floor, assuring her safety. Soon after, the door and much of the wall around it was smashed inward. Her last conscious vision was of some horrible creatures coming toward her. At that point she fainted. By the time she came to, her world had changed. She was in the dark room, surrounded by people she had never seen before. It didn't take long for the true nightmare to begin.

She was fine for the first few hours, keeping to herself, staying near where she had awakened. She found that she had not been injured in any way. She had slept most of the day prior to her capture; therefore she had not eaten in a full day. Eventually, it was thirst that forced her to move. She had quickly learned the consequences of standing up. Keeping low, she crawled toward where others had told her water could be found. On the way, she passed through a group of men, maybe ten altogether, who noticed her immediately.

She had crawled unknowingly into their midst, but would not crawl out for a long while. In the darkness, the room echoed with cries of fear, anguish, or pain. Within seconds, her cries were mixed with the others. She felt hands grabbing her arms, her legs, every part of her, holding her down. Then came what she feared the most. Her lower garment was pulled down and they forced her legs apart. She screamed for help with every breath until someone held a hand over her mouth and neck, choking her. After that, it was hard even to breathe. Her strength ebbed. She stopped struggling.

They entered her ... over and over. While one worked over her, at least five of the others held her down. She could do nothing, but wait for the end. Absolutely no one around her would help. In the darkness, they might not have even known what was happening only a few feet away. Finally, it was over. The faceless men disappeared. The last one removed his trembling hand from her mouth. With his face only inches away, she heard him say, "I'm sorry."

She covered her face with her arms and turned on her side in a fetal position. She cried, feeling so much pain, anger and embarrassment that she wanted to die. Fear finally brought her to her senses. Somehow, she found the missing pieces of her clothing and put them on. Some were torn, but manageable. She crawled as far away as possible from the scene of the attack.

It didn't end there. Six days of darkness, with the fear of being found and assaulted again shattered her nerves. She went without food for four of those days, not daring to leave the safety of wherever she was. The only sustenance she received other than water was a handful of grass-like substance and some half eaten fruit that happened to be thrown in her direction.

When she saw the other people running toward the fruit tree, her hunger overpowered everything else. The rest of the story was known. Now, after finding someone she knew and loved, someone who offered safety and compassion, she could begin to regain her composure. All she needed now was some food.

Gary listened to the story, shaking his head in incredulity. He felt sorrowfulness for her and fury for the men responsible. He wanted to help any way he could, but there was nothing he could do? Colleen would take care of her.

He again set his mind to their surroundings, realizing that something didn't fit. Something was missing. The wall was the only form of architecture he had seen on the planet thus far, but it was incredibly crude for such a seemingly advanced race. It was constructed of dried mud and was incredibly hard. In many places, live foliage and trees actually growing from it. It was obvious that the compound was meant to keep them in, but for what purpose? Where were their cities … their industry, or did they have such things? He was surprised at how little he actually knew about the race. His knowledge was limited to military technology and tactics in battle. He knew that their weapons were in some ways more powerful than the Republics. Their fighters were mostly ineffective against Republic raiders. Their single largest disadvantage was the absence of a radar controlled tracking system for their weapons. The Republic's system on the other hand, was a stable and evening factor. Once laser guidance locked on its target, it did not miss.

It was also believed that their space vessels were unable to attain full light speed. Over the years, none of their captured ships had been equipped with the capability. In the air and in space, the Republic easily held the upper hand, but on the ground, where he and the others would eventually have to make a stand, the odds were frighteningly against them. That fight was in the future.

Gary rose to his feet. First, he had to find his missing friends, if they were even there. Looking at the endless crowd, he knew that it would be easier to find three single stars on the clearest night.

Leon Haute felt sure that he knew what the alien's intentions had been all along. The cargo ship must have been a decoy to attract attention for the time needed to carry out their invasion. If he was right, it meant that they knew about the base on Touchen.

That possibility was the only fact that didn't fit his conclusions. They could not have known. The only other explanation was that the ship stumbled upon Touchen by accident, obviously after losing track of the main force. Fortunately, it had not landed on Belaquin. His memories drifted back to another time, when they first encountered the insect race, a meeting that never should have happened.

They were discovered completely by accident. A geological survey party happened upon the system when they followed up on a routine scanner contact. Initially thought to be a metallic asteroid, they ignored it until it suddenly altered course. They never got close enough to see it, but they were sure it was a ship. The contact led them to an unexplored region. The crew charted a system with at least twenty-one planets, two of which proved capable of sustaining life. One of those two however, proved to be already occupied. The crew managed to remain unseen, but the information they recorded was unbelievable.

Other expeditions followed, to study the only other intelligent life form ever found. There was never any interference. For several months, many trips were successfully completed, but eventually a ship failed to return. Its last transmission led to the conclusion that it had never left Thalosia. A rescue party was sent as soon as possible. What they found raised more questions than answers.

The rescue of the surviving members of the ill-fated mission was heralded as heroic, and the prisoners who returned told fantastic tales. They had been held for several weeks, never dreaming that they would ever get out alive. Most information on Thalosian life came from those survivors. Unexpectedly, a dramatic discovery came about which puzzled all involved. Twenty-one crewmembers were originally captured and held on Thalosia. Seventeen were still alive when the rescue ship arrived. Two additional captives were lost during the rescue, but a total of nineteen humans were brought back alive. What was puzzling was the fact that four extra people were rescued. These four white males had not been a part of the captured crew.

The men appeared to be normal human beings in every respect. They had obviously been imprisoned for an extended time. It was suggested that these men were not from Belaquin and that they had originated from another planet yet undiscovered.

Numerous findings concerning the four individuals aroused speculation. They had no discernible language, but did manage to communicate with one another. Intelligence levels were far below even grade school children. It was almost as if they had come straight out of the Stone Age.

Another suggestion was that they had been captured as children, prior to Thalosia's discovery, and had lived in the compound their entire lives. The men were estimated to be from twenty to twenty five years old when taken from Thalosia. In the first few months, with the proper care, they had learned to speak, read, and write. They had no memories of any place before Thalosia. The mystery of their origin had always remained a mystery.

New theories arose with the recent finding of old Earth. It was a definite possibility they had come from there. If so, this bolstered the belief that there had been survivors other than the Kograns. William Vient had mentioned intelligent, but hostile contacts. They were probably human, but they had never seen or investigated them. There could indeed be a connection.

The rescued survivors had other incredible stories from below ground. The four mysterious men had not been the only other human beings seen. They were rumored to number in the hundreds, ranging in age from teenagers to older adults. None seemed to have the power of speech, and made no hint of recognition or understanding when approached.

These humans were used as slaves, carrying Thalosian eggs from birthing chambers to hatching rooms. The knowledge of these individuals was not released to the public for some time and for good reason. It was the opinion of the Belaquin council at that time, that these humans could not have been from Belaquin, and even if they had been, the Republic was ill prepared for a rescue mission of that magnitude. When the news did break, the battle between right and wrong was long and tedious. In the end, right or wrong, no rescue mission was sent. The knowledge of their existence did however, prompt the long-range missions to search for other life.

The previous rescue mission, unfortunately, brought repercussions that could not have been imagined or reversed. The Thalosians searched for, and finally found the Belaquin system. It was then that the first war began. That had been three decades before. The Republic forces had been decimated. If the aliens had known how much so, they would have no doubt finished the job.

Haute's thoughts returned to the present. He read the most recent report. Between eighteen and twenty thousand missing was the revised estimate. It was impossible to imagine. It had taken over two decades for them to return, but now they had with vengeance. They had repeated history, but this time, they would not survive their actions. There were at least twenty-five Republic personnel included in the missing. He was sure that at least two of them, if they were alive, were already looking for a way out.

The days passed slowly for those aboard the Aquillon. At top speed it took nearly four days to reach the Thalosian system. It was estimated that they arrived roughly two days after the prisoners.

Haute watched Thalosia fill the view screen. He sighed, remembering. He had been here once before and would never forget it. He had been young, ready for action, yearning for adventure, nothing to lose, everything to gain. He traveled here on a rescue mission, the famous mission. He remembered the day very well … the slave pens … the giant caverns. He remembered more than anything, how desperate he was to leave it all behind. The mission was successful in the sense that they got back as many of the surviving prisoners as possible. It was also a failure, caused by inadequate intelligence and unforeseen circumstances. Half their force was lost in the hurried retreat through the forests. They had underestimated the insect's ferocity, as well as their desire to retain their prisoners, which they seemed willing to kill rather than let escape. They did so with no hesitation.

It had been almost thirty years, but he remembered the hills, the same hills where the Shannation people were believed to be held. He remembered the caves leading to hundreds of tunnels, honeycombed with thousands of egg chambers.

It was wondered why humans were utilized for work in those chambers. Did their short life span have anything to do with it? Their livelihood was balanced on a narrow path, forcing them to be careful and precise. It was believed that if the egg hatching time tables were interrupted, for more than one stage, it could cause irrevocable damage. They monitored their laying and kept the population controlled. The Republic knew that if the Thalosians wished to, their numbers they could easily take over all adjoining systems. Their forces would be so incredibly staggering that in a surprise attack, no weapon known could conceivably stop them.

It was Haute's belief that this was possibly what the insect race was about to do. Maybe they needed human slaves to help amass a force impossible to withstand. The Republic could not take that chance. They had to stop them before they reached a stage where they couldn't be. Perhaps they had already reached it. If the Republic forces were being lured into a trap, they would find out soon enough.

He knew in theory what they had to do. The only way to retrieve the prisoners was to travel to the planet surface, find them, and force them from the alien grasp. It was a direct plan, open for change, and riddled with frightening unknowns. To be successful it would take the coordinated effort of the entire fleet and much, much luck. Haute knew the insects tactics, and also knew that many Shannations would never see home again.

Hopefully, finding the people would not be difficult with the Aquillon's scanners. If the thousands of prisoners had been divided into groups around the planet, then the chance of complete recovery was nearly impossible. Haute had argued this possibility to the council, but had been ignored. He believed that the Thalosians hadn't had time for a division, and all would still be held in one region. The reliance on this hope meant everything.

An hour later, in his cabin, Haute called the control room. "This is Commander Haute. Patch me in to the commander of the lead transport vessel."

Commercial transport ships, some twenty-five of them, had followed the seven warships and were just entering the system. Civilian transportation was the main function of these ships in the Belaquin system. In the past week, while waiting for the unfinished Aquillon Three, the transporters, one of every three in existence in the Republic, had been called into service. They were modified to carry extra fuel and were equipped with temporary facilities to accommodate more than one thousand passengers each. They would be somewhat cramped, but there was no other alternative. If everything went as planned, the passengers would have food, water, and medical attention available immediately. In less than a week, the people would hopefully be back with their families.

A moment later, a voice answered Haute. "Commander Haute, this is Commander Hedge, what can I do for you."

"Just be ready, Commander. If we get them out … when we get them out, we'll need you down there as quickly as possible. How far out are you?"

"About three hours sir."

"Good, then I'll be able to start operations as planned."

"Luck to you Commander, I'll position my ships and await your orders."

"I hope to send them soon. Thank you." As the comm went dead, the tired man put his head in his hands, thinking about the hours to come, wishing there was an easier way to do what he must do. There was a special meeting of the Belaquin council soon after the fleet's departure to decide certain delicate issues. He had no word of those decisions as yet, but he did know the subject of the discussion and the possible closure. Whatever it was would be final. There would be no arguing over this great expanse of space. He thought that the questions mulled over by the council should be better off decided by the military men, but what he thought didn't matter now. He must follow the orders, no matter what.

That answer came within the hour. Steven Sievers aged face appeared on the screen in a taped transmission, the only sure way for the argumentative man to get the last word in.

The Aquillon's commanding officer listened to the orders. Initially, he wished to discuss the decision, but after he had heard their reasoning and alternative options, he reluctantly accepted it. The decision was severe, merciless, but admittedly the only way to ensure the future safety of the Republic and its people.

Leaving his cabin, Haute went directly to the control room. As the door opened, no one bothered to look up, each person absorbed in his or her duties. The green and blue planet filled the lower part of the view screen. It looked much like the newly discovered Earth. The beautiful Earth, however, did not provide a home for such a cold-blooded race of creatures. In the past it may have been similar in its ruthlessness, but that had changed, as history would be changed today.

He wondered if the inhabitants below knew that his ships orbited their planet. They couldn't be naive enough to think that humans cared so little for one another that there would be no rescue attempt, or at least retaliation? But then again, maybe they weren't naive at all. Maybe it was the Republic that was naive to think that it could do as it wished. Maybe the Thalosians lay in wait to finish the second half of their plan. Should this venture have been thought out a little more, with that aspect taken into consideration?

It was too late now. It had already begun. In the end, there could be only one outcome. The Republic must prevail. There was little choice in that matter. There was everything to gain, but also everything to lose. He had orders in hand. Even though he agreed with them, it would be a great tragedy to carry them out. In a sense, the Thalosians had sealed their own fate years ago. They had neglected to finish the job. The Republic would not neglect that duty today. He walked slowly to his command chair, sighed and sat down. It was time. "Intra ship communications, fleet wide." His voice was calm, but hesitant, as it should have been.

"You have fleet wide, sir."

"To all Republic ships, this is Fleet Commander Leon Haute. I am addressing every man and woman on this mission. All of you know why we are here. We're here to save our people. Some are our shipmates, some are our friends, and some are our family. This is no doubt, the hardest task we have ever undertaken, but no matter the difficulty ... we cannot hesitate or falter in our goal, not against these beings. Some of us know this first hand. We have been here before and we'll never forget." He looked around the room. All eyes were on him. His voice grew solemn. "Many more our people may die today. There is only one way to change that fact, and that is for us to turn around and go back. If we leave now, we can never go home, and neither will any of the people waiting for us. We aren't here to help them because it's our job. It's deeper than that, I hope."

"Those creatures down there don't care about human life. We do. We have to be strong and unyielding even in the face of death. If we do that, then we will prevail." He paused for a brief moment. "I have received additional orders from the Belaquin council. They have concluded that the Thalosian race has again committed an undisputed act of war. The kidnapping and killing of the people on Shannate was senseless and unprovoked. Upon recovery of our people, a factor four retaliatory strike is authorized and is to be initiated."

It was obvious that the members in the control room couldn't believe what they had just heard. Haute could see reservation in some faces, but agreement in most. He spoke on. "I have no doubt that the Thalosians know we are coming. They may already be prepared. We have to be ready. They killed our people to keep them from being taken before. There's no reason to think that they won't do it now. All ships, all crews ... stand by. Good luck. May God be with all of us today."

CHAPTER 13

▼

On the planet surface, things hadn't gone too badly for the prisoners. On the first day in the enclosure, Gary had spent the majority of the time attempting to locate their missing friends. Unlike on the Thalosian ships, the prisoners were not kept silent, nor were they kept from moving about. These tiny bits of freedom offered an opportunity. Gary walked, yelling Kahn's name, over and over. He had instructed Colleen and her sister to remain where they were so that he could find them again easily.

Kahn was dozing, his head on Deanna's lap, when a voice stood out above the rest. He was sure, even in his half conscious condition, that he had heard his name called. It had been a mans voice and could only be one person. He sat bolt upright. "Did you here that?"

Avraham was already standing. "I heard it, but where did it come from?"

Kahn stood and yelled. "Gary Kusan!"

The response was immediate. "Kahn!"

Deanna jumped to her feet, screaming with joy. "We're over here!"

Within seconds, Gary appeared from the crowd. Kahn met him first and gave him a huge hug that was followed with one from Deanna. Avraham offered a welcoming handshake.

Kahn was euphoric. "Jesus Christ, I thought you were dead. Where's Colleen?"

"She's over on the other side with her sister."

Avraham was concerned. "Kelsey? Thank God! Is she all right?"

"She will be. She's had it kinda rough," he answered. "C'mon let's go before we get moved."

The reunion was rejuvenating. Each party had been sure that the other was lost. They all promised to stay together, no matter what. Together, they waited.

It was still early on the first day when the alien's intentions became clear. Soon after lunch was finished, activity began at the upper end of the pen, nearest the hills and caverns. It appeared that hundreds more Thalosians had entered the pen and were attempting to move prisoners towards the cave entrances. Not many of the frightened people were cooperating. The entrances were slightly uphill from where the Albatross' crew stood, and they could see easily what was transpiring. When people resisted, the insects began to use more forceful methods to move them. They began to beat those closest to them. At one point a large group of thirty or forty men attacked a group of Thalosians and finally overpowered their fewer numbers.

Kahn had the best view, standing high on a pile of wood. He hoped this was the beginning of the escape, but that hope vanished as he and the others watched what happened next. From atop one of the small peaks overlooking the caverns, an abrupt end came to the tiny rebellion. Laser fire poured down on the pen, directed towards the unruly mob. Humans, as well as insects were cut down where they stood. Even some not involved were injured or killed. The area cleared instantaneously, leaving only the dead and injured to be seen. The pen echoed with screams. More Thalosians exited the caverns, walked into the melee of fallen bodies, finishing off any persons still alive.

Gary and the others watched helplessly, horrified at what they had just witnessed. Any idea that he had entertained concerning fighting against the aliens fewer numbers was forgotten. He knew now that there was nothing that could be done. To resist the aliens would bring about certain death.

Then the herding began. Throngs of people moved steadily towards the water, creating a mass of bodies pushing all before them.

Kahn, still shocked by the needless murders, thought fast. "We've got to move."

Deanna moved to stand with Colleen and Kelsey. All three were visibly upset. "What are they doing?" they asked.

Gary thought he knew, "I know they use humans to move their eggs, down in the tunnels," A hint of panic was discernable as he spoke again. "… but we can't be sure. Shit, they could take us down there for anything."

Avraham was the only person in the group still calm among the action. "I don't think they want us all dead, just the troublemakers. If they wanted to exterminate us, they would have done it on Shannate." He looked at Gary. "I think you're probably right. They want us to work."

Kahn spoke his opinion. "That's fine, but what if you're wrong?"

"Then we die down there," answered Gary.

"Or we can resist and surely die up here." Avraham added with finality.

The multitude of people began to move quickly past, crowding closer to the wall. Soon they would be caught up in the mass. Their dilemma was answered by more laser fire from the opposite side of the pen. People, who had already entered the water, trying to swim to freedom, didn't have a chance. The water boiled as laser fire poured into it.

Kahn fought with the dilemma, but there was no choice. To try to escape now was suicide. It would be better to take their chances in the tunnels. "We've got no place to go. Maybe we should just do what they want, at least for now."

The others agreed, locked arms against the crowd and stood, waiting. Eventually, they were forced in the direction of the caverns and into the unknown.

For what seemed like forever, they walked downward into the tunnels. Some of the way was lit, some was not. They stayed together, not taking any chance of getting separated. Gary tried to keep track of the direction, but with the periods of light and darkness, he couldn't be sure of anything. He finally admitted that it was a waste of time.

It was noticed at first, that the cave interior was much cooler than the outside, but the deeper they went, the warmer it became. A constant breeze blew inward from above to gratefully cool the temperature. After a while, they began to meet other people moving in the opposite direction. Each carried dirty white, egg shaped objects, roughly two feet long. Some cried, some spoke, and some smiled, overjoyed to see the new arrivals, but Thalosian guards were everywhere, and the people did not stop.

The smiles they wore looked forever out of place. They were filthy, most of them wearing only remnants of clothing. Their appearance brought horrified expressions from some of the new prisoners, each wondering if they would also be reduced to that state. Avraham was one of those persons. "Where the hell did they come from?"

Deanna, immediately in front of him, shook her head. "I don't know, but they've been here a long time."

Kelsey, arm in arm with her sister, spoke for the first time since entering the tunnels, "We can't stay here. We can't end up like them ..."

Colleen comforted her, but felt sick with the same fears. "Let's hope we're not here long enough."

They eventually reached their destination. An enormous subterranean room lay before and beneath them, hundreds of feet from ceiling to floor and ten times that to the opposite wall. A hundred lights above lighted the chamber floor. It was an incredible sight. Thousands of insects could be seen entering and exiting small openings off the floor. Just as many humans could be seen, entwined among their captors. Only Thalosians came from these outreaching tunnels, each carrying an egg. In turn, a human would take the egg, and follow what the hapless travelers discovered was a seemingly endless cycle. They carried the egg from this chamber to another and returned to begin the cycle again. The Thalosians maintained perfect order.

So that was the routine. They had become a living assembly line of slaves. When half the prisoners were confined to the penned area to sleep and eat, the other half was below in the caverns, working. The insects never tired. They were everywhere, prodding constantly, forcing them to carry the thousands upon thousands of eggs. Soon, the newcomers grew used to the repetitiveness. The shifts were from seven to eight hours in length. The tunnels were filled with people and insects, going back and forth, every hour of the night and day.

Somehow, the crew of the Albatross managed to stay together. They had ended their fourth shift in the tunnels and were heading back toward the surface for a few hours of sleep. Their legs ached from miles of walking and their throats were choked with dust. After carrying the eggs, their arms were like jelly and hung limply at their sides. The Thalosians didn't see it, but there was no need to guard the prisoners as closely as they did. No one had the strength to escape.

As they thankfully reached the fresh air above, they moved quickly to the same area they had rested at each time. They did not return there for its comfort however. Kahn had discussed it with the others and all agreed that there was no chance of getting away while underground. Even if they managed it, they had nowhere to go. The maze of tunnels would be impossible to negotiate. He and Avraham had found a weak point in the wall. It was in an area partially concealed by live vegetation. A small section of the wall had been torn away, obviously an attempt by someone to make an exit through the dried mud, but the digging did not seem recent. The digger or diggers had either given up, or had stopped for other reasons. Kahn and Gary took up where the unknown party had left off. The chance that it could be discovered troubled them constantly while they were below ground, but it was better to chance that, rather than split up into shifts to guard it. Separation was a chance they wouldn't take.

After several hours of digging, the outside of the wall was reached. They could easily crawl through the hole one at a time. Several problems presented itself now. They were on a hostile alien planet, millions of miles from home, with means of escape, but nowhere to go. They had no weapons and had no idea what waited outside the wall. It had been agreed that they should leave during the night hours, but the insects, no doubt, had excellent nocturnal vision.

Even though it was daylight, it seemed the perfect time. The number of guards usually in the area was now low. Only three Thalosians were within a hundred meters, actually too close to chance it. A different decision was made.

"I thought we were going to wait?" Kelsey asked, somewhat uncomfortable with the sudden change in plans.

Kahn answered her. "We were. But night or day, if we've got a good chance, we've gotta go. Avraham's headaches are getting worse. If we go now, we can at least see where we're going."

Colleen added. "He's right sis." She motioned to Avraham. "He needs rest and he can't get it in here. Every time we go down in those tunnels, we take a chance of not coming back out. They might even move us somewhere else. We just don't know."

Kelsey nodded in agreement, even though she felt that if they were caught outside, they would be killed. "You're right; we better go while we can."

Gary noticed that mentally, she had gotten much better over the last couple of days. She still carried bruises from the assault, but at least inside she seemed to be healing. He added his opinion. "Well, if we go, we either have to wait for them to take a break," he gestured towards the nearest guards only thirty feet away, "Or we have to create a diversion."

Resting as still as possible, Avraham spoke without moving. "That might not be so good." The others turned towards him. "Look, I know I've got something slightly wrong with me, but it's not worth getting hurt or killed just to get me some sleep. I think it's going to take a little more than that to fix me, and whatever that might be, is not out there."

Kahn nodded. Avraham but was right, but he was also wrong. Republic forces, if they were able, were coming for them. It was the only hope they had to hold on to. He knew it was possible that Shannate hadn't been the only planet attacked. It was also possible that there may be no rescue coming, depending on how bad the Republic was hit. He forced himself to dismiss both ideas. They were coming, he could feel it. The decision was simple. If they waited in the compound, they would eventually be herded back underground. If the rescue arrived during that time, they might be trapped below, or killed before they could get out. Avraham was right about the diversion. It wouldn't be good to cause any commotion. He was wrong about his injury though. It was far from slight. It was easy to see that he was growing weaker by the day. It would be wrong to wait. They had to go.

Kahn knew that someone needed to make the final decision. He hesitantly elected himself. "All right, here's what we do. We don't wait ... we can't. Once through the wall, we won't be missed, but we have to do it without being seen." The others realized what he meant. It was crucial that no insect or human witness the escape. No one other than their group of six knew of the tunnel. It was imperative that it was kept it that way. If others found out, it would spread like wild fire through the enclosure. Leaving these people behind wasn't what any of them wanted, but it was the only way.

Finally, the chance came. Surprisingly, all visible guards moved away towards the gate, leaving the perfect opportunity. There was no other guard close enough to worry about.

Kahn stood and took a final look around. Most people were sleeping. Some crowded around the food and water. No one seemed to be paying any attention to them at all. Without turning around, he said. "Gary, you go first, check the other side. The rest of you go one at a time. I'll come last."

While the others stood in front, partially blocking their actions, Gary and Colleen slipped through the vine covering and entered the wall. The wall interior was a mass of broken sticks and dried mud. From the outside, it looked sturdy, but was far from it. Once in the small crawlspace, Gary could already see sunlight filtering through from the other side. The crawl was a short twenty feet.

Carefully, Gary punched through the thin outside layer. As he hoped, forest growth grew up close to the wall. The green cover was more than adequate. He poked one hand through and pulled down, scraping away the sides of the hole, making it big enough to permit him to pass. Cautiously, he put his head out. As far as he could see, there was no sign of anyone or anything. He returned to the inside and relayed through Colleen that the way was clear. One by one, they entered the tunnel.

Kahn eventually followed, drawing the vines together to cover the hole. The entire process had taken less than a minute. As far as they knew, no one had seen the escape. They were on their own.

Within minutes, they were moving slowly through the open forest, paranoid that they were being watched, sure that aliens would arrive at any moment. The forest was primeval, the trees massive, with heights reaching well over two hundred feet. Staying hidden as much as possible, they made it across the valley floor to the hills. The farther they went, the higher their confidence became. The way up the steep slope wasn't easy. Some bushes were filled with thorns.

For almost an hour, they pushed uphill and finally the ground leveled out. Also, the forest thinned and gave way to the rows of trees they had seen earlier.

They stood on the edge of a huge orchard. Walking would be easier, but cover was sparse. The clearing where they had first landed was believed to be near. They had decided to find it and remain close to await possible rescue. Finally, exhausted, they took a break, staying in the denser brush to rest. The soft undergrowth and leaves felt wonderful after the metal of the ship and dirt of the pen.

Colleen lay down, just wishing to close her eyes for a few moments. The minutes turned to an hour. When she awoke, she checked on Avraham, who had lain down near by. He breathed heavily, loudly. She shook him gently, but he would not awaken. Kelsey tried as well, but he remained unresponsive. "Avraham won't wake up," she informed Gary and Kahn.

Gary went to their side and checked him. He'd had some medical training, but no more than the rest. He seemed to be breathing fine, but upon checking his eyes, he found one of his pupils much larger than the other. All he knew was that it was another sign of a serious head injury. He shook his head at Colleen. "All we can do is pray that they get here soon, babe, there's nothing else we can do."

It was a unanimous decision to spend the night where they were. No one knew exactly what to do next, but they did agree that they would not leave their friend. If they were forced to move, then he would go with them. Once dusk approached, some familiar fruit was gathered. It held much needed water as well.

The night passed uneventfully. At first light, they found that Avraham had not moved, and still could not be awakened. Kahn made a quick survey, and as far as they could tell, they were still alone in the forest. He decided to make short ventures to see what was around them. Deanna went with him. Only a hundred steps from the others, he stopped and held up his hand. "Do you hear that?"

By the time he asked, the sound had grown loud enough for all to hear. A low whine emanated from somewhere, growing louder, or closer, or both.

Gary, still at the edge of the orchard, recognized the unique sound. "It sounds like …!" The whine was instantly right above them, drowning his words. It was a Republic raider, screaming towards the Thalosian compound. At the speed it was traveling, it would be there in seconds.

Before anyone could say anything, laser fire carried through the trees. Kahn and Deanna moved quickly, but watchfully toward the sound. Their wariness was warranted. They stopped several times as small groups of Thalosians moved hurriedly past. The groups moved roughly in the compounds direction and possibly near Gary and the others, but there was no way to warn them. Hopefully, they would be passed by unseen.

Finally, familiar territory was found. At the edge of the trees, they witnessed an incredible sight. Raiders and shuttles filled the clearing around and between the huge alien transports. Dozens more flew far overhead, some heading towards the valley. Republic troops, after a brief exchange of fire, had captured the Thalosian ships.

Leaving the forest behind, the two former prisoners, delirious with relief, were met by several Republic personnel. The first words out of Kahn's mouth sounded much like an order. "We've got a man back there that needs immediate medical attention."

One man answered. "Uh, okay, but who are you?"

"Lieutenant Bengal, a gold pilot from the Aquillon. We were on shore leave to Shannate when we were taken." explained Kahn.

"You and a lot of others … you escaped?"

"Yes … last night."

"Where's the man you're talking about?" asked an officer, signaling for some troops to come up.

"There are four people straight through the trees. Thalosians were moving that way!"

The officer relayed instructions to the men who had joined them, then spoke again to Kahn. "We have a shuttle waiting for you. It'll be safer there."

Kahn looked to Deanna. "Get on the ship. I'm going to take them to the others."

She started to shake her head, but Kahn spoke again. "There's no discussing it, I will be right behind you. We need to get to them as soon as we can."

She nodded in agreement, kissed him, and turned towards the ships. Kahn turned back towards the orchard, to lead the men to where the others thankfully, still waited. Within minutes, the still unconscious Avraham was aboard a medical ship under a doctor's care.

Colleen and Kelsey were taken to the shuttle Deanna had boarded. Kahn and Gary asked to see whoever was in charge. They were led to an older officer, obviously an infantryman by his dress.

As they approached, Kahn held out his hand to the man. "I'm Lieutenant Kahn Bengal. This is Ensign Gary Kusan. We're gold raider pilots stationed on the Aquillon. We were taken at Shannate."

"Colonel Leonard Rennick, Commander … first ground assault. They say you escaped last night?"

"Yes sir. We got out pretty easy. We didn't know when to expect you guys," answered Gary. "We'd like to help. We've probably got some information you might need."

"It's appreciated. How many of our people are in this location?"

Kahn shook his head. "Thousands ... we don't know for sure. How many are supposed to be here?"

"Estimates show eighteen thousand plus." Rennick answered.

"My God!" exclaimed both pilots.

"What's the plan?" asked Kahn.

"Plan? We are to use whatever measures necessary to get the prisoners out," explained the officer. "That's the plan. Nothing set in stone. There was too much we didn't know. With their type of communication, a surprise attack was impossible. This whole place knew we were here as soon as we hit these transports. There was no way to tell where all of the prisoners were, too many holes."

Kahn nodded. "Do you have contact with Commander Haute?"

"Yeah," He handed him his hand held communicator. "I've got a direct line."

"Great." Kahn took the device and paused; looking toward the shuttles, then spoke to Gary. "Make sure they get out of here. I don't think they should be here when this starts."

Gary agreed and went towards the shuttle. Boarding the steps, he found the three girls seated, being checked by medical personnel. "Any word on Avraham?"

Colleen shook her head. "Not yet."

He looked at Kelsey, who now sported a splint device on her injured arm. "Was it broken?"

She smiled. "They're not sure yet. It might be." She paused, noticing that he was still half dressed. She pulled at the shirt she wore. "Do you want this back?"

Gary smiled, remembering how little she wore underneath. "No, I think you'd better keep it."

Their attention was drawn to a man dressed in hospital scrubs approaching them. Colleen recognized him as one of the doctors that had been with Avraham. He spoke even before she could ask. "We need to get him to surgery. He's got an intra-cerebral bleed. It builds pressure within the skull, which accounts for his unconsciousness. I've given him medication to try to decrease the swelling."

"That's bad, right?" asked Deanna.

"I won't lie to you ... it's about as bad as it can get. I can't believe he's made it this long."

His words cut through Colleen and the others like a hot knife. Her voice was shaky as she asked what she had to, "Is he going to die?"

The doctor nodded. "He could. He will for certain, if we don't get him out of here." His eyes housed genuine sadness. "I'm sorry." He then turned and left.

Colleen turned into Gary's waiting embrace. He tried to comfort her. "I'm sorry, babe." He pushed her away so that he could see her face. He saw reddened eyes, hurt and tired. "Listen to me. You three are going back with him ... out of danger. Kahn and I are staying here for now"" He glanced at Deanna, who nodded her support for at least part of the plan.

Colleen however, didn't support anything. "Why are you staying?"

"We're the only one's who have been down there. You know that. We have to help get those troops in there. The longer we wait, the worse it could be." He looked into her eyes. Tears streaked her dirty cheeks. "I'll be okay. Stay with Deanna and your sister."

Colleen pulled him close, hugging him so tightly he could barely breathe. "You come back to me."

"I will ... I promise. I'll aggravate you for the rest of your life." He kissed her forehead, her nose, and finally, her lips. "I love you," he whispered.

"I love you more," she answered. She watched him leave without looking back, then turned to Deanna and held her, sobbing.

Rejoining Kahn, Gary was tossed a shirt by one of several soldiers who had assembled. Within the last few moments, Kahn had spoken in length to a relieved Commander and had provided several bits of needed information. Information from other sources had also filtered in. All of the prisoners from the pen were now underground, driven there during the initial attack on the Thalosian ships. Raider pilots reported many people dead, again evidently slaughtered for non-compliance.

Rennick explained one of the problems they had anticipated. "We considered blowing up the cavern entrances while most of the people were still outside, but figured that would sacrifice whoever was still below ground."

Kahn confirmed his thinking. "It's a good thing you were behind the trigger. Only half of our people were out."

The Colonel nodded. "Good. Now we have to hope they don't blow the tunnels themselves."

"Then we need to move fast?" Gary added.

"Exactly," answered the older man.

Kahn spoke to Gary. "Are they leaving?" He referred to the shuttle.

"Yeah," he frowned, "I don't think Avraham's gonna make it."

Kahn shook his head. He had already suspected it. "Well, he would appreciate what's going to happen then."

Gary looked puzzled.

Kahn continued, "After our people are out of here, they're doing a factor four on this place. It's all history."

Gary was surprised, not that he disagreed with the extreme measure. "What about the laws?"

"They consider them to be an ultimate threat to the future of our people. The council says this will prevent further retaliation. They killed over three thousand people on Shannate. Look at their egg chambers? If they come back and attack us with those kinds of numbers, they could take Belaquin ... probably our whole system."

Gary agreed. "There's no way we could stop them."

Behind them, they heard a shuttle starting to power up. It was the medical ship carrying Colleen, Deanna, Kelsey, and Avraham. Within seconds it rose and passed over them. Gary waved, unknowing if the passengers saw him. He remembered his promise. The white ship disappeared over the treetops.

A different officer approached them at that point and handed each of them jackets similar to what the infantry soldiers were wearing. "These are energy displacement jackets. They'll stop a short direct laser hit. I won't say you won't get hurt, but it'll keep you from getting killed."

Another soldier brought weapons and harnesses. That man's nametag read Rudolf. "These are the standard issue rifles ... extra packs too. Rennick doesn't want you going in until it's clear in the compound. Raiders have taken out the overhead positions you told him about. Don't know if there are any more."

Kahn had a thought. "Someone said the enclosure was full of Thalosians."

Rudolf adjusted the straps on Gary's jacket. "Right now there's a shit load of them."

"Why not take them out with one of your big bombs or something like that?" suggested the senior pilot.

"We sent raiders in, but ground fire took two of them out. The only thing we have to handle an area that big is a pulser, but we're afraid the concussion might collapse the tunnels."

Kahn's eyebrows lifted. Any typical ground troop would have known that, wouldn't he? He decided he and Gary would do exactly what these men suggested on this trip.

They moved out, following Rennick, staying well behind the bulk of the ground force. The two young men noticed that they walked down the same trail they had followed a few days earlier. They stopped just short of the top of the ridge, allowing a clear, unobstructed view of the compound, roughly five hundred meters away. Smoke rose from several places within the pen and surrounding forest. Other troops continued down the trail, exited from it and disappeared beneath the trees.

Rennick pointed out what they were seeing. "The gate is the only way in or out right now. They've concentrated their defense around there. We're gonna blow it as soon as our guys are in place. We think they're just trying to buy some time, creating some kind of diversion to slow us down. We're going through the wall in at least three other places. Once we're in, you guys will be going down with me. Then the hard part starts."

Gary could see what looked like hundreds of human bodies lying on the floor of the plaza, many near the edge of the water on the far right. He silently thanked Kahn for convincing them to leave when he did. The only moving figures within the walls were alien. He couldn't tell at that distance what they were doing. The openings in the hill were silent. No movement came from the caves.

Below the ridge, in the valley, Rudolf led his squad of twenty men to within two hundred steps of the Thalosian gate. He watched as half a dozen others approached much closer. Those men were to fire the barrage to bring down the obstacle. They stopped, in position and awaited the order.

As Rudolf watched, the unexpected occurred. A searing white explosion rocked the compound and hillside. Even before he could close his eyes from the blinding flash, the shock wave hit him. He felt himself lifted and rocketed backwards along with the men around him.

The blast was tremendous, the concussion felt even by the observers on the ridge above. All trees and vegetation within a hundred yards of the compound gate was swallowed up with fire. Most men within that same proximity were decimated.

Rennick made no immediate move. He used his telescopic headgear to survey the damage. Radio traffic blared, calls for help from below coming through on every channel. He had to admit, he was staggered by what had just happened, but that was no excuse to rush in and be surprised again.

Kahn and Gary were mortified. They had never witnessed an explosion of such magnitude.

Gary was at a loss. "What the hell was that?"

Rennick did not drop his gaze from the gear. "Don't know. It definitely wasn't ours."

"They blew up their own compound?" Gary asked, watching the older officer nod silently.

"Jesus, Colonel, are the pulsers worse than that?" Kahn asked.

"No, they're not. Whatever they used was pretty damn big." Rennick answered.

As the smoke and airborne debris settled, laser fire from a hundred different points reached out from the compound. The gate and much of the wall had disappeared.

In the valley, Rudolf tried to regain his senses. Looking around, all he could see was smoke and fire between him and the Thalosian compound. Most of the forest was gone, trees, bushes and the men who had hid behind them.

Slowly, he realized what had happened. The enemy had blown the gate, and was attacking outside of it now. Streaks of light sizzled past, seeking targets. He could see some of his men returning fire. Figures could be seen coming towards them, walking right past the flames, apparently unaffected by the heat that he could feel even from where he stood. Numerous trees, knocked down by the blast, shielded him. Keying up his communicator, he yelled above the laser fire. "Control, this is Captain Rudolf … what the hell just happened?"

Rennick heard the voice among the others, and answered. "Go to tach three…. Rudolf, go to tach three." He switched channels, listening for an answer.

Rudolf's excited voice came on again, "Colonel Rennick?"

"I'm here Captain. What's your status? Are you hurt?"

"I'm not sure…. I don't think so. Half my men are gone," he said. "Did they set that off?"

"Apparently. If you're not pinned down, you and your men get the hell out of there."

"Affirmative, sir, send out the signal. I'm coming out." He replaced his communicator in its holster, hearing the high-pitched tone sound out. It signaled for all personnel to disengage and retreat.

Rudolf picked out the two insects nearest him, knocked them down with a series of shots, and then ran. He hadn't gone fifty feet, when another explosion detonated to his right. A tree had caught the full brunt of the impact, showering him with thousands of tiny, burning embers; all that remained of the silent witness. Once more, he found himself on the ground, this time with three of his men. Two quickly gained their feet and ran on.

Rudolf grabbed the third man and turned him over, yelling for him to get up. The man beneath him couldn't have answered if he wanted too. Rudolf turned away, releasing the man's jacket. He wanted to throw up. A laser blast had caught the soldier directly in the face, leaving nothing but an unrecognizable mass of charred flesh and bone. The Captain glanced at the man's chest, recognizing the name on the vest.

Wasting no time, he rolled onto his back, and grabbed his communicator once again. "This is Rudolf. Request a strike on the compound gate immediately.

We're being overrun down here!" He could see two Thalosians only ten yards away. They were shooting at something on the ground at their feet. They fired continuously. The Captain prayed their target was already dead. Filling with rage, he fired at the two, unable to watch it any longer. Both insects went down.

Rennick scanned the field. From what he could see, Republic personnel near the gate would be unaffected by a second blast. He couldn't see a living person within a hundred feet of it. He issued the order.

Within seconds, a raider rocketed overhead within a hundred feet of the ground. Descending, it approached the compound. Two small objects were dropped just short of it, exploding on impact with the ground. Waves of invisible force coursed outward through the valley floor, crumbling more of the wall, and killing any Thalosians that stood within two hundred feet.

Rennick waited, watching small rockslides falling from the hills over the caverns. He hadn't wished to use the pulsers, but if the tunnels were going to collapse, they would have done so with the initial explosion. There was no traffic on the radio channels from the valley. From where he stood, he could see no movement inside the pen or from the openings in the hills.

The Colonel started down the trail, telling Gary and Kahn to accompany him. At least fifty soldiers preceded them down the steep slope. He gave orders as he walked. "Spotters, stay sharp. All support move up. Get the medic's in there as soon as it's clear."

The path led them straight into the battlefield. The soldiers advanced slowly. The open trail soon turned into a mass of fallen trees, twisted, entwined and nearly impassible. Giant trees had been thrown down like twigs, exposing, scorched and blackened roots.

Strewn about were the dead, human and Thalosian lying together. The alien's had been literally taken apart by the concussion. White smoke drifted everywhere, making breathing difficult as the men negotiated the desolation. Rennick gave instructions to locate the missing Captain Rudolf.

Kahn and Gary were incredulous. As they looked ahead, they could see what was left of the gate entrance. It had originally been twenty feet wide and was now a gaping hole a hundred feet across.

Three men approached as they reached the compound. Rennick recognized one of them as the missing Captain. He assessed him mentally as well as physically. "Are you hit?"

"I don't think so." Rudolf rolled away his singed sleeve exposing a nasty blackened gash on his elbow. "I guess so. It's not bad, it cauterized itself. The bloods not mine." He referred to the dark wetness on his uniform.

"You're sure?" Rennick pressed.

"Yes sir, I'm fine."

The Colonel, recalling what he had just witnessed from the ridge above, wasn't convinced. "Anyone that survived this, I want checked out, including you, Rudolf."

The Captain did not argue. "Yes sir."

Inside the compound walls, there wasn't much to see. A hundred Thalosians lay in close proximity to the gate area. It seemed there should have been more, but many more lay outside the pen perimeter, scattered in the downed forest.

Raiders entered the compound airspace and drew no fire from the hillsides. Medical shuttles soon followed. Within moments, the floor of the walled area was filled with ships and hundreds of troops. Other than newly arrived Republic personnel, no human remained alive.

Colonel Rennick was eventually lost in the crowd. Kahn and his younger friend watched as the seemingly hundreds of dead men and women were bagged and loaded on the transports.

Kahn shook his head, re-evaluating his decision to return there. He had never been this close to so much death. It was disconcerting. If he made it back in one piece, he would remember this day, and pray to never see another like it. He looked at the raiders passing above him. That's where he belonged. He spoke to Gary. "You know … I don't want to go down there again."

Gary glanced at him and had to admit to himself, "Neither do I, Chief."

"How would it look if we backed out now?" Kahn asked, fishing for support, "It wouldn't be too courageous, would it?"

Gary didn't know how to answer. He wasn't a wise old man with a life's worth of knowledge, but any man would respect the answer he finally gave. "I don't know. I'm not sure if I really know what courage is." He paused, looking toward the caves. "All I know is that I have to go down there and do my best. I know I'm scared. I'm so scared, I want to throw up." He looked at his friend. "If courage is what I feel now.… I don't ever want to feel it again."

Kahn stared at the ground, nodding his head. "When we get in there, we stay together, no matter what."

Gary held out his hand and Kahn took it, firmly sealing the private pact.

As the hour passed, the men sat and watched. During that time, the compound filled with ships and combat ready soldiers, fully laden with weaponry. Did they know what to expect? There was no doubt that they had been briefed, but could they possibly be prepared?

Kahn looked on, proud to be a part of it all. The spectacle of power was indeed impressive. He very much doubted the Thalosians would be so awed.

A lone man finally approached them. He appeared different from the other soldiers. They stood as he came close. The man offered to shake their hands even before he spoke. "Hey, Rennick said I'd find you here. Kusan and Bengal?" The two men nodded. "I'm Commander Jimenez.... SPECAULT.... or special assault. I'm leading the first unit underground. I figured we'd better get acquainted beforehand. I need you both to come with me."

He led them to a shuttle unlike any Kahn or Gary had ever seen. It was smaller than the conventional type, black in color, with many exterior design differences. The man offered no explanation of the ship, simply leading them aboard. Inside the vessel, they found six other men, dressed similarly to Jimenez. The men were readying an unprecedented array of equipment, guns, and accessories. They immediately came to attention as Jimenez entered.

"As you were," he said. They acknowledged his command and continued with their work.

Gary couldn't help notice the uniqueness of each of the six. The men were huge, but not necessarily in height, even though at least two of them were taller than Kahn. It was their stature that he took note of. He had never seen individuals more physically fit. The soldiers were broad shouldered with thick muscles. None wore jackets. The thin suits they did wear were sleeveless and skin tight around the torso.

Jimenez led them into an adjoining room. He sat down, offering seats to them as well. "That was SPECAULT Team one. We'll be the first ones going in, but we don't know what's down there. You do. That's why we need you. Are you up to it?"

Kahn thought about Gary's earlier comments, and gained confidence. "Just tell us what to do."

"Good," Jimenez paused, hesitating for a long moment as he studied them. "I know you both are pilots, Rennick filled me in on that. Have either of you ever been in close quarters combat?"

Gary thought of the experience on Earth, but felt as if that would be tiny in comparison to this. "No sir, nothing like this."

Kahn nodded in agreement.

"We're trained for situations like this, but as well equipped as we are, we've never faced this type of enemy. We can't negotiate, communicate, or anticipate their moves. I won't lie to you; we've never gone up against anything like this, but if things get shitty, we'll adapt and move on. We won't lose it."

Jimenez continued. "We're not sure what's gonna happen down there, but I promise you, getting ourselves back up here alive is our top priority. Those people are important to us, don't get me wrong, but they're not the only ones who want to see their family again, right?" He didn't wait for a response. Rising, he went to the doorway, speaking to his men in the other room. "It's time to join the party, guys."

Each of the six filed into the room, some taking seats, others remaining standing. Kahn had already noted their bulk as well. He respected the dedication that they must adhere to, but he couldn't help thinking that their size, although formidable, may simply make them bigger targets.

Jimenez continued once again. "Gentlemen, this is Lieutenant Kahn Bengal and Ensign Gary Kusan, gold raider pilots from the Aquillon." Glances were exchanged and some nods given, but that was all. "They were underground for a couple of days. Their information may be invaluable to the success of this mission. Any questions pertaining to what we are going to see down there should be addressed to them." He turned to the two pilots. He could tell they were obviously intimidated by the statements, and possibly by his team members. He kept his voice low as he spoke to them. "Don't worry, they're pussycats."

He made his way around the room, stopping briefly beside each man. "This is Geyer ... Trevorne ... Denton ... Simpson ... Racine ... Weaver. I wouldn't trust any of them to date my sister, but I would trust them with her life." The statement brought chuckles from the men, lifting some of the uneasiness from the room. The ice was broken. He spoke on. "Each of us has ten years minimum in special forces service. We use the most advanced weapons known. I doubt if you guys have any idea of what I'm referring to, but you'll know soon enough. We are highly trained in hand-to-hand, explosives, tactics, evasion, and intell. Most importantly, we know how to survive where most would not. That's why we're going in; we have the best chance of survival. I don't expect you two will have to fight, but you have to be ready for anything. Our main mission is to search for and find the main bulk of our people, mark and relay the route for the surface troops. We kill anything non-human, no questions asked; because they're sure as hell gonna try to kill us." He held out his hands, palms up. "That's our story. Now it's your turn. What are we going to find down there?"

Kahn spoke first. "We tried to keep track of the routes we took, but it was impossible. The big tunnels are around twenty feet wide, gradual downhill slopes throughout. It's hard to tell one from the next. There are a hundred intersections and tunnels branching off. The only chamber we saw was the big one where we picked up the eggs. We carried them to several different places, but we always picked them up at the same place. The other tunnels led to chambers that we never saw."

One of the soldiers spoke up. "Is that main chamber big enough to hold eighteen thousand people?"

Gary added. "Easily, it's pretty damn huge."

"How deep are we going?" asked another man.

Gary shook his head. "I don't know. It takes thirty minutes or so to reach the main chamber."

Jimenez thought aloud. "Well, it sounds like this chamber has to be our primary target. If that's where the pick up point was, the laying area has to be close. How did they run it? What was their routine?"

"They lined us up at several places; the Thalosians came out of the smaller tunnels and gave us the eggs. We'd leave the main chamber, always moving up. We'd go wherever they led us, different tunnels, and give the eggs to other Thalosians. They would take them somewhere else. This would go on until they switched us out," explained Kahn.

Gary added. "They divided us up. Half of us would be up here, while the other half was working."

"Another thing ..." Kahn said. "They've got power down there. The main chamber was lighted. Some of the tunnels were too."

"Can they see in the dark?" asked one of the men.

"I'm sure they can," commented Gary, "The lights were probably for us."

"We know they use telepathy of some sort for communication." Jimenez stated. "We're going to have some disadvantages down there." He spoke to his men. "Full gear guys, check your night vision. If we're lucky, our people will be in one place. There's no way we're gonna be able to check every tunnel, but we have to mark them at least." He held up a chrome cylindrical object. "That's what these are for." He flicked the end of the one he held, and it flared, emitting an intense, but non-sparking white light. "They last for eighteen hours. We should easily be in and out by then."

Another man spoke up. "How well can they hear?"

Gary took an educated guess. "Don't know, but at least as well as us."

Jimenez added a comment. "It probably won't matter. As soon as we make initial contact, they'll all know we're down there. It's best to expect a fight going in and coming out."

The two Republic pilots agreed with his prediction. Based on the impressive amount of firearms they'd witnessed in the other room, the team expected the worst.

Jimenez continued his summation. "We can only guess what kind of weaponry we'll be up against. We know they carry rifle type, level two and level three lasers. The twos, we can deal with, but the level threes, we need to avoid." He could see that Kahn and Gary were at a loss. "The level two fires a short, single bolt. Our deflector jackets can divert the blast, and keep it from penetrating. It will knock you on your ass if you're hit directly, might knock you out, but you won't be dead. Their level three is a cutter. If concentrated, it can cut through wood, softer metals, and some rock. I don't have to tell you what it will do to exposed body parts."

The two men listened intently, absorbing any and all advice.

"We know they have explosives. What kind, we don't know. Our mini pulsers should take them out pretty good, if we can get them in range, but we still have to worry about ceiling collapse." He paused to take a message coming in over the Specault channel. It stated that Commander Haute was on his way down.

Fifteen minutes later, he arrived, landing in the compound. He had already learned of the short lived, bloody skirmish.

Rennick met him as he stepped off the ship, bringing him up to date on the progress of the mission, as well as casualty figures. "As you know Leon, all prisoners were taken below ground. We wanted to surprise them, but it just didn't work out that way. We lost one shuttle, two raiders, and thirteen ground troops so far."

Haute was actually relieved when he heard the numbers. "I expected a lot worse Lenny, but this is only the start."

"I know. We're ready for phase two. Specault one is almost ready to go down. You're boys are with them now."

"I would like to see them," Haute requested.

"Follow me." Rennick started through the maze of men and ships. "I never ever thought we'd be back here, Leon."

"Neither did I, Lenny," Haute answered. "Hasn't changed much, has it?"

"No, but we have thank God. We're ready this time."

Haute caught glimpses of the tunnels as they walked and swallowed hard, remembering. "What do you think of the factor four?"

"We shouldn't have had to wait until something like this happened, damn it! We tried to tell'em before!" Rennick raged. "We're gonna lose a shit load of people down here."

"I know … I know," Haute agreed. "It has to end this time."

"Not soon enough for me." Rennick approached the black ship and as he entered, a loud voice was heard. "Officers on deck!"

Everyone within stood immediately at attention. Haute spoke as he stepped in. "There's no need for that, gentlemen."

Rennick smiled, knowing how his long time friend hated some military customs. "Sorry Leon, habits are hard to break. As you were." he said to his men. He introduced his team leader first. "Commander Haute, meet Commander Jimenez, team leader."

"It's an honor to meet you, sir." Jimenez said. His voice held the utmost respect.

"Likewise, Commander. What's your first name?"

"Antonio ... Tony."

"Well Tony, what's the next step?"

"The plan is for your men to try to find the way back to the main chamber. If our people are there, we mark the way and get them out, hopefully, with minimal losses."

Haute added a personal memory. "You know they'll use the prisoners against us?"

"Yes sir, we've heard. We're going to have to play it by ear if it comes to that." He revealed one possibility. "We hope to make them forget about our people."

"And how is that?" Haute asked.

"Start taking away what they care about the most."

Haute's eyes widened with understanding.

At that point Gary and Kahn entered, unseen by Haute. The latter placed his hand on the older mans shoulder, startling him. "Hey, hook this old man up too, he can go along."

Haute turned to see his two friends. Kahn smiled and shook his hand.

"Where are the girls, are they all right?" Haute asked, greeting Gary as well.

"They're fine. They should be back at the Aquillon by now." Gary answered.

"Thank God you're all alright. When I found out where you'd gone and you didn't answer the call back, I figured the worst."

"You always think that," quipped Kahn. "I guess we were lucky."

"Again," added Haute. "Speaking of the ship, did you hear the Aquillon Three was here?"

The two pilots were surprised and impressed. "How? It wasn't supposed to be ready for months."

Haute shrugged his shoulders. "Necessity breeds miracles." He paused, changing subjects. "What about you guys, are you sure you're up to this?" He didn't agree with letting them participate in the entry, but understood the reasoning.

Rennick knew well of his personal relationship with Kahn, but had made the decision to send him anyway.

The two men exchanged glances before answering. "We're all right."

Haute nodded, knowing his opinion wouldn't make any difference. He addressed the entire group. "I think that would be our best option, Commander. Draw their attention to some of their egg chambers, get them to come where you want them and take them out." He cocked his head in thought. "I just hope our strategy doesn't backfire on us."

"What are you thinking, sir?" asked Gary.

Haute repeated roughly the same possibility he had told Jimenez a moment before. "Well, there is a distinct possibility that they could get the same idea. They've got a lot of leverage against us if they decide to use it." He stopped, contemplating. "A lot of things could go wrong."

Colonel Rennick entered the fray. "He's right. If they start killing off our people to keep us away, we may have to accept major civilian casualties. We can't be sure of our options yet. They could be filtering prisoners throughout these caverns. They stretch for miles. What you guys find out down there will tell us how to proceed. Phase two will have to go unchanged for now."

Weaver, one of the SPEC soldiers, had a troubling thought. "Do any of these tunnels connect with each other, I mean at more than one junction?"

Kahn wasn't sure what he meant. "Connect with each other?"

"Yeah, if we receive action from the front, are they going to send their guys around to come up behind us?"

Kahn shook his head, "There's no way to tell."

Weaver looked disgusted at the answer. "Shit, that's great! They catch us in a cross fire in a twenty foot wide killing field!"

Jimenez intervened. "Hey! We've got a lot of unknowns here. That's one of a hundred. Let's just keep our shit together and make sure that doesn't happen."

Weaver backed down, glancing at Kahn. "Sorry man, it's not your fault."

"It's okay. I wish I could tell you more." Kahn reasoned. He understood the man's frustration. He had presented a particularly unpleasant scenario.

Rennick received a message on his communicator. He listened and informed the others. "Motion sensors in the tunnel entrances are negative. You can go in as soon as you're ready. Remember, stay in constant contact. Get in and get out. No hero shit, that's not your job today. Understand?" Several men acknowledged him as he turned to leave.

Jimenez spoke to everyone concerned. "We want to avoid all contact if possible. Rick," he spoke to Weaver. "Suit these guys up. Show them some of the goodies we've got."

Haute knew it was time to be elsewhere. He made his farewell. "Well, I guess this is it." He again shook Gary's hand and turned to Kahn. His voice was low. "You two have been through too much the last couple of weeks. No one would say a damn thing if you stood down now. You know that, don't you?"

Kahn nodded. "We know." He felt a strong urge to leave the shuttle with him, but quelled it. "We do get a break after this, right?" He didn't mean to sound humorous, but it came out that way.

"You guys will get anything you want." Haute took a step forward and embraced Kahn tightly. "I'll see you later." He turned and left the ship.

Kahn stood silently, stunned at the sudden display of emotion.

Weaver didn't give them a chance to think about following. "C'mon guys, time's a gettin short."

Nearly four miles away, on the opposite side of the mountain range, a lone raider was patrolling. The pilot was watching for anything out of the ordinary, patting himself on the back for drawing such an easy job. He was out of the action and was determined to stay on this particular patrol as long as he was allowed.

He could never have seen the small cavern entrance, it was so naturally hidden. What did draw his attention was the glint of sunlight off something shiny below him. For a moment, he hesitated, wondering if he really saw anything at all. He shook his head, sure that he had. He was doing a job. No matter haw lame it was, he might as well do it right.

As he made a loop and returned for a second pass, he realized how important his job had become. He now saw a multitude of insects, each carrying white objects. Eggs, he surmised. At that point his ship was less than two hundred meters away and there was no doubt that the Thalosians had seen him. They began to hurry in all directions, disappearing into the trees. On an open frequency, he spoke loudly. "I found them! There must be a cave. They're carrying out their eggs."

Someone on the other end answered. "Who is this?"

"Sorry … Gibson, blue raider three. There are hundreds of them."

"We've got your position. What about prisoners? Are there any people?"

"Negative, I don't see any, just bugs." He had passed directly over the area, and gotten a good look. He banked again.

His orders came over the radio, "Close it up fast."

The pilot had already started his run, heading directly for the rock wall. All four of the ships laser ports fired into the mass of insects. As he brought the raider nose up, the last of the beams caught the rocky ledges above and shattered them, raining tons of rock and dirt downward. Another loop brought him close over the wrecked cavern. As he neared, he slowed and radioed the main force. "It's closed! I think half the cliff came down on top of them. I don't see …"

Every person within range had been listening to the man's report when the words stopped. The radio simply went dead. After several unsuccessful attempts to re-establish contact, other raiders were expedited to the area. The ship was no longer on the screen. Many noticed a line of black smoke rising in the distance.

On his second pass over the cavern, the careless pilot presented himself as an easy target. At least twenty or so laser beams came at him from the cover of the trees, each one striking home. Gibson cursed his own stupidity as his useless craft fell out of control. It crashed into the rock wall he had just buried.

Moments later, another raider passed overhead. He maintained a safe altitude and speed. His caution however, was for naught. The Thalosians had already disappeared into the forest with their precious cargo.

As the second pilots report came in, Haute consulted with Rennick, who still accompanied him. "What do you think, did they all get out?"

"No way, there wasn't enough time. They know we're coming in though. They're trying to save their eggs." Rennick hesitated. "That's only my opinion of course."

"I value your opinion quite a bit right now, Colonel. What about other exits?"

"There's probably hundreds. That's why we need to get this done. All I can suggest is that we send out some shuttles on the patrols. They're all we have with the scanners we need. They'll be able to pick up anything in the trees."

"We'll send raider escorts with each. I don't want to lose any more."

Rennick knew what he meant. The shuttles were unarmed. "We'll keep them at maximum range. They won't be able to pick up single contacts, but any large groups, they'll see."

Haute nodded his approval. He turned, watching the thin line of smoke drifting upwards. He wasn't personal with a lot of pilots, but he knew this one. He was a rookie, only receiving his commission with the last class. The only reason the young man's name stood out from the others was because it belonged to the grandson of William Gibson, one of the seven men seated on the Belaquin council. He watched the darkness dissipate as it rose, dreading the call he would eventually have to make.

Rick Weaver dumped a black case on the table, opening it to show its contents to Gary and Kahn. They were nearly ready. They wore full body deflection suits, pure black with mirror like detail. They would be armed with nearly the same equipment as the other team members. Their weapons ranged from combat knives to the latest laser rifles. Fire grenades, mini pulsers, shredders, and hand lasers filled the small arms category. Other explosives, to be carried by only two team members, required extensive set up, thus causing extensive damage.

Their packs carried extra communication equipment and power pods that could interchange with every powered device they would take with them, including the lasers. Each man would carry water packets and food rations to last a week.

The rifle weapon was extraordinary. It had numerous fire settings; single bolt, the continuous beam similar to the cutters found in Thalosian technology, and a wide field blast. It gave a short solid pattern covering a ninety-degree angle from the muzzle. Unfortunately, in that setting, the range was limited and a fully charged pod could only deliver five to six blasts.

What the men saw in the case that Weaver had opened was a mystery. He removed one of four identical units from the padded interior, explaining. "We'll need these when the lights go out." He handed the two men their own sets. They resembled helmets, but didn't cover the entire head and face. "These are night vision scopes, the best ever designed, extremely sophisticated. The technology used in these blows the old stuff away. It picks up light particles invisible to the naked eye and works even in pitch. Pretty expensive shit."

Kahn placed his on his head and lowered the face shield. It fit tightly around the sides of his face and cheeks, feeling slightly uncomfortable. He flipped the switch, but it didn't seem to function.

Weaver explained why. "They're automatic. If it's light enough, it doesn't do anything. Your depth perception might be screwed up at first, but your range finder will tell you distance. Its range is up to a hundred meters, depending on the light depravity. You'll get the hang of it." While the two pilots received their crash course in SPECAULT technology, the other team members finished their pre-check and packing. Within twenty minutes, the nine men exited the shuttle. Between themselves and the cavern entrances were Rennick, Haute, and hundreds of soldiers. The compound was nearly silent.

CHAPTER 14

▼

Gary felt a sense of pride as he stepped off the platform, but the fear of what might come, made it hard to move forward. The sun was hot, the black suits absorbing the heat at an alarming rate. He could feel himself starting to sweat. At least in the upper tunnels it would be cooler. As they moved deeper though, he knew the heat would return.

Jimenez stopped just outside the shuttle and turned to face his team. Over the last few years they had been through a lot of good times and bad, but always together. He considered them his brothers, and would give his life, without hesitation, to save any one of them.

He spoke in a normal tone. There was no need for the multitude behind him to hear his words. They weren't for them. "Okay, this is it, last pep talk. Remember what we're here for, evasion, discovery, and withdrawal ... hopefully in that order. If we get in trouble, we get out, no questions asked." He paused as his eyes met with each mans. "We leave no one behind." He knew there would not be. "Let's go."

The mass of soldiers parted as the special assault team moved towards the hill. Words of encouragement were heard intermittently from unknown faces.

Gary walked briskly, Kahn beside him. He could hear the voices, but louder than any words was his own racing heartbeat, seemingly louder than anything else. His heart felt like it was in his throat. Much sooner than he wished, they reached the tunnels.

Jimenez gave his first orders. "We break into two teams, standard deployment. Kusan and Bengal, you're with me in team one." He could see their anxiety. "Its okay guys, we know there's nobody in the first two hundred yards." He then spoke to Gary specifically. "Everywhere I go, you go. Bengal, you are Weavers shadow."

Gary looked at Kahn, remembering their pact to stay together and realizing it may not be so.

Sensing his younger friend was about to protest, Kahn shook his head. Nothing was said.

"You guys said all these upper entrances lead to the same place, right?" asked the Commander.

Kahn answered. "Yes sir, it didn't matter which one we took, they ended up in the same main tunnel."

"Okay, we stay together until then." He turned and walked to the opening. Without a word, each man followed. The tunnels were still lighted as far as they could see. They walked silently, making no sound on the soft dirt floor. Within minutes, they had reached the main central tunnel. It widened to at least twenty meters at its mouth. Within it the lights were dim.

Jimenez spoke quietly. "Alright, we go on night vision now. The lights are on, but we need time to adjust. Switch on your comm units also. We stay together as long as we can, but spread out. I want motion sensors on lead and rear. Ultra quiet advance with minimal voice contact. Racine, you take lead. Geyer ..." He thumbed to the rear. He then lowered his facemask, as did the others. The man named Racine took his portable sensor and flicked it on. After setting it, he proceeded slowly.

Kahn turned on his headgear and was amazed at the clarity. The tunnel, initially somewhat dark, appeared brightly lit and perfectly clear. There was a barely visible grid with a center point within the face shield. Whatever object the center point rested upon was the point from which distance was calculated. The reading, in meters, was visible in the lower left corner of the shield. He immediately noticed what they had told him about the depth perception. It was like walking while looking through a recorder camera. It was awkward to say the least. Hopefully, he would not have to run while using it. They moved ahead.

It was indeed different, Gary concluded, than his other trips through the same tunnels. This time, there was perfect silence, interrupted only by the sound of his own rapid breathing. It was colder than he remembered. Even in the suits, with thirty pounds of equipment, he still caught a chill.

The tunnel grew steeper. Some parts were lit, others not. There was no word from Racine in the lead, and more thankfully, none from the rear guard. Jimenez was careful that they didn't bunch up, maintaining at least twenty foot spacing, one behind the other. They continued downward.

Exactly ten minutes and twenty seconds after Racine took point; his voice came over the comm, startling everyone. "First intersection reached."

"Kusan, move up with me. Everyone else hold." Jimenez ordered.

Within seconds, the two men joined Racine at the tunnels first break. Jimenez looked at the opening in the wall, then at Gary. "Do you remember this?" he asked.

"Yes sir. No one ever went in there, at least not on our shift."

Racine confirmed his answer by pointing out the absence of artificial lighting and human footprints on the powdery floor.

Jimenez nodded. "Mark it and move ahead."

Racine removed a light cylinder, flicked it on and stuck it base down in the dirt. It glowed brightly. Jimenez started a separate counter to keep elapsed time. The official clock had started. They moved on.

Three more similar intersecting tunnels were passed and marked. It was briefly discussed whether or not any human tracks might have been covered to conceal or confuse. Jimenez' decision was that they had not. Decision made … move on.

At the sixth intersection, there was a change from the norm. Human tracks led into both branches. Jimenez ordered everyone to move up. Soon, they all stood assembled. Mission time was roughly twenty-nine minutes.

Jimenez made his thought known. With the temperature in the fifties, his breath created a slight fog as he spoke. "Obviously, this means we split up. Maintain visual contact at all times. We continue as before, lead and rear sensors. I don't know how well our comms will operate through this rock. We should be close to the main chamber, less than ten minutes I'd say. Stay sharp, mark the way. If you find what we're looking for, gather intell if possible and rendezvous back here. We'll mark this intersection with three. Good luck."

Gary looked at Kahn through the headgear. He gave one of his carefree smiles. Gary knew it was fake, but shot an equally fake one back.

Jimenez motioned them to follow him. Racine led the way. Weaver brought up the rear of team one. The tunnel ran without a noticeable slope through five additional intersections. All had signs that people had passed that way, but the openings were much smaller than the main tunnel. Kahn and Gary agreed that the main chamber was straight ahead. The tunnels were marked accordingly. There was still no sensor contacts ahead or behind.

They moved on, only ten feet apart. After twelve minutes of walking, Racine stopped, silently signaling the others to do the same. He shut down his night vision and lifted the facemask, allowing normal vision. He opened his eyes wide, blinking, trying to see something ahead. As the other men watched, they saw him turn towards the rear. He made a cutting motion across his throat and pointed to his headgear.

Gary followed the order and was shocked at the absolute blackness. Instinctively, his body moved backwards to the rock wall, only inches away. The cold stone was reassuring. His body trembled. He told himself that it was from the chill, which shouldn't have been there. Suddenly, the touch of a hand startled him. It finally rested on his forearm. A low voice came through his ear transmitter. It seemed exceptionally loud.

"There's light up ahead." It was Jimenez. Gary looked in his direction, but could see nothing. Finally, after a moment, he began to make out light. It was barely discernable, coming from deeper in the tunnel. "I see it," he answered.

Jimenez's voice came over again. "Team one up." As the others joined them, he continued. "I think we're close." he said quietly. "Emergency traffic only from here on in. Bengal, you go with me."

Kahn moved forward, ready, but reluctant, not knowing for sure what was ahead.

The Commander came close to his face. "You stay right on my ass. We're gonna have a look." He stood from his crouched position, flicked on his scanner and went forward, hugging the wall. Kahn did as he was told. They left their night scopes.

Jimenez hadn't gone a hundred yards when he stopped suddenly, obviously startled by something. Kahn felt a hand encircle his arm and squeeze tightly. He didn't move, having no idea what had caught the man's attention. A whispered, calm voice informed all who could hear. "We've got dead prisoners up here."

Kahn strained, but couldn't make out anything clearly. Remembering his helmet, he reached up, and lowered the visor. He was unnerved at what he could now see all too well. Human bodies, at least a dozen, lay strewn in the tunnel. Two Thalosians lay among them. Kahn was suddenly hit with another conscious realization. Down here, there were no guarantees that you're going home.

The nearest body to him was a woman, only three feet away. She lay on her back, her head turned towards him. Her eyes seemed to stare directly into his. Kahn quickly lifted his visor, the lifeless eyes thankfully disappearing. Jimenez, saying nothing more, led on. Two small tunnels were passed. No light came from them.

The light grew brighter with every meter they put behind them. Kahn could see his silhouette against the curving wall ahead. More bodies could be seen along the route. The scanner revealed no movement from any of them. Jimenez stopped, cocked his head, and held up one hand. He whispered again. "I hear something …"

Kahn heard it as well, thinking it sounded like rushing water. They moved forward again, the light and the sound growing louder. Another tunnel was passed on the left. Jimenez did not mark it. Soon, they passed another on the right. It was also left unmarked.

The sound they heard suddenly became easily identifiable. It was not water. The noise was the roar of thousands of voices rolled together. There was no mistaking it. The portable sensor showed nothing, but they knew it was just a matter of time.

They were right in their assumption. As they followed the wall around a fairly sharp bend to the left, the sensor screen came to life, indicating movement ahead of them. Jimenez crouched and stopped, releasing the scanner to hang at his side. It wasn't needed any longer. Shadows danced in the tunnel ahead of them.

Kahn's breathing quickened. He waited for Jimenez to say something, but he didn't.

The commanding officer of SPECAULT breathed rapidly as well. He had been in intense situations many times, but none like this. He cursed the curve of the tunnel. By the time he got close enough to see their quarry, he would be in plain view, in full light. Should he even attempt a visual confirmation? The people were undisputedly there. How many of them there were however, were in dispute, as well as the number of their alien captors. Intelligence was imperative. He had to try. He turned to Kahn, speaking so low he could barely be heard. "Stay here. I'm moving up. Use your scanner to watch behind us. I'll be right back."

"Watch your ass, sir." Kahn whispered back.

"It's in the rules," Jimenez reassured. Dropping to his hands and knees, he moved forward. He had the unsettling thought that the aliens might have motion scanners as well, but dismissed it, knowing that it was too late to worry about it now.

Kahn watched him inch forward. His scanner read nothing behind them.

Jimenez was meticulous in every movement. He remained as soundless as possible, but the insects hearing would have to be extraordinary for them to hear anything above the background roar.

The wall continued to turn until finally, he saw the tunnels end. As he suspected, there were Thalosians, at least half a dozen, within the small view that he had. Beyond the opening, he could see light, but no people. He studied the insects, only fifty yards away. It was the first time he had ever seen a living specimen. All of them were armed. They did not appear worried about what was possibly behind them in the tunnel. Jimenez wondered why, but only for a moment.

His headset comm suddenly crackled to life. His eyes widened in surprise, but the sound was indwelling, with no possibility of the insects hearing it. A voice came through. "Jimenez, this is Kahn. I've got movement back here ... on my scanner!" His tone was quiet, but urgent.

Jimenez began backing away, touching his own transmitter at the same time. "Racine ... are you guys moving?"

The response was immediate. "That's a negative sir."

Jimenez, now out of visual range of the chamber entrance, got to his feet and walked hurriedly, watching his own scanner. He could see one contact that was Kahn, and many others, much further away. "Son of a bitch!" he muttered. "Bengal, get your night gear on now! We gotta move!"

Kahn was standing and waiting when he rejoined him. If the sensor was right, the contacts were still a hundred and twenty meters away, but moving closer. Jimenez spoke into his comm again. "Commander to team two!" There was no answer, quickly defeating the possibility. Without hesitation, he moved forward towards the contacts. "The last intersection we passed should be between us and them. We have to reach it before they do."

Kahn, wanting to scream, but remained silent, following the man's every move. He heard Jimenez whispering more orders. "Team one, move up to within range of sensor contacts. We might need some flanking fire."

Racine and Weaver understood the urgency in their commander's voice. They moved immediately. Gary followed closely as they nearly sprinted through the tunnel, ignoring the bodies they passed.

Kahn could see that the tunnel straightened ahead of them. The first tunnel opening became visible on their left. Its distance was twenty meters, while the unknown contacts were at seventy, but straight ahead. If the aliens had good nocturnal vision, they could be in trouble. Jimenez didn't slow down, knowing that the tunnel was their only chance. As they neared the opening, the contacts could easily be seen and identified. Thalosians filled the narrow tunnel from side to side, less than a hundred steps away.

What happened next was expected. The two men had no choice but to cross within full view of the approaching insects. The evasion part of the plan was shattered. Screeching and chirping sounds filled the enclosed space, followed by the much louder sound of laser fire. Bolts of light showered broken rock in every direction. It left little doubt to how well the aliens had adapted to their dark environment.

Jimenez pulled Kahn into the narrow opening, stopping to arm the small device he already held in his hand. He said one word to Kahn. "Run!"

All the insects could have seen next was a human arm for the briefest of seconds. For those that were within fifty feet of the opening, it would be the last thing they would ever see. The mini-pulser exploded soon after it touched the floor. It sounded like a clap of thunder in the confined space. Jimenez did not stay to see its effect.

Kahn had no problem following the commander's last order. He ran. His heart felt like it could come out of his chest. All he could hear was his and the Commanders heavy breathing. Eventually, the latter slowed and stopped. He stopped as well, his body grateful for the short rest. He bent over, trying to stifle the urge to cough as he sucked the cold air into his aching sides. He had no idea how far they had run.

Jimenez, even though in great physical shape, was also winded. He took in their bleak surroundings. The tunnel they were now in was much smaller than the one they had just quitted. It measured no more than three meters square and the downward slope was substantially greater. He lifted his visor and waited, holding up his hand, signaling Kahn to try and be silent. There was absolutely no sound. He held up the portable sensor, trying to hold it steady.

A moment passed before Kahn spoke. "Are they coming?"

"Not yet, but they will if they can."

A voice suddenly crackled through the open channel. The connection was poor and the words garbled, but the voice was familiar. It was Racine. Jimenez turned up the gain, but there was too much rock between them. He keyed his transmitter several times, knowing they would not be able to understand any voice traffic. They continued to wait, eyes glued to the sensor screen.

Gary had heard every word that filtered through the head set. Racine and Weaver had been moving since the word came in. He had kept up as best he could, but it was difficult to run wearing the night vision. It was as if his head and his body were separate.

They stopped as they heard the loud reverberation of the mini pulser, knowing at that moment that the game was up. Racine knelt and brought his rifle up, fully expected someone or something to be coming towards them. The echoes faded away.

Gary moved in directly behind Weaver as he stopped as well. "What was that?" he asked, out of breath.

Weaver spoke without turning. "Somehow they got between us. They used a mini-pulser. That's the sound we heard. I knew these tunnels would fuck us."

"Where are they now?"

"Unknown." He gestured forward. "That way, that's all we know."

Racine activated his voice comm. "Team One to team leader, come in." There was no answer. "Team one to team leader." There was still nothing. He faced the others. "If they're still alive, they're out of range."

Gary's heart dropped. It was a dispiriting thought that he hadn't yet considered.

Suddenly, they heard static coming through. The signal was steady and repeated. It was obvious that someone was signaling them. Racine rose and started forward again. "That's them! Come on!"

Kahn sat beside Jimenez, silently wishing that he could turn back the clock. He glanced at his watch. Mission time was approaching sixty-eight minutes. He truly wondered if they would live to see seventy.

The narrow corridor was the blackest black he had ever seen. Jimenez had turned off his night vision and instructed Kahn to do the same. It was a proven fact that depravation of one sense tends to enhance the others. He needed only one of those senses at the moment. Any noise loud enough would echo down the tunnel long before the scanner could pick up anything.

The tunnel held no hint of light. They had passed no intersections. If they were followed, the path would lead straight to them. At this point of their journey, it would be fairly easy to find their way to the surface. If many more turns were forced upon them, especially on the run, then they could find themselves irretrievably lost.

Kahn stared into the darkness. They had only been there a few moments, but it seemed much longer. For the first time since separating, he thought of Gary, wondering if he was as scared.

Jimenez jerked suddenly. "Did you hear that?"

Kahn had not. "No, sir," he answered. Unable to stand the temporary blindness any longer, he reached up and reactivated his night vision.

"Hold on ..." Jimenez listened and heard it again.

Kahn heard it that time as well. Not needing an order, he got to his feet as recognition set in.

Jimenez stood also. He dropped his scanner to his side and reached for something in the side of his pack. Without stopping or turning, he gave instructions to his partner. "Get going." He made no effort to keep his voice low.

Kahn stood rooted in place, as his scanner came alive with activity. He didn't fully understand what was happening or what to do. "Commander, what are we doing?" His words revealed his fear in every syllable.

"You're going down that tunnel. I'm gonna stay here for a minute, then I'll follow. Just stay in this tunnel where I can find you." He gave a quick glance. "Don't worry. Just go!"

Kahn wanted to stay, but withheld any additional argument. As he turned he saw Jimenez jamming something into the soft dirt floor. Shaking his head in disbelief at the situation, he did what he was told.

Jimenez hurried, placing the percussion charge in the sand. Finally, it remained upright. The sound of the approaching insects was unnerving. When it was ready, he depressed a switch, arming it. He had thirty seconds. Moving quickly down the corridor, he counted off. After a fifteen count, he lay down prone, facing the direction he had just come. With his face shield down, the tunnel was dimly lit, the light sensors at maximum to provide even that. Almost immediately, movement came into view. Motionless, he waited.

He knew there were two ways the charge could detonate. The time could run out, or the device could be moved. Five seconds to go. The aliens were on top of it and easily visible in his rifle sights. The timing would be close.

Kahn slowed to a stop, not wishing to go any further alone. He lifted his motion scanner, activating it. Before he could read it, laser fire sounded far behind him. He took two steps towards it when the charge went off. The noise rocked the walls with deafening vibrations, sending him to his knees in pain. Only a second later came the unexpected concussion, which sent him reeling onto his back. A blast of hot air rushed over him, filling the tunnel with dust and dirt. He closed his eyes and rolled over, burying his facemask in his arms. The wind and echoes died as quickly as they had started. The tomblike silence returned.

Only a moment passed before he sat up. He looked up the slope, hoping to see a friendly face. The distance readout was useless in the dust filled space. It could not get a clear reading, hovering between ten and eighty meters. The dirt around him not only made it impossible to see, but also choked him as he tried to take even a short breath. He coughed uncontrollably, knowing that the sound was on its way to possibly to unwanted ears.

Nearly blind and deaf, he staggered to his feet. Pain shot through his back where he had landed onto his pack. He waited, trying to breathe as best he could. Slowly, the dust settled, allowing partial vision.

"Jesus ..." he muttered, realizing the power of what he had just witnessed. Had the tunnel collapsed? It was a demoralizing possibility. "Jimenez!" he called. His voice sounded strange, his hearing obviously impaired by the blast. At that point, any sound was welcome, especially a voice.

The next sound was neither. More laser fire shocked him to a crouched stance. He couldn't tell whether it came from his own headset, or relayed through the commander's transmitter. "Jimenez!" he yelled. "Jimenez!" The firing stopped again. "Answer me, dammit!" he yelled again. Still nothing. He shook his head, fearing the worst.

Hesitating, his mind racing, he mulled over what to do next. Staying where he was would accomplish nothing. What if the Commander needed help? The decision became simple. Raising his scanner, he started cautiously back up the slope. Minutes passed and at one point, the distance readout climbed to an even hundred. Still, there was no sign of anything. Again, he argued his next action. Should he try to contact him by voice? Surely, if he was able, he would have called to him.

Suddenly, the sensor began reading movement, startling him. Elated, but unsure, he brought his weapon to bear at the furthest point of his vision. Fighting the urge to retreat, he stood his ground. Finally, something appeared. At first he couldn't recognize it, but eventually he could tell that it was a walking figure. He could barely see it. His eyes finally focused completely. The readout showed seventy-five meters.

Kahn's mouth opened in horror as the lone figure materialized. He saw more movement behind. Thalosians again filled the corridor.

"No!" he yelled inside. Turning, he ran like he'd never run before. The raw dread of what was following kept his legs moving. More than once, laser fire erupted behind him. Their target was obvious.

He didn't notice the drop off until it was too late. A jolt of sharp pain went through him as his right leg met the ground a foot lower than he anticipated. He cursed as he tried to stop himself, but the steepness of the slope was too much. His hands raked against the walls and floor, grasping at whatever he could. His tumbling body, out of control, finally struck something hard. Finally, his fingers caught. He held on as if his life depended on it.

In the next instant, he realized that it just might. As far as he could tell, from his waist down, there was nothing. The tunnel floor was gone, and he was now hanging, literally by his fingertips. As he took in what was happening, he felt an overwhelming sense of panic rising in his throat. He laid face down, his chest pressed heavily against rock, making each breath short and hard fought. His arms stretched out before and above him, his hands clinging to something unseen. It was difficult to hold on. If all of his body weight were pulling on his arms, he would have already lost his grip. He thought about the extra weight from his pack, but felt that it may have been lost in the downhill fall.

Slowly, he moved his legs to try and find a foothold, but it only increased the pressure on his chest and the pain of his labored breaths. His feet could feel nothing. Desperately, he concentrated to keep his grip from involuntarily relaxing. Looking up he saw only blackness. Reluctantly, he slowly began to accept it. His headgear was gone. No light, no communication, no chance.

Racine slowed his advance, the scanner picking up movement ahead. Suddenly, the sound of a second, distant explosion echoed loudly past. He yelled to the others, "Get down!"

Weaver and Kusan hit the ground as a strong blast of hot air rushed by. Within seconds, Weaver was up again. "My God … that was an incendiary charge."

"Sounds like they ran into some bad shit," agreed Racine. He shook his head, knowing that they would not find pleasantries ahead. They advanced again, movement still showing on the scanner. To add to their confusion, the signals, one by one, disappeared. Within the next minute, the scope was clear. The contacts had either moved out of range, or ceased to move at all.

An opening appeared on the left wall, far too close to be the area of the last contact. They went further. Within another hundred yards, a second and third tunnel intersected the main. They moved on. Scattered throughout and around the fourth opening were the victims of the mini-pulser they had heard earlier. Some bodies were whole, while other rested in crushed pieces. It was impossible to tell with any certainty how many the blast had claimed. Still, there was no movement within range.

The blackness was serene, almost comforting. "For a man about to die," Kahn thought, "I'm pretty calm." He noted that there were no flashes of his life before his eyes, but considered that maybe it came later, at the instant of death. He concentrated on the pain and held on; letting his cheek rest against the cold, rough rock. There was nothing to see but darkness. He closed his eyes, envisioning many things. One image returned over and over. The woman waiting for him was so clear, so beautiful, but so far away. What would she do when they told her? Or would they even know? Would they even find him? That thought above all seemed to upset him more than any other. The thought of dying here alone, lying here for eternity, was most cruel.

Above the pain, he felt something wet running down his left arm, under his sleeve. It tickled as it passed through the hairs on his forearm. There wasn't much doubt as to what it was. It was his blood ... his life ... or what was left of it. He knew he was nearly finished. It was almost a relief.

But suddenly he became angry, gritting his teeth, cursing himself for being in this predicament. He refused to go that easily! He would continue to hold on as long as he was able, even in the face of hopelessness. Maybe, just maybe, the insects would come and pull him up, save his life. Maybe the ground was just below his feet? Maybe it wasn't. He could not take the chance.

His strength deteriorated with every passing second. The pain coursing through his hands was nearly unbearable. He couldn't last much longer.

It was heartrending. There was so much more he wanted to do in his life. Right now, he just wanted to live it. He silently pleaded; ready to bargain with anyone who would listen. He wanted to yell out, in anger, in desperation, but it was hard to even take a breath. His arms screamed for relief. They trembled as he willed every ounce of life into them.

His left hand, his weakest, slipped ever so slightly. The terror, the fear of not being able to last ten more breaths, gave him stamina. He thought of Deanna once more, realizing that he would never hold her in his arms again. Tears came as he considered it.

Unconsciously, another thought replaced her image. He wondered if every person about to die had the same thoughts. Do they think of God? Do they pray to be saved? Did having the thoughts confirm that he was going to die?

To his horror, the same hand slipped again, further than before. He found it hard to concentrate. The pain was subsiding, but only because his arms had grown numb. Why hold on? It was a waste of time. It would be so much easier to let go. Dying would be the easy part. He had always believed that the knowledge of impending death was much worse than the actual act. Falling would be an easy way to go if he fell far enough. Not dying when hitting the bottom would be a horrible scenario.

He opened his eyes with a start. He heard something ... or had he? Was his mind wandering, now that he was on the brink? It had sounded like laser fire.

The high-pitched screech echoed through the tunnel again. He was sure it was a laser! Probably just the damn bugs shooting at his pack, he figured, but he was past caring what form his savior came in.

He opened his eyes, praying to see anything. His lips parted, trying to form words "Help me!" He yelled. Surely someone had to have heard him.

He waited, straining to hear anything. How long had he held on? Ten seconds … ten minutes … an hour? He heard something else, something different. It echoed from far away, maybe a voice? Another drifted in. He could hear words! He took as deep a breath as his chest would allow and shouted. "I'm here!"

Suddenly, there was movement near him. Relief flooded into him. He heard his name called. He couldn't see them, but he could hear them plainly enough. He felt firm hands grip each of his wrists. He was lifted.

In seconds, he was lying on the floor of the tunnel, listening to a familiar voice. It was Gary. He could hear him speaking, but didn't understand. Then, like a door opening, reality rushed back, and with it came pain. His arms hung flaccid at his sides, aching terribly as life flowed back into them.

Gary helped him sit upright. A floodlight came on, casting shadows everywhere. He was shocked at his friend's appearance. Kahn's hair was matted with dirt. His face was red where the skin had been scraped away. His arms were abraded as well, with a gaping half-inch laceration between the knuckles on his left hand. He had bled, but was not now. He looked into his eyes, hoping to see normalcy there. "Are you all right?" he asked.

Kahn coughed, trying to take full breaths. His chest hurt with each inspiration. Finally, he answered. "I will be … as soon as we get the fuck out of here." He looked around; trying to make out the other men, but the light was too bright. "Where's Jimenez?"

A figure approached. "I'm here. At least most of me." He came into view beside Gary.

"God damn … I thought you were dead." Kahn said.

"They got me down for a minute. Some of them got past the charge. I tried to slow them down, but one of them got me before it went off." Jimenez related.

Weaver checked his commander's shoulder, where the laser bolt had burned, but not penetrated the material. The specialized suit had done its job. Jimenez winced as Weaver moved his injured arm upwards.

"Well that charge tore them a new asshole," Racine joked. "It took a bunch of them down."

"It knocked the shit out of me too, though," Jimenez stated. He turned to Weaver, who had finished the short medical evaluation. "Will I live?"

"I don't feel anything broke. If it was dislocated, you wouldn't be moving it." He chuckled. "You're gonna die, but not today."

"Great," answered the dirt-covered leader.

Weaver moved to Kahn's side. "Where are you hurt, other than the obvious?"

"Shit, everywhere I think."

Can you walk?"

"I can run if I have too." He stood with help. A sharp pain shot through the right side of his chest. His breath caught. "Damn ... that felt good."

Weaver palpated the region. "Does it hurt when I press ... or when I let go?" He pushed near the place Kahn was guarding. Kahn winced immediately.

"What is it?" Gary asked, concerned.

Weaver shook his head. "Can't be sure, maybe just a rib separated from the sternum. Could be cracked, too."

Gary smiled at his friend. "Well I guess you might get a vacation after all."

Weaver nodded. "Let me know if your breathing gets worse."

"Well, it's not that great right now, but I can live with it."

"You'll be okay. Let's just get you out of here," said Gary. He saw his friend grimace when he took too deep a breath.

Racine approached, handing him some dropped equipment. "Your headgear seems to be working. Test it yourself as soon as you can. I'll carry your pack."

Kahn began to protest, but felt too out of air to argue, still unable to catch his breath. He shook it off, knowing that he would get better. It would just take a few minutes.

Jimenez checked himself, making sure he hadn't lost anything. "Did you see anything else up there?" He spoke to the three men who had so recently joined them.

"Negative. We passed the one tunnel. It was the only place they could have come through." Racine answered.

"Agreed. Anything from team two?"

"Nothing."

The Commander was concerned about them, but was even more so for his own team. "I hate to break up the reunion, but we need to get out of here. Let's wrap it up."

While the Commander spoke, Gary turned on his own light and investigated the ledge where Kahn was found. What he saw filled him with an overwhelming desire to obey the commander's order, the sooner, the better. "You guys need to see this," he said quietly.

One by one, they joined him on the edge. Kahn stayed further back, but could still see. He had to know. Each man turned on a light, illuminating what lay beyond and beneath.

Kahn gasped at the sight. He felt light-headed as he realized the future that had been so close. If he had let go, he would have most certainly died. It was no less than a two hundred foot fall, but not to the bottom of the cavern. The powerful beams scanned an incredible sight. The tunnel ended where they stood now. The ledge overlooked a gulf so huge that the opposite wall could not be seen. The rays of light disappeared into darkness. What lay below demanded the groups attention.

Below them was death in every conceivable sense. An unimaginable pile of horror covered the floor of the cavern. Bodies rose toward them in a macabre mountain of lifelessness. Most forms were alien, but human remains could be seen as well. Also, there were Thalosian eggs, thousands of them, lying among the dead. The cavern was a massive tomb. It had almost claimed another.

Kahn shook his head, refusing to believe his eyes. An involuntary shudder shook his body as he thought of falling into the sickening mass. "What the hell is this?"

"Their idea of a graveyard," Jimenez answered. "I guess their respect for the dead isn't one of their strong suits. C'mon, let's go."

On the slow climb out, they saw no Thalosians with the exception of the unfortunate few that the fire charge had taken out. About the time they passed that area, Gary, who had stayed close behind his injured friend, noticed something was wrong. Kahn had stopped, pacing in a limited circle, seemingly unable to stand still. "Kahn?" he said quietly. He walked to him when there was no answer. One look told him that his condition had worsened.

Gary grabbed his friend's headgear and removed it. Kahn's eyes were wide with panic. He tried to speak, but his breathing was rapid and short. He grunted with every exhalation. Gary was worried, but his voice remained calm. "Guy's, we need you back here."

Weaver was there even as he spoke. He had heard the unanswered transmission a moment before and had already turned back. Soon, everyone was there.

Jimenez struck a light, bathing the tunnel in brightness. Dead Thalosians lay on the ground around them. He looked to Racine, needing to say nothing. The latter went forward, scanner in hand to stand guard. Both knew the chance they were taking by using the lights.

Weaver could see the distress in Kahn's face. He was pale, sweating profusely, and unable to sit still. "Get his jacket off," he ordered. He opened his own pack, searching for equipment.

Gary and Jimenez did as they were told. The Commander had an idea of what might be happening, but Kusan did not. "What's wrong with him?" Gary asked.

Weaver took a small cylinder from his pack along with an oxygen mask. "He looks like he's hypoxic. He may have a collapsed lung." Even as he spoke, he placed the mask over Kahn's face, connecting tubing to it from the cylinder. A loud hissing sound filled the air as he turned it on.

The distressed man immediately reached up to remove the mask, but Weaver held it firmly. "Kahn, this is liquid oxygen. Breathe it in ... try to slow down. Do you understand me?"

Kahn finally nodded, still wild eyed. He pulled the mask off for a second, getting out two words between breaths. "Can't breathe!"

Weaver nodded back. "I know man, just hang in there. I'm gonna check you out."

Jimenez listened intently for any word from Racine, knowing they were in an extremely bad position. He knew he didn't need to tell his medic to hurry every chance he had.

Weaver retrieved more equipment from his specialized bag. One device he placed on Kahn's right index finger. The other was a stethoscope. With it, he listened to Kahn's chest, both sides, several times. Placing the scope back into the bag, he looked at the Commander. "Son of a bitch ... he's down. His O2 sat is down to eighty two percent. His heart rate is a hundred and thirty."

Jimenez nodded his understanding.

Gary watched and listened, but understood nothing.

Weaver told him in plain English. "His right lung has collapsed." He readied other equipment as he explained. "He's still getting air in, but some of it is getting trapped in the right pleural cavity, blowing him up like a balloon. It's getting tighter, making it harder and harder for him to breathe. He's not getting enough oxygen."

Gary listened, but didn't grasp everything that he had heard. Judging by the urgency in Weavers voice and his actions, he didn't need to ask if it was bad.

Jimenez stood close. "It's called a tension pneumothorax. Weav's gonna fix it, right Rick?"

The medic held up a pressure syringe to the light, measuring a specific dosage. "Yes, sir," He spoke again to Kahn. "Did you hear everything I just told him?"

Kahn nodded, pulling the mask away again. "Can you ... fix it?" He looked calmer, but was still hurting.

"That's what I'm going to do. The oxygen is helping right?" The question was answered with a feeble thumb up. "Great, okay, here's what we're gonna do. This is a morphine injection. It's gonna help you relax, calm you down some more. You're not allergic to it are you?"

Kahn shook his head and shrugged his shoulders.

"Good." He pushed it hard against Kahn's right upper arm. The air powered device swishing as the drug was injected. "Okay, Gary, I want you over here on his right side. Kahn, I want you to do what I say. Hold your right arm up over your head. Gary, you make sure it stays there." Weaver moved to directly in front of Kahn's face. "Look at me."

Kahn looked into the soldier's eyes.

Weaver continued. "I know this sounds stupid, but we have to let some of the air out of your chest. To do that, I'm going to have to stick a needle between your ribs."

Kahn's eyes widened as he listened, grimacing as the words sunk in, His heart beating even faster. Instinctively, he pulled his right arm back down without any objection from Gary. His words came through shortened breaths once again. "You gotta be shittin me?"

Weaver shook his head, holding up a round plate shaped contraption and one of the biggest needles any of the group had ever seen. It measured at least three inches in length. "I wouldn't shit you, you're my favorite turd." Weaver answered.

Kahn had another question. "What happens ... if you don't?"

The response was immediate. "You'll die without it." The tone in his voice was now completely serious.

Kahn felt Gary raising his arm once again. He fought it only for a second, searching for the strength to go through with it. He finally nodded, deciding he didn't like the alternative. He'd been close enough to death already today. "Do it!"

Without another word, Weaver moved close to him, cut his shirt, and began to feel below his right underarm for the right location. Kahn could feel him pushing hard between his ribs, moving downward. Finally he stopped. A sudden cold, wet sensation made him flinch in surprise.

Gary watched in fascination and fear as Weaver readied the needle. He tightened his grip on Kahn's wrist, realizing that the next step was going to be tough.

Weaver, with the site already cleaned with disinfectant, spoke to his trembling patient. "Okay man, here we go. Don't move."

Kahn closed his eyes, forever wishing he had not been a volunteer, at least not today. He gritted his teeth, not knowing what to expect.

The SPECAULT medic was scared as well. He had only done the procedure twice in his life, in a well-controlled environment, physicians talking him through it. He decided to keep that information to himself today.

Weaver, quickly and deliberately inserted the sheathed needle between Kahn's forth and fifth ribs, into the space where muscle tissue, nerves and blood vessels rested. He felt Kahn jump as he did so, and heard a moan escape him, but that was all. He felt the sharp point scrape slightly against the top of the fifth rib. Angling slightly upward, he slid it in to the hub. Holding it with one hand, he pulled out the needle, leaving only a hollow, plastic sheath in place in the chest wall. As the needle cleared, a rush of air followed, escaping through the sheath. Weaver sighed with relief.

He looked at Kahn. "Hard parts over partner, you did good."

Kahn felt an immediate sense of relief as he heard the words. The needle had hurt incredibly. He was sure he'd felt worse pain in his life, but at the moment of entry, he was at a loss to remember when. He nodded back at Weaver, already finding it easier to breathe.

Weaver placed the flat device around the exposed end of the needle catheter. "This valve will keep the pressure from building up again. You look better," he observed.

Kahn found it easier to speak as well. "I feel better. Thanks."

Weaver patted him on the shoulder. "You're still not out of the woods, but this buys us some time. Keep sucking in that oxygen." He glanced at the Commander. "We're ready."

Jimenez nodded his approval.

Kahn was helped to his feet, supported by Kusan and Weaver. He didn't feel remotely well, but promised himself that no matter how difficult it was, he was getting out of the caverns. The light went out, plunging them into pitch once again. Kahn walked with the other men, unable to see. He could not wear the night vision gear with the oxygen mask in place. He didn't have a problem being blind, as long as he could breathe.

Jimenez called to Racine, somewhere ahead of them. "We're coming up."

"Copy that, so far so good." Racine answered.

A moment later, they had rejoined him and moved on. As they neared the main tunnel, the scanners picked up the signals. Low to the tunnel floor, Jimenez and Racine moved to just within sight of the intersection. Some good luck was still with them. So far, the Thalosians hadn't entered the dead end tunnel. From where they lay, they could see several insects moving about the main tunnel.

Jimenez whispered to the man beside him. "Can this get any friggin worse?" Racine didn't answer. He spoke again. "Let's go back."

With the others, out of sight of the intersection, they stood again, scanners tracking. Jimenez laid down the limited options. "We're not gonna get out of here without a fight, so here's the plan. Racine and me will start it. We'll hit them with a few of these first."

Gary recognized what he held in his hand. Weaver had described them earlier. They were called "silent shredders." Their bulbous shape enclosed hundreds of strands of wrapped razor wire, which when propelled with sufficient force, would cut down any victim. Their release was nearly soundless, hence their name.

"If necessary, we'll follow up with some wide field bursts. You guys have to stay close. Once we start, we can't stop. We've got to be out of here in a few seconds at the most. Gary, you have to help him." Kahn, with his mask in place, could only listen. "Weav, you bring up the rear. Drop three or four more behind us, and we run like hell."

"We just gotta hope there's no more of those bastards upstairs." Racine added. Weaver nodded. "What about team two?"

"We'll deal with that problem after we deal with our own." Jimenez explained. "As we move up, we'll try to make contact. Hopefully, they'll be waiting on us." He paused and gave instruction to the two pilots. "Stay sharp and move when we move. Once you hit the main slope, don't stop for anything. Bengal, it's gonna be a bitch. It's uphill all the way." He paused, readying himself. "Let's go."

Hugging the wall, Racine led the way, night vision on. He held his rifle in firing position against his shoulder. He could feel the Commander, tight against his pack, ready with the shredders. Each Thalosian that passed by the entrance was within his sights at least for an instant. He tracked each one as they moved across the opening. Suddenly, two aliens stopped in the entrance. Racine froze in full view of them. They appeared to be communicating, but there was no sound. The aliens stood, looking into the smaller tunnel.

Racine held his breath. His laser sight covered both targets at once. They were so close that if they came toward them, he would have no choice but to fire. If that happened, their fate would be sealed. There was nowhere behind them to go.

Jimenez couldn't see what was ahead, but he knew his man's actions and what they meant. He stood still, waiting. The others, trailing in single file behind, followed suit. In the perfect silence, he could hear the low hiss of Kahn's oxygen mask. He prayed that the injured man would be able to stay silent. Even a cough would be fatal to the team at this point.

As chilly as it was in the cave, Racine still sweat within his mask. It beaded on his forehead and dripped downward, stinging his eyes. Blinking rapidly, he tried to dispel it. Finally, he had to breathe again. His body tensed to hold the rifle still.

An endless moment passed before the Thalosians moved away. For several seconds, no more creatures crossed the opening. Racine moved forward and reached the intersection. He looked to the left, toward the surface and thankfully saw nothing. Hurriedly, he glanced around the corner to the right. The second glance told him all he needed to know. Their luck had run out. The Thalosians were only fifty feet away and moving to them. He knew they couldn't wait. He spoke quickly. "They're coming from the right. We gotta go now."

Jimenez handed him two shredders, already set for five-second delays. Racine popped the tabs, and threw them toward the unknowing enemy. The mayhem was instantaneous.

The approaching insects were mowed down by the blasts, the thin white-hot wire cutting their bodies to pieces. There was little or no sound as the wires unraveled. Any warnings from the insects were literally cut short. Anything standing within twenty feet of the blasts was obliterated. Jimenez stepped forward and tossed two more to the left branch. Upon the detonation of the second two devices, the men moved.

Weaver was the last one out. As he exited the smaller tunnel, he was surprised to see that some Thalosians had gotten to their feet. He seared by his wide field laser burst. As he watched them fall, he could see more aliens in the chamber tunnel behind them. Judging the distance, he set a mini-pulser for ten seconds, flipped off the safety and ran as hard as he could up the slope. Laser fire followed him, one blast striking his pack and nearly knocking him down. He didn't envy the welcome the bugs would receive when they followed. Nor did he pity them. They had brought it all upon themselves.

Even though well out of the danger zone, the sound of the blast made him duck. The concussion passed him as he ran. He didn't stop to see what damage might have been done. The sound of alien agony told him that his timing was right.

As he caught up with the others, he heard Jimenez attempting to contact the other team. Eventually, they answered, stating that they were ahead in the main tunnel. Within minutes, the nine men stood together once again, five of them nearly ready to collapse after the uphill escape.

Kahn fell to his hands and knees, unable to continue. He fought for each breath. Weaver moved to check the decompression site to make sure it had remained open.

Jimenez, although exhausted, knew they couldn't hesitate long. "We've gotta keep going." His lungs screamed for air as well. Kneeling, he set his heavy rifle at his feet. "What did you guys find?"

"We didn't find any people, but Jesus; you should see the egg chambers!" Simpson answered.

"There has to be millions," added Denton. "Unhatched ... just stored up."

Jimenez reluctantly picked up his weapon and started up the tunnel, anxious to see daylight again. His shoulder ached. "We found our people, and we pissed off a bunch of bugs doing it, so let's keep moving." He looked at Kahn who struggled more than any of them for air. "Carry him if you have too."

Two fresh team members assisted the injured man, one on either side. The others doubled up where they had to, carrying the equipment. As far as they could tell, they weren't being followed.

Surface communication stations, which had heard nothing since the team entered the subterranean passage, were surprised to pick up the transmission. "Specault to surface ..." a voice crackled.

"This is surface. Go ahead."

"We're coming out, send down some help. We have wounded and we may have some company in a bit."

"Understood, Specault. Would that be good company ... or bad?" The question was all too legitimate.

"Bad ... definitely bad."

Colonel Rennick was well within earshot of the conversation. Before Jimenez finished speaking, he was issuing orders. Within seconds, a unit of twenty soldiers entered the tunnel. Less than four hundred yards in, they encountered the oncoming lights from Jimenez and his team.

Jimenez relayed information. "There's nothing on our sensors. We dropped a bunch of them at the last contact point. We don't know if they're coming or not."

"Are there any other casualties, sir? Do we need to get anybody else out?" The young unit leader was eager, as well as concerned.

"Negative. Just watch our back until we're out of here." He turned and led the men on the last leg.

Rennick met them as they emerged. He noted that some of them had indeed been embattled somewhere below. They looked like mine workers, covered with filthy brown dirt. He met with the team leader immediately.

The latter removed his helmet, relishing the cool breeze as it met his face and head. Several medical personnel milled around his men, offering fluids and immediate treatment to at least one of his team due to Weavers urging.

He stood upright as best he could as he saw his commanding officer approaching.

The Colonel spoke. "You better not salute, Tony." He wore a smile, obviously relieved to see the team entirely intact.

Jimenez shook his head, running his hand through his hair. "Good sir, I'm too damn tired anyway."

"Haute's on his way for a debriefing. He'll meet us at your ship." He could see the others shedding equipment and clothing. "You've got a few minutes if you want to take it easy."

Jimenez nodded. "We'll be inside, sir."

Rennick watched him go, followed by the others. He called after them. "Tony!"

Jimenez stopped and turned back.

"Did you find them?"

The dust-covered soldier smiled broadly, silently answering him.

Rennick contacted his unit leaders, telling them that phase one was complete, and to ready their men. As soon as possible, they would gather what information they needed from Jimenez and his men, and relay the route to the extraction troops.

As he finished, he saw a shuttle landing nearby. Knowing it would be the fleet commander. Minutes later, they both approached the black assault ship.

Jimenez met the two officers outside the ship. A medic was applying a numbing lotion to his bruised shoulder. He stood as they approached.

Haute expressed his relief that the man was not injured worse. "I'm glad to see you're still with us, Commander Jimenez."

"Thank you, sir. We got lucky. Bengal had a hell of a time, though."

"He's all right, I take it?" Haute asked.

"Thanks to our medic. He's going to need some rehab, but he'll be okay."

Haute was no doubt concerned, but knew there were more immediate issues that had to be addressed. "The Colonel says you were successful?"

"Yes sir. We know where they are. We got close enough to hear them, but visual confirmation was impossible. We just have to hope they don't move them before we can get back down there."

"Agreed," Haute reasoned. He turned and spoke to his long time friend. "Are you ready for phase two?"

Rennick nodded. "As ready as we can be."

Jimenez moved his arm up and over his head, working out the soreness. "It's a pretty easy route. We marked off the secondary tunnels." He paused. "I can go back in if you want me to, Colonel," he offered.

"I don't anticipate needing that, Commander, unless you consider it absolutely vital." answered Rennick. "Or are you just a glutton for punishment?"

"No sir. I've had about enough of that for one day."

"Alright then, I'll get the squad leaders in here and you guys can get this mapped out." With that, Rennick turned to do just that.

Haute remained. "Where are my men?"

"One's inside, sir." Jimenez thumbed towards the ship. "Bengal is already on one of the med-evac ships." He touched the older mans arm as he passed, stopping him. "Commander … they did good, kept their heads. It took a lot of guts to back down there."

Haute paused. "Thank you Commander, I appreciate it."

As he took another step, a different voice addressed him, causing him to pause again. "Excuse me … Commander Haute?"

He turned to see an officer approaching, but said nothing.

The man continued. "Excuse me sir, but there is a man who says he urgently needs to speak to you."

Haute spoke back to the officer. "Who is it?"

"I don't know sir. He wouldn't give his name. He said it would ruin the surprise." His voice was filled with apprehension as he relayed the message.

Haute couldn't believe what he was hearing. "You've got to be shitting me?"

"No sir. I've never seen him before. He's right this way, sir." The young lieutenant was more than eager to let the stranger explain himself.

Haute was adamant. Who would be thinking of ridiculous surprises at a time like this? The officer led the way. As he followed, he looked ahead and singled out a vaguely familiar face amidst the others. Recognition finally took hold. He could not have been more astonished if it had been his own father standing in front of him. The young officer who had relayed the message hurriedly moved on.

The man offered his hand, which Haute readily took. The Commander couldn't stifle his elation. "My God, where have you been?"

The man explained. "Everywhere … nowhere … here and there."

"I can't believe you're here. You left me in a hell of a spot way back when. Everyone thinks I'm nuts."

Ban-Sor still smiled. "I am sorry about that, but I think you understand my position. I could present an interesting problem to your superiors, as well as all your people"

"They wouldn't understand. I don't even understand!"

"Then you can see my point?"

As they talked further, Ban-Sor looked about the compound. He saw the devastation and the pile of dead creatures near the wall. "Uh, Commander, this may sound peculiar, but what is happening here?"

"You don't know anything about this?"

"Well sadly enough, I must admit that I do not know the whole story."

"Then what are you doing here?" Haute couldn't hide his confusion.

Ban-Sor contemplated the question, but was at a loss at finding a suitable explanation. "Commander, some of your inquiries deserve answers, but I find it difficult to discover the words to explain myself."

Haute frowned, mildly unsatisfied. It was just another unanswered question that would remain so. Without hesitation, he changed the subject. "I'm afraid a lot has happened since we last saw each other."

"Apparently. You appear at war?" Ban-Sor said bluntly.

"Unfortunately, we are. One of our planets was attacked, unprovoked, without warning. Thousands were killed, many more taken as prisoners."

"Prisoners?"

"Yes … eighteen thousand people. They were brought here."

"And what do you call this place?"

Haute momentarily wondered how a being who knew so much, could possibly know so little, but answered nevertheless. "This is their planet, Thalosia. We followed them here to try to save our people."

Ban-Sor was intrigued. "Quite an undertaking. I have, in the past, been aware of these beings and this place, but I have to admit, I was unfamiliar with their intentions concerning your people."

Haute offered enlightenment to the man. "We have a long history with them, all of it bad." Ban-Sor said nothing, so he continued. "We attempted to surprise this compound and make an above ground rescue, but before we could do anything, they moved everyone into their tunnels. We've found one of the main chambers. We're pretty sure that the majority of our people are being held there, but we have no idea what we're getting into."

Ban-Sor listened intently. "How do you propose to get them out?'

"We figure it's going to be a hell of a fight no matter what. We may lose a lot of people, but we don't have a choice. The Thalosians have a history of killing captives, rather than give them up."

"And if you are successful?"

The Commander had the feeling that the man already knew the answer. "The Thalosians have committed an unprovoked act of war. They've killed thousands of innocent people. They invaded us once before, but we did not retaliate. It is my belief that they intend to invade again with so much force that we won't be able to stop them." He hesitated before he finished. "We're here to rescue as many as we can, but I have orders to take steps to assure that there will never be another invasion."

Ban-Sor nodded his head and smiled. "My friend, I fully understand the reasoning behind your decisions, but your steps will have to change."

Haute was incredulous. He spoke slowly, maintaining an easy tone, not wishing to upset or anger the being in any way. He realized that he was entering untested waters. He had to keep in mind that he was not addressing a man, and that he really had no clue as to what Ban-Sor was capable of. He chose his words carefully. "Ban-Sor ... I can't just stop what we've started. I have specific orders." The strange man still smiled, as if he hadn't a care in the world. "I can't ignore this." Haute's voice grew serious. "I won't ignore this."

Ban-Sor stood silently, expressionless except for the stony smile across his face.

Haute narrowed his eyes in frustration. "Did you hear me?"

Ban-Sor placed both hands on Haute's shoulders, brought his face close and looked directly into his eyes, still smirking happily. "Here's the deal, Commander. I'll help you get your people back, but as far as your orders are concerned, well, they will have to change. Would you consider that acceptable?"

Haute shook his head, wanting to believe that it was that easy and that he had a choice in the matter. "Of course it's acceptable to me, but I have to answer to other people for my actions. I had a hard enough time convincing myself that you were real. How can you expect me to explain something like this? They think I'm crazy already."

"And are you?" Ban-Sor asked, releasing his grip.

Haute considered the question. Truthfully, he answered. "No, I'm not. I'm just scared. I'm scared for what might happen a year from now, or ten years from now, or after I'm gone. I appreciate anything you can do, but if we leave them here like this, they won't stop. They'll come back and do it again. Believe me, at first I didn't agree with this plan, but I've thought it out. It's the only way to protect ourselves, the only sure way."

"And what of the next race of beings you discover? Will you do the same to them?"

"Of course not, but these creatures have no respect for human life. They kill with no reason, no conscience." Haute's face was red with anger.

Ban-Sor looked about the compound. "If they fail here, they will re-evaluate ... re-think. They know you will be expecting them, and they won't return to your system."

"How can you know that? What do we do if you're wrong? Are you suddenly going to pop in and save the day?"

"You have to trust me," Ban-Sor answered simply.

Haute shook his head, committing his sanity once again to a man he barely knew, but could not say no to. "Before I do anything, I have a request."

Ban-Sor seemed somewhat surprised. "And what might that be?"

"I want you to meet some people." Haute seemed actually animated with the notion. "I mean I want them to meet you, to just see you."

"Go and get your friends." Ban-Sor smiled.

Haute turned and departed, looking back once or twice to ensure that man was still there.

Ban-Sor watched him go, shaking his head in good humor. He simply didn't understand, but how could he expect him to. He and his people were just children in this universe, not able to comprehend the ways of the adults. He surmised that maybe this man that he had chosen, if given the opportunity, might be able to grasp a small part of his surroundings. Maybe he could glimpse the dimensions just beyond his primitive perception. He smiled at the thought. Now that would be an impressive adventure.

He laughed inside, imagining his report to whomever he was going after. The Commander would be angry and embarrassed once again. It would be amusing to watch, but not today; he did not have the time.

Minutes later, Haute returned with Gary Kusan and Colonel Rennick anxiously following. He found Ban-Sor gone again, but wasn't surprised. Shaking his head, he couldn't help being amused. His disappearance, of course, was expected.

CHAPTER 15

▼

Ban-Sor appeared in the dim light of a subterranean passage. He had absolutely no idea exactly where in the cavern network he was, but he could tell up from down. He turned and made his way deeper into the tunnel. Within minutes, he passed remains of humans, and further on, what remained of those inhuman. He could see well enough to realize that nothing alive remained in the tunnel.

Soon, he could make out a muffled roar. A few steps further, he came within sight of the chamber entrance. He stopped to ponder his next move, wondering in what form he should make his grand entry. Deciding to make it dramatic, he kept his human form. As he continued forward, he came within full view of the opening, blinding brightness pouring outward from within. He saw only three Thalosians near the entrance.

Walking boldly toward the three, he was immediately seen. Agitation filled the creature's demeanor as they moved towards him. Without hesitation, they triggered their weapons. A triple set of beams filled the short space between shooters and target.

Ban-Sor stopped, flinching in apprehension at this new untested experience, but to his surprise and delight, all three shots missed badly. One of the blasts struck the ceiling above his head, bringing down rock, dust, and sparking wires as the lighting system in the tunnel was severed.

When the second volley missed as well, he could barely contain himself, nearly bursting out with laughter. He walked towards them again, knowing they couldn't possibly miss again.

He was correct. At a distance of only thirty feet, two of the three actually struck him. The insect beings watched as their shots flung the intruder backwards into the dimness of the tunnel. They immediately moved forward to examine their kill.

The blasts had indeed been on target, hitting Ban-Sor in the upper chest and lower right hip. Much to his surprise, he found himself on the floor of the tunnel. He rose slowly, spitting dirt. He had anticipated the hits, but had underestimated the blunt force of the impact.

Rising to one knee, he groaned in pain, rubbing his chest. Not wishing to be shot again, he raised his hand in protest, and with a whim, froze the aliens in their tracks. As he stood, sharp pain radiated from his buttocks as well. Only then did he remember how vulnerable the frail human form was. Silently, he commended the entire race on their ability to survive with such weakness. Taking his time, he studied the immobile creatures as he made his way past them.

On the surface, Commander Haute again found himself in a unique predicament. He knew what Kusan and Rennick were thinking, but stood his ground. At least one of them had personally talked with William Vient and been told that there had indeed been a stranger with them at their first meeting. Also, there was the unexplained disappearance from the command shuttle and reappearance on Earth; an impossible feat, no matter how they dissected it. Those two facts had kept a shadow of doubt in everyone's mind and kept the Commander in charge. He shook his head as he explained himself yet again.

He could only guess where his elusive friend had disappeared to this time. If he was right, then things could begin to happen very quickly. A part of him fully expected some eighteen thousand people to suddenly materialize within the compound, or even better, to reappear on Shannate. Was the being capable of something so incredible? Either way, the impossible feats would prove once and for all, that this so called figment of his imagination actually existed. In truth, he had no idea what to expect. Regardless, he organized a party of men to start down the tunnel. He also checked with the transport ships. They were ready.

Suddenly, he had time to think. He had orders from the highest authority to wipe this race from existence. Now, an entity, known only to him, had made it clear that this was not going to happen. He could envision his explanation, how inadequate it would be. "I disobeyed direct council orders because Ban-Sor wouldn't allow it."

Sievers would say, "Is this Ban-Sor able to speak for himself? Where is he? Why won't he show himself? I believe we've been through this before, Commander!"

If he went along with this being, he could be risking his entire career and possibly the future of all Belaquins. He had to have proof, and that would again, be Ban-Sor's decision. If he ever saw him again, these points would have to be made clear. Unexplainable actions may do no more than bolster the belief that he was incompetent. Favorable outcomes may suggest that he was lucky as well. To save himself this time, he would need living, breathing, talking evidence.

Two miles away, and some three hundred meters underground, the proof that Haute so badly needed stood at the end of the main tunnel. All other Thalosian guards on the upper level had been immobilized before they could begin to raise their weapons. The chamber lay before him. Nothing in all of his centuries could have prepared him for what he saw. The cavern could have held a small city. It surpassed any preconceived idea that Ban-Sor might have had.

A cloudy fog of moisture and heat rising up from below hid the ceiling. The fog glowed brightly, lit by invisible lights above. On the cavern floor below, the mass of people and insects reached as far as he could see. He stood open mouthed as he took in the amazing sight. He hadn't given much thought as to what to expect in this place, but what he had to do wasn't going to be as easy as he promised.

The first aspect he noticed, concerned numbers. If there were eighteen thousand humans here, then there must be upwards of two hundred thousand Thalosians.

Ban-Sor was overwhelmed by the enormity of it all, and wondered how to handle the problem. It was a fact that many members of the Belaquin race may not be ready to his existence and capabilities. So how does he create this miraculous rescue without arousing suspicion in eighteen thousand eyewitnesses? He had doubts that any of them at this point would question how, but later, someone would.

To simply freeze the aliens, would require more than a logical explanation on Haute's part. Quickly, he decided that the method he had used so far wouldn't be the best solution. It would have to appear to be something more natural, something the majority could find readily acceptable.

His time was limited. He watched several dozen Thalosians moving up both ramps. Even though their facial features were fixed and rigid, they somehow gave forth, seemingly, angry expressions. Could the motionless insects around him still communicate?

Ban-Sor closed his eyes, knowing what he was about to attempt would take all the concentration he could muster. The dull ache in his chest and buttocks, which he had left as a painful reminder of his earlier experience, subsided as he closed everything out of his mind. Within seconds, his human form faded and disappeared as he lost even that small distraction of control.

In the next moment, insect soldiers scurried past and even through what was left of his formless body. They stopped, dumbfounded beside their statue like companions. Then, before they could even take another breath, each of them collapsed.

Shannation prisoners on the floor of the chamber, watched in puzzled fascination as aliens around them began to fall in place. In all visible respects, they appeared lifeless. Within seconds, the only beings still moving on the cave floor were human.

Ban-Sor, without physical body, monitored his endeavor. All of the insect creatures were helpless, as planned. The prisoners needed no coaxing to take their first steps to freedom. They knew the way out. Slowly, they made their way through the maze of fallen alien bodies towards the ramps.

As he watched, he took great care not to loosen his control on the Thalosians. He thought ahead to the next problem, the Republic's plan to destroy this very unique civilization. Why should he care what happens to these clueless, hopeless cultures? Why did he even let himself get involved? The first episode with the Belaquin people had involved extreme manipulation, but he had done it with good intention. In his modest opinion, it had turned out well. He had to admit, he felt truly different with these humans. He found them to be a fascinating species, forever changing and full of surprises. Their history was colorful and entertaining through all their ages. Their cultures, values, and priorities weren't that different from his. Compared to other civilizations, he felt as if he could be swayed in their favor, but this was a sway he could not allow himself to completely be taken in by. He had his own future to think about. It would be dangerous if the elders ever found out. It could prove disastrous for the Belaquin people if he were somehow enticed by them to use his powers in specific ways. The elders would punish all involved, fault or no fault.

He had recently found that he had a conscience and had no desire to burden it with the uncomfortable feeling of guilt. It was wrong in the first place for him to interfere, but to stop now would be more wrong.

He was determined to assist them, at least enough to survive this senseless predicament. He would also assist the Thalosian race to survive, by preventing a senseless vengeful act by the Republic.

The first few people had reached the tops of the ramps and disappeared into the single tunnel that provided entrance and exit. Those who were healthy helped the sick. Those who could walk, instead of running, helped carry those who couldn't. Maybe it was this human compassion that impressed him the most. The measure of it surprised him. Most humans exhibited it in every part of their lives, while other species had none. No … there could be no wrong in it.

The ramps soon filled with the endless stream of people, each one wishing to see the light of the sun one more time. They didn't know it, but a guardian angel of sorts had taken steps to make the wishes come true.

Nearer to the surface, two Republic soldiers manned their assigned station, several hundred yards into the main tunnel. They sat silently, scanning for any contacts from below. Personnel earlier, who had placed portable "suns" along the tunnel, illuminating it from their location to the surface, had accompanied them. When the work was done, they were left alone.

The motion sensors had been inactive since they arrived, but suddenly, they began emitting a steady constant signal. At the same time, sounds came from the darkness below. It was obvious that something big was on its way to them.

The two men took position, nervously readying their weapons. One contacted the surface and advised of the approaching contact. A moment later, they lowered their guns. The sounds, which they could now easily make out, were human voices. In the next instant, at the furthest point of visibility, movement appeared a hundred men and women hurrying towards them. As the first approached, one of the soldiers yelled. "Keep going, follow this tunnel!" The first group passed without slowing. The two soldiers stood against the wall, and watched the multitude pass.

The evacuation, which had moved quickly at first, dragged on for the better part of an hour. Ban-Sor didn't wish to wait, but finally, all living persons were out of the massive arena. As far as the lifeless humans that lay below? He felt no obligation to them. Still, he had to remain a while longer. It would take time to load the ships on the surface.

Commander Haute was incredulous. The sight of the crowds of people emerging from the tunnel was staggering. Many of the transport ships were nearly full. Others were already on their way home. As the people continued to emerge from the tunnel, he wondered if their original estimates from Shannate were correct. Even so, no one took into full consideration a fact that he now noticed. A large number of the people coming from the depths were obviously not from Shannate. Those persons appeared to have been here much longer. He guessed that after this day, many missing person's files would be marked as found, and many more dropped as deceased.

At last, word came from the deepest point within radio contact that no one had passed for several moments. The scouts were awaiting orders. A squad of men was dispatched to search for anyone who might be left. With the numbers involved in the mad rush to escape, it was probable that some injured were unable to make the journey. A search was morally demanded.

As the team descended, Haute wondered what they might find. What had Ban-Sor done with the Thalosian captors? He could only guess. If he never saw the strange man again, that's all he would ever be able to do.

The squad approached cautiously, expecting anything. They had reports from the newly freed prisoners, that the Thalosians were dead. It seemed highly unlikely, yet the fact that thousands of people had just escaped unscathed, supported the claims. Upon reaching the chamber they found the unexpected. In mute disbelief, the twenty men descended the ramps to check for survivors.

Sometime later, Haute was shocked to receive the official report from below. According to the men, after using visual and mechanical means, they concluded that the creatures were indeed dead. Absolutely nothing in the chamber stirred. Even the air was as still as the apparent death it enveloped. Confusion filled the Commander's thoughts as he recalled what Ban-Sor had said concerning his orders.

Haute had an important decision to make. Phases one and two were complete. Only one remained. He had extermination teams ready to do their job, even though it looked as if Ban-Sor had taken care of it. He would use them to at least seal in the unhatched eggs, a task that actually wasn't necessary if the Thalosians were truly dead. Surely, the alien young could not hatch and survive on their own, but this was a subject with no reference.

It was a fact that all the Thalosians were not dead. Possibly thousands had escaped the mountain unseen, thousands that could at that very moment be on their way to the compound to attack. If he withdrew his forces now, would he be charged with deliberately disobeying orders during a state of war? If so deemed, his punishment would be severe. Would Ban-Sor prevent that from happening? It didn't matter. He had to do his duty. If Ban-Sor were sincere in not allowing the Republic to follow through, then he would prevent it somehow.

Another dilemma presenting itself was the possible recovery of the deceased, who still lay below, unidentified and unburied. It had never been believed that this was the only Thalosian stronghold on the planet. If other alien forces were approaching, then the successful rescue mission could still very quickly, turn disastrous. Expedient conclusion and departure was the priority at this point. If they were on their own ground, it would be different.

For reasons unknown, Ban-Sor had already assisted in the final phase, or at least it seemed so. It was time to finish it. His decision was made. "If there are no survivors down there, seal it up and get out."

The team sent down to the main chamber consisted of four men. They had received reports from the scouts who had visited the chamber earlier, that there were no survivors. If that were true, then it made their mission easy.

The team leader stopped their vehicle at the end of the tunnel. He looked at his men and shook his head, knowing they felt as he did. He felt anger towards the squad members who had preceded them. They had been less than truthful in their report to the commander. In the short time they had spent below ground, they could not have made a thorough effort to locate survivors. The task had now fallen upon him and his men. It was a disheartening realization. To search this underground sea of bodies was impossible, far and above the four men's meager capabilities.

The Captain knew he could not leave this place unless he made one final attempt. He needed to soothe his own conscience if nothing else. Wasting no time, he fired his laser several times towards the far wall of the cavern, to draw any attention from below. When the sound died away, he yelled at the top of his lungs, "Is anyone down there?" As his voice faded away, he strained to hear, even holding his breath in case that slight sound might cover up someone's plea for help. Only silence bounced back. It was the loudest sound he had ever heard.

He tried several more times and still heard nothing. Finally, he admitted to himself that it was no use. It was time to finish the job. As he followed the other members of the team out, the young officer turned one last time, silently praying that he was leaving no one to die there. He felt a hint of sadness. Only a day ago, he was ready to kill all of these creatures without a hint of remorse. Now, witnessing so much death, he was overwhelmed. What lay beneath him must be the largest single tomb in the universe, and he was the one chosen to seal it forever. Suddenly, it was a task he would gladly pass on to someone else.

Stiffly, he re-entered the main tunnel. The other men had already moved towards the surface. A hundred feet in, he fired short bursts into the tunnels ceiling. As he hoped, tons of rock finally gave way, quickly sealing the narrow entrance. Choking dust filled the air, forcing him to trot up the slope. The moment the rock came down, the light emanating from the chamber was cut off, plunging him into pitch darkness. Shining his portable light back towards the chamber, he could see nothing. If the tunnel wasn't completely sealed, no one would ever know. He wasn't about to wait around and recheck it. The other men had moved still further ahead to escape the dust. Even straining, he couldn't see the lights of the vehicle. The lantern cast eerie shadows about the tunnel as he walked. Soon, his walk increased to a run as his mind willed him to catch up.

Ban-Sor was not overly upset as he watched the tunnel closed. He had figured as much from the Commander. He was just following orders, having been put in an extremely precarious position. Learning that the cavern was sealed would put his mind at ease. The Commander would believe that he had done his duty to its fullest extent.

The Commander's anxiety had ceased long before the reports reached him from below. The most important part of the mission was complete. He could report to the council, the safe return of the greater majority of the prisoners. The mission had accrued minimal casualties. He found it amusing that he didn't even need to explain the circumstances of phase two. He truly did not know the details of what had transpired, resulting in the release of their people. Phase three could easily be explained as well. There was no shortage of witnesses substantiating that all known Thalosians were dead and the main chamber sealed. He knew that this particular compound was a major site on the planet, but also knew that there had to be others. He held concern for these other locations, but what had happened here would hurt the Thalosians greatly. Ban-Sor was probably correct in his assumption that they would reconsider before repeating this mistake. His only worry now was the possibility that all the Shannation prisoners had not been in this compound.

He could think of no worse fate than for someone to be left behind. Anyone neglected in such a way would surely perish quickly in this lonely alien place. Haute considered the horrible possibility, but there was no way to be sure, until the identified survivors were marked off the missing list. There would be public outcry from families concerned that a loved one was still trapped alive in the tunnels, lost in the darkness. Others would object to the lack of sympathy for the deceased by leaving them where they lay. The Commander would deal with each issue in turn. He would show the grieving families that he understood and sympathized. His own comfort would come from knowing that this was war and that ugliness, inhumanity and irretrievable loss always followed in its wake.

He had sent best wishes with Gary Kusan to carry to Kahn. He had not seen him since he had entered the tunnels. By now, he was safely aboard the Aquillon. He would see him soon enough.

He stood alone on a shuttle entrance ramp. The last of the troops were readying for departure. There was no need for him to remain in the compound, but the bare ground and the surrounding forested hills, although dangerous, seemed more welcoming than the cold walls of the ship above.

Colonel Rennick caught his attention from across the pen by whistling loudly. He was boarding another shuttle and waved as he disappeared inside. Haute waved back at his long time friend, wondering if he thought that he had lost his mind. It didn't matter. This day had gone better than anyone had hoped, and that was all he cared about.

Where had Ban-Sor gone this time, after stepping in to save the day? He couldn't begin to guess. Would he come back again? If a crisis were required for the being to appear, he would just as soon not see him ever again.

A strong gust of wind kicked up dust in the far end of the compound, blowing in his direction. Visible above the hills were dark rain clouds, billowing towards the sea. The fast moving air reached him. He stood and closed his eyes, feeling it gently push him as it passed. The small dirt particles stung his face as they hit and moved on. He welcomed the experience. It would be the last breeze he would feel for the week to come. As he relished the moment, he wondered where his pilot was. He was sure that he was not on board the craft.

As much as he would enjoy standing in the approaching shower, he felt it prudent that he not tempt fate. It was time to leave this place. More than likely, he would never to return and could only hope not to.

Suddenly, something from behind him fell softly upon his shoulder, causing him to jerk with fright. He knew that there was no one inside. Even before he turned, he knew whom it had to be.

Ban-Sor motioned for him to come inside. The Commander hesitated, looking about. The nearest person was at least two hundred feet away, too far to be a witness. He entered the shuttle, his steps grinding on the dusty floor. The shuttle door closed behind him, even though he had not triggered it.

Ban-Sor had seated himself at a table. He spoke as Haute approached. "The deeds of the day are finished my friend."

Haute joined him at the table. "I thank you, but why the change in plans?"

"Nothing has changed. Everything is as I said I would be."

Haute decided not to press the issue just yet. It seemed that maybe his friend had settled in for a long talk. If that were the case, "Would you like a drink?"

Ban-Sor seemed lost in thought for a moment before answering. "As long as it's not rum."

"I don't think we have that," Haute remarked. The dispenser dropped crushed ice into two glasses, followed by mixture number 23. He handed one of them to Ban-Sor. "You saved our people. How ... I can only guess. All I can do is thank you, unless you could tell me a way to repay you."

Ban-Sor took a sip of the glasses contents, immediately pleased at the taste. "Delicious!" he exclaimed. "What do you call this?"

Haute sipped his own drink. "They call it Coca-Cola."

"I must say, it's incredible!" He finished the rest, rising himself to refill the glass. "I didn't do it for reward, Commander. I've already received my thanks from you in one way, and from your people in another." Ban-Sor could see uncertainty in the man's face. "Commander, I know that our affairs have been confusing at the very least. The position I've forced upon you is frustrating, and I apologize. You above all, understand the dispute I could cause. You live in a culture where beings like me don't exist."

"I do understand that. I can handle what others think, but it's more personal than that. You're right. You're something out of a dream, something that can't exist. Of course, I want to show you off. I guess I'm honored, but it's an empty feeling not being able to share you." He dropped his eyes to his glass. "Ban-Sor, I have so many questions. I want to know everything about you ..."

"But wouldn't that make it even more difficult?" Ban-Sor asked.

"Well, maybe, but I don't care. I can't ... not know!"

To Ban-Sor, the man suddenly looked disheartened ... seemingly older. He reached across the table and touched his arm. "Be content in what you know now. In some ways you and I are much alike. We both have great power at our command. The people of your worlds rely on the belief that your wisdom watches over them. You have their respect. If you knew all the things that you wish to, then all that you are would be gone. What is important to you now, would no longer be. You would not, could not, be the leader you are. I'm sorry, my friend, but I won't take that away from you. Your people still need guidance, and they will trust in your judgment." He paused and smiled, looking straight into Haute's eyes. "They will as long as you don't keep telling ridiculous and unfounded stories."

Haute couldn't help but crack a smile at the jest, but still, he felt unsatisfied. Ban-Sor understood his plight, but that fact did not lessen the empty feeling inside him. He knew now, that this being, for whatever reasons, would never reveal what he so desperately wanted to know. "I appreciate your opinion, Ban-Sor, but I'm just a man following orders."

"As many great men in your history were."

Haute shook his head. "I'm glad you choose to put me in that category, but I don't think so."

Ban-Sor laughed. "Really Commander, you sell yourself short."

"A great leader would never have let any of this happen. Without your influence, this would have been a disaster."

"Perhaps, but there's no way you can ever know that, is there?" Ban-Sor answered.

Haute shook his head, again conceding to questions within him. "I'm having trouble understanding something that you did. You said you wouldn't allow us to destroy the Thalosians, but by all reports given to me, you've already done it."

"Your men were accurate. In all appearances, they were dead. In reality, I just put them out for a while. They're probably digging out as we speak."

"Digging out?" Haute exclaimed. The thought was unsettling in the least.

"Of course, you don't think they moved in with the tunnels furnished. If they do one thing well, it's digging."

"Forgive me, but I don't understand." Haute had a hint of distress in his tone. "Tell me again what's going to keep them from coming after us?"

"You've taken care of their ships, correct?"

"These ships … yes. We've disabled them, but they have to have more!"

"Perhaps, but they have more important things to worry about. They will be in no position to accost your people again."

"I pray you're right." He watched Ban-Sor guzzle another glass. Inside, he tried to control his anxiety, hoping that the beings word would be enough. It was difficult to keep in mind that he wasn't the young man he appeared to be. In all probability, he had a Thalosian form and countless others as well. How many others? It was just one of a hundred questions he wished to ask. "Where do you go from here, Ban-Sor?"

The beings eyebrows lifted. "Oh … I'll move on to other unfinished business, as yours once was." Haute asked hopefully.

"You've been sort of a guardian angel to us. Should we expect you to keep watching over us?"

"You never know what the future will bring."

Haute narrowed his eyes as he read into the words. Did they suggest that he might be? He felt he knew the true message being sent. He couldn't mask the disappointment in his voice as he asked his next question. "Will I ever see you again?"

Ban-Sor's half smile faded, replaced by a solemn expression. "It is possible." He hesitated, sensing a feeling he hadn't felt often. "Your people have much too look forward to. They haven't even begun to realize their future, and neither have you. Just let the years turn into history, as this day will. As far as the small part that I had a hand in, well, that is part of our history, no one else's."

Haute listened intently, absorbing the words, as if they would be the last. He spoke of an interesting future. Did he truly know the future? As he looked on, Ban-Sor offered his open hand. Haute hesitated. If this was goodbye, he didn't want to take it. What could he say to prolong this unique beings company? He tried to pick the right words to say, but found none. Finally, he took the hand, perhaps for the final time. "You really can't stay for a while?"

Ban-Sor shook his head slowly and seemingly sadly. "I already have ..." He said nothing for a long moment and then with a sigh, put his farewell into words. "It's been a pleasure to spend time with you, Commander. I have enjoyed every moment, however few there were. Live as close to forever as you can my friend. I hope you can reach out and grasp it. If you do, don't ever let go."

"Forever is a long time," Haute managed.

"It's not as long as you might think." Ban-Sor chuckled.

Haute wanted to smile, but could not. Even as the last words ended, Ban-Sor faded slowly from sight, the firm grip of his hand disappearing as well. He closed his empty hand into a tight fist.

Suddenly, he felt something else leaving him, something he couldn't quite place. Panic struck him as he realized what was happening. His memory was fading, or at least a small part of it. Frantically, he looked around the room, struggling to stop it. Angry frustration filled him. He knew now, that Ban-Sor was relieving all of his worries, simply by erasing any trace of himself from his mind. He closed his eyes, trying to retain something ... anything, but it was too late.

His concentration was broken as the door to the shuttle opened. He stared at the man who entered, his hand still closed in front of him. For a moment, he felt dizzy, his mind seemingly without thought.

The man spoke. "Commander Haute?"

He heard the words, but couldn't form an answer. The only sure thought he could identify was the feeling of helplessness, but why? Other thoughts came, confusing, conflicting. The dizziness made him sit down heavily in the chair beside him.

"Commander," the figure at the door repeated, "Are you all right?"

Like a light being turned on, his surroundings suddenly began to make sense. The man who had spoken to him was now, recognizable. He was a good friend and his shuttle pilot, Mike Roberts. Everything came back with a rush.

The sound of rainfall met his ears, and he noticed the distinct damp smell that only fresh rain could bring. Thunder echoed outside. The sun, which had shone since they arrived, was gone. He noted concern on the pilots face. Had he said something to him? Finally, Haute spoke. "You're wet, Mike."

"Yes sir," The pilot smiled with relief. "It's turned into a mud hole out there. I wasn't sure if you were in here or not. I left the door open, but...."

Haute shook his head. "I must have closed it. Sorry, I don't remember."

"Are you about ready to get out of here? Most everyone else is gone."

Haute hesitated. "Almost; just give me one minute." He rose and walked past the man, stopping upon the ramp outside the ship. The cool rain pelted him. Within seconds, it had soaked his head and shoulders, but he didn't care. It wasn't often he took advantage of a moment like this.

Inside, Roberts remained silent, not fully understanding the action, but envying the older mans ability to find pleasure in such simplicity. Shaking his head, he moved forward to ready the ship for take-off, leaving his commanding officer to his well-deserved minute.

The rain slowed to a gentle drizzle as Haute stood with his eyes closed. He didn't know why, but he felt more alive, more content than he ever had. His thoughts reached deeply. How many more times in his life would he stand alone in a rainstorm? How many more times in his life would he stop and watch a sunrise or a sunset? How could he never have noticed the beauty of so many small things? He took them for granted so often, sometimes every day of his life? How could he forget that every moment once passed is lost forever? He knew that there had to be thousands of them that he had never even noticed, and would never remember.

The rain slowed. He opened his eyes and made a promise to himself to remember more often, and to savor the moments like this one.

Finally, he took a last look around. As his pilot had said, most of the other ships had already left. He turned back inside and closed the door behind him. He had a bizarre feeling, as if something were undone or missing. It was a nagging absence, similar to the frustration of not being able to remember someone's name or the title to a song. But worse, since he could not begin to guess what it was he was searching for.

His gaze fell upon a puzzling sight. On the table at the rear of the shuttle sat two glasses. One was his. He could remember drinking it. But why two? No one was with him before the pilot had come in, or had there been? He wasn't sure. He vaguely remembered talking to someone, but whom? Finally, he dismissed the thought and made his way to the pilot's seat. It was time to leave.

Aquillon One received word of the command shuttles approach from the surface. Preparations had been made to leave the Thalosian system as soon as the vessel was aboard.

The ships medical facility was swamped with military, as well as civilian wounded from the planet below.

Gary Kusan made his way there as soon as he left the docking bay. It took some searching, but he finally found Colleen in one of the surgery waiting rooms. She was alone as he entered. She saw him coming and met him halfway across the floor, embracing him in tears.

"I didn't think you were coming back," she sobbed, squeezing him tightly.

Gary admitted to himself that he had felt the same way for a while. "You can't get rid of me that easy," he answered. Her body felt wonderful. He closed his eyes, burying his face in her soft hair. Compared to the smell of his own body, it was welcome freshness. He had not had the time or facility to shower on the trip back. "Have you see Kahn?" he asked.

She looked into his eyes, wiping her own. "Yeah, Deanna's with him in his room. He's gonna be okay." Tears came again as she anticipated his next question.

Gary knew what they were for and realized that their albino friend must not be doing well. "How is he?"

Colleen tried to speak, but her throat ached from trying to hold it in for so long. Finally, she could. "He's been in surgery since we got here."

"Have they said anything?"

She nodded her head. "They said it was a cerebral bleed, or something ... inside his brain."

"Can they fix it?"

"They can try to relieve the pressure, but they have to stop the bleeding. It's in a bad place, hard to reach."

Gary held her tighter as she started to sob again. "C'mon babe ... we've got the best doctors there are. If they can help him, they will." He felt a change in subject would be better. "How's your sister?"

"She's okay ... a little dehydrated, but okay. Her arm has a hairline fracture ... right here." She touched her own arm just above the elbow. "They put on a splint."

"I know, I saw it earlier. Good. Let's go see her and Kahn for awhile."

Colleen looked to the surgery doors, which had been closed for so long, wondering how she was going to cope. In a way, she figured, this was her fault. She had suggested hiring him to take them to Shannate. Then again, if she hadn't, then someone else would have. She wiped her eyes again, and noticed for the first time, Gary's filthy condition. She frowned in disgust, suddenly catching the unmistakable odor of the Thalosian caverns. "You need to clean up first."

Gary was surprised. "Hey, I'm good! I'm okay."

She pushed him toward the corridor. "No ... you're not. Let's go."

He didn't argue. At least this would get her mind off of Avraham for a while.

An hour later, they approached Kahn's hospital room. When they entered, they found Deanna beside the bed in a chair, asleep. Kahn lay upright in bed, also in unconscious slumber. He was bare-chested, with numerous electrodes stuck to him. A white cloth was wrapped around his ribs. Two intravenous lines connected his left arm to the bags above him. He had oxygen tubing in his nose and hooked around his ears. He seemed to be breathing normally. The heart monitor beeped, signaling each beat. Low snoring from Kahn accompanied the steady rhythmic sound.

Gary took Colleen's arm and quietly led her away. "Let's go see Kelsey. Let 'em sleep.

Minutes later they entered another room, where Colleen's sister was found awake, watching television. Colleen sat down beside her on the bed, holding her sisters hand in her own. "Taking it easy, huh?"

"Always." The young woman's voice was cheerful. The total reversal of circumstances was apparently allowing her to recover in every way.

Gary stood close by, seeing Kelsey in a way he never had. On the trail, days earlier, she had obviously been at her worst, but now, safe and sound with a smile on her face, she was a different person, in more ways than one.

She reached her good arm toward him. Her voice was soft and sincere. "Hi, I'm Kelsey, Colleen's sister. That woman you met before? That wasn't me."

Gary took her hand. "Okay ... well, I'm happy to finally meet you."

She continued, "Thank you for what you did down there."

"You're welcome." He felt embarrassed for a moment. Releasing her hand, he wondered if he had held it too long. Did Colleen think that he had? He shook his head and frowned. The thought was ridiculous.

Kelsey then spoke to her sister. "How's Avraham?"

Colleen could see in her cheery eyes that she didn't have a clue as to the seriousness of his injury. She maintained herself perfectly as she answered. "We don't know. He's still in surgery."

"He's still there?" Kelsey exclaimed. Concern replaced her smile. "He's not going to ...?" She stopped, not allowing herself to even say it.

Colleen shook her head. "The doctors didn't seem too hopeful."

Kelsey dropped her eyes. "That would kill Mom and Dad."

Colleen agreed. "Yeah it would, but let's not count him out yet, okay?"

Gary noted the blue splint, enclosing her arm from shoulder to wrist. It looked extremely uncomfortable. "I heard it was broke?"

She frowned. "Yeah, kind of, I've got to keep this on for five or six weeks. Real sexy, huh?"

Gary widened his eyes, considered speaking his mind, and did it, jokingly. "Well, considering the gown you've got on, I didn't even notice." He received a blind gut slap from the nearer sister. "What!" he yelled. He caught a beautiful smile from Kelsey and smiled back.

Kelsey let her eyes linger on the young man for only a few seconds, but apparently, for him, it was too much. He finally looked away. She had to admit, her sister had found a real winner, at least in the looks category.

Gary, somewhat uneasy, spoke. "Hey, I'm gonna go get a drink and leave you guys alone for a minute. Anybody want anything?" Both women shook their heads as he left.

Colleen voiced her concern with another matter. "How's everything else?"

With no modesty, Kelsey answered bluntly. "You mean … do I have anything?"

"Well, I wasn't gonna put it that way. My God!"

"The vote's still out, I guess. They took tests a little while ago, but they said they wouldn't know for a few hours."

Colleen paused and looked into her eyes. Outside, she seemed normal, but had these last few days taken their toll on the inside? Time would tell.

Kelsey could see all that her sister didn't say. "Hey …" she said, squeezing her hand. "I'm all right believe me. It was hard for a while, but I'm over it. No nightmares, none of that crap. I just want to get back home, if there's anything left. The bastards killed my apartment door, I do remember that!"

Colleen smiled half-heartedly in return. Now she sounded like her old sibling.

Kelsey continued, touching her splinted arm. "I wish I could thank the one that did this."

"I'm sure he'd appreciate that."

"I'm serious. If he hadn't hit me, I'd be dead, right?" she reasoned.

Colleen considered what she said, and nodded her head in agreement. In a twisted way, she was right. The Thalosian, by inflicting the injury, had possibly saved her life. Saviors sometimes appeared in strange forms.

Colleen stood and stretched. "How long you have to stay here?"

Kelsey shrugged her shoulders. "I'm ready to get out of here now."

"If they release you, I'll see if you can bunk with me."

"Is this the ship you're stationed on?" She seemed mildly excited with the thought.

"Where did you think you were?"

"Well, hell, I didn't know ... a ship! I didn't know which one."

Gary rejoined them. "You're aboard Aquillon One, flagship to the fleet."

"Cool. You can show me around later." Again, she locked eyes with him for a teasing moment.

Gary smiled, wondering if she meant him, or both of them. Again, he broke the stare.

Colleen led him towards the door. "Get some rest. We'll see you later."

Passing by Kahn's room again, they saw nothing had changed and continued on.

As they walked, Colleen smiled and spoke. "Don't pay any attention to her, she does that to all my boyfriends."

Gary was at a loss for words. Obviously she had noticed the lingering looks. "Yeah, it made me a little uncomfortable," he admitted.

She chuckled, "As long as you're not uncomfortable between your legs, I don't care."

That was unexpected. "Damn, you don't beat around the bush do you?"

"Hey, you know me; I tell it like it is." She squeezed his hand in hers.

Gary had a thought. 'So how many boyfriends are we talking about?"

He may have hoped to catch her off guard, but she was ready. "Counting you? Oh, a couple of dozen." She dropped his hand and slapped him hard on the butt. "How do you think I got so good?" She couldn't help but feel happy for the moment. He had come back to her in one piece. The moment was short, however. Other worries invaded. How could she feel any joy when her friend was fighting for his life? Before Gary could respond, she spoke again. "Hey, I want to get back to surgery. Do you want to come?"

"I do, but I need to get something to eat first. I'll meet you down there, okay? Did you eat?"

"Yeah, when we got back, I didn't even care what it was, as long as it wasn't fruit."

Gary nodded in understanding "No shit." Just the thought made his stomach churn. He kissed her quickly on the lips. "I'll be there in a little bit."

"Okay, babe ... I love you."

He walked backward away from her down the corridor. "I love you more."

Kahn felt his body jerk. Suddenly, he was awake. It was dark, but not as dark as the tunnels. He may have been dreaming about them, but couldn't quite remember. He started to take a deep sighing breath, but pain caught him halfway through, making him wince in surprise. Now it all came back, the part that hadn't been a dream.

He raised his arm and noticed the wrap around his chest. The plastic piece was gone, and he found that he actually felt pretty good. His hand was wrapped as well. Laying his head back, he retraced what he could remember. He recalled leaving the tunnels and being put on the medship. Someone started an IV on him, and that was it. Nothing else came to mind. They must have knocked him out.

Near his hand was a control panel, lit from within. He touched the button for the bed light. Gradually, it became brighter in the room and for the first time, he noticed the figure beside his bed. Suddenly, he could hear her soft breathing. She was only two feet away. He reached out and gently touched her hair. He felt the uncontrollable feeling of oncoming tears, knowing that he had never loved any woman as much as he did her.

Deanna stirred beneath his touch. Slowly, she leaned over him, wrapping her arms around him, kissing him, saying nothing. She felt the moistness on his eyes and cheeks, and wondered how long he had watched over her. She sat on the bed, her face only inches away from his and stared into his eyes.

Kahn waited for her to speak, anticipating the loving words he knew she would say.

Finally, she said them. "You need a shave."

Kahn sputtered into laughter, holding his side as the pain returned with a vengeance. "Shit! Don't make me laugh!" He winced as he tried to control it.

She moved downward, laying her head on his chest. "You almost did it didn't you."

He had no clue as to what she meant. "Did what?"

"Made me a widow before I was a wife."

Kahn wrapped his arms even tighter around her, letting his headrest against hers, saying nothing. He closed his eyes, content to stay that way forever. Eventually, he spoke. "Where's Gary and Colleen?"

"Colleen was waiting down in surgery, but that was hours ago. Avraham's not doing good. I haven't seen Gary yet." She paused, touching the bandage on his hand. The laceration beneath had already been fused together. "What happened down there?"

"Well, like you said … I almost did it." He shook his head, not believing how close he had come to ending it all. He continued. "We went back down in the tunnels. Jimenez and I got separated from the others. The bugs were coming for us. We made it into a side tunnel and he held them off … told me to run. I didn't want to, but I did what he said. I ran forever. Then I fell hard and the next thing I knew, I was hanging over the edge of a cliff."

Deanna listened intently, trying to picture the events. Kahn hesitated, remembering. His throat grew tight as he relived the fear he had experienced. He licked his lips and closed his eyes, putting himself back in the cavern. His voice trembled. "Jesus De … I was so scared. I was sure I'd never see you again." His body shook as he tried to keep it inside. "I don't know how long I was there. It was dark. There was no sound. It really made me think about a lot of things."

Silently, Deanna decided that this was the last time anything like this would happen. She respected Kahn and his career, but she had plans of her own, for the both of them. Kahn's enlistment would be up in a year, and hers in less than two. Maybe there could be some changes. The last mission and now this incident had cut too close. How many times had they come within inches of losing their lives? She knew it wouldn't be easy to turn him, as gung ho as he was, but he seemed more vulnerable now. Maybe what happened below had changed him. Perhaps she could talk him into taking a trainer position at one of the academies. He would still be flying and best of all it would be shore duty. Oh well, that was something to work on in the future.

Kahn continued, "They finally found me … pulled me up." He pushed her away so he could see her face. "I know you're the only reason I held on so long."

Deanna couldn't hold back the tears. It was the sweetest thing she had ever heard from him. After a moment, she spoke. "They said you would have died if that guy wouldn't have helped you."

"I couldn't breathe. My God … I've never hurt like that before," he related.

"The doctor said you had a collapsed lung and two broken ribs. Your lung has re-inflated … something about relieving the pressure. I don't know exactly what they said."

"I don't care what it was; I don't ever want another one." He felt his ribs under his right arm, finding the tenderness. "Did you see what he did to me?"

"I heard."

"Jesus … biggest needle I've ever seen."

Deanna shook her head in disbelief, not wishing to hear any more.

"How long do I have to stay in here … did they say?" Kahn asked.

"Depends on how you do, maybe until tomorrow."

"Great!" The look on his face showed his disgust.

"Hey, don't push it. I want you back a hundred percent." She stood, leaned over and kissed him. "I'll be back later. I'm gonna go find Colleen."

"Okay, I guess I'll be here." Kahn sighed. "Do they have any food in this place?"

"Call and find out." She moved out the door, turning the lights on fully as she went.

"See you later."

His gaze followed her as she bounced into the hallway. "I'll give you a hundred and ten percent when I get out of here." he muttered under his breath. Studying the control panel, he found one switch that was self-explanatory. He pushed it and held it down.

Eventually, a female voice answered. "May I help you?"

"Uh … yeah. Is it possible to get something to eat?"

"I'll be down there in a minute.… Okay?"

"Okay." He had to admit, if she looked half as good as she sounded, it might be worth the wait. He laid back. There was nothing else to do. He frowned suddenly as he noticed for the first time, the plastic tubing on his face. It looped around his ears and two soft plastic tubes were actually in his nostrils. A second later, it lay on the table beside him, deemed unnecessary by his own diagnosis.

Nearby, Deanna entered the surgery section where she found Colleen waiting. Even before she could speak to her, another door opened down the corridor. A young woman dressed in blue scrubs walked towards them.

Colleen rose to stand beside Deanna. The woman was the first and only person to exit the operating room since the doors had closed hours earlier. As she approached, the two could see her sweat soaked collar and cloth wrap across her forehead. "Are you with Mr. Coleridge?" she asked.

Deanna took Colleen's hand and held it tightly. The look on the woman's face and the tone of her voice was far from hope inspiring. Colleen nodded hesitantly, feeling that she knew what was coming.

"I'm Doctor Jordan," she said. Sighing, she dropped her eyes towards the floor. "I'm sorry …"

Colleen turned, burying her head on Deanna's shoulder. The tears flowed freely. She'd held them long enough.

Deanna felt grief welling up inside, not only for Avraham, but for her closest friend as well. When she hurt, they both hurt. "What happened?" she asked.

The doctor shook her head. "The bleeding was too deep. We couldn't get to it. A lot of things went wrong. We tried, but we just couldn't keep him with us."

Deanna wondered about what they'd been through. "What if you'd gotten to him sooner?"

"I don't think it would have made any difference. It would have been just as hard to get to when the injury occurred."

Deanna held her friend, wishing there was something more she could do.

The woman came closer, placing her hand on Colleens arm. "Are you family?"

Colleen turned, anguished. "As close as he has. I've known him my whole life."

"Again, I'm sorry." Her voice held sincerity.

Colleen wiped her face again knowing that she had done everything in her power to save him. "Thank you. What do we do now?"

"We'll take care of him until we get back, and then other arrangements can be made. Is that alright?"

Both girls nodded in unison. There was nothing else to be said. The young woman made her apologies one last time and left the room.

Deanna hugged her again. "Come on, let's go you've been here long enough."

Colleen walked with her. "I need to tell Kelsey. Gary was supposed to meet me here." She stopped, debating on whether to stay.

Deanna kept her walking. "He'll find us, don't worry."

She was right. Within the hour, he had caught up with them in Deanna's cabin. He had already been to Kahn and Kelsey's rooms in an effort to find them. It was there he learned of Avraham's passing. He apologized for not being with her when she needed him. Soon after, Colleen was nearly asleep, finally allowing herself some rest. After the last few trying hours, she was exhausted.

Gary on the other hand, felt relatively good for now. Hearing that Commander Haute had returned, he decided to see him. Upon arrival in the main control room, he learned that he was in his cabin, preparing a report to precede them home. The report had to hold difficult contents. Common courtesy suggested that he not be disturbed. Instead, he decided to explore the one room on the ship that he very seldom saw.

He joined a female officer at one of the stations. She was studying schematics on two separate screens, each appearing to be views of the Aquillon. As he looked closer, he could tell that they were views of two different ships. "I didn't think they would have her done for at least another six months," he said, startling the woman. She obviously had not seen him walk up.

She nodded her head. "Well, you know engineers. They say they need twenty-four hours for something, when they know they can get it done in six."

"Yeah, I know what you mean." Gary answered, gazing at the screens.

The woman studied him. "You're not an engineer, are you?" She asked carefully, knowing she may have already put her foot in her mouth.

"No ... I don't usually fix things, I just break them."

She sighed with relief.

"Pretty impressive, aren't they?" Gary asked.

"That's an understatement." she nodded.

"Have they got the raiders manned on the new ship?"

"About half ..." she answered.

"Who's flying them?"

"That was a problem at first. Haute shuffled everyone around. He split up our air wing and sent half of them over. He activated flight instructors and reserves to fill in. We didn't know what to expect over here. After what they did to Shannate, he figured it would be bad," explained the officer. "Thank God it wasn't. My brother is one of the reserves."

"They attacked us with small fighters back in the old war. I wonder where they were today." Gary thought aloud.

The woman nodded, wondering the same.

Unexpectedly, Leon Haute entered the room. He was all business. "Status report!"

"All transports are leaving orbit. All remaining ships are signaling a green light."

"Signal all destroyers to escort the transport ships. Aquillon Three to follow." Haute barked.

The orders were sent. A moment later, "Destroyers entering light speed. Aquillon Three is one minute behind."

Haute took his seat. "Message received. Navigation, give us light speed at the earliest opportunity."

The female officer leaned closer to Gary, nearly whispering. "He's not in a good mood."

Gary smiled in agreement. He was not the man he had seen on the planet a short time ago. He decided to postpone his unplanned visit. "Yeah, something's up with him," he added. "Hey, thanks for talking. I'm gonna sneak out of here."

She offered her hand. "I'm Asanda ... engineering department." She smiled broadly, embarrassed from the earlier conversation.

Gary smiled back, equally amused and shook her hand. "Gary Kusan, Gold Raider pilot."

Her smile faded somewhat as he turned to leave. She recognized the name. He was the one from Earth. She shook her head, knowing that it wasn't every day you got to meet a hero.

Hours later, everything was running smoothly. A skeleton crew was manning the Aquillon One. Most of the ships complement slept, having been through long unbroken shifts. It was almost as if nothing had happened. Only the memories of the nightmare lingered. It was the same in the minds of Gary, Colleen, Deanna, and Kelsey. The episode was slowly being put behind them. Kahn had a harder time doing so. He still had the pain to remind him.

The next few days passed uneventfully. Colleen and Deanna spent most of it with Kelsey, making up for lost time, strengthening new friendships, taking care of the most important things.

Nothing was mentioned about Kelsey's traumatic incident on the Thalosian ship. In all appearances, she had seemed to come through the experience unscathed, if indeed, that was truly possible. All tests had cleared her health wise. Colleen promised her that she would never bring it up, especially to their parents, who had never approved of their youngest daughters adolescent lifestyle, or her current occupation. If they knew, they would never let the episode be forgotten. They would use it as another example of why everything about her was wrong. If Kelsey could keep it within her, then she would respect her silence as well.

As for Gary and Kahn, the latter had been released, but was on medical leave for an unspecified time. Gary, like all of the thirty-eight Republic personnel who had been incarcerated on Thalosia, was under psychiatric evaluation for a time. Both situations meant no duty shifts.

Commander Haute had prepared an enormous report to send to the Belaquin council, one that contained many holes. He weaved his way through it as best he could, finally admitting to himself that he truly did not know the whole story of what had taken place on Thalosia.

It seemed that he knew the answers, but couldn't remember them. It was strange. He couldn't shake it. He had resolved to let it go, but it ate at him, never fully leaving his thoughts.

Finally, they were nearly home.

In the control room of the Aquillon One, the navigator spoke. "One hour and twenty two minutes to Belaquin orbit."

The officer in charge at the time smiled with anticipation. Each moment passed meant he was a little closer to his wife and three children. He had drawn duty his first day home, which required him to remain on the ship, but just hearing and seeing them would be better than nothing. The shore leave he had coming up could wait the one more day. He sent word of their approach to his commander's room.

When the wake up call came down to Haute's cabin, he answered it on the first ring. He was already awake and dressed. As always, in Republic tradition, he and all higher-ranking officers on the vessel would be in full dress uniform upon arrival. His uniform shirt and pants were light blue, trimmed in white and gold. A pure white cape, trimmed with gold only, fell across his back. In its center, was the Republic insignia. As he had many times before, he was involved in the tedious process of choosing and placing medals and service emblems. It was impossible to wear them all. Many decorations including service length chevrons would be left in the cases on this day. It was doubtful that he would be greeted by anyone that needed reminded of how long he had served. A handful of non-military pins, given for acts of charity or goodwill would also remain. Most had been presented in thanks for few moments graciously volunteered. The occasion dictated his choices. The most prized of all were his combat medals. The diminutive bits of metal brought good memories as well as bad. Some of them were more than thirty years old.

He picked up a small black box and held it. It represented an episode he wished could be rewritten. Slowly, he opened it, revealing a round gold medallion. Five stars surrounded its outer edge. On its front was again, the Republic insignia. On the back, in words too small to read with the naked eye, was the story behind the honored medal. He didn't need to read it. It had been memorized long ago. Though he never wanted it, he didn't regret the feelings it caused within him. It didn't bring courageousness, valor, or selflessness. It reminded him more than anything else, of an undying friendship, a bond so strong that unfortunately, only death could sever. That friendship was with Kahn's father.

The memories were still vivid, including their last night together. They had talked about their future retirement and how they would open their own business and take on uncomplicated lives of civilians. Their future had been set. Then, in the blink of an eye, everything changed. The very next day, Paul was gone, and Haute was left with the precious piece of metal he now held in his hands. He saw his old friend every time he looked into the young mans face.

He removed the medal and attached it to his chest. It was the final piece to go in place. Glancing at his watch, he sighed. Almost time to go. The intercom sounded as he left the room. "ATTENTION DUTY SECTIONS ONE, TWO, THREE, AND FIVE. PASSENGER SHUTTLES WILL BEGIN TRANSPOR-

TATION UPON ARRIVAL. ALL DEPARTING PERSONNEL MUST REGISTER WITH THE RECALL OFFICE BEFORE DISEMBARKING. LIBERTY FOR DUTY SECTION FIVE WILL CONCLUDE AT 0700 HOURS TOMORROW. LIBERTY WILL COMMENCE FOR DUTY SECTION FOUR AT 0730."

By the time the announcement finished, Haute was already in an el-car on the way to the control room. The atmosphere in the room was one of good humor and casual conversation. It turned to silence as he entered.

The Commander, also in an exceptionally good mood, spoke loud enough for everyone in the room to hear. His voice was stern. "I'll say it again. I hate it when you people do that." He smiled as he continued. "If I wanted quiet, I would have stayed in my room." Mild laughter filled the control room. Someone whistled as Haute found his seat. He shook his head without looking to see who had done it. Whoever it was, they were right to do so. A Republic officer's dress uniform was impressive and prestigious.

With a glance he saw that his ship was no longer at light speed. "What's our position Mr. Taft?"

"Fifteen minutes from Belaquin orbit. All systems on automatic."

"That's what I like to hear. What about the rest of the fleet?"

"At last transmission, Aquillon Three was escorting and also on schedule, a half hour behind us."

"Great. Put us in orbit." He looked about the room as he turned to leave. "Good people, I'll leave all of this with you."

Five other members of the ship's complement were also making plans for their immediate future. Kahn, Gary, Deanna, Colleen, and Kelsey had just entered one of the many hangar bays designated for personnel departure. Not only was the bay filled with Aquillon's crewmembers, it was also the staging area for several hundred Shannations requiring transportation home. Under normal conditions, Touchen would have been the Aquillon's initial stop, but with the large volume of passengers to attend to, Belaquins spaceports were deemed more equipped. The room was a madhouse of chaos and confusion.

Kahn led the others to one of two-dozen lines, one moving just as slowly as the next. He shook his head and spoke to Gary. "This could have been done better."

"Yeah, no shit. We'll be here for an hour." Gary answered.

The girls talked together as they waited, excited to be going to see their families after so long. It was a unanimous decision to get off the ship at Belaquin. It was home and it had been a long time in coming. There was no longer a desire to return to Shannate any time soon. Kelsey would eventually have to return there, but there was no need to go now. Shannate City would not be ready for business for some time.

Arrangements had been made to have Avraham's body transported to the planet, where Colleen's parents had made all funeral plans. As Colleen had told the surgeon before, they were as close to family as the man had. They made it clear that nothing concerning the man's life, or his death would be left to chance.

As they waited patiently, they noticed the drama taking place in the very next line. The conversation between an obviously irate man and the young woman attempting to help him had grown into a loud and heated argument. Apparently, from what they could discern, the man, a civilian, was demanding immediate transportation to Shannate. The poor woman was informing him that there were no direct flights from the Aquillon to the planet. She explained, very politely, that these shuttles were going only to Bentar, and that the first few transfers to Shannate from the Bentar Space Center were already full. As the man maintained his angry objections, the people in his line grew thinner and thinner, until no one stood behind him.

A man in a supervisory position finally arrived and joined the woman behind the counter. His demeanor was stern, but his dialogue was polite. "I'm sorry sir. What seems to be the problem?"

The man, throwing up his hands, seemed somewhat relieved. "Finally!" he yelled. "The problem is this stupid bitch that doesn't know her ass from a hole in the ground."

The supervisor, though in the face of stupidity, remained polite. "Sir, I'm here to assist you, as this woman was. I will do so if you maintain a civil tone. Now … what can I do for you?"

"Civil tone, my ass," the man muttered. He lowered his voice somewhat as he spoke again. "Listen to me. I am the vice-president of Shannate's First Commerce Bank. I have to get back there immediately!"

The supervisor glanced at the numbers already on the computer screen below him. He shook his head and with an irritatingly pleasant voice, said. "Sir, what Kimberly told you before was correct. We can get you on the next shuttle to Bentar, but unless an opening becomes available, you will have to wait there. You may of course, try to hire a private flight if they haven't been exhausted."

There was a hush from the crowd of onlookers as they waited, the suspense building. As expected, the last suggestion brought forth from the man, a stream of obscenities that brought the entire room to attention.

The supervisor and the young attendant stood with broad smiles as they listened, enraging the man even more. They smiled only because they knew something that the vice-president did not. Within seconds, four security men approached unseen by the cursing individual. As they stopped only a couple of feet behind him, one spoke. "Excuse me." His voice was deep and drew attention with the simple phrase.

The man whirled, ready for a fight, surprised, but not intimidated. He was not a man of exceptional size or strength. He seemed rather, someone who utilized his position to acquire. He was even less cordial with the newly arrived authoritative figures. "What the hell do you want?"

"Sir, if you don't calm down, we will have to remove you to somewhere you don't want to be." The warning was wordy, but clear.

"Who the fuck do you think you are? If you think you son's a bitch's can …"

His sentence was cut short by the lead security mans short interruption. "Take him."

The other three men moved as one, allowing time for only a surprised cry from their quarry. Before he could resist, his arms were painfully restrained behind his back and he was escorted from the bay. Applause, sporadic at first, soon grew into a standing ovation as the crowd demonstrated their approval. Screams of lawsuits were lost in the din.

Perhaps it was just everyone's imagination, but the lines seemed to move substantially faster after that. Within the hour, the group of five was strapped into their seats for the short flight. The pilot's monotone voice announced. "WELCOME TO FLIGHT ONE FIFTEEN, DESTINATION BENTAR SPACEPORT, DEPARTURE IN FIVE MINUTES. OUR ESTIMATED FLIGHT TIME TODAY WILL BE THIRTY-ONE MINUTES." Gary, his eyes closed, felt Colleen's hand entwine his own as they waited. He sat somewhat reclined, taking advantage of the comfortable seat. Across from them sat Deanna, Kelsey, and Kahn.

The latter decided that it was much too quiet. He looked at Gary with an amusing thought. "Hey, man, you think Jana missed you?"

Gary did not smile or open his eyes, making no indication that he was paying attention at all.

Kahn continued his antagonism. "She's probably moved out of your apartment by now."

Gary opened his eyes slightly, and gave Kahn a dirty look. He knew good and well where his friend was going with it. "She's missed me about as much as the cops missed you."

Deanna elbowed Kahn in the ribs, partly for trying to get his friend in trouble, but more with understanding of Gary's return remark. "Did you get another damn ticket?" she asked. "That was your last credit, wasn't it?"

Colleen, confused by the conversation, was surprised to hear mention of another girl and her possible departure from Gary's apartment. "Who's Jana?" she finally had to ask.

Kahn ignored Deanna's elbow. "Jesus man, you mean you didn't tell her? I thought you said you'd to tell her?" His voice played the part well.

Deanna wasn't finished. "You can't drive, can you?"

"It's only for six months!" Kahn defended.

"Jana who?" asked Colleen again.

"She doesn't have a last name." Gary answered in his own defense.

Kelsey now entered the conversation. "You don't know her last name?" She added with a sarcastic tone.

"Six months!" Deanna stammered. "What did you do, run over somebody?" She hit him again.

Kahn tried to ignore her, but had definitely felt the last elbow. He spoke directly to her at that point. "You didn't tell her either? What the hell's wrong with you guys?"

Deanna was incredulous. "Tell her what?"

"About Jana!" answered Kahn.

"Who the hell is Jana?" Deanna exclaimed. Even as she said it, she began to suspect that it was all a joke.

Gary looked at Colleen, whose eyes were filled with starts of anger and frustration. It was obvious that she had fallen for Kahn's charade and he'd let it go too far. "She's nobody. She's my apartment computer," he explained hurriedly.

Colleen muttered something in French, which only one of the group might have understood. With that, she got up and moved quickly toward the rear of the passenger cabin. Before any more could be said, she was gone.

Gary tried to get up, but his straps delayed him. "Colleen," he called after her. "Wait, you can't ... it's time to take off!" He undid his strap and rose, looking at Kelsey. "What did she say?"

"You don't want to know," Kelsey answered.

Kahn, who had worn a smile a moment before, now had a sour look. He was somewhat disgusted with himself. He hadn't planned it to end up this way.

As Gary left, he glanced at him and shook his head. "Don't worry," he said quietly.

Kahn nodded, feeling genuinely sorry. He flinched as Deanna hit him one more time for good measure. "Six months!" she frowned.

Gary hurried to follow Colleen. In the rear of the craft, there were only two places she could have gone, the men's bathroom, or the women's. The latter was locked. As quietly as he could, he knocked. "Come on, babe. He was just messing around, you know how he is?" There was no answer. "Colleen … open the door. They're gonna take off any minute."

Bam!! The door hit him in the side of the head, and as he moved back, holding his stinging ear, a hand shot out and grabbed his shirtfront. "Hey …" He yelped as she pulled him into the cramped room and slammed the door.

Gary looked at her in confusion, fully expecting to be chastised relentlessly.

Colleen stared into his eyes from only a few inches away. "Tell me something …" Her voice was low and her breath hot. "Can Jana do this?" She gave him the wettest, deepest kiss she could muster. One of her hands held his head and her free hand moved down between his legs. The kiss lasted a wonderful twenty seconds.

Gary gasped for breath when she finished. He had become one hundred percent fully aroused in half the time that the kiss had taken. Finally, he was able to speak. "No … she can't do that." His breath was fast and deep.

She held him closely, continuing her manipulation down low, kissing his neck. "Have you ever done it in a shuttle bathroom?" she whispered, unzipping his pants. Her hand moved inside.

"Oh my God!" Gary's knees grew weak with anticipation. Her breath was hot and wet against his neck. He knew time was short, but there was no way he could stop now. His hands moved under her shirtfront and began to explore.

Suddenly, the loudspeaker blared once more, startling them both. It seemed that the pilot was speaking only to the occupants of the woman's bathroom. "ONE MINUTE TO LIFT OFF. ALL PASSENGERS MUST RETURN TO THEIR SEATS."

Instantly, Colleen removed her hands. "Too bad, not enough time," she sighed.

Before Gary knew what was happening, the door was open, closed, and she was gone. He sat, incredulous, unable to exit in his current condition. "Jesus Christ!" he muttered.

Before they knew it, they were home. They arrived early in the morning. The sun was just rising when the ship touched down. The high reaching buildings provided a breathtaking silhouette against the brightening horizon. Kelsey made a remark that it was especially beautiful, since the last sunrise they had seen had been over the Thalosian hills.

Leaving the spaceport terminal, Colleen and Kelsey followed Gary to a parking garage, where he led them to a somewhat dusty car.

Colleen looked on, somewhat surprised. She wasn't sure what she had expected. She had never really wondered what kind of car Gary drove. Pilots made decent money, compared to some at least, but he had only just started. Maybe that explained why this particular model hover car was well over ten years old. She had to admit, she loved the older style, but there had to be a sentimental attachment. As Gary inserted his key card, Colleen nudged her sister, and spoke to him. "Is this it?" she said with a seemingly disappointed tone.

"Huh? Is this what?" Gary asked confused.

"Is this your ... car?"

Gary was shocked. "What's that supposed to mean?"

"It's old!" she laughed.

"So what? It's a classic. It's damn near cherry."

Colleen pouted, and Kelsey tried to look solemn as well.

Gary figured they were joking, but he couldn't be sure. French women may have a very different perception of what was important in choosing a vehicle. "Hey ... you guys can ride with Kahn and Deanna if you want?" He suggested. Since Kahn had lost his license and there wasn't room for five in his car, he and Deanna had decided to take the trans-train home.

"No, no, it's okay. We'll force ourselves." Kelsey said. Her perfect teeth gleamed in the low light. She wouldn't say it, but she really was used to much better.

Gary looked at the two sarcastically, shaking his head. "Get in the damn car!"

The next two days were busy to say the least. The reunions between the girl's families were joyous and long overdue. The day of Avraham's funeral was however, a saddening occasion. It was a private service, even though he was known to have hundreds of friends throughout the system. There was no easy way of notification. Other than the Sluder family, most of his closest acquaintances were other pilots. Their whereabouts, with the return of the thousands of Shannations, were unknown. With hundreds of potential private fares, they would be scrambling for business. Avraham would have been ecstatic to be among them. The funeral was thankfully short lived. Over the next few days, the despair lessened.

For the following week and a half, the five friends were together, seeing sights, touring the city and countryside. The time was a welcome change to the hectic weeks behind them.

Kelsey seemed to enjoy her time on Belaquin, but quite to the surprise of everyone, suddenly decided to return to Shannate. She needed to see for herself whether her job still existed, and salvage her personal belongings if possible. At Colleen's urging, she had briefly considered a change to the military, but she couldn't deny her wild side. She had to admit, what she had seen thus far from the military had been wild, but unfortunately the wrong kind. She would miss the excitement and glamour of the casinos. The Republic, in no way could compare.

Three days before the shore leave was technically over, Kahn received a call from Commander Haute on Touchen. He wished to know only one thing. "William Vient is returning home. I am going with him and staying for a few days, at the most a week. I called to invite you, Gary, and the girls to come along. It's not a vacation. We'll be doing a lot of exploration. I'm sure Gary would enjoy a trip into the past. We're taking Aquillon Two. I think you're familiar with that ship, aren't you?"

"Yes sir, I'm not likely to forget that trip." Kahn recalled.

"We'll have a small crew and relief personnel for the people we left back there. It should be a great trip. Are you interested?"

Kahn paused before answering. "I don't know sir, I think I'm gonna pass on this one. I've had enough excitement for a while. If you really need me to go, I'll ..."

"No, no, there's nothing I need you to go for. I just thought you might want out of some of those menial duty station jobs."

"Well, thanks, but those jobs are gonna look pretty good after this last mission."

"I understand." Haute was careful to hide the disappointment he felt. He had his hopes that the young man would go, but understood his decision.

"I'll check with Gary and the others, see what they say, and I'll let you know, all right? Kahn promised. "When are you leaving?"

"In three days. I'm not sure of the time yet."

"I'll get back to you before then?" Kahn promised.

"Good enough." The older man paused and added. "One more thing Kahn ... I'd like to get together with you sometime, away from work I mean."

For a moment, Kahn was confused, but then understood. "I'd like that, Commander."

"I want to talk about a few things, you know, tell you some things you might not remember about your Dad. Things I think he'd want you to know." He found it difficult to talk about. "Okay then … when I get back, we'll do that. I'll see you soon Kahn."

Kahn sighed as he heard the other end of the transmission go dead, thankful that he had not been ordered to go. He knew how Deanna was feeling after his recent close calls. Even though she hadn't brought up the subject as yet, the day would soon come. He knew that she was ready to settle down and maybe have some rug rats. He chuckled at the thought.

What was up with Haute? He had never made a move to actually bond with him before, especially by spending time with him in a non-military setting. Was there something he didn't know?

He was fairly sure what Gary's answer would be concerning the trip back to Earth, but he decided to ask him anyway. When he finally did so, he found he was right. Gary and Colleen were hitting it off very well, more so with each passing day. They were inseparable.

Another day passed before Kahn received a second invitation from the Commander. It was actually a request for him and Gary to travel to Touchen, but only for a few hours. It was promised that they would see something truly interesting. A shuttle would wait for them at the spaceport.

They took the train, leaving the car for the girls. Gary wasn't overly pleased about going, but it was a request from the fleet commander. He couldn't very well refuse. They boarded the transport to Touchen and once there, entered the military base through the bustling merchant town.

Commander Haute was paged and found to be in a research lab near the main hangar area. Again, identification and special clearance was required, but Haute had already cleared them through.

Upon entering, the two men found themselves in the presence of a very unique item. The men knew what it was as soon as they saw it. They had heard about the alien ship captured during the battle above Earth, but had never seen it. The vessel had been kept under tight wraps due to possible contagions or other unknowns. Quarantine had been strict.

The ship was dark gray in color, appearing slightly oval around the edges, domed from front to back and nearly flat on bottom. It measured over thirty feet in length, twenty feet in width, and weighed over nineteen tons. It appeared the shape of an egg lying on its side, roughly cut in half. The exterior shell of this egg had numerous square panels, each with raised ridges resembling a grate pattern. At the bow was a view port covered with mirrored glass, making it impossible to see in from the outside. Various open vents lined the lower edges of the sides of the ship, reaching from near the bow, all the way to the engine ports at the rear.

One small entry hatch was found on top, barely large enough for a man to squeeze through.

Several technicians scurried about, doing what they do best. In this particular case, it appeared that what they did best was to turn the ship into a huge chunk of Swiss cheese. Dozens of holes dotted the ships exterior, opened to reveal the workings beneath. Even in its cut down form, it remained impressive.

The Commander was eventually found seated in the craft's cockpit, obviously intrigued by the ship's fascinating configuration. With all that was going on in and out of the vessel, the visitors had been unnoticed.

"Having fun?" asked Kahn. They had entered the vessel through one of the larger holes made by the investigators.

The Commander was startled, but smiled. "Hey, you got here fast." He placed his hands on what appeared to be the steering mechanism. "Yeah, this is pretty neat." He was like a kid with a new toy. "I wanted you to see this before it was totally pieced out, since you missed it in all its glory."

"You figured right sir." Gary looked about the crafts cramped interior, his heart pounding faster with each new discovery. Just the sight of it exhilarated him. "So this is it?"

The Commander climbed out, allowing an unobstructed view of the cockpit. It was filled with unknown controls begging to be explored. Above and around the control panel was the view port. Everything outside was easily visible through the one-way glass. Gary and Kahn looked for a bit and then followed their commanding officer outside.

Gary made another circle around the ship. "Incredible," he muttered.

"What have they found out?" asked Kahn.

Haute shrugged. "Not much. They took it apart, dissected most of it. Then it got complicated."

Kahn shrugged. "What do you mean?"

"They haven't been able to find a power source." The two men looked at him, unsure of what he meant. He continued. "They can't find a source of power. This is a dead carcass."

Gary heard the end of the conversation. "It looks like it's got a lot of damage. Why would it still have power? What's dead is dead, right?"

"That's not what I mean. These guys can't find anything that would have powered it in the first place."

Kahn was beginning to get the idea. "That's impossible. This thing was knocking the hell out of us a couple of weeks ago, right?"

"Right. It flew, it fired its weapons.... everything, but nothing here works, and they can't find any way it could have."

"Like a non-functional model?" suggested Kahn.

"Exactly." answered Haute.

"What about the pilot?" asked Gary.

"They found no pilot on board. We considered that he might have ejected or it could have been controlled remotely, but that was before we got this new info. We don't know how it flew at all."

Gary had the obvious solution. "Well, it's a Kogran ship. Did you ask them?"

Haute smiled. "The Kograns say it isn't theirs, and they don't know anything about the ship that took you guys to Earth either."

Kahn shook his head. "That's bullshit. Why would someone lead us there ... I mean, they attacked us!"

Haute interrupted. "I know. The Manna admits to firing the missiles, but that's all. He says they never had the technology to go into space. If they had, they would have left before the wars. I believe him. These type ships didn't exist in the twenty-first century. There was no need for them. Even if they had the means, why would they build them?"

Kahn let his memory backtrack to the alien ship. "Okay, yeah, I have to agree. These couldn't have come from the Earth."

"It raises interesting questions," suggested the Commander. "Where did they come from? Who built them, and how in the hell did this one work?"

Gary re-entered the ship, sat in the pilot's seat and moved his hand across the control panel. He spoke loud enough for the others to hear. "So we're talking about a ship that flew with no pilot, no engine and no power?"

The Commander knew it seemed ridiculous, but logic was logic, no matter how bad it sounded. "That's the story."

Gary shook his head, pondering the impossibilities of it.

"A lot more tests have to be run before the final verdict." Haute said. "Let's go see what I brought you here for, let the brainiacs figure this out."

Kahn narrowed his eyes, confused. "You mean this wasn't it?"

"Nope," He pointed towards the floor. "It's downstairs. Come on."

They took an elevator several floors below to another section of the research center. They followed the only corridor there was, and at the end of it found an open doorway. Within was darkness. Small blinking lights could be seen around the room. Haute increased the lighting to a very low level and started to explain the slightly abnormal surroundings that could now be seen. "What we've got here gentlemen, may be the greatest discovery since light speed."

CHAPTER 16

▼

As their eyes adjusted, the room's features became more distinct. They could now see that the blinking lights were actually small control panels.

"We can thank our Kogran friends for these." He referred to several long cylindrical modules or tubes, each seven to eight feet in length and three to four feet in diameter. There were eight of them lying horizontally side-by-side, each one having individual control centers. The tops were rounded and made of glass. Four of them emitted a dull blue light from within. The remaining four were dark.

To Gary, the room seemed like a tomb, the modules like coffins. "What exactly are we thanking them for, sir?"

Haute explained. "The Kograns are survivors. They've proven that. They cracked a secret that we haven't been able to. They had different circumstances driving them, to be sure. They had to make these work or die." He walked to one of the modules. "These devices work perfectly. The Kograns are living examples."

Kahn now knew what they were being shown. He hadn't gotten to see them on Earth. "Sleep chambers," he murmured.

Haute nodded. "They conquered time and death." Maybe we can do it too. The possibilities are staggering. "These chambers can open up the universe for us."

"Are these the actual Kogran chambers?" asked Gary, obviously fascinated.

"No. These are duplicates with a few modifications."

"How do they work?" asked Gary again.

"I only know what they told me. The body is kept hypothermic. The cold slows the heart and brain function to almost nothing. The chamber automatically turns to keep blood from pooling. Muscles are kept active with electrical stimulus." It was obvious he was repeating the technical terms from memory.

Kahn didn't understand everything that was being told them, but grasped the concept. "And you're not dead?"

"Technically, no. There's a lot more to it. You're breathing some kind of specially mixed oxygen. They have to inject you with … anti-coagulants or something like that. It's over my head, but it works."

Gary walked forward, touching the blue glass on one of the chambers. It was cold and surprised him. "These are operational?"

"Yes, these four are … for the past week or so. So far, they seem to be working fine," answered Haute.

As Haute's last sentence died away, Gary's eyes widened and he jerked his hand away from the glass. He felt the hair on the back of his neck stand up as he realized that the three of them probably weren't alone in the room. "How do you know they're working unless someone's in them?"

"You're right. We needed volunteers, and we found some."

"So these have people in them?" Kahn was amazed.

"Four so far. Three of them will come out next month. This first one is a terminally ill patient from Belaquin. She's the real test. She'll be under for six months minimum, maybe longer. Doctors believe that as long as her body is dormant, the disease itself should be dormant. If so, it could be a tremendous breakthrough. If a cure for her illness is found, they wake her up and she starts a new life. The other three, they'll run tests on to see if the process affected them." He paused. "How would you two like to try these out?"

Gary was skeptical. "I don't know about that. What if something went wrong?"

"Very unlikely. Everything … every conceivable problem has been gone over and fed into the computers. If main computer control is disrupted, the backup system takes over. If all power is cut, the mechanism will go automatic and slowly wake up the occupant … only if there is no danger in the atmosphere outside the chamber. The section housing the chambers would be self sufficient, so even if the outer hull is ruptured, the area should remain intact. The variables are really complicated, but the men who are designing them are pretty sharp."

Gary shook his head, confused by what he was hearing. "What you're describing sounds like a ship."

Haute shrugged. "It's possible it may be someday."

Kahn had a question. "How long can someone stay under in one of these?"

"Two hundred years, at least. I think the Kograns can attest to that," he answered. "I won't tempt fate by saying its flawless, but you get the picture. Short of a direct disruption of the chamber itself, it should keep working."

"So you really trust this?" asked Gary.

"Yes, I do." Haute laid his hand on a chamber. "Enough so, that I'm letting them put me in one on the way back from Earth."

"Are you serious?" asked Kahn in disbelief.

"As a heart attack," Haute answered. "Hey, I need to save every day I can."

"Not me. No way," laughed Gary.

"Just wait a minute," began Haute. "Think about it. Imagine what it would be like to wake up in fifty years, the same, as you were when you went in. Look how far we've come in the last fifty. It would be unbelievable."

"It would be something to think about," Kahn mused. "The things you'd see ..."

Gary wasn't as enthusiastic. "Yeah, but what about the drawbacks? Could you leave everything behind? Everyone you knew would be old or dead when you woke up ... if you woke up at all." He couldn't see a decent reason to explore the future, at least not personally. The risk and consequences were too great.

Before Kahn could voice his opinion, the older man jumped in with both feet. "Look, you know I care a lot for both of you. Kahn, you're as close to a son as I have." He took a deep breath. "I'm going to tell you something I shouldn't, and it better not leave this room. Understand?" His serious tone absorbed the young men's full attention. Both nodded. "The Republic has recently started a new phase of space exploration, brought on by what you see here. Like I said, these chambers have opened new doors for us. SPEX is just one of them. I urge you not to talk about this because only a few people know what I'm going to tell you. It will cause uproar with the public when it's released. I'm telling you for one reason. They want our best people on this project and I thought you might be interested."

"What kind of project ... exactly?" Kahn felt he already had an idea.

"What's the longest duration of any SPEX mission to date?" asked the Commander.

Kahn shrugged, but Gary remembered. "Two years out, two years back."

"Roughly. The other two missions have never been heard from. It's been over ten years. Now ... I'm no expert, but that's not a very good track record. Since it was a required subject in the academy, I know you remember what kind of shape the crewmembers returned in. Three of them still haven't recovered from the effects, and may never. None of them were the same as when they left." He paused to catch his breath. "As long as the members of the other two missions have been gone, they don't think they could be mentally stable enough to make it back, if they're still alive."

"I remember reading about it," admitted Gary.

Haute continued. "All right. Now what if a crew was put in these chambers and sent out, scanners doing all the work. If something were found, the crew would be awakened to check it out. Otherwise, they would sleep ... no boredom ... no loneliness ... no homesickness. Those were the major problems for the second mission. The massive storage facilities needed for food and water was another problem. If the crew could sleep ninety-nine percent of the time, those needs could be downsized immensely."

"Sounds pretty far fetched to me," remarked Gary.

"Well maybe. Sounds can be deceiving, but this isn't. A new mission has been researched for years. A ship's already been blueprinted. All the schematics are done; all that's left is the work."

Kahn ran the possibilities over. Could it work? What if it did? What if the crew did find something, perhaps other life with even higher intelligence? It had to be out there. It was ridiculous to think that only they and the Thalosians existed. What about the alien ships? Where did they come from? That was proof enough that other life had to exist. There were probably infinite numbers of other cultures on other planets. To make contact with them would indeed be the ultimate adventure. Maybe the other SPEX missions had survived. Maybe they had found something so spectacular that they had no desire to return. The mission had its temptations, but what sacrifices would have to be made?

Gary was uninterested, but curious nevertheless. "What about the crew? What kind of qualifications are we talking about?"

"Now, that aspect of it has been decided. Qualifications are strictly stipulated. All would have to be volunteers, between early twenties and late thirties, married couples with no children. Pregnant women would not be accepted. All women would be surgically implanted with a sterility agent to prevent children during the mission, completely reversible, of course."

"All members would have to be specialists in one or more of the required fields. They would be physically and psychologically tested. It would be a long process. They want it right the first time." He paused, contemplating. "If I was young enough, I wouldn't hesitate. I've got nothing here to hold me back." He thought aloud. "To wake up in another place, in another time," He sighed knowing it was a dream he couldn't even begin to imagine. "One thing's for sure, someone's going to see it, if not you guys, someone else. Why let them take all the glory? It's the opportunity of a lifetime, and this time it's gonna work."

Gary couldn't deal with the idea of being locked in one of the coffins for a week, much less a decade. The man was right. It would be hard to pass up, for the right person anyway. If what he said was true … if time didn't matter … if years passed with no aging, then it would truly be incredible. On the other hand, nothing in the universe, especially something made by man could be perfect.

Kahn was undecided on how he felt. "How long would this trip last … roughly?"

Haute, for the first time in the conversation, was unsure of himself. "We don't know. They're gearing this mission to be a success. The mission goes on until we find life or the safe point of return is reached. To bring a crew back without making contact, or at least maximizing the effort, would be a waste of time."

Gary added it all up. He knew how intriguing it must sound to his best friend, who was by far, the most adventurous person he knew. There was no doubt in his mind that if Deanna would go, he would gladly volunteer. He had only her to hold him here. His parents were years gone and he had no siblings. Deanna's parents were separated, but she saw both of them fairly often. He wasn't sure how she would respond to something like this.

To ask Colleen would be a waste of breath. She remained close to her family, never missing an opportunity to visit. She had told him once, that there had been a major argument prior to her joining the Republic, prompted by the probability of extended periods away from home. Trying to separate her from her family for more than a few weeks would be out of the question.

It was more or less the same for himself. He loved his parents dearly, and would be hard pressed to leave them for longer then the Republic normally required. This trip had many unknowns, but one fact was blindingly certain. If it lasted as long as it could, he may very well never see his parents again. When a moment moved from present to past … it was lost.

He would never spend another birthday with them, or sit with his Dad, waiting for the fish to bite. He would never again listen to his Mothers stories of the photographs she so carefully kept. He could never tell them how much he loved them. He had never grown tired of those things, and could not imagine giving them up. Hopefully, there were still many years of good times to share.

No … he couldn't leave them. The thought of waking up on a ship, years from now, knowing that they were no longer there, would be too much. No matter how grand the adventure, or how exhilarating the discoveries; he wouldn't be able to cope. Quickly, he shook away the images. Even the thought nearly brought tears to his eyes.

He felt as if Haute still had not fully answered Kahn's question. "So how long Commander?"

Haute knew that if he answered truthfully, the two men would absolutely be turned against the trip, but he had to be honest. Without hesitation, he answered. "Maximum? A hundred out, a hundred back."

Kahn was shocked. "Two hundred years! You gotta be shittin me?"

Gary shook his head and said nothing.

The Commander smiled. He couldn't blame them. As young as they were, they couldn't be expected to understand. They had their whole lives ahead of them. The importance of the mission, as well as the risk, was insurmountable. Anyone who volunteered to go would possibly be giving up everything they had ever known and possibly their lives. No one could guess what was out there. He continued explaining the potential mission plans. "The crew would be sent into the densest part of the known galaxy. We already know that there is other life out there somewhere. The chances of it taking …!"

The loudspeaker blared. "COMMANDER HAUTE, CONTACT CONTROL AS SOON AS POSSIBLE."

The Commander frowned, "Well he sounded excited. Let's head back up."

As they rode upward, each man was lost in thought. One pondered the immediate future. The other two couldn't shake the question of what life might be like two centuries ahead, and the agony that would come with finding out.

Since he would not see the men for a while, Haute wanted one last word. His two guests were quiet, too quiet for their disposition. It was obvious where their thoughts were. He hoped he hadn't placed any undue pressure on them. "Listen guys, I know how overwhelming all this sounds. It's the biggest step you'd ever take in your lives. Any sane man would be scared." He paused, watching the floor numbers decreasing. "The Republic wants to send the best people we can. To me, you're some of the best we can offer. You've proven your worth with your courage and competence. I think it would be a great compliment to you and the girls to be chosen, but a shame for you to miss the chance."

"There are a lot of negatives, but please don't overlook the positives." Still, neither man spoke. The elevator stopped. "Just don't shut the idea totally out. Think about it, that's all I ask. I'll see you in a couple of weeks." He stepped out and walked away.

Kahn sighed as the commander turned a corner. "De would look at this as a good reason to get married."

Gary smiled at his meager attempt at humor, but thought he saw a glimmer of seriousness in his friend's eyes. He saw something else as well. Kahn almost seemed to be waiting for an agreeable reply. What was he thinking?

Without a word, they continued towards the surface and soon were returning to Belaquin. They weren't about to spend their last two days of leave on the all too familiar ice planet.

A day and a half later, Aquillon Two lifted out of her mother ship and waited for the light speed order. Commander Bennett gave it as he entered the control room. He was more than ready for this trip. He deemed it scientifically important, as well as historic. How many individuals got the chance to do what he and his crew were about to do? They had the opportunity to explore a new world, with one difference. They carried ancient maps of this one. They also carried very special passengers who could offer great assistance in the adventure.

The Kogran king, his wife, and their delegates had thoroughly enjoyed their exciting stay in the Belaquin system, but were anxious to return home. There was much work to be done, and for the first time in their lives, they had a peaceful environment in which to do it.

Commander Leon Haute also accompanied. For this voyage, however, he would not be in an administrative position. He was along simply as an explorer, something he had been, in a sense, all of his life, but sadly with few occasions to do so.

The Republic personnel left on Earth had learned much in the past few weeks. As the Aquillon Two grew closer to its destination, the newest reports revealed how much of the Kogran complex had been destroyed two centuries before.

When William Vient read the findings, he was appalled, but relieved. He knew then, how very near he and his people had come to sleeping forever. It made him sick to know that death had been so close. He shook his head. He had condoned the construction of the sleep chambers in the beginning, wishing to take their chances. Since then he admitted to himself that he had been very wrong. They had given his people a second chance at life. Tomorrow, he would start to rebuild what he had yesterday consented to destroy. If this new Republic wished to help him do that, then so be it. These people were indeed a different breed. He could only pray that the past was gone forever.

Finally, the scout ship glided into orbit. The Republic volunteers were overjoyed to hear from home. They had worked hard and accomplished as much as they had supplies for, but had only scratched the surface. The Aquillon Two was laden with replacement supplies and engineers to continue efforts of revival. All knew that the cities, countries, continents, and the world as a whole could never be the same, but in some respects, that fact would be a blessing. Some of the practices of the old would be better off left dead and gone.

Haute was more than anxious to start this newest project. It had been upwards of twenty-five years since he had participated in an exploratory mission. It would be a painstaking process, one that would take much longer than his upcoming stay on Earth. Hopefully they'd make many discoveries before he left.

Before any major changes within the city could even begin, the exploratory phase had to be well in place. There was no wish for any unwelcome surprises. Some preliminary short flights had already been made. Reports from the single shuttle and three raiders that had been left behind were inconclusive. They had scoured the immediate vicinity, but found little. Forms of life had been documented, some familiar, some not, but none that could be construed as intelligent. Their search capabilities had been hindered with inadequate equipment hastily left behind for the task. Now with the help of stronger scanners aboard the Aquillon Two, search on a larger scale could be initiated.

On the first shuttle trip down, Haute and the Manna sat in the cockpit behind the pilots. Their destination was the same great city they had left a few weeks earlier.

They approached from the east, over a broad expanse of ocean. The setting sun on the western horizon, cast a blinding reflection off the water. The city's skyline seemed to rise from the water as they grew closer. The beautiful silhouette mesmerized Haute. Nowhere in the Belaquin system existed a city such as this. Even in its emaciated condition, it rivaled anything he had ever seen.

He wondered silently to himself, how a race brilliant enough to create something so spectacular, could carelessly annihilate it along with their pitiful lives?

His gaze wandered, but repeatedly returned to the most impressive sight of all, the lone tower. It rose hundreds of feet higher than any other, robbing the attention from the smaller structures. He had seen it before. He had looked upon it only seconds before his crash. His hand moved involuntarily to his leg as he remembered.

The black kings' deep voice brought him back to the present. He talked as they flew near the tallest towers. "I thought it was the most beautiful city on Earth. It stretched as far as you could see. Millions of people lived here. It was my home." Haute tried to envision it, but all that could be seen was forest interrupted only by long thin lines of concrete looping and disappearing in the distance. The old highways, once filled with hundreds of thousands of vehicles, now sat silent and unused. "Now look at it. This is all that's left." Vient surmised.

The Commander could only imagine what the man saw in his mind. The city had been changed forever. The forest encroached all the way to the waters edge, and even a short distance further where bridges crossed. They rested unused by any manmade vehicle for almost a quarter of a millennium. The roadways were choked with all that remained of such vehicles, piles of unrecognizable rusted metal, collapsed upon themselves by the elements. They lay in the streets as well, although hidden by the unchecked vegetation. The thought of seeing these and other ancient sights close up brought Haute excitement that could not be matched.

A city this size had been home for tens of millions. It had industries, schools, churches, homes … people working, children playing, black and white together. Granted, discrimination had its place in society's history, but in the last of the twentieth century it had been diagnosed and treated on a small scale. No one dreamed that racism would prove to be the sleeping giant.

The familiar plaza had been cleared since the last visit; enough to accommodate several shuttles if need be. The pilot carefully threaded the ship through the surrounding buildings and dropped nearly straight down to the concrete base. Even as the landing struts touched the street, several Kogran and Republic representatives appeared to greet the new arrivals.

The plaza was dark with shadows from the approaching evening. Haute paused before following the others, wishing to stand alone for a time. He listened for a long while, committing another special moment to his memory. Only the clicking and buzzing of night insects could be heard, their unknown song signaling the end of another day. Tomorrow morning, as they grew silent with the sun, the search would begin.

CHAPTER 17

▼

Kahn Bengal had a completely different search on his mind, the search for truth within himself. He could not get the Commanders invitation out of his head. At first, he had considered and discarded it, but as of late, it had returned to eat at him relentlessly. The pull of adventure and the mystery of the unknown invaded even his sleep. The questions were always the same. What do I really want? What will it cost me?

He already knew the answers. He wanted it all … without any cost. A little over a week ago he was ready to give the girl he loved whatever she wanted. Decidedly, his feelings for her overrode any sense of loyalty to the Republic, but this was different. The future had changed, or at least it could if he wanted. He lay underneath GR1 and daydreamed.

The thirst for adventure had been more than filled for the months now behind him, but what about the coming years? He had never wished for anything out of the ordinary to happen, but on the slim occasion that it did, he couldn't be a spectator and sit and watch. Would a mission into the unknown fulfill his wildest dreams? Could he really be part of it?

He reached for a flow adjuster and accidentally knocked it off the rack onto the floor. "Shit! he cursed. He rolled over and looked hatefully at it, as if to blame it for his indecision. He fumed with disgust. This moment was a perfect example. What was the point of it? He was not a lazy man, but he couldn't stand repetitiveness, busy work that didn't need to be done. He had to admit, downtime in his line of work was a good thing, but it was unhealthy as well. Fighter pilots needed a reason to exist. Skills become dormant with non-use. Was he prepared to possibly spend the next fifteen years filling in spaces on a checklist? No … he was not! He was a pilot, not a calibration technician!

His mind poured over the obstacles. What about Deanna? She wouldn't go. No way. She wasn't the kind to fly off into the history books, or more likely oblivion. He knew how strongly she felt about their future together. He knew the hopes she had for a different life. If she truly cared about me, he reasoned, she would go. Then again, if I care about her, I'll stay.

Dammit! It made no sense. What was most important? Could he go without her? No, he admitted. It wasn't an option. If he stayed, would their future become bitter? Would he somehow blame her for the missed chance? He shook his head. It wouldn't be her fault. How could it be? Fault her for loving him and wishing for a life here? Could he fault her for wanting a predictable future, rather than one with possibly nothing? No … he could never blame her.

What about his closest friend? He was as set against the idea as anyone could be. Was he too young to care about his future? Did he love Colleen enough for her decision to sway him one way or the other?

He leaned back against the cold hard hull, lost in thought for a long while. There were no distractions in the room. His mind suddenly felt as clear as it ever had. After several moments, he finally, nodded his head. "I know what I want," he said with confidence.

Sliding off the gold wing, he noticed the flow adjuster he had dropped earlier. With a smile, he kicked it out of sight under the ship. To hell with it, he decided. I've got a lot of talking to do. With no hesitation, he set off to find his first target.

He found Gary's ship in another hangar, but not the pilot. His tools were there however, so he couldn't be far away. Sitting down, he waited.

Ten minutes later, he still waited, wondering if anyone might be looking for him at his own station. Finally, the younger pilot returned. Kahn spoke first. "Where the hell have you been? I've been waiting for an hour."

"An hour my ass," Gary answered sarcastically. He shrugged, "Sorry, nature called." He gulped the drink he held. "I was getting dehydrated … all this sweating, you know?"

"Give me a break," Kahn laughed.

"What are you doing?"

"I just quit." Kahn said simply.

"Yeah, that would be nice," Gary jokingly agreed. "So what are you striking against today?"

Kahn's smile had deteriorated to a more serious expression. "I'm not kidding."

Gary sat down the drink, laid down on the floor and returned to an open panel on the lower side of his ship. "Not kidding about what?"

"I've made up my mind." Kahn answered.

Gary still wasn't giving the utmost of his attention, but he did pause and look at his friend. "About what?"

"I can't do this kind of shit for the next fifteen years, waiting for someone to hand me a retirement certificate." His voice contained a hint of anger.

"So what … are you getting out?"

"Not exactly," Kahn stared at him, trying to say it without words. His friend didn't get the message.

Gary returned to his work, elbow deep in the bowels of the ship, still oblivious to what Kahn was trying to impress. "You can't quit. You don't know how to do anything else."

"I'm going." Kahn blurted out. He watched the color drain from his friends face as realization set in.

Gary felt his throat tighten. He wanted to speak, but couldn't find the words to say. Finally, he did. "Going where?" His voice held dread.

"Well, I don't know for sure. I guess where I end up isn't as important as when."

Gary felt his heart drop. He pushed away from the open panel. "You're not serious?"

"Like he said, this is an opportunity that comes along only once," Kahn answered. "Have you ever imagined the future?"

Gary couldn't believe his ears. "No," he sputtered.

"I haven't either … until now, but I won't have to imagine it, I'll see it."

Gary had always respected Kahn's decisions, but not this one. He felt anger as he spoke. "Maybe you will, maybe you won't! What if you die out there, then what?"

"What if I die here? What's the difference? Sure there's risk, but isn't that the business we're in? What if this mission succeeds? Think of it. We'd be rich … and famous." He added. "All those years of back pay. We'd still be young. That's when I'll take that certificate."

"I don't believe this," Gary shook his head, letting his body go limp to the floor. "Man, this isn't business! It's not about fame or money! This is about the rest of your life!" He paused, wondering if he was getting through at all. "Some of those people never came back!" Gary's voice was loud with desperation as he tried to make sense.

"This mission will be different. The ship, the planning ... it can make it." Kahn said.

He sounded brainwashed, blind to the possible consequences. Gary's voice remained at a high level. "You don't think the others thought the same thing when they left?"

Kahn shook his head, saying nothing in return. He hadn't thought it would be this difficult, but how could he have known what to expect.

Gary calmed somewhat. "What about De?"

Kahn sighed, seating himself on the raider wing. "I haven't said anything to her yet. Hopefully, she'll think about it. Maybe she'll go."

Gary chuckled. "Yeah...." He stared at Kahn. "What if she won't?"

Kahn hesitated. "I don't know."

They both sat in silence, each wanting the same thing, to change the others mind. Gary again considered what it might be like to leave, even though it still seemed a ridiculous possibility. Immediately, the vision of forever leaving his parents clouded his mind, bombarded his emotions. How could he stand the strain? He remembered when he talked with Colleen the first time, about how hard it would be when they passed away. If they died twenty or thirty years from now or if he left on the mission, the experience would be the same. Was there a difference?

Of course there was! If he stayed, he could spend the last years with them, instead of leaving and consenting to never see them again. It was confusing, but blatantly clear. How could he even consider it? Hell, ever since he'd joined the Republic he'd dealt with feelings of guilt. He knew in his heart that he had not seen them nearly as often as he could have. When had he seen them last? Six ... seven months? He had no excuse for not visiting. He could have easily seen them over shore leave, but did not. They lived far away now, moving just before he'd joined the academy. He had not even seen their new home.

The weekend was coming. He made up his mind. Old plans are out ... new ones are in. A visit was in order.

He looked again at Kahn, who had said nothing more. For a man who knew what he wanted, he looked very unhappy. Even though he still felt objectionable, he offered an apology. "Hey Chief, I'm sorry I yelled," he said. "Go talk to her."

"I think that'd be a good idea." Kahn turned to leave, dragging his feet in apprehension.

"Hey!" Gary yelled across the room.

Kahn stopped, but didn't turn.

Gary smiled. "Don't worry; she loves you, no matter what."

Kahn stood a little straighter as he left the room, whispering silent thanks for the needed encouragement. This was going to be one of the hardest things he had ever done.

After he watched him go, Gary wondered what kind of man it took to make the decision Kahn had made. He thought openly for a moment. Was it feasibly possible for him to make that same kind of commitment? To say no was easy. A yes answer would take courage. His mind drifted back to the Thalosian compound when he had experienced courage before, and the sickening feeling that had accompanied it.

He glanced at the time. Only an hour remained in his work shift. To catch Colleen before she left the ship would require an early clock out, otherwise he'd have to try and catch her at home. Hopefully, she would consider going with him for the weekend visit, but he would have to ask her tonight. Tomorrow would be too late. She might have to change plans in order to go, but he had to ask.

Hurriedly, he shoved his tools in a cabinet and locked up the raider. He ran from the room towards the botany department, where he found her and gladly received her consent to go with him. They would leave the next morning. Deciding to spend the evening together, they went out to eat and then headed over to Kahn's place. On the way, Colleen heard for the first time of the possible future mission and Kahn's abrupt decision. While explaining, he made it clear that he was going against orders from Haute himself by telling her.

Colleen was fascinated by the knowledge of anything so secretive. She was shocked when he told her that she might eventually be invited to partake of the mission. She became intrigued with the prospect, and Gary found himself wishing that he had told her all the details before revealing that fact to her. She had only one question, "When are we going?"

Gary kicked himself. "Uh ... we're not going. You haven't heard everything yet."

Colleen thought for a moment. "Maybe not, but why are you making my decision for me?" she asked sarcastically.

"No ... I'm not. All I meant, is that you need to understand everything first. Then you'll see why." He slowed the car down for a light.

Colleen glared straight ahead, her arms crossed defiantly across her chest. "Just let me decide for myself."

"That's fine," Gary could see that she was angry, but at least she was still talking. He decided to let her alone until she calmed down. Kahn's house was only a couple of streets away. The light turned green. When she still said nothing, he decided it was time to grovel. "I'm sorry. I guess I thought ahead too far."

"I guess so," she answered quickly.

Gary turned the last corner and slipped a glance out of the corner of his eye. In the dim light of the dash, he could see that she was smiling slightly, telling him that she wasn't as upset as she wished him to believe. He cracked his own smile. The weekend was still intact. The night however, was far from over.

Gary shook his head. Kahn's lights were on ... all of them. He obviously didn't care about his electricity bill, though he would bitch loud enough when he had to pay it. He had expected to see Deanna's car, but only Kahn's was there, dust forming on its unused frame.

Colleen was out of the car before it stopped, opening the discussion again. "You say Kahn's going, but we aren't? Why? We've been chosen for this, right?"

"I said the Commander may recommend us, but ..."

"So what's the problem?"

"I'll tell you if you'll just let me!" He ran to catch up, meeting her at Kahn's front door. Opening it without knocking, he yelled for his friend. "Hey Chief ... you home?"

There was no answer.

Colleen was incredulous, noting the completeness of the mess as they entered. "Did somebody rob this place?"

"Do you see anything in here worth stealing?" Gary answered sarcastically.

She shrugged. "Is he here?"

Gary stopped and sniffed the air. There was a distinct odor filling the house. It smelled like smoke. Knowing that Kahn didn't have an automatic food system, he hurried downstairs, "Yeah, he's home."

They found him too far gone to have heard their call, or anything else for that matter. Two large, empty bottles on a table explained his drunken state. Colleen found a smoking pan on the stove in the kitchenette and threw it into the sink.

Gary frowned at his friend, shaking his head in disgusted wonderment. Why does he do this? What reason was it this time? Even as he asked himself, he realized that he probably already knew.

Kahn had passed out on a recliner couch, another half empty bottle between his legs. Gary yelled and shook him forcefully, but the man showed no signs of consciousness. He knew he wouldn't get this intoxicated without good reason, but Kahn seemed to always have good reason. He tried repeatedly to wake him, but it was obviously a losing battle.

Colleen crossed to the other side of the room and opened two windows to let the smoke out, then joined Gary at the foot of the couch. "Is he okay?"

"He will be. Help me get him in bed. Can you get his legs?" As he grabbed under Kahn's limp arms, his face came close to his friends. The smell was overpowering. He looked at Colleen, releasing a long sigh. "You want to switch?"

Colleen grimaced as a waft of air brought the smell of dirty feet below her. "I don't care. Let's just hurry up."

Kahn offered no help as they half carried, half dragged him to the nearby bedroom, where they found his bed under piles of unwashed laundry.

"We're not going to undress him are we?" Colleen asked.

Gary considered the humorous thought, but declined. "He'd kill us for sure." He stood back and observed their work. "I guess he'll be all right here till he wakes up."

"So what do we do now?" Colleen asked.

"I don't know, got any ideas?"

"Yeah ... tell me everything about this secret mission."

Gary was apprehensive, but confident that when all the facts were known, she would agree with him. "All right, let's go find Deanna. Maybe she can stay with him until morning. I'll tell you everything on the way."

At that moment, Deanna didn't want to be found. She was alone, trying to forget the day behind her, but knowing she could not. In all the years since she'd known Kahn, since childhood, they had been through fights, but never like the one tonight.

The loud music surrounded her, the base vibrating her body to the core. It wasn't loud enough however, to block out the words that still rang in her head. She didn't want to think about them, but couldn't help it. What Kahn had said to her, or rather, yelled at her, had hurt her deeper than she could imagine. Desperately, she searched for any excuse to rid him of the responsibility, to convince her that it had all just been a mistake. He had been drinking heavily, but this time he had been different, not the happy, funny person he was usually transformed into.

The tears flowed freely over her cheeks and trembling lips as she relived the episode once more. He had started out talking about marriage, the one subject only she had ever mentioned before. She could remember imagining that maybe the time had come. Maybe he was ready to settle down. Her hopes had soared to the point of no return as she heard the words she had waited so long for. She answered yes even before he had finished.

But even as she said it, she felt as if something wasn't right. Then she uttered the fatal word, "Why?"

His answer wasn't one of love or affection. It wasn't one of the, "I can't live without you" reasons. He answered simply, "Because we have to be married to go on this trip."

Her smile of joy faded to a dull expression of confusion and disbelief as she listened to a lengthy confusing explanation.

Was that it? All she was, after all this time, was a necessary piece of baggage for the next adventure. She couldn't remember everything she'd said after that point. Angry rage clouded the argument. Things were said by both, but not meant. Feelings that she'd never felt before, invaded and overpowered all understanding.

Finally, when they finished, she spoke again, calmly, with hesitation, but sure of her self and her words. She shook her head. "No ... I won't marry you. I can't ... not like this." She had almost reached the door when she heard his last words. She silently repeated them for the hundredth time. "Good! Get the fuck out then! I'll just say goodbye right now!"

Now she stared blankly around the room. In every glance at every happy couple she saw Kahn and herself. Yesterday, everything was perfect.

"This is stupid," she said aloud. It wasn't his fault. He just had too much to drink. His hopes were too high and he wasn't thinking straight. He knew what he had wanted to say, but the words got turned around. That was all it was.

It will be all right, she told herself, wiping away the last of the tears. Everything would be fine. Even now, with this whole screwed up mess, she knew he loved her. She got up from the table, leaving money for the drink she'd only half finished. She felt a little better after her time alone. She smiled weakly as she sighed, knowing that she would love him no matter what.

The chilly night air sobered her fully as she walked through the parking lot. She considered driving back to his place, but it would be no use. He'd be passed out. It was best to let it go until tomorrow. Perhaps he wouldn't even remember the one night she wished she could forget. Getting into her car, she wondered what she would say to him when the time came. Oh well ... by nightfall tomorrow, she would know.

Gary and Colleen searched for a short time for Deanna, but eventually ended up at the formers apartment. Jana's artificial voice filled the room as they entered. "Hello! It's nice to have you back every few weeks."

Colleen's eyes widened. Had she actually heard sarcasm in that voice? "Did you teach her that?" she frowned.

"Not hardly," Gary answered.

"I bet," Colleen laughed.

"I'm serious. You can reprogram a machine. You can't teach it."

"You know what I meant." Quipped Colleen.

Another voice joined the spat. "Gary, you promised not to refer to me as a machine."

He nodded his head and threw up his hands, admitting his mistake. "I know Jana, I'm sorry," he apologized.

Colleen flopped on the couch, shaking her head. The apartment computer was going to take some getting used to.

Gary opened the window panels, looking at the city below him. "You're gonna love Mom and Dad. They live in the country, far away from all of this." He referred to the ceaseless activity below them.

"I just hope they like me." Colleen responded.

"God, you're so paranoid." Turning from the window, he asked. "You want something to eat or drink?" He walked to the bedroom as he spoke.

"Yeah, I guess so. What have you got?"

"We can go out or stay here. Have you ever had Morrocan corry?" suggested Gary hopefully.

"No ... I don't think I've ever had Morrocan anything."

Jana spoke. "How did I know you were going to suggest that?" The sarcasm was present once again.

"Double order Jana, but you knew that too, didn't you?" There was no answer. He smiled, knowing full well that she'd heard him.

Colleen's voice reached him in the other room. "Are you sure Kahn's all right?"

"Why wouldn't he be?"

"Well, I mean ..." She pictured a scenario that dampened her appetite. "What if he throws up, or something?"

"No, he never pukes. He'd feel better if he did, but he doesn't."

Colleen became silent, wondering where Deanna was and why Kahn had drunk so much. They normally would have been together. The smell of something wonderful came from the kitchen. "Why are you so dead set against this mission?" she asked. Little had been said about it as they searched for Deanna. He had stalled long enough.

"Well, there's a lot more to it that I haven't told you." Gary answered.

Colleen looked and listened intently. "Continue," she ordered.

"This mission they're looking at isn't like anything they've ever done before. They're putting the crew in sleep chambers, like the ones the Kograns had."

Colleen interrupted. "Why?'

"Because of the time they might be gone. The last SPEX mission ... you remember it?" He watched her nod her head. "Well, they came back after four years and the crew was kind of messed up. Some of them went crazy from being cooped up so long."

"I remember. So they've got sleep chambers to keep that from happening again. That's understandable. So what will they do, rotate shifts or something?"

"No, the entire crew will be asleep. The computers would run the ship. If something is found, the crew wakes up."

"You've got to be kidding." Colleen exclaimed. The thought of everyone's lives depending on a machine was not a comfortable one.

"Well, I have to agree that it's not a bad concept if it works." Gary admitted.

"How long is the mission?"

Gary smiled inside. He knew that this is where she would balk. "Haute's not sure ... possibly up to two hundred years."

Colleen yelped, almost laughing, shaking her head. "That's impossible! They're full of shit!"

"I know, that's what I said. It may only last a couple of years, though."

"That sounds a little more like it. How the hell could they send anyone out that long? It's ridiculous." Colleen added.

"Now do you understand? That's why I said we're not going."

Colleen thought about the time estimates. She was sold more on the notion that they would never send a crew out that long, whether they could or not. Even five years wouldn't be bad. "Have you ever thought about it?" she asked.

"Of course I've thought about it, long enough to say no." He reiterated the most important part. "He said it could last two hundred years!" He spoke loudly, but politely.

"And it might not!" Colleen's response was in kind. "We might only be gone for a few."

Gary set a steaming bowl before her on the table. "Don't tell me you're even considering this?" He prayed he was reading her wrong.

"I don't know, but I don't think it'll take nearly as long as they say. How could it?"

"I don't know, but that's the drawback. If it only lasted a couple of years, I would consider it, but there's no guarantee." The discussion was turning sour.

"God Gary, there's no guarantee's in life. Who ever told you that?"

"Nobody, but what about the two other SPEX missions sent out? They never came back. One has been gone over ten years. You say there are no guarantees, but I know one ... they're dead." He emphasized the last sentence. Colleen said nothing. The bowl of corry sat in front of her, untouched. "I just think the nega-tives are greater than the positives." He stared at her, silently wishing that she'd agree. "If someone wants to go out for God knows how long, to search for God knows what ..." He paused. "... then there's at least one open seat available. I'll listen to it on the news ... if I'm still around."

"That's the point I'm getting at. If you are still around?" She didn't know exactly where she was going with it, but she needed to be sure. "This is the one chance to be around, to be some kind of time traveler ... at least into the future." For a moment, she waited for an answer, but there was none.

She thought about her own words. What was she saying? She had never been hungry for fame, or wealth, or knowledge, and she didn't feel as though she was now. So where was this coming from? Was she trying to discover his true feelings towards her? Could she put that kind of pressure on him? Should she? If he changed his mind, would she be able to say yes? She spoke without thinking. "What if I went, Gary? Would you go with me?" She sucked in her breath, wish-ing she could take it back. Maybe she really didn't want to know.

Gary nearly dropped the spoon he held in his hand. Did he hear her right? Of course he did. He didn't know whether to take her seriously or not. He hesitated, pretending as if he hadn't heard her, knowing that it was ludicrous. She sat only a foot away.

His brain raced for the right answer. The longer he waited, the worse it looked. He felt in his heart that he would do almost anything for her. The love between them, even though new and untested, was real. Even giving his life for hers would be as easy as breathing, but this ... this was in a way, more difficult. He looked straight into her eyes and asked her the same. "Would you?" Even as he asked, he knew what her answer would be. At the same time, he realized that he had unintentionally put himself on the spot. If she said yes, he would have lit-tle choice but to answer the same. What if she was truly considering going?

He turned away, silently admitting to her that he wasn't ready for this. Her attitude in this whole matter had been totally unpredicted. Could he make the decision now, whether to go and keep her, or to stay here and lose her? No ... it won't come to that. All of this traveled through his mind as he patiently awaited her reply. As expected, she took much less time than he.

"I asked you first." she said simply.

A moment of relief flooded over him, but only a moment.

She suddenly continued, "But yes, I would go with you."

Gary closed his eyes, relief replaced by guilt. He turned back toward her, opening his eyes to stare into hers. He could see the love in them, knowing that she would be giving up as much as he to go on the voyage. Another question burned within him. Would she ever go without him?

He was speechless. She deserved to hear the same words, as much as he wanted to say them, but if she had already committed herself to go … what could he do? A negative answer could end everything with her. If she went without him, the relationship would be over at that point anyway. Both options were unacceptable, but he would not lie to her, or to himself. He could not say yes. If she was only testing him, then he had nothing to lose. The position he found himself in was impossible. For a second, he toyed with a notion that maybe she wasn't expecting an answer. No … the look in her eyes demanded one.

He set down his glass and leaned back beside her. He felt words, right or wrong, emerging as he reached out and pulled her tightly to him. Her head rested against his. He spoke softly. "I want you to know that I love you with all my heart. I would do anything for you. I want to spend the rest of my life with you. I'm sure of all those things, but please … don't ask me … not tonight. I'm all screwed up inside and …"

Colleen stopped him, pressing her fingertips to his lips. "Are you mine?" she asked lovingly.

Gary couldn't help but smile. "Forever …" he answered.

"That's all I need to know." She replaced her fingers with her moist lips and she felt his body relax. It can wait, she thought. Everything can wait.

CHAPTER 18

▼

It was drizzling rain when Commander Haute emerged from underground, but he had expected it. Back home, his shoulder would ache miserably nearly every time the wet stuff fell. Just because he was on a different planet, millions of miles from home, it apparently made no difference.

The sun was up, it was humid, but few rays had touched the plaza. A shuttle, its running lights flashing and floods illuminated, waited for him to board. A couple of men were loading equipment. The shuttle he would take today was different than the first one he had flown over this land in. The interior had been modified with scanning stations and it was being armed in case of unknowns.

Another shuttle had departed earlier, before daybreak, in a westerly direction. His ship would head south along the coast. Their main goal was to seek out the cities, the largest population centers of the old world. By percentages, they were the most logical areas to search. On the other hand, the bombs, as suggested by William Vient, would have targeted these same areas. Therefore, they would retain higher levels of radiation for longer periods of time.

If the city of New York was a typical example however, the scale of devastation might not have been as severe as once thought. It was a fact that many of the missiles sent towards New York City had been stopped short of their target. Whether other cities had similar types of protection available was unknown.

As the first intermittent rays of sunlight broke between the buildings, the second shuttle lifted off and drifted southward along the Atlantic seaboard. A hundred miles above it, the Aquillon Two circled, scanners covering thousands of square miles, searching for and recording anything and everything.

As they rose visibility became poor due to low cloud cover. Weather reports from the mother ship said that it probably would not improve dramatically. Haute sat in one of the bow seats, allowing the best possible view, which still wasn't good. The hot ground below, pelted by the cool water, had released a fine white mist, completely carpeting the forest. Only occasional treetops, some over one hundred fifty feet high, could be seen.

At five hundred feet above sea level, Haute's limited view was far from comforting. Flying half blind wasn't one of his favorite pastimes, but he knew there would be no surprises on this trip. Turning toward the rear, he watched three technicians studying their individual screens. The special scanners were operating on short-range scale, allowing maximum detection capability.

What would they find, he wondered? He was sure there was humanoid life down there somewhere. The Kograns had numerous contacts with them. They were very primitive, considering their reports, and he had witnessed their savagery first hand. The odds were against any mammalian life surviving the cataclysmic changes that this world had gone through. Anything escaping the radiation poisoning would surely have succumbed to the nuclear winter. But had all of that actually happened? If the estimate of destruction and what the post war had brought was wrong, then all bets were off. A great deal of the Earth might have fared better than the city they had just left. Haute believed that the odds were good that they would find other survivors. What they were like and what happened after, was anyone's guess.

He thought ahead to the new SPEX mission being formed and wished that the new scanners on that vessel were aboard Aquillon Two. If so, this search would be a relatively short one. He chuckled, remembering a certain saying. "Wish in one hand and shit in the other, see which one fills up the fastest." It was an old example that still held true.

As they moved down the coast, the rain ended abruptly and the ship was bathed in blinding sunlight. Obviously, the weatherman above was wrong. The air temperature outside the ship rose rapidly and the cold mist hugging the ground began to dissipate. The pilot moved up to a thousand feet and leveled off. Haute was elated at the prospect of being able to see clearly again, but the feeling was dampened by what he now saw.

The devastation appeared complete along the entire coastline. No large buildings, such as the skyscrapers in New York City remained intact. Long beaches, one time beautiful liaisons between land and water were hidden beneath uncountable tons of waste and debris washed up over the decades. Haute was appalled. His hope of finding other inhabited cities was lessened. It was disheartening to think that this was all that was left.

The coastal scenery did not change for miles. Inland, there was forest, thankfully hiding most of the carnage. As they continued, he had the feeling that they were making a futile effort, searching for a needle in a truly immense haystack. On the small scale at which they were forced to operate, it could take years to cover this continent alone. Possibly, he could at least get a rough idea of what other changes had come about from the disaster. The visible changes that they had witnessed so far were extraordinary. The land and the climates, which nature had taken billions of years to establish, had been rewritten by the very life that had emanated from it.

Life itself had been altered dramatically. The unbelievable creatures that had attacked James Pritchart were a perfect example. What events had occurred that could have changed those simple life forms into such monsters? Was it possible for radiation to alter, but not kill? He challenged anyone to explain it. Animal, as well as insect had survived. How had they been changed? Had man been changed so incredibly? Over the next few days, he hoped to find out.

The miles turned into hours along the endless coastline. They encountered only the same wasted land. Scanning of the shallow Atlantic shelf revealed no shortage of life readings, suggesting that the ocean life had rebounded well. On drier ground, there remained no sign of humanoid life. It quickly became clear that animal life in all recorded forms had survived, keeping the scanner technicians double-checking constant signals. Numerous times, they passed and slowed over ruins of great cities, leveled by unmerciful forces, reduced to what they would now forever remain … nothing.

After seeing these cities, there was little doubt that New York had been spared the brunt of the bombs destructive power. Haute had to wonder whether the Kogran city had been directly struck at all.

The first day of the search grew short. At a thousand feet, the approach of darkness was deceiving. The ground was covered with long shadows. Haute watched the sun dip below the horizon, leaving only a reddish glow in the sky. He recalled a poem from the days of wind and sail, some four hundred years past. It assured the coming day would be a good one. He repeated it in his mind. It said, "Red sky at morning, sailors take warning. Red sky at night, sailors delight." His shoulder didn't ache. Maybe the old rhyme was right.

He had entertained an idea earlier in the day, which could be worth checking out. All they required was nightfall. What if the inhabitants they sought were nocturnal, venturing out only under the cover of darkness? If so, they may know the luxury of fire, which at night, would show up easily on the scanners. In this world, fire without lightning would mean intelligence. The only intelligence in this planets history that ever had the ability to produce flame was human. Haute knew that it was a long shot, but reasonably, one they shouldn't pass up.

He instructed the pilot to take a more inland path and to increase altitude. Minutes later, the shuttles automatic lights came on. The Commander disagreed with their suddenness. "Shut 'em off. We don't want to surprise anyone down there."

Their search continued south by southwest. They approached their fourteenth hour. With the Commander's permission, two of the three scanners had been shut down for the night, their operators retiring to the rear compartment. The third man had volunteered to monitor for a little while longer.

Haute noticed that there was no moon on this night. The ground and the sky were one, the horizon indistinguishable if not for the stars. It was an unsettling, but fascinating feeling for him, not knowing what secrets lay in the blackness below. He had grown less than enthusiastic through the day, seeing the same scenery hour after hour, finding nothing. With the night however, came a refreshed sense of hope. The ground below was foreboding; a mystery heightened by the darkness. The star filled sky above beckoned to him with its vastness. There was nothing frightening about its endless beauty. Home was up there somewhere.

Haute stood, stretching his legs for the hundredth time already that day. He stepped back to speak to the man watching the scanner. "Can you increase the settings on your thermal sensors?"

The man nodded and did so.

Time passed and it grew late. Haute leaned back and released an exhausted sigh. He had worn out every comfortable position the bow chair could offer and his eyes burned between each closing. The shuttle was on automatic once again, advancing on a zigzag course, remaining five hundred feet above the terrain. The pilot's eyes were also closing more often and for longer periods of time. Haute had thought it through. The day had limped along much too slowly. He knew what the two men who had stayed up with him felt like. He could ask no more of them tonight. Each of them was no doubt relieved as they heard the long awaited words. "Let's wrap it up guys; we're not going to beat this to death anymore tonight."

Top speed would bring them back to New York in less than an hour. Upwards into space to the Aquillon Two would take slightly less. Haute considered the options and spoke to the pilot. "Find a break in the trees and set us down, Matt."

He turned to the lone man seated in the mid section. "Activate motion sensors. Set them to pick up anything big enough to mess with us."

The pilot's board lit up with a three-dimensional graphic of the ground. Within minutes, he had chosen a site and had descended to a flat area, somewhat wet, but stable. As far as they could determine from the old maps, they were somewhere near a city named "Raleigh" in the state of North Carolina. They would remain there until morning and try again.

Kahn awoke with a start, instinctively closing his hand around a bottle that was no longer there. It took a few seconds, but eventually his eyes focused on a room other than the one he last remembered. Sitting up slowly, he felt incessant pain throughout his head. The room was dark, but some light filtered through the open door from the next room. He closed his eyes and groped for a bottle of pills on the nightstand. It hurt too much to keep them open. Finally, he found it. Strange, he thought, it should have rattled as he lifted it. "Empty!" he groaned aloud. "Oh God ..." He fell backward and rejoined the mess on the bed. This was impossible. No relief ... no transportation to get any, unless? "Deanna!" he called. No answer, "Deanna!"

Suddenly, it all came crashing back. He remembered everything, every crappy detail. He'd really screwed up, worse than ever. He had hurt her badly. What could he say to her to make up for what he had done? It would take everything he had. God, his head hurt.

He needed some help this time. He needed to try to find Gary, but not the way he felt right now. Shoving clothing around on the bed, he found a half comfortable position for his head and lay perfectly still. He wondered momentarily if there was any such thing as a drug delivery service. With the way his luck was running ... probably not. He could wait. Two or three hours more of sleep would help. Maybe Deanna would be here, by then.

Kahn didn't realize it, but he wouldn't be finding his friend for the rest of the weekend. About the time he returned to medicinal slumber, Gary and Colleen were listening to arrival information from an unseen pilot. They were on a commercial flight approaching Brittaan, the planet where his parents now lived. They had left that morning, wanting to make the most of what little time they could spend here.

Gary stared out the window, seeing nothing but darkness. Colleen, beside him, stretched and yawned. "What time is it?" she asked.

He glanced at his watch. "Back home it's three thirty-nine p.m. I don't know about here." Colleen groaned and kept her eyes closed. The flight had lasted over seven hours and she had slept most of it.

Within minutes, the pilot's voice blared again, relaying weather conditions and current time at their destination. It was just before eleven p.m. the night before. Colleen groaned again as she realized that the night here had just begun. They had gained over sixteen hours during the flight, the same time they would lose on the return trip.

The landing was uneventful and moments later, they walked through the gate exit into the terminal. Brittaan's spaceport, tiny compared to Bentar's, was nearly empty. Only a few scattered passengers from the last arrival remained. Gary strained to see beyond the crowd of persons preceding him and Colleen down the ramp, searching for a familiar face. He felt Colleen's hand squeeze his own.

There was nervousness in her voice. "You told them I was coming, right?" It was the fourth time she had asked during the trip.

"God girl ... give me a break." Gary squeezed her hand back, smiling with excitement. "I'm kidding ... don't worry, they know all about you." The crowd in front thinned. His searching eyes found them. "There they are," he finally announced.

Gary happily greeted his mother with a long embrace. It had been months since he did it last.

She looks so young, thought Colleen, but then again, she still was. The woman could only have been in her early forties. Her hair was short reddish brown. She wore glasses. Her face had no wrinkles to speak of, looking much too young to be the mother of a man in his twenties.

After the lengthy hug, Gary went to his father and grasped his hand. He squeezed as tightly as he could, but as usual, his Dad's was stronger. As he looked into his father's face, he noticed many things different. He didn't appear as young. His hair, which had been jet black as long as he could remember, had turned somewhat gray. He now had a mustache and beard, also streaked with gray. It seemed strange. All that was remained familiar were his gold wire rim glasses that he would never trade in for contacts, and his smile.

Colleen was content to wait patiently until Gary could introduce her, but before he could do so, his mother took the initiative. "How are you, Colleen?" She held out her arms and gave the stranger a warm hug.

From that moment, all feelings of apprehension left her, replaced with reassurance. "I'm fine. I'm so glad to meet you," Colleen answered.

Gary finally spoke up. "Colleen Sluder, this is my Mom, Joanie, and my Dad, Kenneth."

The latter stepped forward, also with a hugging hello. "Everybody calls me Kenny." As they hugged, Colleen gave Gary a surprised, but happy glare.

"I'm happy to meet both of you," she said again.

Kenneth reached out and grabbed his son's beard. "What the hell is this?"

"I finally grew one." Gary laughed.

Joan looked the visitors over. "Well, you both look okay. When you told us about Thalosia, we wanted to come. I still feel bad for not coming"

Gary smiled. "Mom, there was no reason to. We were all right." He wrapped a loving arm around her shoulders.

His mother shook her head. "That's all that was on the news for days. My God, all those people killed. You could have been one of them."

Gary sighed, remembering the tunnels. "Yeah, they had more than one chance at some of us."

Kenneth added a haunting thought. "It could have been this planet just as easily. There's no planetary defense here either." He gestured toward the door. "Come on, my bed's calling me." He led the way, his long gone son at his side.

Joan walked with Colleen and again made conversation. "How was the flight?"

"Oh, it was fine," Colleen answered. "I slept most of it. I didn't know what time it would be here."

"Oh no ... well, you'll get tired again. Gary's told us a lot about you. He didn't give us much notice that you were coming."

"Me neither, he asked me the night before we left."

"We haven't seen him since he went to the academy. We wanted to be there for his graduation, but it just didn't work out. It would have been too hard. We talk a lot though. I've got the bills to prove it." They both laughed.

"We're just happy he decided to bring a girl home for once," added Kenneth.

Gary looked surprised. "What's that supposed to mean?"

His father chuckled.

They exited the terminal to the parking lot and approached a fantastic automobile. Colleen knew that Gary liked older vehicles and it was now clear who he got it from. The car was an antique, but in mint condition. It even had rubber wheels, something not many cars had any more. She had no idea what type it was, only that it was a very old style.

Kenneth opened a door, allowing Colleen and Gary to enter. He tossed their carry on bags in the trunk.

Colleen stole a quick word. "Why don't you have one of these?"

"Do you know what these cost?" he whispered. "Besides, this is only a kit car … you know, a replica. Mine is an original," he boasted.

"Yeah, but it's a piece of …!" She began the comeback, but was cut short.

Gary's father interrupted. "So how is old red running? How many years you had that now?"

"Fine Dad, it's still going."

Ken chuckled. "I figured you'd have gotten something else by now." He turned the key and the car's engine hummed to life. "He's right Colleen, this is only a kit car, a replica from the twentieth century. It's a 1979 Ford LTD. I collect old things, antiques, books … the older the better. I've actually got some original items from old Earth itself, over two hundred years old."

Colleen's interest was sparked. "How do you get things like that?"

"You spend a lot of time and money, believe me. I know some of my oldest stuff came off the original ships that first landed on Belaquin." There was undeniable pride in his voice, well justified due to the nature and rarity of his collection.

Colleen found herself looking forward to the visit even more. "I'd really love to see everything." She thought of all the items she could have picked up in the deserted streets of New York City.

"And you will," Kenneth promised. "Like I said, I like the old ways. The things we do, the way we live. I like keeping my feet on the ground …" He glanced in the rearview mirror at Gary, "… unlike my son."

Joan added her two bits at this point. "He's not kidding about that. He won't fly! We haven't had a decent vacation in ten years."

"What do you mean? Every day with me is a vacation," remarked her husband.

Joan rolled her eyes and shook her head. She'd had enough of that conversation.

Colleen spoke next. "My parents collect some antiques, but I don't think they have anything as old as what you have. They like the old ways too."

"Well, we definitely have something in common. I imagine we'll get together one of these days." Kenneth commented. He spoke to his son, changing the subject. "Hey, we've been watching the news like you said, but they don't tell a whole lot after the editing. Are we going to war or not?"

"Well, I couldn't really say anything when I called, but I think it's over for a while." He paused for a moment, glancing at Colleen. "I do have a heck of a story to tell you Dad, one I think you'll appreciate."

"Sounds good, let's hear it."

Gary smiled and looked at his father. "It'll take a while. It's not a five minute story."

"Well, this isn't a five minute drive. We might have time."

"Are you sure you're supposed to be telling any of this?" asked his mother.

"Well, I don't know, but it's all gonna be out in a couple of weeks anyway. I'm surprised it's not already."

"Well spit it out boy. Is it all secret crap?"

Gary knew what he was going to say would shock his father. "We've been to Earth." he said bluntly. Both he and Colleen waited for the coming response. It wasn't what they expected.

His parents exchanged glances, both smiling. Kenneth played along. "You're right," he finally chuckled. "That's a hell of a story!"

Now it was the younger one's turn to exchange glances. Gary realized how it must have sounded. He might as well have said they had been to heaven and back. "No Dad, I'm not joking. We were both there, only a few weeks ago ... the real Earth." He tried to sound as serious as possible.

Kenneth balked for a moment, not willing to give in totally. "So the rumors are true?" He asked, "The Kograns, New York ... all of it?"

"I know it sounds crazy, but it's the truth." He hesitated to go further, but obviously it wasn't the secret he'd thought it was. He noticed distress in his mothers face. She'd no doubt heard stories.

Kenneth was unsure of how he felt. "We knew you were involved with the Thalosia thing, but we didn't know about Earth." He kept eye contact with his son in the rear view mirror. He knew what his wife was feeling. How many times had they almost lost their son in the past weeks?

Colleen glanced at Gary and finally spoke, knowing what his mother's silence meant. She had felt the same, not that long ago. "But that's all over," she began. "No more excitement for a while." She paused. "You'd like it there, Kenny. Everything is antique."

Kenneth Kusan shook his head, imagining. This was something that he had never even dreamed of. In his lifetime, Earth was dead and gone. It was something that had been forgotten.

"My God ..." his father began, finally realizing the enormity of what he was hearing. "Why haven't we heard anything about it?"

"It's still classified for now, especially its location. I guess they don't want a thousand private ships over there until everything's checked out." Gary suggested.

Joan finally spoke. "We heard that the Kograns had survived?"

Gary nodded. "They did. It was unbelievable. Jesus, there's so much to tell you. We were right there in the middle of everything!" The excitement in the young man's voice was evident.

His father listened. He had obviously been through something incredible. "So what's happening now?"

"There was a lot of trouble at first, but it's over. Peace talks were started. A delegation actually came back on our ship. Exploration teams are there now. Commander Haute even invited us to go back with him."

Kenneth contemplated the trip. "I don't think I would have passed on that one," he said candidly.

"We considered it, but we'd had plenty enough adventure for a while. I didn't really enjoy the first trip too much," Gary said. "Can you imagine, Dad ... going back?"

"I already am," he smirked. "I might even fly for that." He caught a dirty look from his wife beside him. "All right, I know you're dying to tell me everything. It ought to be pretty good, but let's save it for morning. If we start now, we won't stop. This old man's tired."

Gary yawned. "Sounds good, I am too." He smiled at Colleen. The interior of the car was dark, now that they had left the airport terminal, but he could still see her.

She saw him and reached across the seat to hold his hand. It had started better than she thought. She felt content ... happy. The weekend would be wonderful.

Gary squeezed her hand as his mother turned to face them both. She started the small talk. "So Colleen ..."

Gary leaned back and looked out the window, only half listening to the conversation. Black forms against the starlit background, moved quickly past. Soon, they reached the mountains, the place where the two people he loved the most had chosen to spend the rest of their lives, and the place that he had only, thus far, heard about. He tried to imagine the coming day, but Haute's words, as well as Kahn's, somehow invaded.

They gnawed at him. He couldn't keep them out. Why? He'd already made up his mind. He closed his eyes and tried to think about something else ... anything else. His mother and Colleen talked on. God, it was great to see them again. It had been far too long. The comfort of being with them finally eased his mind. Within minutes, he was asleep.

As far back as he could remember, breakfast had come early in the Kusan residence. The quiet sound of clinking dishes and the aroma of home cooked food drifted up the stairs to the bedroom. Gary opened his eyes and stared at the ceiling. It was made of genuine wood, a rarity in most homes, and totally absent in his apartment.

The first rays of sunlight were just topping a far away peak to brighten the room. The single window was open, the sound of birds and a breeze filtering through. Had I slept, he wondered? Colleen had, and still did.

He got up slowly in an effort not to wake her. The floor was cold on his bare feet. It was made of hardwood, like the ceiling, narrow strips, polished, gleaming, even in what little light there was. His mother had always believed that a clean house was a must. As he sat on the bed, he squeezed the thick feather mattress, knowing that he hadn't slept on anything so soft in his life.

As quietly as possible, he dressed and started down the stairway, following the smell of ... something familiar. He knew it well, but hadn't had any in months, sausage biscuits and white milk gravy.

As he hit the bottom step, his mother spoke without turning from the kitchen. "I knew this would wake you up."

"Still get up early, huh, Mom?" He stood beside her at the stove.

"I figure I've already slept enough for one life," she answered.

"Sleeping in is one of the few luxuries left though." Gary commented.

"I guess I've done enough of that too. You'll understand when you're my age. You learn to savor each waking moment because those moments are getting fewer and fewer." She stirred the gravy slowly so it wouldn't stick to the skillet. The biscuits lay on a pan, not yet in the oven.

Gary nodded in agreement. "Well, you're probably right, but that's a depressing thought," he announced.

"Well, I can't help that. It's all in how you look at it." She smiled, content in her belief.

Gary noticed the stillness of the house. "I can't believe I beat Dad up."

"You didn't. He's out for his morning walk. It's about the only real exercise he gets anymore." Joan revealed.

"Where at?"

"You can go after him if you want. There's only one trail through the woods."

"Okay ..." Gary yawned. "How long til breakfast?"

"Whenever you get back, I guess. Tell him it's almost ready. How many biscuits do you want?"

All of them, he wanted to say. "Half a dozen will be plenty."

"That never was enough before. I'll fix extra."

Gary was glad to hear it. "Don't let Colleen sleep too late."

A feminine voice from upstairs met their ears. "I heard that!"

Gary smiled. "Do you want to go with me?" he called.

"Where to?"

"The woods ..."

Colleen, lying in one of the most comfortable beds she had ever lain on, smiled, taking in the fragrance from downstairs. "I don't think so. I've had enough woods to last me a while too."

Gary turned, chuckling. "Okay!" He walked outside, "I'll be back."

The air was chilly and the grass wet with dew. For a minute he considered returning inside for a light jacket, but didn't. There was no sound except for the birds. He stopped and took in the scenery. The house was situated on a rise near the top of the mountain. Beyond the house was the valley and lowlands, spread out for miles. Further past the valley were more hills. The impact of man had barely touched as far as he could see. Most of the area was still wooded. A small town nestled in the distance, far down the valley. It was not the city they had arrived in the night before.

He had to hand it to his father. He had the best of taste. This place, this tiny forest clearing, had to be the most beautiful place on this world.

As he explored the yard, he spotted the trail his mother had spoken of. He followed it into the trees. Once he entered the shade, the temperature dropped several degrees. The forest was open, the undergrowth sparse, just opposite of the terrain they had found on Thalosia just a few weeks ago. His father had told him about the mountain last night after they arrived home. He said that this particular forest was comprised of virgin timber. Its massive trees had never been touched by a saw or blade. He marveled at the thought. His father had said it with pride, as if he himself had been personally responsible for that fact. Oh well, Gary reasoned, even if he wasn't before ... he was now. This was his land, his mountain, paid for with every penny he had scratched up and saved for the last thirty years.

Gary suddenly felt very proud of his father. He'd never thought about it before, at least not in this way. Here was a man who had never done anything that anyone would notice. He had started with nothing, maintained a steady job and raised his family. He never wished to make a name for himself or had aspirations of being an important, rich, or famous man. He just wanted to be a good one. At least he had done that well. With hard work, he had acquired his dreams, a house in the hills, a loving family, and the knowledge to be thankful for both.

Studying the terrain, Gary had a strange thought. This planet resembled Earth in so many ways. The plant life, animals, and climate were so similar. It was hard to believe that there hadn't been people here also.

Brittaan had only been discovered three decades ago. It was a planet full of life. What else could the Republic be searching for? Why did they need more? The answer they gave was simply to find intelligent life, but intelligent in what respect?

There was another possibility. Was the Republic pushing the mission for military purposes, rather than scientific? Even though a civilian company financed SPEX, there was no guarantee that the Republic hadn't appropriated some funding. What would be their purpose behind a mission like this? The Thalosians were finished. Was this simply an elaborate search to find another adversary to keep the military intact? It made perfect sense. Why does any civilization need a military presence? Ideally, one is utilized to deter, to protect against, or to attack a hostile entity. Is that presence needed if no enemy exists? His theory had only one flaw. This newest mission had been under way long before the attack of Shannate. It sounded far-fetched, but remained a distinct possibility.

The path he followed suddenly split in not two, but three directions. "Great," he said aloud. Which way? Should he wait here?

A quiet breeze moved the tree branches a hundred feet above his head. Droplets of water fell around him, momentarily breaking the absolute stillness. Rain, perhaps? It was more likely dew from the morning fog. He looked back the way he had come, expecting to see the house in the distance, but there was only the deep dark green. A few sunrays formed long lines of light reaching to the ground. He gave his father unspoken thanks for the trail he had blazed. It was easy to follow. Getting lost would not be difficult without it.

He decided to wait. It was the best choice. His father had to be along soon.

A long five minutes passed. He spent it seated on a dead log he had found. Finally, he rose, coming to the realization that waiting was senseless. His father could sit here all day if he chose to, relishing the peaceful calm, but for him and Colleen, time was limited. He had to admit that he could sit here for hours as well and thoroughly enjoy it. The timing just wasn't right.

He chose a trail and took it. Getting lost was impossible. He would follow it for a while, and if he didn't find him, he'd simply retrace his steps. The worst that could happen is that he would miss him and meet him back at the house. The path led on.

Kahn wasn't sure what to do next. What else could possibly go wrong? Only one thing, so far, had gone right. His headache at least, had left him. Unfortunately, it wasn't all that had left. He had searched for Deanna, but she was nowhere to be found. He wished to try and explain last night's multitude of mistakes. Hopefully, he would be given a chance. When he called Gary's apartment, he received only Jana. She could only vaguely relay his friend's whereabouts. "Unreachable for the weekend," was the message given.

He left numerous messages at Deanna's apartment and tried all of her frequent haunts that he could remember. She had been to at least one of them the night before, but his luck ended there. His options were limited. He needed transportation. His own car was out of the question. If a police drone detected his identification numbers, he would find himself in Bentar lock up, facing the possibly of losing his driving privileges for good. Once he was released, he'd have to answer to the Republic for being absent without authorization. It wasn't worth it. The Belaquin justice system had limited patience with lawbreakers. Punishments today were effective, in stark contrast to the ways of old Earth. Laws were strictly enforced. If caught, perpetrators were dealt with quickly and harshly.

Kahn was frustrated. Where could she be? She hadn't gone with Gary and Colleen, wherever they were. One call to the airport discounted that theory. He entertained the notion that maybe she'd come back to his house, but recounting last night's events strongly suggested that she wouldn't.

Ten minutes of indecision started him walking towards her building. It was likely that she was home and just refused to talk. Sitting at home and waiting would certainly be less strenuous, but this apology needed to be made as soon as possible.

It was his fault. The alcohol and his stupidity was a dangerous mix. Some parts of last night were still vague, but he remembered most of what he had said. Even if she didn't forgive him, at least she would know that he'd made the effort. The walk to her house was far from short. That alone should prove something to her.

He continued on. His plan was a long shot, but what else did he have?

Deanna rolled over in bed and reached for the button to answer the incoming call. She stopped in mid-reach, deciding to wait and let the machine pick up. If it was Kahn, she wasn't in the mood to converse, at least not yet. She especially wasn't ready for another fight, but she doubted that's why he was calling.

It was him. She lay and listened for any trace of sincerity in his message. She was surprised when he filled the entire two-minute recorder. In fact, the machine had to cut him off. When he finished, she rewound it and switched on the visual display, which also had recorded. There he was, in all his humility, speaking words he must have rehearsed. The sentences he spattered didn't come naturally for him. He looked so sad ... so genuinely sorry. It was hard to believe that he was the same man from the night before. Her eyes grew moist.

Suddenly, she felt inundated with guilt. She tried to shake it off, knowing full well that she had not been last night's instigator. She shut off the machine. Again, she told herself that it hadn't been Kahn Bengal last night, it had been the alcohol. She thought about everything they had been through. There were far more good memories than bad. She played the message again, listening intently to one particular part. His voice was soft and loving, his face sincere. "You remember when we were kids? I think it was your thirteenth birthday party. We hid in the closet, and you kissed me for the first time ..." He chuckled, a real smile forming with the memory.

She felt the tears begin again. She had totally forgotten that day. He was several years older than her, but she hadn't cared. She had always had a crush on him. The tape played on. She wiped her eyes as it continued.

"You said something to me that day ... after the kiss. Do you remember? Well I do. You said ..."

She said the words out loud with him. "I'm going to marry you someday." Those words, her own words, cut through her as if she'd said them yesterday. She sighed deeply and turned off the machine. She couldn't do this to him. It didn't matter what he had said, she loved him too much. She had to see him, to just talk it out, whatever it took. She wasn't even sure what he had been talking about last night, just bits and pieces. One thing she was sure of was what she wanted to say to him now. She dialed his number, but received no answer.

Hurried by the thought of what he might do if he didn't find her, she got dressed and headed for the car. As she drove, she tried to remember other things he had said. He talked about a trip. She didn't know when, or where, but he had said that in order to go, they had to be married. Truthfully, that aspect of it was fine with her. She knew the trip couldn't be the sole reason for the discussion. Still, it was strange. What kind of voyage required married couples? It surely could not be a venture sponsored by the military. It was common knowledge within the Republic that marriage between active duty personnel was more or less frowned upon.

She shook her head, perplexed. There was no use wondering about it. She had no information to base a conclusion on. Besides, it didn't really matter. This was a special occasion. The man she loved had proposed marriage. She'd be smart to find him before the idea left him.

Gary had chosen the middle trail. It was no different from the others except that it was maybe worn a little more. More sunlight started to fill the forest. It created shadowy movement where there was nothing. It reminded him of something he'd read about parallel universes. It claimed that occasionally, we have brief contact with these other dimensions either by sight, touch, sound, or other senses. It had given examples. Some were experiences that the common person might have every day. They included the movements out of the corner of your eye, the hair standing up on the back of your neck, the sound of voices or footsteps with no one there, the feeling of someone watching you, goose bumps, cold chills, deja vu. These were all suggested to be subtle glimpses of the other side. The thought was uncomfortable and a little frightening, but wonderful.

As he walked, he marveled at the solitude and the natural beauty. It was easy to see why his father had chosen this place. If personal preferences ran in the blood, this mountain was living proof of it. If he was lucky, then maybe someday, he could raise a family in such a place and take a walk like this again with Colleen.

The trail twisted and turned, crossing several small valleys and ridges, but it was well trod, and he wasn't worried. He hadn't gone that far. Every couple of minutes, he would call out for his father, but would receive only momentary silence from the birds around him. Shaking his head, he grew certain that he'd chosen the wrong path and considered going back. The biscuits and gravy were no doubt waiting by now. As he turned, a faint sound caught his attention. It had always been there, but he hadn't noticed it. It sounded like rushing water and seemed to come from over the next rise. He decided. What would one more hill matter?

He concluded as he topped the crest, that it was well worth the extra few steps. Spread out before him was the most fantastic rock gorge he had ever seen. At one end, further up the slope was the source of the roar. A white waterfall, probably thirty feet in height, fell to feed the stream in front of him. He couldn't believe what he was seeing. Unable to remain where he was, he followed the path to the base of the falls. The falling water created a fine mist in the air. As he drew near, he felt a dramatic drop in temperature. It was as if he'd stepped inside an icebox. The mist was all around him. The moisture clung to his face and arms. Exhilaration wafted through him as he realized that he was possibly only the second or third human being to ever see this breathtaking sight. What could it have felt like to have been the first? It was impossible to imagine. Is this even remotely close to what true explorers experienced? If so, he envied each and every one.

For several moments he watched the water, knowing all the while that he had never been in a place like it. He wondered if something even more breathtaking than this lay at the end of each of the other two trails.

He glanced at his watch. Surely his father was back at the house by now. He knew that he wasn't ever one to wait at the breakfast table, so if he wanted to eat, he'd better make tracks.

Suddenly, with no warning, something strong and firm grabbed his shoulder from behind. His heart was in his mouth. He turned and ducked with a yell of surprise.

Kenneth Kusan burst out with a vigorous laugh.

"Dammit Dad, you scared the hell out of me!" He smiled back. "Why didn't you answer me?"

"Because I didn't know if you were alone or not."

"Alone?" Gary hesitated, puzzled. "Mom said you went for a walk?"

Kenneth interrupted him and turned away. "Follow me," he said simply.

"Where are we going?"

"You'll see."

They left the trail, following no discernable path. The older Kusan talked as they walked. "I'm going to show you something, but with one condition."

"Is this a secret?" Gary mused.

His father ignored the question. "The condition is that you keep this to yourself." He stopped, turned and looked his son right in the eye.

Gary immediately saw that his face held no humor. "Okay, I will."

"You know I trust you more than anyone? A father can tell his son things that he wouldn't dare tell anybody else, right?" He watched his son nod. "This is one of those things. If you don't think you can keep this one condition, we'll stop right now, and go back."

Gary was bewildered, but too captivated to turn back now. He was confident that he could keep it to himself. "Show me."

Nothing more was said. They walked. The forest grew denser, and the going tougher.

Gary noticed his stomach growling. He had left the house nearly thirty minutes before. Would his mother be worried? Was breakfast cold yet? His father gave no indication of slowing the pace. He had to ask. "How far is it?"

"We're almost there," Kenneth answered without turning. Only a minute later, he stopped in a thicket so brushy that they couldn't see further than five feet in any direction. Kenneth smiled. "This is my little secret. Your mother doesn't even know about it yet."

Gary got the impression that what he was about to see must be truly awe-inspiring. His father reached out and moved some vines, opening a rough hole to pass through. Gary stepped quietly, as if sneaking up on what ever it was. Briars caught his clothing as he ducked through.

They now stood in a small clearing, still surrounded by impenetrable thicket. Nothing stood out as Gary scanned in a complete circle, confused. He looked at the man beside him. Obviously his little secret was invisible as well. "Dad, there's nothing here."

"You're not looking hard enough." He pointed to the vine wall in front of them. "Try to see beyond the leaves."

Gary narrowed his eyes, peering into the greenery, thinking it would be easier if he knew what he was looking for. His stomach growled again with a sick bubbly feeling. Suddenly his eyes caught something out of place. It took several seconds, but it began to take form. He stood, perplexed, filled with questions piling up upon one another. He wanted to speak, but found no words. What he saw couldn't possibly be there?

His eyes were riveted to what appeared to be a wall of some kind, nearly invisible behind the green confines. He looked for a clue in his father's smiling face, but saw only the pride of a great explorer ...

Gary walked closer, reaching out to touch it, to prove to himself that it was really there. He found an open place between the vines and touched the surface. It felt rough, like concrete; nicked, cracked and pockmarked, obviously of some age. He stood back to get a better look. The wall appeared to be around nine feet tall. The sides were too densely covered to guess a width. He saw no visible openings in it. Finally, he voiced a question. "What the hell is this, Dad?"

"What does it look like?"

Gary shook his head. "It looks like a wall ... part of a building."

Kenneth walked to the right and parted more branches. "It's a structure of some kind. I just started clearing out on this side. The fronts around here."

If it was possible, Gary's interest piqued even more. His father led the way, eventually finding another clearing. This particular side of the structure was fairly devoid of vegetation, obviously cleared away by his father. Seeing the nearly clean wall left the young man breathless. In the center of the wall was a definite entryway. The opening appeared to be the same height and width of a normal doorway.

"I found this a couple of months ago, after we moved here." He stood beside the open doorway as Gary peered in. It was dark within the structure. "I was making a new trail, got in this thicket and ran right into it."

Gary was spellbound. "This doesn't make sense ... it's so old. Who built it?"

"I've wondered about that since day one. It looks just like something we might build, but that isn't really a possibility. Belaquins only settled this planet eleven years ago."

"This wasn't built eleven years ago." Gary said with confidence.

His father laughed. "No, it wasn't."

"So what then ... someone was here before we were?"

"Evidently. Someone or something." He pointed up the slope through the shrubbery. "I found two other buildings up there, but the walls have collapsed. There's not much left."

Gary shook his head in astonishment. "And you haven't shown this to anyone?"

"Hell no, and I don't think I'm going to. Those scientific assholes would tear this mountain apart looking for anything they could find," answered Kenneth.

"Yeah, but you own this land." Gary offered.

"So what ... you know how it works. If they can't buy you out or throw you out, they'll find a way to force you out. Man's been doing it to each other for thousands of years."

Gary sighed. He couldn't argue with the logic. This could be a significant historical find. Appearance alone suggested it was built by humans, or something humanoid. His father was right though. He would lose this land if the wrong people found out. He could easily see the frustrating dilemma his father had. It had to be hard for him, knowing how important his discovery could be, but not being able to tell anyone. The consequences could be far too severe to chance it.

Gary had a theory. "How many ships left Earth during the war?"

"I'm not sure ... ten or twelve." He nodded his head, knowing what his son was considering. "I thought about that too."

Gary recalled the day he, Kahn, and the girls first set foot in New York. "We saw things on Earth when we were there ..." He shook his head. "... I don't think the people who wrote our history books knew what the hell happened."

"Well, I haven't found anything to suggest that whoever built this was from Earth, if that's what you mean."

Gary thought aloud. "If one of the ships did land here, it should still be here, right?" He tried to surmise an answer, but it just wasn't there. He changed direction. "You haven't found anything inside?"

"No ... nothing. I brought out some lights, but there's nothing here, at least not above ground. It's got a dirt floor. I'm planning on getting a metal detector in there and digging around."

"What if you find something then?"

"You mean something that could stagger our simple lives?" He watched his son nod his head. "Then I will have satisfied my curiosity, wouldn't I?"

Gary frowned somewhat.

His father grew serious. "Son, I don't care what I find in there. I won't lose this mountain. This is my land, and whatever is on it is mine. The only way I'll ever leave it is in a coffin." He turned and entered. Gary followed.

It was dark inside except for a small section in the ceiling near a sidewall that had caved in. Light flickered through it. Seconds later, a portable light was turned on. It lit the room enough for Gary to see that his father was right. There was absolutely nothing in the room except a few dried weeds near the door. It measured roughly ten feet by twelve. The walls and ceiling were clear of vegetation and at quick glance, featureless. The wall on the right sagged outward slightly and cracks were visible where it was beginning to fall apart. Possibly, the thick vine covering was all that had held it intact over the years. There was nothing else to be seen. Gary spoke. "Do you think there's more out there?"

"Could be ... this mountain is big." answered Kenneth. He glanced at his watch. "We'd better get back. You know how your mother is? She's probably got a search party out for us already."

The light went out.

The women were waiting impatiently as the men returned. Kenneth caught the dirty look from his wife, but hid his smile. He spoke before she could. "I didn't say how long I'd be gone."

Joan had noticed both the men's pant legs as they sat. "Don't sit there and pick off those stick tights on my rug," she advised. "Gary, there's some tape up in the cabinet that'll take them right off."

Colleen was curious, even if Joan wasn't. "Where'd you go?" she whispered.

Gary smiled as he retrieved the roll of tape from the shelf. He glanced at his father who sat silently, also waiting for his answer. "It's a big woods, I got the grand tour. My God, there's a waterfall back there you've got to see."

"You went back that far?" remarked his mother.

Kenneth turned, now smiling. His faith in his son was well substantiated. He knew his secret was safe.

Joan came from the kitchen, carrying a huge bowl of gravy. She set it in the center of the table. "We can eat now, Colleen." she said sarcastically. "I guess we can call this brunch."

Gary handed the roll of tape to his father. They looked at each other for a moment, wordlessly exchanging trust in each other.

Kenneth started in. "Well, you two were rattling off some pretty wild stories last night. Let's see how good they are this morning."

Sleep was fitful for Leon Minden Haute. He had finally fallen asleep in the co-pilots chair, reclined in what started out as a fairly comfortable position. So when the high-pitched alarm went off, he was only half asleep. He kept his eyes closed, not ready to start again. He pretended that it was thirty years ago, and he was on a hunting trip with the guys, waking before dawn and heading into the woods. There, they would wait for hours, hoping for a few brief moments of exhilaration. The image faded.

Suddenly, he was fully awake. The tone wasn't a wake up alarm. It was an automatic scanner alert. Evidently, one of them had detected something.

By the time he reached the scanner post, the alarm was off, and everyone was at their stations. He rubbed his eyes, trying to focus on the screen. "What have you got, Jacob?"

Jacob Hyatt, the head scanner officer on the trip, cleared his throat and wiped his eyes. "Heat sensors activated to the northwest of us."

"Close?" asked Haute, noting the direction.

"Only about three kilometers … ground level contact."

Haute smiled. "That's pretty close," he remarked excitedly.

Hyatt punched a couple of buttons to hone in on the exact location for navigation. "The temperature is fluctuating. It's definitely giving off a flame signature."

Haute returned to his chair, adjusted it and sat down next to the pilot.

Hyatt hit another switch. "Coming to you, navigation."

The coordinates transferred to the navigation console. "Got it," said the pilot.

Haute opened the inner screens on the view ports and adjusted the light level within the craft to a minimum. With what little moonlight there was, nothing could be seen outside the craft. "Let's go in quiet. Keep low to the trees." He glanced at the ships chronometer. It read three forty-one a.m. Earth time. The estimated sunrise was still a couple of hours away.

The shuttle rose and within five minutes, was within a hundred meters of the contact. The pilot halted the craft for several seconds above the treetops trying to find an opening to allow visual investigation. "I'm going down," he finally said.

The pilot dropped the craft between the trees, some branches actually touching the sides. He descended to within ten feet of the ground. The craft was completely silent. Five sets of eyes searched the darkness before them. Tiny flickers of flame could finally be made out. The pilot sighed. "That's as good as we're gonna get, Commander."

Haute strained, but could see no movement in the light of the small fire.

Another man spoke. "Sir, I'm reading five life forms in the vicinity of the contact."

Haute was quickly at his side. "Okay, try infrared … see what it shows." A dark screen came to life, relaying a different view. Forest growth, low in temperature, showed up as dark blue, green, and black as the remote scanned the trees. It zeroed in on the fire, which flickered mostly white, but it was the red and orange shapes that drew attention. Haute smiled and said the words he had wanted to say all day. "There they are."

The shapes were motionless. Haute stared at the screen, but could barely remain still. Each of the men in the darkened ship could feel the animation in the air. The range was close enough that the shapes appeared at least to be humanoid. Haute shook his head in frustration, wanting to just get out and see for himself. They had to be human, but they needed some kind of proof to be sure. The fire was obviously made by the individuals around it, but in this world where so much had changed, it was not substantiation enough. The tone in his voice almost pleaded, "Mathew … is there any way you can get in closer?"

The pilot sighed, hesitating. "Maybe a little; much closer and they'll hear us."

"I know, but let's try it." The pilot's last words had given him an idea. He searched the control panel and with the flip of a switch, the inside of the shuttle was rocked with startling sound. The forest around them, looking so peaceful and quiet, was far from it. It was noisy enough, that in the darkness, it was unsettling.

Even within the safety of the ship, Haute found it disturbing. "Is that turned up?"

"No sir."

The amount of nightlife around the vessel had to be great to create such a crescendo.

Haute held his breath as the shuttle inched forward through the trees. He glanced at the pilot, admiring the dexterity he demonstrated. He seemingly had a death grip on the steering rods and an unblinking stare fixed on the proximity scanner. Tense moments passed and finally, the pilot punched a switch and released the rods, his hands stiff and moist with sweat. He sighed again heavily. "I'm sorry sir, that's it."

Haute looked at the altimeter. It read eighteen feet. The distance to the signals was seventy yards. He patted the man's shoulder. "That's close enough."

The infrared patterns couldn't tell them everything they wished to know, but at times, the shapes were unobstructed and had definite outlines. Haute's heart raced. It was the excitement of the hunt he imagined earlier, the thrill of finally seeing an elusive quarry.

He sighed with relief. He had been right. Other human beings had survived, and they had been fortunate enough to make contact on the first night out.

An important question had been answered, but many more remained. Who were these people? He remembered being led through the forest in New York City by the Kograns. One of the black men had mentioned the "tree dwellers". Could these people be a similar group? They no doubt were descendants of some of the war's survivors. What were they like? Had this ravaged world changed them that much? Did they still have spoken language, families and homes?

Still another question that could prove interesting was whether they were black or white? Would color still matter to these people? Did they even know of the war? Maybe the answers would come when they were finally confronted? It would happen soon enough, but not on this morning, not under these circumstances. All Haute wished to do now was to watch and learn as much as possible. There was plenty of time. They found them once and they would find them again.

Suddenly, as they watched, the view of the fire became clear. Someone or something, which had been blocking it had moved. The figures around it were still shrouded by shadows, but movement was now visible within the small circle of light.

They could now see that there were five different individuals. Three continued to lay unmoving, but two others were upright. One moved closer to the fire and for the first time could be seen clearly, though at a distance. It appeared to be a man, clothed in a brown sleeveless garment. He had dark hair reaching at least shoulder length, but had no facial hair that they could see. He appeared to be light skinned. His lower body could not be seen. He stirred the fire, sending glowing ash upwards with the smoke. For several moments he squatted near the flames. At one point, he stood up and seemingly gazed directly at them. Could he sense that something was nearby? Eventually, he turned and left the fire, re-entering the dimness of the circle.

A half hour passed, during which the Commander entertained many future ideas. He cursed himself for not bringing a pair of magna scopes. It most certainly would have been included on a hunting trip, but they had not made the inventory list for this foray. At this range, he could have known the color of the man's eyes. One plan he considered could have been explored much earlier. The forest was boisterous. Would it be feasible to get a man or two close enough to gather more information? It would not be an easy task. He quickly discarded the ides. There were too many unknowns. It wasn't worth risking a life. The right time would come soon enough. The meeting would happen with the right planning.

Haute glanced again at the clock. It would start getting daylight in an hour. There was nothing more they could do here. The decision was made to back out the way they had come in.

Five minutes, and two sweaty palms later, the shuttle pilot flew freely to reposition a half a mile away. They had to sleep. There was no way around it. Daytime searching did allow visual exploration of the countryside, which was extremely important, but little or no human contact would be obtained by doing so. Those contacts were important as well, but day and night searches weren't possible. It would be far too exhausting.

The crew agreed that they should try to sleep for a couple of hours and continue later in the day. If during this short down time, contact was initiated from the outside, ideally by curious humans, then they would have to play it by ear. It could be an interesting turn of events. Word was sent to the Aquillon Two as the sky started to brighten above the tree line. Each man was exhausted, but too anxious to sleep. What would the coming day bring?

By the time Gary and Colleen finished their story telling session, brunch was only a memory. Kenneth and Joan Kusan sat in stunned silence, overwhelmed with what they had heard. So much had happened behind the scenes, so much that they'd not known. The Thalosian threat was hopefully no more. Earth had been found reborn, and peace had been made between the same peoples that had destroyed it. The simple fact that their son was still breathing after all of it seemed a miracle. It was more than enough for one day.

Kenneth considered what his wife had brought up the night before. "Are you supposed to be telling us all this ... I mean, some of it is still classified, right?"

Gary shrugged. "I guess it is right now, but it's all going to be released eventually." The question triggered another thought in the back of his mind. It was one he could do without. The thought concerned the secret trip, the trip that his best friend was probably already packing for.

Just telling of their past adventures had his heart racing. It was almost as if he were there doing it all over again. It was an adrenaline rush! Is this what Kahn thrived on? Is this what he needed more and more? For the first time, he paused and thought about it.

He watched his parents at the table. They were still so young, happy, and content. Old age was by far, the number one killer of today. With an average life expectancy of eighty-six, the both of them, in their late forties, were only halfway there. What if the mission did last only a few years? Would it be so different than being gone as he had been lately? Ten or twenty years would mean nothing to the sleeping crew. For those left behind however, the years would take their toll. The real burdens of the mission ... the concern ... the worry ... the pressure, would be solely on the families waiting for the return. Those loved ones should have as much to do with the decisions as the crewmembers themselves.

Gary looked past the open door to a row of swaying pine trees and thought about his future. Kahn was right in some respects. There were many good things that could come about for the members of a mission such as this; retroactive pay, retirement benefits, system wide fame. If the trip were a success, the crew would want for nothing.

He could have a place like this if everything went well, if he took a risk ... if he took advantage of what Haute called "the chance of a lifetime". Kahn had already realized the possible potential, but why wouldn't he? It was exactly what he wanted; adventure in the unknown ... the possibility of riches.

For an individual with nothing to leave behind, it seemed the smart move. If he didn't go and the trip was short and successful, would he regret not being a part of it?

Colleen's laughter brought his thoughts back into the room. She and her parents were looking at him. His father, no doubt, had told some funny story from long ago. It was impossible to guess which one. There had been many more good than bad. He smiled back.

His thoughts drifted again. Colleen had already revealed that she would go if he did. Had she been sincere? It was no secret that she was very close to her parents, but was that closeness enough to keep her here?

He felt a hand grasp his from under the table. It was hers. She seemed to know that he was thinking about her. Did she also know how dearly he loved her? He squeezed her hand tightly, trying to convey that very message, and received one in return. They both listened as his father rattled on.

Gary noticed something then that he'd never noticed before. His parents were holding hands as well, but theirs rested on top of the table. The simple gesture said so much. Their love was as real as anyone's could be. They had spent over half their lives together, experiencing everything, regretting nothing. They had raised him to manhood, making the memories they loved to tell about. They had withstood the hard times; surviving all the heartaches that life could throw at them. All of these things had formed the undying love they still shared today. This man and woman had instilled their values, knowledge, and love within him. They would go anywhere and do anything for one another, with no hesitation.

He squeezed Colleen's hand even harder, feeling his throat constrict. He knew in his heart that he would do the same for the young woman beside him. He couldn't lie to himself about his own feelings. He already knew the answer to her question last night. If she had already chosen her future and if she asked him, he knew he would be there beside her.

The sudden realization elated him, but at the same time, tore him apart. An uncomfortable feeling welled up inside him. His eyes grew moist with unwanted thoughts. How could he say goodbye to these two people, knowing that it could be the last one? He lowered his head towards the table and rapidly blinked his eyes, trying to stop an inevitable teardrop. It fell anyway. He brought up a hand to catch it, but was too late. His mother saw it.

"Gary? What's wrong?" she asked with concern.

The timing was wrong. Just the sound of her voice upset him even more. He rose with the words and walked to the other side of the table.

Joan stood up, confusion in her eyes. "What's the matter with you?" She stepped close to him.

Gary's throat tightened. He tried to speak, fighting the emotions that accompanied his thoughts. He pulled his mother close, hugging her. Finally, he choked out the words, "I ... love you, Mom."

Joan felt hurt rising in her throat as well, but didn't know why, "I love you too, hon."

"I don't want to leave ..." Gary sputtered, "... but I don't know what to do."

Joan glanced at her husband, bewildered, silently asking for help.

He answered her with a shrug of his shoulders and a shake of his head. He was just as puzzled.

Colleen was saddened, also near tears as she realized what was happening. She knew only then, how much what she said to him yesterday had meant. She had no idea that he had been bothered by it. He had been so careful in hiding it. Without a word, she rose and walked to the embraced mother and son.

Gary stepped back and wiped his eyes. He saw the pain in Colleen's eyes as well. He spoke shakily, still on the verge of tears. "It's not your fault, babe," he managed, hugging her also.

Joan dried her own face. She had begun crying simply because her son was, but the reason was still a mystery.

Gary had regained some composure when Colleen spoke quietly. "I would never make you go ... you know that."

Kenneth overheard the puzzling statement and asked. "Go where?"

Gary released Colleen and spoke to his parents. "We've got a lot to talk about."

Colleen glanced at Gary's mother, who met her eyes with total helplessness. She smiled reassuringly, wondering if she was ready to go through this with her own family. Was Gary considering changing his mind because he thought she would go without him? She had no intention of making him choose between herself and his parents. She couldn't allow him to even think it. This had to be his decision ... and theirs. To put the love they had for one another in the middle was unfair. It shouldn't play a part in this, but she had truly meant what she said to him. She loved him that much. She tried her best to read his emotions and was upset by her conclusions. She couldn't be sure, but the goodbyes may have begun.

A few moments later, they all sat at the table, the dishes cleared away. Gary sighed, unsure of himself and hesitant to begin. Colleen sat beside him, her head resting on his shoulder.

Finally, his mother spoke to him. "Well, I for one would like to know what could upset you this much."

Gary smiled weakly, even though he was far from happy.

Colleen nudged him, "Tell them."

Gary nodded in agreement. "I'm upset because, I ... we ... have a chance to be a part of something really rare and really great."

"Jesus Christ, I thought you were gonna say you were going to prison or something," said Kenneth, relieved.

Gary smiled broadly at his fathers pun. "No ... Dad that might be easier." He paused, but only briefly, regaining his train of thought. "There's a mission coming up. It's pretty important. Kahn says he's gonna go."

Joan shook her head, still uncertain of where the conversation was leading. "I don't understand. Why would another mission upset you so much?"

"Because a part of me wants to go, but I just can't …" Gary chuckled a little. "I know how stupid this sounds. It's just hard. I'm not even supposed to be talking about it."

"Well that hasn't stopped you any other time," said his father.

Colleen felt she could help the situation somewhat. "It's not a regular mission. It's being sponsored by the SPEX industry, jointly with the military."

Joan shrugged her shoulders, feeling no closer to an understanding than she had been a moment before. "And what exactly is the SPEX industry?"

Kenneth reached out and took both her hands in his. "You'll have to forgive your mother. She hasn't been a news enthusiast until lately." He spoke to her. "SPEX is short for space exploration. They're a civilian company, specializing in science and engineering. They build a lot of the ships used by the military."

"They built our raiders," added Gary.

Kenneth continued. "You've heard of them, you just don't remember because they've been idle for the last few years. Stocks dropped … contracts fell through. They've been working for the Republic for the last decade."

Joan thought all of this sounded less than comforting. "So what happened to them?"

"Years ago, they sent ships out to find other life, three separate missions about three years apart?" answered Kenneth.

"I think I remember some of that," Joan's memory was vague at best.

"Well, the first and last ships sent out never came back," Gary added. He watched his mother closely. She looked at her husband's hands in hers, but said nothing. Her face held no expression. It wasn't hard to read her initial feelings on the subject. He could say many things to put her at ease, but he didn't wish to support the voyage in their eyes, at least not yet. He needed to know their thoughts about it from the very beginning. There was long silence before anyone spoke.

His father had always been direct. "What's holding you back?"

"A lot of things …" Gary began.

"I have always supported SPEX, even with their history. Exploration is one of the most important things we can do," remarked Kenneth. "Discovery is a necessity. Without it, none of us would be here now."

Gary nodded. "I agree … it is important." He remembered the beauty of the waterfall that morning, and what he had felt when he first saw his father's secret. "There's no feeling like it."

Kenneth continued. "You've always loved adventure. If you remember, that's the reason you joined the service."

"I remember ..." Gary admitted.

"So ... I still don't see the problem," said the older, wiser man.

Gary looked at Colleen, who was being very quiescent. "There's nothing I'd rather do than go on something like this, but this mission ..." He paused, wanting to be honest with them and to himself. "I'm afraid."

His parents looked across the table, somewhat surprised. "Afraid of what, son?" his father asked.

Gary felt the tightness in his throat starting to return, but quelled it. "Of not ever seeing you again," he sighed. He'd voiced his ultimate fear.

Joan smiled, feeling her emotions building again. "There's going to be a last day, Gary, you know that as well as we do."

Gary knew she was right, but it didn't change the way he felt. "I know Mom ... I just don't want it to be on the day we leave."

"You're afraid you won't come back from this trip, like the others?" suggested Kenneth.

Gary shook his head, and went on to relate the confidence he had in SPEX, the changes the sleep chambers could make, and everything he could remember the commander had said. "No ... I think we'll come back," he finally added. "I just don't know when."

Kenneth nodded, finally understanding. He glanced into his wife's eyes, seeing that she too, understood. "With the sleep chambers, you can stay out longer," he summarized.

"How long?" asked Joan, not sure if she truly wanted to know the answer.

Gary couldn't look at them as he answered. "There's a chance it could last up to two hundred years."

His mother's breath caught in her throat as she inhaled. She covered her mouth in disbelief.

Colleen added quickly. "That's a remote possibility. They aren't sure. It may only last a couple of years." Her remark did not seem to bring relief to the woman across the table. She imagined that if she had a son, even two years would be too long.

Gary didn't hesitate when he saw his mother's reaction. "That's why I was so upset."

Another long period of silence followed. Kenneth rose from the table and walked to the door, looking through the screen to the mountains across the valley. He thought for a moment, about himself and his son, and made a difficult decision. "So you're being selfish to yourself then?"

All eyes in the room widened, but none as wide as Gary's. "What?"

Kenneth didn't turn. "You would give up an opportunity like this, because of one unknown?"

Gary didn't say anything as he tried to discern his father's meaning. He looked to his mother, who normally agreed with her husband, but he could not read her expression. "I'd rather give up this opportunity, than give up my family." He felt defensive. His father's remark had been totally unexpected.

Kenneth turned at that point. "There's no guarantee that you'd be doing that. I think we're gonna be here a long, long time."

"There's the possibility that we won't come back at all," Gary added.

His father chuckled. "That possibility has always been there, son, every time you say goodbye, every time you get in that raider! There is no difference for us. We never know if you're coming back. We think about it all the time. You just never have."

Gary sat in silence, repeating the words in his head, realizing that everything his father had said was right.

"Don't you see? Didn't you think about not seeing us when you were on Earth, or in those tunnels? You could have easily died then!" He paused, out of breath. "This mission is no different than the others ... not to us."

Gary was dumbfounded. "At least I have a decision in this one Dad!"

"You're right! It is your decision, but if you decide against this one, you might as well say no to all of them." He looked to his wife of twenty-three years, still not knowing how she was handling the situation. To his relief, she smiled back at him. It was not a happy smile, but rather an understanding one.

Joan spoke carefully. She knew that what she said might influence a decision that could take her son away from her forever. She would not be selfish. She would not try to hold him back, not from something she knew he would love so much. "We don't want you to leave ... but if you let this pass by ... if this mission is a success ... you'll regret it the rest of your life." She paused, staring into his eyes. She felt a tear roll down her cheek.

Colleen couldn't help it. Her eyes became wet as she watched Gary move to hug his mother. She knew at that moment, what was in their future and that soon, tears would fall with her own family.

The morning passed. Lunch was an exquisite home cooked meal from the town in the valley. The rest of the day was filled with reminiscing and sightseeing, with little or no talk of what was to come in the future. To Gary's joy, his parents were quickly making Colleen a part of the family.

The visit was everything Gary hoped it would be. He had felt so much pressure when he had arrived, but it had been lifted, replaced by a sense of well-being.

He had put thoughts of the mission behind him, but they still lingered. He was incredulous, as well as angry, at how easily he had been turned, but was comfortable with the knowledge that his family was behind him, no matter what.

He wasn't sure in what light he saw the voyage now. Colleen was convinced that the trip could not last more than a few months or years; that other life waited close by, no matter which direction they were sent. Maybe she was right. Maybe he and the woman he loved could indeed have it all.

Whatever the future held, good or bad, the ideals his parents had helped him to realize, made each second more memorable ... more precious.

They spent the evening at home. It had grown cold with the coming of dusk, and Kenneth had built a fire in the stone fireplace that filled one wall of the great room. Some time was spent talking ... some in silence. For a while, they just stared into the bright flickering colors, listening to the wood crackle and hiss. Finally, they retired late, each promising to walk the trails the next morning.

The promises were kept, and with the sun still low in the sky, they set out into the forest.

The two women walked several yards ahead of the men, talking it seemed, about anything other than the beauty around them. Kenneth and his son hung back. They talked as well. "Your Mother and I did a lot of talking last night," Kenneth said.

"Really? We did too." Gary answered.

"We don't want you to think ... I don't want you to think that I was pushing you to leave."

Gary shook his head. "I never thought that."

"Well, I thought it kind of sounded kind of bad when I said it," Kenneth admitted.

"You were right though. It's my decision, but it should be yours too. It affects all of us. I thought Kahn had lost his mind when said he was going. I just couldn't think like he did. I didn't see it. I had no plans to go, not ever, but when you said it, you were right. I was being selfish. I still don't want to go. I'm still scared, but I guess I'm scared too, of how I'll feel if I don't go."

"All of us make choices, right or wrong, every day. Granted, they're not as big as this one, but life is taking chances. If your mother would go, I wouldn't even hesitate to take a trip like this."

Gary stopped, surprised, but envious of how easy his father could make a decision like that. He said nothing.

"We'll be proud of you, no matter what you do. You're my son, but you're a grown man too. Sometimes I forget that. I think we did a good job raising you and we trust your judgments." He looked past his son to the trail ahead where the women had disappeared around a turn. "They'll be to the waterfall soon. We'd better catch up."

He took a step towards Gary to go past him, but the latter didn't move. When he looked into his eyes, he saw no sadness, no doubt, and no fear. What he saw was strength, pride, and confidence. He was filled with the same feelings when his only son spoke.

"Thank you, Dad," Gary said.

Kenneth stepped close and embraced him. "I love you son."

Gary felt it even without the words. "I love you too."

They held the hug as if it would be their absolute last. Kenneth finally released him. Clearing his throat, looking around, he joked. "I don't think anyone saw that, do you?"

Gary laughed out loud.

"Come on, let's see if Colleen's a nature enthusiast." suggested Kenneth.

"She's a botanist, Dad." Gary remarked sarcastically.

"Oh …" he said, caught off guard. "I guess that answers that question." He led the way up the trail, turning momentarily. "Did you tell me that already?"

"Yeah … the night before last."

"Well, you know, I'm getting kind of old …" He turned back, smiling.

Gary followed closely behind, as content in mind and soul as he had ever been.

Deanna checked the flight arrival schedule for the fifth time. She and Kahn had arrived with no time to spare. After finding out there was a ten minute delay, Kahn announced that he had to make a pit stop, making the remark that he felt like he was in labor.

She frowned as he hurried towards the nearest bathroom. "Thanks for sharing," she called after him. She found a seat, knowing that his "labor" would take the entire ten minutes. She waited and thought about the day. As bad as the weekend had started, it was a miracle that she and Kahn were even together on the same planet.

It was early afternoon the day before, when they accidentally ran into each other. She had found him walking towards her apartment, ready to do whatever he had to do to change the remains of the night before.

Within moments after the unplanned reunion, apologies and acceptances were over. Kahn had one request afterward. He asked her to drive to a beautiful lakeside park, near the cemetery where his parents were buried. Then, while they strolled along the waterfront, he suddenly knelt before her, took her hands in his and spoke from his heart. "De ... I know I messed this up the first time, but I'm asking you to give me one more chance." He produced a ring from his pocket. "I'm asking you to please be my wife."

She would never forget how she felt at that moment. She was filled with elation and apprehension. All she could think about was the night before. During the talk that followed, he'd said he didn't care about the mission that it didn't matter anymore. She hesitated, wondering whether he was being truthful, but within, knowing that no matter what the future held, she would not say no.

She pulled him up to a standing position in front of her. He slipped the ring onto her finger.

Kahn smiled, satisfied with the fit. "I bought it before I even knew about the mission."

It was all she needed to hear. She threw her arms around him and giggled with joy. He had his answer. That night, they spent together, talking about the times to come. To Kahn's amazement, during the long talk, she consented to consider the mission, knowing how much it meant to him.

Her thoughts faded as Kahn's bathroom break ended. It surprisingly lasted only six of the ten minutes. She commented as she rose to meet him. "That had to be a world record."

Smiling and pain free, he let out a well deserved sigh. "Damn Chinese food ... runs through me like water."

"Thanks again. That's more information than I needed," she frowned.

"Hey, you need to know everything about me, my most intimate details."

"I can't wait. Come on, we're still twenty gates away."

"They'll wait!"

"I know ... I just want to find out what's so important. Didn't they say anything?" Deanna inquired.

"Nope ..." Kahn answered.

Deanna's eyes narrowed. "You'd better not be lying ..." she warned.

"I'm not!"

They walked as quickly as the crowds would allow. It was late on the weekend and it seemed as though everyone was either flying in or already in the spaceport. Gate 37 was their destination. When it finally came into view, they could see only a couple of dozen new passengers arriving. Finding their two friends required only a glance in that direction.

The normal greetings were exchanged.

"So what did you guys do all weekend?" asked Gary, "After your ass sobered up." He and Colleen of course, knew nothing of the fight their friends had been through.

Kahn smiled. "I wondered how I got in bed." He put his arm around Deanna and pulled her against his side. "Oh ... we did a lot of talking."

Colleen slung her light bag over her shoulder. "Well, so did we."

Deanna couldn't stand it any longer. "You guy's got married, didn't you?"

The stunning statement brought forth incredulous looks from Gary, Colleen, and even from Kahn.

"What?" stammered Colleen.

The expression Deanna saw on her face discounted the assumption. "What then? I know you told Kahn something!"

Gary squinted. "No we didn't!" he said. He turned and started walking away, adding nothing more to his answer.

Kahn's mouth fell open in disbelief, expecting something that didn't come. He followed. "Well tell us now!" he called after him.

Gary stopped and turned back, giving Colleen a wink. She smiled back. "Well, I don't know for sure yet, but I hope I'm speaking for both of us. We're thinking about taking Haute up on his offer."

Kahn's expression didn't change. Several seconds passed. "What offer?" he asked honestly.

"The mission that you're so hot to trot about," Gary answered.

Kahn stopped and put both his hands on his head. "Jesus Christ, you gotta be kidding me? Two days ago you wouldn't even talk about it!"

Gary stopped as well. "I know. I don't believe it either. We talked a lot about it. Dad and Mom think I should go. They made me look at it a whole different way." He looked at Colleen and took her hand. "It was hard, Chief."

Kahn was speechless as he listened to his friend. The tone of his voice towards the end was sullen. He nodded his head in agreement. He could in a way relate to the pain Gary would feel. He had felt the same with the loss of his own parents. He'd lived with the hurt for as long as he could remember. It never went away. He shook away the thought as he'd done many times. This wasn't about him. He put his arm around his best friend's shoulders. "It's gonna get harder, bud. I can't say I'm sorry you changed your mind though."

"I figured you'd be happy."

Kahn nodded. "Hey, we've got some news too."

Colleen guessed quickly. "You guy's got married?" she asked jokingly.

Deanna smiled sweetly. "No, but we're going to!" she blurted out, holding up her new ring.

Colleen was overjoyed. "Oh my God!" she squealed. The hugging of course, followed.

Gary held out his hand. "I'll be damned. I knew you had it in you, but I didn't think you ever let it out." He leaned close to him, whispering. "You did ask her, didn't you?"

"Yeah," Kahn answered, "… twice."

"Well congratulations." He shook his hand, then turned and hugged Deanna. "It's about damn time …" he whispered.

Small talk followed as they left the spaceport. As luck would have it, the foursome passed Deanna's car first, and hesitated there long enough for her to try and start it. For whatever reason, it failed to do so. She looked at Kahn, who found no humor in the situation, since she was his only transportation. "This is your fault!" she told him.

"What the hell are you talking about? How could this possibly be my fault?"

Gary interrupted. "Come on."

They continued on to his aged classic, which proved reliable once again. They talked as they drove, about the many things that their futures might hold, and whether the plans were set in stone or not. Kahn informed Gary that he believed Deanna was willing to go as well. "What about Colleen?" he asked quietly. "Are you sure she wants this?"

"Well, I think so," he whispered. The girls talked loudly in the back, not remotely paying attention to the conversation in the front. "She said she would go if I did" He thought for a moment. "When she said it though, she knew I was dead set against it." He paused with a new revelation. "Jesus … I hope she doesn't change her mind now."

"Has she talked to her family yet?" Kahn knew that aspect would mean everything.

"She hasn't had a chance yet." Gary slowed the car, noticing something up ahead. He strained to see in the distance.

"Well, she's got plenty of time." Kahn also looked ahead. "Looks like a wreck."

Flashing lights and strobes penetrated the blackness around the freeway, blinding anyone approaching the area. Numerous emergency crews were there, fire control, medi-vacs, and trauma units. By the looks of it, it appeared to be very bad.

Human police officers directed four lanes of traffic into one to bypass the scene. Vehicles crawled past, the drivers, no doubt, trying to catch a glimpse of something they didn't see everyday.

Gary was no exception. There appeared to be three separate vehicles involved; two small cars, and one truck. The truck was one of the large heavy haulers, measuring at least one hundred feet long and weighing tens of tons. It now lay on its side. It looked like it had somehow rolled, catching one of the cars underneath. Large wrecker equipment, with the aid of anti-gravity units had lifted the hauler off of the ground.

Underneath, there was a mangled, unrecognizable lump of wreckage. Firemen had somehow cut away the crushed top of the car, folding it backwards over the rear of the vehicle, allowing medical personnel to approach. They didn't appear to be working on anyone, but how could anyone have possibly survived. The third vehicle rested nearby, damaged, but not badly. Several people stood around it, but none seemed injured.

Gary glanced in the rearview mirror as he neared the scene. Seeing no one behind him, he came nearly to a stop next to a policeman. Gary had to ask, "It looks pretty bad?"

The man looked friendly enough, but gave the impression that he would rather be anywhere but in the middle of the road. He nodded. "It is. The truck drivers were alright, but there's two dead in the car, man and a woman, we think."

Before more could be said, headlights suddenly appeared behind them, coming up fast. The foursome watched from only twenty feet away, as two of the firemen unfolded a sheet and draped it over the car, covering the remains until they could be removed. The officer spoke again. "You'd better move on."

Gary did so.

Deanna was solemn. "Oh my God ... can you imagine?"

Kahn shook his head. "They didn't feel anything ... they couldn't have."

They drove straight to Kahn's home. The fatal wreck remained the topic of conversation. Once there, the host invited all to spend the night. Gary saw Colleen visibly flinch in apprehension at the thought, but upon entering the home, they received a shock. It was nothing like the home they had been in only two days before. The home was nearly spotless. Deanna had provided the initiative and Kahn the work.

As Gary and Colleen considered Kahn's offer, they talked more. It was suggested at Gary's urging, that they should continue their regular work routines until they could again speak with the commander. Kahn frowned at the idea, knowing that the man was not due back for weeks, but consented. They also felt it prudent not to speak to anyone else concerning their future plans. The time would also give Deanna and Colleen a chance to think the subject through. Even though both seemed to support the men's decisions, they knew there was much more to be done.

The evening grew late, and their flights left early. Gary and Colleen had to turn down Kahn's invitation, needing to ready for the morning trip back to Touchen. The four friends parted ways for the night.

CHAPTER 19

▼

Four weeks passed before the fleet commander returned home. His report had nothing significant enough in it to set a special meeting with the council. He decided to wait until the next one was scheduled. All data collected over the month long exploration was available on disc. All recorded footage would describe what words could not, concerning the current state of the planet. The council members could review the discs at their leisure and make their own conclusions from them.

It would be their responsible for releasing information to the news networks. Haute, looking at the first mission as a whole was in a way satisfied, but also disappointed. All attempts to communicate with the primitive humans had resulted in failure. It was determined that these elusive individuals were mostly nocturnal. Contacts found at night became untraceable with the coming of the day. These incidents and the lack of visible dwellings suggested possible underground habitation. With the limited number of contacts consistent in the same area however, it was only a guess. The one Republic death attributed to these primitives had occurred in broad daylight. Did this suggest daylight ventures? There were still more questions than answers, but the mission had only been the first attempt. There was still ninety-nine percent of the planet to be explored. Other missions would follow. Peaceful contact would hopefully be accomplished at some point.

The Commander had made good on one experiment at least. He had allowed himself to be placed in a sleep chamber for the trip home. He found it a unique experience. As he expected, he had some anxiety prior to being put under, but discovered upon awakening, that it was unwarranted. He admitted afterward, that he felt more rested than he could remember.

The process had only one uncomfortable aspect that he would change. If possible, he would just as soon stay asleep for the short period during body warming. The post sleep hypothermia was horrible. Perhaps it could be improved in time. Overall, he gave it his complete approval.

Soon after his return to the ice planet, he made a visit to an area he had not seen in over two years. The area carried a special level clearance and operated on a need to know basis. Absolutely no one without it could enter. He initially reached the section via elevator. He exited and approached a large pressure door at the end of a short corridor. Two well-armed security men guarded the door. He was surprised. Things had changed since he was last here. The guards were an added feature.

Haute approached, nodding a greeting to the guards and spoke into an identification panel. "Leon Minden Haute ... Commander ... clearance 0-4-1-2-0-3."

The computer processed the input, eventually answering. "IDENTIFICATION RECEIVED. VOICE COMMAND RECEIVED."

One of the guards extracted a blue key card and placed it against a screen. The door slid aside to reveal a cubicle, slightly smaller than a normal elevator. Haute stepped in, the door closing behind him. The right hand wall held another computer panel. This was the final fail-safe measure. He followed the screen instructions, though still familiar from past visits; right eye open against the provided lens ... right palm on the lower panel. This provided the system with a total of three separate checks, voice, retinal and handprint. If all were correct ... fine. If not, the subject would be trapped within the cubicle, awaiting release or arrest, whatever the case may be.

Haute let the computer scan. He felt a slight twinge of apprehension, waiting for the one time when the machine would malfunction or misread. Once again, he was unjustly worried. "IDENTIFICATION ACCEPTED," the machine stated.

The cubicle turned, rotating one hundred eighty degrees to reveal another door that opened at once. Exiting into a cross corridor, he turned left and finally reached his destination.

He stood on an upper level balcony of a round hangar bay. It was immediately obvious that dramatic changes had taken place in the past two years. Overwhelming the center of the bay, where before there had been nothing, was a ship.

He gazed silently at it. The blueprints he'd seen almost five years ago didn't touch the enormity of what he saw now. He could still remember when it was just an idea jotted down on a piece of scrap paper. Now, it was real, as real as the metal railing he gripped in front of him. He stood nearest the rear port side. As he circled the railing, he approached the bow, noticing gold letters emblazoned upon it. They read, "Explorer Two." For a time, he'd kept up with reports on the progress of the project, but he couldn't remember having seen one for several months. He regretted being less than truthful with Kahn and Gary concerning the mission, but he'd never dreamed that construction had come this far. From his current vantage point, he couldn't be sure about the interior of the vessel, but the outside looked nearly finished.

Workers milled around the room, making their way through a maze of machinery, parts and equipment. There had never been a deadline for completion. The mission was far too important to force hasty mistakes.

If one word had to be used to describe the ship, it would be streamlined. A deep blue mirrored finish sent reflections across the room. Her new design perhaps marked a new era in shipbuilding. The master of operations had chosen from numerous scale models, put together by the most brilliant builders in the business. He based his decision on the vessel that could potentially fulfill all that the mission required, most importantly, to safely sustain the crew for the duration.

Haute remembered how the creator had described her years ago. The ship would have a triple hull, made of the strongest material known. The metal would be ultra expensive, costing nearly half the provided budget. New expulsion shields would be used on the mission. At full strength, they would deflect even large asteroids weighing tens of tons. Anything of that size however, would be detected long before the shields would be required. The crew should be well protected from any intrusion, hostile or accidental, but who could possibly imagine what waited where the vessel may be going.

Haute had listened and tried to envision what now lay before him, but he knew now how short he had fallen. The ship was unique in every way, from its outer skin, to its living heart, the crew, which perhaps would be the most distinctive part of all.

Haute's thoughts were interrupted by someone's approaching footsteps. Turning, he recognized the master builder himself. The man was Richard Happine, a retired pilot and an old and trusted friend. Broad smiles lit the faces of both men as they shook hands.

"Leon Haute, how the hell are you?" The voice was deeper than the man's soft features.

"Fine, Rick. How about you?"

"Oh, I'm still here, I guess." He sighed and laid both hands on the railing. "It's hard to believe, isn't it?"

Haute stood admiringly beside him. "Yeah, I have to admit, I was a little surprised when I came in."

"I was beginning to think you weren't coming back. What's it been, a year?"

"It's been two since I've been down here. I saw you at that banquet, about a year ago, I think." Haute recalled.

Happine nodded. "Yes, the sportsman's banquet. I remember. I won that spotting scope, which is still in the case, I hate to say."

"I've been pretty busy too, but that's no excuse. I should have come down before now."

"Oh, it's alright. I'm kinda glad you were busy. Your trip to Earth gave us a breath of fresh air. Those chambers will change the entire project. It's a major change, but definitely one we can live with."

"How long are we looking at?" Haute asked.

"Until the test flight?" The master builder pursed his lips as he figured. "Uh … we're way ahead of schedule. Maybe only a few months."

Haute was floored. "My God!"

"Yeah, we would have been done sooner, but we had to do a lot of rework on the interior. Some minor structural changes have to be finished, but it's going good. It was tough, changing everything."

Haute felt excited as he thought again of how much the sleep chambers would revolutionize the mission. They gave it a much higher chance of succeeding. "This one's gonna come back, isn't it?" he said with pride.

Happine nodded with the same enthusiasm. "It should … unless we've screwed up somewhere along the line."

"Bite your tongue," Haute said. "Is that possible?"

"I can't see it, but we don't know what's out there, do we?" Happine reasoned.

"No, but that's why we're going."

Happine smiled. "She'll come back. I wouldn't send her if I didn't believe it." He could see Haute's eyes wandering over the blue ship before them. "Well, you want to go in?"

"I thought you'd never ask."

Happine led the way to the main floor. He started the tour by taking him completely around and under the vessel, dodging equipment, talking as they went. "When do you plan on recruiting the crew?" asked Happine.

"I've started talking to a few, but I didn't plan on releasing any of this to the public for quite a while."

"Well, you might as well get the ball rolling."

Haute sighed. "Yeah ... no time like the present. I can't wait to start arguing with the protesters."

Happine laughed. "I know ... I know, but they've had us by the balls long enough. It's time to get on with it. You're pretty popular right now. A lot of neutral people will get behind you on this."

"I hope so. I just hope I'm up to it." Haute reached up and touched the ships belly.

"You're tough enough old man," laughed his friend. "... but time's a growin short. It's gonna take a while to screen all the applicants"

"You think there will be that many?" Haute frowned.

"You'll be surprised. You still have the specifications we agreed on?"

"Yes I do," Haute answered. They approached another stairwell, this one leading up into the ship itself.

"Good. We have to stick to it. It'll make or break this trip. The ship is pretty well predictable. It can be controlled. The crew is the wild card, the one part we can't be sure of."

Haute nodded, understanding what his friend meant. The human factor was the possible flaw in every mission, the uncontrollable free will to make the wrong decision.

Happine continued as they entered through the lower hull near the bow. "There's no doubt in my mind that these past trips failed due to human instability. Don't get me wrong. It wasn't their fault," he hurriedly added.

Only a step behind, Haute now stood inside the ship. "Whose fault was it, then?"

His friend of thirty some years, looked back sadly. "I think it was mine."

Haute frowned in confusion and disagreement. "I think you've been sympathizing with your protesters too long. How is it your fault?"

"I knew all the risks before I sent them out, Leon," he answered. "Hell, I knew they would probably fail."

"I don't believe that. I thought about going on one of them. I looked over the material. They all knew what they were getting into before they signed on, just like I did. There was an equally good chance they'd succeed."

Happine shook his head. "With the equipment they had, the limitations ..."

"Hey, it was the best we had," Haute argued.

Happine thought for a moment. "Then why didn't you go?"

Haute shrugged. It had been a long time ago, but he could remember well. "I don't know. I guess I was already afraid of what we knew was out there, much less what we didn't know about." He looked at the virgin vessel around him. "I wouldn't pass up the chance again, I'll tell you that."

"I guess you're not afraid anymore?" Happine asked.

"I guess not," Haute admitted.

Happine sighed, shaking his head. "I'm just so excited, not for me, but for the end result. By God … I'd like to see it!" he exclaimed.

"Good or bad?" Haute smiled.

"It won't be bad. Not this time." Happine said seriously.

Haute was relieved to see his friend's old confidence. "Well, like I said, I've contacted a few individuals. I can't guarantee they'll make the grade, but I think I'm a pretty good judge of character. They're good kids … young … adventurous. You wouldn't believe what they've been through."

"I take it they're members of your crew?" assumed Happine.

Haute thought about the question before answering. "They're more than that. Two of them are gold pilots. I'm gonna hate like hell to lose them if they decide to go." He looked at his friend, knowing he would appreciate his next words. "They saved my ass back on Earth, Rick. I'd put my life in their hands tomorrow if it came down to it."

"They sound like what we need." Happine suggested.

"Yeah … it's just too damn bad there aren't enough of them to go around."

Happine nodded his agreement and gestured toward another door leading into the main deck area. The tour began.

The ship was large. It was two hundred seventy-five feet long and narrowed to less than seventy feet wide to cut what resistance it might experience. Its design would meet a multitude of specifications including speed, maneuverability, and durability. Crew space had to be limited, taking only one third of the interior. The two thirds remaining consisted of engines, storage, and fuel, the latter of which required nearly twenty five percent of total area.

The passenger compartments consisted of four accessible levels. It was upon the lowest level that they stood now. They passed into a large area that spanned nearly the width of the ship. The room had a large elevator platform allowing access from beneath the ship. It was the main entry for storage supplies to come on board. Hundreds of boxes and containers filled the central area, waiting to be moved into place. On either side of the room were the standard emergency escape pods installed on all sizable vessels. They were equipped to hold five persons each and there were a total of four on each side. Hopefully, they would never be needed. The room also contained two airlocks, one on each side.

They walked aft ward, passing through a short corridor. Happine stopped and explained that particular section. "On both sides, here and in the bow section are the main sensor housings. They can be entered from this deck only." He led further to the rear. Directly in front of them was one of two elevators on the ship, each providing access to the levels above them. Numerous hatches and ladder ways also connected each level in case of lift failure. The builder did not lead him any further rearward on the lower level, describing only fuel cells and bulk storage areas.

They entered the elevator and moved upwards. Level three was completely bypassed. It held additional fuel cells, storage areas, and the main weapons compartment at the bow. They stopped on deck two and stepped into a corridor that led to both sides and forward. Happine spoke. "This forward section is the medical unit including surgery, x-ray and laboratory departments. It also has a research hub covering more scientific fields than I can think of."

Happine turned right off the elevator and passed through a thick pressure door, which stood open at the time. Haute noted that the room they entered appeared to be medical in nature. The tour guide bypassed a description and then entered the most central section of the ship. For the first time, Haute saw what he had described to Gary and Kahn only weeks before. He stood, trying to envision the finished product.

His friend interrupted. "This is the heart of the ship, Leon. This is where we had to change all the structural components." He pointed to the middle of the emptiness. "The chambers will be here, thirty of them. This entire section is self contained, separate from the rest of the ship. Over here are the secondary control spaces." He pointed to various places in the room. "Two other airlocks will lead outside and into the main spaces. The whole ship can be run from here if necessary." His voice held pride. "We designed her well, Commander."

"I'm impressed ... believe me, Rick."

"Once we get the chambers in, we're going to test the alarm systems, the wake up phases, let the computers run a series of mock disasters, that sort of thing."

"Well take your time. I'd rather run behind schedule, than have this mission flop before it starts."

"You know me; I'm not the hurrying kind." He paused as some technicians walked through. "I need this job as long as I can get it."

Haute laughed, "You and me both."

Happine chuckled, "Come on, let me show you the rest." He led out the aft pressure door into another corridor and entered the other elevator. Within a moment, they stood on the upper deck. Upon exiting, they turned forward and entered another large room. Unlike the rest of the crew spaces, the compartment looked nearly finished. It was an elaborate lounge, kitchen and dining area in one. It was truly extraordinary, measuring at least sixty feet in length and forty wide. Corridors exited the room, leading to the crew's private quarters. Upon investigation, Haute found them to resemble those on the Aquillon, although smaller. The accommodations catered to two persons each.

A short walk took them straight to the main control room. The room was filled with stations unlike any Haute had ever seen. There was no central command chair. The pilot and copilots seats faced the view screen before them, with four separate stations behind. Happine hit a switch and the large rectangular screen retracted to allow direct viewing through the forward windows.

Haute sighed and sat in the copilot's chair. He wanted to speak, but was too overwhelmed with the entire experience.

Happine placed a hand on his shoulder. "I know ... but we need you here."

Haute nodded with actual sadness. It was truly going to be the adventure of a lifetime ... and he would miss it.

A week passed, one which the Commander spent most of with the master builder. They went over details down to the slightest item, until Haute knew the ship nearly as well as his friend. He also grew to share the same enthusiasm as to its ability to accomplish what it was designed for.

On this particular morning, he had returned to the Aquillon, where regular duties awaited. One of those duties he did not look forward to. The meeting had been set with the higher-level associates of the SPEX Corporation. After that, the joint mission would be announced to the public. Protests, bad press, and even legitimate threats were predicted and prepared for. Hopefully, with the new mission specifications included in the release, support would grow rapidly. One aspect that could help credibility with some of the more adamant individuals against SPEX would be the announcement that the Explorer Two would also be equipped as a rescue vessel. The projected route for the new mission would be through the same territory the last SPEX crew had explored. There was a good chance that the new scanners might bring some closure to the questions in the minds and hearts of that crew's families.

After the news release, the recruitment and tedious selection of the new crewmembers would begin. Haute could actually look forward to that at least. He was only one voice in the selection process, but it was the only hand he would play in this saga, and he would do his best.

He figured it was a waste of time, but he wished to touch base with two individuals before the announcement. Maybe the number needed for the Explorer Two crew could be reduced to eighteen.

In seconds, an el-car took him from the hangar deck to the control level. A stack of routine reports was introduced to him upon arrival in the main control room. He had not been there for five weeks. After hurriedly looking over the papers, the subjects of which repeated over and over, he came to an assumption. No news was good news.

He looked at his watch as he spoke to the communications officer on duty. "Ships message, Lieutenant." The man grabbed a pen. "Find Kahn Bengal and Gary Kusan and have them report to my quarters at 1000 hours. I need a code twenty five on that also." He turned and left. Before he could make it to his cabin, a voice came over the air answering his request. "CODE TWENTY-FIVE COMPLETED." The men had been located and the request acknowledged. The Commander entered his quarters to wait.

The meetings main topic was delayed for several moments after the two young pilots arrived. It became a tale telling session on Haute's part, based on his recent adventure on Earth. He enjoyed revealing some of the secrets uncovered on the long lost planet, but finally he came to the purpose of the reunion. It was time to begin the process of uncovering secrets held elsewhere.

"I won't beat around the bush with you guys. I really don't have the time. In a few days the Explorer Two mission goes public. I asked you about it before, if you remember?" He paused, seeing surprised expressions from both.

Gary interrupted. "Excuse me sir, but why so soon?"

"It's not that soon Gary. I have to apologize to both of you for something. I spoke to you earlier about a ship that SPEX might build. That wasn't the whole truth."

Kahn knew where Haute was heading. "They've already started?"

Haute nodded, "Five years ago."

Gary was somewhat dismayed. "How long before it's finished?"

"Maybe a few months." Haute answered. In his defense, he added. "I had no idea they were as far as they were. I thought they were still a couple of years away from completion."

Neither man spoke.

"Regardless, we're going to start the weeding out process to find the right crew. I would like preliminary numbers before I start. To put it bluntly, I need your answers pretty soon." The blank looks on their faces told him that he was wasting his breath. "I want you both to know, I didn't ask you this just for the hell of it. By no means do I want to get rid of either one of you. You are two of the best men I've ever commanded. We've been through more in the last few months than most see in twenty years of service. I would gladly put my life on the line with either of you. I don't want to let you go, but this trip … the possibilities are incredible. What you discover may affect the future of everything we know. That's a little more important than my personal feelings, I'll tell you." He sighed. "You know the benefits, and you know the risk involved, so I need an answer from you, at least in the next couple of days." He frowned, wishing he didn't have to push, but he knew they had already thought about it. "If I had more time, I'd give it to you, but I don't. That's all I've got gentlemen. You know how to reach me." Both men rose together. It seemed to Haute that the younger of the two wanted to speak, but for some reason, didn't.

Kahn spoke for himself and his friend. "Thank you, sir. What you said means a lot to us. We'll give you our decision as soon as possible."

Haute nodded. "I appreciate it. I know this decision involves more than just you two, so make sure it's the right one." They exited, the door sliding shut, leaving perfect silence in the room.

Haute shook his head. He knew what they had to be thinking. He envied them for having the opportunity, but didn't envy what it could cost them. A decision for him would be easier. He had a family as well to leave behind, the Republic, but that family would surely still be here if he returned. Their families might not. A decision to go would be heart wrenching, but those are the kind of individuals needed for a mission such as this, men and women who could make those kinds of choices and follow through. He dismissed the thoughts. He had too much to do.

Only a minute after the departure of his visitors, the door buzzer rang, startling him. He walked to the door and opened it. To his astonishment, the two men who had just left stood before him. The obvious was voiced. "What the hell are you doing?" he asked.

Kahn had a solemn face. "Well, we don't think it's fair that we keep you waiting for a decision we've already made."

In Haute's eyes, Kahn's demeanor said it all. "Well, I'm truly sorry to hear that. I hate for both of you to miss it." He dropped his gaze to the floor.

Gary spoke up, equally as forlorn as his friend. "Yes sir, we hated it too, but that's one of the reasons we've decided to go."

Haute was already nodding his understanding of their decline when he caught the unexpected statement. He looked at them again and found them smiling. "You sorry son's a bitches." He stood aside and ordered them back into his cabin.

The next few moments were spent in a whole new light. Haute talked end-lessly, describing the ship and what to expect in the upcoming months. "You realize, you still have to pass the requirements. You can't just raise your hands and get to go."

Gary shrugged. "I've never failed a test in my life, Commander." He turned to Kahn. "Have you?"

Kahn was caught slightly at a disadvantage. "Well ... I wouldn't go that far."

The Commander chuckled, so overjoyed that he could barely contain it. "I have no doubts about either of you. So the girls have consented to go?"

"Ninety-nine percent," Kahn said.

"Great," Haute said. "You know how they change their minds though."

"Hey, they know who the bosses are," quipped Kahn.

Haute rolled his eyes. "Yeah, too bad it's not you two."

Kahn, feeling confident, had a question that had been waiting for five long weeks. "Commander, what exactly is going to be required of us, I mean, since we've officially volunteered?"

Haute narrowed his eyes, unsure of what was being asked.

"What he's asking is if we still have to go to work until we start testing?" Gary added.

Kahn laughed in an effort to disguise how bluntly the translation had come across. "Well, I didn't mean that exactly ..."

The Commander thought for a moment. The ship was still several weeks away from finishing, and he knew that there would be months of additional technical training before departure, all entirely dependant upon their being chosen in the first place. The question was actually legitimate. "I'll tell you what. I'll put you on temporary leave for a couple of days to talk to the girls. Take them somewhere and tell them where we're at." He couldn't help noticing that the two men resem-bled children that had just gotten out of school for the summer. "I trust you'll notify Miss Sluder and Miss Wilkens?"

"Uh ... no, actually, we weren't going to say anything to them," answered Kahn.

"Not for a couple of days or so anyway," added Gary.

"You really don't want to live long enough to go on this trip, do you?" Haute joked. He turned to a console and dialed up the duty masters office. "This is Commander Haute, confirmation number, 2-2-3-2, requesting temporary leave orders for four individuals."

The voice on the other end acknowledged the request. "All right, sir ... sub-jects names, please?"

Haute relayed the names and waited for the return confirmation codes, which he jotted down and handed to them. "You're official. Don't get in trouble. Let the recall office know how to find you."

Kahn nodded. "Thank you, sir."

"This is highly irregular. I can't guarantee I won't be calling you back."

Both nodded their understanding, repeated their thanks and said their good-byes.

The two men hurriedly put their workstations in order and made their way to the hangar deck to travel to Touchen. They looked forward to breaking the news to the ladies, who were somewhere below the planet surface. They saw a lone figure manning the departure station as they approached.

The officer on duty seemed less than thrilled to be there and was even less so when she found out that she had to do something. She swung her legs off the desktop and sauntered up to the counter, mumbling something beneath her breath. Finally, she spoke aloud. "What do you need?" Her tone was less than cordial. Her nametag read "Captain Tierra Pinnick."

Kahn almost spoke his mind, but knew full well that it could land him in the brig if he did. For a moment, he recalled an episode concerning the vice president of a Shannation bank. Keeping that in mind, he responded in a jovial tone. "Yes ma'am. We need a transport back to Touchen."

The woman shook her head and threw a logbook on the counter. "You know the drill. I need your work release and confirmation code," she remarked sarcastically.

Kahn clamped his jaw tightly, and held his tongue, contemplating. One more word and he was going to report her to the Commander himself, higher rank or not, but then again, maybe she was just having a bad day. "Confirmation code, 9-0-7-1." He waited in anticipation as she wrote in the book, and then added. She would really love this. "And we don't have a work release." He could barely repress the urge to smile as he glanced at Gary, who watched in silence.

She had moved to a computer terminal as he said it, punching in the four numerals, only then realizing exactly what she had heard. Immediately, she hit the cancel button. For the first time, the men saw what could have been construed as a smile. "If you two think you're leaving this ship without one, think again." She turned her back and returned to her desk. "I'll see you at quitting time."

Kahn continued to smile, but Gary did not. He had never run into this situation before, and had no idea what they were going to do.

Kahn waited until the woman was comfortably seated with her feet once again on the desktop. He even waited for one last remark.

She looked up after a moment. "You're still here?"

"You just erased Fleet Commander Leon Haute's confirmation code. You'll have to call him to get it back since I don't remember what it was. We have his personal permission for the transport. The work release waiver was on the screen."

It was almost comical to watch the Captain's smirk change to a look of horror. Within ten minutes, a mini-transport was on the way to the planet's icy surface, with two amused passengers aboard.

They searched for the girls in the plant solarium where they were supposed to be studying new species of plant life brought back from Earth. They were instead, directed to the other end of the complex, where they found them teaching a new class. Knowing that the men's interruption was far from normal, the girls dismissed the class to an early lunch, and they found a place to talk. An emotional hour later, the lunch and the talk were over. The decisions were made.

Soon after, on the trip to Belaquin, Gary closed his eyes and lost himself in a multitude of fleeting images. He was not tired, but he had seen ships like this one too many times. It was time for a change. They had tried to coax the girls to leave Touchen with them, but leaving the class half finished would not be prudent or fair to their students. They promised to meet with them that evening.

He thought of the talk they had just finished. Colleen and De had been surprised and somewhat disappointed. They'd thought there was more time as well. It was hard, but they didn't falter in their decisions. Hopefully, at least four positions could be considered filled aboard the new SPEX vessel.

It had been difficult. The girls finally admitted to themselves that it was real. It was no longer just a topic to be discussed sometime in the future. The future had suddenly and unexpectedly arrived.

Deanna had already mentioned the voyage to her family weeks earlier, sugar-coating it with the joyous news of her engagement to Kahn. Colleen had also talked of it on her last trip home, but had not gone in depth with its details. It was something she had needed a little more preparation for. She wasn't sure exactly how, and wouldn't know until she did it.

Gary shook his head, thankful that his dilemma was already over. The departure date was still far away. It left plenty of time. It was unknown when they would be recalled to begin the selection process, but he had already promised himself that afterward he would be going back to his parent's mountain. Maybe he and his Dad could do some exploring. Who knows what they might find?

It was a full three days before the Republic contacted the foursome. They were to return to the Aquillon and resume their duties. Commander Haute contacted Kahn several days later. The mission had been released to the media and the volunteer list grew immediately and considerably. He assured Kahn that the chances of he and the others making the final cut were good, but the selection was to take much longer than anticipated. They were to continue working until contacted again.

The SPEX mission made headlines throughout the system and filled hundreds of hours of airtime on the news networks and talk shows. Seven long weeks passed before the call finally came. Kahn received notification while at Deanna's parent's home while on weekend liberty. With the notice, came special delivery packages for him and Deanna. They contained official congratulatory letters from the Republic and SPEX, notifying them of their appointment to their individual positions. Also included, were their schedules for the next several months. The packets contained no information concerning any other crewmembers.

An accompanying order directly from the commander instructed Kahn to return to Touchen within forty-eight hours. On the next day, after a four-hour wait, Kahn and Deanna flew out of the tiny airport near Deanna's hometown of New Harmony. The wait was twice the actual flight time to Bentar, where the next morning, they would catch a final transport to Touchen. They still had eleven hours left of the forty-eight when they finally landed in Bentar. Some of it would need to be devoted to sleep. It was close to midnight when Kahn checked his home messages. The first was from Gary, saying that he and Colleen had been contacted as well. The second was from the commander. It said, "Kahn, I called you back for the Explorer test flight scheduled for noon Monday. Meet me at 0800 for your security clearance. Don't be late. I'll see you in the a.m."

The aforementioned a.m. arrived much …

"Too early," was Gary's answer to Colleen's question of the time. "It's five-twenty," he grumbled sleepily. He had showered late the night before so he could sleep later. He felt as if it hadn't made any difference. Exiting the bathroom, he pulled on his uniform pants and sat down on the bed.

Colleen groaned and turned toward him, rubbing her eyes. The blanket fell away, leaving her breasts uncovered. "Why are they starting so early?" she asked sleepily.

"I don't know. He must have a good reason." Gary sighed, admiring the view. He shook his head, knowing that seeing her like that could cause problems.

Colleen saw him staring and made no effort to cover herself.

Gary glanced at the clock and decided that he had a couple of minutes. He moved up on the bed beside her and draped his arm around her waist. His head rested on her warm chest. "I guess he wants to show us the ship first," he said "Which is probably a good idea."

"Wouldn't you rather stay here?" she suggested in a teasing tone. She had nothing to lose. Her tour would not be for some time yet.

He softly pinched one of her nipples and thought seriously about the invitation, but only for a second. "Oh God ... I can't." He moaned, rolling off of her, searching the bed for his socks. He looked at the clock again, desperately trying to refigure his schedule to come up with a few free moments, but there were none to be had. If he'd known, he may have set the alarm for earlier, but she wasn't normally a morning person. That, as opposed to a shower, would have been worth getting up for. Again he wondered if he had the time.

No, he admitted decisively, now's not the time to start bad habits, one of them so perfectly called a quickie. He found his socks. "Believe me, babe," he groaned, "There's nothing I'd rather do, but I cannot be late for this."

She got up and moved to him on her hands and knees, giving him a slow, deep kiss after closing the gap. "How long is this gonna take?"

Gary sighed deeply, fighting his urges. "I don't know. They're starting so early ... maybe all day."

Colleen kissed him playfully. "Well let's hope not."

He stood, putting space between them. Just the sight of her on the bed made him crazy.

She sat back, thankfully covering up. "I'll keep my motor running."

Gary chuckled, shaking his head. "Just don't run out of gas." He put on his shirt and hat. Walking to the door, he turned, winked and left.

Minutes later, he pulled up in Kahn's driveway. Kahn exited the front door immediately. He had actually been up and waiting. Gary called out his open window. "You ready?"

"I'm ready for this ..." Kahn answered eagerly.

Gary nodded. He knew his friend looked forward to this day more than any other. He had to admit, he felt the same.

In less than two hours, they walked the bustling corridors of Touchen control. The Commander was found and the three men took time for breakfast, something that two of the three very seldom experienced. Kahn remarked that on any given morning, the urge to sleep overpowered the urge to eat. Twenty-five minutes after eight, they finished and proceeded to the security center where clearance passes and identification readings were recorded. By nine, they entered a corridor that Kahn and Gary had never seen before. Two security guards waited at its end.

As Gary walked, he noticed his palms were cold and clammy. His underarms were uncharacteristically wet as well.

The security team was friendlier than the one Haute was used to. They were quite talkative as they went through the routine. With the first check finished, they entered the cubicle and proceeded with the secondary security measures. The door slid aside after its rotation was completed. A moment later, they stood against the railing.

The room was filled with a hundred people clearing away equipment, disconnecting ductwork and wiring, and cleaning up. One man actually hung below a platform positioned over the bow, wiping off the glass view port.

Haute remained back a little, and let the two men look on in admiration. "This, gentlemen, is your ship, the Explorer Two," he said proudly.

Kahn was speechless. He'd never seen anything like it. "Fantastic," he finally muttered under his breath.

Gary said nothing, letting his gaze wander over the glistening blue hull.

Enthralled, they looked on for several minutes. Finally, Kahn began the long walk around the ship, via the catwalk they stood upon. They made nearly the complete circle without a word being uttered.

Haute spoke as they neared a stairwell. "You guys about ready to go down there?" Both men answered with surprised looks. "I know ... dumb question," he added.

As they descended and drew close to the hull, Gary let his hand slide against the cold metal. It felt truly strange. "What the hell is this made of, Commander?"

"A new titanium alloy. This is the first ship ever made with it. It's been hematized, or something like that, supposedly decreases resistance. Nothing sticks to it, not even water. It's like a permanent super wax job."

"Feels weird," said Kahn, running his hand across the smoothness.

"Who gets to fly her this morning?" Gary asked.

"The master builder, Richard Happine, and another guy I've never met. I don't even know his name. They've been in the simulator for weeks."

Kahn shook his head in disbelief. "This is too much. I've been waiting all this time and now ..."

Haute could relate. "She's special ... no doubt about it. Do you understand the notoriety of her name?" He gestured to the letters on the bow.

"Two hundred years ago, the first ship to land on Belaquin was the Explorer One." Gary answered.

Kahn, of course, had known the answer as well. The Explorer One was as well known to the people of today, as the Pilgrim's Mayflower had been known to school children of yesterday. "I wonder if this ship will be as famous?" he asked.

"I don't know. I hope I'm still around to find out," Haute answered seriously.

His words made Kahn think of something for the first time. When the day to leave finally came, he might say goodbye to this man for the last time. He had thought him more as a mentor, never as a replacement for his father. He still remembered vague images from his childhood. Some became vivid in his dreams. At times, he wasn't sure what was real and what wasn't. He remembered one thing very well. He had loved his father and mother.

He could not deny the respect he had for Leon Haute. The man had been there for him countless times. Sometimes it had been hard to separate personal and professional feelings. To leave him, would by far, be the most difficult part he would deal with on this venture.

He was suddenly brought back to the present by the Commander's voice. "Let's go up. We've got some time before they're ready."

Haute, upon entering the ship, was shocked by the changes that had occurred just in the last two days. Everything appeared to be in place. The miles of electrical cords, the ventilation tubing, tools, and containers of material waste was gone, leaving the decks clean. He was thoroughly impressed.

The two men who followed him were intrigued by every wonder shown them. The tour was brief, but thorough, ending in the main control room.

Two men were already seated within, one old and one young, both facing a complex display of screens and controls. The older man noticed the three visitors entering the compartment and turned to greet them.

The Commander introduced the two raider pilots to the master builder, and in turn, was introduced to the remaining man.

His name was Eric Danielson, perhaps thirty years old, a civilian pilot for the last ten. It was clear from the start that he, Kahn, and Gary would get along.

"Gold Raider pilots!" Danielson exclaimed, extending his hand. "God, I envy you. I tried to be one, passed all the entry exams."

Gary took the offered hand. "So what happened?"

"They said I was color blind," he explained. "You believe that shit? I didn't even know it."

"I didn't know that made any difference," confessed Kahn.

"Yeah, neither did I. I guess I can't see certain shades ... red ... green ... purple."

Gary frowned, trying to imagine.

"It's messed up," Eric shrugged. "They won't let me fly a raider, but they'll let me fly this. Makes you wonder, doesn't it?"

Kahn concurred, "No shit."

Happine sat down where he had been a moment before. "Eric and I have been living in the simulator for the past two weeks. We've gotten pretty good at all this."

Gary shook his head at the endless array of buttons and switches. It was a far cry from a raider. "Sounds like fun," he remarked with a hint of sarcasm.

"You'll be having some of that fun here pretty soon," said Haute.

"He's right." Happine gestured towards the control panel. "Each member of this crew will know the basics of manual as well as auto flight procedures for this ship. You two, of course, will go far more in depth. Bottom line, you're both going back to school. There are certain fields that everyone will be trained in ... navigation, chamber operation, some medical, ship computer basics, etc."

Haute was amused at the men's reactions with the mention of schooling. "It's not going to be a picnic by any means."

Over the next hour, the two "veteran" Explorer pilots explained on a limited scale, the operation of the vessel, but all in the room knew that only practice made perfect.

Gary, forever inquisitive, voiced a question to the master builder. "Mr. Happine, I read the acceptance packets, but I need to know something ... at least your opinion on it." He felt that if he could place stock in anyone's opinion, it would be this mans. Happine had envisioned the mission and brought it from dream to reality. He, no doubt, knew the answers. "How long will we be out there?"

Happine thought for a moment before answering. "Well, our experts indicate ...!"

Gary interrupted. "No ... not the experts. I know what they say. I want to know what you say ... just you." The other three men waited also.

"My personal opinion?" Happine asked.

"Or your best guess."

"To tell you the truth, Gary, I'm afraid to make a guess. I've been wrong before."

Haute remembered. "On the first mission," he related.

Happine nodded. The expression on his face held disappointment and regret.

"What about the last one?" asked Danielson.

"I'm not wrong on that one, not yet. It hasn't been ten years."

Gary felt disappointment as well, but tried not to show it. He had hoped to hear something feasible from him, something he could draw some estimate from. Inside, he realized the futility of a guess. The unknown is truly unknown. That was a simple fact. The theory, or guess he sought, would have to be based on situations in a controlled environment. The environment where they were headed was far from controlled.

Happine sensed the discouragement in the young man. "There are too many factors involved son, especially with this new ship." He paused, contemplating. "I'll give you an example of some of the things we've had to think about. Try to imagine. Say we send you guys out. You are traveling at light speed ... okay? You travel at that same speed for forty-nine years, still sleeping."

"Back here, technology has advanced so much that now we are capable of speeds fifty times the speed of light. We launch another ship in the same direction you went. In only one year, it catches up to you. You are awakened, contacted by a ship and crew that didn't even exist when you left. The question has been brought up. If we think you're going to be gone that long without finding anything ... why even send you? Why not wait fifty years until technology catches up, and send one out then? You see? There are too many unknowns. Until we figure them out ... we can't know."

Gary nodded with understanding. The man had given him a complicated, but fascinating answer.

"Hell, we don't even know how fast she'll go yet," added Haute.

"That's gonna change real soon," stated Danielson. "We've got a green light."

Happine was visibly surprised. "Already?"

Danielson punched an order into the terminal before him. "These guys are ready for us to get outta here." He smiled. "Checklist on line."

Happine motioned for the three visitors to have a seat, and began checking his own screens. "This takes about five minutes ..." He turned and gave them a quick look. "Then we fire'em up."

The two men went over the list, flipping switches and turning dials, one of which dimmed the control room's interior lights. The only illumination came from the glowing display of controls. For a moment, it was like they were already in space. Happine's hand moved over the panel. The darkness gave way to blinding light the view port's black tint faded away.

A low hum, barely audible to the passengers, signaled the engines beginning their warm up. To the technicians outside the vessel in the hanger bay, it was drastically different. The bay was filled with a high-pitched whine, the decibel level actually high enough to cause injury to anyone unprotected.

Happine constantly checked the panel, finding readouts within normal range. He had a strong feeling of apprehension. He knew that his co-pilot must have been feeling the same. It was brought by the fact that they were no longer in the simulator. The pre-flight check and warm up were the same. The apprehension was from what was to come.

The simulator had assisted in the learning of procedure to familiarize the individual with controls. The ship should perform nearly as it did in the simulations, but in the pilot's minds, the unmistakable difference was clear. Their feelings were fully warranted. Their bodies knew what was real and what was not. The simple mistakes made before today had no consequences. Any made now ...

Methodically, they continued until the check off list was complete.

Happine glanced at Danielson's board, stating. "All grids are nominal. Computer control confirms."

Danielson nodded. "I agree."

In bay control, a hundred technicians monitored the ship, checking their own lists. The whine from the ship vibrated the thick glass that separated them.

Happine could see the men across the way as they gave the thumbs up. He called them over the air. "Control, how do you read?" he asked.

"Loud and clear, your warm up looks good."

Happine agreed. "Everything reads great on our end."

"Are you ready for elevation?"

He took a deep breath. This was it. "Affirmative control, commence elevation."

Kahn watched it all, his heart racing. Was he having second thoughts? These guys had never flown this ship. In fact, no one had ever flown this ship. Decidedly, it was too late to bail out now. The mission's risks had begun.

Loud hissing came from somewhere within the ship. Happine recognized the sound as various outer doors pressurizing and sealing shut.

"All hatches sealed," confirmed Danielson.

The five men in the cockpit couldn't see it, but above them, the bay ceiling was retracting, revealing a vertical shaft leading upward, five hundred feet to the surface.

In the Explorer, a slight jerk was felt, signaling upward movement. The catwalk surrounding the blue vessel sank below the men's line of sight. Two minutes into the escalation, Danielson increased engine output, as he had done fifty times in the simulator. The hum grew louder until readings reached the appropriate level.

Happine started the external heaters positioned around certain moving parts. Most of the ships exterior coating was moisture resistant, but on this particular morning, according to the reports, surface weather was unusually savage. It would provide the first harsh conditions to test that degree of durability. The heaters were probably not needed, but he was taking nothing for granted. Another moment passed and the lift stopped. Immediately, a bell alarm began sounding.

Happine glanced rearward, explaining the unsettling noise. "It's just the surface platform opening up." The alarm stopped.

Even as he said it, clouds of snow began blowing by the view port, swirling within the shaft. None came to rest on the glass. Again, the jerk was felt as the ship rose. When they stopped again, there was no mistaking where they were. They had risen into the middle of an ice storm. Visibility had become nil.

"Another beautiful day on Touchen," Kahn smirked.

Happine glanced at the outside readings. "Yeah, we've got a mild fifty-seven degrees below zero, with a sixty mile an hour breeze."

Control had rotated the lift off platform to face the vessel into the gusting storm. An experienced pilot in his own ship, or a seasoned Touchen merchant could lift off in any direction, but the pilots in the Explorer Two were neither.

Happine checked the readouts for the tenth time. One was an enhanced landscape imager, allowing the viewer to see a three dimensional picture of the surface terrain around the ship. On all sides were the smooth lines of featureless snow covered hills. The merchant town was somewhere behind them, hidden by the storm.

Happine donned a voice-operated headset, leaving his hands free. He wiped them on his pants before taking hold of the control stick. He knew this was the hard part. A ship this size, in this storm, would be a challenge for any pilot. Switching off the headset for a second, he glanced at his copilot, wet his dry lips and said. "You sure you don't want to do this?"

Danielson smiled. "The first time? No … you go ahead."

The older man returned a half-hearted smirk. "Control, we are awaiting your clearance." He studied the scanners himself, and saw only a couple of contacts, miles to the south of their position. Their paths would not intersect.

"Clearance given. You are good to go."

The engine whine again grew in intensity, finally reaching a pitch too high to hear. Loose surface ice and snow was melted and blown away as the force from the lower engine ports strained to push the ship upward.

The two pilots glanced back and forth across the panel. Danielson read the gauges. "Thrust is ready."

"Release the mags," ordered Happine. He referred to the docking magnets that still held the ship to the pad.

The magnetism gradually decreased and abruptly, the ship jumped upward and slightly backward. Surprisingly, in the strong gusts bursting through the valley, the ship held fairly steady.

Danielson checked the ships tracking. They were moving steadily upward, now several meters above the pad. "Clear on the three-sixty." Excitement filled his voice.

Happine, the stick vibrating in his hand, was excited as well, but did not let his concentration waver. His eyes were glued to the trim and angle indicators. "Jesus Christ, this would be a hell of a lot easier if I could see something," he said, obviously frustrated. "Retract the gear when we hit two hundred feet. That should help."

Kahn gripped the armrests tightly. He wondered if he'd feel better behind the stick himself, even with no training.

Happine pulled the stick up and pushed slightly forward, watching the altimeter numbers rise. The ship lurched back and forth as the outside wind buffeted it.

His co-pilot watched the level indicators change dramatically, but he didn't need a monitor to tell him that the ship was difficult to keep steady. "Outside gusts over one hundred. Do you want the gyros?"

Happine answered quickly, "Not yet." He pushed the stick further forward, gaining speed rapidly. The rocking decreased considerably.

"That's better," Danielson sighed.

The vessels creator momentarily locked the stick, keeping the ship on a smooth steady rise. He finally exhaled with well-deserved relief. "God, I hate this planet."

The surroundings grew brighter as they climbed, the freezing ice storm gradually giving way to relatively clear sky. The shearing wind died away as well. Minutes later, the sky changed from blue to black. Stars appeared out of nowhere.

The main engines were shut down. The Explorer Two floated freely. Happine gazed in awe at the beauty before them. The inky blackness was riveted with thousands of tiny pinpoints of light. He felt a hand on his shoulder and turned.

"How long has it been, Rick?" Haute asked.

"Too long. I forgot what it looked like from this seat."

"It's the one thing that never changes." He stared out the window in silence for a bit. The beautiful void had countless beginnings and no ends. Time and space were constant companions, neither able to outlast the other. It was intriguing and frightening, but irresistible.

Danielson had seen the view much more recently. "Well boss, this is a really touching reunion, but I've got a hot date tonight, so what's next?"

"You wish, youngster. Does your wife know about it?" Happine received a smile. "All right, plot the initial course we agreed on, and we'll get on with it."

Gary moved closer to the younger pilot, watching him bring up a schematic on the navigation screen. "What have you got planned?"

Happine answered instead. "More than we have time for, actually. We'll get as much done as we can. Firing up the new scanners is probably the most crucial test today, long range as well as short range. We'll make our initial speed tests at the same time."

Danielson added. "We have to check the auto guidance. Any discrepancy would make it a short trip. Once we're put under, it's all we've got. It has to be perfect."

Haute explained further, "The computer should ideally alter course when correction is needed, and then return to the original settings. There's really only one way to test it."

Kahn had a suspicion as to how. The ship would have to head directly towards something and wait for the computer to do its thing. "And if it malfunctions, you mentioned something about a short trip?" he asked.

"We've got back ups, six separate systems. They digest the input. If there's a disagreement between any of them, then the ship is automatically shut down, and brought to a stop. At that point, you guys will be woke up to check it out." Happine stopped talking long enough to reset a selector knob on the communications board. The digital readout changed. He turned and handed the men three cordless headsets. "Put them on, you can listen in."

The Commander was puzzled. "Listen in to what?"

Happine hadn't switched on yet. "We've switched off the mainline Republic transmitter."

"Which puts us where?" Haute asked.

"Another system we need to check. We're set up on a new communications link up. We kept it under wraps so far."

"A new frequency?" Haute continued. He'd evidently missed it on the flight op reports.

"New everything. We're on a private channel exclusive to this ship through a separate transmitter. No one can monitor us. The power of the booster is incredible."

Haute was surprised. He had no problem admitting that he was a selfish person. He didn't necessarily need to know every last detail, as much as he wanted to know. He also realized that this was not solely a military mission, but they did play a major role in it. If this new type booster proved worthy, then the Republic would obviously want a foot in the door.

Kahn was a bit indifferent to the new information as well. "I didn't know this mission was that big a secret anymore. Why the hush on this new frequency?"

"Well, it's not that big a deal. You're right, the mission's not a secret, but this test flight is. Not very many people know we're up here." Happine explained.

Gary quipped in. "But everybody with a scanner can see us."

Happine continued, "Sure they can see us, but they don't know who we are. We're not in any system libraries, and we won't have any communication on the open lines for anyone to listen to."

Haute shook his head. "I still don't understand all the secrecy."

Happine may have been the only man in the room that did know. "We couldn't take any chances. We've received warnings from unknown sources, direct threats on the crew and the ship, sabotage … the usual stuff."

Haute suddenly became extremely interested. "Why haven't I heard about this, Rick?"

"We knew they'd come, but they didn't come until yesterday."

Haute nodded. "Pretty coincidental, don't you think? Threats yesterday … test flight today?"

"Not necessarily. For them to know we're out here, then it has to be someone on the inside." The man defended, "I know my people Leon. These threats are random."

"You admit it's a possibility though?" Haute pressed.

"Yes, I agree, it always has been." Happine reasoned. "I wouldn't risk this ship and crew if I wasn't sure."

Haute nodded, though still upset. "You know I trust you, but I would like to know about any others."

His friend nodded in agreement. "Understood." With the touch of a switch, the new frequency was activated. As expected, a silent band was all that was heard. He turned to the others. "Now we wait."

Below the icy storm, anxious persons in Explorer control watched for any-thing out of the ordinary. The flight path had been preplanned and the lone con-tact on their scanner screen was exactly where it was supposed to be. A lone man at the communications center switched off the open board. Turning the fre-quency to another setting, he depressed the transmitter. "Outpost eleven, this is Touchen flight control, please come in."

There was a slight delay before a voice answered. "This is outpost one-one, go ahead Touchen control." The man sounded indeed puzzled. The person on duty at the remote outposts normally prompted communication, not the other way around. His communications computer scanned all known channels, but he had never heard traffic on the numeric figures before him.

"One-one, who am I speaking to?"

"Lieutenant Atkinson."

"All right, Mr. Atkinson, this is Lieutenant Criss. You'll have a small cruiser coming through your sector in a few minutes. You've probably got it on your scanners right now. This is a vehicle operating under special orders. It is of new configuration and no identification numbers are displayed. You have standing orders to let it pass and re-enter our system. This authorization is order number Tango-Sierra, four two two. Do not attempt to make contact. You may respond only if they contact you first. The order should be coming up on your screen now. Do I need to repeat any part of this transmission?"

"Negative, control. I've got the ship on my grid. Any idea how long they'll be out?"

"Unsure, a few hours, we expect."

"Understood, Touchen control, I'll pass down the orders if necessary." Atkin-son frowned in uncertainty as he killed the transmission. This was very irregular, especially while the entire system was on high alert. It didn't seem right, but everything appeared legitimate. The scanner was on audio alert. It emitted a two-tone beep as an object entered minimal scanner range.

He checked the approach readout once again. Whoever it was, they were right on course to pass through the checkpoint. He looked out, scanning the stars to find the one spark of light that could be the vessel. The outpost stations were all pretty much the same. Each had a domed glass roof, allowing the duty watchman to see in all directions. It was like working in a planetarium, except the starry view was genuine.

Finally, he saw it, one light moving among the others. As the seconds passed, the light grew in size, gaining shape, finally taking on the distinct curves of a craft. The lieutenant squinted. The rays from the distant sun glinted off of the ships blue skin, shining far brighter than any star. The shine was nearly blinding, but the officer's eyes widened nonetheless. The man from Touchen control had not exaggerated. His descriptive term "new configuration" was correct. He'd never seen anything like it. Without prior warning, it would have been construed as alien.

He stared unblinking as the ship passed within a few hundred yards. Reaching down, he triggered the recorders. He wanted the oncoming duty officer to see this. He wondered what this new ship was, who was in her, and where they were going. They were pointed into a rather remote region of space, normally traveled by long-range merchant and unmanned mining carriers. This ship definitely wasn't one of those. He guessed it to be military, although its appearance lacked the ominous look of the warships of today. He shrugged. It could be anything.

He watched as long as he could, until it disappeared again within the stars. With the vessel gone, he felt the returning tedium, dreading it. He played back the tracking tape to check the copy. There was the extraordinary ship again. On the screen, he highlighted a certain section, magnifying and enhancing the same area. This time, he saw the letters on the bow. Enhanced again, they became readable. "I'll be damned," he said aloud. Everything suddenly made sense.

By the time the Explorer Two reached outpost eleven, Touchen was far behind. Once in free space, Happine increased speed to one quarter light-speed.

Danielson checked the basic long-range scanners and announced. "We're totally clear according to the factory installed." He shook his head. "It's like looking through a cheap video-scan." He referred to the hopefully, soon to be outdated sensors.

Happine agreed. If the restructured scanners performed as anticipated, all current long-range systems would be severely outmatched. Today's shakedown cruise would make or break the challenger.

"Go ahead and switch over, Eric. Let's see what we can see," suggested Happine. He was more than anxious to see the fruits of his labor. He had been involved in every aspect of the design of this magnificent structure, including the untested hardware. The scanners were a critical piece of the puzzle, but there were several pieces to the whole, any of which, if missing or flawed in their operation, would spell failure.

Danielson made the change and listened as all hell broke loose within the control room. Scanner alarms went off at once. Loudly and clearly, they marked themselves off the checklist.

Happine's hands hesitated over the control panel, unsure of where to go first. Finally, he managed to turn off most of the unwanted noise. He was noticeably unnerved. "Sorry guys, we didn't really expect that."

"What the hell happened?" asked Kahn.

"Scanner alarms ... they were set on audio instead of visual. They're set for a lot of readings, metalloids, energy, organic, anything it doesn't recognize. The damn things work! When we switched over, they did what they were supposed to."

Gary nodded in understanding. "We're still too close to our own system."

"Exactly," said Happine. He pointed out the scanner readouts. The monitors were filling with seemingly hundreds of separate contacts. "We're too close to everything. Look at this." He said with awe. "The range is incredible. We didn't really know how intricate they were or how far they'd reach. I wouldn't be surprised if your old friend Earth accounts for a lot of these readings."

Haute was astounded at the thought.

Happine continued. "All scanners are basically the same. They tell you what you've got and how far away it is, but the closer you get, the better they read. We've pumped up the power, which increased the range. The older systems couldn't handle the added juice. They got hot. It created interference and gave false readings. We modified the insulation and cooling systems and finally came up with what we've got here. The computers were upgraded as well. They argue over the information and you either get a course adjustment, or you don't. It's complicated, but you'll get a crash course on it in a couple of months." He glanced at the speed indicator. It read one-quarter light speed. "Let's try it." he decided. "Inch it up to L-one. I'm gonna shut down the lateral and rear long-range scanners. We just need to know what's in front of us for now."

"That's what I've been waiting to hear," Danielson sighed. He checked the forward scanners once more and then slowly eased the throttle forward. Reaching the desired position, he locked it. There was no discernable change in the feel of the ship as it accelerated.

Happine held his breath. Would she hold up? Was their design as good as they hoped? So many things had to be more than right, more than the minimum requirements. Stress levels were critical. Any structured object underwent a certain degree of stress at high velocity, even in a void. With the speeds the ship might reach, that stress had to be monitored and controlled at all times. In less than fifteen seconds, the computer verified light speed.

Hesitantly, he looked to one of twenty digital readouts. What he saw put his mind at ease. He could breathe again. Hull stress was nearly non-existent. He stole a glance at his co-pilot, who wore a broad smile. He'd already seen it. No words were needed. The first step was behind them.

Danielson's smile faded abruptly. "What if it's wrong?"

Happine's arm straightened between them, squeezing his co-pilot's cheeks with a more than firm grip. "You really want to die a young man, don't you?" He turned to face Haute. "I told you she'd be quick."

Haute knew that he had just witnessed a new record for light speed achievement. "You have my attention."

"How fast will she go?" inquired Gary.

Danielson answered. "We don't know yet, but we will."

Happine turned back to the tasks at hand. "Okay ... let's try some simple maneuvers, some ups and downs, and some twenty degree turns."

Danielson was having the time of his life, animated by the success thus far. He fed coordinates into the navigation computer.

At light speed, the Touchen system dropped quickly away behind. With short-range scanners, the outpost soon faded and vanished from the screens. Utilizing the old systems, at light speed, time of contact to visual was roughly twenty minutes. The new scanners range was only a machines untested guess.

Haute stared ahead into the blackness filled with flickers of light. He remembered the old movies he used to watch, when light speed was a fantasized notion. No one knew what it felt like ... what it looked like. In the film director's imagination, the stars would appear and slide away to either side. It looked realistic enough, even though far from real. In today's reality, the stars did move past, but their movement was so miniscule, that it's nearly undetectable to the human eye. To reach many of the stars, even at light speed, would take years. The few stars that did move discernibly past however, were much closer. They were the small suns that provided light to the Belaquin system. The unusual proximity of the stars in the system formed what astrologers called a bright spot in the galaxy, the same bright spot that had beckoned to the travelers from Earth so long ago.

Haute shook away the thought. To try to imagine the infinity around him was utterly impossible. Did it end out there somewhere? Not likely. The good book, which he most certainly believed in, said that there truly was none. If there were an end, to find it would be less than desirable. No ... they would never find it. God didn't have that in his overall plan.

Silent moments passed as the Explorer Two performed simple maneuvers. Happine saw no problems as the ship performed flawlessly. "Let's put scanners on maximum."

Eric gave a doubtful look. "Won't we still read ...?"

"Probably. Forward and forty-five degree laterals only."

Danielson followed the order. As expected a majority of new contacts listed on the screen.

"Okay guys, here's your first lesson in scanner language." Happine motioned them to come up to the panel, which they did eagerly. "All right, we've got a lot of separate contacts here, most of which you'll be able to recognize after your training."

Kahn looked on and grimaced. The scanner screen was a mass of tracking lines and numbers, none of which made the slightest bit of sense. Happine caught his confusion. "Think you can sort that out?" he asked. "Well neither can I. That's why we've got the brains built in. All we have to do is turn this into our language." He punched a series of buttons and spoke to the ship itself. "Explorer Two, scanner data inquiry. Audio, please."

The voice that answered sounded like a living person. It was a female of course. "SCANNER DATA AVAILABLE."

Gary smiled when he heard it. It reminded him of Jana. It reminded him also, that he'd have to eventually release the apartment. She was only a mass of circuitry, but even so, she seemed alive. How would she react to the news? He felt saddened by the thought. It was awkward that he could feel this way about a machine, but she was more than that. Saying goodbye to her would be difficult in an unusual way.

Happine continued. "Composition of closest contact now within scanner range?"

"CONTACT ONE, NON-ORGANIC, METTALLIC COMPOSITION, TITANIUM, MAGNESIUM, COPPER, IRON ..."

"Stop." he interrupted, "Is it a known structure?"

"AFFIRMATIVE. IDENTIFIED AS A CLASS FOUR ORE TRANSPORT BARGE."

"Stop! Description and course?"

"BENTEEN CORPORATION ... IDENTIFICATION HIGH BOY. SEVEN, THREE, EIGHT. ONE MILLION METRIC TONS. SPEED, POINT ONE TWO FIVE LIGHT. COURSE ..."

"Stop! Estimated time to intercept?"

'ONE HOUR, SIX POINT THREE THREE MINUTES AT PRESENT SPEED."

He turned to the others. "Anything else you want to know?"

Gary was impressed, but confused. "Don't our computers tell us that kind of stuff now?"

"Not at this range, they don't," defended Happine. "That's the nearest ship to us. The others are a lot further away. The furthest we could detect anything before at this speed was twenty minutes."

Kahn brought up a good point. "I see a sharp decline in scanner tech's in the near future."

"Well, I don't know about that." Richard answered. "I don't think we're ready for a complete takeover." He took another look at the stress reading. All levels were minimal. He took a deep sigh. It was time again. "Move her up, Eric," he said, still watching the readings. "Real slow ... I bet we get a reading now."

"L-two?"

Happine nodded.

Haute and his fellow passengers had already found their seats once again. They all knew what was about to happen. He stared out the forward view port, expecting anything.

Happine's gaze was unwavering as he listened to the engines increase in power. He watched the numbers rise. Soon, seemingly too soon, the computer beeped three times, confirming to setting. The engine whine subsided once again to silence.

Happine shook his head, suddenly filled with awe and personal pride. His face revealed both emotions as he spoke to the other four men in the room. "Well, guys, we just made history. We're moving faster than any human being ever has." Only silence followed his words. He looked at the readouts. The stress level was still low. The Aquillon Two, which he had also helped build, topped out at one and a half the speed of light. She registered heavily into the stress category at that point. It was better than he ever expected. "I can't believe it."

Haute rose and laid his hand on his friends shoulder. "Why can't you believe it? You built her didn't you?"

The Lieutenant on outpost one-one glanced intermittently at the strange ships position on his scanner board. It had maintained the same course and had increased its speed to light velocity. This action of course, had been expected. At that speed, it would stay in range another fifteen minutes. He closed his eyes for a moment and leaned back in his chair. He promised himself that he would not watch the clock as closely today.

The moment seemed to grow long and he suddenly opened his eyes. Angrily, he sat back up. He had dozed off for at least five minutes. Rising, he decided to make some coffee to wake himself up. He had done well all night and during the early morning, but his relief wasn't due for another hour. He could make it until then.

Minutes later, he sipped the hot liquid. Almost a passing thought, he checked on the only contact he had that shift. He glanced at the three-dimensional schematic of the space around him and saw ... nothing. The ship was gone.

Wide-awake, he checked the clock again. It had been only nine minutes. He checked the initial contact time to confirm it. The ship should still be on his board. "That's impossible ..." he muttered. There was no shortcut out of the sector. There was no way to explain it, but the mysterious ship, and all aboard her ... had vanished.

It was past midnight when the soft sound of an alarm woke the Captain from his half sleep. A ship had appeared on the scanner. "Shit ..." he mumbled. He had hoped to make it through the watch without a hitch. Nothing had been scheduled to be coming in. He wasn't even supposed to be here.

The person who was supposed to be there had showed up in his office with a medical slip excusing him from duty. So instead of ruining someone else's evening, he called home, explained to his wife, and took the watch. He would be working seventeen straight hours, but it was easy duty and it paid time and a half.

He checked the monitors and started the flight recorders. The contact was on a freighters course, but it wasn't a cargo ship. Maybe it was the new ship Atkinson had recorded. He'd surveyed the tape, as well as the orders that accompanied it, and had agreed that it was a very strange situation. The ship was approaching at light speed. Whatever it was, he'd see it in eighteen minutes.

Maybe he should close his eyes again. He was stuck here and the only thing he wanted to see right now was the inside of his eyelids. He decided against it, wondering if there was a hidden camera watching him. He chuckled, maybe he should have thought about that before he closed them the first time.

Happine eased the autopilot back to manual. They had dropped below light speed for the first time in over twelve hours. The checklist was done, every test having been completed. He leaned back in his chair and stretched his aching joints. He turned in his seat, exhausted, knowing that he wasn't alone in his pain. It had been a fatiguing, but exhilarating trip.

This ship ... his ship, had made him proud. It had surpassed all of his dreams. He could barely contain himself when they doubled light speed. If someone had told him what would happen in the few hours following, he would have laughed in their face. In those hours, a new breed of space travel had been born, a breed to put all others to shame.

He recalled the excitement. Stress was registering at forty-four percent when the ship finally reached top speed. What the computer read was the unbelievable.

Haute was incredulous "This isn't possible," he stammered. The lever rested at maximum thrust, registering just under the level six setting. He stared forward. The view had changed. Many of the stars could be seen moving toward and past them.

Happine gripped his chairs armrests. They, at least … felt real. What was happening now couldn't be. They were moving over a million miles per second. No one spoke. Indeed, there weren't words that could express what they felt.

Several seconds edged by, until Danielson broke the death like silence with an amusing note. "Well, I guess we can check off the speed test, huh?"

His words preceded a multitude of system checks including automatic course changes, mock contacts and many others. One that had to be flawless throughout the test was the flight path recorder. Without it, the return home could be their final quest, as well as a probable epitaph.

Finally, the tests were finished, and after so much time, so was the crew. They still had a long way home. Happine, alone in the control room, brought the ship to a complete stop. He marveled at the moment. They were in space that was considered untouched … unexplored. They had exited the freighter lanes and entered regions never before charted. After a while, knowing the others were exhausted as well, he sighed and urged the ship to full power. Even at that, Touchen was hours away.

During the trials, they discovered that the new scanners at full speed gave only a maximum of ten minutes notice on small contacts, twenty on larger readings. Happine set the helm to slow to light speed well before contact with the Touchen system. Anyone who happened to see them would be alarmed with a contact moving five times faster than anything known.

The hours came and went. He glanced through the open door to the rear of the room. He was alone. The other men, at his urging, had retired to more comfortable surroundings to get some rest. He had considered it himself, but declined the whim. He relished every moment.

It seemed as if he and his creation were alone in this magnificent empty stillness. His throat tightened with the thought. This was the first and last voyage he would ever make in his handiwork. It seemed a great misdeed that his history with the ship would end there. More than ever, he wished he could be a part of the distinctive crew. He thought of a question recently asked of him, and how he hadn't been totally honest in his answer. Gary had asked him how long they might be out. He said he didn't have an answer. It wasn't totally a lie. He hoped differently, but believed, that even if he lived to be a hundred, he would not see their return. But, how could he tell someone that; someone that was leaving family behind? No ... he would not answer honestly. It wasn't a deliberate act of deceit. The truth was, no one but God knew this ships future.

The sound of movement came from the rear. Someone was coming up. It was almost time to wake them anyway. Outpost elevens scanners would probably pick them up soon.

Desperately, he took a long look around, committing to memory everything that his eyes took in. In another hour, this maiden voyage, these few hours of adventure, would be just another memory. It was one he would remember to the end of his days.

The corridors were dimly lit for the evening. Gary drug his feet as he walked. He was exhausted. He hadn't slept in almost twenty hours. He'd spent much of his time on the ship exploring. He tried to catch a nap on the way back from Touchen, but had only made it worse.

Colleen wouldn't be up, not at this hour. He wondered if she'd be angry with him for being gone so long. It was a possibility, but surely she would know that it wasn't his fault. The fact that his clothing didn't smell of smoke, and his breath of alcohol, should help the situation. He should have called.

He arrived at her apartment door, and punched in the code. The panels slid aside, the noise making him grit his teeth. He had never noticed it being that loud before. Inside, it was nearly pitch. The soft music that usually played while Colleen slept was absent, leading him to wonder if she was even there. Maybe she and Deanna had hooked up for the day and ended up over at her place. He didn't want to turn on the light in case she was there. Slowly, he groped his way to the bedroom, feeling his way along, hoping he wouldn't knock anything over in the process. A few familiar shapes started to develop as he reached the door he sought. The clock on the mantle sent an eerie glow across the room. He squinted and finally saw Colleen lying on the bed. Now that he had his bearings, he inched forward. Unbuttoning his vest and shirt, he let them drop to the floor, keeping her kept his eyes on the bed. So far, so good; she hadn't moved. After removing his boots, he dropped his pants. As they reached about knee level, he yelped in horror as he felt something sharp poke him on both sides of his back.

Instinctively, he tried to turn, but with his pants around his ankles, he did nothing but fall onto the bed. As he fell, another yell met his ears. He recognized the voice immediately, but it was too late. His heart was nearly out of his chest. "Jesus Christ, Colleen, what are you doing?" he whispered loudly. His body shook involuntarily.

"What am *I* doing? You scared me to death!" she answered.

"I scared *you* to death ... I about pissed my pants." He was no longer whispering. There was exasperation, as well as embarrassment in his voice. Quickly composing himself, he followed it up. His voice was calm. "Babe, what are you doing up?"

Colleen couldn't help but smile in the darkness. She knew he wasn't too mad. Slowly, she walked to him, dropping her robe to lie with his clothing. As she drew close, he tried to sit up on the bed, but she pushed him back. "Lift your feet," she said. As he did, she pulled off his pants and threw them into the darkness.

"Uh ... I might need those tomorrow," Gary smirked.

She didn't answer. Instead, she leaned onto the bed, her knees on either side of his legs, and put her hands on his shoulders. She kissed his chest, then his neck. She let her nipples barely brush against him as she moved.

He tried to relax, giving himself her. He felt himself start to arouse, and was sure she felt it also. He smiled, enjoying the moment. God ... she turned him on. She always had. Her long hair floated softly around him, each strand's touch sending shudders through his body. Finally he could take it no more. He reached up, trying to push her up and away. As he did, her fingers curled inward, pressing her nails against him. The pain forced him down again. She moved beside him, her fingers tracing sensuous trails from his torso to his knees. He drew in a short breath and held it tensed. As her touch left him, he released it with a heavy sigh. Shaking his head, he decided he'd had enough.

He sat up quickly, grabbed one of her wrists and pulled her roughly back on top of him. Bringing himself to a sitting position with her on his lap, he kissed her breasts, his hands caressing her neck and the small of her back.

Colleen let her head fall back, offering herself totally to his touch. She took in every movement, her nipples already rigid in anticipation, moaning with pleasure, happy that she'd waited up for him. She had longed for real love from men over the years, most of them older, supposedly better, but never, had found emotion like this. Gary was the one; the only one she would ever need, or want. She knew she would do anything to keep him, and would give up everything to keep from losing him.

Gary laid back and entwined her long hair in his fingers. He pulled her down against him, and with one quick motion, rolled her beneath him. He kissed her deeply, then stared into her eyes for a full minute.

Colleen finally spoke. "Well you've got me. What are you gonna do with me?"

"What do you want me to do?" Gary asked back.

"Oh ..." She paused, thinking. "How about something perverted?" she whispered.

Gary chuckled. "So now I'm a pervert?"

Colleen kissed him again, slowly, softly biting his lip. "All men are perverts."

Gary moved to lie alongside her, never taking his eyes from hers. "Do you know how much I love you?" he asked quietly.

Her playful demeanor took a back seat as she became as serious as he. "I think I do."

Gary took a deep breath. "Colleen, I love you with all my heart, more than anyone or anything. I think I knew it the first time I saw you. You are everything I've ever wanted. I will be faithful to you as long as I live. I'll do my best not to hurt you, or ever make you cry." He paused for a long second. "I will love you until I take my last breath, and even after that if I can." This time he would stay silent, waiting for her to say something. He wondered if she would cry, but a sniffle from her darkened face told him she already had. She pulled his face to hers, touching her cheek to his. He could feel her tears.

Colleen held him close, surprised at the unexpected baring of his soul. Between sobs, she finally spoke. "Those almost sounded like wedding vows."

Gary closed his eyes in relief as he answered in a whisper. "That's because they were, babe." He pushed away from her, found her left hand, and slipped something he had held hidden onto her finger.

Colleen became breathless as she felt, rather than saw, what he was doing. Had he said what she thought he had? She sat up quickly, fumbling for the light. In an instant, it was on, and she blinked, looking upon the most wonderful thing she had ever seen. The single marquee diamond sparkled for the first time into her memory. "Oh my God," she stammered. She broke down, unable to speak further.

"Will you be my wife, Colleen?" Gary asked, satisfied that he already had his answer.

"I love you so much. Yes!" she cried.

The early morning hours rushed past. They made love as if it would be their last time ... like they had their first time. Afterward, they lay silently in each other's arms, milling over their own thoughts, not realizing that each wondered the same. What would the future bring? Some of it they knew. Some they did not. Eventually they drifted off. The morning was nearly over. The clock above them was nearing five.

CHAPTER 20

▼

Kahn groaned and gritted his teeth, shutting off the alarm for the second time. Thirty minutes ago, it had broken his fitful slumber, but he'd done some hasty figuring. If he skipped the shower and breakfast, it would give him at least a half an hour. With a flip of a switch, he was again dead to the world.

There would be no resetting this time. He had to be in class in a short twenty minutes. Another mind-numbing day spent at a desk. This day, combined with seventy-one similar days, made up over two months of mission preparation to this point. Not in his wildest dreams or wildest nightmares had he never imagined that he'd be ensnared in school again. He had loathed even the thought, whether it was teaching, learning, or whatever. He had not been the best student in the academy, at least outside the ships. That was no secret. It was not a pass or fail course. Grades had been tracked, and his hadn't been that high. No matter how long it took, the material had to be learned. He had to admit that even pilot training had much to be desired. Simulator flight time was the exception. Flying was his dream. The Republic raider was his first love.

Regrettably, there would be none on this assignment. As of now, he may have already spent his last minute in the Republic gold.

Grudgingly, he rose from bed and staggered to the bathroom to take care of the morning routine. Looking in the mirror, he rubbed his eyes and studied his face. His five o'clock shadow was right where he had left it. It was two days old now. Should he mow it or not? He decided on the absolute minimum; that being to shave his neck, making it look like a beard in the early stages. It seemed as though he started a new one every week. He liked the look, but Deanna didn't care for the scratchy feel.

He glanced at his watch. She would be in class by now, telling the instructors that he might possibly be late. Maybe she felt it was her duty to protect him, to cover for him all the time. She acted like a wife already. That had been the central theme of their more recent conversations. Marriage was an exhilarating, yet frightening scenario. Had he run all this time because he was scared of it?

He slapped cold water onto his face. It was rudely awakening. He had been awakened to many things lately. The running was over, regardless of the reasons, and he was fine with that. Deanna had caught him.

The door buzzer went off. It was Gary. He grabbed a hairbrush and looked for his uniform shirt on the way through the bedroom. He found it in a pile on the floor. He'd forgotten to hang it up. The wrinkles didn't disappear when he shook it out. "Son of a bitch!" he muttered. His other two shirts were still at the cleaners. Five minutes more would make a lot of difference. He pulled on the shirt as he opened the door. His friend stood patiently outside.

"Oversleep?" Gary asked.

"You could say that," Kahn answered. "Give me a second, I need my shoes."

Gary saw the wrinkled shirt and unshaven face and shook his head. That was Kahn and this had become standard operating procedure. He'd never been a neat individual, but at least his uniform had been. He'd changed. "Make it a quickie, we're late."

"They'll get over it!" Kahn retorted angrily. He held regret as he said it, but he was upset. He hated when someone voiced the obvious. No, that wasn't it, he admitted. It wasn't Gary's fault. It was the monotony … the same time in the same room, day after day. "I'm sorry man. I didn't mean to yell at you." He apologized, shaking his head, disgusted with himself. "It's just these damn classes. I mean, half this shit we don't need to know!"

"I know it, but it's no different than any other school we've been through! Hell, you had to go through this same shit in flight school … remember? Velocity plus resistance equals whatever? Why did we have to know that?" He paused, upset as well. "You dealt with it then, chief, just deal with it one more time. Why are you letting it piss you off so much? There's no way around it. We all have to do it!"

Kahn said nothing as he pulled on his socks. With his next breath, he became aware that they were the same ones he had worn yesterday. The smell was overpowering. He smiled, mildly disgusted with himself and looked at his friend. "You know something?"

Gary's eyebrows lifted.

"Everything you said is right. I'm the one who wanted in this. Nobody forced me." He chuckled and changed the subject. "I'm a real scumbag, you know it?"

Gary, wishing his friend would finish dressing while he talked, was shocked at the unexpected revelation. "What?"

"I'm a scumbag."

"Well, I wouldn't say that ..." Gary disagreed.

Kahn interrupted him in mid sentence. "I don't know how you guys put up with me."

Gary came to a sudden realization, one he had never noticed before. "How do we put up with you? Maybe we like you because of the way you are."

"Well I don't like me ... I haven't for a long time." Kahn came through the door, wrinkled shirt, socks and shoes in place, nodding as he walked. "I won't be late tomorrow."

The selection of the Explorer Two crew was history; twenty-two men and women ... eleven couples. Some were already husband and wife, while the others had made the commitment to be joined soon. Each crewmember had been thoroughly checked out. Professional, as well as personal backgrounds was scrutinized. Psychological profiles were prepared and studied. One means or another brought all attributes and weaknesses forth. Each also received a complimentary medical physical unlike any they'd ever seen.

Each person was well educated and experienced in his or her individual fields. Although unplanned, the crew was split down the middle, consisting of eleven military and eleven civilian members.

The hundreds of interviews had been time consuming and arduous for all involved. They had searched for unique individuals. They needed responsible persons willing to take the biggest step of their lives with only one guarantee. They would be guaranteed the promise of the unknown. Apparently, these brave twenty-two were content with all that was asked and given. Many had admitted during the interviews that their only reason for wanting the trip was the opportunity to see the future. Most gave the impression that they believed in the historical and scientific importance of the mission as well.

Three additional months passed. The official news release of the crew's identities was made. The entire Belaquin system became aware. The Explorer Two became a name spoken in every home, school, and workplace. It became immediately difficult for the members. The twenty-two volunteers were propelled into the media fire, becoming overnight celebrities sought after by every news agency in existence. They called them pioneers, retracing the paths of those who had never returned. Most said this type of behavior demonstrated the bravery and fearlessness that made Belaquins what they were.

Others, and there were always others, called it reckless, irresponsible, and suicidal. The support was obvious and easily outnumbered the un-silent skeptics. Many remained detached from the events unfolding in front of them. Some tried desperately to derive anything they could from the short moment of something new. Several agencies took polls to ask what people thought. They presented a simple question. Would this crew come back ... or not?

Gary didn't care for the polls, the attention, or the so-called fame. It didn't fit. Personally, he felt that it took too much of his time, which was growing shorter by the day. More than once, he'd grown angry with the reporters with their constant prying; the protestor's gnawing away at whatever they could think of. "Why spend so much money on space travel, when there are so many problems here? Why not spend it on the ones who need it, the homeless, the sick, the dying?"

Statements of that sort caused the greatest annoyance, because in his heart, he knew they were right. He just couldn't say it. The public relations experts had coached them how to answer questions; what to say, what not to say, how to respond to something not anticipated.

The most uncomfortable feelings were prompted from more personal inquiries. "What about your family? How can you leave them? How do you feel about never seeing them again?" He didn't need the constant reminding. It troubled him often and it hurt more than enough.

The last goodbyes were growing nearer. It seemed ominous, more real than ever before. The time of departure, anticipated by some, dreaded by others, now had a date. In his case, the dreaded day was less than two months away. School was out. It was hard to accept. So many things still had to be done in the little time left. The last month was free. The members of the crew would be allowed to spend it as they wished. His wish was to spend the final days with his family. Colleen had voiced plans to do the same. Even though they would be newlyweds by then, the decision to be alone with their loved ones was not a difficult one.

Lately, all he could think about was his parents. He was thankful that they supported what he was doing. Without that support, he wasn't sure he could do it. More than once he had serious thoughts of dropping out, but he knew that wasn't possible.

There was heartache ahead, but there would be happiness as well. His wedding day was only a week away. It was to be a double ceremony. He and Kahn had done so much together over the last few years, why should this occasion be any different?

Gary stood alone in the observation room aboard the Aquillon. He stared at the stars, only a layer of glass separating him from them. They seemed so close. Soon enough, he would be lost among them. He'd been there for over an hour, watching in thoughtful silence, hoping to catch a shooting star or two. Strangely enough, with the wide view of the sky he was afforded, he had seen only one.

Space had always fascinated him. The shooting star was no exception. The end of the stars life actually happened years ago. The sight of it, even though traveling at the speed of light, had just now reached him. If he had blinked, he would have missed it. Was he the only person who had seen it in that brief instant? Would some other being, on the other side of the galaxy, see the same sight years from now?

He thought again of the wedding. Was he ready? Was he happy? As far as Colleen was concerned, he was sure of it. He hoped beyond hope, that she didn't have the notion that he had asked her only because of the mission. Nothing could be further from the truth. He'd considered it long before Haute ever mentioned the Explorer Two.

The plans for the weddings had been rushed. They had spared no expense, since all related costs were generously taken care of by SPEX. This being the case, the said costs were substantial.

Gary stepped to the window and reached out, laying his hand flat upon it. Even though it was warm in the room, the glass still felt cool. It only suggested what lay beyond; cold, loneliness, emptiness, but he knew there had to be more.

He thought about the three previous missions. He had studied the files over and over. All were fascinating stories. The first crew was surely lost. Something had gone wrong. It had been too many years. No one could anyone feasibly survive that long, not with the limited supplies on board. It wasn't even a consideration. If that crew had not discovered a planet that could sustain their lives, then their fate was clear.

The second mission hadn't fared well either, but they'd at least made it back. Whether it had been deemed a successful mission or not, didn't matter. It was a miracle that the crew had managed to return at all. There were in horrible condition. Some were still functional, mentally as well as physically, enough so to make it home. Many of the others had suffered severe psychological trauma, losing all sense of reality, becoming a danger to themselves and the others. One had tragically murdered two crewmembers and committed suicide, nearly taking the ship and the rest of the crew with him.

Earlier physicians had seen it and documented it long before, on the original trip from the desecrated Earth. They had called it "space dementia". Extreme paranoia, hallucinations, and severe depression were common terms seen in most of the reports. When those ships launched, the circumstances had been significantly dissimilar. Many necessities were overlooked in the hasty preparation. Indeed, in the final days, there wasn't time to diagnose each potential problem and prepare solutions. It had become a load and go situation, to where, no one had the faintest idea. All they knew was that if they wished to live, they could not stay where they were.

The Belaquin system was the bright spot at the end of the universe for those weary travelers. The supplies on some ships had nearly given out, forcing divisions of other's supplies, in turn putting all ships in jeopardy. Difficult situations were faced and courageous individuals were forced to make impossible decisions. Hope had remained unwavering. The survivors willed themselves to stay alive; not individually, but as a whole, and agreeing that if they were to die, then all would die together. Hundreds of books had been written, telling the historic tales from that desperate time.

Gary felt honored to follow the example set by those long dead travelers. Perhaps he could write his own place in history. Could he live with the same spirit that they had? Did he have the same desire to succeed? For them, to succeed was to survive ... to fail was to perish. He longed to go back for just one moment with his ancestors, to see it for himself.

His dreams of the past were suddenly interrupted. Another star streaked across the distant heavens and blinked out. He had been looking almost directly at it. As short-lived as it was, in a way, it seemed fulfilling. It seemed as if it was meant only for him.

Commander Haute looked over the test results, confirming his personal expectations. The scores were high enough to prove that the crew had taken them seriously. The tests had been geared to reveal trouble areas in the member's psychological profile. Understanding these areas was essential. No chances could be taken. The only unanswerable question was whether the long period of sleep would change those profiles. Again, it was hoped that the Kograns would be the example.

The sleep chambers had performed impeccably. The volunteers shut within them for several months were the same coming out as they were going in. All agreed that the worst part of the experiment was the apprehension prior to going under.

Congratulations were in order. They had done it right the first time. At this point in time, it looked like the original crew list would stick. All the persons selected had surpassed all requirements. He picked up the files to study them yet again. The first four belonged to Kahn, Gary, Colleen, and Deanna. They had been the first to volunteer. He placed their files aside and moved on.

The fifth belonged to the primary Explorer Two pilot, Eric Danielson. At thirty years of age, he was near the mission average. Danielson was a skilled pilot and as he said before, could possibly have made it into a raider. Other parties had decided his future however. In the civilian community he had made his mark, piloting nearly every type ship at one time or another for Conquest Airlines. He had made a good life with them for the better part of twelve years. His flight record was unblemished. He had received a second offer from the military only a few years earlier to fly supply ships, despite his vision problems, but declined due to personal reasons.

Haute read the reasoning Danielson had voiced and smiled in understanding. Money had been the instigation for that decision. Everyone knew that a military man wasn't a rich man. He saw a handwritten footnote. It read, "Fighter pilot or nothing!"

Next was Eric's wife, Melissa. Haute had grown to know Eric quite well, but had not had the occasion to spend a lot of time with his spouse. He remembered some things without the file. She was a certified therapist in psychology and mental health, the latter of which could possibly be needed in great abundance at some point during the mission. She was also thirty years of age and had been married to Eric for four and a half years. Eric was her third husband in the last eight. Those years had played a large part in the molding of her career and eventually had brought her name to the pages he held.

Less than a month after her first marriage, her husband was diagnosed with prostate cancer, succumbing to the deadly disease less than three months later. She was of course, devastated.

Her second marriage, a year later, also ended in only a few short months, thankfully in less tragic circumstances. Its abrupt ending was brought about by Melissa after discovering her new husband's part time job brought in absolutely no additional income after the first three weeks. This fact prompted her to follow him to his supposed new place of employment, where he was caught red-handed with another woman. Divorce papers quickly ensued, and were just as quickly signed.

These events, coming in such a short span of time, drove the young woman to seek help. She visited a mental health facility to which she was never admitted, but in fact, later became the director of. She met Eric a year later, and he became her third and hopefully final partner in matrimony. She and Eric had no children, but had agreed to try after the coming historic adventure.

Gary Kusan's official title for the mission was co-pilot and assistant navigator, but the main navigator's name was Tony Jarrell. Haute had recognized the name immediately on the initial volunteer list. He knew him because he had once commanded him.

Jarrell had served two and a half years of 4.0 duty, but it was all he wanted. He fulfilled his contract and resigned. He had worked for a year as an intelligence specialist on Olania, a station Haute had assisted at for a short time. The staff there was comprised of civilians and military officers only. Jarrell had been a lieutenant upon leaving. He finished his tour in navigation.

When he left the service, he pursued his father's footsteps, stationed on a rescue unit as a firefighter paramedic. His performance there had been exemplary as well. Now, at age thirty-six, he would follow different footsteps; steps leading down an unknown path. His position in the crew was crucial. As navigator, he would be laying the invisible breadcrumbs to follow home.

His fiancée of four years had agreed to follow the path with him. She had kept the last name of Cottier from a previous marriage. Her first was Cherie. She and Tony had finally set their wedding day, which Cherie stated during one of the interviews, was long overdue.

Haute liked the twenty-six year old girl from the first moment he'd seen her. She had thought that certain mission requirements were a bit backwards. When he'd asked her why, she'd replied, "You want to put eleven married couples on a ship together for how long?"

Haute agreed. She had a point, from a jokingly pessimistic side. Humor like that, even though not a pre-requisite, would be welcome on this trip.

Her specialties were biology, geology, and physiology, and she would be virtually alone on this trip in those broad fields.

The Explorer Two medical staff comprised five persons. The team consisted of two medical doctors, two nurses, and a general practice surgeon.

The doctors were a husband and wife team. They were general study physicians skilled in all facets of the fragile human body. They also carried experience in emergency medicine and procedures. The two of them were active duty Republic personnel, schooled by military and civilian physicians alike.

Scott Simpson, at thirty-seven, was the oldest member of the crew. His work partner was thirty-three year old Julie, wife of ten years. Haute noticed her birthday had passed since the papers had been printed, making her thirty-four. They hadn't been the only doctor husband and wife team to apply. In fact, more physicians had volunteered for the two available spots than all the other openings combined. Why so many were attracted to the mission was a mystery. To make matters more difficult, many applicants easily surpassed the higher-level qualifications. The final decisions came down to the personal interviews, which had very little to do with mission standards. They were based simply on the couple the interviewers were most comfortable with.

Haute felt no guilt concerning the choice. They hadn't scored the highest overall, but the decision had been unanimous except for one board member who relied strictly on the numbers. One section of the curriculum they had scored exceptionally higher than the others in was the diagnostic scenarios. They required intuitive decisions based on little or no positive information; something that they might encounter on this type voyage.

On a more personal note, the ten-year team had tried to have a family for nearly the entire span of the decade, experiencing and overcoming three separate miscarriages. The one child they did have died at age two months from complications prior to birth. These two individuals had been through the worst that parenting could bring. They had endured devastating events that could linger for life. They admitted that they still had heartache, but the committee saw only the strength they demonstrated in being able to live through it.

Haute scanned through the remaining files. He recognized most of the names, but his memory didn't bring forward the faces.

Two nurses would assist the doctors. Both were female ... both comfortable in their positions. The first was from Belaquin, born and raised by a farming family. Her name was Karista Overbay, a beautiful girl, twenty-one years old. Haute felt she could have been a model if she wished, but she was proud of her job and had aspirations of possibly becoming a physician. Like her father, a farmer for forty years, what she had chosen to do with her life, she would do for the rest of her life. She held a nursing degree as well as one in medical laboratory technology. She was solidly set for her later years, but then the opportunity of a lifetime presented itself. She wanted financial stability in her future. If it succeeded, this trip would no doubt give her that.

Michelle Updike made up the other half of the nurse's staff. She was a civilian, older than Karista by four years. She held the same certifications, but had at least three years more experience. Now, after several months of advanced training, their far from simple duties were greatly enhanced.

Michelle had been married less than a year when the SPEX mission was announced. This was her second marriage, the first having gone sour at the tender age of eighteen. She had waited, absorbed in obtaining her degrees before even thinking about another lifelong relationship. In her more adventurous life, she moonlighted as a martial arts instructor and held second-degree black belts in two separate styles.

The last member of the medical team was also a physician; a surgeon no less, and the husband of Nurse Updike. Michael was tops in his field. His selection into the crew was nearly elementary.

Only one other qualified surgeon had attempted to make the roster, and he hadn't quite met the criteria. That subject was over the age limit, worked jobs in three different cities in the last three years, and offered less than exemplary credentials. At the time of the interviews, he had numerous negligence lawsuits hanging over his head, each of which he was more than eager to exonerate himself from. It seemed to the panel that the man was simply looking to escape a future, rather than find one. In fact, the only requirement that he did fill was the no offspring category. To sum it up, he was not the sleek, upstanding professional being sought.

On the other hand, Updike would probably have taken the position easily, regardless of the numbers running against him. There had been so many letters of recommendation sent to the board that the selection committee hadn't bothered to read them all. He was the best of the best. No one who knew him personally ever dreamed he would volunteer. He was a well-known figure in the medical world and medical journals called him a true hand of God, at home on the operating table, no matter what he was presented with.

In all respects, the mission would be extremely fortunate to have so skilled a member, but Haute had an uncomfortable feeling and had voiced it to the other members of the committee, in essence, suggesting that something wasn't right. This man had everything he could want, one of the wealthiest volunteers by far. One question put to him was why would he give it all up? He answered simply, that his financial future was well taken care of, and even though he loved saving lives, whatever work he may perform on this voyage, if chosen, would be his last.

His wife Michelle brought to life a more personal issue concerning her husbands reasoning. As talented and confident as he was, the pressure he lived with was overwhelming at times. He wasn't perfect. He'd lost patients on the tables. Each one seemed to take a piece from him, a piece that saving a life back could never replace. He wanted out before he had nothing left. At age thirty-five, he impressed the committee as being one of the most intellectual men they had ever met. He also impressed them with his courage to give up all that he could be. With the right investments, by the time they returned he would be whole again.

Another name that caught his eye as he studied the pages was Robyn Carmichael, the daughter of Charles Nathaniel Carmichael, member of the Belaquin council. Haute shook his head in disbelief. How did she ever get his permission to take this trip? Her father had been a relatively silent objector since the project started, at least according to the media. "No comment" was the most common term heard from the man. It could be construed as good or bad. With his years in politics, he had become smart enough not to give any information that could be manipulated or misquoted in any way. In the public eye, he probably seemed pleasant enough. It was too bad they hadn't caught wind of his more private self.

Behind the scenes, he was different. Haute thought him a bastard and always would. He'd received a bad enough taste from the man to last a lifetime. There was no doubt in his mind that the feeling was mutual. Everyone knew that he considered him a back stabbing prick, relentless in his pursuit to create hardship. He actually seemed to enjoy it. One member of the council once said that the man's soul purpose in life was "to piss people off".

Haute chuckled. It shouldn't have been that big a surprise to see the woman's name on the list. Truthfully, she probably couldn't wait to get away from him. Was it too far fetched to wonder if she was selected because the members knew he was against it?

That wasn't the case however. She was well suited for her position. For the past four years, she had been a computer specialist from Bradstreet Techtonics, a manufacturing company for the Republic. She had probably worked on some of the Explorer Two's programs, unbeknownst to her, of course. She had a unique design for her work, as did all programmers and would no doubt eventually recognize it, with or without her father's blessings.

Her fiancée of six months, Kevin Jordan, was also from Bradstreet, where up to now he had been the executive program director for several of the firm's major contractors. He had held that position for two years. His thirtieth birthday was approaching. When asked why they wanted this mission, they answered the same ... adventure. Haute hoped the young couple wouldn't be disappointed.

Two vital positions were the chamber technician spots. Volunteers were plentiful since several young people had joined the new and exciting field. The only drawback was the lack of experience. No one had been involved with the chambers long enough to gain any.

The first chamber tech eventually chosen wasn't an original volunteer. She had waited almost until the last possible moment. Hers had initially been one of the "one wants it, one doesn't" situations. In this case, Jeannette King, one of the first to join the Republic's Prolonged Sleep Study program was happy with her new career, and hadn't even considered the Explorer mission.

David King, her husband, wanted it from the start, even with his wife's disinterest. He had been heavily involved in the design and construction phases of the Explorer Two and no one knew the ship better. He had begged Happine, who he knew personally, to keep him in the running for ship's specialist, even though he had never officially volunteered; all the while promising that his wife would come around. Personally, Happine didn't have a problem with the request, but professionally, he could not honor it. King had done extremely well on the entrance exams he was allowed to take, but to ask the board to hold open two positions was asking the impossible. There were too many applicants for the chamber technician positions. Happine gave him no guarantees.

David made good on his promise, but his constant nagging hadn't changed Jeannette's mind. A routine trip to her obstetrics doctor had done what her husband couldn't. The King couple had everything they could want; good jobs, a nice home, friends in an upper class society, and many other perks enjoyed by families with a better than average income. Their marriage was missing only one vital ingredient. They had never experienced the joy, nor collected the precious memories that only children could bring. For years, they'd tried with the same sad results. The specialists had run the usual tests, and found the problem to be within her. Their diagnosis stated that she had a severely decreased level of egg production. At first, it was still possible for her to conceive, but the odds were greatly against it. They still tried. Two years later her physician revealed that during that time, her fertile egg output had ceased.

Her fears were at last realized. Her physician, who she had grown close to over the years, was a trusted friend. He would have given her even one chance in a million if he could have, but her prognosis was final. Jeannette would never ever bear children, at least not without outside intervention. Her body could physically bear and deliver a baby, but it would have to be from another woman's egg. She didn't feel it would truly be hers, and she didn't want that. Kevin made it clear that he would follow her wishes, whatever they may be. Less than a week after the doctors disheartening news, her wishes changed dramatically. The very next day, her and her husband's names were on the Explorer Two's volunteer list. Doctors deemed her medical condition to be no threat as far as the mission was concerned. Jeannette was excited with the possibility that by the time they returned, medical advances could have an answer for her condition. Jeannette was thirty, David ... twenty-nine. They were young. They still had plenty of time. The rest of their lives was history, or at least would be.

A ship's specialist is essentially a part of the ship itself. They are apprentices to the builders themselves, as necessary as the engine that powers it, or the steering rods that steer it. They know his or her vessel as well as anyone can.

The Explorer Two would have two of them at their disposal. The first would be David King. The second was Thomas Goldman, "Tommy" to his friends. He was thirty-four years old. His most distinctive feature was his height. He was an inch taller than Kahn, and tipped the scales at two seventy-five. Just looking at him was intimidating.

Indeed, the commander, recalling the interview, had felt uneasy when first seeing him. Goldman's voice was deep and commanding. It reminded Haute of William Vients. He fully expected a sore, if not crushed hand from the original meeting. It wasn't the case however. The man's disposition was immediately opposite of his appearance. He was kind, with controlled strength; a nice a man as he'd ever met, although contrary to the character he portrayed.

Goldman's face was well known throughout the system. He was known best as a cold-blooded killer. The man had mutilated scores of persons, slaughtering men, women and even children. He was heartless, pitiless, having no remorse, no conscience, and no fear. He could tear a man's head off and stuff it in a pillow without a second thought. He'd done it before.

Haute shuddered, recalling some of the more horrific images as he reviewed his file.

Goldman had been in three films, a continuing saga of a serial killer being sought by an unrelenting cop. The directing was exceptional, the special effects realistic, and the storyline surreal. The films hadn't been blockbusters, but the gore and suspense had held their own.

He had made dramatic changes in his life. He no longer was an actor. Over the last year and a half, he had worked hard to learn more and more about his seemingly sole purpose in life, the Explorer Two. He had personally overseen the installation of the specialized engines aboard the vessel. That had been months ago. More recently, Goldman had attended to more urgent personal matters. He had terminated his contract with his production company before it would normally have expired, abruptly bringing legal action against himself.

The lawyers representing the film industry were powerful. They made one thing clear. They had no intention of letting go of the box office star. The killer owed them one final slaughter before his screen rival finally ended the pursuit.

Little did they know, Goldman had prepared for the upcoming legal clash. He had an incredible out of court settlement to offer in an effort to keep the battle short. It headlined the entertainment sections of all magazines and papers. If necessary, he would hand over all personal assets, as well as all future profits from the three previous films, the latter of which would no doubt provide substantial returns. His offer, with the help of the Republic's legal resources, would surely defeat, or at least appease McCraney Films Unlimited. Everything however, was in a judge's hands. The decision was still forthcoming.

Tommy wasn't alone in his troubles. His partner in the quest for the mission belonged to his twenty-five year old, soon to be bride, Kelly Jacqueline Taylor. They'd been engaged for two years, having met during shooting of his third film. Miss Parker soon discovered that the life of a movie star had much to offer, and also much to be desired.

One of those desires was for some privacy in their lives. The only place she could gain any of it was at work. There, she had a totally different life in the arms of the Republic. Her specialty was high performance, high output machinery. The Explorer Two's main drive would be right down her alley.

Her current duty station was the Aquillon. This meant, of course, that she and her fiancée hadn't been together much during the last several months. Taylor had over a year to go on the ship. When faced with the chance to possibly make the change, she jumped at it. It was her chance to make a real life with Tommy. She totally supported him in his decision to leave the limelight.

Her accomplice in grime was also a military man. His name was Wayne Montgomery. He was currently designated as an advanced engine specialist, and he would have an edge over Taylor, at least in the beginning. While she had been shooting about the stars for the last year, he had assisted with the finishing touches on an unheard of engine type, one he would hopefully never have to touch again. That engine of course, belonged to the Explorer Two. Montgomery was twenty-eight years old.

There was one person in the crew that had no specific physical tasks to accomplish. His job was to analyze every detail of the mission, evaluate and decide, logically, what could or should be done.

Phillip Powell would be the mission psychoanalyst. He had the credentials. He had spent years in college, majoring in fields that most students could not. He had challenged himself with the most difficult courses possible. At thirty years of age, he was one of the youngest professors in the university system.

Powell was unmarried, the wealthy bachelor so to speak, but that would soon be ending. His wife to be was one of the registered nurses, Karista Overfelt, who had actually survived two semesters of Powell's "logic" course. Apparently, he had convinced her that it was logical to become involved with him. So here they were.

The last file belonged to the second sleep chamber technician, Patricia Joice. Pat was drastically different from the other women on the mission, at least from Haute's point of view. She lacked the professional front the others flaunted and presented another side. The first facet of her personality that anyone would notice was her energy. It seemed to Haute that she bounced, rather than walked, everywhere she went. She seemed to have an incessantly happy disposition, evident in her smiling face, which she wore at all times.

She was a beautiful girl and young; only twenty, and just recently that. Her body was muscular and taut like a dancer's, but petite, standing only five feet two.

The Commander had to admit, he'd had disturbing thoughts about the girl. He felt himself attracted to her in more than a casual way, and he knew why. Miss Joice had a flirtatious persona, and it had been aimed at him from the start. It wasn't his imagination. It happened far too often to be accidental.

He shook his head and pushed the thought back, as he'd done a hundred times before. It didn't matter. Whether she was somehow attracted to him or not, she would be married before the week was out. The lucky man was engine technician, Wayne Montgomery.

Haute closed his eyes. If he'd met someone like her twenty years ago, would it have made any difference? He had dated, but never committed. Would he regret not having children? He had no close family, only distant relation from parts now unknown. The fact didn't bother him that much. He had grown used to spending holidays alone. It was his fault. He still received the invitations, but something usually came up and he didn't go. The something was never overly important, but it didn't take much. After so many unanswered attempts, most would have given up, but the cards and letters came nevertheless. Was it because of his elevated status, or did they really care that much?

He had evaluated his life many times over the years. He knew he would change a lot about it if he could, but not the job. He loved it; the responsibility, the pressure. He lived and breathed it. Maybe he couldn't function without it, though lately he had contemplated giving it a try. Perhaps he would ... perhaps soon.

Haute closed the files. He'd read too much. His neck muscles ached. Hopefully, a headache wouldn't follow. He glanced at the calendar on the wall. The mission launch date was coming soon. It signaled the start of a great adventure. Was he anxious to see it? Truthfully ... no. For him, it would be the end of another adventure.

CHAPTER 21

▼

Kahn reached into his vest pocket and took out a small packet containing some tablets. He had put them there the night before, just in case. Sighing in relief, he popped two of the blue pills into his mouth and chewed them. He turned to Gary, who stood before a full-length mirror. He wore a shiny black tuxedo with tails that reached to his knees.

As he shook his head at his friend's meticulous nature, he caught his own reflection in the same mirror. He had to admit, he liked what he saw. It was his first time in a tux and he savored the moment. Finally, he spoke. "You want some of these?"

Gary turned, recognizing the contents. "Hell yes … give me a couple."

"They work." The queasiness he'd had a moment before was already subsiding. He glanced nervously at his watch. "Jesus … it's almost time."

Gary looked at his best friend, who also happened to be his best man for the day. Actually, they were each best men. They had decided to have it that way; a very distinctive way. He looked at his own watch, nodding his head. "I know," he answered. He took a deep breath and blew it forcefully out. "Are you ready?"

Before Kahn could answer, there was a quiet knock on the door. It opened slightly and a man peered in. It was the minister who would be performing the ceremonies. "It's time."

Both nodded at the older man. They had only met him two weeks ago. He was from Deanna's hometown, where he resided over a small church frequented by the Wilkens family.

Opening the door fully, they followed him down a narrow hallway to another closed door, where he turned. "Just do exactly what we did last night." he urged.

Gary, in front of Kahn, turned to face him in the dim light of the corridor. He hesitated before he spoke, just taking in the moment. "Thanks chief ..."

"For what?" Kahn asked.

"If it wasn't for you, I never would have met her."

Kahn smiled, remembering more than that day. "Thank you, too."

Gary was puzzled. "For what?" he chuckled.

"Thalosia ..." Kahn said simply.

The younger man nodded in understanding.

The minister opened the door. Kahn reached out his right hand, which Gary took, but a handshake wasn't enough, not for this occasion. He stepped forward and embraced his friend. "I love you, brother."

Gary felt closer at that moment than they had ever been. He slapped Kahn's back. "I love you too, man."

A moment later, they entered the ceremony room. The music started as they took their positions. The church they stood within was near Deanna's small hometown of New Harmony. It had been chosen by all involved, as the simplest and most beautiful. It was well over a hundred years old and rested on the wooded banks of a large lake. It was barely large enough to accommodate the families and friends who had been invited.

Gary stood facing the pews filled with people, a large part of them his family. His parents sat only a few feet away. He recognized aunts, uncles, and cousins, some of whom he hadn't seen for years. He tried to make eye contact with each and every one of them.

Soon, the soft and unfamiliar music stopped and a new piece began. He knew this one well, as everyone did. It was the wedding march. At the same time, movement caught his attention from both sides of the back of the room. Two brides appeared, escorted by their fathers. Long, white, flowing trains following each measured step. The dresses shimmered in the sunrays as they passed by the windows.

Gary's eyes moved to meet Colleens ... and never left them. He swallowed, trying to hold steady and straight. His left knee began to tremble, but stopped as he tightened his stance. He felt breathless. Never had she looked so beautiful. He was filled with pride and the comfort that he would never forget this moment.

Deanna had done well until her father, with tears in his eyes, kissed her and told her that he loved her. As he left her beside Kahn, she couldn't stop the wetness that clouded her vision. She blinked her eyes to clear the tears, not that they would ruin the occasion.

She held Kahn's hand tightly. She'd waited her whole life for this day.

The minister spoke of love, commitment, trust, faithfulness, and other qualities of a good union. She listened intently to every word, praying that he was describing all that was in their future. Only time would tell.

Colleen stood with Deanna on her right and Gary on her left. She waited patiently, hand in hand with the wonderful man who had asked her to be here with him on this day. She didn't move. She barely breathed, wishing to stay in this special place forever; wishing to keep the feelings she experienced during these few moments.

She had cried earlier, when her father Michael finally took her arm to give her away. The simple gesture hit him hard. He whispered to her, that it was one of the hardest things he would ever do; that he would always be her Daddy, and she would always be his little girl … his "pooky bear". He had said it with tears streaming down his cheeks. To see him cry nearly broke her heart.

She stared into Gary's eyes, trying to read his thoughts. She saw only love. If there were any second thoughts, they were buried deep inside. She ridded her mind of everything but the sincerity in his eyes, the touch of his hands, and the words spoken by the respected man before them.

Kahn listened to the words as well, trying his best not to look nervous. It was hot and binding in his suit jacket, especially around his neck. He hunched his shoulders ever so slightly to try to ease the pull of its weight. He felt a squeeze from the woman holding his hand. He squeezed back, noticing that his hand trembled. Hopefully, she wouldn't mistake it as sign of apprehension or fear.

He felt neither. Maybe he had for a long time, but not since the day he admitted to himself and her, what his heart wanted. Her parents sat directly behind them. They had complimented him on the way he looked that afternoon and for the first time since he'd met them, he felt true warmth from both. They had always been friendly enough, but he had always sensed that they felt their daughter could do better. Deanna thought he was ridiculous. What he did for a living was honorable, holding the highest rating a Republic raider pilot could have. He attributed their new outlook towards him to the personal renovations he'd recently attempted. At least it all fit.

Before the ceremony, he'd noticed a lone figure seated in the back. The man was nearly unrecognizable in the clothing he wore. He was fairly sure he had never seen Leon Haute dressed as a civilian. He thought about all they had in common, similarities in life. Summed up, they were the same. He and his father's best friend were adventures, leaders, and loners. In his case, the latter was about to change.

The minister spoke on, finally asking for the rings and their promises to one another. As suddenly as it began, it was over. Photos, hugs, handshakes, and congratulations followed. The reception lasted long into the night. It was private as well, even though the media, kept in the dark at least for a while, did manage to sneak some publicity shots for the papers. It was no matter. Nothing could dampen the joyous mood that carried the newlyweds into the following few days.

Gary awoke to the sound of an unfamiliar voice and a hand shaking his shoulder. He became instantly awake as he remembered where he was.

The voice was pleasant. "Sir, we'll be landing soon. You'll need to belt in." The words came from a stewardess he had talked to earlier in the flight.

He felt somewhat embarrassed. "I'm sorry. I must have really been out."

"That's no problem. Thanks for flying with us, Mr. Kusan." She moved to check other passengers. Yawning, he stretched his arms and legs as far as he could. He sat in anticipation, closing his eyes again. It felt good, enough so that it would take little effort to return to a dream state. He complemented himself. He had hoped he could spend the flight catching up on some sleep. He checked his watch. Six and a half hours had passed. He would easily make it through the coming days.

He and Colleen had spent their wedding night and the two days after, in a small lakeside cabin, fully stocked with everything they could want; all provided to them by sources unknown. It was peaceful and romantic. They had access to a boat, a fireplace, and privacy. They didn't even know whom the cabin belonged to. It was explained away as an anonymous wedding present.

Now, after leaving his wife with his new in-laws, he had made good on his promise to himself, that being to spend the last days with his Mom and Dad. They had flown to Belaquin for the wedding, his father actually enjoying the experience, but they had preceded him in returning to Brittaan by two days. He had tried to convince them to wait one more day to leave, and offered to cut short his limited honeymoon to accompany them, but his mother's reasoning made sense. If he left early, the cabin getaway would be wasted, and if they stayed, they wouldn't be together anyway.

Gary was surprised to see find father waiting alone in the terminal. "Where's Mom?"

"Hair appointment ... ten o'clock." Kenneth frowned at the idea. She had it done just before the wedding and now again.

Gary checked the time. "It's only nine o'clock though?"

"You think she can show up at the salon without fixing her hair first?"

Gary nodded. "That makes sense."

"We're supposed to meet her for lunch," his father explained.

Gary yawned again. "Good, I missed breakfast. Hell, I missed the whole flight."

"I don't see how you can sleep on one of those things."

"I thought you'd changed your mind about flying? Mom said you liked it."

"You're mother has a strange sense of reality, son."

Gary laughed.

Kenneth led the way to the car and they headed towards the hills. As they passed through the small valley town, he pointed out a beauty salon. "That's where she's at."

Gary watched him pass without slowing, "Aren't we supposed to meet her?"

"Not yet, we've got something to do first."

He drove on, up into the mountains. Within twenty minutes, they were home. His father popped the trunk and Gary helped carry some groceries in. Putting his on the table, Gary sighed. It was good to be there again, even though it hadn't been that long. "Anything cold in here?" he asked, referring to the food items.

"Don't think so, I didn't pick the stuff out, I just pushed the cart." Kenneth answered. "She would have reminded me if there was."

"Where to now?"

"The grand room. C'mon."

Gary followed him down the steps into the large central room. Every time he saw it, he was impressed with its construction. The cathedral ceiling peaked twenty feet above the hardwood floor. The entire wall facing the valley was paneled in glass. The huge fireplace against the left wall rested cold and dark.

His father walked to a large cabinet where he kept many of his smaller valuables. Kenneth took a key from his wallet and unlocked a drawer. He removed a wooden case and placed it before Gary on the table. "Open it," he said.

"What is it?"

"Just some new ... old stuff I got recently."

Gary looked at the case. The wood was burnished and smooth, polished to a brilliant shine. His father had never taken the cheap route, no matter what it was. He clicked the brass latches and slowly opened the lid.

The box held five metal items. He identified three of them at once. The other two, he couldn't place. All were obviously old, as his father had already said. He reached to touch them, but hesitated.

Kenneth read his mind. "Go ahead."

Gary smiled and removed the first and largest item. It was a small silver spoon in immaculate condition with only one blackened blemish on the handle. Its handle design was elaborate. On the back was the name of the apparent manufacturer. "J. Lay and Co."

The second item was a length of linked gold chain, less than an eighth of an inch wide and approximately five inches long. There was no clasp and no markings. It might have been part of a necklace at one time.

The third item was an earpiece from a pair of eyeglasses. It was gold in color, but corrosion was thick in some areas, hiding any markings there might have been.

After examining each piece, he replaced them in the case, exactly as they had been before.

The identities of the remaining two objects were a mystery. One was a bent, tubular piece of metal three inches long, also about an eighth of an inch in diameter. It had been broken on each end by what appeared to be repeated bending back and forth.

The last bit of metal was flat, thin, and circular, not unlike a coin, but it too was encrusted with corrosion, with no discernible markings visible. Gary looked each one over and placed them back. He looked to his father, who sat silently. "Very nice. Do you know history on any of them?"

"No, I haven't had time to follow up on the spoon. It's the only one with anything to go on."

"Do you have any idea what these are?" he gestured to the last two items.

Kenneth picked up the round item. "This ... I can't even begin to guess. It could be a coin, but I'll have to get it professionally cleaned." He placed it back, and retrieved the bent metal tube. "This, I'm fairly sure, is the inside of an ink pen. That's the only decent guess I could come up with."

Gary nodded, going along with the notion. "Where did you get them?"

"They all came together, locally."

"I bet they were expensive, the spoon especially." Gary guessed.

"Actually, no ..." Kenneth answered.

"How much?" Gary hoped he wasn't being too questioning. His sense of the value of these precious things might be drastically less than his fathers.

"Free."

Gary chuckled. "Yeah, right."

Kenneth said nothing.

Gary closed the box. When there was no further input from his father, he smiled and said. "You didn't get these free!" He didn't phrase it as a question.

"I most certainly did," smiled his father. "But technically, I'm still in the hole for the price of the metal detector."

Gary's eyes widened with realization. He shook his head. "No ..." he began, "... you gotta be shitting me?"

Kenneth rose, taking the box back to the cabinet drawer, followed closely by his son, who still could not grasp the concept. He re-locked the cabinet. "That's what I've found so far in the first building, but there's more up there, I guarantee it."

Gary couldn't believe what he was hearing. "Dad ... these are from ... I don't get it."

"All I know son, is that there were people here a hell of a long time before I was."

Gary walked slowly to the wooden staircase leading out of the room and sat down on it, as confused as he had ever been in his life. The room was silent as he entertained possible answers. Finally, he spoke. "They had to have landed here ... before Belaquin?"

"Maybe, but if they did, they would have stayed here," Kenneth suggested.

"But if after, there would be records saying so." Gary paused. "There is no record of this planet until a few years ago."

"Maybe one of the ships from Earth got separated from the others."

Gary asked the obvious. "Yeah, but where's the ship?"

Kenneth sat down beside him. "It's not here, that's for sure. It could have taken off again somehow."

Gary finished the theory. "And they never found Belaquin."

Kenneth thought of the secret filled hillside, where he had spent many hours. He shook his head, wishing he had some answers. He glanced at his watch. "We better get going. She might have got in early." He stood, moving back up the steps.

Gary stood, perplexed. "Dad ... this is important!"

"I know it is, bud." He stopped in the kitchen and turned back for a second. "Believe me, I realize the significance of this. I've thought about it quite a bit. I just haven't decided how to handle it yet."

"Did you show all this to Mom?"

"Yeah, I took her up there. She knows all about it."

"What does she think?" Gary pressed.

"She says it's my decision. Big surprise, huh?" He continued towards the car outside. "She doesn't want anything bad to happen to this place, but she thinks someone needs to try and find out what happened here."

"I agree with her," Gary said.

They started back down the main road to town. "I'm not ready to call anyone yet." Kenneth sighed. "There's more that I haven't told you."

Gary was all ears. "What?"

"When I was digging, I found something I couldn't show you," Kenneth answered.

"What, Dad!" Gary squirmed in his seat.

"I've uncovered the top of a stairway going down," he finally said.

Gary sat in complete silence, imagining the possibilities. "My God ..."

His father smiled. "You feel like getting your hands dirty?"

Gary's face was incredulous, his voice eager. "When can we start?"

"We'll get to bed early, and go up tomorrow."

Gary felt exhilarated with the invitation. What might they find? Silently he wished they could go now, but he would not voice it. There was plenty of time.

Linda Sluder opened the window beside her chair. The sun had just come up. She could see its rays on the yard and road outside. They lit the kitchen as well. She'd asked her husband Michael, when he had built on the two-room addition twenty years ago, to put the windows above the sink to face the sunrise. She loved how the sun reflected off the wind chimes hanging outside, sending a cascade of colors through the glass. The chore of dishwashing took time. If there were little kids running around, she could watch them at the same time.

A breeze filtered through the screen. It was cool now, but she knew as the day wore on, she would have to close the window and turn on the air. It was supposed to be hot, but being summer, it was expected. She sipped her coffee, noting that it tasted rather strong this morning, but she couldn't complain. She hadn't made it. Her husband had risen even earlier than she, wanting to get some chores out of the way before the kids got up.

She looked forward to this special day. For the first time in a long time, all of her children would be together again under her roof. Kelsey was already there, having arrived two days before the wedding.

Her son Chad would be there that evening. Of everyone, he had objected the strongest to his sister's future plans of travel. He lived two and a half hours away, but stayed close in other ways, visiting every weekend.

It was her daughters that had traveled the farthest. But it didn't matter, for the next few days, they would be together, saying all that needed to be said.

She stared out the window in thought. Colleen, her oldest daughter, her first baby girl, was leaving. She'd left many times before, but not like this. Would she come back this time? Just the thought brought sorrow to her heart. It was truly possible that she might never see her again. How could she have ever supported her daughter's decision?

She knew why. That's what parents do. They can't run their children's lives forever. You make choices concerning your kids, some bringing joy, some tearing you apart, but you live with them, not because you think they're right, but because they've reached the stage of responsibility. That stage deserves a measure of respect.

She'd cried many tears over her decision and knew that more would follow. The hard part was yet to come, in less than two weeks. These next few days would be precious.

Her husband had taken the week off, as all the family had, to make the most of what little time there was left. She looked forward to that evening, when the kitchen table would be surrounded by the persons she loved most in the world, each of them laughing, reminiscing, and more than likely arguing. Each had their place at that old table, always the same. She sighed. That's what memories were made of.

Someone entering the room interrupted her thoughts. It was her oldest girl, hair a mess, nightdress kicking up with each step, eyes barely open. She smiled as Colleen shuffled through the bright sunrays and knelt beside her chair. She placed a hand on her daughter's head as she lay it down on her lap. Softly, she stroked her black hair, trying to remember the last time she'd done it. Nothing needed to be said, each perfectly content with where they were.

Linda closed her eyes and for a few moments, traveled years back to the same house … the same room … the same chair. Her same little girl was seven or eight, curled up on her lap, sleeping soundly. She'd tried to stay awake for her Daddy, but he'd worked too late. She was his girl, no doubt about it. Where he went, she went; what he did, she did. No father and daughter could have loved each other more.

On this night, it was Mommy who had read with her in her favorite book, helping her pronounce some of the harder words. The two of them had their special moments when Daddy was gone, and they had secrets that only two little girls could share.

She rocked slowly in her chair, watching her sleep. With the lights off, she could see the brief flashes of fireflies floating across the yard. Colleen had been out there not long before. She caught as many as she could and put them in a jar that now rested on the table beside them. For a moment Linda wondered. Would she remember little instances like these in fifteen or twenty years, or would they be lost in time like so many others?

She looked lovingly at her grown up girl, remaining still except for the movement of her hand. She was afraid to look away ... afraid she would miss a single moment like this one, especially when so few may be left. The moments passed. Colleen's breathing grew deep. Apparently, she was again asleep. Did she still dream of fireflies?

Suddenly, without stirring, her daughter whispered, just loud enough for her to hear. "Mom ... I'm gonna miss you so much."

Linda smiled, tears instantly filling her eyes; tears that had been on the brink for too long. She answered when she could, her voice trembling. "I'll miss you too, baby doll," she sniffled. "I'll miss you too."

CHAPTER 22

▼

The final days slipped past, each member of the Explorer Two crew eventually finding his or her way back to Touchen. The deadline for reporting was three days before lift off. The early return date was made for a specific reason. It had been set to allow the crew to return their attention to the ship and the mission.

The last goodbyes had been said. Many had shared better times with their friends and families than they ever had. The time spent with them would be the last before launch. Each of the crew had been urged to bring their most personal belongings with them. There were nearly no restrictions on what those items could consist of, though one individual joked about bringing the first car he'd ever owned. He received the answer he expected and settled for photographs.

The first day after returning was used by most of the crew to cry on one another's shoulders, to reflect back, and to accept. None would be permitted to leave the underground complex until they did so aboard the Explorer Two. This was a strict stipulation with only one exception, if a member should resign their position. The mission psychologists fully admitted that it was a distinct possibility that one or more could lose it near the end and not be able to follow through. Each member was evaluated on the second day and seemed relatively confident and in good spirits. The third and last day passed uneventfully.

"Explorer Two, this is control. We have you on course heading zero, two, niner, point seven, four, sierra. Do you concur?"

"Affirmative control, heading two, nine, seven, four. We should be approaching a visual with outpost seventy-two in about ten."

"Okay, do another system check and give us a call back in ten."

"Roger that," answered Danielson. He turned to his co-pilot, shaking his head. "Is this for real?" he asked.

Kahn's first impression was that this was another joke, but there was no humor in Eric's voice. This time, the man was serious. "It's as real as it is gonna get," he answered.

Danielson turned back to face front, staring into the blackness, expressionless.

Kahn started the system check, control had requested. It would be the final one before they left the Belaquin system.

He and Danielson were alone in the control room. The others were in the back or below, doing whatever. Kahn wondered if the mood was as solemn throughout the ship. He glanced to his left at the pilot, who was strangely quiet. In the glow of the control panel, he was surprised to see a tear roll down the man's cheek. He bit his lip and considered saying something to him, but didn't. What was there to say? Each of them would have to deal with it. Each should have already dealt with it. Maybe they thought they had.

His tears weren't the only ones that had fallen that morning. Kahn had felt his own eyes moisten as he watched some of the others earlier. He had to admit, he had a tough time as well when he said farewell to the only person whom he would truly miss; the man, who had attempted to fill a huge hole in his life. This morning he realized that he would miss him very much. Finally, with concern, he spoke. "You okay?"

Danielson broke from his stare and quickly drew his hand across his face. "Yeah ... yeah, I'm fine. I just ..." He stopped in mid-sentence, turning away again.

"I know," Kahn said. "It's gonna be hard on all of us. We'll make it, though."

Eric chuckled with a slight sniffle. "That's what my Dad said. He said he didn't know how, but we would."

"He's right."

Danielson thought back, thankful for the time he had spent over the last week at home. It had helped dispel some of the guilt he felt, but there was much more that still remained. He knew he hadn't been the model son the last few years. He had let the business of life interrupt what was really important. Family should have been first, but in his case, he'd let it take a back seat. He'd let weeks pass at a time without even calling. When he had the chance, he would put it off, telling himself there was plenty of time; that his life and his parent's lives were just too busy. It sounded like such a sad excuse. Now, he realized that it was.

He sat in silence, remembering. He'd told them how sorry he was for handling it the way he did, and that he wished he could do it all over again. He would change a lot of things. He'd left his Dad and Mom a video-letter, taped that morning, revealing the last of his apologies, his regrets, and his hopes. His biggest hope of all was that he would see them one more time, just to tell them again how much he loved them.

Kahn felt more should be said. "You know, I don't have my family anymore, but I know how you feel. I thought I forgot a long time ago how to really hurt ... inside, I mean. I was wrong. I guess we don't forget, do we?"

"I don't think I can." Eric answered, lowering his eyes. The tears had ceased. "I don't think I really want to."

Finally, after taking what seemed like an eternity, the info screen between the two men revealed that the computer had finished the systems check. All readings were normal.

Eric cracked a half-hearted smile. A part of him had hoped that something would be wrong, so they could turn around and be delayed another week. Another part was thankful that he didn't have to go through it again.

Kahn watched a short-range scanner contact move into the visual field. As they moved closer, it became easily recognizable.

Danielson slowed the craft to nearly a stop as they approached the outpost. It looked the same as all the others. He turned the ship, and passed closer than they should have, slightly below the structure.

A lone man stood behind the curved glass, watching in awe, knowing full well that he could be the last person to ever see the magnificent blue vessel. It glided majestically past, only a few meters away. Corporal Brian James would have a story to tell his children that evening.

As he watched, a light came on, illuminating everything within the ship's cockpit. Two men could be seen, both whom he recognized from the many news broadcasts he and the whole world had watched. Both of them raised their hands to wave. He held up his arm for a brief moment and then moved it to a Republic salute over his chest. One of the men was still military.

James was suddenly glad he had volunteered for today's duty. He had no idea he would be in the position he was in now. He felt privileged to have this personal moment with the brave crew. Past this tiny outpost was the void. Was it bravery ... or recklessness to venture out into it, knowing that they may not return? He didn't have what it took, but he respected those that did.

He held his lone salute until the two pilots could no longer see him. As the vessel slowly passed, he could see other windows along the side. The interior was brightly lit. He thought he might have seen others, moving about inside, but couldn't be sure.

The glow of their engines grew smaller and finally disappeared. James turned off the recorders, made a copy of the tape and placed it in his case. The original tape would be a historic item, something for the Belaquin archives one day.

The copy, he would carry home; a personal treasure for him and his family. It might be valuable as well some day. He'd heard rumors about how long the ship might be gone, and couldn't help wonder if an outpost would even be here to welcome them back.

The first few days of the mission passed quietly. The crew kept to themselves, allowing those who needed it, time to adjust. Some spent time stowing equipment, situating work areas to meet personal tastes and making their cabins a little more like home. As the first week ended, the adjustments were nearly complete. The shock of leaving had seemingly been abated.

Gary took his dinner tray from the galley and joined Kahn at a table, exchanging greetings with Mr. and Mrs. Montgomery on the way. As he sat, he noticed his friend's somber expression. "You gonna eat or what?"

"Or what, I guess," Kahn drawled.

"What's the matter?"

"I don't know … just not hungry tonight." He dropped his fork on the plate. The food was more or less untouched.

Gary downed a couple of bites, speaking as he chewed. "You sick?"

Kahn shook his head, leaning back in his chair.

"You ready for tomorrow?" asked Gary, trying to come close to what was troubling his friend. Kahn acted like he didn't want to be bothered, but he reasoned it was his duty to antagonize.

"Yeah, I guess."

"Yeah, I can tell you're really excited about it." He couldn't keep the sarcasm from his voice.

Kahn looked at him, finally smiling. "Okay, smartass." He could never stay upset too long with Gary around. "I just thought there would be more to it. All this hype and we just go to sleep?"

Gary nodded, knowing exactly what he meant. "There will be more to it when we get woke up."

Kahn rose to leave. "Yeah, right," He walked away without another word.

Gary chewed and thought about what Kahn had said.

The ship had been fully automatic from the point they'd left mapped regions. They were even past the planets visited by the mining companies, who were notorious for traveling the furthest. The positions of pilot, co-pilot and navigator for now had become unnecessary. Maybe that was the reason for his friends' sour mood.

The crew was ready for phase two of the voyage. Today, the final medical exams would be given, and tomorrow, the preparatory procedures would be performed. That day was sleep day.

Gary sat, thinking about his friend's state of mind. He wasn't sure himself how he felt about the coming day. He held it with dread somewhat. There was one possible aspect of the coming future that he could have problems coping with. In the event of contact or a problem with the ship, he was one of the six individuals who would be awakened. How would he react with what they might be confronted with? There was major discussion in the months prior to launch, whether the crew should even be allowed to know the length of time they'd been gone. One argument stated that time passage, if excessive, would be too much for them to deal with. The same side offered the suggestion that if the mission time were withheld until their return, there would at least be outside resources available to help.

The other side argued that to deprive human beings of something as important as the passage of time could be even more damaging and even cruel to a point. As it should have been, the crewmembers had the final vote. After hearing all the pertinent summaries, it was unanimous. They would know.

It was this that Gary dreaded the most; seeing the mission clock for the first time. Regardless of the reason for the awakening, it could be a crucial point of the voyage. Some might voice the idea of going back, even if the contact was less than what they hoped to find. Would professionalism and duty override the more personal human side? Which would he choose?

Tony Jarrell turned, feeling the warm body of his wife lying next to him. He readjusted the covers, moving up against her and slipping an arm around her waist. She stirred, but her steady breathing continued, interrupted only for a moment. He lay as still as possible, timing his breathing to match hers. She faced away from him. His face nestled in her fresh, clean hair. It was still damp in some places from the late shower she had taken.

For several moments he lay awake. He still hadn't opened his eyes. He was afraid to. He knew the alarm clock was within five minutes of going off ... it always was. It wouldn't have bothered him on any other given morning, except that these last few moments alone with Cherie were dearer to him than life itself.

Today was the day they went under. The experts said it could be even more difficult than the day they left Touchen. At the time, he was sure that nothing could have compared to that pain and anguish. Now, the same feelings began welling up again. A week and a half ago, he had said goodbye to everyone he knew. Today, he would have to go through it again ... with Cherie.

He pulled her closer and his lips started to tremble. He shut his eyes tightly, trying to stop the inevitable tears, turning his face into the pillow to keep quiet. This time there was no stopping them. He tried to hold his breath, but couldn't. A soft moan escaped his clenched lips as he released his breath.

He felt her stir and turn toward him. He opened his wet eyes to see the dark blurred features of her sleepy face.

She wore an understanding smile as she spoke. "Oh sweetie, I thought we got over this last night?" She moved her hand across his face.

Tony sniffled and gained some control. It was hard for him to speak. "I'm sorry. I didn't want to wake you up."

"What time is it?" Cherie asked, stretching, forcing the stiffness from her muscles. No matter what time it was, she knew she would not be returning to the blissful slumber.

Tony reluctantly turned to look at the clock. This morning, his assumption had been wrong. It would be another three hours before the alarm would sound. "Four-thirty." He answered.

"Oh ..." Cherie groaned. She finished her stretch and embraced him, "Still sad?"

Tony couldn't believe the tone of her voice. It was as if she didn't care. He found his voice again. "Doesn't this bother you? Don't you know this could be the last time we're together?"

Suddenly, her loving embrace was gone. "Tony, I don't have a problem with this. You, of all people, shouldn't either!" She sat up on the bed. "Who wanted this mission so bad?" Her tone had turned almost angry. "I'll tell you who wanted it ...!"

"I know ..." he said sharply back. He calmed just as quickly, "... who wanted it!" He knew this wasn't a good start for the day, this one especially. "I guess I thought I could handle it. It's so hard ..."

Cherie calmed down as well, sorry that she had raised her voice. "I know it's hard, but there's nothing we can do about it. What do you want to do ... start a mutiny?"

"Don't be ridiculous."

"Then don't be afraid of it. If you didn't trust these people, you wouldn't have started this." Cherie said.

"I'm not necessarily afraid ... I'm just looking at the possibilities."

"I understand. They need to be looked at, but we did that a long time ago. We're rehashing everything all over again. Sure, we could die, but I really don't believe that will happen, do you?" She saw her husband sadden. She hugged him again. "Do you?"

Tony felt the pain in his throat again. "I just don't want to lose you."

"You won't ever lose me ... you know that." She kissed him lightly. "Well, maybe for a minute."

He watched her roll from the bed and slip on her gown. "Where are you going?"

"I've got cotton mouth. Do you want anything?" Cherie offered.

"Whatever you get," he answered. "Hurry up."

A moment later, she was in the dimly lit corridor. The floor was carpeted, but she tiptoed anyway. The ship was quiet. Passing through the main crew lounge, she stepped barefoot from the soft carpet to the cold bare floor of the kitchen area. She scanned the beverage panel, made the selections and started back to the cabin with two glasses.

She stopped when she felt the welcome carpet and took a drink. Turning toward the corridor, she took a step. Before she could take another, a sound from somewhere behind her riveted her to the spot. Suddenly, she became aware of how scant the garment she wore was. "Wonderful," she thought, "... somebody's going to see me." She turned quickly, smiling in premature embarrassment to see ... no one.

The sound had to have come from further toward the bow of the ship. The only compartment there was the control room, and only a few persons were authorized in the room at this point of the mission.

Suddenly, she heard it again! She placed it this time. It definitely had come from the corridor leading to the control room. She had always had a suspicious nature, but this time, another emotion crowded in, one of strong apprehension. She was presented with a dilemma, investigate or retreat to the cabin?

She didn't dwell on the decision long. Setting the drinks on a table, she paused long enough to dial down the light in the dispensary unit. If anyone was in the control room, she had no desire to alert them with her shadow.

She now stood in the short corridor leading to the bow. Once again, she heard the sound. This time, she was so close that it startled her. It made her hesitate, but didn't discourage her. A cautious moment later, she could see the doorway to the control room. It was open!

The interior of the room was black. Only the lighting from a couple of systems boards lit the room. As far as she could see, no one was there. She frowned, puzzled. For a moment, she stood in the doorway and watched the stars slide slowly past. She thought of what her husband had said just yesterday; how after only a week and a half, they were in uncharted space. The ship from the second mission was found to have inaccurate navigational files. It was impossible to tell exactly how far they'd gone. It was estimated that the Explorer Two would have to travel five months before they would pass the point where they had turned back. It was confusing to her, but she didn't really need to understand. Thinking of her husband reminded her that she had a mission of her own to take care of.

As she moved her gaze from the starry heavens, noise and movement made her tense with fright. Her pulse raced, her eyes wide and searching. The urge to run was overpowering, but why? Whoever was in the room was no stranger. Still, she wasn't supposed to be in there. Another cautious step allowed her to peer around the corner of the bulkhead. At first, she saw nothing, but the same noise repeated, allowing her to pinpoint it. A faint blue glow lit the back starboard corner of the room.

As she watched, she saw movement again. Eventually, she could make out the form of a person and also finally recognized the sound. The person was rapidly typing on a keyboard. It looked like they were seated at the navigation console, but she couldn't be sure. The typing continued.

Finally, she could take it no longer. The fear of being discovered was too much. In seconds, the light in the dispensary was reset, the drinks were retrieved, and she was back in her cabin.

Tony knew something was wrong the moment she turned on the light. "What took you so long?" he asked.

Cherie set the glasses on a table and crawled back onto the bed. "I've got to ask you something."

"What? Can I have my drink?"

"Just wait! Is anyone supposed to be in the control room?"

Her voice was excited, but he paid little attention to her. Instead, he got up and got his drink. "What? Who?" he asked, somewhat irritated.

"Anyone!" she persisted.

Tony asked again, "What are you talking about?"

Cherie repeated herself, sounding each word separately and loudly, "Is anyone supposed to be in the control room?"

Tony thought for a moment, narrowing his eyes. "I don't think so, why?"

"Because someone's in there, that's why."

"Why the hell would they be in there now?" He looked at the clock. "It's supposed to be locked up."

"The door is wide open, hon. I didn't ask what they were doing."

"Did you see anybody in there?"

"Yes ... somebody was in there." Cherie watched him start to shake his head. "It was dark, but I'm sure they were at your terminal."

Tony's interest was now aroused. Why would anyone be at the navigation station? Maybe she thought she saw someone and didn't, but she wouldn't have mistaken an open door. He consented to the possibility, but could think of no reason at this hour of the morning, for someone to be in there. Only four persons were allowed in the room during automatic flight patterns, and he was one of them. "Alright, stay here. I'll see what's going on. I'm sure it's nothing."

Jarrell exited the cabin with a potentially open mind. He was sure she must have seen something. As he reached the bow corridor, his openness to the situation dropped considerably. The door was closed. He frowned, somewhat disappointed, but he had to consider that just because the door was closed now, didn't mean it wasn't open five minutes ago.

He walked to the door and punched in the code. Once inside, he flipped on the overheads. Attentively, he scanned the room, looking for anything out of place, but found nothing. His station was how he had left it. He sighed with relief. Quickly, he dowsed the lights and locked the door.

He wondered what he should say to Cherie. A part of him doubted what she thought she had seen, but she had never been prone to imagining things. He would investigate further by checking with the other three men. Maybe there, he would find the simple explanation, if there were one.

Patricia Montgomery, maiden names Joice, made the final adjustment on the oxygen saturation monitor, watching it climb to its recommended percentage. She sighed. Only one more step remained. She needed to code in the alarm settings to the main computer, and this chamber would be finished.

A woman's voice from behind her gave her a start. She recognized it immediately. It was Jeannette King, her new friend for the last several months. "How long did it take him?" she asked.

"He fought it quite a bit ... fifteen minutes or so." Pat answered, smiling in recollection.

"Well, he looks pretty content now," she observed. "Good looking guy, huh?"

Pat nodded with raised eyebrows, but said nothing. The fifteenth crewmember had just been housed within the chambers. Pat marked the name Michael Updike off the list. Only seven names remained, her own next to last. She put the clipboard and pen back on the shelf and started with Jeannette across the room. "How many more have we got?" asked the latter.

"Five, plus you and me." answered Pat as she began set up on the next chamber. As she worked, she noticed the return of a feeling she'd had all day. Was it anxiety? Was it fear? Whatever it was, it was uncomfortable. She had to ask. "Are you scared, Jeanie?"

Her friend didn't look up. "Damn right. You'd have to be crazy not to be." She paused in thought. "Not fifteen minutes worth, though."

"He didn't seem upset at all. It really shouldn't have taken that long."

"It can though. Remember what they said? When your conscious subsides, your subconscious takes over. He was scared ... he just didn't know it."

"Shit ... I'll probably take an hour," Pat mused.

Jeannette laughed. "Don't worry, babe, I'll give you a knockout dose. You won't feel pain or anything else, I promise."

"You're such a pal."

Together, they entered the medical center, where the remaining crew of five waited. They had been prepped earlier. The Simpson team had finished up with Tommy Goldman, Deanna, and Kahn, and was about to start on one another.

Pat directed her attention to the modestly clothed bronze giant, marveling at his physique. She'd been impressed with him from the moment she'd seen him. His muscles were defined, perfected by years under the weights. She knew the work it took to maintain a body such as his; a body such as her own, but the attraction was purely professional. She had no desire to let it go further than mutual admiration. "Well big guy, are you ready to take the plunge?"

Goldman got a strange feeling. "You look like you're enjoying this."

"You look like you enjoy breaking people in half." Her smile didn't falter. She coaxed him to follow.

Goldman slid off the table, naked except for the shorts he wore. White electrodes spotted his body. "What I do is only an act."

Pat stopped and let him walk past. As he did, she reached out and patted one cheek of his hard butt. "So is mine."

Jeannette looked at Kahn and his bride of only two weeks. They stood together, looking silently into the chambers that held their best friends. They'd seen them go under a short time ago, watched the goodbyes, knowing their own was coming. Gary and Colleen were fine now … no more apprehension, no more tears. Finally, she spoke. "It's time, guys." She hated to say the dreaded words.

Deanna said nothing. She looked into her husband's brown eyes, wondering if she could say goodbye. This man was truly her reason for living. The changes he had made in the last few months proved to everyone close to him that miracles could come true. She had already loved him the way he was, the sloppy, obnoxious, impatient, but occasional sweet man that he used to be. Now, the thought of being separated, even by only a few feet was killing her.

Kahn couldn't find the words either; not at first. He saw the pain in Deanna's eyes and the effort to hide it. If anyone was prepared for what was to come, it was her. She had been their strength all along. He wasn't about to give her a reason to break down now. His own pain screamed to be let out, but was stifled. He forced a smile, false as it was, and answered. "We're ready."

Moments later, in the chamber room, Kahn shook Goldman's hand as the latter was slid into the chamber. The drug given him had already begun to work. He doubted the man would even remember the gesture.

Jeannette moved another chamber out from the bulkhead, the seven-foot long glass shield rising upward to allow easy admittance. Its interior was brightly lit. The unblemished white sheets reflected light around the room. They looked to Kahn like elaborate coffins.

He looked at Goldman once again. He was unconscious, lying motionless, his bodily functions brought nearly to a standstill. Kahn tried to see something … anything to suggest that the man was still alive, but there was nothing, not even a perceptible rise in his chest to mark his breathing.

He suddenly felt sickened, but suppressed it. For a moment he was sorry. He wished he could stop right now; to not go to sleep. More than anything, he wished he didn't have to say goodbye to the woman before him. He stared wordlessly into her eyes.

He watched her face sadden with the anguish of the moment. Her legs lost their strength as he held her in his arms. Her tears fell freely onto his bare chest. It took all he had not to follow her example. His eyes grew moist. "Its okay, De. Don't do this. It's gonna be just like sleeping overnight. You won't even know it." His voice was almost a whisper. He put his hand under her chin and lifted her face. He looked into her eyes and brought his lips to them, gently kissing each one. He found her mouth and kissed it, feeling her lips tremble against his. "I love you …" he whispered, "With all my heart … I love you." He kissed her again.

Deanna held on with no intention of letting go. Kahn glanced at Jeannette, who stood next to Deanna's chamber, waiting patiently. He could see in her eyes that she fully understood. She'd gone through it many times this day, once with her own husband. Kahn was in no hurry, so he let her hold on as long as she wanted. He held on tight as well. Finally, she began to weaken, accepting the inevitable. At that point, he reluctantly took her arms from around him. "Come on baby … it's time."

Her sobs diminished as she let him go. She formed the words, "I love you," but no sound came from her lips. Turning, she moved slowly away, still holding his hand.

Jeannette helped her into the chamber, where Deanna sat while her electrodes were connected. Kahn knelt at her side and helped her lay back. With the touch of a switch, the pad on which she rested conformed to every curve of her body, filling every space beneath her. As Jeannette hooked up the intravenous line, Kahn held her hand. She had stopped crying, relieved that it was nearly over, but her eyes were still red and moist.

She watched the women secure the catheter line to her arm and fasten straps around her chest, waist, arms and legs. Deanna already knew what they were for. First, they kept any involuntary movement from disconnecting the electrodes or the IV catheter. Substantial movement such as a seizure like episode would set off the alarms anyway. If not secured, extremity movement from simple dreaming had potential to set them off. The second reason was to support the body during the chamber rotation process, preventing blood pooling, bedsores, etc. Careful regulation of temperature would prevent perspiration, which could lead to prolonged moisture and possible breeding grounds for bacteria. There had thus far not been any sign of such activity in Kogran or Republic cases, but for this mission, no stone had been left unturned, and there had been many stones.

Jeannette moved close to her, speaking quietly. "Okay, Deanna, we're ready. I'm going to give you some medicine. It's gonna make you sleepy. When you wake up, you'll be with him again." She saw worry in her eyes. "Believe me, I've done this myself. It's just a long relaxing nap."

Deanna squeezed Kahn's hand as tightly as she could and didn't take her gaze from his. She felt the tears coming back, but this time they weren't from pain. They were tears of relief. She knew this man loved her and no matter what, nothing would ever change that.

The seconds passed. She began to feel strange. Soon, she felt that she was losing the ability to think clearly. She felt panic and fought against the sleep that threatened. She concentrated all her thoughts on the man beside her. Kahn's face began to blur and she finally gave up, closing her eyes. She was content in knowing that the last face she saw was his. For a while, in the darkness, she could still see him.

Kahn watched her go. Even after her teary eyes closed, she still held tightly to his hand, but soon he felt its strength fade away also.

"She's out," said Jeannette. "She's the fastest so far."

Kahn nodded. He watched her finish the system calibration and replaced the chamber within the wall. At the same time, she brought another out. Suddenly, it was his turn.

He flinched as the needle pierced his forearm.

"Hurt?" asked the woman standing over him.

He hesitated. It hadn't really. "A little … it just surprised me. I've been stuck with bigger before." He would never forget the Thalosian tunnels. Was he as scared then?

"Oh really? Well, hopefully, you'll only have to get one more before this is over."

"What do you mean?" Kahn asked, confused.

"One now and one more after we find what we're supposed to, and head home."

"I kinda had in mind, having this one and sleeping for the round trip," he joked.

"Kinda be a waste, wouldn't it?"

"Yeah, it would. It's not what we signed up for, is it?" He watched her press the switch that would inject the medicine. Within seconds, he felt a warm sensation travel through his arm.

Jeannette's voice took on a more serious tone. "Kahn, how long do you think we'll be out here?"

Kahn frowned. How many times had he been asked the same question? He could already feel the numbness invading his being. Concentrating, he forced himself to relax. "Forever …" he finally answered. He felt so sleepy. Did she hear me, he wondered? Did I even say anything? His thoughts drifted to the conversation he'd had that morning with three other crewmembers. He'd been asked if he'd been in the control room earlier that morning. He, of course, had denied it, but so had the others. Who had it been, if anyone? And what were they doing?

His mind shifted to a different image … Deanna. All he could see clearly were the last few moments he had spent with her. Now he fully understood her fear, sadness and tears. He felt his own emotions well up. If he could just relax for a few more seconds, it would be okay. It was so difficult … so hard to think. One by one, the last moments faded away. Eventually, her beautiful face faded as well, replaced by blackness, leaving him alone ...

Jeannette watched his departure from consciousness, trying to decide whether his last word was his true opinion or a humorous guess. It didn't matter. Everyone had their ideas based on absolutely nothing.

She went through the same system checks and put the chamber back into the wall. As it slipped into position, she took one last look at his face. Something caught her attention and she moved closer.

On his face was a single drop of water, tracing a shiny path over his cheek. She swallowed hard. What were his last thoughts ... his last wishes? She looked to the next chamber. He was thinking of her. There was real love between these two people, and truth, and honesty. They still carried a bright flame.

She could remember long ago, when she and David had been that way. Their love wasn't gone, but the flame had somehow dwindled. They hadn't planned it that way, but it happened. He called it "normal". That might be true, but she missed it nevertheless.

As she looked back to Kahn, she watched another tear follow the same path as the first. Suddenly, she wanted to wake her own husband and tell him a hundred special things, but she knew it was far too late. She would say it all when this was over ... if she remembered. She sighed. Forever was a very long time.

CHAPTER 23

▼

The lights flickered and finally stayed on, lighting the small room with a dim glow. The Captain entering the room made a mental note that three of the five overhead lights were out. He continued to a control panel, where he checked a short list of readings. He was familiar with the routine, having been there a half a dozen times over the last year. Looking about, he noticed tracks where he had just walked. The dust on the floor was heavier than normal. He made another note to have the ventilation checked. Writing down the numbers, he stepped onto the elevated central platform and checked it.

He had volunteered when offered this simple task. Not everyone had the distinct privilege of entering this room. He put the palm of his hand against the curved glass top of the sleep chamber. As he moved it across the surface, the dust fell away to settle elsewhere. A soft blue light illuminated the person within.

The features of an aged man were distinguishable in the dimness. He had seen him many times before. The man had been there for as long as he could remember. The captain, of course, knew his history and how important he had been. The fact that he had been here so long was witness to that. Not just anyone was allowed to be suspended in sleep state. They either had to have terminal disease, be extremely wealthy, or have enormous status.

The man he studied had to be in his seventies, or had been when he was put under. He would be much older now. The face was wrinkled, framed with a pure white beard. There was no visible movement anywhere on his body. Electrodes covered his torso, legs, and arms. Clear tubing ran from the sides of the inner chamber to disappear into either arm, providing him with what little sustenance his body needed.

The Captain chuckled and shook his head. The methods of preparation for sleep state had been so primitive back then. He had to admit though, they were sufficient. The chamber readings had remained unwavering for years.

He moved his hand again, wiping more dust from the glass, revealing the nameplate. It would be the last time he would ever see it. His retirement was up soon. He sighed. It was hard to believe that he had only been a child when the chamber had been placed in the room. He wondered … could he have done what this man did? No … not when he had a family that he loved so deeply. This man had none.

He touched the bronze nameplate and read it aloud, his words eerie in the small space. "Leon Minden Haute, Fleet Commander, Republic Forces." His service dates were printed as well; the year he took command and the year he relinquished it.

He'd had the opportunity to read the reports, learning the circumstances of the man's decisions. He'd been one of the creators of the well-documented Explorer Two mission. Some time after the ships departure, he had announced his retirement to take care of personal matters. His details of his actions over the next few years were sketchy. It was known that he traveled extensively, but the whereabouts were usually unknown. When he finally did come out of seclusion, he published his biography and made a special request of the Republic that he had taken such good care of for so long. He requested to be placed in a sleep chamber, to be awakened only upon return of the Explorer Two. The grateful Republic, of course, honored his final wishes.

The Captain wondered if the man would ever again walk Belaquins beautiful countryside far above them. He hoped for his sake, that the man would get to see a sunrise and sunset at least once more, feel the tickle of snowflakes touching his face, or experience the innocent joy of a laughing child.

He had read his touching novel, amazed at how deeply it affected the reader's senses, enlightening them on how important life's simple treasures were. His story was fantastic in a way that the reader, at times, couldn't be sure whether it was fact or fiction. The story was dedicated to someone Haute had forgotten about for a long, long time.

The Captain sadly turned away, heading for the stairwell leading from the underground vault. As he took the first step upward, he recalled what the dedication had said, and remembered how no one, including himself, had known what the words meant. He had memorized it. "My long lost friend … I had forgotten you for so long, but that is what you willed me to do. What I have not forgotten is what you said to me the last time I saw you. You told me to live as close to forever as I could; to reach out and grasp it and never let go. I've tried my utmost to do just that, and I hope that I have found a way. If I am ever honored to meet with you again, I will thank you for opening my eyes to what is truly possible in this universe, and for enriching so many aspects of my life. I miss you, my friend. Until I see you again, Ban-Sor, I pray you sleep well.

The End

978-0-595-46817-1
0-595-46817-9

Printed in the United States
122194LV00002B/3/A